JOYCE CAROL OATES

YOU MUST REMEMBER THIS

PERENNIAL LIBRARY

Harper & Row, Publishers, New York
Cambridge, Philadelphia, San Francisco
London, Mexico City, São Paulo, Singapore, Sydney

A hardcover edition of this book is published by E. P. Dutton. It is here reprinted by arrangement with E. P. Dutton, a divison of NAL Penguin Inc.

First PERENNIAL LIBRARY edition published 1988.

Library of Congress Cataloging-in-Publication Data

Oates, Joyce Carol, 1938–
    You must remember this.

    I. Title.
PS3565.A8Y6   1988   813'.54   87-46320
ISBN 0-06-097169-X (pbk.)

---

88 89 90 91 92 FG 10 9 8 7 6 5 4 3 2 1

FOR JEANNIE AND DANIEL HALPERN

CONTENTS

YOU MUST REMEMBER THIS

PROLOGUE

June 7, 1953

She had been waiting for a sign to release her into Death, now the sign was granted.

She swallowed forty-seven aspirin tablets between 1:10 A.M. and 1:35 A.M. locked in the bathroom of her parents' rented house.

She swallowed the tablets slowly and carefully drinking tepid water from the faucet.

She knew to go slowly and carefully not wanting to get overexcited feverish not wanting to get sick to her stomach.

Better to light a single candle than to curse the darkness her father often said but she preferred the darkness.

She stood five feet three inches tall in her bare feet, she weighed eighty-nine pounds.

She was leaving no message behind.

Her tight fist of a heart beat hard, in pride in growing ecstasy she half believed it could never stop.

She had read about the subject at the library, she didn't intend to make the usual mistakes.

She waited until the others were asleep, she'd always been practical shrewd sly, Enid Maria thinking her own private thoughts.

She began to feel bloated from so much water but the nausea was only in her head.

She'd taken a long dreamy bath earlier that evening and washed her hair while the others were watching television: Arthur Godfrey. She could hear laughter far away downstairs.

She'd powdered herself with talcum powder, shoulders breasts belly even between her thighs quick and rough. Stark-white sweet-smelling Jasmine Princess from Woolworth's.

She was thinking of the undertow at Shoal Lake, that eel-like coil of icy water sliding up her body. The sun had been beating hard on her head, the water warm, even sluggish, she'd thought at first the icy water might be a fish or a water snake, it slid swiftly up her legs then disappeared.

The warning was, if you swam in that part of the lake and the undertow got you you wouldn't have time to cry out for help.

The water like an icy slippery eel had slid up her body then disappeared. She'd kept on swimming.

She remembered her sister Lizzie the other day singing "Wheel of Fortune" along with Kay Starr on television.

She dressed herself like a bride to die in her white cotton nightgown from Sibley's with the wide lace straps threaded with a narrow white satin ribbon. A white satin ribbon at the neck too, fixed in place by a safety pin.

She had no pity for the face in the mirror. The bony ridges of her chest, the familiar delicate bones.

She had no pity for the small breasts faint and hazy through the fabric of the nightgown as if seen through frosted glass.

She remembered the sky at Shoal Lake above l'Isle-Verte mottled and luminous like old wavy glass. She remembered the island that was two islands, two halves of an island, above the lake and below the lake in the colorless water.

She remembered the smell of tobacco smoke.

She remembered his voice, Don't tell anybody will you.

She remembered her father teasing her, lifting her in his arms long ago, his whiskers scratching her face.

She was an honor student too smart to die by accident.

She was in control. She didn't believe in accident.

She gagged several times swallowing the pills, by then she had lost count but she knew there would be enough.

Her mother had said, Are you sick Enid, is it your period again so soon?—peering frowning into her face.

Her mother said, Do you have cramps Enid, let me get you some aspirin.

She had toweled her hair then let it dry loose on her shoulders. Chestnut-red crackling with static electricity. She brushed it slowly getting out all the snarls. She hated snarls. Tiny clots of hair in the brush she pulled out of the brush, quickly dropping them into the toilet bowl, her eyes averted.

She remembered a mourning dove the boys had caught in the vacant lot then dosed with gasoline then lit with a match. The bird's wild wings flapping flying in looping crazy circles, ablaze, its beak opened emitting a terrible shriek. It flew up into the air higher and higher then suddenly fell to the ground.

She said, I didn't tell anybody.

She remembered kneeling at the communion rail at St. James's, her eyes shut her fingers gripping one another tight, she hadn't been able to thrust her tongue forward like the others.

She remembered the communion wafer melting on her tongue. You weren't supposed to chew it, just let it melt.

Only say the word and my soul shall be healed.

She was wearing around her neck: a necklace of tiny mother-of-pearl beads a gift from her sister Geraldine, a thin gold chain, a thin silver chain with a religious medal on it the Virgin Mary stamped on it, a confirmation gift from her Uncle Domenic who was a priest.

She lived at 118 East Clinton Street in Port Oriskany, New York, the east side of the city near the railroad yards and warehouses and the big factories along the lake—General Motors, U.S. Steel, Stubb Central Foundry, Swale Cyanamid. Mrs. Stevick, hanging wash in the back yard, complained of the stink in the air but most days you hardly noticed. The white sheets were dirtied the worst.

She was a virgin. He hadn't touched her there.

She didn't believe in God, she believed in Death.

She'd been waiting for a sign, now the sign was granted.

She hid the empty aspirin bottle in the wastebasket beneath the sink, she turned off the bathroom light before opening the door—be slow! be quiet! take your time!—she went back to bed slipping into bed holding her breath, but her sister Lizzie sleeping close by snoring faintly didn't hear.

She was fifteen years old. She was very happy. The date was June 7, 1953.

I
THE GREEN ISLAND

November 1944–
June 1953

1

Not once upon a time but a few years ago. Last year. Last week. Last Thursday. On Union Street, on Cadboro, up in the Decker project, up behind the high school in that alley. In Kilbirnie Park. Out by the reservoir. In the middle of the night, at six in the morning. In broad daylight.

The Buehl girl in ninth grade with the frizzed snarly hair her eyes slightly crossed, nobody wanted to sit near her because of lice, then they were saying somebody's got her pregnant was it her own daddy? then they were saying somebody got rid of it was it her own mommy?—aborted with a coat hanger, maybe it was an ice pick, she didn't die but they didn't let her back into school and afterward the family moved away: went where? Good riddance to bad rubbish even the teachers at De Witt Clinton said, and Mrs. Stevick, who'd heard the worst of it from Father Ogden's housekeeper. Then there was that family in the Decker project, one or another of those low ugly asphalt-sided barracks, a GI with a Bronze Star medal it said in the paper, Sunday morning he cut everybody's throats with a butcher knife not even sparing his eighty-nine-year-old grandmother, tiptoed in the

9

dark just before sunrise taking his time, six people altogether, but with himself he just slashed his wrists and arms, wasn't dead when the police came. And then there was that thirteen-year-old girl locked up in a house on Niagara north of Clinton: she'd run away from home they said—a farm around Foxboro, Olcottsport—met some guy at the Greyhound station downtown, he brought her to this house he and his buddies were renting together, then they wouldn't let her go kept her locked up did things to her all kinds of things, what would you expect? Up and down the block it was known *something* was going on in that house, a half-dozen motorcycles parked on the street some nights, car doors slamming any hour, bottles smashed on the sidewalk, people were afraid to complain, a week, ten days, twelve, finally somebody did complain and the police broke in and found the girl, took her to St. Joseph's, she was unconscious, she'd lost so much weight they said in the papers, quoting a doctor, she was a "living skeleton." Also she was covered in cuts, scabs, cigarette burns, one of the guys arrested told the police the girl gave them a hard time, that was why they punished her sometimes but they didn't mean anything by it, they were going to let her go.

("Living skeleton"—Enid kept thinking about that. Said it out loud, shaped the words in silence. "Living skeleton." Staring at herself in the bathroom mirror, naked, regarding with clinical distaste the jutting collar bones, the knobby shoulder bones, the thin pale envelope of skin rippling over her ribs. Yes she saw it, yes it was there. Her mother was always trying to make her eat though she *did* eat all she wanted, all that wouldn't make her sick, she'd grown two inches in a year, now she didn't want to grow any taller.)

One morning a few years back, she couldn't have been more than eight or nine, she was at her father's store, Daddy was waiting on some customers up front and she was poking around in the books and magazines he kept near the back, old mismatched volumes of the *Encyclopaedia Britannica,* mildewed damp-smelling back issues of *Life, Collier's, Saturday Evening Post,* there were children's books she sometimes read when she was visiting Daddy for the day but this morning she was leafing through *Life* staring at photographs from the war, she knew her Uncle Felix had been in the war, her cousin Joe Pauley who had died, then she saw photographs of extermination camp victims, emaciated men in uniforms that were comical, striped, "living skeletons" of Bergen-Belsen they were called, Buchenwald prisoners staring at the camera through barbed wire looking so calm, so quiet. There were piles of the dead along a country lane, there was a little boy in short pants her age squinting at the camera looking as if he might smile hello, it was all so calm and ordinary. Enid turned a page and then she was staring at the face close up of a boy who had died trying to squeeze beneath a barn door through a space of—was it three inches or so? so small!—a face smudged and broken yet beautiful in sleep, in death. Enid stared. Enid wanted to memorize. This was a face she would often see in her lifetime but it meant her no harm, it brought with it the conviction simple as a lock clicking into place that the human world was wrong, she'd been born into it by error.

Daddy came seeking her out, she was so quiet; she smelled his pipe tobacco but didn't look up, no she wasn't crying no she wasn't upset, her mouth felt cold that was all, she didn't look up at Daddy though he spoke to her, it seemed she could not look away from the face of the dead boy until he released her. That head—that human head—so improbably forced beneath a door! Those shut eyes, that dirt-smudged mouth! Daddy snatched the magazine out of her hands saying, You shouldn't be looking at such things, they're not for your eyes. He sounded angry at first, panting, sucking at his pipe, but really he wasn't angry, she knew to stay quiet and his mood would pass.

They always spoke of it as their house at 118 East Clinton but it was only rented, two-story gray shingleboard that needed paint, the roof and chimneys repaired, in fact it was a duplex they had to share with another family, Mr. Stevick was saving up to make a down payment on a house of their own but it wouldn't be on the east side, maybe out by Prudhoe Park where some of his relatives lived. It was only meant to have been temporary, the Stevicks living in this neighborhood so close to Tuscarora, so close to the factories on the lake, that smell from U.S. Steel was the worst, grit everywhere you couldn't help but breathe, but there was Swale Cyanamid where Mr. Stevick had worked during the war so he was an expert: the real poisons in the air you can't even detect.

Most of the buildings on the block were duplexes nearly identical with their own, some of them shabby and rundown, eyesores, a few newly painted with plots of grass tended out front, up the street was the Union Commercial Corrugated Box & Handling Company, a long low concrete building painted a shade of gray so faint it was no color at all. The box company was of virtually no interest to the neighborhood children, even its windows were opaque with a thick film of grime, but its parking lot was surrounded by a six-foot wire mesh fence they enjoyed climbing, it was broken in parts, badly rusted, their mothers worried they'd get tetanus from it, that meant lockjaw, still it was a game of sorts—climbing the wire fence when no one was there to stop them, breaking it down in stretches. Enid learned to jump six feet to the asphalt pavement not even crying out in surprise or pain, landing on the balls of her feet, her arms extended for balance.

Beyond the parking lot was a vacant lot, perhaps two acres of scrubby trees and bushes, broken glass, debris, rubble strewn among the tall grasses; there were large burnt patches where neighborhood boys had set fires. (For the hell of it on summer nights!—somebody would turn in an alarm, the firemen would arrive within minutes, the fire truck with its shrieking alarm; that meant an hour or so of excitement and nobody was ever caught.) The lot was crossed by numerous paths leading down the steep slope to the canal and to the narrow plank footbridge that spanned the canal perhaps twelve feet below the railroad trestle. The footbridge was maybe five feet wide and shaky and if a train came by the noise was deafening, terrifying, the planks of the footbridge vibrated and it was natural to think the bridge would fall apart and you'd fall into the canal far below and drown—along this stretch just north of downtown Port Oriskany the canal walls were thirty feet high just solid rock face and nothing to grab hold of except scrubby little trees that would break off in your hands. It had the look of a nightmare and Enid dreamed of it often.

The vacant lot was a place for wild rough games, games the girls didn't always want to play, once the boys caught a boy named Jimmy Schultz pulled down his pants and underwear and rubbed dirt, mud, leaves on his genitals, another time they caught a mourning dove, sprinkled gasoline on it and set it afire—the bird flew up, its wings flapping, it turned in circles, shrieking, ablaze, then suddenly it gave up, it fell straight down to the ground just a patch of burning feathers. Later that day Enid's brother, Warren, came over to bury it, said afterward it wasn't anything but some burnt stuff but he buried it anyway—felt sorry for it. Enid hadn't come back to watch.

By night sometimes people dumped things in the lot, broken-down iceboxes, wrecked chairs, torn and scorched sometimes blood-stained mattresses—the boys made jokes, saying, Hey you know what *that* means! Once in a while raw garbage was tossed down, even out by the sidewalk so you could see it and smell it, and Mrs. Stevick was furious almost in tears: Some people are just *pigs*. Some people don't deserve to *live*.

Even Warren who was big and husky and strong, aged eleven, didn't go near the lot after dark—he didn't belong to the Clinton Street gang. The story was, though, the worst things that happened there didn't happen to boys.

There was a story Geraldine heard in ninth grade—a soldier on leave and a woman were found dead one Sunday morning in a parked car above the canal. They'd driven through the lot to the very edge of the precipice, made sure the car was hidden behind trees, fixed a length of hose to the exhaust pipe, and let the motor run all night, filling the car with exhaust. They poisoned themselves, Geraldine told her sisters, with carbon monoxide.

"Why would anybody do that?" Lizzie asked.

"For love," Geraldine said.

"Yes, but why?" Lizzie asked. At the age of nine she was a big-boned girl with a wide blunt almost-pretty face. Brown eyes narrowing in derision.

Geraldine said evasively, "One of them was married to somebody else. Or maybe they were both married to somebody else."

"Okay but why do *that?*" Lizzie said.

"Because they did! Because it's what some people do, stupid!" Geraldine cried.

The soldier had stuffed the window opening around the hose with his army jacket—or was it navy? Geraldine couldn't remember for sure—then the two drank a bottle of whiskey, smoked cigarettes, half lying in each other's arms with the car radio playing, the woman's head resting on the man's shoulder when they were found. In the morning the car's gas tank was empty and the motor was off and they were both dead.

"Okay but *why?*" Lizzie persisted.

"For love, asshole," Geraldine said.

Lizzie and Enid explored the lot when nobody was around, looking for evidence, but they found nothing—only broken bottles, debris, scorched mounds of earth. No car tracks: only bicycle tracks on the paths, muddy and rutted. Most of the hill was lushly overgrown, scrub oak and scrub willow, flowering weeds taller than their heads, in late summer the earth had a ripe rich slightly rotting odor. The air hummed and glittered with insects. "Why would anybody want to kill themselves," Lizzie said in contempt, "—look how *nice* the water is!"

The canal was sluggish and mud-colored, said to be polluted, but from certain angles its surface reflected the sky and shone with the varied colors of the sky in small perfectly measured shivering waves. Like music, Enid thought. Except there was no sound. It *was* beautiful wasn't it, why would the lovers have wanted to die?

That evening Enid asked Mr. Stevick what was carbon monoxide. He glanced up from the newspaper, staring at her perplexed and unsmiling, asking why did she want to know *that?* She just wanted to know, she said. Well, it's fumes from a car exhaust, Mr. Stevick said. Car or truck, whatever. Exhaust fumes. It smells. It stinks. It's dangerous to breathe. Why do you want to know? She just wanted to know, Enid said, retreating.

Years later when she knew she must kill herself she looked up carbon monoxide in a volume of *Science Digest Handbook* in the branch library on Huron Street. But there wasn't much information: *A colorless odorless gas. When mixed as it commonly is with automobile exhaust nothing can be detected but the automobile exhaust—the poison itself has no smell.*

Mrs. Stevick told funny rambling breathless stories you didn't know whether to believe. Mr. Stevick laughed and said they should be taken "with the proverbial grain of salt," then he'd apologize if she got angry, make a show of kissing her on the cheek though at the same time he winked at the children so she couldn't see—poor Momma with half the family laughing at her! A man followed her off the trolley, she said. A man spoke to her in the butcher shop in some language she didn't know, she thought it might have been French. The telephone rang and when she answered it nobody spoke, when she put back the receiver it rang and rang and when she answered it—the same thing.

Many years before when Geraldine was still in diapers, Warren not even born yet, Mrs. Stevick went to visit a girlfriend on Parmalee Avenue where it wasn't built up at that time, just country really, fields and cows, no pavement, her friend's grandfather was this Captain McCarn, a retired police captain in his eighties at least, the poor old man had had a stroke, couldn't talk, his mouth permanently twisted so he looked as if he were smiling but it was a queer bitter smile: it went right through your heart, Mrs. Stevick said.

Those days, Hannah Stevick was still fairly slender, she had a plain fresh face a healthy skin, her fair brown hair shone from brushing, one hundred strokes a day as her mother'd taught her, she wore it neatly plaited and wound around her ears like earphones—there were pictures of her from that time the girls giggled over. Momma looked so young! But it was certainly Momma, staring suspicious at the camera, that frown line already puckering between her eyes.

This Captain McCarn, Mrs. Stevick said, he followed her everywhere with his eyes, didn't say anything except mumbling, she had the notion her girlfriend was embarrassed by the old man but the visit went well enough. Mrs. Stevick and her girlfriend each had babies under a year and many things to discuss, but then: she had to go to the outhouse at the bottom of the garden, brought along Gerry, whose diaper she changed, then she sat in the outhouse for a few minutes, a dank little cubbyhole of a place—like upright coffins, they used to be—everybody these days below a certain age was spoiled, having bathrooms all their lives. Then when she was about finished she knew there was something wrong, something strange, she couldn't figure out what it was at first, then she saw it—a long straw moving up and down in the crack of the door by the hinges! Her skin prickled, her blood just ran cold, she knew it was the old man out there spying on her but she couldn't stand up and pull up her underpants, she was trapped, she had to sit there just dying so ashamed, and now Gerry was starting to fret and the straw going up and down up and down, the most awful thing! She couldn't say a word. Just couldn't say a word. Then after ten minutes the straw dropped away and she knew she could come out but still she was afraid—just couldn't move for a long time. What could you do about an old man like that?—some sick old crazy old lecher that was a retired *policeman?*

Sure enough when she opened the outhouse door and peeked out there was nobody in sight, not a soul, but she knew the captain was in hiding close by, she could feel that man's eyes on her all the way back to the house. And poor Gerry crying and kicking knowing something strange was going on!

So she told her girlfriend, hot and shamed and nervous, she had to get home; no she didn't explain a thing just wanted to get out of that place as fast as she could. So she packed up and left. Took the trolley back to Union Street where she and Mr. Stevick were living then. After that awful time she only saw her girlfriend once or twice, naturally she never ventured out to Parmalee Avenue again. However long Captain McCarn lived to terrorize other women she never knew and never asked.

"Now you know why I tell you girls," Mrs. Stevick said severely, "never trust the police. Any policeman out on the street, he smiles at you, says something friendly, don't you believe it. *I mean what I say.*"

* * *

Warren's story for years was how he'd been a witness to a terrible accident on Tuscarora Street, a boy run over and killed by a truck.

He was in seventh grade at De Witt Clinton coming home from school with two other boys on the block, a November day when it gets dark early, not cold that day but very windy, lots of grit and stuff blowing in the air, and there was a Negro boy maybe ten or eleven years old pedaling his bicycle south on Tuscarora headed toward Clinton, a wobbly stripped-down bike a little too big for him; still he was going fast, weaving in and around traffic, wool knit cap pulled low over his forehead, a boy Warren didn't know from school or anywhere else. Then it happened that some white boys, teenagers—from the Decker project most likely because that's the direction they ran in—started chasing the boy, shouting, threw something at the bike, the boy lost his balance or maybe the front wheel hit a pothole and down he went in front of a coal truck barreling along too fast to stop if the driver had even seen what was happening, which evidently he didn't. When he sounded the horn, threw on his brakes, it was already too late—he'd run over the boy and the bicycle, the truck's front tire ran over him, caught him and the bicycle both up under the fender and dragged him along for a short distance, there wasn't anything to stop it!

Warren told the story staring and breathless, panting, his color high and his eyes shining with tears of excitement. He began to stammer slightly—it was poor Warren's curse, it aroused Mr. Stevick to exasperation but there was nothing to be done—trying to explain how fast the accident had happened, how you can be halfway looking not thinking about anything much not really *seeing* until suddenly something happens and everything is changed. That was how it was: the white boys running after the boy on the bicycle then the bicycle going down then the truck then the boy crying out then the truck's horn and the air brakes then it was over, the boy was crushed and dead—blood spilling out of his mouth, ears, like you'd squeeze paint out of a tube.

Warren kept saying again and again how fast it had happened, he couldn't really make sense of it. First the boys running; then the Negro boy falling; then—was it the truck going over him before he screamed, or was it the horn sounding first, or was he already dead then, the bike twisted up under the fender dragged along the street? Then it seemed there was a pause—nothing happening—then people began to shout, just words like Hey! Stop! What the hell's going on there!—gawking to see what had happened. The white boys cut through an alley and ran like hell not looking back, nobody Warren or his friends knew by name but he'd seen them around, high school boys probably, they surely didn't go to De Witt Clinton. By this time Warren was by the Negro boy thinking maybe he could help?—he helped in emergencies and household crises, Mrs. Stevick was always yelling for him—he had the idea he could get the bicycle up and working again, he was dazed and dopey not understanding the boy was actually dead though you could see he was *probably* dead, that big tire going over his chest and shoulders, squeezing the life out of him. Everything happened so fast, Warren said, swallowing down his stammer.

Now all sorts of things took place: people came running over, the truck driver jumped down from his cab acting crazy, saying it hadn't been *his* fault, the kid had cut in front of him, then he saw Warren and told him to stand back, get out of the way—Get out of here you fucking kids you done enough!—punched Warren like you'd punch a dog to get him moving. All the while the Negro boy was lying there half under the truck bleeding to death the truck driver was going after Warren, saying it was his fault—him and his friends—that was whose fault it was! So Warren was just astonished. Warren couldn't say a word. There were people all around now, men who'd been unloading crates in the street, secretaries from the Teamsters' office running out in their high heels with little screams and gasps, he was being pushed out of the way, the truck driver's attention was diverted, Warren decided to run like hell, get out of there before the police came, because how could he prove who he was?

That is—how could he prove who he wasn't?

Telling the story he began to cry, he was clumsy, shamed, thirteen years old and he never cried now, a stocky boy with stiff springy chestnut-red hair like his father's, brown eyes delicately flecked with hazel and gold, the sockets deep-set, the lashes fine, colorless. He said, again and again, They shouldn't have scared him like that, should they? And, Why did that man blame *me?*

He kept saying, as if it were a discovery of his own, It all happened so *fast.*

The main thing—Mr. and Mrs. Stevick agreed for once—was that Warren wasn't to tell the story outside the family.

Sure as hell he isn't going to wind up any witness for the police, Mr. Stevick said. I know all about the police!

Enid was six years old at the time. She listened to her brother, halfway frightened that all he felt—all he'd seen—might flood over her as well, his grief like a rush of water, waves, overwhelming her. She wouldn't be able to breathe, she'd drown!—standing so near, listening so hard, a child with the habit of staring intently, frowning as if things mattered too much to her. Absorbed deeply as she was in what she saw and heard she was slow to wake, to return to herself. But what *was* herself?

Warren stopped crying, he was ashamed, disgusted with himself, still he felt sick to his stomach, said he didn't want supper, he was going upstairs to do his homework then go to bed. But after supper Mrs. Stevick took him a plate—meat loaf with a hard thick ketchup crust, fried potatoes and onions heavily peppered—a glass of hot milk laced with honey which was Mrs. Stevick's specialty when any of the children were sick—and he ate it all hungrily, sitting in his pajamas on the edge of his bed. His eyes were red-rimmed, the lids puffy. In his pajamas he looked younger than thirteen despite his husky shoulders and long limbs. While he ate Mrs. Stevick sat with him crocheting, her fingers moving swift and deft and the needles flashing. She had been having health problems that fall—the doctor thought it was a kidney infection, she'd had a number of infections since her last pregnancy—but she felt well enough that night keeping Warren company, not talking. When the children were sick Mrs. Stevick was nearly always sympathetic, she herself was sick so often!—it was health she had learned not to trust, waking up energetic and happy, looking forward to the day, then about noon you'd pay for it—you always paid for it, extending yourself unwisely. Also she seemed to think it was weakness for a mother to acknowledge her children's affection, it would make them think less of her—her own mother had been the same way.

Downstairs they listened as usual to *Fibber McGee and Molly* thinking Warren would come downstairs, it was one of his favorite radio programs along with *The Shadow, Jack Benny, Grand Central Station, Mr. Keen,* "tracer of lost persons," but even when Fibber McGee's closet shelf crashed down as it did every week and the Stevicks erupted in laughter Warren stayed away. Mrs. Stevick said flatly, "He'll get over it—he's just pretending now."

There were numerous stories, not all of them for children to know, about Mr. Stevick's younger brother Felix—his half brother really, born twenty-one years after him to his father's second wife. Felix was a professional boxer, a middleweight, locally famous—the newspapers were always printing his picture: on the front page if he'd won an important fight. The sportswriters called him "Felix the Cat," which Lyle Stevick thought a vulgar silly name but then wasn't boxing vulgar and silly—certainly it was crude. He didn't approve of Felix's way of life in and out of the ring, not because he was jealous or envious—not at all—but because it was a careless immoral life bringing injury to others.

Felix's own mother had kicked him out of the house when he was sixteen and he'd lived on his own more or less ever since. He'd done well in the Golden Gloves amateur tournaments, then he'd turned professional aged eighteen and kept on doing well, winning all his fights, before enlisting in the U.S. Army and going off to the Pacific where—as Mr. Stevick said—his luck held. Only consider: In August 1945 Private First Class Felix Stevick was one of several thousand men aboard a troop transport ship in the China Sea bound for Japan—the war had escalated into its wild kamikaze phase, Iwo Jima, Okinawa, more to come—when Harry Truman ordered the A-bomb dropped on Hiroshima *sixty-six thousand people killed outright* then three days later Nagasaki *thirty-nine thousand killed outright* and five days later World War II was over!—and Felix Stevick's life was spared, a week before his twenty-third birthday. That was his luck.

Lyle Stevick often said if it'd been *him* and *his* luck old Harry Truman would have postponed dropping the bombs until after Lyle's ship had landed in Japan and everybody was wiped out. But Felix the Cat—bless him—always landed on his feet.

(In defiance of her parents Geraldine saved newspaper pictures and clippings pertaining to Felix Stevick, even taped his photo on the inside of her closet wall back along the side where Mrs. Stevick wasn't likely to notice: *Felix "The Cat" Stevick* in white boxing trunks with black trim, muscled shoulders, arms, torso, fists in sparring gloves raised to mid-chest, his handsome face unsmiling, unreadable. Whether he was matched with worthy opponents or no, Felix Stevick rose rapidly through the middleweight ranks and at the peak of his career was number-four contender for the world title, then held by Rocky Graziano. After his terrible defeat in 1948 and his "retirement" from the ring Geraldine took down the photo, threw away all the pictures and clippings—but by then she was in love with a boy named Neal O'Banan, crazy about a boy named Neal O'Banan, in fact impregnated by Neal O'Banan and soon to be wed.)

* * *

What was the secret about Enid's Grandfather Stevick who'd died many years before she was born?—something shameful, nasty. Something Enid's father didn't want his children to know.

He'd been mayor of the city from 1912 to 1916. Only imagine: a Stevick mayor of Port Oriskany! And a Democratic congressman in Washington for two terms before that. (It was the "reform-minded" men in his own party, Mr. Stevick said, who'd driven his father out of office—broke his heart really, the pious sons of bitches.) Though Lyle and his older brother, Domenic, had never actually lived in the house because Karl Stevick had divorced their mother by then, Lyle sometimes drove the children on Sunday afternoons past the mayor's official residence on Grover Park: a large foursquare limestone house with numberless windows, a heavy slate roof, an imposing portico like something in a movie. When Mr. Stevick got drunk he often talked of his father, angry and hurt and baffled, hinting at something his father had done, something that "took guts" but was maybe "a terrible sin"—it was years before Enid learned that her grandfather had killed himself. But the reason Lyle was angry with his father was because he'd left his mother for another woman, a "showgirl" named Ursula Mohr, a glamorous platinum blonde many years younger than he and *that* Lyle could never forgive. Walking out on his family, his wife and two boys. Taking up with a woman like that—a classy version of a whore. And having another baby by her, the old fool.

That was Felix, Ursula Mohr's son. All you could be sure of, Mr. Stevick would say, making a joke the children didn't quite grasp, was that he was *her* son.

Before going into politics Karl Stevick had been a Port Oriskany businessman, moderately successful; after being forced out of politics he began to speculate rather flamboyantly in real estate in the city and up in the Adirondacks, he invested in a downtown speakeasy (the notorious Lulu's), he even invested in several club fighters with short-lived careers. (One man was so badly beaten in a match with the one-eyed middleweight Harry Greb he died ten days afterward without regaining consciousness.) At his peak Karl Stevick must have been worth several million dollars, Lyle calculated. But it all came to an end in 1929.

And by Christmas of 1930, that most cheerless of all holiday seasons within memory, he was dead: aged sixty-two. Dying of cancer of the kidneys, with a frame like Lyle Stevick's, wasted away to less than one hundred pounds where once he'd weighed nearly two hundred, he had managed to talk one of his girls into bringing him his .22-caliber "good luck" revolver as he lay in his hospital bed hooked up to numerous life-giving tubes and a catheter. (The catheter had been the final humiliation.) He told the girl he wanted the gun for sentimental reasons only but as soon as she left him alone Karl Stevick shot himself cleanly between the eyes: one squeeze of the trigger and it was over. He'd been ashamed of his illness, in its late stages he'd forbidden even his wife Ursula to visit him, even his sons, Lyle and Domenic (though Domenic was by this time a fully ordained Roman Catholic priest) and Felix (just a child—eight years old). If you can't run the game your way, cut your losses and get out, he'd often said. So he did.

The twenty-year-old girl—on his payroll as a secretary—was charged with aiding and abetting a suicide; the incident drew a good deal of sensational publicity but the girl never came to trial. And within eighteen months after Karl Stevick's death his widow Ursula remarried.

This was Lyle Stevick's obsessive story, the one he kept circling back upon, but the children had to piece it together over the years—like one of those large complicated jigsaw puzzles Aunt Ingrid had for weeks on a table in her house, rather dark somber fussy landscapes of European settings with cows, rivers, fleecy clouds, streaming rays of sunshine and much dense foliage; you picked up a piece shyly, tried it, put it down and tried another, until finally something fitted together as if by accident and you could try again. Mrs. Stevick said it wasn't good for the children to hear about their Stevick grandfather, but Mr. Stevick told her he'd talk about what he wanted to talk about.

At school however when the Stevick children were asked were they related to whoever "owned" the Stevick Building on North Main Street they always said no they weren't. (This twelve-story office building with its once-elegant marble façade was all that remained of what Lyle Stevick called his father's "visible empire"—sold off long ago by the widow.) Once in grammar school Enid's teacher asked her was she related to the man who'd been mayor of Port Oriskany a long time ago, and as heads turned in Enid's direction she sat still and stiff, staring at the top of her desk, and said, No. No she was *not*.

Lyle Stevick always slept soundly—snoring his head off as the family complained!—except when he didn't sleep soundly at all, when he suffered from an old terrible nightmare he'd had since the age of twenty-nine when Karl Stevick shot himself.

This was the dream: Lyle is in a room somewhere underground with ugly white walls pressing in on him, a low ceiling coming down, everything glaring and dazzling in white, a kind of weird silvery-white, and in the next room though he can't see him his father is lying on a table (like the tables in the mortuary at St. Joseph's Hospital, but Lyle Stevick hadn't known about them until the early forties when he did volunteer work there), his father is dead *yet still watchful,* stone dead but *his eyes are open, but he can't get to him.* In the white-walled room he's nearly blinded, he can't breathe, he knows he will die but he can't move and he can't cry out for help except to whisper, Oh dear God, Oh Jesus, Mary, Joseph!—and the light increases whitely, blinding, the tile walls and the ceiling are pressing close, he can't bear it, he knows he will go mad, *he can't bear it.*

Then abruptly he's awake. Awake and lying in his own bed, his heart beating hard, terrifyingly hard, pajamas soaked in sweat and that panic taste in his mouth—for a minute or two not really knowing where he is though Hannah is sleeping beside him, he's restored to himself again, his body, his muscular coordination, his ability to scream for help should he want to scream for help. Yes, he has escaped the white-walled room again, he has narrowly escaped going insane, but he knows it's there waiting for him and his father too, cold, stiff, dead, waiting, those terrible eyes of his open, waiting for his son to close them.

In the bedroom Lizzie and Enid shared at the upstairs rear of the house there was the prettiest wallpaper—pale yellow with thin curling strips of roses, tiny red roses, and fine-etched greenery like embroidery slightly frayed. Like something in a picture book!—so pretty, so fascinating to look at. The wallpaper was water-stained now and bulging in spots, Mr. Stevick and a friend had put it up years ago, drinking ale and kidding around and finally impatient with smoothing the damned paper flat; it was hard work papering walls, Mr. Stevick told his wife afterward, *you* should try it sometime. But Enid didn't at all care about the bulges and water stains, she loved the wallpaper just as it was.

Tiny red roses. Tiny feathery green stems and leaves. Soft pale yellow in the background like mist, like the color of the sky early in the morning. Enid lay in her bed not asleep but not quite awake, hearing music in her head, staring into the wallpaper which was where the music came from, some place far away, far in the past too; inside the wallpaper was a pathway, many pathways, everywhere she looked if she looked hard enough there were pathways, curving mountain roads, places to hide, rivers, trees, mountains, cliffs, lakes, islands like in the Adirondacks where Mr. Stevick took the family sometimes in the summer; then suddenly she was seeing the canal from the embankment, the lapping water mixed up with the music, and she was alone on the footbridge frightened a train might rush by overhead before she could get off, but no train ever came wasn't that the promise?—not here in her room in her bed lying perfectly still allowing the music to wash through her, feeling her soul slip thinly from her into the wallpaper where there was no harm, never any danger, that was the promise. Or she was in the vacant lot where she wasn't supposed to be by herself—there was the warning, the worst things there happened to girls—the tall grasses confused her, the paths were the wrong paths and she could hear Momma calling down the block Enid Enid *Enid!* the voice faint but still angry. Or she'd find herself at school. In the playground before the doors opened. Not dressed right—in her pajamas or her underwear. Cracks and tarry smudges in the asphalt underfoot, like the cracks and smudges in the wallpaper, while waiting in the girls' line for the Negro janitor to unlock the door. But she was in no danger, she was safe, the secret paths pulled her back, no one could follow.

On the bulletin board at school there was a large map of Port Oriskany and "outlying areas" printed by the Civil Defense Bureau showing FALLOUT ZONE, INTERMEDIATE ZONE, SAFE ZONE. There were red concentric circles you could study—10-MILE RADIUS (limit of total destruction), 20-MILE RADIUS (limit of heat and shock), 30-MILE RADIUS (little if any immediate effect), 60-MILE RADIUS (all clear). The map was in the wallpaper too, she could see the circles, the arrows, the outline of the lake, the snaky movement of the canal. If the bomb was dropped it would be dropped on the factories by the lakeshore, which meant some of the East Side was within the 10-MILE RADIUS circle, though De Witt Clinton Junior High School itself and the stretch of East Clinton where the Stevicks lived was inside the 20-MILE RADIUS circle. That was good, they said. That wasn't too bad, they said. Enid lay very still feeling the music inside her chest, in her throat, in her fingers, though when she'd tried to play piano at the Pauleys' house that old upright with the yellow keys some of them broken, sticking, it had sounded silly—just a child fooling around—

and Momma'd whispered for her to stop. She wasn't asleep but she wasn't fully awake, her heartbeat was quick, secret, she was running up a flight of stairs in the wall, then she stumbled and almost fell, her leg muscles twitching—or riding Lizzie's bicycle out in the alley not able to get her balance right—or pushing pushing herself squeezing herself by inches beneath a door, or was it a wall?—some kind of barn or shed—through a tiny space at the bottom squeezing herself to get through to get out her eyes shut tight with the effort her jaws locked together to get out, to get out, to get out.

2

Late September, 1947, the morning of the day Enid's father took his children downtown to the Armory to see their Uncle Felix box for the first and only time in her life, she happened to overhear her parents speaking in sharp raised voices in the kitchen. She was only nine years old but she knew as if from instinct that the disagreement had to do with Mr. Stevick's wanting to do something with the children Mrs. Stevick didn't want him to do.

They were quarreling about the boxing match. They'd quarreled about it earlier, days before. And in that morning's *News Transcript* Mrs. Stevick read that local fight experts were picking Felix Stevick's opponent to win over him—granted, Felix *was* a flashy boxer, and a local hero—the bookmakers were giving 3–2 odds which meant that Felix was going to lose and probably going to be hurt and she didn't want her daughters to see it.

Felix could even be killed, Mrs. Stevick said. How could he risk taking their daughters to such a thing?

In a voice of mock calm Mr. Stevick told her that the odds— "About which you know nothing, Hannah"—had originally been 2–1 in favor of Mel Watkins; now they were narrowed. That meant something didn't it? The smart money was beginning to shift to Felix—that meant something didn't it? Watkins was number-four contender in the middleweight division but he'd lost his last two fights and Felix who was number seven hadn't yet lost a fight and everybody Mr. Stevick had talked to around town believed Felix had a good chance of winning if he didn't fall into the trap of fighting Watkins's kind of fight and not his own. "If he gets hotheaded he's through but if he stays cool he'll be all right—*he* knows that," Mr. Stevick said, but Mrs. Stevick interrupted to say she didn't care about any of that—she wasn't following him, wasn't listening—she just didn't want her little girls to be exposed to seeing their uncle hurt in some terrible way. Now she'd had time to think it over she didn't want them to see anybody hurt, Felix *or* the other boxer; the Armory itself was a terrible place to take children—all those loud brutal men shouting and carrying on.

"Hannah, you've never seen a boxing match," Mr. Stevick said evenly. "You know nothing about it—nothing."

"I know how I *feel*," Mrs. Stevick said, her voice rising. "I know what's *right*."

Mr. Stevick said he was no great fan of the sport himself—"If you can call it a sport"—as Mrs. Stevick well knew. Nonetheless this was a special occasion, all of Port Oriskany was caught up in it, Felix Stevick meeting a top-ranked opponent and if he won he'd probably have a title match within the year—that was the way these things worked, allowing of course for some *sub rosa* dealing. No really good, no nationally known athlete had ever come from this part of the state: Felix was everybody's hope.

"The fact is, Hannah, Felix sent over tickets and it would be small-minded of me not to accept. He's making an effort to be decent, to be friendly—I have to meet him at least halfway," Mr. Stevick said. He spoke to Enid's mother as if he were explaining something to a very slow child. He was a furniture salesman—he'd been a salesman nearly all his life, one kind or another—now as Enid listened she could hear that side of him shift forward, buoyant, hearty, bullying, subtly contemptuous. Always subtly contemptuous behind that smile. "Felix and I have had our disagreements God knows but he's making an effort now and it's the least I can do, to accept. You must know that."

"It's one thing to take Warren, but—"

"Look: the Pauleys and the Rosskys are going. Lillian is going—says she wouldn't miss it for the world. If she goes why the hell can't *you?* And I'm sure the girls will be there, Annemarie, Dinah—"

"*Your* relatives."

"What do you mean, *my* relatives? What kind of a tone of voice is that—coming from *you* of all people? *you?*" Mr. Stevick said derisively. It was a household joke of a kind, Mrs. Stevick's kin—an old joke. But Mr. Stevick let it pass. "And afterward there's a supper at De Marra's restaurant—assuming my brother wins."

"And what if he doesn't?"

"They don't think along those lines, those people. They're always going to win."

"The Armory is a terrible place and you know it."

"But the girls want to go—ask them."

"I don't care what they want!—Enid especially. Enid's too young."

"Enid *wants* to go with her daddy," Mr. Stevick said. "Ask her."

"She's too little to know what she wants."

Enid was in the living room crouched by the stairs around the corner from them but she could picture her mother's flushed face, the wide cheekbones, eyes pinched at the corners, narrowed. Momma would be standing with her feet apart, arms wound in a loose fold of her apron as she did when she was nervous and talking fast, not always knowing what she said. Close up you could feel the heat coming off her, and the smells that were hers—something rich, milky, biscuity, over-sweet—were intensified. At such times she lashed out stammering but accurate and meaning to hurt as she did now, saying, "You! Call yourself a Catholic! Call yourself a father! *His* brother! You hate Felix and you want to see him hurt and you want your own children to see—"

At this Mr. Stevick must have struck something with his fist, a counter, the kitchen table, Mrs. Stevick gave a scream and he was on his way out of the kitchen his footsteps heavy as if somebody were pounding the floor with a hammer. Mrs. Stevick shouted something after him but he kept going, wouldn't turn back, he always said at such times he had to get out of temptation's path or Hannah would regret it.

If he hadn't ever belted that woman in the mouth, he always said, shaking his head, smiling, it was no thanks to *her*. *He* was the one who maintained his self-control.

Enid tried to hide but her daddy caught sight of her and for a moment she thought he'd shout at her too but then—this was how Mr. Stevick was, you couldn't ever predict—but then he smiled. Just smiled. Like she was his little girl and he exempted her from harm. Sucking hard on his pipe, releasing a nimbus of whitish smoke, his face too was flushed, mottled, pleasantly heated in anger. Not a word to Enid but just a wink as he slammed out of the house, that wink of his meaning Daddy and his littlest girl have a secret understanding and

Momma is excluded, Momma is a fool—out there in the kitchen shedding helpless tears, her face hidden in her apron.

That evening in the Armory Enid pulled at her father's arm to ask him why the boxers wanted to hit each other like that—why they stood up there letting themselves be hurt. Mr. Stevick laughed and said, "Honey, they don't feel pain like *you.* They don't feel anything much at all."

Enid wondered, Could that be true? When it looked as if they were being hit so hard?

The Stevicks had come into the big arena in the middle of a preliminary match between two young featherweights who pursued each other around the ring punching and slapping and clinching with an air of desperation as people in the audience shouted. They were hardly more than boys, it seemed, wearing nothing but swimming trunks, and their ribs showing, and sweat on their backs. Mr. Stevick had "ringside" seats—in fact they were five rows back from the ring—amid a noisy beery contingent of relatives; Stevicks, Pauleys, Rosskys, others. Lyle Stevick was noisily welcomed—everybody liked their daddy. Geraldine went to sit with her cousins and Enid sat between Lizzie and Mr. Stevick, blinking and staring, unable to take in everything at once, there was so much to see—and so much noise—and there in the ring in front of them the young boxers were swiping at each other with their red gleaming gloves and Enid felt her bowels cramp thinking it was something you shouldn't see but there it *was*—and people not especially paying attention except when they started to punch hard in flurries of frantic blows.

Mrs. Stevick had cautioned Enid she'd better hide her eyes if something bad started to happen—which it would—put her fingers over her eyes *and keep them there.* Enid Maria was the smallest child among the relatives—Dinah Pauley was Lizzie's age, a big brash girl like Lizzie—and there were other children in the arena but nobody small as Enid. There *were* women—Mrs. Stevick had said there wouldn't be, in such a place—and some of them were screaming like the men.

And all the while people were milling in the aisles, squeezing into their seats, vendors were selling hot dogs, French fries, drinks, it wasn't like church or the movies where you had to be quiet and respectful. So much *happening.* So much to *see.* The place was filling with smoke that stung Enid's eyes—cigarette smoke, cigar smoke, that dense suffocating smoke from Mr. Stevick's pipe he never seemed to notice made other people choke. But Enid sat close to him. Enid squeezed close. She was shivering, already feverish, thinking her daddy had brought them to a place that was public but also secret where anything could happen. Anything could happen and people would watch: that was why they'd bought their tickets. To watch.

The main bout, Watkins vs. Stevick, ten rounds, middleweight contest, didn't begin until after 9:30 P.M. It was late but Enid felt as wakeful as if it were early morning.

Long afterward—very likely, for the remainder of her life—Enid would recall the profound shock of seeing her Uncle Felix in the ring: her Uncle Felix, whom she'd known as teasing, funny, friendly, boyish, appearing suddenly in that noisy public place, the object of so much cheering and attention. Was that Felix?—*that* man? She would not have recognized him. In a white robe that was silky and glossy, trimmed in gold, like a woman's robe—sweat glittering like jewels on his skin, and his hair wet—shadowboxing and feinting and dancing about as if he were alone, unobserved, while in fact thousands of people were watching him—looking nowhere else but at *him*. Already his fans were wild for him, already Lizzie was jumping up and down screaming "Felix! Felix! Felix!" as if she'd gone crazy.

Enid was to think the fight lasted a long time, a terrible long time, but in fact it ended in the fourth round—less than twelve minutes of actual fighting. She was to think her uncle had been hurt, since by the end of the fight he was bleeding from a cut in his forehead, but Mr. Stevick said no, she shouldn't worry, Felix was trained to take punishment and bleeding was nothing to him—not that kind of bleeding anyway. A few quick stitches, said Mr. Stevick, and good as new.

When the bell sounded for the first round Felix moved across the ring at his opponent so quickly Enid couldn't see what was happening. It was all so fast, so blurred and fast—the boxers' gloves, arms—the boxers' legs—the thud of leather against flesh—the sounds of their shoes scraping against the canvas. By the shouts and cheers of the crowd Enid guessed that important blows were being landed, points being made, the crowd was on Felix's side and the crowd seemed elated so Felix must be doing well but she couldn't really see, she was too frightened. She knew that, if she looked, she'd see something she wasn't supposed to see. And it would be too late then to hide her eyes.

Except: there was the young man who was her uncle, near naked in his white trunks trimmed in gold, his body covered in swaths of hair—crouched, stalking—dancing to the left to avoid his opponent's long jab—then darting inside with a flurry of short blows, bulling the man back toward the ropes as the crowd erupted in excitement. Which blows landed solidly, which were ineffective or missed, it was difficult to see. By the time the bell rang signaling the end of the round Enid had shut her eyes tight, but around her everyone was saying that Felix was ahead, wasn't he? Wasn't that Felix's round?

Mr. Stevick's pipe had gone out in the excitement so he relit it soberly, leaning across the girls to tell Warren that in his opinion— "Of course I'm no expert"—the round had been even. Felix got in some tricky shots, that was his style, hit and run, jab and glide, but Mel Watkins had gotten in some solid blows of his own, rib-cracking blows, which the referee and the judges had surely noted. Watkins at thirty-one was an old ring veteran, he'd fought Zale and Graziano and gone the distance once with Ray Robinson of all people; he was cagey, tough—the most dangerous kind of opponent: ringwise was what they called it. Whereas Felix was twenty-five, which wasn't young, for a boxer, but the Mattiuzzios had brought him along cautiously, until tonight he hadn't fought a really dangerous opponent and you could see that for all his fancy side-to-side moving and his fast hands and feet he had a lot to learn. "Also, the crowd has him too excited," Mr. Stevick said gravely. "He'll walk into a punch and get nailed."

With his pipe Mr. Stevick pointed out to the children certain associates, as he called them, of his brother's: that was Felix's trainer in his corner, that oldish white-haired man leaning over him; that was his manager, squatting next to him; there, across the way, seated in the first row, was Felix's old high school pal Vince Mattiuzzio and next to Vince his father, Leonardo—the man who owned the boxing club that sponsored Felix. And there was the grandfather, Giulio Rimi, who owned a few shares of Felix too. And one or two other men whose names Mr. Stevick didn't know—"We don't run in the same circles." And that woman in black, black silk dress, black hat slantwise on her head like Bette Davis or Joan Crawford—that was Felix's current lady friend, Irene Mercer. Divorced wife, or maybe they were just separated, of a man named Otto Mercer, a big-deal businessman who owned property all around town. "Of course I haven't had the honor of being introduced to Mrs. Mercer," Mr. Stevick said in a voice heavy with irony.

Enid and Lizzie stood to get a clearer view. The drifting smoke was so thick Enid had only an impression of a face beautiful as a face on a poster, dead-white skin, red lips; beneath the stylish hat a tight roll of hair that shone like a copper penny. "She's pretty," Lizzie said. "She's like a movie star."

"She isn't pretty," Mr. Stevick said curtly. "She's cheap. She's common. She's even a few years older than Felix."

Enid stared. She wondered how Mrs. Mercer could sit there so calmly watching Felix fight—if she loved him, the way women loved men in movies. If she wouldn't want to see him hurt.

Several times in the next two rounds the boxers stood toe to toe trading punches, bringing many in the crowd to their feet, including the Stevicks and their kin. Such screaming! shouting! when Felix opened a cut over Watkins's right eye! Seeing the bright splash of blood Enid knew Momma was right, she shouldn't have come here tonight. But even Mr. Stevick was shouting now as if he couldn't help himself. "Felix! Felix! Felix!" The strange yearning collective cry rose from all parts of the Armory and rang in Enid's head and Enid was tasting something black in her mouth staring at the man who was her uncle bearing down on his dazed opponent, pummeling him with a dozen swift blows, continuing to hit him when he tried to stall by clinching, striking a flurry of short hard blows to the ribs, to the small of the back, dragging down on his shoulders as if trying to make his legs buckle beneath him. His legs were gone, Watkins—that was what they were saying. And they were saying, chanting, "Kill him! Kill him!" but Enid clamped her hands over her ears and didn't hear.

The gong sounded. The boxers were seated in their corners. Mr. Stevick leaned over Enid and asked was she all right?—or would she like Daddy to take her out into the lobby?

Enid shook her head, no.

The next round began and Enid, squinting through her fingers, transfixed, saw a blow of her uncle's strike the other man on the side of the head, a terrible blow so that sweat flew like sparks in the bright lights and again the crowd was wild and Enid thought how she hated everybody in this place—not just in this place but everybody—all the world. The corpses piled alongside the road and the marching soldiers, the Nazis with their funny insignia and Hitler with his mustache Mr. Stevick made fun of but where was the fun? where was the joke?—these people, her father, her uncles, cousins, screaming "Kill him, Felix! Kill him!" and Lizzie and Warren, even Warren, like maniacs beside her. Watkins fell to the canvas and Felix ran on his muscled springy legs to a neutral corner and you could see now his forehead was bleeding above his eye, he'd been butted, his opponent's head had struck him in one of their clinches so now he was wiping blood from his face with his glove and looked surprised, disbelieving, *his* blood?—like he'd never seen it before.

Between the rounds Mr. Stevick bought Coke and orange crush for them and beer for himself—all the relatives were drinking beer, even the women—and wiped Enid's face and asked was she okay but forgot her at once, wiping his own face which was gleaming with sweat. He'd taken off his coat, undone his shirt collar. The air in the Armory was hot and close smelling of spilled beer, French fries, smoke—an oily smell too like lotion. "What did I tell you, Lyle!" one of the Pauleys shouted over. Mr. Stevick grinned and made a sign with his thumb and forefinger, shouting back, "What did I tell *you!*"

Most of the relatives had made bets on the fight but Mr. Stevick was close-mouthed, whether *he* had or not.

When the new round began Felix rushed his opponent at once. Gave him no rest and no chance to clinch or slow the fight down—you could see the man was tired now, breathing through his mouth. But Felix was hot, Felix looked as if he'd just begun, could fight all night, nerved up and exuberant and posturing for the crowd at whom he never looked. There was an exchange of blows—lightning-quick—then a powerful left uppercut of Felix's in a tight short arc and suddenly Watkins was back against the ropes as if trying to grab hold, awkwardly, clumsily, on his way down but he couldn't fall, unable to protect himself against the punches raining upon him, head, midriff, ribs, jaw, until at last Felix on his toes balanced just right struck him a left hook, lifting his chin from beneath, shaking free a rainbow of moisture, a flying skein of blood—and the man slipped free of the ropes, his knees gave way beneath him, and he was down, down on his face, the kind of fall that meant it was all over and the referee began his count methodical and final but Watkins wasn't going to get up—the fight was over and Felix Stevick was already dancing about the ring raising his gloves in triumph. And now the Armory did go wild.

Amid the din a bell was ringing signaling the end—like the bell on the altar during mass, Enid was thinking. You feel it go through you. You hear it without really hearing.

"My God."

Mr. Stevick, looking drawn, dazed, said the place was "claustrophobic" and he couldn't breathe, clamped his pipe between his teeth staring at the lights, then turned to lift Enid roughly in his arms. Let's get the hell out of here, he was muttering, but where was Warren? where was Lizzie?—and the goddamned aisle so crowded, so much jostling you couldn't get through, half the riffraff in Port Oriskany piled in here tonight. He should have known better, he said. Hannah was right.

The relatives wanted to go to Felix's dressing room right away to congratulate him but everybody else in the arena had the same idea and Mr. Stevick, belching beer in Enid's face, said first no, hadn't better, then changed his mind said why the hell not?—it's a celebration. But after many minutes of pushing and shoving in a crush of people in a poorly lit corridor that had the feel of being underground, they couldn't get through—was the way blocked? *was* this the right way?—Lyle Stevick, standing at his full proud height, his natty black fedora on his head, trying patiently to explain to a security policeman that he and his family were expected in Felix Stevick's dressing room; *he* was in fact Felix Stevick's older brother; and this man here—Felix's uncle Stefan Rossky, arguing drunkenly with someone at his side—was expected too. They were all expected. Impatient with the man's stupidity Mr. Stevick tried to push through but another policeman was blocking the way, and there was a mammoth bald man in the way too, the corridor was ringing with voices loud as in the arena and Warren held Enid's hand tight so she wouldn't get lost and even Lizzie was scared being shoved so roughly by people who didn't so much as glance at her to take note she *was* just a young girl. It didn't seem to matter that Mr. Stevick spoke loudly and with ironic authority like someone on the radio, the police were trying to clear the corridor using their billy clubs, shouting at everyone to leave by the nearest exit where the doors were open leading out into a back street—"Get moving! Get moving! Move right along there!" Warren picked up Enid, grunting, and managed to push his way through and Lizzie slipped along in their wake and finally Mr. Stevick appeared outside looking mortified, incredulous—he'd been poked in the chest by a cop wielding a billy club, he said, he and his children herded out into the street like cattle, *it was an insult he would never forgive.*

Somehow they got out of the crowd, shoving and brawling and some pretty foul language there, but Mr. Stevick gathered his children except for Geraldine who was riding with the Pauleys and Christ! he was furious, Jesus Christ! slamming into the car and the key in the ignition and out of the parking lot, driving up Niagara in wild bursts of speed, the children frightened of him and subdued, the way he liked them. He braked at the canal bridge, then sped up again so the posts rushed by, he wasn't drunk but was in that frame of mind, telling them the Stevicks had one and all been insulted that night at the very hour of Felix's triumph, they must remember to avoid such occasions in future, such gatherings of riffraff, like the Church tells you to avoid the occasion for sin. You can be sure, he said, thumping the steering wheel, that Felix had engineered it on purpose. Oh yes. Keeping his closest relatives away in preference to strangers, that Mercer woman and those Italian backers of his, Eyetalian wops, sons of bitches, scum of the earth; Felix was even beginning to look like them with his hair greased and slicked down, and how mean how nakedly barbaric his performance tonight, even if you concede boxing is a low vicious primitive sport did they note how Felix had continued to hit his opponent where he'd opened that cut? in the man's eyelid? tried to make it bleed worse? the eye already swollen and hemorrhaging inside no doubt and Felix jabbing at it nonstop, it served him right *he* got butted and took some rabbit punches too the referee didn't call, now he'd rise to number-four contender probably, that was how it worked, though the ranking was all crooked anyway as everybody knows, a matter of deals and manipulation and *maybe Watkins had even thrown the fight* if the Mattiuzzios got to him, but the newspapers would never pick up on *that* possibility, oh no, it'd be a cold day in hell when that happened. So in the morning paper front-page photos of "Felix the Cat" and more talk about Port Oriskany having a world champion sometime soon, pundits comparing their hometown boy to Graziano and Zale and Robinson enough to make you puke, frankly—all it suggests is that this part of the state hasn't anything worthwhile and decent to be proud about. "Felix the Cat"!—Jesus!—and Felix was so immature so vain believing the crap everybody shoveled at him, the sportswriters with their hyperbole and hysteria comparing him to Billy Conn because he was good-looking and "classy" and most of all white but what was so classy about his performance tonight?—a lot of posturing and showboating for the crowd. You could see Watkins had landed some good solid body blows early on and Felix would be feeling them for days, big welts and bruises and that cut in his forehead, he'd been so vain about his face even taunted an opponent once in an amateur tournament, offering him his chin, saying, C'mon fight, that was the kind of arrogance in him he'd have to pay for one of these days, and pay for with his blood—just wait and see.

Well he didn't know, Felix didn't, what boxing was really about 'cause none of them did, too much adulation and the women hot for them and seeing your picture in the paper all the time like that, it gave you erroneous ideas about the universe—obviously. But *he* knew. Lyle Stevick knew. In his student days—"Such as they were!"—he'd studied the great philosophers, such men as Hobbes and Schopenhauer who saw the world clearly and without illusion, there was Schopenhauer saying we are all in the grip of the blind Will, the Will of nature which their pious Uncle Domenic would never acknowledge, seeing the Will as God—*the Will as God!* a sorry notion—always demonstrating the fact he didn't listen to Lyle's logic, just shut his mind down as they'd been trained in the seminary, hear no evil see no evil say no evil, oh no. Self-righteous prigs in their priest's costumes the skirts the turned-around collar so perfectly white and starched, knowing the faithful will swallow down their most imbecilic and self-serving pronouncements, out of the pulpit *ex officio* they had the word of God knowing the faithful would obey out of fear and ignorance and desperate for something to believe, willing to ruin their lives by marrying too young, willing to mortgage their souls having children too soon, "as many as God sends," but you didn't see people like Felix Stevick eager to marry, selfish bastard, immoral and scandalous, and his own mother who wasn't exactly a saint had washed her hands of him, couldn't control him—just as well he's a boxer, he'll get his head broken one day soon, and that's that, like poor old Joe Louis, but Felix the Cat won't wind up in *that* company no matter how many deals are made. Christ, he'd thought Watkins might be dying the way he couldn't move and they were passing ammonia under his nose poor bastard, but he himself Lyle Stevick was at fault for bringing his children to such a place, exposing them to such a spectacle, but it would never happen again *never again* no matter if Felix fights for the middleweight title, no matter if he wins the title—which he won't, Graziano will murder him, now *there's* a real gutter fighter, Eyetalian making no bones about not knowing how to box, just slug—and they certainly weren't going to De Marra's tonight—Freddy De Marra, another greasy wop—he wouldn't give Felix the satisfaction of turning him and his family away twice in one night, consider the subject closed.

Mr. Stevick braked the car to a jolting stop by the Ferry Street underpass, there was the Canal House Tavern close by and he'd be, he said, only ten minutes, fifteen at the most, they could entertain themselves, couldn't they, listening to the radio but don't for Christ's sweet sake run the battery down or he'd warm their asses, and they'd better keep the car doors locked too, considering the neighborhood.

And if anybody comes by, any drunk for instance prowling around or looking in the car windows, just blow on the horn and keep on blowing and Daddy will be out at once.

Told the frightened children, Lizzie you take care of Enid, and Warren you take care of your sisters, and Daddy will be right back. Got it?

He was gone more than an hour but by then Enid was asleep, drifted off to sleep in the back seat of the car while Lizzie and Warren fiddled with the radio dial and talked about the fight, falling asleep in jerky patches like steps going down, like the crumbling cement steps going down into the cellar back of the house where a stale dark odor rose. She twitched and woke, couldn't remember where she was or why, opening her eyes wide hearing the radio, or Lizzie's loud voice; maybe she was getting sick again, burning with fever, and Momma would be upset—Enid had had measles once and a temperature of 104 degrees and Momma was angry at first, then, kneeling by Enid's bed, she whispered *Hail Mary full of grace* and begged the Virgin to spare her baby, thinking Enid was asleep and couldn't hear—and now it seemed Enid was getting sick again, seeing lights falling from the sky startling and blinding, the bell ringing, her uncle's body exposed when he took off the white robe, so much of it covered in dark hair like an animal, his chest, his thighs and legs, even part of his back, his muscular arms; then the boxers came at each other as if they'd been pushed from behind looking only at each other, seeing nothing else, and the sound of the gloves hitting flesh was a sound she couldn't stand to hear though hadn't Daddy told her the boxers weren't like her? But she could taste the trickle of blood, the back of her tongue was coated with something slimy and red, she couldn't swallow, she was gagging, suddenly wide awake, and Lizzie was leaning over the seat saying Oh God you're not going to be sick are you? if you are open the door!— then she was all right and sleeping again, the side of her head on the prickly arm rest and again the lights falling through the air and again the men's gloves, the flying skein of blood like a streamer, confetti—a man in a white silk robe trimmed in gold his face cross-hatched with blood whom she didn't know and who didn't know her.

3

Once there was Enid Maria and there was Angel-face but Enid Maria knew very little about Angel-face while Angel-face knew everything about Enid Maria. Sometimes for the sheer hell of it Angel-face scrambled Enid Maria's bureau drawers to confuse her, mislaid her homework to terrify her, lost her library books so she'd have to pay a fine; she even, sometimes, punished Enid Maria by losing her lunch money—*you* can do without, *you* don't deserve to eat. Enid understood it was dangerous to walk along a busy street in Angel-face's company because Angel-face might decide suddenly, whimsically, to cross the street—smiling and doing any damn thing she pleased. And she could get away with it!

The "good" girl, the honor student at De Witt Clinton Junior High, was Enid Maria Stevick, named for her father's mother who had died many years ago. (A good woman, Mr. Stevick would say, sighing—a martyr.) Enid Maria: it *was* a pretty name. The other girl, Angel-face, was Enid too but sly wriggly hot-skinned treacherous, with eyes like delicious chocolate candies and an innocent watchful expression, delicate-boned as a bird (hadn't some old fool said, eyeing her?) and sneaky. The other girls called her Honeybunch, Dolly, Sweetheart, Kitten, but Angel-face they decided suited her best.

Bring Angel-face along, they suggested to Lizzie.

Send Angel-face in first, they said, giggling—"*She* can get away with murder."

Even if she wasn't well Enid Maria rarely missed a day of school—it was a matter of pride. Each year elected secretary of her class and each report card A's and A+'s and didn't the teachers adore her!—sweet-faced and shy, one of the *reliable* students. Sundays and Holy Days of Obligation she attended mass at St. James's and took communion with the Stevicks, careful to allow the communion wafer to melt on her tongue. She went to confession Friday afternoons, kneeling in the dark that was like a child's hiding place, murmuring breathy little sins that were mainly just words appropriated from the prayer book with the opalescent cover her Uncle Domenic had given her—there were lists of venial and mortal sins in the back for the scrupulous sinner to scan. Enid said her acts of contrition as rapidly as she could, said the rosary too as rapidly as she could, drawing the cheap plastic beads through her fingers while Angel-face derisive and bored prowled the church staring rudely at worshipers. All Angel-face did was wait for the ceremony to end. The bell's ringing as the Eucharist was lifted reminded Enid of the Armory and of her Uncle Felix but this bell was more delicate, tremulous, a sweet chiming sound like music, no reason for Enid to hide her eyes or stiffen herself against shock.

Oh shit, Angel-face said, yawning, grinning—when is this going to *end?*

Now that Geraldine was married to Neal O'Banan and living on the West Side, Enid Maria was Momma's favorite when Momma had a favorite. She was surely Daddy's favorite—though he liked to tease Lizzie, razz her he called it, and between him and Warren there was a special understanding, a seriousness he maybe didn't have with his daughters. At mealtimes he'd question Warren about his studies as if trying to trip Warren up on facts, dates; he'd prod Warren into talking—"conquering" his stammer. But most of the time Lyle Stevick didn't take much notice of his children because his mind was elsewhere. He worked, as he said, long hours at the store. Day in, day out. Only the Sabbath as a respite.

Mr. Stevick owned a furniture store—secondhand or "bargain" furniture mainly. He was caught up in worries about paying his rent and customers who tried to return items they'd damaged, not to mention customers who tried to sell him stolen goods. He was always feuding with his landlord, a German—"No secret he's a Nazi." The old building he rented on Lock Street was a constant heartache to him—rotting shingles and unreliable furnace, the damned cellar that flooded with every heavy rainstorm, the termites, mice, rats. Each Sunday he recruited Enid to help him scan the business-rental ads in the *News Transcript*—how he'd love to tell that fat Kraut he wasn't renewing his lease—but of course it wasn't that easy.

When Mr. Stevick wasn't tearing his hair out as he said over the business he was civic-minded: considered it the duty of every citizen to keep a constant eye on the men in government, federal, state, county, "Those leeches who'd bleed us all white if they could." It was his habit to write letters frequently to the *Transcript* and the *Evening Herald* on an old Remington office machine he kept at the store.

Meticulously revised, buttressed with facts, figures, statistics, quotations (Samuel Johnson, George Bernard Shaw, Mark Twain were favorites), Lyle Stevick's letters were models of their genre and his friends and kin wondered why one of the papers didn't give him his own column on the editorial page. How scathing his wit, how blistering his logic!—denouncing the Oriskany County Board of Supervisors, City Hall, the U.S. Internal Revenue, the failure of the Republican-controlled Eightieth Congress to "cope with inflation," the "political cynicism" of Harry Truman's installation of loyalty oaths for government employees—"Before we know it the U.S. will be copying the U.S.S.R." When Truman's Attorney General issued a public statement to the effect that there were Communists everywhere—in factories offices butcher shops on street corners even in private business—*and each carried in himself the germs of death for America,* Lyle Stevick composed his most brilliant letter but neither the *Transcript* nor the *Herald* would publish it. Mrs. Stevick strongly disapproved of his mailing it—what if he got arrested? what then?

And Enid worried he *would* get arrested: storm troopers banging on the door as in a war movie and her daddy carried away.

Angel-face avoided Daddy, guessing he wouldn't much like *her*. But Enid Maria perched on his knee, he'd read to her from his stack of books, reminisce about his boyhood and the days of Mayor Stevick before the war. Lizzie was jealous—Mr. Stevick and Lizzie "grated on each other's nerves" as he said—and he criticized Warren for "getting ahead of himself" (whatever exactly that meant, Warren didn't know). When Geraldine dropped by the house big-bellied in her maternity clothes he'd drift off into the alley, smoking his pipe, leaving her and her mother to talk—he'd stop for a drink at one or another of his taverns and wouldn't return for hours. But he adored Enid Maria. How he adored Enid Maria! When she brought home her report card he'd make a show of examining it carefully line by line, praising his little sweetheart but asking aloud in a Jimmy Durante voice of what earthly use would brains in such a pretty little girl *be*.

4

"Think of it as a game," Lizzie said.

"And if you're caught—remember you're alone," Lizzie warned.

"Just act your own sweet self, Angel-face," Nelia said, squeezing Enid's wrist, "and nobody's going to think nothing."

That was the season pop-it beads were all the rage, you made necklaces and bracelets short or long as you wanted, a single strand or a half-dozen loops. Lizzie had pearly pink beads and frosted white, now she wanted black, jet black, and the dangling earrings to go with them, a nice black belt too, one of those wide shiny elastic belts that pinch your waist in so you can hardly breathe but it looks damn good, hips and breasts starkly defined. In a gold filigree frame on the girls' bureau was a sexy black-and-white photograph of Rita Hayworth—*To Lizzie, love, Rita!* in Rita Hayworth's own signature—with luscious wet pouting lips, sleepy seductive eyes, hair all frizzed crimped curled, the ends upturned, oh she was gorgeous wasn't she? Lizzie just wanted the Christ to *be* her but sort of herself too at the same time. Rita Hayworth was wearing black pearls it looked like, a half-dozen strands rippling over her big breasts straining tight in a silver lamé blouse. Oh shit, said Lizzie, laughing, if I could look like *that!* her husky breathy voice trailing off into silence.

And she wanted some decent perfume, she said. She didn't like Midnight Sin in the milky blue bottle, it smelled too sharp; Daddy sniffed the air pretending to be a hyena or something, saying Who stinks in here? his idea of a joke. Lizzie was going to pour it down the toilet.

In the gang there were: Lizzie Stevick and Nelia Pancoe and Rose Ann Esposito, who was Jerry Esposito's younger sister—Jerry had taken Lizzie out a few times to the movies, roller-skating; he was older, seventeen or eighteen, he'd spent six months at the juvenile facility at Red Bank for car theft, now Lizzie never saw him any more, God damn him. And sometimes their cousin Dinah Pauley came along, poor fat Dinah who got out of breath so easily. And sometimes Lizzie's sister Enid came along, Enid who was Angel-face, looking so sweet, shy, scared—like butter wouldn't melt in her mouth, Nelia Pancoe said, in her hillbilly drawl that always seemed to mean more than it really did.

Downtown on Main Street after school, the most strategic time was just before five when the stores were crowded the salesclerks tired and ready to end their shifts, eyes glazed with fatigue looking right at you sometimes not seeing a thing: Sibley's, Montgomery Ward's, Kresge's, Woolworth's, Grant's, the big bright fluorescent-lit Rexall drugstore on Niagara, and Port O'Call Fashions, the discount Norban's on Union Street. They drifted in together in twos and threes, the plan was to meet twenty minutes later in the women's restroom at the Greyhound bus station a few blocks away. Remember to act natural, Lizzie said in a low urgent voice. The store detectives were trained to watch kids who acted "suspicious," which meant any Negro kids who came in without their mothers; they couldn't watch everybody at once. If worse came to worst, Lizzie told Enid, just drop what you have on the counter and walk away fast; don't run, just walk away fast, think of it as a game.

Enid would push through the doors, her eyes misted over in excitement, her throat tight with the need to keep from laughing, always the interiors were warm, busy, bright-dazzling like a carnival. Now it will happen, she told herself, now it begins and can't be stopped: like the undertow at Shoal Lake. Like making love, she thought—you let a man or a boy begin then he wouldn't stop, maybe couldn't stop—so Lizzie said—until it was over.

And dying would be like this too, the only hard part was at the beginning when you made your decision.

A few years ago when she never meant to steal, wouldn't have thought of stealing (not Enid Maria, not *her*), she walked off by accident with a book from out of a bin of 99-cent books in Kresge's, just by accident; she had set down her schoolbooks so she could browse, the books in the bin were all jumbled together, had torn cellophane wrappers, they were by writers of whom she'd never heard, mystery novels mainly, still she wasted ten minutes or so browsing through them looking for something she might like. As in the library, looking for a book to open, leaf through, stop and read a line at random the way some people did with the Bible, words to change your life maybe, though they never did. So Enid looked through the books for a while then drifted away, then out on the street she discovered she had picked up one of the books along with her own schoolbooks, which meant she'd *stolen,* she could be *arrested!* She ran back to Kresge's to return the book; terrified, she tried to explain to a salesgirl what had happened, she'd done it by mistake she hadn't meant it, and the girl took the book from her and tossed it into the bin with the others, no more ceremony than that. Stealing by accident had frightened Enid—she thought of a world cracking open, fracturing along invisible fault lines where you did things you didn't intend and learned of them only afterward when it was too late. Stealing on purpose was different.

Lizzie and Nelia strolled away swaggering, big cheerful girls with quick eyes, red lips, an air of nerved-up play. It was part of the game that they would snub Enid if she approached them now, in the stores they just didn't *know* her. So she made her slow sly way, ignoring them too. In Grant's in Rexall Drugs in Sibley's with the lady shoppers in the big bright Norban's where recorded music was piped in overhead she usually carried Lizzie's old fake-leather shoulder bag into which items might be easily slipped, she wore Lizzie's old maroon corduroy jacket with the spacious pockets, Angel-face on the prowl. And if she was caught by a store detective, what then? and if the other girls ran off and left her behind, what then? These were chances she must take. Now it begins, she told herself, now it can't be stopped.

Over the weeks the older girls marveled at her, Lizzie declared herself impressed, among her trophies were a pair of white plastic harlequin sunglasses a tube of pink lip gloss a key chain with a rabbit's foot gold hoop earrings pearl earrings rhinestone cluster earrings a simulated red leather wallet a small purse-sized plastic hairbrush several pairs of stockings a pair of good kidskin gloves she gave to her mother (saying she found them on the street) some silver lead pencils some tiny glass animals for the bureau in her and Lizzie's room. Enid's fingers moved of their own volition, it seemed, while her heart beat in erratic flutters. But this was Angel-face who couldn't be stopped!

Once in Sibley's Enid lingered by herself after the other girls had left, moving along the aisles like a sleepwalker, drifting by the costume jewelry counter, pretty gold chains gold earrings gold bracelets inlaid with glass jewels, a treasure bin of pop-it beads of all colors, there they were. The salesclerk asked could she be of any service and Enid Maria politely sweetly said No thank you she was just looking, her silky chestnut hair was brushed back neatly from her face and secured with silver barrettes, she wore a white blouse with a clean collar and a green cableknit sweater Mrs. Stevick had knitted, Angel-face in her best disguise. Covertly through her lashes she watched a salesclerk waiting on a customer, her vision was sharp, all her senses sharp, it was like pushing through a time warp as Mr. Stevick might say, finding yourself in another galaxy! Her fingers were icy, stiff, maybe she was trembling, still her hand snaked out it was too late no it wasn't too late but her fingers closed over the beads now suddenly it *was* too late she was dropping them in the shoulder bag and someone called out sharply across the aisle, "You! Miss!"—but Enid was already walking away, quick and unhesitating Enid was walking away, her heart rocked like a pendulum walking her away her lips were drawn tight against her teeth, she was thinking calmly, Now it begins, now it begins; they were calling after her, "You there, miss—you in the green sweater!" and though she believed afterward she had not panicked, nonetheless she pushed clumsily past two women shoppers entering the store and then she was out on the street and then she was running in the harsh cold air, she knew to grip the shoulder bag tight against her ribs to keep it from swinging loose, she knew to run close like a rat against the buildings, then to turn into the alley between Grant's and Scanlon's Shoes; she was running, she was running breathless and laughing, oh sweet Jesus, Angel-face could run forever she would live forever nobody dared touch her.

In the smelly unventilated women's room at the Greyhound terminal they were waiting, a little worried, Enid was ten minutes late at least; then she rushed in panting, giggling, her eyelashes beaded with moisture, her face sickly white, and Lizzie grabbed hold of her half angry asking, Was she all right, did something go wrong?—and still giggling, breathless, she opened the bag so that Lizzie could see the gleaming black coil of beads. And Lizzie tossed away her cigarette into the sink to hug Enid, she was so relieved just delighted, Christ they'd all been worried! Now the others crowded around, Nelia and Dinah and Rose Ann, all nerved up, high, shrieking with laughter, crowding around sweet Enid Maria with her loot.

Nelia stopped to kiss Enid almost on the lips, left a smear of bright lipstick. *"You're* the damnedest cutest thing," she said in her sly hillbilly drawl.

Mrs. Stevick was in the hospital for fifteen days, she'd had her gallbladder removed; now she had only to get back her strength, lying there in the high cranked-up hospital bed listening to one of her radio programs or reading a magazine—*Woman's Day, Coronet, Catholic Home Messenger, Saturday Evening Post.* Her doctor said she was coming along well though she had lost a good deal of blood during the surgery. There were inky bruises around her eyes, tight lines bracketing her mouth, Enid saw for the first time how her hair was fading to

gray, to no color at all. She looked like a stranger there in the white
nightgown in the high white bed smelling like nothing of the house
at 118 East Clinton, but the surprise for the family was how well she
liked the hospital. She didn't have to do a thing hardly lift a finger for
two weeks, she said wonderingly—it wasn't like coming to the hospital to have a baby!

Mr. Stevick visited her once a day though hospitals made him
nervous, he said—he'd done volunteer orderly work in this very
hospital, St. Joseph's, during the war but still it made him nervous, he
hated the smells in particular. Maybe he just knew too much! Mrs.
Stevick had a fair number of visitors but didn't seem to mind being
alone. When Enid came to visit her after school she was always listening to *Ma Perkins* on the radio; then came *Stella Dallas,* so her time
was occupied.

Enid gave her mother a get-well card and a bottle of cologne—
Eau de toilette du bois—from the Rexall store. It was part of Angel-face's
loot: strange to see it being turned, examined, in Mrs. Stevick's fingers
as if she *did* suspect. Mrs. Stevick thanked her, even dabbed some of
the cologne on her wrist, delicately beneath her jaw, a girl's half-shy
gesture long unpracticed. Before Enid left she said again in a wondering half-reproachful voice how nice it was just to be alone sometimes,
just to rest. She hadn't known she was so tired.

Time for Angel-face's ears to be pierced, the girls said. Specially since
she got all these nice earrings.

They did it one night at the Pancoes' when both Nelia's parents
were out. Enid wasn't going to mind the pain but she worried about
the size of the needle: what if Lizzie's hand slipped?

Lizzie said her hand wasn't going to slip. Just sit still.

The radio was turned up high, the Fontane Sisters, then Nat King
Cole, "Mona Lisa," then Frankie Laine's "Mule Train" which Enid
couldn't stand. They sat Enid at the kitchen table, draped a towel over
her shoulders; the faster you do it the less it hurts, Nelia said practically. She scalded a long darning needle in the flame of a match, then
Lizzie took it from her. Shouldn't they have iodine or something for
the germs? Nelia said, so she went off looking for iodine. Now the
radio was playing "If I Knew You Were Coming I'd've Baked a
Cake"—the happiest song of all.

The Pancoes lived in a first-floor apartment in the Decker project,
a few blocks north of East Clinton. The project covered a full city

block, asphalt-sided buildings like barracks, a little beaten-down green space meant to be a park, the rest of the space between the buildings paved in concrete. The project had been subsidized primarily for veterans—Mr. Pancoe had been in the navy—and many of its tenants were Italians, Hunkies, or hillbillies like the Pancoes from West Virginia, people with five or six or seven or even more children in their families. There were six children in the Pancoe family counting Nelia, the oldest at fourteen. She was a rawboned girl with a broad handsome ruddy face, big muscular haunches, a rope of dirty-blond hair in a loose braid falling down her back. She was moody and dangerous at school, she got in fights, she'd failed eighth grade, but with her friends she was good-natured, lots of fun. She and Lizzie were best friends, she had some good friends like Rose Ann, Dinah, but Enid she liked to say was her "heart." She'd tried to teach Enid to dance to radio music one day but she danced too close and too tight, Enid got nervous; another time she asked Enid would she like to practice kissing: "I'll be the man," she said, showing her gums, grinning like it was half a joke, "any old man you want!" Enid pushed her away trying to make her own joke: "I don't kiss *funny*," she said.

Lizzie was having trouble getting the needle through Enid's earlobe, maybe the damn thing wasn't sharp enough. Nelia wiped away the blood. Enid sat curiously still not shrinking from the pain but moving into it, concentrating on it, her eyes closed, her eyelids quivering; she thought of kneeling at the communion rail taking the communion host on her tongue in a state of mortal sin, she thought of Hell and of pain promised for eternity but what *was* eternity? Pain was here, pain was now. You felt it in the flesh and it was you.

She was thinking of Warren at boot camp in Fort Rawling, New Jersey. She missed him more than she'd expected—didn't after all miss Geraldine much. In his last letter he told them he'd probably be sent to an army base in Japan and then to Korea: President Truman had pledged American arms to South Korea which meant American soldiers "which means Private First Class Stevick." It seemed that the good people of South Korea were being threatened by a Communist invasion from the north and a "line had to be drawn" in Asia as it had been drawn in Europe—that was the only thing the Russians understood. So Warren said; so Warren was told. Before he'd left for New Jersey, Enid had stared at him thinking him strange already—changed—his look brisk and efficient, *assured*—not like Warren Stevick at all. Enid asked wasn't he afraid, wasn't he worried something might happen to him if they sent him to the other side of the earth, but Warren cut her off, saying quickly no of course not.

He didn't have to think was he afraid or not, he just followed orders. Did as he was told.

Enid thought of the man her Uncle Felix had knocked out at the Armory—what sort of pain was *that?* She'd seen his face contorted, blood pouring from his eye, he'd been hurt no matter what her father said. And then there was Felix himself so badly injured in his last fight—twenty-eight stitches in his forehead, hospitalized for a brain concussion—he'd quit boxing forever. First one man was hurt, then the other.

Lucky the fool wasn't killed, Mr. Stevick said.

When both Enid's ears were pierced the girls held cotton batting against the tiny holes to soak up the blood. Lizzie said contritely she should have numbed Enid's ears with ice cubes first—she'd forgotten. "Oh, fine," said Enid. "Thanks a lot." Lizzie then dabbed her ears with iodine and rather clumsily worked in gold studs, breathing warm against Enid's face; then when it was over Lizzie and Nelia kissed her, saying she was a brave little Angel-face sitting there like nothing was happening. Like she wasn't even there at all.

You were supposed to turn the little studs twice a day which of course Enid did, Enid Maria was always scrupulous about such duties, a dozen times a day she examined herself in one or another mirror impressed with that flash of gold in her ears—so glamorous, so *adult*—which was why men sometimes glanced at her in the street, on the bus, sometimes stared rudely at her without knowing what they did. Embarrassed, her face warm, Enid looked carefully away pretending she didn't see but she liked it, oh yes she liked it and she'd learn to like it a lot more, Angel-face promised.

As soon as her ears healed she'd be able to wear real earrings like the older girls but why weren't her ears healing?—it was past the time. Both earlobes ached, particularly the left, even the left side of Enid's neck sometimes, she lay awake unable to sleep because of the pain, too proud to wake Lizzie up and tell her, too stubborn; she knew she deserved this she knew she deserved whatever happened whatever beat quietly in her blood, and finally her entire head ached and there were shadows under her eyes and her English teacher Mrs. Stutzman asked her what was wrong, was she in pain? was she ill?—then seeing her inflamed ears sent her to the school nurse who removed the studs—*not* gold, the nurse said—and treated the wounds with io-dine. Who did this to you? the nurse asked. Does your mother know about it?

Gradually the swellings went down, the tiny holes healed over until they were hardly more than pinpricks in the flesh. Enid examined them in the mirror, disappointed, pinching to feel some sensation—her earlobes were numb now. Or so it seemed.

5

"This is the happiest day of my life."

The bride's eyes brimming with tears like water in a shallow container the slightest agitation would spill. Yards of white shiny satin, *so* white—and a tulle veil (her Grandmother Rossky's)—tiny pearl buttons at the nape of the neck and on the sleeves—a snug-fitting bodice but the stomach and hips conspicuously looser.

Like Gerry Stevick, they whispered. *You* know.

How many months? Two, three—

Oh, at *least.*

But Annemarie Pauley on her wedding day was shiny-faced, defiant, the prettiest Enid had ever seen her and surely the happiest: standing on the steps preparing to toss her bridal bouquet as her cousins and girlfriends clamored "Here! over here! *me!*" and she was laughing and at last the tears did spill over, running swiftly down her powdered cheeks.

The fragrant white bouquet—carnations, tiny tight rosebuds—sailed out over their heads but none of the girls caught it, instead to everyone's surprise (and embarrassment, disappointment) poor dull-witted Albert Rossky managed to snatch it out of the air with a look of childish glee. What could you do? Albert was Annemarie's cousin, thirty-nine years old with the mind of a ten-year-old, annoying but harmless.

Lizzie growled in Enid's ear, "Shit. She said she'd throw it to *me.*"

* * *

They were drinking a rowdy toast to the bride. To the groom. To the parents of the bride and to the parents of the groom. The champagne tasted, Enid thought, of flowers, sunshine—she'd never tasted anything like it.

A few tentative swallows and already she was laughing. It was a day *for* laughing.

They were drinking a toast to the bride's Grandmother Rossky, her bluish hair so tight-permed the scalp looked pinched, next the groom's grandmother, then the bride's grandfather, then the groom's grandfather, an elderly man with an alert smiling toad's face—the Zieglers were a curious lot, not so friendly at first as if thinking maybe their boy was marrying beneath him but by degrees Lyle Stevick was warming them up, Lyle Stevick the man to count on in such situations—and the table erupted in laughter at a witticism of the old man's Enid didn't hear. Next a toast to Private First Class Warren Stevick aged eighteen years ten months who was being shipped overseas October first and who would celebrate his nineteenth birthday somewhere in Korea—as Mr. Stevick informed them to Warren's acute embarrassment—and Warren was urged to his feet, blushing, thanking them for the tribute, trying to respond to the noisy gaiety of the moment but at a loss for the right thing to say, and Enid dug her fingernails into her palms hoping he wouldn't stammer. He didn't stammer but he sat down abruptly in the midst of a sentence, forgetting to take a ritual sip of champagne and the table applauded anyway, he *did* look handsome in his dress uniform, his hair cut short and shaved up the back of the skull, his posture stiff, self-conscious, a posture that belonged to the U.S. Army and not to him, and relatives who hadn't seen Lyle's boy for a while were frankly astonished at the change—he'd lost twenty pounds at Fort Rawling, his shoulders his upper arms even his neck looked thicker, stronger. You almost wouldn't think it was the same boy, would you, one of the aunts said, marveling, and Enid didn't know whether to feel annoyed or proud.

Now Mr. Stevick made a toast to the memory of his nephew Joe Pauley who had died in the service of his country defending the American flag along with countless thousands of other American boys, Joe Pauley would never, he said, be forgotten by those who loved him, and Mr. Stevick's eyes shone with tears but he was smiling his broad white salesman's smile so Enid knew it was all right: he was in control. Everyone joined in the toast even the groom's people who had no idea who Joe was, only that Joe was dead, and Mr. Stevick spoke passionately of the mysteries of history and fate and the inscrutable ways of Our Lord, and Lillian Pauley, Joe's mother, crushed a paper napkin to her mouth, and Annemarie at the head of the table looked as if she was about to cry, and silly Dinah who'd had too much champagne, and there was the shock of Frank Pauley, Joe's father, swerving to his feet so moved he had to go to Lyle Stevick to shake his hand—or was he going to embrace him?—both men big, broad-shouldered, going to fat and ruddy-skinned as if they'd been too long in the sun. Enid felt her eyes sting with tears like the tears that spilled out sometimes during a movie, taking her unawares—quick tears that came and went but left her shaken. She was too young to remember her cousin Joe but they'd been told of him countless times, he'd died so young in a Japanese prisoner-of-war camp on the far side of the world—Pampanga Province, but Warren hadn't been able to find it on the map. The nicest kid you'd ever want to meet, Mr. Stevick always said, that's the hell of it. There was wayward family bitterness of a kind impossible to articulate over the fact that Joe, who'd been such a sweet-natured boy, had died and Felix Stevick, who was Joe's uncle even though he was Joe's exact age, *had* come back—hadn't been taken prisoner, or much hurt.

Leave it to Daddy to get half the table crying, Enid thought, casting a look in Warren's direction which he didn't intercept, except of course Momma sitting stiff and embarrassed staring at the food on her plate, a big chunk of wedding cake, saffron baba covered in heavy whipped cream, she had at least laid down her fork when the toasts began but wouldn't drink her champagne—thinking her husband was making a drunken fool of himself and how could he be stopped? Enid watched her mother resentfully. Why was she so cold!—so stubborn! She was a fleshy woman, not fat, with an oddly smooth unlined face, fifty years old (Enid calculated) and not unattractive; had a flair for sewing but no eye at all for making herself up the way the other women did, a little lipstick at least wouldn't hurt, a little rouge like Aunt Lillian—Lizzie had begged her, "Just today, Momma," but no: not Hannah Stevick. It was a fixed idea in Mrs. Stevick's mind too that her husband's family disliked her, used every opportunity they could to snub her, make her feel like dirt because she was the daughter of country people outside Olcottsport and the Stevicks could claim some distinction by way of old Karl Stevick—"that terrible old man" as Mrs. Stevick referred to him when Mr. Stevick wasn't around. The cruelest story was that Hannah had tricked Lyle into marrying her when he'd really been in love with another girl. (And you know what "tricked" means.)

Enid shivered with repugnance, thinking of such things. It was a distasteful notion—her middle-aged parents once young enough for *love*.

First the solemn high nuptial mass at St. Anne's, then the wedding brunch at the Pauleys', then the enormous reception at the Knights of Columbus hall on South Main Street—more people than Enid had ever seen together at a private social event, someone said there must be two hundred guests, a tent striped like a candy cane in the back and a five-piece band playing fox trots, waltzes, polkas all afternoon like something in a movie. A platform had even been set on the lawn for dancers should they want to dance in the hazy mid-September heat.

Enid had been too young to be caught up in Geraldine's wedding but *this*—this was something very different. Dinah's sister Annemarie marrying a boy named Ziegler and the Pauleys had talked about nothing else for weeks, or was it months: Annemarie's wedding dress, Annemarie's bridesmaids and their dresses, Annemarie's wedding gifts, Annemarie's honeymoon, and so on and so forth. Dinah spoke so excitedly you'd have thought *she* was the bride.

(Maybe to puncture her cousin's self-importance or maybe just out of curiosity Lizzie asked if Annemarie and her boyfriend "had to get married"—and Dinah stiffened and said she guessed that wasn't any of Lizzie's business and Lizzie shot right back saying, Don't get your back up, Dinah, look, everybody knows Gerry had to marry Neal O'Banan *she'd been three months pregnant if a day* and look how happy they were now, the new baby and all. And Enid protested, saying that Gerry had *wanted* to get married. And Lizzie said scornfully, That's what *I* said, stupid.)

That morning Lizzie fixed Enid's hair as she'd promised, a glamorous upswept style copied from Debra Paget in *Screen World*—French twist, bangs, curls, ringlets. Handing Enid the mirror she said, "How's that, Angel-face?" and Enid regarded herself with—surprise. And pleasure.

In the movies female beauty meant power, its locus was the face, the body—Enid stared at her reflection in the mirror and wondered had she a chance.

And her dress—a hand-me-down of Geraldine's but Mrs. Stevick had altered it, blue glazed cotton with a layer of gauze over the skirt, wide belt with a cloth-covered buckle, bodice richly embroidered in white and dark blue flowers that seemed to spring toward the eye as if they were real. Enid wouldn't have wanted to admit how she loved the dress, what hope she had for it, she thanked Momma with tears in her eyes and Momma seemed embarrassed, even annoyed, that *was* Momma's way—couldn't take gratitude or a compliment head on. People kept telling Mrs. Stevick she sewed so well she could be a professional dressmaker—"seamstress" was another word, foreign to Mrs. Stevick's ear—but she merely laughed, irritated and confused by the suggestion. Women didn't work unless they had to. The only woman with a job among all the relatives was Hannah's older sister, Ingrid, who was a widow and hadn't any choice—fifteen years now at Carleton Brothers on her feet eight hours a day.

Even Angel-face was impressed by the wedding ceremony. At first. The stately bridal music, the crimson carpet laid down like something for royalty, the many bouquets of flowers on the altar, Annemarie in her beautiful long full-skirted white dress walking up the aisle on Mr. Pauley's arm slow and dignified and her face shining with pleasure—all brides are beautiful, Mr. Stevick had said, and maybe it was true. And even Frank Pauley in a suit he'd bought, not rented, for the occasion; Uncle Frank you'd expect to burst into laughter in the presence of certain of his buddies—dressed like he was, with even a white carnation in his buttonhole.

There was some envy in the family regarding Annemarie's groom, the young man she'd "caught"—a boy in his mid-twenties who was the only son of the owner of Ziegler's (Restaurant & Bowling Alley) on Stubb Boulevard.

By degrees Enid's interest began to ebb, her thoughts began to drift, there was Angel-face yawning and moving restlessly around the church, Angel-face scarcely listening to the priest's womanish high-pitched Latin and the altar boys' murmured responses. Not intimidated by the vaulted ceiling, the solemn bell-ringing, the smell of incense. What had it to do with *her?* was invariably Angel-face's question, and a reasonable question it was, Enid acknowledged, as she knelt on a cushionless wooden bench, a rosary threaded through her fingers meant to link her to—whatever it was meant to link her to. God, maybe. Other people. Enid's own self, her soul.

Years ago Enid's Uncle Domenic the priest had catechized her smilingly as if bringing her good news. Who made the world? he'd ask and Enid knew to say God made the world. And why did He make the world? Uncle Domenic asked. And why did He make man? And why did He make *you?* His black costume his perfectly creased black trousers his starched white collar and always he smelled faintly of shaving lotion. Mr. Stevick called his brother "Father" as a joke, teased him about certain lady parishioners over in Foxboro and about putting on weight around the middle—"But then I guess God allows *some* indulgences, right?" Uncle Domenic laughed politely, a thin hissing sound.

It was known that every morning of his life since Karl Stevick's death Domenic Stevick had said a mass for his father's soul but to what purpose? Enid wondered. The Church taught that suicides are absolutely damned—in Hell, not in purgatory. Hell's the place you never get out of.

Enid was twelve and a half years old now, not so easily duped.

The cavernous old church vibrated with sound, wave upon wave of organ music, chords like hammer blows. Always at mass Enid drifted with the music, flexing her fingers as if she were the one who made it: an Enid Stevick no one knew, up there in the choir loft, hidden from the congregation. But when the music came to an end— the stops were always abrupt, jarring, it was as if a platform of a kind had collapsed, or the lights in a darkened theater were switched rudely on—the harsh but wonderful music silenced and now, how disappointing! how banal! ordinary human sound resumed. So Angel-face smirked at the priest's singsong voice, was not impressed by his fancy vestments, the swinging of the chalice, the power of the Eucharist. Angel-face prowling the church feverish and impatient staring at the other worshipers' faces asking *Why, how, what is it, where?*

And there was Felix Stevick whom no one had seen in months and some had not seen in years suddenly making an appearance at the Knights of Columbus—double-parking his new Studebaker convertible out front as if he didn't plan to stay long. The car was a brand-new '51 model metallic gray with maroon trim and a dazzling amount of chrome and Felix himself was looking good, not at all shamefaced or battered since his defeat, he was in the company too of a young woman of striking looks—a stranger no one had ever seen before. Neither Felix nor his mother had come to the wedding service or the Pauleys' brunch, hadn't even been courteous enough to reply, Lillian Pauley complained, though RSVP was gilt-stamped on the invitation.

But here he was. As if nothing had changed greatly in his life. Seemed to take for granted the way people stared at him, their looks of admiration or disapproval; he was handsome, swaggering, in high spirits, his fingers closed casually about his girl's bare upper arm and the girl was just Hedy with no last name, a singer "out of Cleveland" working at the Eldorado Club where they'd met—and what did it mean, what kind of insult was it, the relatives would ask afterward, Felix bringing a woman like that to a family gathering?

Hedy with no last name: bone-white bleached hair coiled and curled and her lips dark like Joan Crawford's, elaborately made-up eyes, a prominent beauty mole on her left cheek. She was young, not much more than Annemarie's age, but smiling and self-assured, you might say even a little arrogant, basking in the attention in her snug silvery-satin skirt and diaphanous black blouse with the V-neck, stiletto heels that threw her pelvis forward and emphasized the curve of her tight little buttocks. And there was Felix in a creamy-colored jacket with fashionable wide lapels, sharp-creased dark trousers lightly pegged at the ankles, a white silk pleated shirt, a silk tie of silver and maroon stripes—to match the Studebaker, maybe. Now that he'd quit boxing Felix wore his hair long, past his collar, oily scented wavy black-brown hair carefully combed—sculpted, it almost seemed—into a pompadour. He wore gold cuff links and collar studs and a wrist-watch with a wide gold band and even a ring on his left hand and his shoes had a subtly pointed toe, gleaming black, expensive. Enid watched as Felix and Annemarie embraced—as Felix kissed Anne-marie, gripping her head with his fingers spread in her hair, rumpling her veil. Annemarie was drunk on champagne and when she laughed there was a sort of happy violence in her laughter new to Enid.

Mr. Stevick had thought his brother might be scarred—"perma-nently disfigured"—from the beating he'd taken out in Detroit at the hands of a brawler boxer named Corvino, but so far as Enid could see the only really visible mark was a thin white scar above his right eye snaking through the eyebrow, raw as an exposed nerve. He looked fit as ever, springy on his toes and smiling his easy boyish smile, shaking hands with the men and embracing his many aunts and cousins as if he was genuinely fond of them and took it for granted they were fond of him: and how could they resist.

And all the while Hedy looked on bemused, smoking a cigarette. Does he fuck you? Angel-face wondered. Do you like it, does it hurt?—does it feel good?

Felix politely kissed Hannah Stevick on the cheek and shook Lyle's hand, murmuring they hadn't seen each other in a while, and made his way to Warren asking when the hell had *he* joined up, or had they drafted him?—Christ, he said, time goes fast, you can't keep track of the wars. He seemed a little unnerved by Warren in uniform or maybe it was the way Warren had changed. Geraldine came to hug him and he hugged her in turn, hard, shook hands with Neal O'Banan whom it didn't seem he'd ever met before; then came Lizzie high on champagne to throw her arms around his neck saying she hadn't seen him in a long long time, why didn't he ever come to visit? Felix looked around as if seeking out his other niece but though he saw Enid he didn't seem to recognize her and that hurt. But Lizzie dragged her forward so Felix hugged her too, kissing her high on the forehead asking her how old she was now, was she in high school yet? His breath smelled of whiskey.

The band was playing a boisterous version of "I Love You Truly" again, how many times had they played it this afternoon, Felix pulled Annemarie out to dance, the two of them laughing together while others stood watching, Felix and Annemarie clowning around like kids, Felix's feet tangled in Annemarie's gown and Annemarie feinted a blow at his chin, then after a while she struck a dreamy pose, her cheek against Felix's, and it might have been a real dance, nighttime and a romantic setting not the Knights of Columbus with so many people so much commotion and the smells of barbecue and beer.

Next came "Melancholy Baby" and Felix danced with Annemarie's mother, Lillian, Mrs. Stevick's age or older but the woman could dance!—then "Beer Barrel Polka" fast and furious and Felix took off his coat and tossed it on the grass, pulled his niece Dinah out onto the dance platform, Dinah in her pink bridesmaid's dress chunky and perspiring, shrieking with laughter. The polka was loud, fierce, comical—dancers tripped over one another's feet—but when it ended everybody wanted it played again so the band obliged and this time Felix charged across the floor with Lizzie, their arms outstretched like battering rams, Felix's oiled hair disheveled and Lizzie's upswept hairdo coming down, a brassiere strap showing white at her shoulder.

Then Felix danced with Hedy, the two of them laughing together, pressing together, no matter the eyes following them. Then Felix danced with Stefan's mother, Mrs. Rossky. Then he noticed Enid watching and asked her to dance: C'mon, he said, when she held back, pulled her out and Enid consented in a wave of panic, scarcely hearing the band play "As Time Goes By" which was one of her favorite songs—she was mortified by self-consciousness, legs stiff as crutches.

But Felix was a good sport, Felix was enjoying himself, gripping his niece's icy fingers in his and pressing his hand against her back, slightly drunk, smelling of whiskey, beer, hair lotion, humming under his breath. It was said of Felix Stevick that you never got to know him, the man he was behind his smile and bared teeth, he'd given his mother a hard time and *she* was no pushover, he'd walked away from his career when people were saying he shouldn't, shouldn't give up, not so fast. But he did, he said, what he wanted to do. He didn't do what he didn't want to do; it was as simple as that—that was his life.

Enid kept losing the beat, tasting mortification and terror, and Felix, amused, patient, helped her start again, humming loudly, telling her to loosen up honey didn't she know how to dance?—and Enid saw the scar in his eyebrow like a piece of white string and scar tissue around his eyes too—pearly flesh that, catching the light, shone like another kind of skin, an elderly person's, or a baby's. When the news came of Felix injured in Detroit, the first loss of his boxing career, Enid had thought, Well yes—you deserve it. She remembered the night in the Armory and Mr. Stevick's rage and there'd been bad blood between the brothers ever since.

The dance ended and Enid walked quickly away, looking at no one. She'd had enough of dancing, enough of these people—and herself, most of all herself: Enid Maria in her blue dress and silly high heels. Her very bowels writhed with repugnance.

Enid Maria you poor sad cunt, Angel-face said coldly. Why don't you die.

———————

In the airless women's room on the second floor of the hall she locked herself in one of the stalls desperate to be alone. She waited to be sick, or to burst into tears, but nothing happened. Her veins and arteries and all her nerves were a many-branched tree of quivering radiant light like pain.

At one of the sinks she ran water from a cold tap onto her wrists, dabbed at her face with a wet paper towel. In the pocked mirror a narrow-faced narrow-chested young girl of startling ugliness with a fanatic's damp glassy eyes but it was wiser Enid knew not to look; more merciful. She'd been deceived all that day among so many attractive young women and girls.

She saw that her dress was stained too—one of the tiny embroidered flowers marred with a pimply blemish she tried to scrape off with her nails.

Climbed to the third floor, pushed through a door into a barnlike space used for storage—the temperature must have been above ninety here, her skin prickled with heat. A drone of flies and wasps, strands of cobweb hanging from the ceiling. Cartons, boxes, folding chairs, card tables, coat racks, against the opposite wall an old upright piano partly covered by a dusty canvas—it felt right to Enid to be here, alone and safe. She looked out a window at the party on the lawn below, so many people milling around and that big striped tent like a circus tent, children running wild. The grass was littered with papers. The band was playing "Rum and Coca-Cola." Beyond the stucco wall at the rear of the property was a residential neighborhood of one-family brick houses, then a church, some stores; miles away the Stevick Building visible through the brown haze that lay low over the city. The haze drifted downwind from the lakeshore factories, gave the glassy blue lake a look of dreamlike distortion as if it were being seen through a tinted lens; as if, squinting in that direction, you couldn't get your vision clear.

Enid sat at the piano bench. Didn't give a damn if her dress got dirty—the wedding was over, the party ending. It seemed like a very long time ago she'd bathed and washed her hair trembling with excitement and why? to what purpose? "Another day, another dollar" was one of Mr. Stevick's deadpan sayings, meant to be funny.

She struck a few notes on the keyboard but they were tinny, flat. In grade school she had taken piano instruction twice a week in a special program arranged for her by the director of music for the public schools, but the lessons ended when she went on to De Witt Clinton and in any case there was no piano at home for her to practice on. Mr. Stevick said no Stevicks had the slightest musical talent—he'd always liked to sing but wasn't even good enough for the parish choir.

Enid lazily picked out one of her old exercises. Czerny. Triad scales, chords, running her thumb up and down the keyboard until the cuticle began to bleed. The piano was a wreck, ivory keys discolored, many of them broken, mute. How does a piano come to this, Enid wondered. Abandoned. Forgotten: just junk. Something enterprising Lyle Stevick might buy for $50 and try to sell for $150. That was his business, his life's trade.

6

It was a coarse dirty love, she felt it sharp between her legs. Shy about touching herself, then she couldn't stop. Her teeth tore at the pillowcase, her eyes rolled in her head. Afterward the pillow was damp with her saliva, her nightgown damp with sweat. The smell of the bed made her slightly sick.

How hard the heart could kick yet not burst: a muscle gone mad. Like the secret muscles between her legs frenzied and racing, contracting against her fingers. Each time Enid Maria thought she would die but she never died. There would be no end to it.

She was tireless, ferocious, monkey-nimble!—on the long flat gymnasium mats smelling frankly of dirt, abrasive to the touch, she did handstands and cartwheels her knees perfectly straight toes pointed outward, she flew it seemed from one end of the mat to the other, she did somersaults, she did headstands so expertly the gym instructor used her as a model, chiding the other girls: Watch Enid, do it the way Enid does it, like *this.*

There was Enid Stevick kneeling eagerly, lowering her head to the mat so that her hair spilled down, hands positioned just so, head positioned just so, then she raised her smooth slender legs until they were in the air, unwavering, high, straight—effortless it seemed—ankles together, toes pointed—performed *One, two, three!* as Miss Holland snapped her fingers.

Shit, the older girls complained, Stevick's double-jointed.

On the trampoline she was wilder yet, more flamboyant, showier, none of the girls dared jump higher, no one would risk such somersaults, such dives, head tucked under and chestnut hair flying, legs spinning, flips in one direction five-six-seven at a time then in another as rapidly; Enid could land flat on her stomach her chest, her arms outstretched (a tactic forbidden by Miss Holland, for fear of "ruptures"), then fly up as high as six feet to twist, turn, and land again on her stomach and chest, eyes narrowed against the stinging slapping pain, lower lip caught in her teeth. The other girls cheered, whistled; Enid's hot! they called out, Stevick's hot!—not eager for their own turns to come but content to watch her bounce high and higher still, risking her neck. She was feverish, radiant with concentration, oblivious to her audience and to anything beyond the trampoline canvas itself, the old gymnasium at De Witt Clinton Junior High School with its stink of Lysol, floor varnish, locker room mildew, and perpetual dripping damp in the showers; even Miss Holland had to shout to get Enid's attention: Didn't she know she could break an arm doing a stunt like that? As a safety precaution the girls in gym class formed a circle around the trampoline, hands gripping the metal rim in case the performer suddenly lost control and fell into the springs or in the direction of the floor, but Enid Stevick flew so high, Enid did such manic flips and twists and improvised monkey routines, who could save her if she had an accident?—the girls were prepared to leap back to save their own heads.

One afternoon after school Lizzie Stevick came to see what Enid was doing, she'd heard some things about her crazy younger sister; she stared in amazement, she *was* impressed, then turned away smirking— "I got better things to do with *my* ass, thank you!" But Miss Holland was proud of Enid, Miss Holland was thinking maybe she had a real athlete here, a gymnast, a trampoline artist she could help train. If only Enid wasn't so headstrong, so indifferent to counsel, shying away from people who had her best interests at heart.

Miss Holland was an olive-dark youngish woman in her thirties with a leathery skin, small hands and feet, a rare quick smile, a voice like a chainsaw the girls said when she lost her temper, which was never less than once each class period. She loathed teaching at De Witt Clinton on the East Side of town, made no secret of it, the older bigger girls talked back to her boldly, insolently, mocked her just out of earshot, left the locker room strewn with soiled towels, Kleenex, even sanitary napkins, defaced the walls with lipstick—FUCK SHIT EAT ME HOLLAND. They lied outrageously about when they were having their menstrual periods so they weren't required to change into gym clothes and sneakers and take a shower at the end of class. As if I give a damn about any of you! Miss Holland sometimes shouted, moved to tears of disappointment and rage.

Enid Stevick was her pet, it was a pleasure, she frequently said, to see somebody do something well for a change; still she lost her temper with Enid too. For taking unnecessary risks, not listening to instructions. She *could* break an arm. She could break a leg, her collarbone, her neck. In the midst of one of Enid's trampoline performances Miss Holland made her stop and get down: Enid was flushed, overheated, her blouse was sweated through, her eyes looked wild and unfocused. Miss Holland commanded a girl to trot off and fetch a towel soaked in cold water, then she wiped Enid's damp face with it, brushed her hair off her forehead and drew it back into a ponytail, fastened it with two or three deft turns of a rubber band. The other girls watched in silence. Enid's flush deepened. Miss Holland adjusted the ponytail, held Enid at arm's length examining her critically, then gave her a little nudge and said, "All right, Stevick, continue, show us all you've got."

("She's queer for you," Lizzie told Enid, "talks about you in the other classes, did you know?" Enid shrank from her sister's mocking smile, no she didn't know, she didn't really know what *queer* meant and didn't want to be told. She said blushing, "You're crazy," and Lizzie said, laughing, "Just don't let her get you alone in the shower.")

Lizzie and the other girls had boyfriends, Mick Hamill, Jack Nicolaou, Jerry Esposito, who had the use of his brother's 1947 Dodge sedan while his brother was in the army. Lizzie told Enid she'd better stay home, there wasn't any place for her; stay home and do your homework, Lizzie advised, these guys aren't for *you.*

Enid didn't want to stay home, she was afraid to stay home but Lizzie wouldn't listen. Write a letter to Warren, Lizzie said. Do your homework.

Why was she afraid?—it had something to do with the wallpaper, some days. But why, why, she didn't know, the wallpaper was her special place, her refuge, she could wander amid the lakes the rivers the islands, she wasn't really in danger of getting lost.

"I wouldn't be any trouble if I came along," Enid said stubbornly.

"Yeah you'd be trouble!" Lizzie said.

"I could have a boyfriend too," Enid said.

Lizzie was admiring herself in the mirror, turning her head from side to side so fast her hair whipped. She licked her red-lipsticked lips, pursed a kiss at the mirror. "Yeah you sure could," she said vaguely. "That's just it, Angel-face."

The wild weedy vacant lot on East Clinton overlooking the canal. The tall straggly grit-darkened weeds, scrub trees, an old dumped sofa the boys set afire then doused with water but it smoldered for hours, the stink of burnt rubber from tires too that had been set afire in the long humid August evenings. Burdock, chicory, tiny purple asters Enid picked in a bunch to bring home to Mrs. Stevick, who wasn't feeling well, but in an hour they went limp, began to wither. In the lot in the wind-flattened grasses paths crossed and recrossed one another following the bumpy contours of the land, some paths were trickier than others, more hidden, along one the boys had toiled digging holes like jungle booby traps, the idea was someone would come running unknowing and stumble and break his leg. There was a wider shallower hole with sharpened sticks set at angles meant to be spears or bayonets; here the idea was a Jap booby trap seen in a movie: the victim runs along not looking where he's going, turns a corner, trips and falls onto the spears and instantly he's dying, dead, stabbed through the gut. Weeks passed and the sticks were knocked askew, the shallow hole turned to mud.

One day Enid was cutting through the vacant lot on an errand for her mother, she heard shouting, ran to the canal bank in time to see a pack of neighborhood boys dangling another boy off the footbridge over the water thirty feet below: the boy's name was Bobby Kroetz, he lived three doors down from the Stevicks, he was thirteen years old and in Enid's homeroom class at De Witt Clinton, he was white-faced, terrified, one boy held his left wrist and another held his right, he screamed at them to pull him back up, not to let him fall, but they held him there dangling, laughing hilariously, then seeing Enid they called out, Hey Enid, want a swim with Bobby? want a fuck with Bobby? and Enid stood not moving, not even frightened, just watching them waiting for it to end. They would drop Bobby by accident!—he would fall into the filthy canal water and drown!—and Enid would be a witness. Her brain was dazzled, she seemed to see herself there squirming in his place, she felt the terrible vertigo the panic flooding her veins but she couldn't speak as Bobby was speaking, pleading for his life. And finally of course they pulled him back up onto the planks and he lay stomach down too weak to stand, sobbing to himself while they jeered, teased him for having pissed in his pants, and next day he wasn't at school, and the day after when he saw Enid he stared at her with such hatred that she recoiled: she knew he wished her dead.

It was only a game, Enid told herself.

It was only a game and can't hurt.

The game, the games, perpetual, unremitting. Childhood and the years beyond. Eleven, twelve, thirteen years old. Fourteen years old and still at De Witt Clinton, still a child, Enid Maria learning the many things it is wise to fear.

The vacant lot in which she sometimes wandered in her sleep. The alleys leading off East Clinton each so distinctive, known by heart. The asphalt schoolyards, the railroad yard at the far end of Cadboro, the empty boxcars, the tall rusted chain-link fences, the parking lots for Diamond Chemical Company, Empire State Heating & Refrigeration, Inc., Union Commercial Corrugated Box & Handling Company, workers streaming out at 5 P.M. five days a week. There were mysterious cars abandoned on side streets and gradually stripped by neighborhood boys of tires, wheels, parts. There was the dead end of Packer Street behind East Port Oriskany High School. The YMCA pool where Enid still swam, sometimes, on Saturday mornings though Lizzie no longer went. She liked it that the bright turquoise water, so choppy, smelling so of chlorine, was a place where Death was possible yet it was a place too of play, splashing and diving. The high tiled ceiling rang with shouts, the water slapped hard against the sides of the pool, Enid Stevick dived tireless slick and squirmy as an eel, dived and dived, swam the length of the pool as many times as her lungs and her shoulder muscles allowed; at last the water chopped and slapped inside her skull, her eyes were threaded finely with blood, she'd have to pull herself out of the pool barely able to climb up the metal steps, she staggered with exhaustion with satisfaction!—now nothing could matter, nothing could startle or hurt, for hours. The game itself was suspended.

Tokens dropped in the till, the bus rattling over the Decker Boulevard bridge, the look of the canal on winter mornings!—the surprise of the steep rock sides laced with ice glittering in the sun, mist rising thinly from the narrow channel of broken churned ice, steamy smoke like breaths from freighters and tugboats below. Enid leaned to the bus window transported, staring, her eyes narrowed in the pain of such brilliance, such beauty, all her senses were alive, aroused!—she might have been memorizing such visions as her own. For where was Enid Maria Stevick except in such visions, such moments of suspension? Through her astonished eyes the world flooded untouched by grief or fear as if *she* did not exist at all.

Then there were the civil defense drills at school, not very different from fire drills except in this instance it was the atomic bomb that had been dropped (somewhere along the lakeshore strip of factories most likely: where else?) but it was all routine, the pupils filing noisily out of their homerooms pushing and giggling, herded into the lower corridors where they crouched by the lockers, kneeling, bent over as far as possible, forehead to the floor and fingers laced tight together against the back of the neck. The back of the neck was thought to be a particularly tender part of the body requiring protection from the A-bomb blast: the radiation was invisible but swift and deadly, like x-rays perhaps but fiery, the sun's heat many times magnified. Enid had studied photographs of atomic bomb detonations, the famous mushroom cloud the sky ablaze; she asked her homeroom teacher what good it would do to follow the drill if the bomb had already fallen, and if it hadn't yet fallen how would anybody know to do the drill? and her teacher said vaguely, a little impatiently, that these were standard procedures, precautions everybody should take.

It was probable the Russians would drop the bomb—or try to drop the bomb—sometime within the next few years: that was the result of spies having stolen away American secrets to give to them but ordinary informed citizens could still protect themselves if they took intelligent precautions and did not panic at the time of attack. Students in the Port Oriskany public schools were given civil defense pamphlets—*What to Do in Case of Atomic Attack: The First 24 Hours*—to read and to take home to their parents but most of the pamphlets were tossed away, littering the streets and sidewalks around the school.

It was a game, Enid reasoned, it couldn't hurt, though she studied the pamphlets, she memorized certain of the passages: *If you know the Bomb's specific dangers you can learn the steps to escape them. In fact your chances of living through an atomic bomb attack are much better than you may have thought. At Nagasaki, for instance, almost 70% of the people a mile from the bomb lived. And today thousands of Japanese survivors live in new houses built right where their old ones stood! A population that has PLANNED TO SURVIVE will survive in even greater numbers.* In the end Enid too threw the pamphlet away.

There was tall skinny big-knuckled Mick Hamill who learned to call her Angel-face, he had hair like broom sage, shrewd shifty jokey eyes, he was sixteen years old, he'd quit school on the very day of his sixteenth birthday, now he was doing odd jobs in the neighborhood helping to unload trucks down by the waterfront, waiting until he could join the navy—that was all he wanted: to join the navy. He had an older cousin stationed in the Yellow Sea on an aircraft carrier, Mick hoped the war wouldn't end too soon, he wanted to be a fighter pilot, just wanted to get into uniform and take off. There were many girls who liked Mick because he wasn't quite so rough or crude as the other boys, he had one steady girlfriend, Rose Ann Esposito, sometimes they necked in public, on the bus, in the alley behind the school at noon, Enid wondered how Rose Ann could let him kiss her—Mick with his wide silly dirty grin, making sucking noises with his mouth meant to be obscene. He had taken Lizzie to the movies a few times, roller-skating too, but Lizzie said he wasn't always so nice, he could get a little rough sometimes, he was best as a friend. But Rose Ann was in love: Rose Ann wore his jacket, his identification bracelet, a heavy gold-plated signet ring on a chain around her neck. One afternoon Mick dropped by Nelia's where the girls happened to be, Mick's family, hillbillies like the Pancoes from West Virginia, lived in the Decker project too, Mick just dropped in bringing them presents and the girls crowded around the tall lanky slope-shouldered figure in a corduroy jacket and oil-stained jeans as Mick grinning passed out silver cigarette lighters as if he was dealing cards, one for each of them, then some rings with bright-colored glassy jewels, Jesus he had a pocketful! Is this Christmas? the girls asked—what *is* this? Mick said he was just feeling generous. They asked where he had picked up these things and he grinned sleepy-eyed like somebody in a movie with secrets he couldn't tell.

Enid's ring was metal light as tin meant to be gold, it had a dime-sized stone meant perhaps to be a ruby, it *was* attractive. Mick slid it on her finger himself, it was too large even for her middle finger, she'd have to wind tape around it if she wanted to wear it. The girls made a show of kissing Mick to thank him but Enid shrank away, not wanting to kiss him. Mick teased her asking didn't she like him, why didn't she like him? Enid blushed, offering to return the ring, but Mick was only teasing. "It's for you, Angel-face," he said, winking.

She had not especially wanted the ring but she wore it for weeks with adhesive tape wound around it, white tape that gradually became filthy and frayed. Sometimes she sat in school, her elbows on her desk her hand raised to her face, and by bringing the ring close to her eye she could secretly look through the stone's glassy prismatic surface to see reflected in miniature the classroom behind her—rows of desks, the windows, the faces of her classmates who had no idea she was watching them. It was idle, it was surreptitious, a way of passing the time, still there was something hypnotic about it, staring into another dimension as if through a tiny window where colors were faded to a dull shadowy red. Sometimes too she could see her own eye—her own eyeball—though the focus was so close and queer her eye began to ache. Why should I come back? Enid wondered, mesmerized. But of course she always came back.

Mick Hamill wasn't her boyfriend, Enid had no boyfriends, she dreaded being touched but even more the need to talk, to say things that were lies. One winter day, however, Lizzie's small gang of friends was returning from downtown across the footbridge when they heard a train rushing up behind them; they started running to get across before the train sped by overhead—laughing, squealing with the pretense of fright—but Enid panicked, Enid went stiff-legged, the others kept on running, leaving her behind, she was too frightened even to call out after them, not even Lizzie looked back. The train rushed by, boxcar after boxcar, a violent noise like thunder but so loud she was inside it, deafened, she couldn't move she was paralyzed she was gripping the railing in terror, it had something to do with the canal below, the way the water could be seen moving swiftly beneath her feet between the planks of the bridge while the train roared above her on the trestle; this was Death, this was Death, Enid suddenly realized, she had to grip the railing hard as she did or she would be swept over the side, she might climb up and throw herself over the side, it was going to happen!

Then one of the boys, it was Mick Hamill himself, came running back to get her, stooped, hands pressed over his ears. "Hey, Angel-face!" he shouted. "Wake up! Move your ass!" Laughing he grabbed hold of Enid to wake her from her trance, slung an arm around her and yanked her loose from the railing, forced her to walk fast, half run, one arm tight and heavy about her shoulders, with his free hand he rubbed the underside of her jaw, rubbed her neck, played at unzipping her jacket, all done quick and light, Mick was clowning, showing off, he'd rescued Enid Stevick from—what? The train would be past in another minute or two, there wasn't the slightest actual danger, only the noise, the vibrating of the bridge, yet there was Enid ashy-white, the blood drained out of her lips, big dark dilated eyes. Afterward Mick claimed he could feel her heart beating like crazy, she was a trapped bird and he had her there, he could have done anything with her he wanted, he said gloating, that sweet little cunt.

7

The first time Warren was wounded in Korea, in mid-January 1951, they sent him to a hospital in Yokohama; he was able to write home two days later assuring the Stevicks he was all right, he was fine, leg injuries mainly, flesh wounds, shrapnel in his right knee but the doctors were confident he'd be discharged in a week, then he'd have a few days' furlough in Tokyo before being shipped back to his company. *Please don't worry about me,* he wrote, *I'm getting first-rate medical attention, the hospital staff is wonderful, it's great to sleep in a real bed for a change!* The tone of these letters was invariably sunny, boyish; in one of the letters Warren listed the food he liked best in the hospital: bacon and eggs fried chicken meat loaf apple pie chocolate and vanilla ice cream both, *Pvt. Stevick hasn't eaten so well in a long long time.*

He didn't write again for many days after Yokohama and Tokyo, then it seemed that the letters were changing; rarely did Warren speak in the first person, he spoke instead of *Pvt. Stevick,* sometimes even *"Pvt. Stevick,"* as if this were a fictitious character to be lightly mocked, derided. "Pvt. Stevick" doing this, "Pvt. Stevick" doing that, "Pvt. Stevick" and his misadventures in wartime. He spoke in a similarly light tone of the men in his company, some of whom were his friends and some not; they had names like Jerry, Bud, Ed, Mitch, they were from Rhode Island, Tampa, Florida, the State of Washington, Detroit, Michigan, Anchorage, Alaska, there was even one young man who'd attended East Port Oriskany High School for a year and he and Warren knew some people in common, a coincidence, wasn't it? And there was Sergeant Callaghan, nicknamed Hammerhead, a big tall guy from Boston he'd been in a German prisoner-of-war camp during World War II, he had two Purple Hearts and a Bronze Star, he was decent, fair-minded, tough, Pvt. Stevick was afraid of him but had to admit he respected him.

Sometimes there was no mention of Pvt. Stevick and his fellow soldiers, the letters reverting to an earlier tone; the writer might have been an intelligent schoolboy scrupulously listing the things he saw, recording them for a distant audience. The Korean terrain was tirelessly described: mountains valleys woodlands hills, hills with steep rock cliffs, hills with terraced rice paddies on their lower slopes, mountains capped with snow, mountains pitted with shell craters and scarred with white phosphorus and napalm. There were villages or the remains of villages made up of tile- and thatched-roof huts, roads that were mud when it rained and gritty suffocating blinding dust when it had not rained for several days. Many times there were no roads strictly speaking but only lanes, cattle trails, paths. The winter landscape was primarily snow, evergreens, stunted scrub oak, grassy hills bleached to brown. In these letters weather was meticulously noted and Enid began to look for clues in the weather—bright sunshiny days, days of hailstorms, blizzards, strong deafening winds, melting ridges of snow above the roads and again the roads turning to mud, then again roads that were rock and dust. There were rushing swollen mud-brown rivers, low freezing temperatures and then unexpectedly warm temperatures, the sun ablaze in an empty blue sky. It was a beautiful country, Korea, Warren said numerous times, underscoring the word *beautiful* as if he expected his family to disagree.

Warren rarely spoke of higher-ranking officers, only a few times in months did he mention General MacArthur, nor did he discuss politics except to say *There isn't any choice Pvt. Stevick has resigned himself: if the UN (the US!) loses in Asia then Europe is next.*

Mrs. Stevick one day said that the letters were not Warren's, they didn't sound like Warren, but no one agreed with her, the thought was too terrible.

In a rising voice Mrs. Stevick asked was it possible they had another boy writing home in Warren's place? that he had actually been captured by the Communists and somebody else was writing in his place?

At first Mr. Stevick laughed at her, told her she was crazy, she'd been listening to too many hysterical programs on the radio, reading too many overwrought stories in *Reader's Digest* and *Catholic Family.* Then seeing that she was seriously upset he tried to calm her, reason with her, Enid and Lizzie tried too: of course this was Warren, this was his handwriting wasn't it!

(Though in fact Enid had noticed over the months that the handwriting in Warren's letters had altered significantly. By degrees it was becoming stiff and left-slanting with long straight blunt *l*'s, *t*'s, *j*'s, a look of tension, impatience. Frequently the tissue-thin stationery was torn from the pressure of Warren's pen.)

"It doesn't *sound* like Warren," Mrs. Stevick said plaintively.

There were numerous radio programs Mrs. Stevick listened to faithfully that were both a consolation to a mother with a boy in the service and a source of keen anxiety. Among them was *America Watch*, broadcast out of Chicago under the auspices of the American Community of Christian Churches every weekday at four; it was interdenominational but once Cardinal Spellman was a special guest on the program and once Senator McCarthy himself, speaking passionately and angrily to his radio audience about the threat of Godless Communism at home and abroad. In *Catholic Family* there was a popular column of many years' standing devoted to the stories of mothers of soldiers killed, maimed, or missing in action (in both the Korean conflict and in World War II), their devotion to the Virgin Mary and the ways in which the Virgin Mary gave them strength. Mrs. Stevick read each column, clipped it out of the magazine, filed it away in a kitchen drawer. In none of the columns were fears precisely like Mrs. Stevick's discussed but the column gave her consolation nonetheless.

Mr. Stevick was in the habit of disparaging such sentimental nonsense, it was all church propaganda, he said, ways of soliciting money. He knew, he knew, wasn't his own brother a priest? One day Mrs. Stevick said in a sudden rage, "*What* do you know?"—turning upon her astonished husband, her hands clenched into fists raised awkwardly at shoulder level, trembling—"What have you ever known about anything, *you!*"

In the late winter and early spring Warren's letters were often fragmentary and incoherent, punctuated with place names that were exotic yet familiar, so often did they appear in the newspapers—Pusan, Taegu, Chorwon (where in fact Pvt. Stevick had been wounded; now he was back again), the Naktong River, the Han River, it seemed the UN forces were crossing and recrossing the same terrain, the same imaginary lines on the map (the famous 38th parallel for instance), now he spoke of Seoul the capital city (lost to the Communists then won from the Communists then lost to the Communists then won from the Communists!), a sad city, Pvt. Stevick observed, a tragic city one might say, the civilian population vanished or dying or dead, no food no electricity no sanitation, only UN vehicles in the streets, UN soldiers afoot everywhere. In March, however, flowering shrubs began to blossom—forsythia, azalea of gigantic sizes, bright savage colors—yellow, flame-orange, crimson, purple—Warren underscored the colors, the point of his pencil tearing at the paper.

The letters arrived unpredictably—two weeks and not a single letter, then three letters in a single mail delivery. Enid thought it a bad sign that Warren no longer acknowledged their letters to him, never

66

commented on their news or troubled to answer their questions. He spoke in the third person exclusively now, Pvt. Stevick hoping no one back home "seriously" missed him. He was really all right, he was contemplating staying in the East forever.

("What does he mean by that?" Mrs. Stevick asked, frightened. "It's just a way of talking," Mr. Stevick said vaguely, taking the letter from his wife's fingers to read and reread it. "He's joking, maybe.")

Warren was still describing landscapes, the effect of bombing, napalm, on villages, rice paddies, he spoke at unusual length about MacArthur and the General's "doomed campaign" to bomb and blockade Red China "just to save a few American lives." He spoke of Chinese soldiers captured who had not known where they were! or who they were fighting! thinking they were somewhere in China fighting the Chinese Nationalists. He spoke of North Korean soldiers, South Korean soldiers, Communists, anti-Communists, all a scramble, a scrimmage, nobody knew what he was doing except following orders: that was the only significant thing. The Korean landscape was not empty after all, Enid now realized, as Warren's earlier letters had suggested, it was swarming with soldiers: UN troops of so many nationalities!—Belgians, Greeks, Filipinos, French, English, Dutch, Turks, Americans. The sky was not empty but tirelessly crossed and recrossed by jets. There were M-1 rifles, hand grenades, carbines, tanks, mortar, napalm falling from the sky. There was "enemy" fire and there was "friendly" fire. And the amazing Turks about whom legends arose—fearless and indifferent to pain (their own or others'), calmly picking shrapnel fragments out of their bleeding flesh, treating bullet wounds with a slap of mercurochrome. The Turks were ideal soldiers, Warren said, they fought until they were shot down or blasted to pieces. And the Koreans themselves, "our Koreans"— hardy cheerful smiling little people, uncomplaining even in the very midst of carnage—he'd seen Koreans taking virtually no notice of the dying close about them, or the dead, so long as the victims were not members of their own family. Maybe it's their religion, Pvt. Stevick speculated, you can't feel another's pain unless you try, and why try? Squalling infants pocked with shrapnel wounds, children with eyes burnt out by napalm, children with limbs torn off, why try to feel their pain?

Enid noticed that Warren never spoke now of the men in his platoon, no more jocose news of Mitch, Jerry, Bud: the kid who'd gone to East High, even Hammerhead was gone, mysteriously replaced by "Sergeant Mayo" from Alabama who had "single-handedly" wiped out more than two hundred of the enemy since the start of the "conflict," he had three Purple Hearts, a Silver Star, a Bronze Star, and now he wanted a Distinguished Service Cross—he'd get that one if it killed him, he joked. Sergeant Mayo instructed his men helpfully in the use of the M-1 in place of the carbine, which shoots impracticably fast, what's the point of killing a man with thirty rounds of ammunition, wasting that much good ammunition if you can do the job with one or two rounds; and there's the art of the bayonet too, the point kept extra sharp, sticking Chinks when they're down but not quite dead to finish the gooks off, once you're in the clear and they're lying there there's no danger, the reward says Sarge is sticking 'em and sticking 'em as long as you want.

Mr. Stevick was upset as his daughters had never seen him, wondering could they get Warren's letters before the letters were actually delivered to the house?—before Hannah opened them? He saw now the situation *was* serious: whoever was writing those letters wasn't really their son; Hannah had to be protected from them, and the U.S. Post Office would have to cooperate.

Then in a day or two it happened that General MacArthur was relieved of his command, April 11, and a week later Warren Stevick was wounded at the battle of Imjin, airlifted this time to a hospital at Taegu; the letters of Pvt. Stevick were mercifully suspended.

8

November 30, 1951: a day in which Lyle Stevick's life was to be irrevocably changed though to him it offered at the start every appearance of simply another of his days, ordinary, dull, slow, you might say snail-paced . . . the air tasting of metal and factory, chemicals and yeast from the Tuscarora Street distillery . . . almost enough, Mr. Stevick thought, but only *almost* enough, to make a man drunk. The hours passed as usual at STEVICK'S BARGAIN & UNPAINTED FURNITURE ("Almost Anything Under the Sun Bought and Sold") at 1109 Lock

Street: business as usual cause for neither celebration nor despair, he'd made a few canny transactions, cleared perhaps $45, a half-dozen customers before noon, which was in fact not at all bad, but nothing worth comment except perhaps the "political discussion" with a hot-headed old geezer named Lelord Muer: an incident too ridiculous to note in any detail though after his arrest by Port Oriskany city police Mr. Stevick would be required to recall it in the most painstaking detail.

And to contemplate it, in one way or another, for the rest of his life.

It happened like this: Lyle Stevick managed to sell, after no little effort, a table lamp and (slightly soiled) shade for $12 to an elderly white-haired little snapping turtle of a man, one Lelord Muer of whom he'd never before heard, no former customer of his, surely; and while wrapping the lamp in a newspaper he caught sight, as did Muer, of a headline about the Rosenbergs, and he and Muer began discussing the case—Muer passionate in his conviction that the Commie Jews deserved the electric chair "or worse," Mr. Stevick thinking the situation "shameful," a "miscarriage of American justice"—then they fell to discussing rather heatedly the recent much-publicized dismissals in the Port Oriskany public schools, then by some precipitate leap Mr. Stevick was never to comprehend they were debating the relative sizes of the United States, Russia, and Red China. And Lyle Stevick could not resist hauling down a world atlas from a shelf to prove to the blustery old fool that *the Union of Soviet Socialist Republics and the People's Republic of China constituted a significantly larger land mass, in toto, than did the United States.*

Mr. Muer stared bewildered at the maps with the pop-eyed incredulity of a comic-strip character. He mumbled something Mr. Stevick did not hear; then said well maybe there *was* something to it—but much of the Commie land was useless wasn't it? Steppes, tundras, mountains, Siberia, Tibet—

"Simply a matter of geography, Mr. Muer," Mr. Stevick said quietly. He valued his relations with his customers, even his senile crank customers, so he was careful about keeping a note of triumph or derision out of his voice. "Incontestable."

So Muer went off carrying his lamp and shade but must have brooded over the incident the rest of the afternoon, the old bastard, must have worked himself up to a pitch of patriotic emotion—or was he simply crazy? suffering from senile dementia?—for at 6:10 P.M. as Lyle Stevick sat at his desk at the rear of the store doing some financial figuring, smoking his pipe, popping Sunkist raisins from a little box into his mouth, two young policemen arrived with a warrant for his arrest. The charges were "suspected subversion" and "promulgating of Communist propaganda."

"You—aren't serious!" Mr. Stevick exclaimed faintly, looking from one to the other. "A warrant for *my* arrest?"

Yes the policemen were serious, they were brusque, matter-of-fact, in no mood to debate the issue: there was the warrant in hand and if he was Lyle Stevick he was under arrest.

Mr. Stevick examined the document with shaking fingers. His heart was thumping in his chest, terrible pulses beat in his throat, his head, his very eyes—it was a wonder he didn't have an attack right then.

Both policemen were alarmingly young, hardly older than Warren, it seemed. And so unfriendly: Lyle Stevick wasn't accustomed to people not smiling at him when he smiled at *them*. The world was atilt when that failed to happen. . . . One of the officers held a nightstick and the other a pair of handcuffs, there were pistols boldly strapped to their thighs. "This can't be serious really," Mr. Stevick said but dared put up no resistance, no not the slightest, as, with the stiff caution of an elderly man, he moved to obey orders. So rattled he left his pipe behind smoldering on top of his desk, his hat, his gloves, would have forgotten even to lock up the goddamned store had not one of the policemen curtly reminded him. He might not be back, he was told, for a while.

It could not be happening!—Lyle Stevick locked in the rear of a squad car like a common criminal. Behind a wire mesh barrier. Lyle Stevick arrested, taken bodily from his place of work, hauled away into the night. He sat in a trance of oblivion, his heart clutching, his eyes burning as if a terrible bright beacon already shone into his face. Did they truly think he was a Communist? a spy? a dangerous subversive? In his panic he could not have said what a Communist was . . . what crimes he might have committed in all innocence . . . he knew only that he was a good man, a decent man, a Catholic husband and father fifty years of age, he deserved to be treated with more kindness than this.

In the summer of 1950 a Senate investigative committee headed by the conservative Democrat Millard Tydings had examined Senator Joseph McCarthy's much-publicized charges of communism in the federal government (eighty-one "documented" cases in the State Department alone) and found each and every one of them fraudulent: this, as it turned out, incredibly, preposterously, *at the very start of the Senator's rise to power.* Lyle Stevick was baffled as in subsequent months the presumably disgraced McCarthy dominated headlines in his crusade against Communists—Communist sympathizers, pinks and dupes and "probable spies" in responsible positions—in the upper echelons of Truman's administration no less!—the charges, the headlines, went on and on. If Lyle Stevick went to mass he was likely to endure passionate sermons from the pulpit extolling Joseph McCarthy, that brave fearless bred-in-the-bone Catholic patriot, and condemning his enemies who were atheistical, traitorous, "progressivist," and virtually ubiquitous. Embittered right-wing nonsense, Mr. Stevick thought it, and he supposed he could understand it from an ignorant parish priest in his late sixties (after all Father Coughlin had had quite a following hereabouts in his time) but how on earth to explain the vehement pro-McCarthy editorials in the Port Oriskany *Evening Herald,* which was a Democratic newspaper? How to explain the week-after-week obsession of national magazines—*Time, Life, Saturday Evening Post, Reader's Digest, Coronet?* Each time Lyle Stevick picked up one of these magazines he came upon articles so fueled with anger they fairly leapt off the page—"Reds Are After YOUR Child," "Commies Plot Assault on U.S. Schools," "Commies in the Pulpit," "Trained to Overthrow: The International Lenin School in Moscow." He could not believe that any halfway intelligent person took such things seriously—and yet! Surely it was obvious that Joseph McCarthy and his cronies were liars and bullies, mere political opportunists, yet, absurdly, the Senator's star continued to rise, to rise and rise, as others sank, or were destroyed: not even old Harry Truman could stop him now. Not even J. Edgar Hoover could stop him, now.

There were arguably ambiguous cases, of course, that dragged on and on to great publicity: Alger Hiss, and Fuchs the "atomic spy," and Julius and Ethel Rosenberg sentenced to death in April 1951 for "passing atomic secrets to the enemy." But confused with these, as in one of Hannah's Friday night casseroles in which days'-old ingredients in new and startling and not always definable combinations appeared affably mixed, were hundreds maybe thousands of other cases, private citizens denouncing and exposing one another in complaints to their local police or even, if inspired, to the FBI: a Socialist alderman here in the city forced to resign (he and his family having received death threats), the Democratic mayor currently under malicious attack by his own city council for his Fair Deal–New Deal loyalties, a Unitarian

minister arrested and held without bail for twenty-four hours for
having given an "inflammatory" sermon about civil rights, a professor
of Asian studies at the local university fired by the university's board
of trustees for "suspected subversion," some six hundred books in
categories "subversive" or "inclining to subversion" removed from
the Port Oriskany public library and its branches, loyalty oaths and
denunciations and firings in the public schools, a vigilante bonfire (as
the newspapers described it, not with disapprobation) in Kilbirnie
Park and books by Dreiser, Twain, Jack London, Whitman, tossed
into the flames, one of Lizzie's teachers suspended for teaching Thoreau's "Civil Disobedience" to her class, one of Enid's teachers fired
for merely questioning the weekly civil defense drills. . . . It was the
world of the mad Don Quixote, Lyle Stevick thought, it was the world
of the vicious little Lilliputians examined by Lemuel Gulliver, yet it
was *this* world and one was (wasn't one?) obliged to live in it.

Mondays and Wednesdays without fail Lyle Stevick wore a freshly
ironed white shirt to his store but the arrest came, unfortunately, on
a Friday. His shirt was somewhat rumpled, the collar frankly soiled,
the necktie he'd plucked from his closet was not one of his more
attractive ties (black and mustard-yellow stripes, cheap glazy material,
a Christmas present from one of the children he'd never had the heart
to throw away), his shoes waterstained and scuffed. Still he was wearing, by chance, the good brown gaberdine suit, and the good black
wool overcoat, he looked all right, he looked respectable enough
though obviously—ah too obviously!—nervous: reaching repeatedly
for his pipe which wasn't in his pocket, drawing a hand shakily across
his head, feeling with surprise the scalp, the smooth hairless terribly
exposed skin that reminded him he was no longer a young man, no
longer handsome vigorous young Lyle Stevick with a full head of hair
he'd taken for granted as he'd taken his life, his freedom, for granted.
Hadn't he thought in those years he would live forever!

He had no Communist leanings, it was absurd to think so: he'd
never to his knowledge even set eyes upon an actual Communist let
alone spoken with one, consorted with one. Maybe the police would
give him a lie detector test and send him home?

But the arrest was like an assembly line—or was it "Lyle Stevick"
who was the assembly line—going on without recourse to a man's
wishes, a man's heartfelt protestations of innocence, his condemnation
of his accuser, his threats to sue for false arrest. At police headquarters
on Union Street he was booked, fingerprinted, made to empty his

pockets, he was frisked, searched, treated with an impersonal disdain that wounded his soul, he was told to sit told to stand told to move along told to keep his hands at his sides told to wait first in an unheated fluorescent-bright corridor seated in a row of silent arrested men nearly all of them Negroes and handcuffed, then for fifty minutes in an airless windowless room thinking of, what was the title, that terrifying story of Chekhov's in which a man, a doctor, winds up in the very mental ward he'd consigned others to in his apathy—"What difference does it make?" he'd said to his patients and now, and now, he himself was trapped . . . oh God *trapped* like an animal.

Then Mr. Stevick was summoned from the room and, at last, given over to two plainclothes police—lieutenants in suits and ties. His heart lifted foolishly—maybe he'd have a chance, more of a chance, with men in suits and ties? But the lieutenants were unsmiling too, you might even say rude. Informing him he could telephone his lawyer if he wanted and he tried to joke saying there was no such thing as "my" lawyer, he didn't trust lawyers and in any case why should he pay a lawyer money when he was innocent?—but the policemen were not amused. He chose not to telephone Hannah (couldn't bear the thought of it!) so telephoned Domenic instead, trying to speak calmly, providing facts, information, resisting emotion since what was the point, resisting asking Domenic to pray for him for what, dear Christ, was the point. Then he and the others were joined by a senior detective named Scheier, introduced, Mr. Stevick thought rather threateningly, as a specialist in subversion, Communist agitation, Red plots and so forth, and the dreaded interrogation began.

It was to last five hours with only a single break for the arrested man.

Afterward Lyle Stevick was unable to recall the sequence of questions, partly because they were cyclical, often repeated in slightly different words, as if to trick him. He was unable to recall the number of times he repeated the same facts about himself—his father's name, his father's occupation, his having been baptized and confirmed in the Catholic Church, his line of business, the names of his wife and children, his brother who was a Roman Catholic priest, his place of residence on East Clinton, the ridiculous circumstances that had led to Lelord Muer's filing a citizen's complaint against him, above all the fact that he *was not* a Communist *had never been* a Communist or a Communist sympathizer. He'd been—and they could check—a registered Democrat since 1922, the first year he was qualified to vote. His interrogators seemed to be following his words, a stenographer was even taking them down, yet Scheier and occasionally one of the lieutenants interrupted to ask again and again about his "connection" with Russia and Red China: Why did he know so much about these countries? Had he ever visited them? Did he have relatives, friends, acquaintances who had visited them, or lived abroad?

And why did he stock books like the atlas, and all those encyclopedias, the *Britannica* for instance—wasn't that a foreign book—*if he was running a furniture store?*

Mr. Stevick tried patiently to explain. He knew nothing about Russia and China, really. He'd never left the United States. Had no relatives, friends, acquaintances who'd visited any Communist countries or lived abroad except during the war but surely that was different? The books had been bought along with furniture and household goods, he was in the secondhand business after all, no other reason. Still Scheier said several times, "Quite an extensive library you have there, Mr. Stevick!" as if he understood the arrested man was lying, playing games with him. Scheier was a short squat barrel-chested man with a creased face, resembled thugish Gene Fullmer though he had pale blue seemingly intelligent eyes, bald as Lyle Stevick himself which might count in Mr. Stevick's favor though damn it he *was* short, a man no more than five foot six couldn't help resent a man six feet two inches tall. It must have been that Scheier was bored with his task or annoyed that the interrogation was yielding so little information since he kept returning to the matter of the books, why so many *books* in a *furniture store* Mr. Stevick?—reading off a list of titles a subordinate had provided him with, *The Decline and Fall of the Roman Empire, Look Homeward Angel, Alice in Wonderland, The Wealth of Nations, Selected Tales of Nathaniel Hawthorne, Jean-Christophe, Bulfinch's Mythology, The Metropolitan Opera Guide, The Wisdom of China and India, One Hundred and One Years of Entertainment, The Lives of the Great Explorers, The Call of the Wild, A Primer of American Birds, Gone With the Wind, A Tale of Two Cities, The Devils, The Illustrated Shakespeare.* The technique was very like Senator McCarthy's but the air of angry conviction was lacking.

(Mr. Stevick cringed at the Dostoyevsky title—but his interrogators were in possession, evidently, only of titles; they had not troubled to investigate the books themselves. So, suspicious as *The Devils* sounded, it had not been identified as a Russian work. There was that small blessing at least.)

"And who are your associates, Mr. Stevick?" Scheier asked several times, fixing the accused man with a knowing smile. "Your friends? Who read the same sorts of books, and have an interest in the same sorts of things? Maps of foreign places, and all that?"

Mr. Stevick sat stubborn and silent, knowing he was expected to name names; to save his own neck by accusing others. But he would *not* accuse others.

"No one? Nothing? Not a one?" Scheier asked.

"No one," Mr. Stevick said.

"You're absolutely sure? No one?"

"No one, sir."

"That," Scheier said, expelling his breath in an irritable hiss, "I find damned hard to believe."

In the end, ironically, it was Warren who saved him—the fact that Lyle Stevick had a twenty-one-year-old son who'd served his country bravely in Korea fighting the Communists; a boy awarded not one but two Purple Hearts. The policemen listened respectfully as Mr. Stevick spoke of Warren, recounting the woundings at Chorwon and at the battle of the Imjin River, emphasizing the fact that Warren had actually been given up temporarily for dead at Imjin. Thus far the poor boy had had three operations to remove shrapnel fragments from his flesh, even an operation to reduce fluid in his brain and yet another operation was scheduled for January—plastic surgery on his mutilated face and jaws. Also, Mr. Stevick said, his voice trembling, a tiny particle of shrapnel had worked its way into Warren's left eye and the vision had badly deteriorated.

There was a pause. Scheier and the lieutenants stirred restlessly, and offered their commiseration. Lucky, Scheier said, the boy is alive today.

"I give thanks to God," Mr. Stevick said, "for that very fact."

Still, he continued, Warren's attitude was remarkable. He was a *good* boy—always had been. Even in pain he never complained, rarely suffered from depression like so many other ex-GIs, he was talking about going to college next year if things worked out. . . . Once the doctors took out the catheter Warren's spirits had lifted dramatically: the kid was damned happy to be alive.

Again the policemen commiserated with Mr. Stevick. Scheier volunteered the information that, at that very moment, he had a nephew somewhere in Korea, private first class, his brother's boy, it was a goddamned shame wasn't it about MacArthur, the way things had gone. "And they don't even have the balls to call it a 'war'!" Scheier said, making a spitting gesture.

"It's a tragedy," Mr. Stevick said shakily. He wiped his perspiring face. "It's damned *sad,* sir."

Following this exchange the tone of the interrogation lightened: Mr. Stevick understood that a crucial point had passed, he'd made it, thank God he'd made it, he was childishly grateful, craven you might say, but grateful that his captors had decided to have mercy on him, that even with their superior power they would not punish him—*this time he would be spared!*

Though they didn't, as if for form's sake, let him go for another hour.

Arrested at 6:10 P.M., released at 12:25 A.M., immediately he telephoned Domenic with the good news then took a cab up to Lock Street too weak too dazed too disoriented to face Hannah yet, there'd be time for that later. What he needed was a drink, and his pipe. Some precious solitude and in any case his car was at the furniture store, he'd have to drive it home. Thoughts came rapid, flooding, choking—he'd never be able to sleep that night. He'd never be able to sleep again.

Police had evidently done a quick casual search of the store. They had moved furniture around, broken into his desk, left piles of books spilled underfoot. Lyle Stevick kicked the books aside, he wanted only to know if his bottle of Early Times was safe and it was, there in his lower desk drawer, though the sons of bitches had forced the lock. His hands shook badly as he poured a few inches into a coffee mug. He drank; he sat heavily in his swivel chair, sweaty inside his overcoat but shivering too. By night the store looked different, unsettling, the familiar colors bleached out, the shapes of old eyesores queerly distorted in shadow. It was like looking at a family scene and seeing strangers. Sofas that had been on the floor for years, baby bassinets, a tall Victorian highboy by the stairs, a grandfather clock. . . . Sometimes at night working late or just sitting dreaming at his desk he heard mice scuttling close by, perhaps he heard rats, a sound as of nails clicking on the floorboards; sometimes the aged timbers of the building shifted and creaked in the cold and the noise was like a spike in the heart but it came to nothing.

He was fifty years old. He was exhausted, worn down, finished. They had broken him, humiliated him. *All things yearn to persist in their being,* Spinoza had said—he believed it was Spinoza who'd said that— and it was true, it was true, therein lay mankind's shame.

He drank whiskey and prepared a pipe; still his hands shook, his thoughts came in a wild self-mocking flood. The smell of the sweet strong tobacco was a consolation, however: the first taste, his mouth filled with heat and smoke. He was safe, he *was* spared.

For many minutes he sat there at his rolltop desk in his overcoat, sweating, shivering, his thoughts leaping and darting out of control. He wasn't going home: he couldn't face Hannah and the girls. If he went to bed he wouldn't be able to sleep and if he slept he'd sink into that old dream of his, that old nightmare that left him weak and terrified, helpless as a child. The white-walled room, the unbearable pressure of the walls, the glaring lights, his dead father lying close by, eyes open, waiting for Lyle to close them. Except his father wasn't really dead he could close his own eyes couldn't he!—Lyle Stevick hadn't the strength to touch him, he was worn out, worn down, emptied even of pity.

Karl Stevick had left Lyle and Domenic and their mother one terrible January day in 1911. He'd had his women, his whores, eventually he married a pretty blond showgirl many years his junior, he had a third son, by then he was finished with politics, he hadn't that much longer to live. *Requiescat in pace,* Lyle thought bitterly. He remembered as a boy the hours—the evenings—of walking aimlessly in the city, downtown, along the canal, out along the lake, in residential neighborhoods, staring at lighted windows, trying to see inside, guessing at strangers' lives. Even the meanest houses and slum tenements had seemed places of exquisite mystery to him, places of refuge, sanctuary. He hadn't anywhere to *be,* those evenings, those hours, years and years of wandering, it seemed, not knowing what he did, knowing only that his father had left them and that he was alone, he'd be alone the rest of his life.

The galling truth was: though Karl Stevick protested he loved his sons, he had never loved Lyle or Domenic half so much as he loved Felix, the son of his folly, his old man's infatuation. His old man's lust.

And what of that? Why did Lyle Stevick care?—he was himself a father now, an adult, such things should be far behind him forgotten, covered over in time. Perhaps he had lived too long.

That low quick throb of gratitude, that craven writhing of his soul—*this time he would be spared!*

But would he?

He drank whiskey in the dirt-encrusted mug, he smoked his pipe quickly, waiting to be soothed to be calmed to *be,* he would not recall being made to empty his pockets as a uniformed clerk stared without interest, he would not recall the shame of being frisked! searched! like a common criminal. He had had the opportunity many times that night to name other people to the police, to "implicate" others, an opportunity some frightened men might have seized to save themselves or to punish old enemies or friends. Lyle Stevick would not have condescended to such an act, not to save his soul—or would he?—after all, the interrogation had not lasted much beyond midnight.

And if they had threatened him with physical violence, what then?

And if they had threatened him with public humiliation and exposure, what then?

Taped on the wall behind his desk were calendars going back to 1943, yellowed cartoons clipped out of magazines, several of Mr. Stevick's hand-lettered admonitions—CAVEAT EMPTOR, IF THE FOOL PERSISTS IN HIS FOLLY HE WILL BECOME WISE, BETTER TO LIGHT A SINGLE CANDLE THAN TO CURSE THE DARKNESS—some of his own cartoons drawn in India ink, his own version of Jiggs and Maggie, Popeye, Dick Tracy, the children's favorites the Katzenjammer Kids; he'd amused and surprised his family in the old days with his flair for such trifles, even Hannah was drawn to laugh at a teasing version of herself as Blondie—oh, Daddy could perform miracles in those days. Now if he went to the trouble of hand-lettering signs they were for practical purposes in the store: CONTINUOUS SAVINGS! "BETTER THAN NEW!" INVENTORY SALE—LAST 3 DAYS! XMAS SALE IN PROGRESS! In the front window was a sign he'd made years ago, his favorite, red balloon letters on a yellow surface, $TEVICK'$ FOR $AVING$! It was clever and it caught the eye, drew people in. Perhaps.

An odd blunder of fate that Lyle Stevick was in the secondhand and unpainted furniture business, wasn't it; he'd drifted into it by accident in the early thirties when other prospects had failed, a partnership in a men's haberdashery downtown, an investment in a real estate company made with Karl Stevick's assistance, suddenly he was no longer a young man, he was a married man with one, two, three small children, a wife who cried in secret when she believed he couldn't hear. The Immaculate Conception he'd called it—the first pregnancy—hoping to hide his shock and despair behind a smiling face, but his brother Domenic that self-righteous prig hadn't thought it amusing, had turned from him in shame not wanting to hear, to know. Damned asshole seminarian with all the answers—in Latin! Try to talk to him, try for consolation from him on the subjects of love, sex, accident, fate. Hannah was a virgin *and* pregnant when they married. Christ he'd been a virgin himself, why not admit it?—sitting dazed in a lecture hall at the university listening to a philosophy professor speak briskly of the world as idea and the world as will, sheer seething writhing yearning will, yes, old Schopenhauer knew the lure the irresistible temptation of Woman though the bastard had been too shrewd to succumb. Lyle Stevick in love with the daughter of a Polish Jew, a well-to-do furrier with a shop on Main Street where Sibley's was now (the girl's name was Elisabet, pale shimmering hair features delicate as etched glass a smile that seared his soul *but don't think of it*)—young Lyle Stevick in love with one girl but triumphant only with another.

His father had told him bluntly the Jews wouldn't have had him anyway. Marry your own kind, then when the kissing's over you won't have *that* to fight about.

Lyle rose unsteadily from his desk, took his bottle of Early Times and his pipe, and made his way carefully to the rear of the store, careful not to bump into the sharp corners of things, not to knock anything over; he knew the way by heart, a narrow path through a maze of tables, chairs, floor lamps, plush sofas smelling of mice and dust, still the darkness could confuse him, Scheier asking those questions again and again over and over confused him: Oh, please let me go. Have mercy. At the cellar stairs he switched on the light and stood for a moment blinking and trying to keep his balance. He wasn't drunk—he'd always been a man who held his liquor well—but he hadn't eaten for hours, that was the problem, the whiskey had gone to his head. Christ, he didn't want to topple head first down the cellar stairs, break his neck, and be found next day by his brother or poor Hannah herself.

When he felt more in control he descended the stairs carefully, once a fat s.o.b. customer had crashed through two steps on the stairs going to the second floor, fortunately the steps were at the bottom, fortunately the fat slob wasn't hurt, no lawsuit, though he'd had the temerity to be angry with Lyle, indignant. Now in the cellar Lyle was breathing air so familiar it was a consolation actually, ashy and wet and sweetly foul like spoiled meat, the smell of cobwebs, mouse and rat turds, the damp cold earthen floor. Ashes to ashes, dust to dust. Here he was. There were serious drainage problems down here, it was an impractical place to store furniture but he hadn't any choice, where could he move to he'd pay so little rent and why trouble to move anyway—he was exhausted, worn out. *Dei gratia.* His family and his tribe of relatives knew Lyle Stevick as a vigorous tireless ebullient soul, a go-getter, the uncomplaining head of a difficult household, but the truth was otherwise, Lyle Stevick was otherwise, phony and tattered as these Christmas decorations in a heap on the cellar floor. Green plastic tree from Norban's, strings of snarled tinsel, angel's hair in messy clots.

A warrant for your arrest, the young policeman had said.

Almost faint with anticipation, he drank trembling from the bottle.

Perhaps Christmas 1951 would not be a problem for Lyle Stevick after all.

The rope, the rope—hidden behind a packing case, neatly coiled, good strong sturdy rope it was though not very thick, not clumsy to knot. Approximately eight feet long, more than he needed. He loved the rope's splintery toughness between his fingers, the consolation of its weight, its very smell. On Ritter's scales he'd weighed—oh Jesus was it two hundred five pounds the last time? still he'd had a big breakfast and lunch that day, stripped to his underwear feeling like a fool his stocking feet on the doctor's scales, sucking in his breath as if that might make a difference. . . . He tossed one end of the rope over a beam, wound it around the beam several times deftly, expertly, making certain the rope was tight, snug, couldn't slip loose. He tested it hard, pulling on it, grunting. Bits of dirt and grime fell into his upturned face.

Then he turned away, heart pounding. For the moment that was enough.

He spread a newspaper on one of the bottom steps, sat down. His breath was steaming slightly, his pulse fast. With numbed fingers he lit up a fresh pipe. Took another swallow of whiskey. Contemplated the rope—the dangling rope—its shadow resting lightly on the wall behind, vague as a smudge on the damp stone. The rope was motionless of course but it had the look of being about to move. From somewhere close by came a faint sound of trickling water and far overhead the creaking of aged timbers in the cold, but these sounds too were consolations, here he was.

All things yearn to persist in their being save for those liberated from the blind brainless pitiless Will.

He'd sit here in secret in his place of refuge waiting for the prompting of his soul, his thoughts would leap and dart and finally drift where they would, as always. No one knew of this sanctuary.

If the telephone rang upstairs—was it ringing? ringing and ringing with "Father" Domenic's persistence?—he did not hear. Half closed his eyes, seeing again the subterranean mortuary at St. Joseph's, those white-glaring walls, the lights; 1944 and he was a volunteer orderly doing his duty for the war effort and no longer a boy, but that damned refrigerated air the stink of ammonia and disinfectant the stink of Death overcame him, he felt as one struck a violent blow to the heart, utterly benumbed. The occasion of his first death, that day: a woman patient who'd died in the night and Lyle's simple task was to sponge the body, to clothe it in a shroud of coarse pulp paper, taking care not to rip the paper along the lines of its grain, then to wheel it into the corridor down to the elevator to the mortuary, not once allowing himself to think that the "woman" (Mrs. Faxlanger, aged seventy-two) in room 558 had promptly become a "body" on a cart. How abruptly, how irremediably!—"she" was now "it."

He'd known then that all the philosophy in all the books, all the poetry and wisdom stored in libraries, the knotty eloquence of man's language could not contest that fact.

A young nun seeing his sickly white face came forward calmly to assist him, spoke quietly to him; she helped him wheel the cart and the body into the mortuary, helped him lift the body onto a metal drawer pulled out of the wall, then he pushed the drawer back in and closed the door, panting, shaking; the task was done.

There was a consolation however—children don't know.

Children are innocent, they don't know do they?—as long as they don't know there's a part of Daddy that doesn't know too isn't there?—when his children were young when they came to spend a morning or an afternoon at the store, a lark it was, Jesus he'd gotten a kick out of that, visiting Daddy, playing amid the furniture, a treasure trove for them you could tell, and sometimes Enid would sit fully absorbed for an hour or more at his desk reading one of the children's books piled in a messy stack against the wall, yes he could remember her reading *The Snow Queen* one winter day and he'd teased her about being a snow princess. Enid was so beautiful at that age so delicately boned her eyes so beautiful he often observed her in secret, in pride, a gloating greedy pride: Enid Maria, the last of his children and the one he loved best. Some months back sitting in this very place he'd tormented himself half pleasurably with the worst possibilities of his life—the deaths of his children, his wife—yet equally terrifying the possibility that he would be powerless to protect them. Was there a greater horror, a worse nightmare?—a father powerless to protect his children. Jesus, his nerves tore like silk at the thought of one or another of them injured, abused, but he'd dealt with Warren's situation sensibly enough, and when they were naughty in the old days he'd sometimes been roused to a blind rage against them, even against Enid—had to admit it, even Enid in one of her tantrums, her dark dilated eyes slitted against him, two or three years old and fired by a demonic energy, that was a dangerous age. Enid and Lizzie both, he remembered them playing a game of hide-and-seek in the store, their squeals of laughter their muffled cries impudent thumping on the stairs they tried to frighten themselves in mirrors they clambered under beds ran amok upstairs though Daddy had told them no, what if they broke something? what if a customer came in? what if they hurt themselves? *Lest ye become as little children again ye cannot enter the Kingdom of Heaven* but Lyle Stevick gritted his teeth, made an effort to calm his rapidly rising anger, hearing his daughters crashing overhead. At last he'd have to excuse himself if he was waiting on a customer, he'd go to the foot of the stairs and call up to them, they'd always stop immediately, freeze giggling and big-eyed where they were, but Daddy wasn't deceived he knew their play would begin again as soon as he withdrew, his threats of punishment—"I'll warm both your bottoms!"—were part of the game. If there was no one in the store he might be drawn into going up there himself, half in anger half in caprice, setting his pipe in an ashtray; he'd been younger then, climbing the stairs two or three at a time to seek out his naughty little girls to set them squealing in terror and delight crawling like small animals making the floorboards creak raising puffs of dust he could often detect. "Enid! Lizzie! *I'm coming after you!*"

9

Now that he'd never again be in training, now that he was a businessman—part owner of a resort hotel, in fact, in the Adirondacks—Felix Stevick smoked as frequently as he wished. Puerto Rican cigarillos were what he liked best, long, slim, tapered, hand-wrapped in brown paper, expensive. His particular brand was sold at only a few tobacco shops in the city; when he drove out weekends to Shoal Lake they weren't available even at the Saddleback Inn, so if he wanted to keep them in stock—if he didn't want to be forced to smoke ordinary American cigarettes—he had to bring his own supply. He was a rapid rather nervous smoker, smoking both cigarillos and cigarettes in short distracted puffs, then stubbing them out half smoked or tossing them away still burning. He didn't really approve of smoking, he said. But what the hell.

Puerto Rican tobacco was supposed to be superior to American tobacco, mild, light, sweet-tasting, worth the higher price, but the smoke was so strong it made Enid's eyes sting, it seemed to her nearly as disagreeable as her father's pipe tobacco. Still, she asked her uncle if she could try a cigarillo for the fun of it.

Felix said "No" at once, he wasn't even amused by the request. Enid persisted rather childishly, "Why not?" and Felix said she'd only look cheap, women didn't smoke cigarettes like these. Still Enid persisted. She meant to tease her uncle as she teased her father, just slightly pushing at his tolerance, she was bright bold insouciant, trying to extricate the package from his shirt pocket. But Felix fended her off as one might fend off a small annoying child; he laughed and walked away, leaving her by herself. That was her uncle's power, Enid thought, stung; that was the power of being adult—to walk away.

"Look cheap?" she called after him, not showing the angry hurt she felt. "Why would I look cheap? In whose eyes?—*yours?*"

Geraldine said, scolding, "Those things are practically cigars, Enid, you couldn't smoke one if you wanted to."

Geraldine said, seeing her sister's face, "Honey, you'd only make yourself sick."

The cigarillos came in a slender cardboard package, not a paper package like American cigarettes. It was embossed with the shapely figure of a female Spanish flamenco dancer—black hair piled high, one arm curved seductively above her head, crimson skirt raised to show a bit of petticoat and black high-heeled shoes. The morning after Labor Day, packing to return to the city, Enid discovered one of the packages in a drawer of the cheap deal bureau in her room; she drew her thumb slowly over the raised figure, stood for a long moment with her eyes closed, her mouth gone dry and numb; yes, she remembered having picked up the crumpled package from the beach below the O'Banans' cottage, she hated to see a beach littered no matter where, empty soda bottles, napkins, pages from the Sunday newspaper; she remembered picking up the crumpled package her uncle had tossed carelessly down but she didn't remember bringing it back to the cottage, she didn't remember hiding it in the drawer.

She threw it away in the trash ashamed, she wouldn't have wanted her sister or her brother-in-law, even her three-year-old nephew, to see.

Late summer 1952, the last two weeks in August, Enid had come to Shoal Lake to stay with the O'Banans in their rented cottage. She kept Geraldine company when Neal was out fishing, helped with little Neal Jr. and the baby, spent a good deal of time swimming, bicycling around the lake, lying on the beach. Neal O'Banan was wonderfully generous with his Stevick in-laws, inviting his wife's fourteen-year-old sister along on their vacation—in fact he'd invited Lizzie too, even Warren for a weekend, seemed genuinely disappointed when they couldn't come. Neal was from a big Catholic family (five sons, three daughters) and liked to say he never minded a crowd.

He intended, God willing (and his wife!), to have a big family himself.

Lizzie said of their brother-in-law, *"Doesn't* he remind you of Daddy!"

Enid's reply was evasive, subtly resentful. "No one reminds me of Daddy," she said.

Enid was shy of Geraldine at first, there was a considerable difference in their ages and they'd rarely been alone together in the past ten years. At the age of twenty-three Geraldine was a fully mature woman very much married, very much a mother: her air of warm heated fleshy self-assurance sometimes set Enid's teeth on edge. She was an attractive woman, her fine clear skin lightly dusted with freckles, her eyes rather small, close-set, watchful, a pinch of extra flesh beneath her chin, plump shoulders and arms, heavy breasts. Her dense springy hair was worn now in a poodle cut, a cap of tight curls, so new a style, so severely short and shaved at the nape of the neck, she drew attention at Shoal Lake without being aware of it. In Enid's presence she fell into the habit of chattering, thinking aloud it might have been, as if she imagined her younger sister to be lonely simply because she was so very quiet. Geraldine's voice was sunny, uninflected, overbearing in its ebullience. How happy she was!—how fortunate *she* was!—with Neal and Neal Jr. and eight-month-old Andy, whom everybody adored.

Enid watched her covertly, thinking, But is she *my* sister?—what does it mean? Do we love each other?

Enid recalled that week of mysterious tension at 118 East Clinton before Geraldine's engagement was announced, that week of quarrels, tears, Mrs. Stevick's strained pinched face, an edge of fury to Mr. Stevick's booming joking voice, doors slammed, Geraldine's high heels clattering on the stairs. Enid had been ten years old at the time and had not understood, still did not understand entirely; she hadn't wanted her older sister to marry and move away, she'd been fascinated, made rather anxious by the sustained commotion, the telephone calls, the mystery never explained but simply resolved with the wedding, the nuptial mass at St. James's. Most of the preparations were made in haste by Mrs. Stevick and Mrs. O'Banan, Neal's mother, who became fairly friendly at that time, then lapsed into indifference toward each other afterward. But Mr. Stevick grew fond of his brash young son-in-law, Neal was so good-natured, so tireless, he had the smile and handshake of a born salesman, a glint of smiling aggression in his eyes. He had been two years ahead of Geraldine in high school, a football player; he basked still in the glow of a local reputation, men admired him, men stopped him on the street in Port Oriskany even now to shake his hand, he grinned in embarrassment and blushed like a kid but Geraldine teased him—he adored it! After graduation Neal went to work for his father, who owned a large hardware store at the Grand Shopping Center; he seemed to be doing well, with a mortgage on a three-bedroom ranch house in Lakeshore Meadows south of the city and a 1950 Plymouth sedan and now this vacation at Shoal Lake in the village of Shoal Lake, not in one of the cheap shantylike cottages stretched along the southern shore where Lyle Stevick had brought his family in the past.

Not that the O'Banans' rented cottage was large or new or particularly attractive, it was just a summer place of varnished logs, with somewhat shabby furnishings, a small gas range in the kitchen, a pleasant view of Shoal Lake looking toward l'Isle-Verte and Grande Isle, rather thin walls, doors difficult to close. Going to the bathroom was an experience of intense embarrassment for Enid when the others were close by; trying to sleep in her cubbyhole of a room was yet more painful if Geraldine and Neal made love as they frequently did on the other side of the wall. Enid pressed her pillow over her head, her heart beating slow and sullen: how vulgar! she thought, how I hate them! she thought, how can Gerry like it?—for Gerry clearly *did* like it.

Enid asked Geraldine what it had been like to have her babies and Geraldine shrugged, looked away, said it was nothing *really,* she'd forgotten most of it to tell the truth, they'd doped her up good, though she remembered being in labor, she remembered a lot of pain, but it was a dim vague pain as if it'd happened to someone else, someone on the other side of a screen, you know?—eleven hours for Neal Jr., six hours for Andy, maybe the pain wasn't always just dim and vague, maybe at times it was pretty bad, but to tell the truth she didn't remember. "When you wake up, you know, there's this *baby,*" Geraldine said, her mouth twisting as it did sometimes when she was taken by surprise or when she was about to say something cutting, sarcastic, not knowing perhaps what she might say. "They give you this *baby* and it's *yours.* And it's yours for life!"

Enid thought Neal Jr. bratty much of the time though there were quieter times when he was sweet, suddenly darling, you just wanted to hug him; but the baby she adored, the baby you couldn't help adoring, warm and squirmy and luscious in his bath, kicking and flailing his plump limbs, splashing water Enid hardly minded; it sur- prised her that she hardly minded, not even the stink of diapers was really bad once you got used to it. It struck her as an amazing fact that she was this infant's aunt, he would grow up thinking of her as Aunt Enid, he'd never know *her* at all.

Holding the baby Enid thought she could be its mother, after all she was old enough now, think of the girls in the neighborhood who had been or were "in trouble," the latest rumor was Rose Ann Es- posito but Lizzie said flatly it wasn't any rumor it was the truth, poor Rose Ann!—nobody knew yet if the son of a bitch would marry her. Enid said she wouldn't marry anybody she didn't want to marry or anybody who didn't want to marry her and Lizzie said yes she would and Enid said no she wouldn't and Lizzie said, Okay then, what would you do, just have the baby by yourself? and Enid said hotly, I'd run away, and Lizzie said, Okay, but you'd have the baby anyway, smart- ass, wouldn't you, and Enid said, I'd run away, I'd kill myself, and Lizzie, seeing the look on Enid's face, dropped the subject. She herself was in love with one boy one week and with another boy another week but she didn't want to get married at all right now; she said she wanted a career in show business.

Enid missed Lizzie up in the mountains, the two might have aligned themselves together against Geraldine, so very much the fe- male boss of the household, worse than Mrs. Stevick in her kitchen, giving Enid orders in a sweet lilting voice when Neal was around, calling Enid honey, sweetie, as if they'd always been close. It was Lizzie who had cruelly observed that Gerry nine months pregnant looked like a boa constrictor that had swallowed a hog, yet she hadn't seemed to *see* herself, she'd gone around looking so damned happy, so damned *proud*.

The third day at the lake Enid got badly sunburnt swimming on a bright clear but not especially warm day, her face her shoulders her back in particular. Geraldine scolded her, gave her aspirin, rubbed Noxzema carefully into her pinkened skin as she lay on a wicker sofa on the veranda of the cottage, her eyes closed but her vision leaping and blotching, with waves with sunshine with the sound of a radio from the cottage next door. She was weak, dizzy, feverish, slightly sick to her stomach, rather frightened: disoriented. She recalled having felt like this after that curious experience on the footbridge, she'd managed to get home, then half fainted on the stairs, had to drag herself to her room, to her bed, her heartbeat fluttering and wild; she was sick for two days and Mrs. Stevick nursed her, scolding, saying she didn't dress warmly enough she didn't eat enough she was too thin to be in good health a serious bout of the flu could kill her and she'd have only herself to blame. Enid knew she would never be able to cross that footbridge again, it was a risk she must not take, not any bridge on foot, not even the wide busy Decker Boulevard bridge, if she walked close beside the railing that was the danger, if she could see the water below that was the danger, the tug the pull the impulse to climb over the railing and fall, drown; she must take care never to be guided by a will external to her own.

Do it! now!—came the voice.

Now, quickly! Before someone sees!

But of course there was no voice, there *was* no voice, she heard nothing really. Only the sudden violent twitching of her muscles, the sudden violent yearning to die. And what aroused in her that terrible storm of panic was her own immediate resistance to the impulse. For *she* did not want to obey *it*. *She* was superior to *it*.

Away at Shoal Lake in the mountains there were no dangerous bridges she had to cross on foot, no dangerous heights, by bicycle she was safe, her speed kept her going, the principle was perhaps the very principle that kept the bicycle from falling over: sheer motion. Might it be a law of physics? Enid wondered. So long as you are in motion you don't fall. There was the undertow at Shoal Lake, the numerous ghostly undertows, but she never swam alone now—she swam off the beach below the O'Banans' cottage, she swam out to the float, she dived a good deal, with so many people around a lifeguard always on duty she was quite safe she could not drown even if she wished and she did *not* wish.

She remembered Lizzie once saying years ago, Why do a thing like that?—meaning dying.

Why do a thing like that?

Still: there was the possibility of being suddenly swept away by an impulse, a voice deep in her muscles and bowels urging, Do it! now!—urging, Do it! you can't be stopped!—and the Death-panic would sweep over her, leaving her stunned, cold, her very soul struck dumb. The Death-panic was not the desire to die but her resistance to that desire. When she died she would die by her own hand, she vowed, by her own choice, she would not give in to the urgings of a will external to her own even if the will was God's. *She would not.*

Enid opened her eyes, startled by the sound of an outboard motorboat on the lake. She was startled to see that she was where she was—on the porch overlooking the lake. There was the immense plain of water spread flat like a sheet of bright metal, the cloud-streaked sky reflected in the waves, islands that looked as if they were floating weightless— l'Isle-Verte, Grande Isle, Isle à la Motte, others too small and insignificant to have been named. Shoal Lake was said to be the largest glacier lake in the western Adirondacks, six miles long and a mile and a half wide, bounded by forests of cedar, balsam, hemlock, Scotch pine; black spruce in moister soil like the soil around the O'Banans' cottage. Enid loved the names: Shoal Lake, l'Isle-Verte, Mt. Tahawus (visible to the north), Gray Peak (to the east), Blue Mountain, which she'd never seen, Mt. Marcy, Boreas Mountain, lakes she'd noted on the map—Kiwassa, Saranac, Champlain, Placid, Rainbow, Tear-of-the-Cloud—the names, the mysterious sounds had the power at times to fill her with vague cravings or were they half-submerged dreams impossible to define. She wanted—so much! She wanted so much she would never have.

From the village most of Shoal Lake looked wild, even desolate, but there were numerous colonies of summer cottages built along the southern shore, some expensive resort hotels, there were millionaires' camps hidden from sight, in fact Enid's grandfather Karl Stevick had built a large house in the village in the twenties, which had long since passed out of the Stevicks' hands. A shame, Lyle Stevick said, that his brother Felix, who wanted to invest money in Shoal Lake, hadn't any interest in reclaiming the old house.

(For Felix had surprised the family by announcing he intended to invest in a resort hotel up at Shoal Lake somewhere on l'Isle-Verte: he was going into the hotel business, about which Mr. Stevick said grimly he didn't know a damned thing.)

Geraldine came out to join Enid, asked how she was, said she *did* look better; Geraldine sat heavily sighing on the top step of the porch, she lit up a cigarette, launched into her cheery thinking-aloud, Enid had come to see that her sister used such interludes to plan ahead what she'd serve for supper, what she needed to buy at the A&P in the morning; her life was a litany, a rosary of tasks she said with zest. Geraldine was wearing slacks and a brilliant blue halter top that strained against her rather remarkable breasts, her face and shoulders were pink, freckled, her waist slightly flaccid. She had gained perhaps thirty pounds during her last pregnancy and had not lost much of the excess weight. At such moments when they were alone—the baby napping, Neal Jr. out with Neal Sr.—Enid hoped they might talk of serious matters: Mr. Stevick for instance, who seemed to be drinking a good deal these days, who'd become embittered and strange and unfunny in his jokes since his arrest; Mrs. Stevick, who complained of fainting spells, being unable to breathe, headaches, and so on and so forth but who wouldn't see a doctor; why didn't Geraldine ask about Warren, who *was* greatly improved, he'd be going away to college in a few weeks, or about Lizzie, or about Enid herself; why was it always this rambling thinking-aloud, only asking Enid her opinion from time to time out of a hurried politeness, then scarcely listening to her reply?

". . . porterhouse steaks Neal's going to barbecue. And potato salad Enid you can help me with, okay? Fix some hardboiled eggs out of the fridge. And there's bread. And some of that fudge ripple ice cream you know, God that's *my* downfall, that stuff is so good, Neal's got a sweet tooth too, his mother says all the O'Banan men have sweet tooths but I don't want him to get fat or anything, they say when a man has built up his body, I mean muscles, they have to keep the muscle tone just right or it turns to fat; poor Daddy, I wouldn't want Neal to get a belly like *that*. It's all from drinking beer, that kind of a belly. . . . By the way, I got a call from Felix just now, he wants to take us all out to dinner or something, he's coming up next weekend. Isn't that thoughtful?—it's just like Felix, isn't it." She paused. Smoked her cigarette. Ran a hand through her tight crisp curls. "I wonder what his life is like now—Felix's, I mean. Not boxing any longer. Of course it was dangerous, Neal says it's more dangerous than football, he'd never get into the ring with another man unless he was pretty sure he could knock him out! It's the only sport Neal says where you just hit or get hit, you have to like hurting other people, that's the main principle of the sport, even the champions are in danger Neal says. But I think he and Felix will get along, don't you, Enid?''

Enid said vaguely, pretending to be sleepier than she was, "Oh, sure.''

For months there was a rumor that Felix Stevick was going to invest in a new gym and health club on the south side of town in partnership with his friend Vince Mattiuzzio, then it seemed he was making inquiries about other kinds of property in the city—bowling alleys, restaurants, motels along Lakeshore Drive and Nine Mile Road—then it happened that he and a man named Sansom (an Albany businessman of whom no one in the family knew a thing) had bought a hotel on l'Isle-Verte! It was a once-glamorous lakefront hotel of some two hundred rooms, the old Rideau Inn, damaged by fire in 1949 and on the market ever since. By the time the Stevicks heard the news, Felix and his partner had already made a substantial down payment on the hotel, taken out a thirty-year mortgage at three percent interest, and were accepting bids from local construction firms for the renovation, which was going to be costly. Their plan was to open the Rideau Inn (capitalizing on its name and reputation) in the summer of 1953.

Lyle Stevick talked of little else for days. His brother going into the resort hotel business! in the Adirondacks! Where had he gotten the money? How could he afford such a purchase? And what of operating costs? maintenance? For the past few years since quitting boxing Felix had had no visible source of income that anyone knew of—even his mother was said not to really know what he did—he drove an expensive car, he dressed well and lived in a fancy apartment in a postwar building on Niagara Square; where the hell did the money come from? Was it from playing cards, gambling on the horses, on boxing? One of Lyle's Rossky cousins said he'd heard by way of a real estate agent in town that the asking price for the fire-damaged Rideau Inn was a cool $87,000—and beyond that was the cost of renovation, insurance, and so forth; Felix was going to get knocked on his ass as he'd been knocked on his ass by that bastard Corvino in Detroit.

Since Annemarie Pauley's wedding reception Lyle and Felix rarely met and then only by accident. Lyle Stevick felt he was being snubbed and by who, for Christ's sake?—a man all washed up before the age of thirty? He didn't bear Felix any grudge however, live and let live, some day Felix would need his blood kin and maybe his blood kin wouldn't be available, that was all. In the meantime he hoped Felix wouldn't get in debt and into serious trouble.

Felix apparently drove up to Shoal Lake that weekend but business appointments prevented him from visiting the O'Banans. He did however telephone late Sunday night to ask if Neal would like to join him in a poker game at the Saddleback where he was staying; it seemed Felix had somehow struck up an acquaintance with businessmen in the area who liked to play, also there were some hotel guests who wanted to be counted in, the situation looked good.

The Saddleback Inn on Grande Isle was generally considered the finest resort hotel in the Shoal Lake region. Sure, said Neal O'Banan, flattered, he'd drive right over. Neal greatly admired Felix Stevick, interrogated Geraldine and Enid about him—what had he been like while he was still boxing, how much money did they think he'd earned, had it affected him very much losing the way he did? Neal O'Banan thought boxing was the sport he'd have liked to do most if he'd had the nerve for it. If he'd been, maybe, a slightly different person.

The day following the poker game at the Saddleback, however, Neal said very little about the game or about Felix Stevick. He had a hangover, slept past eleven, was subdued, sullen, irritable; no one dared ask him how the night had gone: had he won or lost. (Lost, Enid thought. That's obvious.) That evening Enid overheard Geraldine and Neal talking heatedly, they were in their bedroom, the door shut; Enid was on her way outside but couldn't help hearing Neal's voice, then Geraldine's, then Neal's suddenly loud, nasty, *I don't need your goddamn advice, God damn you!* and quickly Enid left the cabin, ran barefoot through pebbles and prickly weeds down to the beach—*He lost,* Enid thought with a queer tinge of satisfaction. *That's obvious.*

Years ago when the Stevick family vacationed at Shoal Lake, Lyle rented the same cottage each summer, owned by a friend of a friend who was kind enough to charge them a little less than they might have paid elsewhere. Of course the cottage was hardly more than a "glorified shanty" as Mrs. Stevick invariably said—a cramped kitchen that always needed cleaning, antiquated plumbing, creaking floorboards, ill-fitting screens, and a roof of hammered tin; no bathroom at all, just a smelly outhouse to the rear. A single door for the entire cabin opening out onto a narrow plank porch overlooking the incline to the lake, a path that was part sand, part rock, part thistles, so steep you could twist your ankle if you weren't cautious. And the neighbors: Mrs. Stevick invariably had her difficulties with *them*.

But the lake was so wonderful, wasn't it.

Momma, wasn't it?

By night, lights winked along the shore of l'Isle-Verte where the yachts were moored, in the distance Grande Isle, then Isle à la Motte, which even by day had the appearance of unbroken pine forest—just wilderness. Most mornings a chill gauzy mist lay over the lake which burned away by nine or ten o'clock so that the islands were defined slowly, one by one, finally the mountains in the distance; always there was the nervous slap of waves against the rocky beach and the sharp odor of the pine trees close about the cabin mixing with sleep, dreams. At home Enid had snapshots of Shoal Lake taped to the wall above her desk, she amused her daddy by packing her suitcase a week ahead of time. To be there! to be away! Half asleep half awake, she lay in her bed swimming arm over arm, her small muscled limbs eager for the water's resistance, she was quick lithe sly as an eel swimming safely past the undertow, swimming by moonlight through the flattened waves toward l'Isle-Verte. Stars glittering overhead, a bone-bright moon.

Shoal Lake was like certain kinds of music Enid came upon by accident, turning the radio dial—so beautiful it hurt her nerves.

Mr. Stevick's father had owned thousands of acres of land in the Adirondacks years ago; the big house he'd built for himself and his second wife still stood on the edge of the village in an exclusive area off Black Spruce Lane. A retired millionaire was said to own the house now but he'd erected a twelve-foot redwood fence to shield the property from the street and a wrought-iron gate invariably padlocked when Lyle Stevick drove the family by to look. One day, Mr. Stevick said, he would make arrangements with the owner of the house or the caretaker to let them in—after all, he'd never seen the house himself. Would they be selfish enough to refuse him?

The day of the visit never came. Enid's father let the matter drop, and she always wondered whether he'd made his request and been denied.

One August however when Enid was seven years old and Lizzie ten, they explored the property alone, trespassing by way of the beach. Enid was fearful of being caught but Lizzie said why not, come *on*, nobody's going to stop us, and nobody did. Their grandfather's old house was large, imposing, but rather melancholy and run-down, not so very different the sisters thought from the big old fancy houses out West Clinton where well-to-do people used to live, any number of windows so queer and narrow, and sloping roofs, and chimneys, and rotting fretwork along the eaves. The shingle boards were a dark weatherworn brown. Red climbing roses gone wild and straggly in the garden, grayish-pink gravel in a curving driveway but weeds poked through it, a long shabby wharf with no sailboat or yacht, only an old rowboat partly sunken in the water. Everywhere underfoot were brambles and wild purple grapes so ripe the air hummed dangerous with bees. Enid blinked hard wanting to memorize all she saw—she'd thought it was important somehow, maybe her father would ask her about it one day—but Lizzie kept saying, Is *this* it? Is *this* it? in a voice that sounded cheated. She picked up a handful of pebbles and threw them.

They looked up to see an elderly man in a wheelchair being pushed by a nurse onto a second-floor porch; the man was bundled in sweaters and a blanket, he wore a wool cap pulled low on his forehead, looking silly and sad in the sunshine. It was August—it wasn't cold! As the sisters stared he turned his face toward the sun, sat blinking, blind-looking, his skin very white. Lizzie tugged at Enid's arm—the nurse had seen them—but Enid stood rooted to the spot staring up at the elderly man. She thought he might recognize them if he saw them—wasn't he someone *they* knew?—a frail old man wrapped in a blanket on a warm summer day, slumped in a wheelchair. The nurse was calling sharply, "Go home, go home, girls." Her voice wasn't angry but it sounded strong, confident. "This is private property, girls, please go home."

As a boy Felix Stevick had spent summers at Shoal Lake in the house on Black Spruce Lane but, no, he hadn't any interest in revisiting it. "Really? Why not?" Geraldine asked him. "Why should I?" Felix said. "But aren't you curious?" Geraldine asked. "Curious?" said Felix. "Why? It's just an old house."

Labor Day weekend and Felix had come finally to take Geraldine and Neal and Enid to dinner at the Shoal Lake Yacht Club, then to drive them out to the Rideau Inn. How did *he* get to use the club, Neal O'Banan asked Geraldine, don't tell me your uncle is a member! So when Felix came over the first thing Geraldine said was she'd always thought the Yacht Club was for millionaires, not people like themselves. Felix smiled and corrected her: "For millionaires and their friends."

Initially there was some strain between the men, Neal not quite so open and relaxed as usual, but Felix gradually won him over, directed most of his remarks to Neal and appeared genuinely interested in his answers. The men were drinking beer, Geraldine had a fancy summer drink, Enid had club soda with a twist of lime in a tall frosted glass, an elegant-looking drink that gave her inordinate pleasure. She stared at the other patrons on the terrace, their expensive sports clothes, their shoes, the ways the women wore their hair—so casual, sometimes tied back with scarves, but so attractive—the quick flash of gold, jewels. Even the waiters were striking: black men, not young, who carried themselves with soldierly pride, uniformed in spotless white. Here, close up, were the beautiful boats they'd only seen from a distance all those years, bobbing in the water, taking the warm orangish cast of the light, the declining sun, hulls and sails softly illuminated. Enid wished sharply that her mother and father could be with her, to see *this*. Even as she knew they'd disapprove: Momma with a cold dismissive shrug, Mr. Stevick with a defensive quip. "All that glitters is *not* gold."

Enid had a sip of Geraldine's drink, then another—"It's delicious!"—and they warned her not to be fooled, the vodka hasn't much taste, what you're tasting is orange juice.

If Neal had lost money at poker the subject never came up. They talked about Neal's business, which was hardware; about politics, and Port Oriskany, and people they knew in common. Felix eyed Neal frankly, maybe it was his old ring style of looking another man directly in the face, asked him was he happy these days? settled down like he was? did he miss football? and Enid noted that Neal O'Banan, who usually behaved as if he was somebody very special, spoke to Felix with a sort of wary apprehension as if not trusting him, or not trusting himself to give the right answers. Though Neal was much the larger man there was a feeling between the two of subtle rivalry, something of the feeling Enid sensed between Neal and Mr. Stevick but sharper here and more intense, since Felix was only a few years older than Neal. But he was in charge, taking them to dinner, taking them *here*—where the very prices on the menu stunned the eye.

Neal said he missed football, yes, missed the excitement and the team and, you know, being put on the spot like that—having that kind of tension and responsibility and knowing what you did in the next two or three seconds really mattered. He shook his head, didn't look at Geraldine, said, "I guess it's like guys coming back from the war—regular life, real life, it's kind of a letdown." He asked Felix did he miss boxing and Felix didn't answer at once, as if the question annoyed, or insulted. Then he smiled, showing his white teeth, and said, "Hell no, I don't miss boxing; when you give up boxing you get the world back—the world's what you've been missing without knowing it." It was the most Enid had ever heard her uncle say at one time—quiet, quick, but something furious in his tone. Neal O'Banan didn't ask another question.

Enid narrowed her eyes watching her uncle. He was wearing a white linen sports coat, a shirt of pale blue stripes open at the throat, amber-tinted sunglasses, a wristwatch with a fancy platinum stretch-band, the gold ring. "What kind of a man wears a ring?" Mr. Stevick would ask, jeering. His hands were smaller than Neal O'Banan's but the knuckles were prominent and Enid recalled having heard that boxers' trainers or doctors sometimes injected the backs of their hands with a painkilling drug before a fight. She recalled the man who was her uncle in the ring in the Armory beneath the lights being wildly cheered as he battered his opponent into submission but she could not see that this man, smiling, warm, sociable, was that man. The other man was inside this man maybe—had to be—but it wasn't a fact to be seen, or comprehended.

Her uncle's real life moved in quick nervous ripples beneath his talk and his smile and the way he looked at you, composed his face. The man you saw wasn't there and the man who was really there you couldn't see. Mr. Stevick once said that Felix's problem was he hadn't any soul—"any human soul"—but Enid knew now that was just a way of her father saying his young half brother wasn't *him*.

On the way to the old Rideau Inn on l'Isle-Verte the men talked about Felix Stevick's new car, a royal blue Packard hardtop with a V-8 engine, beige leather interior, wide whitewall tires. Neal O'Banan up front beside Felix was admiring as a boy—slapped the back of the seat saying there was nothing like the smell of a new car, was there? "Goddamn more fun selling cars than hardware," he said. Felix demonstrated the engine's fine calibration, how quickly he could accelerate from 0 mph to 50 mph. Geraldine and Enid cried out in happy alarm: the speed limit on the narrow asphalt road was 30 mph, as low as 15 on curves. But Felix had no trouble handling the road.

And there finally was the Rideau Inn behind a high stucco wall and a wrought-iron gate—padlocked, but Felix had the key—an enormous structure, fire-damaged but still impressive, both glamorous and sinister. The O'Banans marveled over it but Enid stared in silence, feeling now for the first time how Felix had gone beyond her father, beyond her father's world of petty sales and deals and inventories and rentals—that shabby rented house on East Clinton. To lay claim to this: how was it possible?

She understood Lyle Stevick's bitterness. Tasted it in her own mouth.

Felix left the Packard parked at the roadside and led them in. The building was like nothing Enid had ever seen close up, dated yet modern—"modernist"—with a salmon-pink façade, six slender columns supporting the portico, a flight of stone steps leading to a square blunt double door of hammered metal meant to suggest—what?—the door of an Egyptian tomb? The slate wall had been badly fire-damaged, much of the handsome façade scorched and streaked as if with tears. Moss grew in bright green patches on the roof, weeds and flowering thistles had long since poked through the fissures in the paved forecourt. Several of the black shutters had fallen or hung askew on their hinges, twined with poison ivy and Virginia creeper.

So quiet here. Sad. Angel-face thought, The scene of the crime.

The hotel had been built, Felix said, in the twenties, meant to be a Mediterranean villa. He and his partner, Al Sansom, were going to change the name to Villa Rideau—thought it had a little more class.

Inside they were hit by a powerful stench of burnt wood, smoke, damp, mildew, rot. Still the O'Banans were admiring—Geraldine in particular. ("It's like something in a movie," she told Felix, "but I don't remember which one.") They stood in the lobby craning their heads. The oval ceiling was shadowy with grime and cobwebs but impressive—a large many-branched brass chandelier hung from its center. One of the walls was decorated with a fresco depicting a tropical island floating in a turquoise sea—vaporish and lush with trees, plants, flowers. The fresco was like an illustration in a child's book, Enid thought, stylized and dreamy. You stared and stared and couldn't figure it out.

The electricity wasn't on, Felix said, so they'd better make the tour quick before it got dark. He'd lit one of his fancy brown-wrapped cigarillos and his mood had become more intense, impatient.

Enid trailed behind the adults, staring intently as if memorizing this remarkable place. It reminded her, didn't it, of an opening, a crack or a fissure—a way in. Or was it a way out. One of the mysterious paths in the wallpaper beside her bed she'd followed in her sleep except this *was* real, for all its strangeness—the lobby opened out into a sitting room of rich-paneled walls, outsized leather sofas and chairs, an enormous fieldstone fireplace stuffed with debris. And beyond it a dining room overlooking the lake—so beautiful in its design and proportions Enid stood transfixed. She imagined herself eating—dining—here, her hair tied casually back by a scarf, a bracelet gleaming on her wrist. If her uncle owned the hotel they'd be invited up here, wouldn't they? If—

You'll never be invited up here, Angel-face observed, and you know it.

In the gigantic kitchen Geraldine exclaimed at the size of the stoves, the ovens, the work counters and cupboards!—never seen anything like it. There was an odd hard violence to her admiration as if she expected Neal to challenge her.

The kitchen was the most seriously damaged of the rooms they'd seen. An entire wall had collapsed, there were mounds of debris, exposed wires, the smell of burnt wood and burnt grease. Felix flicked ash from his cigarillo onto the floor and told them, amused, that this was where the fire began—"But it didn't take hold exactly the way the owners wanted."

Geraldine and Neal professed surprise. "You mean the owners set it?—it was arson?" Neal asked. "For the insurance?"

Felix shrugged as if the question was too simpleminded to answer.

"Did they get away with it?" Geraldine asked.

Felix said, "Sure."

Out back, on the beach, they breathed in the fresh air with relief—it was just past sunset, cool, each evening the wind seemed to die down at this hour, the lake looked subdued as if chastened, with its waves flattened, flat. Yet there was a subtle rhythm to the slapping of the water, a hidden melody. "Sansom and I own this too," Felix said— meaning the stretch of beach. But suddenly he'd become bored, indifferent.

"Well," said Neal O'Banan, hands on his hips, "it really *is* something, this place."

"Is it?" said Felix. He laughed pleasantly and tossed his cigarillo out into the water.

Geraldine begged Felix to drop by their cottage next day, have a swim, stay for a barbecue supper before he drove back to Port Oriskany, but Felix said no, hadn't time—then around 6 P.M. he showed up after all. He'd checked out of the Saddleback, he said, and was actually on his way home; couldn't stay long. But in fact he was to stay at Shoal Lake until well after dark.

He'd brought the O'Banans three bottles of red Italian wine, several six-packs of beer. Even presents for Neal Jr. and for the baby—things he'd picked up in the Saddleback gift shop, in haste. A foil-wrapped package of chocolate cigarettes for Enid but she tossed it away indignant at the joke: she wasn't a child.

Felix and Neal and Enid went swimming while Geraldine lay on the beach with the boys, leafing through the Sunday paper. Felix swam negligently, not fast, his arms, his shoulders, his back sharply muscled, hair streaming water, whorls and tufts of dark hair on his body streaming water. He told Neal he was in poor condition these days but he swam better than Neal, who'd gained ten or fifteen pounds since his marriage, and Enid, falling behind the men, wondered how it felt to have inhabited your body, your very flesh, as a weapon—if you ever got over it, were able to forget. The quick swing of the arms, the power of the fists to hurt—did you ever forget?

She wondered did her uncle see other people in opposition to him, as opponents. Or just the men.

After the barbecue supper the men drank a good deal of wine and beer and Geraldine too got a little high—"tipsy" as she called it—and Felix gave Enid a boxing lesson on the beach, still in his swim trunks, Enid still in her swimsuit, though they were done with swimming for the day. Angel-face poked her way forward, cheeky, giggling, having drunk two or was it three cups of the dago-red wine while Enid Maria stood aside abashed and alarmed at her behavior. Strangers drifted over to watch the impromptu lesson but Felix ignored them, focusing on Enid, demonstrating a left jab, a left hook, left hook to the head, left hook to the body—"C'mon, Enid, let's see it! let me have it!" he said with a mixture of gravity and horseplay that made everyone laugh. Except Enid: Enid didn't laugh.

It was remarkable how without seeming to move, almost carelessly, Felix was able to fend off her wild blows—and she meant to hurt, she was striking as hard as she could. But nothing she did had any consequence though she tried to imitate Felix's stance, the positioning of his arms and hands, the movement of his feet. "Here's a right cross to the chin, sweetheart, light and easy, see?—here's a straight right to the body—here's a left inside uppercut; sweetheart, keep that guard *up,* don't just stand there in front of me; see what's going to happen?"—lightly grazing Enid's chin, breasts, belly with his loosely clenched fists. He reminded Enid astoundingly of a juggler: it was all so easy, his movements: yet she couldn't imitate him, couldn't begin. His blows swept by her like dream blows she'd have had to slow, freeze, to imagine their power, and how they would hurt. Her own fists rang with pain as they struck his forearms, fists, elbows. "Hit me in the face, I can take a punch," Felix said, laughing, but each time Enid sprang at him he slipped aside, quicker on his feet than she was—but how was that possible? He outweighed her by sixty pounds. He was drunk, or nearly. And he stood before her with the stinking cigarillo clamped between his grinning teeth—she wanted to send it flying.

By this time the horseplay was getting rough because Enid was determined to hurt her uncle, at least to land a solid blow; the laughter from the little ring of spectators was galling to her and she didn't give a damn for Geraldine scolding, telling them they'd better stop before somebody got hurt. Felix was saying, "C'mon, try this, like this, no, like *this,* honey: watch me," but no blow of Enid's found its target. "Keep moving, keep up that jab, keep in motion, get hot," Felix said, laughing, teasing. Enid's hair was sticking to her forehead, her skin feverish, Enid Maria in her coral-pink two-piece bathing suit from Grant's with the tiny green seahorses on the bodice, small hard breasts, small hard buttocks slim as a boy's, and her legs hard with muscle, she'd studied herself in mirrors half her life in despair and hope knowing it's power you need, oh, Jesus, power; if you're beautiful you'll have it over other people, over men, you'll be loved, desired, never have to die.

Felix was getting careless and some of his blows were beginning to sting, he could ward her off even as he appeared to be moving backward or shifting sideward, strike her snake-quick from two, even three angles seemingly at the same instant, leaving her incredulous, frustrated—caught her an open-handed blow on the jaw that frankly dazed her and in a frenzy she sprang at him, flailing and kicking, her eyes maddened, teary, her hair in her face, and he saw he'd maybe gone too far, he said, "Okay, sweetheart, that's it—enough for the first lesson"—he was laughing then startled, annoyed—"hey, you little bitch!" as Enid slipped through his guard, pummeling like a windmill, panting and feverish and using her nails and there at last went Felix's cigarillo flying—and everyone laughed. She hit him several times before he managed to grab her wrists; it was wildly amusing, hilarious—she'd split his lip and it was bleeding in a fast thin trickle down his chin; then suddenly she was sorry, breathless and sorry, repentant. Sticky hair in her face and one of her shoulder straps slipped off her shoulder so she was tugging it up, deeply embarrassed, but Felix didn't much mind the blood, wiped it away with the back of his hand, licked it away, the lesson was over, he said, Christ, he was thirsty, was there another Bud in the cooler?—he'd had enough of boxing for tonight.

Enid ran up to the cottage, went to wash her face and her sweaty underarms, sand sticking to her backside and she'd had enough too, hadn't she—pretending not to hear Geraldine's voice raised sharp and reproving behind her.

What happened after that was never clear in Enid's memory in its chronological sequence, though she was to contemplate it, you might say she was to think fairly seriously about it, for a long time afterward.

"Want to go for a ride, sweetheart?"

Uncle Felix with his car keys in hand, Felix with his hair newly combed, sly and jokey and not-serious as he'd been most of the evening, his words slurred from drinking. "Want to be my sweetheart, sweetheart?" he asked, staring at Enid as she'd seen men stare at her in the street or on the bus, looking quickly away.

Angel-face prodded her, yes.

Geraldine would be annoyed if she slipped away, leaving her with cleaning up from supper, but Felix was saying he needed to get in the car, cool off, he got restless staying in one place for too long; also, they'd run out of beer—*"That's* serious."

Was he maybe too drunk to be driving?—but he handled the Packard smoothly as ever, speeding along the narrow curving road where the shoulder was dangerously soft, sandy; if one of the car wheels slipped off the road they'd skid but Felix held the car steady and Enid beside him wasn't worried. People by the roadside waiting to cross, bathers, picnickers, children about to dart in front of the speeding car, but Felix tapped his horn and cleared the way and Enid could see it was all right, they weren't in any danger.

He asked did she have a boyfriend.

No, Enid said.

No boyfriend? No?

No.

He glanced at her, amused, or was it something other than amusement, Enid couldn't look at him now, knowing maybe what she might see and not wanting to see it.

Why not? he asked. You're old enough, aren't you?

Enid was turning the radio dial, listened for a minute to Frankie Laine, who was one of Lizzie's favorites—rich low anguished bawling voice you didn't know whether to laugh or cry, something twisted in your heart.

Her hair was whipping in the wind from the opened windows. She felt good, felt like laughing, the fruity taste of the wine and a man, a stranger, gripping a girl's head in his hands and kissing her, a sight you shouldn't see. Yesterday, the redwood deck of the Shoal Lake Yacht Club beneath a striped sun umbrella overlooking the lake and the millionaires' boats, tonight beside her Uncle Felix speeding along a lakeside road, Enid Maria in her Uncle Felix Stevick's new Packard, the royal-blue finish gleaming, the dashboard glittering; she didn't require Angel-face to nudge her into understanding her good fortune. Felt a queer sensation—a sense of rightness, being in the right place—or was it a spell flung over her like a net pulling and tugging and why should she resist, knowing it was right? Why not? Felix asked again in a louder pushier voice but she'd forgotten the original question.

Dinah Shore singing. A song about love, losing your one true love, crying yourself to sleep, the memory locked forever in your heart.

Enid was going to ignore Felix's teasing, she'd learned to ignore Daddy's teasing when it grated against her nerves; the trouble with him is he forgets we're not children any longer, Lizzie complained hotly. Enid was staring at the cramped little cottages close by the roadside feeling a thrill of superiority—and pity—clotheslines hung with towels, bathing suits, laundry; now they were passing the very cottage—the shanty—Mr. Stevick used to rent two weeks every August until the summer they stopped going forever. Momma's health was the reason supposedly and Lizzie said sarcastically, What a load of bull, it's just her getting her own way; anyway, all Momma did was bitch at them those two weeks, scrubbing out the oven, scouring the goddamned kitchen like it was her own and not just rented, nagging the girls to help her—well, shit on her, said Lizzie, *I'd* rather stay home. And Lizzie had her boyfriends, at home.

Beyond the cottage was the lake—glittering water like a snake's scales through the darkening pines. The smell of water too, almost sunset, darkening, but in open spaces the sunshine reappeared, bright, glaring—Enid blinked as if she'd forgotten the time, where she was.

Back at Gerry and Neal's there was Enid Maria helping as usual with the baby's bath, lifting the baby's small warm squirming body, frightened of dropping him for what if, dear God, she *did*—what then? The slippery skin, soapsuds dribbling down her front. The baby's tiny perfectly formed genitals—and Enid Maria turning her eyes shyly away, couldn't help herself. Geraldine and Neal whispered together sometimes when she could hear, made allusions, jokes, still crazy for each other like newlyweds, like those simpering jokes about newlyweds, eyeing each other as if they couldn't help it, no matter Geraldine's kid sister was there. Then their bedroom noises: oh, Christ, won't they ever stop? Enid clamped her hands over her ears, pressed the pillow over her ears, she hated them they were pigs, pigs—Geraldine making noises like that, like Enid had never heard before, then daring to face her next morning as if nothing had happened. But: Enid wasn't there with them. Enid had washed her face, brushed the snarls out of her damp hair, changed to a cotton skirt and a pullover nylon sweater, pretty little white ribbed sweater, sleeveless, over her bathing suit. Want to go for a ride, sweetheart? he asked, joking, not-serious, he'd come up to the cottage looking for her, Want to be my sweetheart, sweetheart?—like a refrain from a jukebox song. And why not.

Why not.

She hadn't heard Geraldine calling after them asking where they were going, aren't you going to help me clean up, Enid—pressing her knuckles against her mouth to keep from laughing. Before she'd left home Lizzie told her, Don't let her boss you around up there, she just wants a housemaid and a baby-sitter, and Enid said, Don't worry, I won't.

The bitter red wine had gone to her head but the air was clearing it. Thoughts flying like confetti out the window so she dissolved in breathy laughter and Felix asked what was funny but she said she didn't know. And started in laughing again. Felix said, Aren't you silly.

He stopped at a package store in the village, bought two more six-packs of Budweiser, opened a can and drank from it thirstily as if, funny man, he hadn't drunk anything in hours. Asked her did she want a taste, honey, and Enid said no. Enid said hadn't you better worry you'll get a beer belly like Neal or my father, and Felix only laughed. Enid felt the heat coming off him, wondered was his lip swollen where she'd cut it. He hadn't held it against her, that cut. Or slapping the cigarillo out of his mouth so people laughed, but Christ it *was* funny and that started her in laughing again.

Felix decided to take the long way home through l'Isle-Verte, let's see the hotel again, there were a few things he said he hadn't showed her the day before. As he drove he passed the beer can to Enid, telling her take a sip, take two, once you get used to beer you'll like it, so Enid tried but the taste was bitter as always—as bad as a mouthful of smoke. They crossed the bridge—a narrow humming vibrating bridge the kind you can see through, the water a short distance below and that's frightening, but Enid didn't allow herself to look: looked straight ahead. The sky was brilliant with light and color; my God how beautiful it is, Enid thought, the lake shivering, the waves shot with light—so beautiful it hurts. She thought, This is the happiest day of my life.

But suddenly she was chattering. Heard herself chattering. Like a schoolgirl reciting facts to impress—she and Warren once memorized most of an Adirondacks State Park pamphlet and she knew to tell her uncle that the base rock of the mountains was one billion one hundred million years old—think of that. Then came the Ice Age, sheets of ice like mountains, glaciers big as cities gouging out valleys and damming up rivers, cutting into the sides of mountains—that was why the Adirondacks were supposed to be so unusual, the bedrock knocked askew and split in fault zones. There was a drawing she'd seen of sheets of ice pushing down from the North Pole breaking and squeezing everything out of shape, had he ever seen it?—no?—or drawings of the glaciers?—no?—Enid speaking quick and bright and urgent, Enid Maria who knew all the answers at school. She wondered had the beer gone to her head too but she hadn't had more than two small mouthfuls. Kept wanting to laugh. Interrupting her recitation with laughter. She loved the names, the special names, she said—*kettle holes, drumlins, kames, eskers, valley trains*—they were sort of like poetry, weren't they, or music—*kettle holes drumlins kames eskers valley trains*—but she wasn't sure what they meant any longer. The word *glacier* too—

Felix said, We won't stay long, Enid.

Parked his car in the same place but brought Enid around to the rear of the hotel instead of the front. The old hotel tall and gloomy like a building in a movie in which something was going to happen or had already happened, the camera would take you to it. Once out of the car they reverted to their earlier mood, teasing and joking as they had earlier, at the cottage. Teach me how to box, Uncle Felix, Enid had said, is there any special trick to it?—and Felix said, Hell no, any shithead can do it, obviously.

This beach was pebbly and littered with debris but there was the lake, the surprise of the lake at sunset, waves like thousands of mirrored surfaces at a slant, broken, quivering with light. Enid waded splashing in the water, hiking her skirt to her thighs as Gerry'd done the other day in that sundress of hers, the poppy-and-green cotton, showing her freckled back and tight as a bra over her breasts, aware of both Neal and Felix watching. Now Felix wandered off though Enid was talking to him, she noticed he was gone, she was rubbing her eyes watching the sky in the west where the clouds were massed and riddled with light—felt a pang like sorrow, that she might start crying. So happy.

Where was he?—she ran along the beach like a small child splashing and kicking looking for him, then caught sight of him around the side of an old boathouse, was he urinating in a corner?—she turned away stung, disgusted, why were they such pigs, Daddy making so much noise in the bathroom and sometimes not bothering to close the door tight, Neal O'Banan in the cottage in the tiny bathroom, that long splashing in the toilet bowl like you'd imagine a cow or a horse. Boys in the neighborhood unzipping their pants in the alley, peeing in the weeds in the vacant lot, how she hated them all, wished them dead—but in another minute Felix caught up with her, taking the steps to the terrace two and three at a time as if nothing was wrong. And what *was* wrong—it was just what people did, men did, normal behavior. Enid Maria should be used to it by now.

Felix asked did she like his hotel. Was she going to come stay there sometime?

Enid said sure.

Enid said, swallowing, I don't know.

What don't you know? Felix asked, nudging her.

Still wearing his swim trunks but he'd put on a shirt, sleeves rolled up to his elbows. He had a key for one of the rear doors—by magic unlocking it, no trouble, and they stepped inside, a little quiet at first as if they were trespassing, the odor of burnt wood and rot in waves after the open air, a smell of darkness too, gathering night. Then Enid pushed against Felix, running to escape him. Hide-and-seek!—it would be a game of hide-and-seek like they'd played in

Daddy's store when they were children—Enid and Lizzie and sometimes Warren.

Enid eluded Felix running for her life turning corners banging
her shinbone stifling her laughter, she was breathless with laughter,
squatted behind a chair no time to think there on her haunches panting and elated pressing her knuckles against her mouth to keep still,
or was it to keep from sneezing—this damn dust. Felix passed by only
a few feet away, calling out, Enid? honey?—but couldn't find her.

Looked for her calling her name, Enid sweetheart little girl little
bitch! aren't you a little bitch!—stumbling and cursing, laughing, but
she was too smart squatting in her hiding place then crawling hands
and knees to another squeezing herself under a low-lying table breathing in the dust her knuckles in her mouth. Enid honey? Where are
you, honey? Then he was on the stairs stomping his feet to get her
attention, calling her name in a teasing singsong, you'd never think
of Felix Stevick like this, playful as a child, a rowdy noisy child,
whistling and stomping on the stairs to get her attention because it was
just a game—all in play. He cupped his hands to his mouth, calling
out, Enid, hey honey, *don't* follow me, calling back down the stairs in
a voice like Daddy mocking, challenging, *Don't* come up here, don't
open the wrong door if you do; and for a few minutes Enid couldn't
make up her mind how to proceed: suddenly the place was quiet. So
quiet. If this was a game of hide-and-seek Felix had cheated, he hadn't
found her so it wasn't his turn to hide, he'd cheated.

It was nearly dark where she was hiding. She crawled out, brushing her hair out of her face. So quiet. There was a smell like her
father's store, that terrible cellar where the drains clogged, a place
they weren't supposed to play. Earth, stone, cobwebs, trickling water.
Mr. Stevick told Lizzie and Enid to keep the hell out of the cellar but
naturally they'd crept down as soon as his back was turned.

She was thinking she'd go back out onto the beach and wait for
him there, or sit in his car fiddling with the radio. But instead she
found herself at the stairs. Tiptoeing up the stairs. Felix? she whispered. Uncle Felix?—where *are* you?

Upstairs it was quiet. Nobody in sight. Don't open the wrong
door, he'd warned, but what did that mean, exactly? The doors to the
hotel rooms, one after another, and all closed. Looking as if they were
locked but maybe they weren't. She tried the first door, opened it,
leaned in—Felix? A spacious room with a tall window, no drapes or
curtains, the panes shiny with grime but the window faced west and

the sky was still light, orangey clouds tinged with black like topological maps.

Felix . . . ?

No one here. Not in this room. Bedsprings and a rolled-up mattress, bureau mirror reflecting a small pale hunted face that seemed to be floating in space.

She shut the door quietly, stealthily. Tiptoed to the next door, the next room. Felix . . . ? Turned the knob, her heart beating hard, quick and hard the way she liked it, saw a room like the first, except here the bureau with its hefty oval mirror was against a different wall. She was thinking, So this is what a hotel room looks like, the real thing. She'd never been in one before.

God damn you, Felix. Where *are* you?

She told herself she'd try just one more door, one more room. If he wasn't there she'd run downstairs, she'd wait for him in his car, her heart was beating a little too hard now it was like the first tentative steps out onto the footbridge when you thought you heard a train approaching, so quick and fluttery a heartbeat you almost can't breathe. Still she went to the next room put her hand boldly on the knob saw the brass number on the door 188 and wasn't it a familiar safe number for some reason so she turned the knob and pushed the door open. And there he was, waiting.

10

Two days later back in the city he telephoned. Enid happened to answer the telephone, she answered it in fact on the first ring, turning her back to noise out in the kitchen. Felix's voice was low and quick, hurried, all he had to say was that he'd been drunk out there and hadn't meant what happened.

It wouldn't happen again, he told her.

Enid said nothing. In the kitchen Mrs. Stevick was frying something, hot splattering sizzling grease, Mr. Stevick was talking loudly, complaining or was he half joking about something in the newspaper or was it something that had happened to him that day at the store. Enid said nothing, listening to her uncle's low nervous voice; he was assuring her he'd been drunk he hadn't known what he was doing it was just something that had happened out on the island and it wouldn't happen ever again. Then after a pause he said, "Don't tell anyone, Enid."

"No," said Enid. "I won't tell anyone."

We are living in one of the great watershed periods of history, Adlai Stevenson was saying. *This era may well fix the pattern of civilization for many generations. . . . God has set for us an awesome mission: nothing less than the leadership of the free world.*

The radio voice was a joyous revelation—taut, bell-like, clear, strong. For all its subtle playfulness it was strong. A voice of immense practicality and wisdom. And authority—how many times was the man interrupted by applause! Simply to listen was to know. *That's him,* Warren Stevick thought, hearing the voice for the first time. *That's the one,* Warren thought calmly, yet his eyes filled with tears, he instinctively hid his face.

It was September 1952. Warren was newly enrolled as a freshman at Cornell University, he roomed alone in a shabby boardinghouse on North Seneca Street with a half dozen other "older" students, he was supremely ready to fall in love.

His life was all fragments and shards, bits of bone, shrapnel, flesh, he even had a put-together face as he called it—the seams about his jaw weren't perfectly aligned even after two operations, the left eye glared milky and near-useless, the bright plastic teeth attached to their partial plate were perhaps *too* perfect to be believed.

Perhaps no one noticed, no one greatly cared, thus why should he care? He gave thanks to God hourly for being alive.

Better to light a candle than to curse the darkness after all.

* * *

At the Imjin River in Korea in another life he had been Private First Class Warren Stevick of the second platoon of George Company of the second battalion of the Twenty-seventh Infantry Regiment of the Twenty-fifth Infantry Division of the United Nations Armed Forces under the command of General Douglas MacArthur. At Imjin, Private Stevick had died in a cataclysm of fire and mortar so immense it filled the universe without sound and without pain, his soul swiftly departed his body, distinctly he recalled afterward the extraordinary sensation of his soul hovering over its former body, contemplating it with pity and revulsion, the broken bleeding flesh meant to be *him.* Yet the soul awakened dazed and incredulous and wondrously refreshed in another life in this clumsy put-together body which would be the necessary vehicle of his Incarnation, hence never to be despised or scorned or even pitied. *You are the one,* Warren was told. *And you are one of many.*

He had understood then that his injured body would not fail, though his every breath was forced by a respirator and tubes ran down his throat and up into both nostrils, tubes were attached too to his arms and legs, his heartbeat was monitored, his eyes swathed in bandages. His body would survive because it was ordained he would survive housed in its warm flesh because he, Warren Stevick, was one and he was many and his life's task was so very simple he would never have thought of it himself—Warren Stevick the honor student, proud of his report cards and their A's and B+'s!—*he must help reduce the suffering of humankind which is a suffering primarily of the flesh, the consequence of a tragic misunderstanding of man's relationship to his brothers and sisters on earth.*

In the hospital at Taegu the doctors were not confident he would live yet Warren was eager to speak with the Catholic chaplain; his eyes were bandaged, tubes ran into his nostrils, yet he insisted upon talking: his voice was elderly but unyielding. "This means," Warren said, "the end of war, the abolishment of the weapons of war, the revelation of a common bond that one flesh is all flesh just as one spirit is all spirit that is God." The chaplain, whose face Warren was never privileged to see, allowed him to speak for some time, then spoke himself in a soothing if forceful tone of the dogma of the Church, the sacraments of the Church, the mystery of the Incarnation of God the Father in the flesh of Jesus Christ His Only Begotten Son. And Warren said, "But I don't mean Jesus Christ exclusively, Father! I mean all mankind, all men and women, *all* mankind." He was speaking excitedly, incoherently, he sensed the chaplain's embarrassment and irritation, he knew he was disturbing other patients in the ward, those who wished merely to drift in their morphine coma or to die without the agitation of words; still Warren said, "We must reduce human suffering here on earth in the flesh!—in our lifetimes!" Eventually the chaplain grew tired, he blessed Warren and moved on.

But it was so very simple he would never have thought of it unaided: Warren Stevick had been accursed by his own self-involved *self*-obsessed soul.

And now I am born again, he thought, his eyeballs moving jerkily behind their tight bandages. And for what . . . ?

In America in Port Oriskany in the veterans' hospital on North Union Street, Warren underwent surgery "successfully," his family was told; he would not die, he might very well make a recovery, a nearly complete recovery, but they must be realistic, the Stevicks were cautioned with a light emphasis upon the word "realistic" —after all, Warren had suffered an extraordinary physical trauma, a protracted physical trauma, which could not fail to have emotional consequences.

His priest-uncle Domenic visited his bedside, listened to Warren's halting talk of the terms of his Incarnation, seemed baffled, embarrassed as the chaplain in Korea, told the Stevicks afterward that he hoped his nephew wasn't drifting away from the Church: he seemed to have been infected by an Oriental sort of mysticism or pantheism over there. In a number of awkward episodes Warren talked with his father of his experience, his hopes for the future of mankind etc., and while Lyle Stevick appeared to be intensely interested at first, deeply moved if a bit puzzled, the conversations trailed off into mutual uneasiness, silence. He was able to match certain of his son's remarks with the names of certain philosophers—Plato, Aristotle, Marcus Aurelius, Kant, Schopenhauer, Pascal—but his information did little to assuage Warren's urgency. Unable to smoke in the hospital room, Mr. Stevick sucked on his unlit pipe nodding sympathetically, vaguely, telling Warren he would soon be out of the hospital and back home where he belonged, *there* his life would fall into place.

With his mother, Warren knew even in his drugged state to speak only of concrete things, memories—favorite foods, the weather, family news of a benign sort. He already felt guilty at having frightened her with his near-death, he didn't want to upset her further.

After he was discharged from the hospital, Warren fell into the habit of talking with Enid because she was the only member of the family who seemed not only capable of understanding but interested in what he said. And she was so much younger than he!—it amazed him to see how quick she was to take him up on issues, to ask him questions, to draw him out. At this time Enid was fourteen years old, a small-boned rather intense girl, high-strung and easily moved to laughter or to anger, quite intelligent, Warren sensed, though there was something disagreeable, perhaps disorienting, about her intelligence. Her eyes were bright and quizzical, frequently narrowed, the eyeballs themselves slightly protuberant seen in profile. In repose her delicate mouth often looked wounded, almost ugly, as if a tension was gathering inside her that frightened her.

But she *was* beautiful. Involuntarily Warren thought, Poor Enid!

As an outpatient at the VA hospital Warren was obliged to return four times a week for therapy intended to rebuild the badly atrophied muscles in his shoulders and thighs. He had the use of a lightweight aluminum walker, eventually he needed only a cane, but Enid frequently volunteered to accompany him on the bus. The trip was arduous, involving a transfer at Clinton and Union. Repeatedly they drifted back onto the subject of Warren's "death" in Korea. Enid wanted to know precisely how it felt, how he'd known what was happening, why he was so certain it had happened at all. It meant, didn't it, that he had a soul but what *was* a soul?—if it was housed in flesh as Warren insisted. "Everything that happened might have been a hallucination," Enid said. "It wasn't a hallucination," Warren said calmly. "But how do you *know?*" Enid persisted. She spoke not looking at him, her face just perceptibly averted, her mouth curious, pained. "How do you know you're awake now," Warren said, "and not dreaming?"

He had meant the question to be rhetorical but Enid sat pondering, frowning. Finally she said, "But I don't know!"

In that other life in that other dimension Private Stevick understood that the cycle of his being was rapidly running out. His soul so carefully baptized by the hand of man in the service of the Divine was mere water spilling noisily into water like the rain- and mud-swollen spring rivers his platoon had to cross in pursuit of the invisible enemy or in retreat from the invisible enemy. This enemy awaited them like night, like time itself waiting to obliterate the flesh. It was a matter of corrosion, of wearing away.

Private Stevick's face dissolved first, then the faces of his family to whom he wrote his disjointed letters.

What fascinated: the flooding rivers bearing in their crazed momentum a mix of uprooted trees, parts of huts, fences, the bloated carcasses of cows, oxen, goats, human carcasses too, so mangled and misshapen it was not necessary even to pretend pity.

What was once human quickly became mere water rushing into water, filling the universe with a delirium of purposeless motion.

South of Chorwon in the mud and pelting rain there was a battle in which Private Stevick had not died. Afterward the chaplain recited the names of the dead and those believed to be missing, intoning the names, the syllables, as if by this solemn means the absent men might be evoked. Then he told a story from the book of Ecclesiastes about a city under siege and how after all hope was seemingly lost a good and wise man appeared to save the city; yet in spite of his heroism the good and wise man was very soon forgotten. In a hoarse aggrieved voice the chaplain addressed the company, telling them of the sacred obligation to remember not just now, today, at this time, but in the weeks and months ahead. "I want to share with you the knowledge that we the living must be worthy of the sacrifice of our fallen comrades," he said. "We the living are the only link in the precious chain between the past and the future. We must honor the past, we must honor the dead who have died that we and our countrymen might live. We must hand on to future generations all that is sacred of the past, then with God's grace we will be worthy of our comrades' sacrifice today. Remember they have died that we might live!" he said passionately, tears shining on his face and his graying hair blowing in the wind. "That America might live!"

Private Stevick stood dry-eyed and antagonistic, unable to weep even for his own impending death.

Now in his awkwardly assembled body stitched and braided with the scars of incisions, Warren summoned back such episodes without pain or grief as if they had happened to another man. But he felt a strong tug of sympathy for that man: we are one, we are many.

Such things he would like to tell Adlai Stevenson. If they met, if ever the two of them happened to be alone together. *We the living are the only link in the precious chain between the past and the future.*

But there was another Warren Stevick determined to be practical, shrewdly pragmatic. His instinct was that politics is fundamentally the art of the pragmatic, of altering the world, what good was idealism if not linked to activism?—he'd read and admired Thoreau as a boy of thirteen. So he joined up with the Young Democrats of Ithaca, New York, immediately after hearing Stevenson's speech, and amid an army of like-minded tireless Stevenson supporters he quickly emerged as outstanding in his commitment and zeal. His guiding principle was a simple one: Adlai Stevenson is a great man, he will be a great President, but he must be *elected*. So Warren stuffed envelopes hour upon hour, distributed flyers in the city, typed up lists of names, addresses, telephone numbers, rang doorbells, wrote editorials for the campus newspaper analyzing both the Democratic and the Republican party platforms. He helped organize a public debate in which these issues were discussed, he appeared before the St. Thomas More Society to defend Stevenson against charges of immorality (Stevenson was a divorced man), he even debated the Socialists. His friends warned him against falling behind in his classes, jeopardizing his scholarship —in fact he had two scholarships—but Warren was confident he could do everything that needed to be done: he'd sweep floors at campaign headquarters, he'd clean out toilets, and did, in the service of the great man!

The early years of the fifties might fix the pattern of civilization for many generations, Stevenson had said, and Warren believed this to be so. What task then was too petty, too demeaning, too without reward, if it aided in the election of Stevenson to the presidency? *What thy hand findeth to do, do it with all thy might.*

So Warren Stevick entered the sphere of *doing,* so distinct from that of *being,* yet following naturally from it. Of what value after all was *being* if it remained locked within itself, self-referring, self-enhancing? He had never much liked the saints who preached an ecstasy of mere inwardness, the communion of the self's soul with God and the obliteration of the world.

He was working too for an Ithaca lawyer in his mid-thirties, a strong Stevenson man campaigning for a district congressional seat. His grades didn't matter set beside a task of such magnitude, yet if he failed a subject or two he could make it up the second semester, he didn't doubt his newfound strength or the rightness of his goal.

Adlai Stevenson had begun his campaign strong and continued to grow in strength as the weeks passed. The man was indefatigable, it seemed, alert, confident, amused, and passionate, supremely well-informed and so marvelously articulate this was a radiance of personality indeed!—in the Midwest, in New England, in Texas, in Oregon, speech following speech revealed him as a man supremely talented for campaigning, for addressing large crowds but also for speaking into and through the rather quirky rather unpredictable new medium of "television" itself. Even his critics had to concur—there had never yet been a television personality quite like Adlai Stevenson. *What* he said and *how* he said it were uniquely joined, his glistening eyes, his warm smile, then his sharp anger when he spoke out courageously, accusing Senator Joseph McCarthy of being himself un-American, in truth a disgrace to America; he dared take on his hugely popular opponent, General Eisenhower, by charging him with political expediency—for was not Ike without moral principle to shrink from defending his old friend and comrade General George Marshall against absurd attacks of having "surrendered" China to the Communists? To which Ike and his staff of speechwriters could make no coherent reply.

Warren and his friends watched Stevenson at every opportunity over the television set at campaign headquarters, he bought a cheap radio so he could listen to political news at any hour day or night, the radio on a bookcase close beside his bed. Stevenson's star was rising! Stevenson would win!—yet Warren thought it troubling, baffling, that after Richard Nixon was publicly exposed for taking bribes, voters continued to support Eisenhower over Stevenson; yet more inexplicable, there was an upsurge in popular support for Nixon himself: a man revealed by way of television as callow, hypocritical, mealy, manipulative, very clearly a liar. Oh, so very clearly a liar!

Though Eisenhower had begun his campaign weak, even bumbling, he was ending it with a surprising strength—a professional soldier's stratagem, as it would afterward be disclosed. Stevenson was no less Stevenson than before on his good nights, but at other times he appeared to be tiring, his humor less genial, rather more sardonic, even bitter, he was baffled himself—he, Adlai Stevenson, so clearly Eisenhower's superior in every way, trailed his opponent in all the nationwide polls! Yet more dismaying, heartbreaking perhaps, was the fact that the discredited Richard Nixon—the hypocrite "little man" who preached purity and Americanism but practiced corruption and political subterfuge—was now himself drawing enormous crowds across the United States quite independent of Eisenhower!

In October Nixon and his cohort Senator McCarthy appeared frequently on television to accuse Stevenson of being "soft" on communism, or was the Democratic candidate—as McCarthy maliciously suggested—actively pro-Communist? "Birds of a feather flock together," McCarthy said with sly leering gravity, then again no less cryptically, " 'By their fruits ye shall know them!' " Now it was General Eisenhower's campaign promise that as President he would go personally to Korea to help bring about a truce, now political cartoonists even at relatively liberal newspapers were merciless with Adlai Stevenson's receding hairline, his prominent forehead—"egghead," a wonderfully cruel immediately popular term just coined by the political columnist Stewart Alsop. "Egghead, egghead," what did it mean?—it meant derision, it meant contempt, even loathing, it meant loss.

Yet when Warren finally heard Stevenson speak in downtown Syracuse near the end of the campaign he fell yet more deeply under the man's spell. No matter that Stevenson's face was lined with weariness, no matter that his powerful voice sometimes faltered, all that Warren had believed from the start was true: Adlai Stevenson was a great man he must be elected President of the United States he *would* be elected President of the United States. Even so late in the campaign the crowd was clamorous, joyful, interrupting Stevenson countless times with applause, no matter that the man had made most of his points before, no matter that, as he suddenly admitted in a frank level voice, he was now running scared—as that apt old political expression would have it.

That only meant, Stevenson continued passionately, that he must work harder during the next several days right up to the eve of the election, and he was willing to work hard as he hoped they knew by now; he was willing to work damned hard.

Warren applauded, standing swaying on his feet with the others, the many rows of men and women their eyes bright with tears their faces ecstatic; he felt half drunk, punchy, his hands ached with the wonderful violence of clapping. If only such a moment could last forever! if only—forever!

Afterward Warren was taken backstage to meet Stevenson by the lawyer who was campaigning for Congress, it was a surprise to see that close up Adlai Stevenson did look his age, those marvelous eyes so quick with life bracketed by lines and soft bruised skin; and how very diminutive a man he was, standing flat-footed on an ordinary floor with other men surrounding him. Warren himself was feeling rather faint tonight, for the past week or more he'd been working hard at campaign headquarters eight, ten, twelve hours a day, he'd stopped going to classes, hadn't had time even to check into the university medical center for a blood test (he suspected his white blood count had dropped again, he knew the symptoms), ate no more than one hurried and tasteless meal a day. Still he knew that the evening in Syracuse would be one of the great events of his life whether Stevenson won the presidency or not and he meant to savor it, to value it precisely, even as he experienced it.

Amid a hubbub of voices and jostling admirers Adlai Stevenson shook Warren Stevick's hand, his handshake was firm, unhesitating, his manner forthright and warm. There was opportunity for little more than a minute's conversation, during which time Stevenson adroitly drew out of Warren the fact that he was a Korean veteran a scholarship student at Cornell, that he came from Port Oriskany, New York—an old Democratic stronghold though the party machinery in that rough city, Stevenson said wryly, was nothing much for Democrats to be proud of, was it! Warren then told Stevenson in a rush of words that he was a great man—the greatest American of his time— and that the campaign he'd led had been a great campaign no matter its outcome. And the smiling fatigued man shook his hand a second time and thanked him.

And that was that.

Mr. Stevick insisted upon placing a $25 bet with Warren: not just that Ike would win but that Ike would win in a landslide.

Mr. Stevick was a faithful Democrat who intended to vote the straight party ticket as usual but he knew, he said, which way the wind was blowing, he could smell it from afar.

Since the humiliation of his arrest Mr. Stevick's humor was harsh and jocose, unpredictable. He seemed not to understand or to wish to understand what the election meant to his son. "Adlai doesn't have a chance, no man of intelligence and sensitivity has a chance in this country," he said. "You know what the great American philosopher P. T. Barnum said about the United States!"—not caring that Warren was silent at his end of the telephone line.

On election night Warren watched the returns on television at campaign headquarters, his eyes aswim in tears of anger and incredulity, how ashamed he was not of his candidate—not of his own efforts—but of America! of American voters! The loss was so much greater than the Democrats had anticipated. Even as the campaign ended it had been difficult to believe that loss was inevitable, a matter of numbers, statistics; prominent on one of the walls at headquarters was the famous photograph of Harry Truman on the morning of November 3, 1948, holding aloft the Chicago *Tribune* with its gloating mistaken headline DEWEY DEFEATS TRUMAN: remember that the polls can be wrong! But now in 1952 the news was very different, television announcers were speaking excitedly of a landslide, the most dramatic national victory since FDR in 1936, there could be no amusing mistake to be set right in the morning.

By 11 P.M. it was reported that thirty-nine states had gone for Eisenhower, a mere nine for Stevenson. More than six million popular votes separated the candidates and there was the promise of more, much more to come! Repeatedly the map of the United States was shown on the screen and repeatedly the newscasters gave their reports, made their gleeful predictions, spoke of Ike's "absolute victory," Ike's "crushing victory," Ike's "sweep of the country," Ike's "landslide" ("the most dramatic since FDR in 1936": oh yes), until Warren felt sick, drained of all feeling except shame. Lyle Stevick in his coarse lazy cynicism had been right all along.

At 11:30 P.M. Adlai Stevenson appeared on television to read his formal statement of concession.

He was the very man Warren had met in Syracuse, the very man!—now trim, gracious in defeat, good-humored it might almost have seemed, for he knew well how America adores a winner and despises a loser, how closely America scrutinizes its losers to gauge the depths of their injury and humiliation: Is the wound mortal? yes but does it *hurt?* As if to concede to such expectations Adlai Stevenson paused after the reading of his formal announcement—suddenly one was allowed to see that this was a man in defeat, a man stunned and exhausted by defeat—in a very different voice Stevenson told the anecdote that would be repeated countless times after this election night which Warren would remember all his life: Asked by a journalist how he had felt after an unsuccessful election, Abraham Lincoln said, Like the little boy who stubbed his toe in the dark, he was too old to cry but it hurt too much to laugh.

But Warren Stevick did cry, he gave himself up clumsily to grief, awash in humiliation, shame, anger, for what did anything matter now? The greatest American of his time had been scornfully repudiated by his fellow citizens.

Warren left the others shortly after midnight, went to his boardinghouse to his room to his unmade bed, that he might lie in the dark like a wounded animal; his left eye behind its thick magnified lens had been aching for hours, its vision nearly gone, his bowels were sick, cold, he wanted no commiseration, he wanted only to be alone with his grief. But he was so exhausted he soon fell asleep. Slipped in a queer zigzag delirium into sleep. He saw a Negro child on a bicycle pushed into the path of an enormous truck—a coal truck it was—he heard the blare of the horn the terrible squeal of the air brakes he tried not to see but there was the small body twitching, the bicycle mangled, the splatter of blood. When he woke the vision was still with him, a shard of nightmare he couldn't remember—had it been real had it happened was it only Warren Stevick's dream?

12

Felix I want you to love me.
Anything you do to me—it's what I want.
I love you Felix, I would never tell anyone.
She invented a code to write in her notebook, if Lizzie or Mrs. Stevick discovered the book they wouldn't be able to read it, they wouldn't know, Felix and Enid's secret was safe. *I will never tell anyone* Enid wrote. She hid herself away in her room, her skin gave off a sickly clammy heat. When she was with other people she frequently stared at them blind and radiant, her eyes dilated with passion.

He was out of town they said, he'd become a real businessman they said, borrowing money, making investments, maybe he would form a company of his own for tax purposes. Enid was careful not to ask about him too frequently especially if Lizzie was close by for Lizzie would guess, Lizzie would know, hadn't she always been in love with Felix herself? In school there were certain familiar windows certain familiar angles of vision, chimneys, patches of roof, fire escapes Enid came to associate with Felix and her thoughts of him, just stepping up into the Decker Boulevard bus, just hearing the bus's pneumatic brakes released and of course her own reflection in a lavatory mirror as she washed her hands, scrubbed her hands; she scrubbed her hands a good deal sometimes, her face as well, then she blotted them with paper towels slowly, not wanting to disturb the obsessive rhythm of her thoughts.

At Shoal Lake on l'Isle-Verte in that room in the old Rideau Inn a man had been waiting on the other side of the door Enid opened, he'd pulled her inside swiftly and unhesitatingly, he'd known what he wanted and what he was going to do, even what he wasn't going to allow himself to do, yet in his excitement in the frenzy of his passion he might have snapped her neck—her backbone!—it could have happened in an instant if she had resisted.

Want to be my sweetheart, sweetheart? Felix had said, teasing, but she hadn't been listening, had she.

Still she'd gone upstairs. She'd opened the door.

His fingers were impatient, tugging down the straps of her bathing suit he was sucking at her breasts, biting her flesh, trembling with excitement, his body was all muscle and heat pushing against her, she realized in her trance of astonishment that he was part naked prodding and then pumping himself against her in quick hard thrusts he'd lifted her skirt he was grinding himself against her belly then between her legs the crotch of her panties, then it was over, his breath expelled from him hard, abrupt, surprised, angry, sweat ran in rivulets down his face, down his chest and back, Enid was embracing him without knowing what she did, then in the embrace she tightened her hold, she clutched at him to keep from crying out.

She had felt the warm semen pulsing onto her belly, she'd known what it was.

Still he said nothing. He seemed hardly aware of her except as a presence, a body giving him some small unwitting resistance, his will was dominant, all-obliterating. Enid understood that he was detached from her and from the rather anguished mechanical act he had performed, even as he stood swaying drunken against her, his arm crooked around her neck locking her in place, his hot shamed face in her hair, still he was somehow separate from her, saying her name, her name, so sweet so sweet so sweet—he swallowed a belch and Enid smelled beer.

Her eyes were open, staring. She was staring sightless as the sky darkened by degrees, the clotted clouds thickening, ridged with black. Now she could hear the lake again, dull spent waves, at dusk most days the wind died down and the lake became flat, merely rippling, shivering in motion. From somewhere up the beach came the sound of voices, gay drunken voices, waves of laughter so faint and chancy they might have been distant music. Now Felix had taken her hand, he was closing her stiffened fingers over his penis to stroke him hard again.

13

There was no hour when she began to think consciously of suicide but there was a day in late autumn—November, the week before Thanksgiving—when she realized she had been thinking of it for a long time.

Not of suicide really but of death: Death.

She was riding on the crowded overheated 4:20 P.M. bus taking her home from school along Decker Boulevard, she was sitting beside a heavyset Italian woman of about her mother's age, her schoolbooks were in her lap, her gym clothes in a soiled paper bag, she had not wanted to take an earlier bus because two of her friends—Enid had friends in high school, Enid Maria was pretty, mildly popular—were riding on it and she wanted to be alone to think of Felix Stevick as she so frequently did; then suddenly she understood she was not thinking of him at all but of death of dying of Enid Maria Stevick dead.

And the tight clenched muscle in her chest relaxed. Like a fist slowly spreading its fingers.

Now the broken-off parts of her life, the fragments, bits, puzzle pieces, began to fall into place, to assemble themselves, as invariably they do once we are under the enchantment of Death.

Still, Enid knew she must wait for a sign.

She would not act until she received a sign.

But now she was so bright, hard, fired with strength and energy, she arranged Lizzie's bureau drawers as well as her own, she helped her mother with housework, she began to anticipate almost with excitement the simple mechanical repetitive tasks of the housework she performed in her mother's presence, Enid so very daughterly, pliant, childlike in her submission to Mrs. Stevick's will. But at times her eagerness to help in the kitchen especially aroused some antagonism in her mother, her mother's nature was one that resisted generosity in others out of fear she might then be required to be generous herself.

On the Decker bus she often gave up her seat to older passengers or to women with young children, she was nervously alert to the needs or near-needs of other people. It pleased and excited her to see the space she'd occupied taken, the emptiness where she had been so readily filled in.

Felix I want to die, Enid wrote on a sheet of notebook paper, her blood coursing in hard stubborn surges, *I love you so much.*

And before her courage failed she slipped the paper into an envelope, addressed it to her uncle, stamped the envelope and ran out to the corner to put it in a mailbox.

When she came back coatless and out of breath, that queer radiant sheen to her face Mrs. Stevick gripped her by the shoulders and said in an ugly rising voice, "What is it? What game are you playing? Is it some boy? Some boy hiding out there? Are you turning into a slut like your sister? *Tell me!*"

But Enid was innocent, Enid had nothing to tell.

Even after she died the notebook could never be deciphered. Enid and Felix's secret was safe.

She wondered if she should write him another letter to assure him the secret was safe, then decided against it. One letter from Enid when he didn't love her, had no interest even in fucking her again, was enough, a second letter would be vulgar, tacky, he'd toss it away without opening it and she didn't want to tempt him to such an act.

Christmas 1952: the Stevicks at 118 East Clinton got their first television set.

It was Mr. Stevick's surprise gift for the family, an eleven-inch portable Philco with a simulated walnut cabinet, they could place it on a table in a corner of the living room adjacent to the corner of the living room their neighbors used for their television set, the volume turned up high enough to drown out their neighbors' television volume.

Everybody was getting a TV now, if you can't lick 'em, join 'em, Mr. Stevick said contemptuously. The set was secondhand but he'd decided to bring it home and not sell it at the store, he didn't intend to watch much but the rest of the family might like it.

Now the machine hummed nightly in the shadowy living room, its small screen glowed with an eerie atomic radiance, pale, bluish, ghostly, flickering. During the daytime Mrs. Stevick set up her ironing board so that she could watch whatever chanced to be on, she was deeply moved to see Senator McCarthy in person on the floor of the Senate, she could try to guess the answers to quiz show questions: What is the longest river in the world? What are the dates of the Crimean War? Who was the "Swedish Nightingale"? Her sister Ingrid came over once or twice a week to watch, Lizzie stayed home more often or met her boyfriends at other times, Mr. Stevick sat in his old leather chair, a magazine or a book open on his lap, yes he really was reading though he glanced up now and then to see what was going on, what sort of foolery the studio audiences were in an uproar about, there was Uncle Miltie simpering in a woman's taffeta evening gown, staggering in spike-heeled shoes, there was Lucy fluttering her inch-long eyelashes at Desi, there was Phil Silvers in his army officer's uniform smirking and leering, there was Ed Sullivan rubbing his hands together—like a funeral director, Mr. Stevick said—Ed Sullivan grave and smiling clearing his throat; best of all there was Arthur Godfrey and his troupe—"Awful" Godfrey, Mr. Stevick called him but in truth he rather liked Godfrey's wit, he recognized something sly and mean beneath it which corresponded to his own.

And there was Groucho!—of course. Groucho wriggling his fantastic eyebrows, sucking lewdly at his cigar, if Lyle Stevick would admit to any TV favorite it was Groucho Marx and Lizzie and Enid were partial to him too, perhaps because he reminded them of their father when they were children.

Since she was going to have a career in show business—singer, dancer, actress, she didn't yet know which; maybe she'd be all three!—Lizzie liked the variety shows best. She was particularly excited by Ted Mack's Original Amateur Hour though invariably resentful of the talent. (Wasn't Lizzie Stevick just as good?) Lizzie had a strong full throaty voice like Kay Starr, some said, or was it Patti

Page, or Dorothy Collins so sweet and girlish or Peggy Lee who was sexy sly insinuating—Lizzie could imitate them all depending upon her mood.

(But her career was slow to begin. Mr. Stevick refused to allow her to take singing and dancing lessons because he "feared for her morals.")

Evenings that winter Enid did her homework with the door to her room ajar so she could hear the sound of the television downstairs—it made her feel less lonely. She didn't want to join her family but she wanted to know they were there as they'd be there after her death.

Sometimes she looked up from her work, stricken with a curious kind of happiness. Hearing laughter downstairs—downstairs at 118 East Clinton! It was amazing. It was unprecedented. It would not have been possible without television.

Enid was struck too by the fact that the television screen, so unlike the movie screen, sharply reduced human beings, revealed them as small, trivial, flat, in two banal dimensions, drained of color. Wasn't there something reassuring about it!—that human beings were in fact merely images of a kind registered in one another's eyes and brains, phenomena composed of microscopic flickering dots like atoms. They *were* atoms—nothing more. A quick switch of the dial and they disappeared and who could lament the loss?

Shortly after Christmas Day there arrived a quite unexpected present: a small but heavy crate of Florida citrus fruit (brightly dyed navel oranges, seedless pink grapefruit), figs, mixed nuts, chocolates, and foot-long candy canes, mailed up from Neiman-Marcus in Miami Beach and addressed to *The Stevicks*. The enclosed card, a shiny embossed Santa Claus, was signed *Felix Stevick* though it looked as if he hadn't signed it himself.

"What is *this!* Why the hell *this!*" Mr. Stevick exclaimed.

He was baffled and offended by Felix's gift, refused to let the subject rest. Why did his brother do the cockeyed things he did, what were the man's motives? Did he in fact *have* any motives?—Felix had never so much as sent them a card in the past, he'd ignored them all for years, scarcely remembering to congratulate Lyle on the birth of his children. And now *this.*

Felix just wanted to show him, Mr. Stevick said, that he could afford it—not just a gift from a fancy store but the fact that he was down there, while the rest of the family was suffering in the cold. Or maybe it was simply that like other boxers—the breed was known for such quirks—Felix Stevick was generous when the spirit moved him that way and the meanest son of a bitch on God's green earth when it moved him another way.

"His secret is he doesn't have a soul like other people," Mr. Stevick said seriously. "He isn't all *there.*"

"The way you're going at those nuts, Daddy, sure looks like *you're* all there," Lizzie observed.

And to Mr. Stevick's embarrassment it was so: without seeming to know what he was doing he'd devoured nearly the entire container of mixed nuts himself. His favorites were cashews and Brazil nuts—he'd left the peanuts untouched.

Enid wanted nothing of Felix's gift, not even the sweet pink grapefruit, not even the kiwi fruit which was like nothing the Stevicks had ever seen before—it took them a while to work out how the fruit should be eaten. (Mr. Stevick had tried biting into it but the skin was repulsive.) Eventually Enid ate some of the oranges since they were mixed in with oranges from the A&P in the refrigerator but by that time she'd put it out of her mind that they were from her Uncle Felix, that they had anything to do with him at all. But by then she wasn't eating much, in any case.

Enid asked Warren had he ever wanted to die, for instance when he was first hospitalized in Korea, or afterward when he had time to think, to really feel pain and remember what had happened to him, how terrible people were; had he ever regretted the fact that his soul *had* reentered his body? (Enid never doubted that what he'd said was true. Warren was incapable of lying.) Enid's question appeared to be spontaneous but Warren was evasive answering it, busy packing a suitcase, tossing in clothes, books, papers; he intended to leave next morning on the 7 A.M. bus for Ithaca and hadn't much time for distractions. (All vacation he'd spent in his room working, writing papers and studying for examinations in courses he'd been failing at midterm. He had let everything slide working for Adlai Stevenson: and look what it had gotten him.) So Warren had little enthusiasm for taking up this question of all questions of his sister's.

He said quickly, "I don't think so. No."

"You never have wanted to die?—never?"

"*No.*"

Seeing Enid's look of hurt at his tone he went on to tell her that when people are badly injured as he'd been they don't want to die because they're incapable of forming the thought of "dying"—of "death." That belongs to consciousness. That belongs to volition. "Also I had the idea that God would refuse any soul that came to Him before its rightful time," Warren said. "It sounds absurd now—sounds insane. But I couldn't think coherently then. The entire belief in God, the edifice of religion—*our* religion, I mean—it's all rather insane. But I shouldn't say such things," he muttered, "and upset you."

Though he could see, couldn't he, that Enid wasn't upset at all. That she was staring at him, her lips slightly parted. Listening so intently she'd forgotten to breathe.

"Sorry," he said, dismissing her, turning back to his packing. It looked as if he was eager to get away.

For women the most common methods are, in order of popularity: pills (barbiturates, aspirin); gas and carbon monoxide poisoning; drowning; slashing of wrists; leaping from heights; gunshot. For men the most common methods are: gunshot; hanging; gas and carbon monoxide poisoning; pills (barbiturates, aspirin); leaping from heights; drowning; poison (arsenic, rat poison etc.). Women more frequently attempt suicide but men more frequently succeed.

She thought a good deal of her Grandfather Stevick—daring to shoot himself in St. Joseph's Hospital in his bed beneath a crucifix—knowing he must die and wanting only to take control of his dying.

Yes, that was it, Enid thought. Control.

The Rosenbergs for instance. Yes, the Rosenbergs—you had to admire them. Sentenced to death in the electric chair with the proviso that *if they confess* the death sentence will be lifted, *if not* they will die. And they astound and thwart their prosecutors by *not confessing.*

Immediately after the judge's sentencing they had burst into song in their detention cells—Ethel sang an aria from *Madame Butterfly,* Julius "The Battle Hymn of the Republic."

In her notebook in her secret code Enid wrote of the Rosenbergs, copied remarks of theirs out of the newspapers, inscribed their names lovingly. According to Warren, who was infuriated by the decision, what Judge Kaufmann had done was a travesty of justice *intended to be such.* No one had been sentenced to death under the ridiculous Espionage Act since its passage in 1917! Could any government be more cynical, more manipulative, more tyrannical while priding itself on its democratic heritage!

But Enid loved the Rosenbergs because they wanted to die and because they were going to die by their own decision really. That was their secret—their triumph. To die together to force their enemies to commit murder to assert their love for each other for all eternity.

Julius & Ethel
Ethel & Julius

She counted the months on her fingers. The weeks. June 18, 1953, the scheduled date of their execution, wasn't far off. She wondered if she would outlive them—if she could bear her life that long.

In April a boyfriend of Lizzie's named Tony Sapio was killed in a car crash on the John Jamieson Expressway when his car careened across two lanes of traffic to slam into the concrete road divider. But the coroner discovered he'd been shot in the shoulder by a high-powered rifle. Police theorized the shot had been fired from the Grand Street overpass but there were no witnesses. The incident had occurred in midafternoon of a Tuesday but there were no witnesses.

In Lizzie's crowd, at East High where Tony had been a student a few years before, nobody talked of anything but Tony Sapio and who might want him killed!—wasn't it known that Tony's father and his older brothers were in the rackets aligned with the powerful Rimi family but Lizzie never wanted to talk about that, Lizzie knew nothing about that, she wept and spoke only of Tony: of how sweet he'd been to her, the presents he'd given her, the places they'd gone in his jazzy Pontiac Catalina. It was true that Lizzie Stevick couldn't claim to have been a steady girl of Tony's—he hadn't any steady girl, he was too restless—but she'd been crazy about him. Sort of. In love with him off and on. He could be nasty sometimes, he could be rough, but God he *was* sweet. And now he was dead.

So Lizzie mourned him, cried and cried, her face powdered dead-white, her lipstick darkish maroon like death. Even her perfume gave off a wild frantic odor of grief. In the halls of East High, Lizzie's girlfriends surrounded her jealously to comfort her while other students stared—maybe in envy. Enid seemed hardly to know her sister now Enid wasn't Angel-face any longer, now she'd turned away from that and their lives were divergent; God, Enid thought, seeing Lizzie around school, *is* that my own sister?—glamorous, hard-faced, sophisticated. Lizzie had a "reputation" at school it was best not to consider, but much of it, Enid thought, was just exaggeration, rumor. Surely it had to be.

Lizzie had teased hair, spit curls, bangs that fell to her eyebrows.

Her eyebrows were drawn on thick and bold and emphatic as Elizabeth Taylor's. On school days she wore tight sweaters or orlon blouses so thin you could see the straps of her lacy slip and brassiere, frequently she wore a black elastic belt that cinched her waist in tight, showed her hips and breasts to advantage—the amazing amplitude of her young body. Enid wasn't jealous but Enid was sometimes intimidated watching her dress, watching her examine herself in their mirror; then at school she'd see Lizzie at a distance with her pack of girlfriends as formidable as she, the boys who hung about them rough and daunting, though Lizzie's "serious" romantic interests were older boys long out of school with cars and money to spend. Lizzie wore a ring Tony Sapio had given her on a chain around her neck. Several days in succession she wore the scarlet satin jacket with black leather trim Tony had given her—his own jacket, Lizzie claimed, which he'd outgrown and wanted her to have. "It's hard to believe Tony is dead," Lizzie kept saying. In her wallet was a dime-store snapshot of Tony she showed to anyone who asked to see it: Tony Sapio handsome and cruel-looking like a thick-jawed Frank Sinatra with sideburns and oily pompadour cresting over his slightly blemished forehead. He always wore his shirt collar turned up in back in early-fifties punk style.

His murderer, or murderers, would never be found.

"I can't believe it—that he's dead," Lizzie said, staring into the mirror at her drawn pasty white-powdered face. "Enid, I can't *believe* it."

Then one day Enid found the scarlet jacket on the floor of their closet, it must have slipped from a hanger or maybe Lizzie hadn't bothered to hang it up, just tossed it into the closet as she sometimes did her clothes. Enid liked to clean the room when her sister wasn't around—and Lizzie wasn't around very often—she'd become nervous and obsessive about the closet in particular, wanting it neat: the shoes in neat rows, no dustballs, fallen clothing, things "lost" in the corners.

She picked up Tony's old jacket, slipped it on, examined herself in the mirror. A bright lurid pretty scarlet color—shiny, rather cheaplooking, fake leather too—but the jacket had style of a kind. Enid was amused seeing herself in it though it was far too large for her, too large even for Lizzie; Jesus, what an eyesore, Mr. Stevick said, shielding his face when Lizzie appeared in it downstairs, don't you girls have anything decent to wear!—but Enid liked it, there was Angel-face grinning for an instant out of the pale hunted face in the mirror, then disappearing, gone.

* * *

She never crossed the canal by the footbridge, refused even to cut through the vacant lot, these were degrading memories as of a distant childhood spent in illness, squalor, humiliation. She was growing up she *was* grown up nearly, fifteen years old in April, a sophomore in high school, withdrawn from the sordid Clinton Street neighborhood even as she was obliged to live in it: Enid Maria Stevick biding her time. She was waiting for a sign to release her.

Still she thought sometimes of the footbridge, the loose-fitting planks, the rush of water far below, that swaying sickening movement that was like a lever prizing loose her soul, and the deafening racket of the train, the boxcars, the long line of boxcars rattling and shaking the very air in thunder. . . . To die in such a way, to throw herself over the railing to drown in the filthy canal, how easy, how effortless, yet it would be an impersonal death, not Enid Maria's own.

She went to see movies by herself in the afternoon in secret, Gloria Grahame in *The Bad and the Beautiful*, Shirley Booth in *Come Back, Little Sheba*, Hollywood melodramas that left her headachey, ashamed; once out on the street the intensity of the films remained with her, she felt suddenly a muscular impulse to do something quick and violent and irreparable, pretending to be crossing the street not turning her head stepping in front of a bus a truck it might be over in a second Enid Stevick killed at once and no pain: Now! Do it! But immediately came the reaction, the resistance: her body flooded with panic and her thoughts annihilated, she stood unmoving, rigid, even her eyes sightless waiting for the attack to pass.

This was the Death-panic, she'd learned to call it.

The Death-panic: that she would kill herself, that she would be killed clumsily, suddenly, with no deliberation, or that she would *not* be killed but mangled and crippled, a public spectacle, an object of pity and scorn.

She was Enid Maria Stevick, *she* was too smart too crafty to die by accident!—so she instructed herself.

As for certain thoughts that flooded into her head at certain unanticipated moments—she half believed they might be someone else's thoughts, some force some power maybe it *was* God urging her to die.

When he'd driven them back along the narrow silvery bridge from l'Isle-Verte to the mainland to the village of Shoal Lake, Enid had watched the skimming pavement, the blur of water to her right;

her hands had been clasped tight in her lap, her fingers still sticky with his semen, she'd thought then that she might reach over and wrench the steering wheel to the side, quick and hard before he could stop her, they'd crash into the railing but probably wouldn't have broken through to fall into the lake, yet it all passed swiftly and in silence, he sensed nothing, he seemed hardly aware of her now urging the car above the speed limit for the bridge, impatient to get her back to the O'Banans. But the Death-panic hadn't flooded her then, not really. She'd been too weak; she wouldn't have had the strength to die.

Upstairs in the bathroom Enid counted eleven bottles of prescription pills of varying sizes, three for Lyle Stevick and the rest for Hannah Stevick. Some of the prescriptions were years old, others fairly recent. Mr. Stevick suffered from high blood pressure and frequent indigestion, Mrs. Stevick suffered from a shifting variety of ailments including migraine headache, inflamed gums and eyelids, fatigue, female problems, rheumatism; also indigestion, "nerves." Yet so far as Enid could make out there was no prescription for barbiturates in the medicine cabinet: barbiturates, the method of choice for suicides.

There was a generous bottle of Bayer aspirin, however. Always a bottle of Bayer aspirin and sometimes a second in reserve in the cupboard beneath the sink; Mrs. Stevick took aspirin too when her other medicines didn't seem to help.

Enid wouldn't buy her own, that would make it seem premeditated.

In early June as the date of their execution approached, the Rosenbergs were often in front-page headlines in the *Evening Herald,* there were editorials supporting the court's decision, columns by Westbrook Pegler, who argued that the government's next step was to make membership in the Communist Party or its "covert subsidies" itself a capital offense and put to death all persons who were guilty. Enid read the stories in dread, praying the Rosenbergs wouldn't suddenly weaken and confess.

The sign she awaited came to her on June 6.

Often on Saturday mornings she took a bus downtown to the public library, which was one of Enid's private places—went there alone, never with Lizzie or another girl—then afterward walked five or six long blocks south to Niagara Square. This was a newer area of Port Oriskany, razed and renovated since the war. Swanky neighborhood, Mr. Stevick would say in his drawling sneer, where the newest apartment building, built 1950, was fifteen stories high, brick and limestone and opaque glass with a simulated marble façade at ground level and ornate iron grillwork on the lower windows—the building in which Felix Stevick lived. There was even a green awning at the entrance, *The Niagara Towers* scripted in elegant flowing white.

Enid never went inside this building. Never thought of it.

Instead she sat in the square on one of the benches trying to read a book, then after a while she'd find she wasn't reading because her eyes had misted over or she was staring at the apartment building across the street. He had never replied to her letter, of course, she hadn't expected any reply, any acknowledgment of her grief. He'd forgotten what happened at the lake and if he happened to see his niece Enid Stevick sitting there in the square he wouldn't have understood her purpose. Nor did Enid know what she wanted of him.

Yet she was drawn to the square, she was drawn to such episodes of debasement and futility. Like those saints, male and female, they'd learned of in confirmation class, passively offering their bodies to their torturers, offering no resistance—here is my heart here is my tongue my bowels do with me what you will. And their torturers did, ah, they did!—burnings, mutilations, dismemberings!—for the glory of God.

Sometimes an elderly madwoman in a winter overcoat sat on one of the benches tossing bits of bread to squirrels and pigeons, chattering to them as if they were her friends. When pedestrians came by, or rowdy boys on bicycles, the creatures fled in panic but returned shortly to repeat the cycle, cautious at first, watchful, then devouring bread greedily as the old woman chattered at them scolding and affectionate. Enid watched the woman with sympathy and revulsion but the old woman took no notice of Enid.

Sometimes instead of taking a bus back home Enid hitched a ride.

Saved herself a dime though it was risky: if the driver turned out to be someone who knew her, then word might get back to the Stevicks and she'd be in trouble. She'd stroll half on the sidewalk half in the street, a thumb shyly raised should any driver take notice. Walking slowly up Niagara in no hurry to get home, maybe eastward along Grand to Decker Boulevard, it wasn't that unusual in these years for schoolgirls to be hitching rides in Port Oriskany though it was rare to see a solitary girl—that might attract notice. But Enid was always alone. Enid liked being alone. She liked the edgy sensation, the feeling of not knowing who might stop his car and she'd run to get in. And if the driver was a man she didn't know who'd pay no attention to where she wanted to go but drive where *he* wanted—to the expressway, for instance, and out beyond the city limits into the country— what then?

But the rides Enid had were always friendly, easy, innocuous— immediately forgettable.

And when she arrived home Mrs. Stevick might say, "Where were you all day?" and Enid would answer, "At the library, Momma, didn't I tell you?" not the slightest note of insolence in her voice as there would be in Lizzie's. But Mrs. Stevick knew better. Mrs. Stevick always knew better. She heard insolence when it wasn't there, on the surface, but *was* there, in the heart. She sensed not the thoughts her youngest daughter actually had but the thoughts she didn't allow herself to have precisely because Momma, staring at her suspiciously, could read her mind. It was to this deeper level of discourse as to another Enid Maria that she'd respond, saying "Were you!" with a bitter sort of pleasure. She did no more than glance at the books cradled in her daughter's arms like precious cargo, knowing them mere props, signs of subterfuge.

A chilly June afternoon in a light rain Enid was hitchhiking by the Niagara Street bridge when a car braked suddenly to a stop and she saw that the driver was her Uncle Felix—signaling for her to get in. And not smiling.

She hadn't recognized the car, hadn't been prepared, had he bought a new car again so soon?—and afterward she would wonder whether her uncle had stopped because he recognized her or had he stopped just to pick up a young girl hitchhiking alone in the rain.

"Get in! Close the door!" Felix said. And he still wasn't smiling.

Enid sat stiff, not looking at him as he drove across the bridge, a cigarette burning in his fingers, ashes sprinkled on the seat and floor.

He was nerved up, angry. "Does your father know you hitch rides?" he asked.

"I don't know what he knows," Enid said.

Felix said, "It's cheap and it's asking for trouble—I don't want any niece of mine doing it."

The car smelled new—that heady pungent smell of new leather. But the air was thick with smoke.

"Don't you know any better?" Felix asked.

Stiffened in opposition to him, Enid said nothing. She made a pretense of glancing through one of her library books and by degrees her uncle's anger subsided. Still, he was driving fast—going north on Niagara through intersections as yellow lights changed to red. Wanted to get her home and out of the car.

Rain began to drum on the roof, on the windshield. Enid took comfort in the swift mechanical motion of the windshield wipers, the way the glass cleared, then gave itself up to the splattering rain, then cleared again—it was hypnotic. She would have liked to turn on the radio but didn't dare. Her senses were keenly alert, she felt her bones brittle as glass, the very balls of her eyes staring hard and brittle and blind as she continued to turn the pages of her unseen book. *I never told anyone* she wanted to tell him, *who would I tell?*

Already they were beyond Washburn Street, turning east on Clinton, and now numbing familiar sights passed blurred with rain dreamlike in succession—the Ajax car wash with its big yellow sign, the White Tower restaurant at the corner of Clinton and Lock, the Esso service station where Mr. Stevick had had a quarrel with the mechanic, then Carrier Furnaces, then the Clinton Street Bank of Port Oriskany, then blocks of brick rowhouses mean and cramped and then slightly larger houses, duplexes like the Stevicks' covered in shingleboard in gunmetal gray or dark brown or green, with wide porches and steep slanting roofs and small plots of grass or no grass at all, just scrubby soil, weeds. Mrs. Stevick had seeded the lawn in front of their house but it was mainly dandelions now. Without knowing it Enid had begun to cry. Enid pulled a soiled tissue out of her purse and wiped at her eyes. *Who would I tell?*

Felix didn't take her all the way to her house. He parked in the street a block away.

Didn't turn off the car motor. The windshield wipers continued switching back and forth, a great pale cloud of exhaust emerged from the rear. Felix lit up another cigarette and tossed the match out the window. He said in a voice that was oddly affable, relaxed, "You must know it's low class to hitch rides, gives some people the wrong idea."

Enid shut her book. "I do what I want to do," she said.

"Showing your ass out on the street."

Enid was crying and it made him angry, that was why he was trying to keep his voice light; she could feel the tension between them palpable as the charged air before an electrical storm. She looked at him, seeing his dark narrowed eyes, the pale scar in his eyebrow smooth as a piece of exposed bone. She said suddenly, "I didn't tell anyone," and he said at once, half joking, "Didn't tell anyone what!"— and she swallowed hard and went silent. He looked away, face twitchy in disdain, began to tap his fingers on the steering wheel so she could feel his agitation, his rising fury. "Look, you know I was drunk up there, I *told* you—I'm sorry for what happened Jesus Christ I'm disgusted I'm not that kind of a shit really!—taking advantage of a girl your age my own brother's daughter I'm not that kind of man," he said in a rapid voice, a murmur, his face darkening with blood, and Enid sat in a trance, her mind extinguished as if knowing what would come next, the words that would leap out of him next, harsh, hateful, no transition between one tone and the next, "You led me on, acting the way you did fooling around the way you did you knew damn well what you were doing didn't you!—and now I see you out on the street hitching rides!—also I've been hearing about your sister Lizzie, things like she was mixed up with that asshole kid Sapio that fuck-off him and his brother both the old man can't handle them they goddamn deserve whatever happens to them, but look: I never did anything like that with any girl your age before it was just something that happened because I was drunk because you led me on, then that letter you sent—what the hell kind of a thing was that, that letter—from you—I threw it away, what kind of a shit do you think I am? Do I have to spell it out?"

Enid made a sudden movement as if to touch him or was she simply shrinking back from him, and Felix struck out at her by instinct, a hard stinging slap on the side of her face with the back of his hand, lightning quick, she hadn't seen it coming and her head knocked against the window and for an instant she was stunned, astonished— then she hid her face in her hands, crying like a small child. So ashamed, so ashamed. And she'd known beforehand, she'd known all along—so ashamed.

Felix didn't touch her again. Would not comfort her, wanted her gone—revulsed by her. He lit another cigarette, he let her cry for a while, then said, "It's stopped raining," though in fact it hadn't quite stopped yet. "You can get out now, Enid. Get out."

II

ROMANCE

June 1953–
February 1955

1

The sisters were playing together above their father's store. It must have been a slow dull Saturday—a rainy Saturday—many years ago. Through a crack in the floor they could spy on Daddy from above as he stood speaking with a customer, there was the faint gleam of his scalp through his hair, there his rapid gesturing hand. How his voice rose, his laughter! He had a hearty matter-of-fact tone with his customers, even with strangers he'd never seen before. That was the trick, he said, of salesmanship.

The furniture store was a treasure trove, a child's kingdom. Through the grimy front windows of the second floor Lizzie and Enid could stare across Lock Street to a big long yellow sign with black letters—MO STEINBERG'S SEPTIC SERVICE & SEWEROOTER (CLOGGED PIPES—DRAINS—SEWERS OUR SPECIALTY)—at the rear they could stare out onto a weedy vacant lot heaped with broken concrete, then the rear of a boarded-up warehouse they were forbidden to explore. In their games of hide-and-seek poor Lizzie often wandered perplexed and resentful for many minutes not knowing where Enid was hiding. It wasn't fair, Enid was so small!—once she managed to crawl inside a rolled-up rug remnant, not minding the filth, another time she crouched beneath a chair with a chintz flounced skirt Lizzie passed by unsuspecting a half-dozen times. But Lizzie got her revenge by slamming the door to an old icebox her sister was hiding in; then she ran away excited, she didn't intend to let Enid out until she was good and ready, *that* would teach her a lesson. "Where's Enid?" Daddy asked and Lizzie said, "*I* don't know!" But after a few minutes she changed her mind and ran back and opened the door and there was Enid curled up, her arms hugging her knees tight her eyes shut pretending maybe to be dead. Lizzie screamed at her to come out!—even then she wouldn't open her eyes right away. Afterward she told Lizzie she hadn't needed to breathe, she just closed her eyes and went to a place where she hadn't needed to breathe.

Now it was Enid's hoarse rasping breath that disturbed Lizzie's sleep. And a smell too of tainted air, something altered, the window was open a few inches and the wind had changed, blowing now from the east bringing a familiar chlorinelike stink from Diamond Chemical, a fainter odor too from Goodyear Tire. Lizzie was confused, seeing for a moment a tall fire-rimmed smokestack belching smoke, then her eyes were open and she was fully awake, frightened of something in the room. Close by in the other bed Enid was breathing as Lizzie had never heard anyone breathe before, strangely, long shuddering choking breaths punctuated by silence: Lizzie could count a beat of three, four, five, *six,* then Enid gasped horribly for air as if she was drowning, there was a wet catch or click in her throat, terrifying to hear. For a long moment Lizzie lay frozen, then she whispered "Enid?" and leaned over to switch on the lamp.

She was never to forget the sight of her sister there in the damp twisted bedclothes, her face contorted, her eyes rolling white in their sockets.

In a panic Lizzie called out, "Enid! *Enid!*" trying to wake her. The breathing stopped then began again, hoarse and labored, choking, the wet gurgling catch in the throat horrible to hear. Lizzie stooped over her sister, pulling at her shoulders, but Enid lay limp and unresponding, a thread of saliva on her chin. The bedclothes gave off a rank sweaty smell, Enid's lips were drawn back from her teeth in a grimace.

She's dying, Lizzie thought.

She's been poisoned, Lizzie thought.

So it was Lizzie who saved Enid's life.

* * *

Mr. Stevick telephoned St. Joseph's emergency service at 2:25 A.M. saying his daughter was in convulsions, the ambulance arrived at 2:33 A.M. and he rode with Enid to the hospital, leaving Lizzie and her mother behind. It all happened with a vertiginous swiftness—the ambulance out at the curb, the emergency crew on the stairs, men lifting Enid unconscious from her bed in her sweat-stained nightgown while the Stevicks stood back, staring, appalled.

Now Lizzie and Mrs. Stevick were getting dressed, they would not be going to the hospital until morning but it took them a very long time to get ready, it seemed to take many minutes to walk from one room to another, Lizzie began to take her hair rollers out then forgot what she was doing, standing in a daze of incomprehension. Mrs. Stevick wandered clumsy and weeping from her bedroom into the girls' bedroom then back into her own, it might have been an asthma attack, she said, sometimes asthma attacks are fatal one of her cousins when they were children down in Olcottsport died of an asthma attack in the middle of the night only seven years old her aunt never recovered, you never recover from such a shock, but once she'd seen a man in a fit thrashing on the floor of a trolley they said afterward it was an epileptic seizure *that* was the most horrible thing she'd ever seen. Mrs. Stevick was crying, whimpering, dear God dear Mary don't let my daughter be an epileptic don't let her die. In her long wrinkled nightgown with her graying hair in a frowsy braid she looked like an overgrown girl, save for the papery creased skin and the soft heavy swinging breasts. Her eyes darted wetly, half maddened with fear.

Most of the upstairs lights were burning at 118 East Clinton, a good many of the downstairs lights; next door the Schultzes were angry at the commotion and began to thump on the wall as they sometimes did and Lizzie in her slip whirled and slammed her fist against the wall crying, "God damn you, let us *alone!*" Then almost immediately the telephone rang, it was Mr. Stevick at the hospital trying to speak calmly, saying they were pumping out Enid's stomach he couldn't get a straight answer from anybody how serious it was—was his daughter going to live.

Lizzie had picked up the phone. Mrs. Stevick stood plucking at her arm saying, "Is she dead? Is Enid dead?" and Lizzie cried, "Momma, *no!*"

It was a night she would never forget. Yet she could remember it only in patches, broken-off pieces.

Mrs. Stevick was sick with a headache could barely walk and went to take some aspirin only to discover the bottle missing, then Lizzie found it in the wastebasket beneath the sink neatly hidden under some wadded Kleenex, an empty bottle, not a pill remaining, so that was it, she thought stunned, so that was it!—she pushed past her mother, ran to the telephone, she knew she'd better call the hospital, even if they were already pumping out Enid's stomach they should be informed.

Aspirin: a bottle of aspirin.

But *why?*

Mrs. Stevick seemed somewhat relieved, her panic trance began to lift, she said Enid must have woken in the middle of the night with a headache, felt sick didn't know what she was doing took too many pills by accident, the doctor always warned Mrs. Stevick too many of them could make you sick.

"Yes, Momma," Lizzie said tonelessly.

She went to look for a note, didn't they sometimes leave notes explaining? Mrs. Stevick joined her poking through Enid's things, Enid's half of the bureau Enid's half of the closet the drawers of Enid's desk; midway in the search Lizzie was flooded with nightmare horror remembering that between her mattress and bedspring she'd hidden some money some $20 and $50 bills also some platinum-plated cigarette lighters several switchblade knives with eight- or nine-inch illegal blades her boyfriend Eddy Carlisle had given her to hide away for a few weeks just as a precaution but there was no reason to look in that particular place and in fact Lizzie found Enid's notebook not even especially hidden in one of her desk drawers, that school notebook Enid always seemed to be writing in, lying on her bed utterly absorbed, not interested in coming downstairs to watch TV, having to be called twice for supper. Lizzie didn't give the notebook much thought, she didn't give her younger sister much thought, she'd supposed the notebook was a diary maybe or maybe a story Enid was writing, Enid was the kind of student who always did extra assignments at school though her report cards were all A's even occasionally A+'s, Lizzie just couldn't understand that kind of mentality. She just couldn't! Once she asked Enid what she was writing and Enid said with that shivery little twitch of her nose that meant she was being intruded upon, Oh, nothing. And even shielded a page with her hand, as if Lizzie wanted to read it.

Still, it was something of a shock to see that the notebook was all in code.

Mrs. Stevick pulled it from Lizzie's hands to examine it. Her forehead crinkled in disapproval, suspicion. Page after page she turned in slow astonishment trying to read what Enid had so fastidiously printed in block letters. DKWMXQT YUIZ TLLAQDJ—what *was* this what kind of a language what kind of a trick all nonsense words you couldn't read a thing, wasn't this just like Enid.

By 5:30 A.M. Enid was out of the emergency room and in the intensive care unit, Mr. Stevick telephoned to say, her condition was said to be "critical but stable"; now at last he began to sob and Lizzie was crying too, sobbing unable to stop. "It's all right, Daddy," she heard herself say, "it's all right, Daddy, they won't let her die." A flame of bitter hatred ran through her for Enid hiding away in the bathroom poisoning herself and for what, for *this?* "Daddy, they won't let her die," Lizzie said.

She and Mrs. Stevick were to leave for the hospital in a cab later that morning. Lizzie telephoned Geraldine, then her Uncle Domenic to tell them the news, then she risked a quick call to Eddy Carlisle though it was still early—"Honey you won't believe what happened here last night"—swaying sick and dazed on her feet, telling the story as she'd tell it many times in many different versions. Enid was alive only because Lizzie had come home early, she'd originally planned to stay overnight at Nelia Pancoe's where there was going to be a party but then the party was canceled because the Pancoes were going to be home that night after all, this wasn't a story Lizzie could tell at 118 East Clinton nor was it a story she would ever tell in Enid's presence. She had saved her sister's life, she alone was responsible. "That's why Enid doesn't always like me now," she sometimes added with a hurt little laugh. "She knows not to trust me."

2

She was forty-eight hours in intensive care, then they moved her into a private room; still they had to feed her intravenously, there were tubes attached to both her arms and the insides of both her ankles. Your daughter has very small veins, one of the nuns said.

The Sisters of Charity: long spotless white robes rustling as they walked along the corridors, rosaries clicking softly at their waists, those splendid white starched wimples framing their faces so tightly you couldn't see a strand of hair. Of course the hair was cut short, shorn, maybe some of the older nuns were nearly bald, wearing their headgear so tight so many years. When he'd been a volunteer orderly here Lyle Stevick had fantasized certain of the younger nuns naked beneath their habits but in his fantasies they were always hairless, bodies smooth as porcelain dolls. He wasn't the kind of Catholic to be intimidated by nuns though he had gone to parochial school.

The doctors intimidated him, however. Asking with ill-concealed irony how such an "accident" could have happened. Asking whether the Stevicks were certain Enid had left no message behind? no note? were they absolutely certain? If what she had done was intentional it meant she had tried to kill herself, it should be reported to the police. There is always the danger too, Mr. Stevick, that she will try again.

Mr. Stevick sat stricken but composed, knowing he must choose his words with care. Don't let any of them talk you into committing her to a psychiatric hospital, Felix had warned. They might give her electric shock treatments. They might diagnose her as schizophrenic; they might never let her out.

Not that he needed such advice from his younger brother or from anyone, Lyle Stevick hadn't been born yesterday. One of his Weir in-laws had been locked up in the State Psychiatric Hospital at Mercerville since 1915 for having threatened a tax assessor with a shotgun, he'd been a recluse of sorts living alone on a small farm—harmless, really, Hannah said—but once the authorities got hold of him and started testing him he was finished. (He couldn't tell them who was President of the United States or Governor of the State of New York, didn't even know the date, the day of the week. The diagnosis was "paranoid schizophrenia.")

In the first interview with the doctor after it was determined that Enid Stevick would live, both Mr. and Mrs. Stevick were closely questioned. The doctor's name was McIntyre; he wasn't of course the Stevicks' family doctor, he'd simply been on emergency service in the early morning hours of June 7. Mr. Stevick couldn't help but feel some slight animosity toward the man because even with Hannah present he seemed to be withholding the proper degree of warmth, solicitude. Also he was young—which meant younger than Mr. Stevick—perhaps only in his early forties, with a prim little mouth and unsmiling eyes. In his neat white physician's coat sitting behind his desk, a silver crucifix conspicuous on the wall behind him, he reminded Mr. Stevick of a priest withholding his blessing as in a poker game a player might withhold even the semblance of acknowledgment of a winning hand. Jesus Christ Almighty, Lyle Stevick wanted to plead, my little girl nearly *died!*—and now I'm being interrogated by the Gestapo.

It was Enid's story that the overdose had been an accident.

She didn't recover consciousness sufficiently to talk for nearly forty-eight hours, then she'd been only intermittently coherent, answering questions put to her by Dr. McIntyre and Mr. Stevick in a faint feeble hoarse voice. Words issued from her with excruciating slowness, she seemed to shape each syllable with all the strength in her body, straining with effort, then lapsing into exhausted silence. It was appalling for her father to see how fragile was the life sustained within her, how chancy the pulse that continued its slightly erratic beat, the heart monitored by way of a mechanical bleeping machine close by the bed. Her skin was translucent, the wings of her delicate nose waxen, in a single day she'd lost eight pounds and her eyes looked bruised, blackened. Her blood pressure was still dangerously low, McIntyre said, the lining of her stomach raw, bleeding; he'd cruelly warned of possible kidney failure, of "irreversible" damage to the liver, in fact her heart had stopped beating in the emergency room several times. In so weakened a state she could not have lied, Mr. Stevick reasoned, surely she wouldn't have had the presence of mind to fabricate a story, in any case his little girl *didn't lie,* saying at first that she couldn't remember what had happened, then gradually it came back, she said she had woken in the middle of the night with a severe headache she'd gone to the bathroom half asleep and taken some aspirin tablets she didn't remember how many then later in the night she woke up again her head aching bad so she went back very sleepy and groggy and took some more tablets no she hadn't counted them it was all confused mixed up with sleep and wanting to get back to sleep, how badly she'd wanted the headache to go away.

Was she lying? Lyle Stevick would stake his life on it, *she was not.*

Yet he knew to keep his voice controlled and affable, deferential was the way doctors liked to be treated, little gods they were in the hospital worshiped by the nurses all billowing and brisk, white as starched angels in their medieval attire. Well, it could turn a man's head!—some of the student nurses, nuns or otherwise, were real beauties. During the war when the male population was so depleted Lyle Stevick heard fantastic lurid rumors of liaisons between doctors and lay nurses (even the name comically appropriate), there was one rather ugly doctor popular and much admired, a good Catholic husband with nine children, whose exploits were particularly enviable, also a tale less amusing of the chief of surgery himself so drunk or morphine-dazed he had to be forcibly prevented from performing surgery upon more than one occasion. So Lyle Stevick knew with whom he was dealing, he swallowed down his true self, his salesman's proud gruff slightly antagonistic self, let's face it he was back in the interrogation room at police headquarters answering questions calmly and intelligently, not seeming to notice his wife weeping beside him, he couldn't be held responsible for Hannah's emotional instability.

Yes, doctor, he said politely; no, doctor, he said politely; I don't think so, doctor, he said firmly. Lyle Stevick hadn't been born yesterday.

He was wearing his good brown suit, a freshly-ironed white shirt, a carefully knotted rust-red necktie, his trouser cuffs were soiled but McIntyre wasn't going to notice sitting behind his desk. Hannah was dressed as if for church in a box suit as she called it, the jacket square and buttonless, a drab dark-blue material, shapeless on her corseted but shapeless body. She wore her summer hat of glazed straw, also dark blue, fastened with hatpins atop her steely brown-gray hair. And though she was not wearing her white crocheted gloves she held them clutched in her lap along with her handbag. She wept for a while, then sat holding her handkerchief against her nose. Mrs. Stevick too believed her daughter's account of the incident, of course she believed Enid: she and her youngest daughter were particularly close. In a slow halting voice she told Dr. McIntyre perhaps more than he wished to know of Enid's companionship about the house Enid's eagerness to help with household tasks Enid's good manners her high grades ("She was 'Outstanding Girl' in eighth and ninth grade both at De Witt Clinton") her cheerful personality her fondness for her sisters and brother, no she hadn't any boyfriends yet *that* was a relief. Also Enid was deeply religious she took after her mother's side of the family in that regard, never missed mass on Sundays or Holy Days except now and then if she didn't feel well Enid did have a tendency toward headaches, migraine headaches, menstrual headaches, she took after her mother's side of the family in that regard as well. As Hannah spoke Mr. Stevick glanced at her, startled but much admiring her peasant craftiness. But then he was always being surprised by the members of his family, wasn't he.

There was, after all, that ambiguous troubling clause in the Blue Cross–Blue Shield insurance regarding "self-inflicted injuries" which along with "acts of God" were not held accountable by the claims office.

Mrs. Stevick was saying in a firm emphatic voice that there was no suicide note, no message left behind, and Enid wasn't the kind of girl to have attempted such a thing without leaving a note behind explaining. "I looked everywhere in her room, her sister and I turned the room upside down—I know about things like this, doctor, believe me—but there wasn't anything, just my daughter's school things, her notebooks and papers, that was all. No," she said with a queer sort of clumsy dignity, lifting her chin, her voice trembling, "there was nothing. What happened was an accident and it will never happen again."

Mr. Stevick noted the delicate moment in which Dr. McIntyre decided to believe Hannah. He was nodding, listening to her; then he nodded more sharply, lowering his gaze as he made rapid notations on a sheet of paper. He was a good generous man after all, a father himself and doubtless a good Catholic, Mr. Stevick had noted framed snapshots on his desk showing one, two, three, four, could it be five smiling beaming children all quite young?—and a sturdy good-looking woman with a haircut like Geraldine's.

Still it was cruel of him to say as a parting shot, "Your daughter is so sick, I'm sure *this* will never happen again."

The second interview was much briefer, matter-of-fact. Dr. McIntyre appeared to be in a rush, he simply wanted to speak with Mr. Stevick by himself, leading him out of Enid's room, strolling down the corridor in the direction of the visitors' lounge though they never arrived there, the conversation wasn't that long. He had, he told Mr. Stevick, examined Enid fairly thoroughly now, he'd done an exam just in case, and his daughter was still a virgin, nor was there any sign of venereal infection or disease, sometimes in cases like this—accidental overdose or not—it turns out the girl is pregnant, keeping it a secret from her family, that sort of thing, it's standard procedure to examine them, Dr. McIntyre said, laying a sympathetic hand on Mr. Stevick's arm, seeing perhaps the look on Mr. Stevick's face. "In this case it's good news, Mr. Stevick," he said, easing away, "I thought you'd like to know."

Lyle Stevick stared after him. Numbly he said, "Thank you, doctor."

Thank you you lecherous son of a bitch.

3

"Enid? *Enid*—"

The first sight of his sister in the high cranked-up hospital bed in the intensive care unit of St. Joseph's tore through his heart, though certainly Warren Stevick knew what he should expect to see, he'd prepared himself for the worst yet hadn't thought he might not recognize her. There was Enid barely alive, tubes in both her nostrils distending the flesh, tubes in her forearms, her ankles, wires attaching her to an electronic heart monitor, it was the apparatus of Warren's own devastation, the mutilation of his own soul; he could not bear seeing Enid caught in it.

He stared. He stared. So wasted, so papery-white, child-sized again as if she were ten years old, a flicker of consciousness just discernible in the eyelids' quivering and in that ashy dampness about the mouth. . . . How could she have hated herself so much, to have wished to punish herself so horribly!

"Enid—?" he whispered.

He was told she might be able to hear him, she might be able to respond, she'd been talking fairly coherently earlier that day, she'd recognized her parents and her sister Lizzie. She was going to live, Warren had been assured, the crisis was over.

Yet it seemed to Warren they might be mistaken, she looked so ghastly.

"Enid? It's Warren—"

He hoped to arouse a moment's recognition in her, he was suddenly desperate to stir the most minimal the most fleeting acknowledgment of his presence.

"Enid honey—"

She lay unresponsive as if at the very edge of death. How she was being punished, Warren thought, for whatever it was she had thought she might do in her innocence.

He recalled her asking him about the trauma of his wounding. His woundings. Asking about his soul slipping out of his body. Warren had misled her, perhaps, his experience in the war had rapidly retreated from him and was now like a dream uneasily bracketed by sleep. It might have been another's dream told to him long ago.

Mr. Stevick and one of the nurses were assuring Warren that she could hear him, very likely. She knew he was there.

He stood some distance from the bed, shy of coming closer. Afterward he was to remember the conviction he'd had that she was in fact dying, slipping away from them. No matter the bright blipping of the heart monitor regular as a metronome set at a fast speed. No matter that she breathed unaided, her lungs filling with air, expelling air, the beat irregular but rhythmic. And if she died perhaps it was his own fault.

He was overcome with grief, guilt, rage, suddenly he lost control and said, "Oh, Enid—*why? Can* you hear me?—*why?"* and his father's fingers closed, gripping his arm tight enough to hurt.

He was silenced at once. He knew better.

Yet it seemed Enid tried now to wake, to rouse herself, her eyelids struggled to open but the effort was finally too great. Her life slumbered deep and secret within her, a trickle of life, mere life, precious, incalculable.

Under his breath Warren murmured, *"Why—!"*

Out in the corridor he began to cry fiercely, he didn't give a damn for the spectacle he made or for his father's disapproval, his father's silent seething rage. He wanted Enid to have heard even if she was dying. He wanted her to know that he knew, he was close to her as her own soul.

That was the first day, the most precarious episode. Warren was to stay in Port Oriskany over a week and never again did he lose control.

Geraldine had telephoned him at his boardinghouse in Ithaca to tell him the news, he'd taken a bus home as quickly as he could, convinced en route that he would arrive too late, Enid would be dead. An overdose of aspirin, Geraldine said, and Warren said excitedly, Do you mean she tried to kill herself? Enid? and Geraldine said, No, it wasn't that way, don't *say* that, it wasn't that way at all.

Enid was going to live, Enid was going to be all right, it was an accident, an accidental overdose. Warren listened and tried to make no judgment, this was a time of anxious benign lies after all: you just wanted to get through it. But it was a time too of surprising even exhilarating demonstrations of generosity, affection, love. A time of giving comfort and being given comfort in return. Warren embraced tearfully by his Aunt Ingrid, Warren shaking Frank Pauley's hand, Uncle Domenic solemn and gracious and a source of genuine solicitude in his priestly black costume, aunts, uncles, cousins, neighbors, Felix Stevick anxious to know what he could do for the family, was there anything Lyle needed?—the two of them conferring in the corridor about the price of hospital rooms. Felix wanted to make up the difference between what Lyle's insurance would pay for a bed in a semiprivate room and a bed in a private room, he wanted his niece to have the very best care, he said emphatically, the very best care St. Joseph's could offer. And Lyle Stevick was in no position to decline the offer. Lyle Stevick was deeply grateful.

It was the only time within Warren's memory, he thought, the two had been so close. For they *were* brothers after all.

And Lizzie and Geraldine made it a point to be attentive to their mother and to their father, even to Warren: eyeing their brother critically, worriedly, how is *he* taking all this?—poor Warren who probably wasn't very stable yet himself.

There was only one member of his family with whom he'd been able to talk in recent years, Warren realized.

Damn you, Enid. How could you.

Days passed, hours excruciating and prolonged as days passed, Enid was out of intensive care, Enid was eating soft-solid foods now, Enid had contracted a hospital viral infection and was reattached to a tube feeding her antibiotics to drive down her alarming fever. Could one die of a mere unprovoked fever?—one could, one could. Mrs. Stevick herself was close to collapse.

Enid's eyes were yellow as if with jaundice, her skin so sensitive from hyperesthesia the slightest touch gave pain.

How then could Warren reproach her. How could he trust himself alone in the room with her.

Why did you do it, Enid! Poisoning us all!

Still, it became by degrees a matter of practical arrangements, scheduling visits to St. Joseph's, having cafeteria meals there at noon, then dinner maybe in one or another Union Street restaurant. Mr. Stevick favored the Chop House but Mrs. Stevick was upset by the prices, she thought too the food was carelessly prepared. She hated and distrusted restaurants on principle: it was one of her stories of how she and Ingrid had worked at the Algonquin Dairy when they were girls, of how filthy the place was back where customers couldn't see, you wouldn't believe it, and the Algonquin has such a nice reputation even today. When Felix took the entire family out to dinner at the Gondola on West Grand Mrs. Stevick couldn't enjoy her food, kept thinking of her poor daughter in the hospital, she said, and of how it probably was in the Gondola's kitchen. These places are all alike, she said.

Warren was waiting, he believed, for the proper moment to speak, the perfect equilibrium of emotional forces; then he would ask his father (or Domenic, or Lizzie, or Geraldine) how long they hoped to maintain the pretense that Enid had not attempted suicide. That what happened to her had fallen from the sky chancy and un-premeditated as, say, a flowerpot off a high windowsill.

Though it was a truth Warren had picked up somewhere that things once said within a family cannot be unsaid. And things done but never named might well be forgotten.

Always his family seemed to be eluding him, nervously fending him off even as they asked with apparent interest about his college life: his studies, his professors, his friends in Ithaca, the organization to which he belonged (The National Committee to Secure Justice in the Rosenberg Case) and was he seeing any nice girls? any nice Catholic girls? In Warren's very presence Mrs. Stevick spoke of him with the vehement hope that he would settle down soon, find someone to marry soon, before it was too late. Warren laughed but didn't dare ask what his mother meant. Too late?

He would be twenty-two years old in November.

Warren knew not to upset his mother by bringing up the subject of Enid, but now even Mr. Stevick was difficult to approach. He was bluff and blustery and loud and ebullient in one mood, sour and depressed, exhausted, in another. He whistled under his breath, hummed, sang nonsense tunes ("Yes! We Have No Bananas") around the house, was always lighting up his pipe, fouling the air with smoke, even as Warren was trying earnestly to talk with him; or he fixed Warren with a look so bleak and weary, so defeated, Warren fell silent out of pity. He knows, Warren thought helplessly. But: does he *know?*

It was Warren's idea that Enid see a psychotherapist after she was discharged from the hospital. (Later he was to learn by way of Lizzie that Dr. McIntyre had recommended the same thing, he'd offered to make a referral.) He tried to explain to his father that in 1953 there was nothing exotic or shameful about psychotherapy—a number of Korean veterans including Warren himself had had psychotherapy sessions at the VA hospital—sometimes it was helpful, at the very worst it was harmless; what was there to lose? But Mr. Stevick was angered by the suggestion. There isn't any mental illness in our family, he said.

Not once did Warren say the word *suicide,* not once *attempted suicide,* though he risked his father's further anger by hinting that what had happened to Enid once might happen again: sometimes there was a pattern. Enid had almost died, after all, and you might argue that there was a trauma there to be dealt with, exorcised, as after combat in war, a physical memory lodged in the flesh as well as the spirit.

Mr. Stevick looked at him oddly. As though he had never seen Warren before, had never really heard him speak before. As though the experience might have been a novelty at another time in his life but merely perplexed and wearied him now.

"The fact you seem to want to ignore, Warren," he said slowly, shaking his pipe in Warren's direction, "is that your sister did not die. She did not die. And now the wisest procedure is simply to forget."

Warren tried to reason with his Uncle Domenic, with whom years ago he'd been fairly close; now their relationship seemed strained as if Domenic understood that his nephew had drifted dangerously beyond the reach of his blessing: wasn't Warren studying history, politics, non-Thomist philosophy at Cornell?—wasn't Cornell itself notoriously liberal and secular?—atheistic? He had no doubt but that Warren was neglecting his religious duties, if he'd been going recently to 7:30 A.M. mass at St. James's it was only to accompany his mother, that sort of thing. But Domenic was too tactful to bring the subject up, perhaps too hurt. Like all priests of Warren's acquaintance he seemed to believe that any estrangement from the Church among members of his family was a direct repudiation of him. Not anger or sarcasm but deep mute hurt was the consequence.

But Uncle Domenic strongly disapproved of Warren's suggestion. Psychotherapy—or psychology, psychiatry, psychoanalysis, whatever you called it—it was based upon atheistic principles, was it not? dwelt upon sexual matters, did it not? He knew something of Freud, he'd read some startling articles on Freud and Freud's followers, he'd read enough to be disgusted, repelled. If Enid needed any special counseling, he would want to see her himself; he'd already spent many minutes with her in prayer; and there was always Father Ogden at St. James's, a good man, a reliable man, he'd known Enid since she was a baby, hadn't he baptized her in fact? Hadn't he baptized Warren too?

Warren said flatly, not troubling to hide his disappointment, "I don't remember."

As for Warren's sisters, Geraldine was impossible now to talk with, anxious and chattering about her boys, her husband, her in-laws, Neal having disagreements with his father for whom he worked and what if—he's so hot-tempered—he up and quits? And now that Enid was going to be all right, what about their mother?—what about the terrible strain on Momma's nerves? Since Korea, Warren was made to feel uncomfortable in his older sister's presence, he thought it might be the fact he'd been wounded, the scarred flushed look of his lower face and his magnified, swimming eye, she had never quite gotten around to inviting him out to the house to dinner though Neal seemed friendly enough: maybe she thought he might frighten the four-year-old? the baby? In any case she wasn't going to help him with Enid, with *that,* she simply refused to talk about it. And Lizzie was no better, she thought the less attention Enid got the better because Enid just hated being fussed over, being touched or talked about or looked at, she'd close up tight the way they said a clam or an oyster did, you know?—a shell snapping shut.

Warren asked Lizzie bluntly if Enid had left behind a note or a letter, and Lizzie stared at him shocked—how could Enid have known to leave a note behind when the overdose was an accident? Then did she leave a diary behind, anything like that? Warren asked. (He had wanted to search Enid's half of the room but both Lizzie and Mrs. Stevick opposed him. They had already looked through everything, they said.) No, said Lizzie, no diary, anyway, wasn't Enid going to be all right? wasn't she almost herself again? trying to catch up on her schoolwork in the hospital so she wouldn't miss her final exams. "Isn't it just like Enid," Lizzie said, shaking her head, smiling, "to worry about grades in the hospital!"

Felix Stevick too was offended by the idea of psychotherapy for Enid. His response struck Warren as both puritanical and crude: "You don't want some stranger fucking with your sister's head, do you?" he said, staring at Warren.

Uncle and nephew had met by accident on one of the hospital walks, between lawns that shone unnaturally green fed by busy mechanical sprinklers. It was nearly 7 P.M. but the air was moist and fresh, the sky a summery watercolor blue. Warren, on his way home, hadn't recognized his uncle at first, it was Felix who greeted him, smiling, tapping his shoulder lightly with a fist, waking Warren from his trance. (He had spent several hours in Enid's room, in her presence but not really with her; there were constant interruptions from nurses, other visitors, the most tiring a long chatty visit from their Aunt Lillian and Cousin Dinah. Yet Enid, perversely, had seemed to brighten in their company.) Felix immediately asked after Enid, he seemed rather high-keyed, expansive, he hoped to visit her for maybe ten minutes, he said, then he had to drive up to Shoal Lake where there were last-minute problems with the hotel. "How is she? When will she be discharged, do you think?" Felix asked.

"The doctor thinks sometime next week," Warren said.

Felix was wearing amber-tinted sunglasses, a white linen sports coat over a dark shirt open at the neck, dark-blue impeccably creased trousers and sporty canvas shoes. His hair grew over his collar very black, sleek, carefully brushed, the shadow of his beard showed faintly on his chin, cheeks, upper lip. As always Warren felt exalted and uncomfortable in his young uncle's presence.

For some reason Felix seemed eager to talk. He even offered Warren one of his long thin brown-wrapped cigarillos though he must have known Warren didn't smoke. He asked him about college, his plans for the future, he was going to be a lawyer maybe?—no?—Lyle had seemed to think so at one point. They'd have to have a beer together sometime Felix said, talk about Korea. He'd never sat down and talked with him about Korea, Felix said with regret. He stared at Warren as if he had more to say but thought better of it. Embarrassed, rather pleased, Warren said slightingly, "I don't think much about the war any more." "Yes," said Felix. "It's all you can do."

As they spoke Felix rocked slightly on the balls of his feet, his manner was keenly yet pleasurably alert, he had still a natural athlete's ease in his body, a muscular confidence Warren recognized but had never experienced. There was something innocently sensual about the way Felix smoked his cigarette, exhaling smoke from both nostrils as he laughed. And he liked to laugh. He liked to touch people—laying a hand on Warren's arm in quick emphasis of one or another remark he made. Warren recalled watching Felix spar with a friend at the Mattiuzzios' gym one day years ago; he'd been hypnotized by the boxers dancing about each other, lashing out with their lightweight gloves so swiftly one could barely see from where a shot had come, where it had been aimed, at once there was another, another, another, and all the while the men were circling each other caught up in a ferocity of concentration powerful even to witness. This was sparring, practicing, not real fighting, a kind of elaborate play. Warren stared fascinated, wondering how they could keep it up as they did, what would be the weight, even, of one's arms? the strain of being always on one's toes? every nerve keenly alert, razor sharp? Warren began to feel dazed and exhausted just watching them, trying to anticipate their next moves. Of course Felix was far more skilled than his opponent but he carried him along; several times the bout was interrupted by laughter, Felix thumped his friend's shoulders with loud slapping thwacks then cuffed his hair, the men were streaming sweat and breathing hard yet not really tired. And at the end they'd embraced for a moment, clearly they were fond of each other, respected each other. Warren who was nine at the time understood that there would be no context in his life in which he might embrace another man. To do that you would have to hurt him first.

Yet Warren was always uneasy, as an adult, in his uncle's presence. Everyone liked him—so Warren resisted liking him. He'd heard, too, ugly tales about the man told and retold about town, rumors of course but surely there was a kernel of truth. It was an open secret for instance that Felix had spent some time in a U.S. Army stockade in Manila for fighting with an officer. He'd once smashed the windshield of a South Side boxing promoter's car with a tire iron. Nastiest of all the stories was that Felix Stevick was said to have broken a woman's jaw after she'd shot him with a .22 caliber revolver!— nicked him in the forearm. Complaints against Felix were invariably withdrawn, charges dropped by the authorities, Mr. Stevick believed his brother had been arrested a number of times over the years but never spent a single night in jail—never came before a judge. He was friendly with a police captain or two, just like Karl Stevick in his day. And he and his Italian associates had the right contacts downtown.

The only moderately honest thing in his brother's life, Mr. Stevick liked to say, was his boxing. And look what came of *that*.

Felix asked how the family was taking it and Warren told him the truth more or less and they fell silent listening to the lawn sprinklers and Warren said half angrily, "Look, everybody knows it wasn't an accident—*couldn't* be an accident."

"What?"

"Swallowing most of a bottle of aspirin tablets."

"Then what was it?"

Warren looked at him, his left eye misting over. "You know what it was."

"No I don't," said Felix. "What was it?"

Warren took a step backward. Felt a wave of weakness, nausea. Guilt. "Just—not an *accident.*"

Felix stared at him as if he didn't hear. Adjusted the tinted glasses as if to get Warren better into focus.

"That's why I think a psychotherapist is—"

"That's a serious accusation to make against your sister, Warren," Felix said. His mouth twitched in a kind of a smile.

"It isn't an accusation," Warren said quickly.

"Yes, it's serious," said Felix.

Now the man had turned cold, mean; contemplative. Staring at Warren. Sizing him up. He was about to say something further, then changed his mind, said goodbye brusquely, and left Warren standing on the path looking after him. At the street Warren turned to look back, thinking his uncle might be watching him, but he'd disappeared into the hospital. The mechanical sprinklers tossed their skeins of water lightly in the air, delicate rainbows emerged and faded above the grass, which was so green it almost hurt the eye. Damned grass doesn't look real, it looks like funeral parlor grass, Mr. Stevick had said, making his shuddering disgusted sound that invariably shaded into a joke of a kind. Imitating Arthur Godfrey maybe. Groucho Marx.

At a family gathering years ago when Felix Stevick was riding a string of boxing victories that looked as if it would never end—Port Oriskany's own Billy Conn, the newspapers crowed—someone asked him whether he'd ever hit a man as hard as he could. And Felix's answer was one Warren had never forgotten: No, of course not, you never hit anyone as hard as you can, anything you do is never the most you might have done.

"Also," Felix had added, as if he was speaking to someone particularly obtuse, "your man is in motion. In the ring."

But what was the point, Warren wondered, of hurting another person? That fundamental principle—*hurting another person.*

In Korea he'd known for a while. But now he'd forgotten.

Each time he used the men's room at St. Joseph's, Warren studied his reflection in the mirror, rehearsing the words he would say to Enid when he had the opportunity at last to say them. He was drawn childlike and trusting to new mirrors, in public places especially— mirrors which had never framed Warren Stevick's disfigured image before.

He'd never been vain about his looks before the shrapnel, hence why be disturbed now?—not all young women were repelled by him.

After two operations his lower face still looked wrong. The flesh was rough and minutely rippled as if not entirely healed but it was healed. Cosmetic surgery under the VA wasn't intended to perform miracles, they told him, nobody looks like Cary Grant so don't expect it and Warren did not expect it; Warren was grateful for what he had. The left eye was nearly useless but there was the right—after all. Think if he'd lost both. As someone said, one eye is a thousand percent better than no eye. Also the plastic teeth glued to their removable aluminum plate were of better quality you might say than his own teeth had been, as real teeth. There was that to consider.

The subtle asymmetry of Warren's face was repeated like a fault line through his entire body. One shoulder just perceptibly higher than the other, the backbone a little curved. Pain like waves of heat in summer appearing, disappearing—it had something to do with the barometer probably. In damp air his joints swelled and ached, the right knee in particular. In another year he would need more surgery on that knee, they told him. In general he'd become so accustomed to a certain degree of pain—headaches, eyestrain, backaches, rheumatic muscular aches—he scarcely noticed any longer. When it got too bad he took aspirin, knowing to buy it in its cheapest most utilitarian form, *acetylsalicylic acid.* No wonder drug quite like aspirin, the doctors said, but Warren had never had the urge to swallow down fifty tablets.

Should he ever want to die he knew how it might be done swiftly and irrevocably: a bullet at the base of the skull, the cerebellum where the primary life activities were located.

One bullet would do it. You wouldn't in any case have a chance for two.

Suddenly, easily, he was saying, "Were you very unhappy, Enid?"

And Enid said at once, "What do you mean? Unhappy when?"

She was sitting propped up in her hospital bed smiling quizzically in his direction. It was the sixth day of Warren's visit and they were alone together in the room; Warren estimated he might have as long as a half hour. Mrs. Stevick had intended to come with him but she'd felt too exhausted and had sent him on alone. Enid's skin was tight across her cheekbones, the flesh beneath her eyes still discolored, but the eyes themselves were clear, her hair newly washed and brushed, shining, a fine brownish-red on her shoulders. Almost herself again as the Stevicks persisted in saying.

"Before," Warren said.

"Yes? Before—?"

"Before the accident."

Warren wondered if unconscious in her bed in the intensive care unit Enid had heard him ask *why, why* in that accusatory voice, *Enid, why?*—at a moment when she might very well have been dying.

Now he kept his voice level, undemanding. He wasn't even nervous so far as he could judge—he wasn't stammering.

Enid's gaze shifted from him but her expression was unchanged. Her lower lip caught in her teeth in a half smile. Only three or four days ago she had been a small frail hunted beaten creature awash in pain, now they had given her sustenance, fed her veins, brought her back to fullest consciousness. Already her face had acquired a stark ivory-pale beauty, all that had belonged to childhood had abruptly vanished.

Warren understood. Enid's soul had turned inward to husband its strength, she had drawn her own rich secret sustenance from the dark. Such death watches were nourishing to the spirit even as they were devastating to the body. He understood, he had journeyed to that lightless imageless utterly silent place himself.

Yet he continued with an embarrassed persistence. "Whether there was, you know, anything unusually upsetting that had happened to you, anything . . . you could tell me about. If you were terribly unhappy. If you had any reason . . . to be unhappy."

The bedclothes were drawn up neatly to Enid's chin, she lay unmoving beneath them, her very body listening, alert. Her thin fingers plucked at the sheet, she was smiling aslant, her lower lip caught hard in her teeth, but she wasn't quite able to look at Warren.

So rarely had they been alone together they felt almost shy in each other's presence. The hospital room was the most public of places: at any moment anyone might appear in the doorway. There was a young nun named Sister Mary Elizabeth whom Enid particularly liked and who was fond of Enid, a woman with severely pitted cheeks who nonetheless carried herself tall as an Egyptian princess in her elaborate white habit, Warren knew Enid was waiting for her to enter the room to take her temperature, to take another reading of her blood pressure, to save her from this difficult conversation with her brother. So he repeated his question.

"Enid—? You can tell me. I give you my word I won't tell anyone else."

Enid shook her head wordlessly, looking away. He imagined he saw her eyes fill with tears but perhaps it was a trick of the light—the slanted June sunshine, too cheery for these circumstances.

Warren swallowed down his frustration. He knew he was being disagreeable in pursuit, staring at his sister so bluntly with such undisguised love. He knew, he knew! yet he could not help himself. He suspected there was a secret she might suddenly almost casually reveal if she were not coerced.

But the hospital room, the sunlight, the bustle in the corridor close by—why was most that was visible of life inappropriate, Warren wondered, to the deepest starkest reality? to tragedy itself? Here was a fifteen-year-old girl who had hated life so desperately she had tried to kill herself; now a copy of a geometry textbook lay face down on her bed, her nails were polished a pearly pink because Lizzie had wanted to give her a manicure, her hair was fastened back from her face with gleaming mock-gold barrettes. The windowsill close by Enid's bed was lined with greeting cards and a miscellany of gifts including a wicker basket of tinfoil-wrapped chocolates in the shapes of animals and a small stuffed panda adorned with tiny bells. There were long-stemmed white roses past their bloom, petals detached and fallen onto the sill, there was a small pot of yellow azaleas wrapped in festive shiny aluminum foil. Several visitors had brought Enid rosaries—lying now neatly coiled in front of the greeting cards. Neal O'Banan's mother had donated by way of Geraldine her hardcover copy of *The Robe,* which she said she'd read two or three times, she'd found it so inspiring—she'd heard that Enid Stevick was a reader, she liked serious books, she'd be certain to like this.

Warren got nervously to his feet. Began to pace—stood at the window for a moment—then sat down close by Enid's bedside wanting to seize her hand, her wrist. He asked her again had anything happened to her? anything at school? at home? She hadn't written him a letter for weeks, he'd been so caught up with the Rosenberg petitions and other things to tell the truth he'd scarcely noticed. He wanted to take her thin wrist and grip it hard, stroke the blue vein on its underside; dear God, what if she'd cut her wrists?—no mistaking that for an accident.

"Are you in love, Enid?" Warren asked.

She didn't reply at once. Now she seemed clearly tired—a

shadow darkening her face in opposition to him. "I don't think it's that important—to need to talk about it."

"About what?"

"About this."

"Yes but what do you mean?—'this'?"

"People's emotions. Things they do."

"What things?"

"Being happy, being unhappy—it's so silly," Enid said. "It isn't important."

"Then what is important?" Warren asked half in dread.

Enid shrugged and looked away.

"Then what *is* important?" Warren persisted.

"I don't know."

"Why do you say it, then?"

"I don't know—you're making me tired."

She glanced toward the door awaiting Sister Mary Elizabeth. They didn't speak. Warren knew to keep still, not to provoke her, he could see he *was* making her tired, he was going about this in the wrong way. His clumsiness, stammering, bullying.

Enid said finally, *"Your* life now, the way you live—you don't care about your*self,* it isn't just your emotions and what you like or don't like or—Are you really going to Washington?"

"I'm not going anywhere," Warren said. "I'm staying here. I want to talk to you."

"I'd go to Washington if I were you," Enid said dreamily. "Tell me about it—what you're doing. Your friends, people you work with. The Rosenbergs."

Reluctantly, knowing she was leading him off the subject, Warren told her about The National Committee to Secure Justice in the Rosenberg Case—the campaign for clemency, as it was called—thousands of signatures on petitions, thousands of telegrams and letters sent to Eisenhower, there'd been large rallies, demonstrations, vigils, U.S. embassies were being picketed abroad and flooded with petitions and appeals, the Pope himself was said to have taken a stand for clemency, to have made a direct personal appeal to Eisenhower. It was true, Warren admitted, that American sentiment ran heavily against the Rosenbergs, virtually every American newspaper and publication favored the execution, yet over the months many thousands of citizens were being convinced by the committee's arguments—the trial as a whole was unfair, unjust. At this moment there was a twenty-four-hour vigil outside the White House. The immediate goal was simply to get another stay of execution, then perhaps the death sentence itself commuted, a new trial granted with someone other than the prejudiced Judge Irving Kaufmann presiding.

Many of the people involved in the effort really had no opinion as to the Rosenbergs' "guilt" or "innocence," Warren added. They simply thought the entire proceeding had been unjust.

Enid was staring at him, listening intently.

"Do you think they want to be saved?" she asked.

As if he had heard that question numerous times, Warren said patiently, "Enid, how do I know what they want or don't want?—and what has it to do with *them*, finally? Some of us want a new trial, that's all, we want everything reexamined, new evidence admitted, new witnesses, new testimonies, above all a new judge. Whether the Rosenbergs themselves 'want' to be saved might be said to be irrelevant."

Enid appeared rebuked, chastened.

Now clearly she was tired, her eyelids drooped; as Warren watched the spirit seemed to be draining out of her. He had failed, the conversation was over. She said, in a queer bright wandering voice, "It must be like being caught up in a flood or an avalanche . . . an Ice Age . . . a glacier sweeping down carrying you with it, you and so many other people . . . all those petitions, rallies, vigils. That's what I wanted to know. The way your life is, the way it's gone. It must be like God if you could believe in God," she said.

Warren kissed his sister goodbye. "Yes," he said ironically, squeezing her chill little hand. "If you could believe in God."

Next morning, June 17, Warren left Port Oriskany on the 6:20 A.M. Greyhound bus for Washington, D.C. He had a ten-hour ride ahead but he would arrive well in time to join in the night-long vigil at the White House (in which, he'd read in the *Transcript*, nearly three thousand people were participating) in support of clemency for the Rosenbergs. Did they want to be saved, did they want stubbornly to die? It was not individuals who mattered in this case but justice, humanity, compassion, truth.

Dozing on the bus, Warren dreamed of the city to which he was going as a place of tall glimmering spires, white marble monuments, the gold-gleaming Capitol dome itself powerful as a heraldic sun. The city was a floating island, white and chaste and serene, punctuated by leafy interludes, rich oases of green. His heart was stirred with excitement, hope!—and when he woke startled he thought it quite likely that the Supreme Court would grant another stay of execution, perhaps until the fall. Perhaps the terrible sentence would be commuted altogether: after all, the eyes of the entire world were fixed on Washington. You didn't really require God, Warren thought, for clemency.

4

Domenic Stevick had tracked him down, phoned him at the gym where by chance he was sparring with a young pro boxer, told him the news about Lyle's youngest daughter, and the first thing he said was, "Jesus Christ!—is she going to live?" and the second thing was, after a beat or two, "Did she leave a note?"

Even as the words came out he knew what a shit it meant he was, if he hadn't known before. *Did she leave a note. Did she say why.* But Domenic said sharply, no she hadn't left a note, what kind of a question was that?—the girl had taken an accidental overdose of aspirin tablets, she hadn't known what she was doing. And, yes, she was going to live. They'd acted fast, got her in the emergency room before it was too late. "I thought you should be informed," Domenic said, "since the girl is your niece."

"Yes," said Felix.

"You might want to drop by the hospital or the house—see if there's anything you can do for Lyle and Hannah—"

"Jesus, yes," said Felix, though he didn't know what he was saying, felt a sick sensation in his knees which meant his legs were gone, "sure, yes." Did they know? Did anyone know? *Had* she left a note they hadn't found yet? "But she's okay, you said? She's going to live?"

"She's going to live but she isn't okay," Domenic told him in his priestly reproachful voice, the voice Felix always associated with the self-righteous son of a bitch. "She was fighting for her life until just a few hours ago."

Domenic Stevick—"Father" Stevick, whom Felix scarcely knew—scolding him as if he was a kid, not thirty-one years old, as if he was Domenic's actual brother, not half brother, and gave a good goddamn about what he thought, priest or not, going on about how he'd had "a good deal of difficulty" locating Felix, first he called Felix's apartment at Niagara Square a half-dozen times on Sunday and again on Monday and no luck—didn't Felix live at Niagara Square any longer?—then he called Felix's mother, then Sansom & Stevick, Inc., even tried the Rideau Inn or whatever it was, at Shoal Lake, but never got through, finally it was Lyle who said try the gym, the Mattiuzzios' gym, they'd know where he was. So he did. And just by chance Felix Stevick was there.

"When I talked with your mother she said she hadn't seen you or heard from you in weeks. You could be anywhere, she said." The remark was uttered as a reproach in itself—no need to continue.

Felix understood he was supposed to say he was sorry but he said nothing. He was testing the strength in his legs, waiting for it to return. His head crowded with thoughts like hornets bright-glinting in the sun, buzzing, darting, feinting at him; he'd let them sort themselves out before he knew what to do.

It would take a while before it sank in, exactly. Enid had almost died, had almost killed herself, and because of him.

She had said in that letter she didn't want to live but he'd thrown it away, crumpled it angrily in his fist. He hadn't given it the right interpretation maybe. He hadn't thought she was serious—hadn't thought that at all.

Anything you do to me—it's what I want.

Sure he'd crumpled it in his fist and tossed it away, damn her, just—God damn her. Wanted nothing more to do with her. And now this.

Overdose of aspirin, almost died—God damn her. Trying to manipulate *him.*

"Domenic—thanks. Thanks for calling."

He hung up before the conversation was really over but he couldn't take it another minute. Just couldn't take it.

He'd been sparring with Jo-Jo Pearl, the Mattiuzzios' young welterweight who was also Felix Stevick's protégé—you might say—when the call came. Didn't even know who "Domenic" was at first and only when he got upstairs to Vince's office where he took the call did it hit him. Bad news. Family news. It crossed his mind that Lyle had had a heart attack or was already dead and he'd miss him—nobody quite like Lyle.

Had time to grab only a towel, now he was dripping sweat and shivering, teeth practically chattering with the shock. Vince took one look at him and poured him a drink, handed it to him, wordless, and Felix swallowed it down. "Family trouble? Somebody died?" Vince asked. Felix shook his head, no. Staring at a filmy patch of sunlight on the plush burgundy carpet feeling his mouth tug into a kind of smile— the kind you make to throw your opponent off—waiting to know what you're going to do.

"Your mother?" Vince asked. Ursula was the only relative of Felix's Vince knew.

Again Felix shook his head, no. Made a gesture meaning he didn't want to talk but he'd have another drink—yeah, thanks.

He was sitting on the edge of Vince's glass-topped desk. Couldn't have said really where he was though he was staring out the window at the smog-heavy sky, traffic moving in several directions on the John Jamieson Expressway, east, west, south, north, funneled about a tightly coiled cloverleaf. The expressway was only a few years old: the motion of its traffic pleased Felix's eye. He felt his kinship with it. He could calm himself watching it, not thinking yet what he'd have to do, how he'd face them or if he could face them—her—at all. Not from this window but from the roof of the building another flight up you could see Lake Oriskany a mile off, the waterfront buildings, lake freighters, smoke. Even in summer the air was rough, gusty, foul, invigorating with its smells—sulfur and yeast and rubber and chemicals and motor exhaust, sometimes a strange sweet-chalky odor, sometimes too an odor of something sharp and orangey like overripe citrus fruit from the smokestacks of Diamond Chemical. Except for those years in the army in the Pacific, Felix had lived in Port Oriskany all his life: there were times when he felt his soul outside him in the very air, the incessant winds from the lake, the gritty smells. He had a sudden powerful urge to climb the stairs to the roof. Run up there, throw the door open.

He must have made a sound of some kind. Vince stared at him quizzically, said, "Felix, is there anything I can do?" and Felix roused himself, wiping his face with the towel, kneading his eyes hard; Felix said, "No thanks, Vince, I'm fine."

He left Vince's office, shutting the door harder than he'd intended. He would have to see her—right away. He'd shower and drive up to the hospital and see her, and in the first instant of seeing her, he thought, he'd know.

Poor kid, almost dying. Because of him.

Poor Enid. His niece. And because of him.

Trying to manipulate *him*.

And if she'd left a note and they found it, what then? Turned it over to the police, what then?

Took a long shower. A long time under the hot steaming water and a long time under the cold water. One of Felix's old places of refuge.

Where he'd hidden away from talk of him after his fights, talk flashing bright like swords, the very air afire. How brilliant Felix had been et cetera how far he'd go et cetera which of the top contenders he was ready for right now et cetera when he'd known he hadn't been brilliant he'd only been good, fairly good. Quick on his feet and both his hands fast but that wasn't going to be enough and when he was alone he knew it, which was why he needed to be alone but was frightened of it too. All the things they said of him, all the claims they made—he was the one who'd have to live it, nobody else. Alone in the ring with his opponer and nobody else.

He shut his eyes, lifting his face to the shower nozzle. Seeing that blow that came so unexpectedly, so against his will—slapping her with the back of his hand. Only a few days ago. And now the hospital. Ambulance called in the middle of the night and the emergency room, the intensive care unit, now she was "resting" and "doing as well as can be expected" considering the physical trauma.

Suppose she died, Stevick, then what? Then—

Then he'd kill himself?

Kill himself.

Get loaded and drive out the expressway get the car up to ninety and slam into an abutment—over in seconds. Nobody knows. Nobody gives a damn. The stretch of concrete above Nine Mile Road. After 2 A.M. the expressway is empty, not a soul.

He wondered if the blow had left a mark on her face. If anyone asked her about it. And what she'd said.

And at the cottage, that night. After he'd dropped her off. What she'd said to Geraldine if Geraldine had questioned her.

I won't tell anyone, Felix.

I would never tell anyone, Felix.

If he killed himself there'd be a front-page headline. Former pro boxer, middleweight contender, maybe a photograph—Felix "The Cat" Stevick grinning in victory, glove raised. A long time ago but they'd dig out the photo, run an obituary. And all his old enemies would see it and feel good all morning. Even his old friends.

In the car a few days ago, the rain drumming on the roof and the tension between them, thinking, She's your own niece, your brother's daughter, but he'd been angry, outraged, and then she started to cry and he'd wondered could he control himself, his excitement, the heat in his groin wanting to make love to her but this time to really fuck her as she deserved. Little bitch teasing him—provoking him. Her squirmy sweaty body in the little-girl's bathing suit, the strap slipping off her shoulder. Looking at him with those hot eyes. By the time he'd come there behind the door he'd been hard for an hour, he was aroused now in the shower remembering how he'd finally grabbed her, grinding himself against her, his first orgasm like a blow to the pit of the belly leaving him weak-kneed sucking for breath. The second time had been easier—sweeter—he'd been more in control, guiding her fingers, squeezing and stroking himself by way of her pliant fingers, again he couldn't have stopped but there hadn't been the danger to her he'd felt before—that he might do something crazy to the girl he'd never be able to undo.

At the same time he couldn't believe he was doing it—any of it. Standing off to the side astonished, not even disgusted or ashamed, just not believing he was capable of such a thing.

On the beach they'd fooled around the way you do after a few beers, not meaning anything by it, or anything much, it was all pretty funny, everybody laughing and in good spirits, and Felix had been feeling good too, he missed not having any family sometimes like this, Sundays and holidays at the beach just lazing around swimming and lying on the sand fucking around the way they'd done except the girl got too excited too carried away he could tell and he'd been worked up too but it should have ended at that point, Felix should have known somebody was going to get hurt.

He'd been coming to the Mattiuzzios' gym for many years, he might have thought of it as a home of his if he'd been drawn along the lines of such thinking.

Except for the six or seven months after he'd quit professional boxing, when he'd stayed away. And his wartime years.

His father had brought him there as a young boy. Crecca & Mattiuzzio's Athletic Club it was then, a single floor of a bleak-looking cinderblock building on the corner of Huron and Fourth in a neighborhood of Italian restaurants and taverns, small grocery stores, butchers, gas stations, cheap hotels, and rooming houses. Vince Mattiuzzio's father, Leonardo, had a number of local business interests, among them the promotion of prizefights in Port Oriskany—he and his friends brought a number of famous boxers to the city including Gene Tunney in a non-title bout, Jack Sharkey, Harry Greb, Mickey Walker, Jack Dempsey himself after he'd lost his title and was fighting exhibition matches. And Max Baer—Felix's father had loved Max Baer. And Jimmy Braddock. And Primo Carnera of course, matched with one of the club regulars. They'd laughed about that for years.

Felix's father had taken him to an exhibition match between Mickey Walker, then middleweight champion of the world, and one of the club's young boxers, when Felix was seven years old. The match was a friendly one in theory except Walker seemed to lose perspective when he was in the ring and a lucky left hook from the young boxer that drew an enthusiastic response from the crowd offended him so bitterly he let loose with a barrage of hard blows as if he'd wanted to kill his opponent, and the fight had had to be called in the third round. Walker was a thickset almost pudgy man with a pudding face who resembled a clerk more than an athlete—the "Toy Bulldog," he was popularly called—a mean vicious son of a bitch if he was crossed or thought somebody was getting the better of him.

Felix climbed atop a chair to see better. He was excited and frightened, sensing that something was going wrong—somebody was being hurt. The shorter man was hammering away at the taller man, driving him backward across the ring by the force of his body blows, then catching him in the head, battering his head, a dozen unanswered punches before the young man fell into the ropes and the referee called the fight. There was silence in the room as if somebody had died and Mickey Walker, suddenly magnanimous in victory, went to help his opponent to his feet, threw his arms around him in a florid sentimental gesture, sheerly Irish, belligerent and affectionate. The fight was over but the world's champion was hugging the young man he'd so badly beaten as if they were brothers.

It had all happened so swiftly—Felix hadn't quite understood what it meant. Only that it meant something important. And that he wanted it for himself.

"People do what they want to do—no more and no less. That's the secret no one wants to admit."

So Karl Stevick told Felix. His tone was cynical but not bitter— amused, rather. Karl Stevick was an amused man.

Even in his final, terrible illness he maintained his amused tone.

Telling his young son things the boy wouldn't understand until years later.

Felix learned that his father had another family—other sons. He loved them too, he said, but he'd had to leave them because he fell in love with Felix's mother. Before she was, strictly speaking, Felix's mother.

"Why?" Felix had asked.

"Why?—why what?"

"Why wasn't she my mother?"

"Because you weren't born yet. You were ready to be born but you weren't, yet."

"But why?" Felix asked. He was a child but old enough to sense danger here, a hint of a time when *he* had not seemed to exist or to matter. His father had other sons, he'd had another wife, he wasn't to be trusted.

Eventually Felix was introduced to his older half brothers, Domenic and Lyle, but he never met his father's first wife. (Her name was Maria. She lived for years in a residential hotel on Eaton Boulevard, always sick and always asking for money, according to Felix's mother.) Domenic went into the seminary, then became a Catholic priest; Lyle went into "business" but was forever begging favors of Karl Stevick—loans, advice, introductions to helpful people. The Church did not recognize divorce so Karl Stevick was a "bad" Catholic, a sinner, and his second wife Ursula wasn't his wife at all but his concubine, his whore.

Felix was to learn, to his chagrin, that *he* was illegitimate in the eyes of the Church: a bastard.

"And it can't be changed?" he asked his mother.

This was after his father's death. His mother said indifferently, "Why do you care? Is it your pride? *I* don't care so why should you?"

Why should he? Felix wondered. But still, he did.

Karl Stevick died of a self-inflicted wound to the head while hospitalized with cancer, dying of cancer, in fact—he'd forbidden his wife and young son to come see him in his final days. That was *his* pride. But there was scandal too about another woman, a young woman said to be his girlfriend, she'd brought the pistol to him in the hospital and was arrested as an accessory to his crime and Felix's mother was never to forgive his father for the betrayal and the embarrassing publicity. "Just as well," she'd told Felix with an angry laugh, "—now I don't have to mourn."

As a boy Felix Stevick thrived on opposition, resistance. When he was alone he played like any child, oblivious of his surroundings—he fantasized, those years, a twin self with whom he chattered and conspired, but when another consciousness intruded upon his he came awake, alert, alive. His mother, his mother's housekeeper, a neighbor child—the sudden assertion of another's will in relationship to his own excited Felix to combat: within seconds he was flooded with emotion and purpose. An obstinate child, he was called. A bad child. Impossible to control.

"He takes after his father," Felix's mother said. It was not meant to be a compliment but an abrogation of blame.

Even before his father had taken him to see Mickey Walker in action Felix had liked fighting with other boys. Fighting was the most concentrated form of play, wasn't it?—you never got restless or bored or turned your back and walked away. As a child Felix was livened by a remarkable precocious strength and malice, not throwing punches wild and swinging, standing flat-footed like a street fighter—he knew how to jab to keep an opponent from him, how to feint, how to slip punches, how to hurt with the most direct blow. He didn't mind being hit either, or even hurt—seemed rather proud of his cuts, bruises, blood-encrusted nostrils.

Karl Stevick was of an age to be the grandfather of a son young as Felix which was why, perhaps, he so indulged him, "gave him his head," made little effort to discipline him. He didn't want Felix to be a boxer but he was sure the whim would pass—after all you have to be fairly desperate to risk getting maimed or killed for so little, at least at the outset of a career. Look at Dempsey, look at old Jack Johnson, Mickey Walker himself, even Gene Tunney, who'd been a slum kid regardless of how he refashioned himself after he became famous. Harry Greb had nearly killed Tunney once in a light-heavyweight match: if Tunney hadn't been desperate for money he'd have quit boxing forever, after that beating. All the really good boxers have been poor and I mean dirt-poor, desperate-poor, Felix's father told him, and you're not in that category. You're not hungry enough to make it to the top.

Which turned out to be true—eventually.

But Felix took his heroes directly from the boxing world, he measured all men, all male behavior, against that world—which was a twin or mirror world of the "real" world and far more significant. If he wasn't to be Mickey Walker the world champion, he'd be the young man who dared climb into the ring with Walker for three amazing rounds, locally famous for the rest of his life for a single lucky left hook that caught the champion on the jaw and set him back on his heels. What did it matter what happened, finally, how badly or publicly one was injured—there, in the ring, elevated above the crowd of ordinary men, even injury was meaningful.

Felix liked it too that, in boxing, if you're hit it's because you deserve to be hit, meaning you aren't able to defend yourself against your opponent, meaning you should never have entered the ring with him, meaning you deserve all that happens to you even death—nothing is accidental. He saw nothing like it anywhere else in the world.

He wasn't the kind of man to think about the past, to brood or mull things over. Why? What's the point? What you can see when you look around is all there *is*—the past is gone, dead, buried. Still, he wondered sometimes what old Karl Stevick would have thought of Felix "The Cat" Stevick. He'd have winced at the name, and laughed; he'd been a good sport. He'd have been caught up as so many were in the young man's prospects. He'd have made bets—and made money, up to a point. Felix had a spectacular professional record of 29 wins 0 losses with 25 knockouts—no matter if the Mattiuzzios had handled him with more than usual care, matching him primarily with club fighters or over-the-hill boxers of some distinction Felix had no trouble in outboxing and outpunching—no matter, he *was* good. Up to a point. As Billy Conn himself had been good, very good, up to a point—the moment when he decided to try to knock Joe Louis out instead of winning the heavyweight title *merely* as a boxer.

Of course Felix had had some difficult nights, before Corvino. He'd won matches like the one with the Negro Oscar Ellis knowing he hadn't come near to defeating his opponent—only outdanced him, outboxed him, outsmarted him. It wasn't the same thing as defeating him—the men who'd taken him the distance knew that. Still Felix thought he had a chance—everybody thought he had a chance. Look at Tunney outboxing Dempsey for instance. Look at Tommy Loughran. Benny Leonard. "Gentleman Jim" himself.

The long long upward climb so dizzying, ecstatic, it seemed a plunge into the very sky without boundary or limit, then the abrupt ending—the end—that night in October 1948—Detroit, Michigan— two minutes into the eighth round of a ten-round fight. Felix made the great mistake of his career which turned out to be the final mistake of his career, getting angry with his opponent getting emotional trading punches standing toe to toe "man to man" slugging it out and

Corvino was stronger, tougher, meaner, built like a bull and tricky in ways Felix knew but had never confronted, never in the confusion and heat of an actual fight, and his forehead was gushing blood, blood in his eyes, and he was breathing through his mouth, lost his mouthpiece and after that he didn't know what happened except he was finished. Why did you do it for Christ's sake, Felix? Vince screamed at him in the very ambulance, Why for fuck's sake did you do it!—but Felix didn't hear, he'd gone to a place where he wasn't required to hear. His trainer, his manager, his backers—he wasn't required to hear what they had to say. So this was Felix's personal story, his legend, how he'd been suckered into a brawl with Gino Corvino of all people, who was built to take punishment as Felix Stevick wasn't, he'd been sleepwalking for two or three rounds, hit repeatedly in the gut and the referee seeming not to notice, a haze of pain and blood pouring down his face and chest splashing onto Corvino's chest and the referee's white shirt, blinking to get his vision clear he saw things double, or distended, shifting out of focus like objects reflected in water, and the strange thing was he didn't feel pain, much—only knew the bell was ringing when the assault abruptly stopped. Box him, Felix, for Christ's sake! his trainer begged, not knowing or not wanting to know that Felix was incapable of boxing by that time, just his body going through its elaborately rehearsed motions, arms and gloves no longer able to protect him from the terrible things that were happening to him, low blows and kidney punches and elbowings to the gut, rabbit punches to the base of the skull when they clinched and even after the butting which was called an accident Corvino used his laces on Felix's eyes both his eyes bleeding, swollen half shut, lucky they said afterward he didn't lose the right eye, but then finally it was over: didn't see the punch coming or even feel it, one of a half-dozen punches he hadn't seen coming. He wondered what Karl Stevick would have thought, seeing his son take those blows before he fell to lie insensible for three, four minutes as if dying or dead—many in the arena had thought he was dead—his mind gone, tasting a trickle of blood in his mouth that seemed to be draining from up inside his skull. He'd seen his death like an opening, an entranceway, hazy with light, but chill. He saw it and tasted it.

At St. Joseph's he stood outside the doorway of room 419 where his niece lay in a bed, asleep, it seemed, or unconscious, IV tubes stuck in her arms and her arms thinner than he remembered. Her face was a pale blurred oval turned from him but there was Hannah Stevick sitting by the bedside and Lyle standing, his back to Felix, perspiration in a triangular stain on his white shirt. It was a shock to see that Lyle was going bald—his scalp showing through the baby-fine graying hair. And that, from the back, he looked so middle-aged, stooped. They didn't get along but Felix liked the man well enough—just didn't want to get mixed up with him.

A semiprivate room—Felix counted three other beds. Why the hell hadn't Lyle arranged for a private room?

Felix thought, I'll pay for it!

But he couldn't enter the room. Couldn't speak. He'd climbed the stairs instead of waiting for the elevator but now he couldn't enter the room—dreaded Lyle or Hannah noticing him because just seeing his face maybe they'd know. Maybe Geraldine had told them something. They weren't fools.

And did he love her?

And was he really to blame?

(Maybe when she recovered she wouldn't remember what had happened between them?)

His mind was empty, extinguished like a flame blown out—that quickly, terribly. He couldn't have spoken five words even to confess what he'd done.

He supposed he did love her—in a way. Seeing how she'd suffered, had almost died, for him—for the idea of him—which no other woman or girl had ever done. There was that, *that* was incontestable. Her skin so pale, the tubes stuck in her arms her ankles even her nostrils—it was the real thing, he knew, he'd come close himself to dying. Domenic had said over the phone that the "crisis" was past but Enid had had an "extreme physical trauma." The lining of her stomach was bleeding and other organs might be affected, it was too soon to know.

Still she'd had her way, almost dying. To punish him.

Or to call him here.

Which no one else had ever done, though women had threatened to kill themselves because of him—had threatened to kill Felix too, which was another matter.

He didn't love her but there was this connection between them now, this bond. A blood bond as if between two men who'd fought each other to a draw. Or say one of them beat the other decisively but the losing fighter fought a courageous fight and pushed himself beyond his limit—the winner was forever in his debt.

Yes, she'd had her way. But he wasn't going to enter that room.

St. Joseph's Hospital—the nuns in their starched white habits, their faces framed tightly in white—reminded him of his father, his father's death. So many years ago. He'd come with his mother several times until Karl Stevick decided suddenly he didn't want them to see him again, so ravaged by cancer. It wasn't him any longer anyway he'd said, all that's over.

He could see Enid Stevick in her hospital bed but from this distance he couldn't have said was she living, was she dead. Knew if he touched her skin it would be clammy as death in any case and seeing his face maybe they'd know—Hannah, if not Lyle; the woman was no fool—so he turned and began to walk quickly away, not really knowing what he did. He'd see her—them—another time. Behave decently and normally—another time. He'd offer to pay for a private room if doing so wouldn't offend his penny-pinching brother, which it probably would. Another time.

"Felix, is something wrong?—you don't seem like yourself."

Al Sansom's wife laying her hand on his arm, her polished manicured nails. A faint scent of perfume delicious and warm and Felix shook his head, no, of course not, and drained the first of the three martinis he planned to drink, trying to focus his attention on a glossy flyer fresh-printed that opened to eight narrow pages of color photographs and columns of print, creamy-white letters on black. Hot off the press, Al Sansom was saying, advertising "the most beautiful resort hotel in the Adirondacks THE VILLA RIDEAU: Grand Opening scheduled for Summer 1953."

"Wouldn't guess how damned expensive something like this is," Al Sansom said. "Kind of thing you glance at and toss in the trash without reading." He'd had to hire six people not even counting the printer to get the job done right, they were printing up five thousand copies and distributing them all over, particularly New York City. Travel agencies et cetera and some direct mailings. "What d'you think, Felix? Looks good, eh?"

On one of the pages the word *luxery* caught Felix's eye. "Is that how it's spelled?" he asked. He didn't know: the world of print rarely engaged Felix, he skimmed newspapers and magazines not to read but to extract facts, information, news. Al and Claudette puzzled over the word too, Al thought it might be one of those words spelled different ways—a French word made into English—but Claudette who'd once been a legal secretary said she thought it was a typo.

"Typo? What's that?" Al asked.

"Typographical error," Claudette said.

"Which means—?"

"An error in the type. An error in printing."

"Meaning?"

"Meaning what I said!" Claudette exclaimed. She was an extremely attractive young woman well accustomed to the semi-hostile flirtatiousness of men but her husband's blustering manner often confused her. She glanced at Felix as if for confirmation. "It's an error that's nobody's fault, exactly."

Al Sansom was holding the flyer to the light, scrutinizing it. His eyes were small, suspicious, damp, his handsome ruined face took on the reflected gloss of the printed pages. "All errors are somebody's fault," he said irritably. "Only 'acts of God'—as our friends in the insurance racket say—are exempt. And we know why."

He tossed the flyer down on the table as if he'd seen enough and signaled a passing waiter for another round of drinks. Martinis for him and his partner, sloe gin fizz for his wife. "What the hell, our clientele won't know how to spell 'luxury' either. Nobody will notice."

Felix and the Sansoms were having drinks in the cocktail lounge of the Onondaga Hotel, where the Sansoms always stayed when they visited Port Oriskany; Felix was supposed to have dinner with them that evening. But it was difficult for him to concentrate on Al Sansom's conversation, which was a kind of monologue punctuated by questions, a litany of complaints delivered in an amused deadpan voice. He was thinking of Enid in the hospital—thinking of Lyle and Hannah. What he'd done and was he sorry and would it happen again.

"—such a beautiful hotel, a pity if it burns down before it officially opens," Al said in an undertone.

"That isn't funny, Al," Claudette said.

"Who said it's funny? It's tragic."

"You shouldn't say things like that where you might be overheard."

"Well, I was only joking. You know I was only joking." He looked at Felix in mock appeal. "Felix knows I was only joking, don't you?"

"Sure," Felix said.

"Still, *you* weren't laughing either, Felix, were you," Al said. "Tell us why you weren't laughing—is it because the fucking place is going to be a disaster?"

Felix said, "Let's drop the subject."

"The most beautiful hotel in the Adirondacks and we've sunk a small fortune in it already and the 'grand opening' has already been postponed twice and it looks as if it will have to be postponed again. Nothing funny about its burning down. Am I wrong? Am I drunk? Don't look at me like that, beautiful one," Al said to Claudette. "You know how I feel about you looking at me like that in the presence of another party."

Felix half closed his eyes and saw something—someone—approaching him. One of the Sisters of Charity. Billowing white robes and the comforting click of a rosary hanging from her waist. There was a crucifix on the wall above his niece's bed; he hadn't noticed it at the time but he could see it clearly now.

Al Sansom sensed Felix's thoughts drifting and spoke more emphatically to get his attention while as if absentmindedly he stroked his young wife's fingers, made small caressing circles on her skin as if in code. Uneasy in Felix's company at times but at other times rather familiar as if he'd known his partner for years when in fact he barely knew him at all. Barely knew him at all, which was the way Felix wanted it.

There was a day when Vince Mattiuzzio said to Felix, What about the resort hotel business?—up in the Adirondacks? and Felix said carelessly, Why not? For months he'd been casting about for something to invest his money in, something to do with his life, a 15 percent investment in Jo-Jo Pearl and the possibility of investing with Vince in a new athletic club in one of the suburbs but still he needed something more. The Adirondacks, Shoal Lake, l'Isle-Verte. Hadn't been back in years and hadn't much cared that Ursula had sold off his father's property without consulting him—the way she did most things. Why not the resort hotel business? There was a reason of course for Vince's bringing up the subject as if he'd just now thought of it but Felix wasn't curious about the reason. In the days when Felix was their fighter, the Mattiuzzios would tell him who they'd matched him with and Felix never asked why, why a certain match and not another. There was always a reason and he trusted them not to trouble him with it. Now he was in business—or wanted to be. Had money and had to make use of it. He'd been driving around town inspecting properties for sale—apartment buildings, restaurants, vacant lots, places he believed might arouse in him the idea of ownership. In some men it was a fever, an addiction. Pride, honor, happiness, a reason for getting up in the morning, manliness itself—an extension of one's soul, maybe, a visible emblem of power. But Felix never found anything he wanted to buy. Felix looked, Felix made inquiries, but he never found anything he wanted to buy. It was like the days when he'd been locally famous and he'd had all the women he wanted but hadn't wanted them, much.

Vince said, There's a lot of money to be made in the resort hotel business. Vince smiled, saying, This guy Sansom—he's a kind of joker in the deck. You know? We get you in but you don't acknowledge us and he won't ask questions either.

When they first met Al Sansom shook Felix Stevick's hand and said, "Love. At. First. Sight." He was a man with a sense of humor, wanted you to know that right away.

His passion was real estate, he told Felix. Because it's *real*—you can see it, walk on it, build buildings on it, you can sell it when the time's ripe for selling. Ripeness is all, he told Felix with a heavy wink. Knowing when to buy, when to sell.

"You were an athlete, I've been told. Boxer?—yes?—then you can understand the value of something durable, permanent. That doesn't wear out."

Felix stared at him. He'd never disliked anyone so much in his life. "That's right," he said.

Al Sansom was a fussily dressed man in his mid-fifties married to a woman much, much younger—Felix Stevick's age. His third or was she his fourth wife. Intelligent yet given to coy insinuating smiles, an air of mystery, secrecy. His credit with banks and loan companies was excellent but there appeared to be an aspect of his general character, his trustworthiness it might be said, that was in doubt: so Felix was to learn months afterward. (Sansom had had dealings with the Mattiuzzios years ago, or with friends of theirs, that had turned out badly; this too Felix would learn after he became Sansom's partner.) The man had a faintly pink, flushed skin, nothing at all like Felix's olive-dark skin, his nose was somewhat swollen, with prominent nostrils, nothing at all like Felix's narrow Roman nose, yet something about him—his eyes, the bony structure of his face—reminded Felix of himself. Looked more like Felix than Felix's own father, was that it?

Felix supposed he'd look like Al Sansom when he was Sansom's age. If he drank too much. If he lived that long.

Now Al was on his third martini, scattering cigarette ashes on the cocktail table, speaking lyrically of Shoal Lake, l'Isle-Verte—what a beautiful unspoiled part of the world it was—and what a privilege to develop it. "The Rideau is only the beginning for Sansom and Stevick," he said. "You just wait. We're having our problems now but you just wait."

"That's right," Felix said.

"Make us both multimillionaires. Billionaires. Wait and see."

What did you do, what thoughts did you think, Felix wondered, if your daughter had tried to kill herself—fifteen years old. Seeing Lyle Stevick's broad stooped back. Sweating through his shirt.

Al was telling Felix and Claudette about an experience he'd had up at Shoal Lake last week—damnedest wild wacky terrifying thing.

Seems he was driving over the bridge to the mainland alone in his car, early evening about 8:30 P.M., and suddenly he sees something hovering over the lake maybe a mile away to the north, an airplane sort of, but not really, sort of disc-shaped and flat with lights that glimmered the way they do through mist or rain, sort of blurred, but everywhere else the air was clear. That really struck him: *everywhere else the air was clear.* "Actually I don't believe in flying saucers—UFOs the air force calls them. Probably I just saw something reflected in the water." He grinned at Felix and Claudette, awaiting their response, but they had none. He said, "Too many goddamned things we have to believe in right now that strain our credulity. No room for flying saucers from another planet."

"Al, you're so funny," Claudette said. She laughed easily, or with a semblance of ease, when she'd been drinking. "Al, you're so *wise.*"

"Wise old man," said Al glumly. "Felix, what's your thought?"

Felix hadn't been listening. He shifted his shoulders in an elaborate shrug and shook his head. No.

"Felix my right-hand man. Felix meaning 'joy.' "

A light-skinned Negro in a white dinner jacket was playing a cocktail piano, singing in Cab Calloway style: "Stormy Weather," "These Foolish Things," "Blues in the Night." The melodies blended together, no one seemed to be listening. Now "Hong Kong Blues," with his shoulders hunched, his face screwed up, eyes shut, and Felix made an effort to follow the punchy tune, the comically despairing words. *Kicked old Buddha's gong. Leave Hong Kong far behind me. Happiness once again.*

Couldn't have said why he was angry with Sansom except he was angry, mild kick of his heart and a wash of adrenaline like alcohol in his blood. Jesus he'd like to punch the man in the face: one swift right and the cartilage of his nose would go.

He was thinking that Vince Mattiuzzio had not lied to him about Al, simply hadn't provided him with all the information he had but that wasn't lying, Vince never lied to Felix because they were friends. Close as brothers except they weren't. Also Leonardo liked him, even after he'd let them down. And old Giulio. Saying Felix was the most beautiful boxer he'd ever seen, which meant he didn't know all that much—but had a warm heart. What do you want to know? Vince might ask evasively. Why do you want to know? Say the county prosecutor takes it in his head to serve Felix Stevick with a subpoena, say Felix finds himself testifying before a grand jury investigating "racketeering" in upstate New York—whatever "racketeering" means—Felix testifies under oath he doesn't know a goddamned thing. Which is the truth, isn't it. Real estate transactions—hotel and motel ownership—wine and liquor distribution—vending franchises—road construction—trucking—entertainment—auto dealership—boxing—harness racing: Felix Stevick knows nothing of "racketeering" in any of these activities.

Were you ever approached by anyone to throw a fight? the bastards would ask and Felix would say contemptuously, I wasn't that kind of fighter: I was being groomed to win a world title.

Al excused himself to go to the men's room or was it to make one of his mysterious telephone calls. Felix and Claudette were left alone with nothing to say except Claudette kept up a gay thin uneasy chatter knowing she hadn't Felix Stevick's fullest attention tonight but not knowing why. A striking woman with honey-brown hair falling over one eye, dark-lipsticked lips, a warm clear healthy skin. The first time she and Felix had met they'd established their attraction for each other immediately, but tonight Claudette sensed something wrong and perhaps she too was slightly angry.

"You just don't seem like yourself tonight, Felix, *is* there something wrong?"

Felix shook his head, no.

Though he never thought of Al Sansom's wife at any other time, when he was in her presence Felix was reminded of those wartime photographs of Hollywood actresses—Betty Grable, Rita Hayworth, Veronica Lake—and of those lost embittered years of his young manhood, his life as a soldier in the U.S. Army sentenced to years of combat in the South Pacific, nearly dying, shitting his guts out with dysentery, exhaustion, despair. Nineteen years old when he went in, twenty-three when he came out: lost years. He'd boxed some in the army but his opponents were pushovers and it tore his heart to think how he was being cheated—what Ray Robinson, Joe Louis, Tony Zale had done by the age of twenty-three. And through it all the Hollywood glamour girls were smirking at him, moistening their lips and smiling at him, at him, inviting him to do to them what he could.

Did he give a damn for Hitler, Mussolini, Tojo?—there were plenty of other guys to fight them. Felix Stevick was a private person, had his own life's goal.

"—hope he didn't annoy you with his jokes. Sometimes I just don't *get* his jokes and I'm his wife."

Felix said, "Well."

"He likes you very much no matter how sarcastic he gets. Likes you *very* much 'cause he says he can trust you."

Claudette spoke earnestly, confidentially. It was an affectation of hers to seem, or actually to be, breathless. Tonight she was wearing a white summer knit dress with a low neckline designed to show the tops of her pale soft breasts; when she leaned toward Felix to touch his arm she gave off a sweet fragrant odor. Felix was aroused by her as naturally she intended but he was thinking of the lake, the woods, the Villa Rideau last summer—smelling of smoke, ruin, the corridor stacked with furniture and the two of them running crazily like kids except she *was* a kid, the girl, his brother's daughter he'd taken advantage of. He'd been drunk but he'd needed to get drunk to do what he'd wanted to do.

Warning her not to follow so of course she'd follow!—wanted it as bad as he did but not knowing, maybe, what it was.

The Negro pianist was playing "Paper Moon" in mock-pretty style when Claudette began speaking about her beliefs—what she believed in. Stressing life, she said. No formal religious beliefs, wasn't a churchgoing Methodist like her family, still she knew there was a God, a spirit governing the universe. The crimson drink had gone to her head, she was slightly high, very prettily high, her wavy hair sliding across her cheek; breathing quickly as if she needed to speak fast before Al returned, she told Felix she'd hoped to start a "second family" with Al but it didn't seem to be working out. Felix asked what she meant and she said, I love Al but it doesn't seem to be working out. Then a pause, and the cocktail piano like background music. You get to expect it, seeing movies.

She'd had a baby girl, her first marriage, and the baby died within a week and her husband seemed to blame her and to tell the truth she blamed herself sort of, isn't it strange how the mind works, how it goes against what you know is reasonable. Eighteen when she got married, nineteen when Lily was born and died, then she and her husband separated, got divorced when she was twenty-three and she'd thought her life was over, why not end it, did some drinking and made some mistakes with men, the kind who take advantage of you when you're down. Then picked herself up again, went to secretarial school in Albany and got a job and actually went years without seeing any men, she was scared of men, then finally she met Al Sansom who took one look at her and said, Somebody hurt you bad, didn't he?—and she'd burst into tears. He was a kind, kind man—wasn't at all sarcastic and jokey as he acted in public—still, he had a short temper sometimes, his health wasn't good. She'd wanted to start a second family, Claudette said, her voice trembling, but Al didn't want any more children, had grown-up children from his other marriages always in trouble and always asking for money. You got to be young to make certain mistakes, Al always said.

She believed in life, though. *She* did. Human beings are here on earth to love one another, not destroy one another, to bring forth new life in the image of God, didn't Felix agree? Felix shook his head, smiling, and Claudette asked almost pleading, *Didn't* he agree? Felix said he hadn't any idea why human beings were on earth. "Maybe to fight?" He laughed though he wasn't in a laughing mood.

"That isn't funny," Claudette said pouting, laying her hand lightly on his, reprovingly. "You know you don't mean it," she said and Felix felt the blood rush into his face. Instinctively his fingers closed tight around the woman's hand, she winced at the pain and at his saying sharply, "Don't touch me if you don't mean it."

He telephoned St. Joseph's Hospital and was told at the switchboard that Enid Stevick was in "good, stable" condition and that visiting hours began at 11 A.M. the next day. Telephoned the Stevicks at 118 East Clinton and after eleven rings his niece Lizzie picked up the phone sounding sleepy, frightened, she didn't recognize Felix's voice at first, telling him her mother and father were still at the hospital, asking him what time was it?—she'd lain down on her bed and the next thing she knew she'd fallen asleep. Lizzie was eager to talk to Felix, oh God, she said, it was the most awful awful thing hearing Enid like that, breathing so hard, I just knew she was dying and they said her heart stopped in the emergency room, that meant she *could* be dead right now—what did you do up in the woods, out in the country, where you couldn't call an ambulance? Lizzie began to cry and Felix dropped another coin in the phone when his three minutes ran out, he asked after Lyle and Hannah, how did they seem to be taking it? and who was Enid's doctor? and how did Enid seem, herself, did she understand what had happened? what did Lizzie think *had* happened? Lizzie said, oh Felix it was just so awful I think she did it on purpose but Momma and Daddy—they think it was an accident. Felix shut his eyes, trembling, knowing if they were together Lizzie would be pressing herself in his arms, hadn't his nieces always adored him—Geraldine, Lizzie, Enid—there was Geraldine a married woman looking at him smiling with the knowledge of what men and women did together and for each other, and watchful too at the lake because of Enid's behavior, sisters sense these things, don't they, always a little jealous of each other. Lizzie was saying, "Think if she'd *died,* Felix—" and began crying again and Felix was going to ask about a note, had Enid left a note, but he decided not to: they'd have found it by now.

Or Enid would have told them by now. If she intended to tell.

He'd walked out on the Sansoms saying he couldn't stay to have dinner with them, if that meant he was rude it couldn't be helped. At 11 P.M. due at Freddy De Marra's for a poker game but he wasn't going there either. He got in his car and drove and stopped for his first drink at the Diamond Horseshoe on Nine Mile Road where the bartender knew him but respected his privacy, always gave him, or offered him, a drink on the house, they'd talk boxing or cars or mutual acquaintances, some of them they hadn't seen in years, some of them probably dead. After the Diamond Horseshoe, Felix headed north on the Jamieson, feeling good; this was what he wanted, this was what he'd been headed for, momentum bearing him along.

You could say it was like memory: like the boxing matches going back to when he was fifteen years old weighing one hundred thirty pounds which he could recall in sequence, in vivid cinematic detail if he chose. Strange, though, how in memory you see yourself from the outside—on film. Like memory as if all this had happened before too, the girl he'd raped but hadn't quite raped but he *had* and it was what he'd always been afraid he would do. Asked Vince once did he ever think like that, along that line, and Vince misunderstanding said, Yeah, sure, I think every man would like to, at least once.

Fulton, Marietta, Timber Lake, Unionport . . . he exited from the expressway now driving north and east, speeding through towns posted for 25 mph, half hoping a local cop would try to give chase. Maybe Lebanon: the Lebanon Inn with its parking lot half filled, pink flashing neon sign: but no he didn't feel like stopping yet. Drove on to the next little town, then the next, Spragueville, Oconee, passing tourist cabins gas stations rinky-dink little stores spread out along the highway; now he was forty miles out of Port Oriskany where people didn't know him. Turned into the cinder lot of a tavern called Club 55 a quarter mile from the Pendleton Raceway, hadn't he been in Club 55 on one of his army leaves?—he remembered the stock-car track close by. Yes, and he remembered he'd had a good time.

Slipped on his tinted glasses though it was night. Ran a comb through his oiled hair, turning his head from side to side regarding himself in the mirror; Felix Stevick was vain of his good looks, pleased too his nose wasn't dented or even flattened, twenty-eight stitches in his face but there was only one scar really and it could have been worse: could have lost the eye. Corvino and his manager were sorry as hell for what had happened, Corvino wasn't a bad guy outside the ring, said the butting just happened—"These things happen." OK, said Felix, no hard feelings. They were worried maybe the Mattiuzzios would get even with them and maybe the Mattiuzzios did, or the Rimis; Felix was out of it and didn't know or want to know. Settle your own quarrels. I'm walking away with my life.

Stood at the bar drinking an ale scanning the crowd, he was getting excited at the prospect, moving a little with the jukebox beat and taking his time looking around. Mainly men, hicks, a few women, no one he knew or who knew him.

Drifted about with his glass and bottle, and at the far end of the bar there was a girl in a Spanishy white blouse with an elastic neckband tugged down over her bare shoulders, red curly hair, white skin the kind Felix was crazy for—Susan Hayward in some movie, he'd only seen the posters—and she was with a big guy maybe six foot two weighing maybe one hundred ninety pounds: fat arms covered in dark hair, heavy shoulders, a day laborer or a farmer possibly, he'd been in the navy, there was a tattoo on one of his forearms. Felix thought, Why not?—he'd be giving the bastard at least thirty-five pounds.

He made no secret of it, looking at the girl the way he did. Open, obvious. Not smiling because he was serious and eventually she got self-conscious, casting Felix a sidelong nervous smile but he ignored the smile and she nudged her boyfriend whose name was Robbie, Felix had overheard; okay, Robbie, how about it?—the big guy's face flushing dark with blood.

Felix didn't push it immediately, turned aside as you naturally would and ordered another ale, pretended to ignore Robbie and the girl, then after a minute or so casually turned to look at them again, at her—his gaze a hook catching at them, pronged hook in an open eye: now only Robbie was watching him. Twenty-five years old in a faded green T-shirt straining against his big torso, the neckline stretched from his big hard head. Robbie had tried for a country-chic look, ragged sideburns and greasy hair in a pompadour, slick DA quills behind. Well it wasn't all muscle, there was fat too around Robbie's waist, the neck thick but not from strengthening exercises, he'd come swinging at Felix and Felix would slip it and give him something fancy, a straight right to the windpipe, an inside right uppercut with his full weight behind it—no, he'd try for the classic solar plexus punch you never get a chance to throw in the ring, just under the heart and your opponent drops as if dead. Or maybe he'd chop up Robbie's face, carrying him as long as he could, working his jab, circling him in the parking lot—it would be in the parking lot, car headlights turned on—wouldn't want to seriously injure the sucker, that meant an ambulance, state police, trouble. But if Robbie got lucky and landed a few good shots, if Robbie'd ever boxed in the navy, what then?—Felix was giving him thirty-five pounds and a couple of inches on his reach for sure so if he knew how to box he'd kill Felix but Felix doubted that was the case. Not here, not tonight.

Then Robbie's girl spoke earnestly to him, leaning to his ear, pulling him away from the bar, Let's go home honey, she'd be saying, she didn't want any trouble, wouldn't even glance back over her shoulder at Felix in a flirty reproachful farewell 'cause he'd scared her—something tight, mean, vicious in his face. So that was that.

Fuck it, Felix thought. Heart beating so rapidly his breath came short, pained; he'd never felt so much alone.

Halfway back to the city he stopped at Joe's Marietta Café, dialed Lyle's number from a pay phone. One A.M. and the poor bastard was probably in bed exhausted from the vigil but Felix had to talk with him. Had to hear his voice.

A dozen rings and Lyle finally answered, voice cautious, fearful, Felix knew he was expecting the hospital with bad news so he said quickly, "Lyle?—it's Felix," but so softly Lyle couldn't hear. Lyle was saying, "Hello? Hello?" in this vague dazed quizzical voice Felix had never heard before and Felix meant to speak, standing with his hand cupped to the receiver, but the words didn't come or he hadn't prepared what they would be. Shouts and laughter and jukebox music from the bar and Felix said, "Lyle?—" then his voice failed him and Lyle said with mounting anger, "Look, who the hell is this?" waited for a beat or two, then slammed the receiver down.

Felix stood listening to the dead line, just stood there listening, wondering how long he'd stand there, not even drunk but in fullest consciousness, fully himself, wondering how long he could take it.

5

The Supreme Court granted a stay of execution for Julius and Ethel Rosenberg—of not quite twenty-four hours. Each died in the electric chair at Sing Sing shortly after 8 P.M. on June 19, 1953. There were no last-minute confessions.

Enid was not to read an account of their deaths until she left the hospital the following week. Even then she came upon the article by chance in a copy of the Port Oriskany *Evening Herald* Mrs. Stevick was using to soak up water beneath her washing machine in the basement at 118 East Clinton. Reading and rereading the article Enid surprised herself by her reaction: she began to cry bitterly. But they had done it!—they had escaped. Still she was crying, she cried thinking not only of the Rosenbergs who were dead but of Warren—how he must have felt, how he must feel. As the time for the executions approached the four hundred pro-Rosenberg pickets keeping their vigil in front of the White House were taunted and threatened by a crowd of nearly seven thousand anti-Rosenberg pickets with signs of their own held high— BURN COMMIE TRAITERS! NO PARDON FOR JEW SPIES! 2 FRIED ROSENBERGERS COMING RIGHT UP! At 8 P.M. the anti-Rosenberg pickets erupted into cheers as at a New Year's Eve celebration.

"Poor Warren," Enid said, letting the newspaper fall. She was grateful she wouldn't have to see him for a long time.

6

So you want to love me, Felix said.

So you thought you'd kill yourself to punish me, Felix said in a voice just loud enough for Enid to hear.

In the hospital room when they were alone together he stroked her hand in secret, slowly he drew his fingers along the curve of her waist, her thigh. She felt his touch through the bedclothes, staring at him weak with love. At these times he said nothing, a kind of trance was upon them both, a languorous blood-heavy extinction of their minds. She saw he was angry with her, he was sick with desire for her, the rest of the world was distant, obliterated. Enid felt a shuddering sensation of the kind she had felt sinking into sleep, into Death. Except she had not died. They had hauled her back as one might haul a fish out of the water with a net. So you thought you could escape us!

You're never going to do that again, are you, Felix said.

Enid's lips moved numbly. No.

Are you?

No.

Are you?

No, Felix.

And they stared at each other half perplexed, trembling with anticipation, a desire so keen it must surely have charged the air in the room and anyone blundering inside would have known. Felix's color was high, warm, his smile seemed involuntary, he was the one who had brought Enid Stevick the twelve creamy-white roses wrapped in tissue paper and smelling of cold; he was the one who had brought the Swiss chocolates in the plump red satin box there on the window-sill for Enid's visitors to sample. Of all Enid Stevick's relatives the nuns were most taken with her young Uncle Felix.

He promised her he wouldn't hurt her he wouldn't really do anything to her until he thought she was ready, no matter that Enid, crying her hot spasmodic tears, squirming eel-like and ravenous in his arms, demanded love, adult love; she *was* ready, she said, the taste of wine oddly dry in her mouth, sweat running in rivulets down her sides. Felix stroked and caressed her, he kissed and tongued and sucked her breasts, her nipples, he liked even to suck her underarms, he liked her sweat, the tastes of her body—there was nothing of her body he didn't adore! He might kiss and nuzzle the soft rather bruised flesh of the inside of her elbow, the flesh behind her knee, he kneaded her buttocks, the small of her back, her belly, always he stroked and kissed and tongued her between the legs, he loved making love to her in any way he might, rubbing his erect penis in its thin tight rubber sheath slowly between her legs, slowly slowly again again again kissing her with his tongue deep in her mouth until Enid couldn't bear the powerful waves of sensation, orgasm overcame her quick and terrible, her eyeballs rolling in their sockets and her lips drawn back in a death's-head grimace from her teeth. She heard herself cry out helplessly, crazily—the delirious words *I love you I love love love you* or no words at all, only frightened sounds like those of a small child being beaten. Their faces were hidden from each other, Felix's weight on her was profound as the very weight of the world, she wanted it never to be lifted.

Sometimes it was a glass of red wine he urged her to drink, sometimes straight vodka, he gave her only a shot glass of vodka it was such powerful stuff he warned but it should loosen her up. And it did.

He was risking jail for her, he must be crazy, he said, baring his teeth in a mirthless laugh, but what the hell: it was something they needed to do. When they weren't together he seemed to be thinking about her all the time, he'd wake in the middle of the night thinking of her, he knew what that meant, it meant this, and this, and this, *this*—he was going to teach her to like it as much as he did.

Elsewhere his life didn't interest him. The hotel at Shoal Lake was doing fairly well in its first season, better than they'd expected; he was bored with it however and had to be moving into other things, investments, he had a few ideas he was working on, he'd see. Sometimes he talked to Enid about his life, particularly about his boxing career or the prospects of Jo-Jo Pearl's boxing career, but he didn't like her to question him. There were afternoons, entire hours, when he didn't talk to her at all, he was all feeling, emotion, desire, rarely did he respond to anything she said at such times, very likely he didn't hear.

Repeatedly he cautioned her: she wasn't to expect anything from him, not anything, did she understand, yes honey but do you *understand*, he'd give her things, presents, sure, he was crazy about her wasn't he, he was paying for her piano lessons, hoping Lyle wouldn't get suspicious, that wasn't what he meant, he meant he just wasn't making any promises. It wasn't love it was just something they needed to do, he didn't intend to harm her but he wasn't making promises of any kind, did she understand, this isn't a relationship that can last. And Enid said, reckless, teasing, to show she wasn't hurt: Except I'll always be your niece, won't I.

In the beginning it worried him, their close relation, being blood kin as they were, not once did he say the word "incest" nor did Enid allow herself to think much about it. It was just a word out of the dictionary! The main thing about being blood kin, Felix said, was of course you didn't want to have children and she wasn't going to get pregnant, that was damned sure.

Though in a few months he stopped worrying about their blood tie, or talking about it. Maybe he even liked it, he hinted, that she *was* his niece—it showed how much of a shit he was. He'd always wondered.

Still he was superstitious about seriously making love to her. Breaking her hymen, penetrating her as deeply as he could. Wouldn't it then mean too much to them both! She'd be getting married someday, he said. Enid said, hurt, I don't want to get married—I love you. Felix took such remarks lightly, he didn't really hear. He said, Sure you're going to get married someday, sweetheart—what else are you going to do?

Another time he told her he didn't want to ruin her life. And Enid said her life was already ruined, wasn't it—she had only him to make it well again.

7

At the start of the affair in midsummer of 1953, Felix made it a point to take Enid out of town whenever possible, to motels and tourist cabins north along the lakeshore as far away as Mattawa or Oconee, thirty miles from the Port Oriskany city limits. With the passage of weeks and then months he grew less cautious, even at times irrational: he always chose a motel beyond the city limits but he was apt to settle for one of the new motels strung out along North Decker Boulevard—the Bel-Air, the Americana, the Sleep-E-Hollow, the Great Western—not minding that the nearest of these was only a few miles from Enid's high school and from East Clinton Street. He rarely took her to a "good" motel because he reasoned the management would be more suspicious, he tried not to return to the same place too soon, he had a dread of someone recognizing his face. Yet after one of her Saturday morning piano lessons he arranged to meet her at the Onondaga Hotel where he bought her lunch at the Café Chez Carmen—it must have been a special occasion.

Enid remembered that particular day, that lunch, she'd had to play and replay the scale of A-sharp minor for her piano instructor, he was a marvelous teacher but exacting, humorless much of the time, a former concert pianist and vain about his standards. As she and Felix sat in the crowded buzzing restaurant like niece and uncle on a holiday outing Enid's fingers secretly depressed ghost keys against the table's edge. Up and down the keyboard, the tricky scale of A-sharp minor.

Not for some time would Felix allow her to visit his apartment on Niagara Square, his concern that they might be seen together was far greater than hers, which made her laugh but also made her feel hurt, careless.

Didn't he love her? Was he ashamed of her?

Felix said, I don't know what I feel.

She would lie in his arms and bury her face in his neck and tell him of the mistake she'd made—believing Death was her friend, something of her own. But Death had no presence. No being. There was just the body in its struggle like being drawn down by an undertow while you were still conscious and alert, knowing you would die not in peace but in agony, sucking water into your lungs, dying even as you were struggling to live. No escape once the process began unless at the very bottom of the lake there was escape—the rich black muck, oblivion. But you couldn't reach it unaided, that peace, you had to drown first. You had to die.

But they found you and hauled you back. A gasping thrashing fish out of water—so ugly! You'd thought dying would be something secret and private, hidden away in your bed, but they stripped you naked and forced a long tube down your throat and vacuum-sucked your guts out, then stuck you with needles under bright unwavering lights. Like being turned inside out, on display. And all of it what you deserved.

She'd thought it was her very life she wanted to kill, but it was only Enid Maria.

Still—she'd recovered. During her convalescence she regained the weight she'd lost and a few pounds more, her breasts slightly fuller, her hips, a pinch of flesh at the small of her back Felix liked to caress. Once your pride is broken your body is a sort of sleeping infant ravenous for nourishment from any source.

From any source.

Felix had said in the hospital, Look—promise me you won't try it again.

Felix said, You've got guts but what's the point of it?

When he made love to her if the sensation wasn't too fierce and sharp immediately, if she wasn't tensed against his hurting her, she sometimes felt her mind drift free, and break: she was being drawn down by the undertow but it had no terror for her, it wasn't the undertow at Shoal Lake, those icy rivulets like eels or snakes caressing her body. It was like a slightly quickened breath a feathery accelerated heartbeat, her vision was gone though her eyes might be open, every muscle in her body yielded and tensed, and yielded and tensed, there was a beat not at first her own but her lover's, a beat, a beat, an ever-increasing beat, only at the very end was she roused to consciousness, and panic—always it was the first time just as the beds they lay in were the same beds, the walls enclosing them the same walls, she breathed in delirium with the smell of disinfectant and Air-Wick, the sight of a solitary hair in a bathroom sink meant that not long before she had been grabbing and clutching at Felix, she went wild scratching at him, calling his name, hating him, wanting to draw him into her, deep into her, the orgasm was so terrible because he kept himself from her, gripping her buttocks tight, kneeling over her, cautious, straining, his forehead furrowed in sweat, he brought her slowly and then swiftly, pitilessly, to orgasm with his mouth, then trembling pumped himself to an orgasm of his own, just nudging the mouth of her womb with his stiff penis, her tight little cunt, he didn't want to hurt her he said, he thought he might injure her she was so small; still it drove him crazy, he loved it, he'd never guessed a girl her age could feel such things strong as any adult woman he had ever known. He wondered could she feel what he felt.

Enid's mind was extinguished, she wept, she did hate it; for a very long time she couldn't move, it was like waking in the hospital but knowing you were paralyzed, your muscles locked still in sleep, in stupor, while the world kept its distance. She couldn't draw a breath wholly her own, not Felix's, half asleep she imagined he was breathing her breath for her, lying heavily against her, oblivious of her, as if they had fallen together from a great height. By degrees her frantic heartbeat always calmed but this too was Felix's heartbeat. He gripped her tight, one arm awkwardly beneath her the other cradling her neck; if he slept he drew her down into sleep, the undersides of her eyes burned as she made her way through a grassy field or slope, the grass vibrantly green! so wonderfully green! and there she stood shielding her eyes against the glare of the sun on the lake, in the lake was the sky which always consoled her, Heaven and Earth in one plane. She saw in the water a shadowy reflection not her own, she stared, she stared, she began to weep with desire, a need so desperate it could scarcely be borne, like the pleasure that rose so violently between her legs that was Felix's to give or to withhold.

He had fallen asleep kissing her. But the kiss meant so little, it was one of many thousands.

Those kisses tasted of Enid's own body but also of wine or vodka or Johnnie Walker Scotch whiskey Felix carried in a silver flask with the handwritten engraving *To Felix the Cat, January 1, 1948, love Irene.*

"Who is Irene?" Enid once asked.

"Was," said Felix curtly. He didn't like to be questioned.

Sometimes when they woke Felix laughed softly, he felt so *good.* His body which seemed to Enid beautiful was bathed in a luminous pleasure that was sweat, he loved to sweat, he was convinced it was good for you, most things are good for you was Felix's conviction, he astonished Enid and made her laugh wildly being tickled, crazily tickled, tonguing and nuzzling her armpits, he loved the fine silky red-glinting hairs, he forbade her to shave her underarms, if you do the hair grows back rough and sort of razorish, he said. Now a woman's legs—he liked a woman's legs smooth.

Oh Jesus, already he had half a hard-on but it was getting late, he had to get her home, or did he.

* * *

Enid watched her lover aslant. Or by way of a mirror. Even a little drunk, giddy, standing naked herself, her hair disheveled, she found it difficult to face him to allow him to see her staring—it was like looking into too bright a light.

Felix's handsome face darkened with blood, hair in his eyes, the muscular beautifully formed flesh of his torso, his thighs, his springy legs, hair in uneven dark patches on his chest, belly, at his groin. He was unmindful of her and supremely confident in his body, padding naked, barefoot, genitals swinging loose like fruit.

(Like fruit!—but so delicate. She thought too of the skin of an unfledged bird. A creature fallen from its nest, its skin hardly more than a membrane, a network of tiny veins. The creature itself a sac of blood and organs, an unopened eye.)

She'd grown up in a city landscape which meant: clumsy drawings or scratchings on the pavement, on walls and doors, lockers at school, *cocks, pricks,* so many thousands floating disembodied and faintly comical, there were crude attempts at female genitals as well but the symbolism was uncertain, even a girl might stare in innocent bewilderment not knowing what the circle with its harsh vertical line was supposed to mean. But the *cocks,* the *pricks*—you learned not to look to be embarrassed or ashamed or frightened, stretches of pavement your vision glazed over unseeing. But why, Enid had wondered as a child. Why were the drawings drawn, why such effort? Lizzie said it was just kids with dirty minds, not to pay any attention. And the words *fuck, screw, shit*—just kids with dirty minds, Lizzie said, assholes that don't know any better.

The Stevicks were reticent about such things, such things *were* dirty—thinking about them even involuntarily constituted a venial sin to be confessed to Father Ogden in great embarrassment. They were shy of exposing their bodies, even Enid and Lizzie growing up took care to undress with their backs to each other, Enid had only rarely glimpsed her mother in her slip and then by embarrassed chance. She would have been mortified seeing her father undressed—the very thought made her heart pound.

But Felix wasn't at all self-conscious, Felix was quite without shame, he loved his penis, his cock, Felix and his cock were one, erect and trembling with anticipation. But he hated the thin medicinal-smelling rubber contraceptives he was obliged to wear, afterward he peeled them off with disdain and Enid might find one or two in the bathroom wastebasket if there was a wastebasket, sometimes just on the floor of the bedroom kicked amid the scattered bedclothes. Still, he didn't want to get her pregnant, he worried about it more than Enid did, if he didn't wear a Trojan he'd have to come on her belly and what he liked, what he was crazy for, was pushing himself inside her as far as he could without hurting her too much, just pushing, pressing, stretching her tight little cunt, it was only a matter of an inch or two, or three, but Jesus how he loved it and Enid being so small so like a child her ass small enough to be gripped in his hands—this excited him greatly, more than he could have guessed.

Felix would penetrate her as far as he could, then a little farther, until Enid began to bite her lips to keep from screaming or maybe she did scream and he'd press the heel of his hand over her mouth but that was it, he'd stop, he'd stop, through her sticky eyelashes she could see his face in orgasm warm, rapt, dreamy, the face of a bliss she could barely imagine.

It feels good, honey, but it isn't love.

One evening at supper Mr. Stevick asked Enid sharply what she was thinking about—her face showed she sure as hell wasn't listening to or thinking about *him.* And Enid blinked, seeing both her parents and Lizzie looking at her, Lizzie's sly smile; Mr. Stevick had been going on in a tone difficult to interpret—comical? despairing?—about atomic bomb testing, the newest thing is H-bomb testing, H meaning *hydrogen,* meaning a lot more people killed at impact and after. Enid said in a quick embarrassed resentful voice, "Nothing." Mr. Stevick said, hurt and cheery, " 'Nothing will come of nothing'—Lear to his impudent daughter."

She had been thinking of Felix: how she adored him, it might have been a time when she hadn't seen him or even spoken with him for some days, he called her when he could but he forbade her to call him—he gave her his telephone number but said, Don't use it! "Nothing," Enid said stiffly. In truth she had been thinking of her lover's face when he made love to her, she'd been thinking of his cast-off condoms, how someone would find them cleaning the room, the "maids" in many of the motels and tourist cabins were in fact the owners' wives, even their young daughters, how like used toilet paper or Kleenex the condoms were, disgusting or maybe just the usual debris to be picked up, thrown away. Felix's milky semen bunched there heavy at the tip of the translucent rubber—picked up, thrown away.

* * *

Enid had been out of St. Joseph's and was "herself" again as every-body noted for some time when she realized the Death-panic was gone; now she'd died and the worst had happened and Felix loved her, she could recall the sensation sometimes distinctly—walking too close to a high window or a railing, glancing down the stairwell in her piano teacher's apartment building to the lobby five flights below—but it wasn't the panic itself, only its memory.

Still she couldn't bring herself to cross the canal by way of the footbridge. Not yet. Not now. Nor did she cross through the vacant lot on any errand at all—she knew the worst things that happened there didn't happen to boys. And wasn't Felix always telling her don't hitch rides, don't walk home from school alone, stay out of alleys or back streets—you look too good for something not to happen to you.

Enid's piano teacher was Mr. Lesnovich, Anton Lesnovich, yes, the man was expensive and it had been difficult to get him to take her, she was only beginning, really—and at her age!—but he's the best in town, Felix said, Felix had done some inquiring, made some tele-phone calls, the irony was it had been his own mother, her husband rather, who'd helped—some connection or other having to do with contributions to a local chamber music group in which Lesnovich was involved. Musicians are temperamental but fair-minded, Felix thought, or anyway that's what he'd been told; also they make so little money, most of them, they're grateful for small favors. Like ex-ath-letes brightened by seeing their names mentioned in a sports column now and then. Lesnovich had been a solo performer at one time but only locally, he'd never made any recordings that anybody knew of but his reputation was excellent and if he charged a lot he was worth it, nothing but the best for Felix Stevick's young niece.

Felix was paying for the lessons of course—at $15 an hour no-body would expect Lyle Stevick to pay for them—and he'd also bought Enid a piano, a small trim Knabe spinet, the pretext being that the piano was secondhand, something one of Felix's friends no longer wanted, he got it at a bargain $250 while brand new it was worth ten times that much. This Lyle Stevick could appreciate, he wasn't as likely to take offense at his brother interfering with his family. Jesus, that *was* a bargain, a Knabe so cheap and it looked brand new in fact, not a scratch on it, perfectly in tune.

Felix was pleased that Lesnovich took Enid on as a pupil, that he thought she had some talent at least, but he didn't seem particularly interested in her progress, didn't ask about the lessons or what she was playing; she soon saw that that side of her life wasn't very real to him. He was more concerned that Enid's father not suspect what was going on between them.

Enid said, "No, Daddy takes it for granted." Rather cruelly she said, "He tells everybody you feel guilty and you owe it to him— trying to make up for all the years you treated him like dirt."

Okay, honey, this time we won't stop, Felix said. He'd dosed her with Johnnie Walker for which she was developing a taste and the door was bolted and chain-locked, the blind drawn down carefully past the windowsill, the shabby brown-spangled curtains yanked nearly closed, out on the highway an occasional car, the grinding of a truck changing gears. Just take it easy, honey, Felix said, and you'll be all right. But he knew to fold the towel over twice and slip it under her hips.

Oconee. Or Mattawa. Or was it Spragueville—the Bide-a-Wile Tourist Court, the Sleep-E-Time Motel. Low rates, off-season rates, VACANCY. Inside, the familiar stale smell of insecticide, the thin bed-spread cigarette-scorched, spidery rust-colored stains on the ceiling. Outside was Route 55 looping up from Port Oriskany how many miles to the south, running through farmland desolate in winter, running beside the enormous lake and the lake was the color of pewter and choppy, raw this afternoon but beautiful too, saw-toothed chunks of ice at the shore. Driving up, sitting close beside Felix, saying nothing for a long time, Enid watched as snow began to fall lightly, glinting like mica. No sun, just clouds, a uniform gray like a ceiling pressing low but she was suffused with happiness like sunlight. And the air so fresh and cold and wet each breath drawn in sharply hurt, each breath felt good.

Once begun this time it wasn't to be stopped.

Felix gripped her buttocks and drew her toward him, his vision filming over as if he were going blind. With the first stab of pain Enid shut her eyes hard, not wanting to see his face.

. . . love you. Love love love love you.

Yes, she tried loving him as he'd taught: legs, knees weakly embracing him, panicked fingers on the bunched-up muscles of his back.

The pain was like nothing she'd ever felt before. A knife entering and reentering her pushing deeper each time scalding her insides but he wasn't going to stop. Her mouth was ugly with the strain of not crying out, sweat gathered in tight little beads on her forehead. A wild crazy ride. She wasn't drunk enough. Felix was fucking her half to death.

When it was over he lifted himself from her, blood on his penis, the damned condom was torn, oh Christ, he said. His breath caught in his throat, saliva gleamed at the corner of his mouth. She knew he'd loved it and she tried not to despise him.

He wanted to take her to a doctor. He knew a doctor, he said, back home. She seemed to be bleeding pretty badly, he might have torn her insides. Enid said it was all right. She thought it would be all right. It *would* be all right for Christ's sake just let her go—she went into the bathroom shutting and locking the door behind her if the goddamned sliding lock really worked. Her fingers felt cramped as if she'd been lying on them. Her mouth was numb and ashy, drained of blood, reminded her in the mirror of a fish's mouth.

Still her eyes shone in elation, triumph. No one would ever hurt her like that again.

Wad after wad of toilet paper, her hands shaking, then she flushed the paper down the toilet trying not to see, the blood was a clear thin red, not dark and clotted like menstrual blood at the start of one of her periods. The insides of her thighs were chafed raw, the pain was a dull throbbing burning going a little numb. So this is it, Enid thought.

Oconee. Or was it Mattawa, Spragueville. A rust-stained toilet bowl she'd seen many times before, stray hairs gathered in the shower drain, strangers' voices lifting and falling away outside. Someone starting a car in the parking lot. She waited until the bleeding seemed to stop, then used more tissue paper, then washed herself tenderly, awkwardly, it puzzled her that her hands were still shaking now everything was over.

Light and teasing, vaporous, there came a dream—she knew, dreaming, it was a dream—that she had to get home, they were waiting for her at home but she was miles away, she didn't even know which direction home was. What had she done, what had been done to her!—a man's weight heavy upon her, one arm slung across her belly in sleep. On a road somewhere nearby cars approached, then receded, diesel trucks shifted their gears on a long slow grade, then the country quiet again and she was half asleep her muscles twitching her eyeballs moving jerkily in their sockets she had to get home but she couldn't move.

In the wallpaper with its creases and wrinkles, its mysterious hollows and ravines, footpaths, forests, floating islands—there she was wandering utterly alone. The dime-store mirror taped to the inside of her locker door, a reversed world over her shoulder through which the figures of her classmates and friends passed oblivious of her, not knowing how she observed them. And hadn't she had a magical ring years ago? Hadn't Felix given her the ring? Held close to her eye the glassy jewel trapped a tiny rectangle of the world, reversed, over her shoulder, emptied of her presence. That was its extraordinary significance—it did not contain her, it knew nothing of her. She had tried to enter it once but she had failed, the crossing was too difficult.

"Enid—?"

Felix was shaking her, she woke dazed and groggy, her heart pounding, not knowing where she was. He stood above her gripping her by the shoulder, shaking her so hard the bedsprings rattled.

He sat heavily beside her, asked was she all right? he'd showered, his hair was damp and slickly combed, a cigarette burned in his fingers and Enid even in her confusion could sense how he was trying to disguise his worry. But of course she was all right. She was always all right. Felix kissed her eyelids, her mouth, rather roughly, he said they'd better be going she'd better get dressed did she need any help?

Halfway home they stopped at a tavern. Felix had a beer and Enid needed to use the women's restroom; the bleeding had started up again, she felt it seeping hot and sullen in her loins, now there were dull intermittent cramps in the pit of her belly. Through the cheap Masonite door of the restroom a country-and-western song came twangy, sweet, insinuating, in rhythm with her pain. Again she used wads of toilet paper, again her hands were trembling. Her sensation of triumph had faded.

She was thinking of the drive up earlier that day, Felix nervous and excited but saying very little, he'd hit a patch of ice and the car went into a brief skid. Then some miles along as Felix approached an intersection a farmer in a pickup truck edged out rather incautiously—he was supposed to have stopped, Felix had the right of way—but Felix bluffed him out and sped through and the men sounded their horns, quick easy spasms of anger. "Fucker," Felix said to the rearview mirror.

They spoke very little on their way to Spragueville to a shabby cinderblock motel close beside the highway advertising OFF-SEASON RATES, PRIVACY GUARANTEED, SINGLE & DOUBLE BEDS, VACANCY.

The night before Enid had read in the newspaper that Felix's boxer Jo-Jo Pearl had won a "close" decision in Pittsburgh but when she asked Felix about it he said only that Jo-Jo had a lot to learn. Enid asked when was he going to take her to see Jo-Jo box, hadn't he promised her he would, and Felix said he'd take her sometime, maybe, if the circumstances were right. He didn't think it was a good idea for them to be seen together in public just yet, anybody who knew him would know. Know what, Enid said half tauntingly.

She'd been in the smelly unheated restroom so long waiting for the bleeding to stop, leaning against the sink, her head now aching fiercely and her eyes filled with tears, one of the waitresses came in asking was she okay?—her boyfriend was getting worried about her.

"Yes I'm okay," Enid said. Her voice came out mocking, the word *okay* emphasized, it was a word she hated and rarely used. "Tell him I'm *okay*. I'm coming right out."

When she returned to the table she saw that impassive hooded look of his, that pretense that nothing was wrong he was supremely in control, Felix Stevick idly peeling a label from a beer bottle, giving her his easy smile, except he was getting worried, wasn't he just slightly worried, he was thinking maybe his girl would end up going to a doctor, not a doctor of his acquaintance, maybe she'd get through supper that night or maybe not, maybe she'd crack suddenly, Jesus was she going to crack, hysterical and crying, telling her mother first then both her mother and her father what had happened, who it was who'd fucked her, tearing up her insides so she was bleeding like a pig, yes and he'd loved it too every second of it he'd been more excited than she had ever seen him and nothing she could have said or done was going to stop him at the end, he'd raped her and he'd loved it but it wasn't going to remain a secret. Yes, Felix Stevick seemed to understand this, half rising from his chair as she sat down, he seemed to anticipate it all, looping his arm around her shoulders bringing his mouth against her ear like any lover bland and affectionate trying not to get anxious about what was coming next. Enid was going to tell her parents, she was going to tell the doctor, she was going to tell it again and again, eventually she'd be forced to tell it while a police stenographer took it all down, that was why he was beginning to look anxious, wasn't it, the arrogant son of a bitch.

She was shaking, shivering, her face burned, the skin was papery-thin waiting to be ignited, Felix hesitated then asked if she was still bleeding and Enid said quietly, "If I'm bleeding I'm bleeding, what does it have to do with you?" Enid said in a quiet low rushing voice,

"Why do you want to know? What business is it of yours? If I'm bleeding I'm bleeding, what does it have to do with you?" She looked at him in hatred, in loathing, she was saying less quietly, "You son of a bitch. You bastard. I know *you*—you bastard. I knew you all along. I knew you last year. I mean at Shoal Lake—I knew you then. You filthy son of a bitch, getting me drunk taking me to that place trying to fuck me standing up, then you made me—"

Felix tossed a $5 bill down on the table, Felix was walking her out of the tavern carrying their coats. Once they were in the car he made no effort to quiet her, said nothing, hardly troubled to fend off her several furious blows against his shoulder and the side of his head. As he backed out of the parking lot the white-walled tires of his DeSoto Deluxe spun and threw up gravel, then he was off on the highway, accelerating, headed for the city.

Enid fell asleep then; when she woke the sky was massive and darkening and Felix was signaling to exit the John Jamieson Expressway at Nine Mile Road, the air gritty from U.S. Steel on one side, the Goodyear Tire smokestack rimmed in flame on the other. Now she spoke quietly. "I don't think I want to see you again, that's all." And Felix said after a pause, "Yes, that's right, I think you're right, Enid."

8

For her sixteenth birthday Felix gave her a heart-shaped pendant about the size of a quarter, sterling silver trimmed in gold on a thin gold chain. He left the gift wrapped in plain white tissue paper in a box from a local jeweler's with Mrs. Stevick. Enid was given it when she came home from school.

"*Isn't* it beautiful!" Mrs. Stevick said in an accusatory voice. "Take it out, Enid, put it around your neck, what's wrong with you?"

The date was April 9, 1954, nearly five weeks since they had last seen each other. In all that time they hadn't spoken either, but that night Enid telephoned him.

* * *

He wanted her to know, he said carefully, that the necklace didn't mean anything, she wasn't to think it meant anything, did she understand?—and Enid said yes, she understood. She'd understood all along.

9

It was a season of apprehension, slow-gathering crisis. Lyle Stevick felt it in his bones and in his lungs, in the very pit of his belly, yet he could not have said from which direction the lethal blow might fall: he could not have given a name to his terrible dread. The frequent televised testings of the Bomb (that blank terrible screen erupting into light, steam, smoke in silence) had the power to frighten him as mere printed photographs had not, he was following with intense interest the Army-McCarthy hearings (eventually to run for thirty-six days), yet he did not believe these external matters could account for his waking nearly every morning out of a thin unsatisfying sleep with a sense of having narrowly escaped some catastrophe, his old hated dream of the white room perhaps, the featureless glaring white-tiled room. He'd wake to the taste of dread, scummy and stale in his mouth, he'd begin coughing immediately, waking poor Hannah, staggering doubled over to the bathroom racked with the need to purge himself of a poisonous clotted phlegm lodged deep in his insides. Not out of his lungs but out of his very guts he imagined the violent spasms issuing. What is it! what is it! what is it!

Hannah too was frightened, said it was from him smoking that pipe of his all the time, anybody with a brain in his head could figure it out, Lyle told her scornfully he didn't *inhale* the smoke for Christ's sake, but she nagged him to see Dr. Ritter so finally he capitulated, made an appointment, then broke it on the sly the next morning: one call made from home with his wife close by, the other made from Stevick's Furniture, afterward he felt gay and exhilarated as a child dismissed early from school. In any case the coughing spells always diminished as soon as he left 118 East Clinton.

"Nothing like canceling a doctor's appointment," Lyle Stevick said to one of his pals where he had lunch, lunch and a few beers, the Cadboro Tavern where Lyle Stevick was well-known and liked, where you could get knockwurst on rye and corned beef and cabbage and meatballs and sauerkraut and Stroh's on tap. "Nothing like it, right? for setting a man up all day."

His pal was his own age, early fifties, but looked a hell of a lot older, tiny veins exploded in his nose and eyeballs slightly bulging, threaded too with blood, Lyle thought he hesitated a bit before clapping a hand on Lyle's shoulder and saying loudly, "Damned right."

Why drive all the way downtown to see that asshole Ritter, pay him $25 for the same old self-righteous crap, he knew he was overweight by a few pounds, he knew he had a belly, a ring of fat around his waist, wattles and sad loose cords beneath his chin, he knew he had problems with his blood pressure, but the real problem was a liking for salt—food just didn't *taste* without it—and beer and coffee and God knows what all else on that printed list Ritter had given him, he'd filed it away long ago and hadn't seen it since. He was taking blood pressure pills every morning of his life he complained last time he went in, why didn't the damn things do the trick? Ritter told him the pills only brought the pressure down a few points, the rest was up to him. It was up to him too, Ritter said, chiding and pompous, twat-mouthed old bastard, if he wanted to keep smoking that pipe when it was bad for his heart and his lungs and his mouth, just the other day he'd lost a patient, an old friend too, died at St. Joseph's of cancer and the cancer'd begun in his mouth, he'd been smoking a pipe for forty years just couldn't give it up—and on and on, but Lyle Stevick had stopped listening. There were just some things in life, he thought, you can't listen to. Your mind just naturally shuts off.

It was like that too with the war scare. Every day a headline in the newspaper, every day the NBC news, the Soviets are demanding, the U.S. is protesting, the Soviets have exploded X, Y, Z, the U.S. has exploded X, Y, Z now double-Z, crises in East Germany in Yugoslavia in Hungary in Africa in Indochina, never forget Red China, never forget Nationalist China, Eisenhower has said, John Foster Dulles has said, Khrushchev has said, Bulganin has said, there is Vice-President Nixon, there is Senator Joe McCarthy, there is the new ultimate war weapon exploded back in February, the super-weapon called the hydrogen bomb or the H-bomb or the fusion bomb or the thermonuclear bomb. Lyle Stevick read fascinated that this colossal bomb used the heat of an "ordinary" atomic bomb to set it off, you could vaporize an entire South Pacific island with it, you could tear a hole two hundred feet deep in the ocean floor with it, you could toss up a giant fireball three miles in diameter, release a cloud of radioactive dust twenty-five miles into the stratosphere with it, one of the television announcers said with solemn excitement that the blast of a single H-bomb was as powerful as the sum of all the bombs dropped on Germany and Japan during World War II *including the two original A-bombs.*

Think of that!—if you could.

But of course the hydrogen bomb would never be used, its development was only a defense strategy.

Much talk too in the newspapers, magazines, on television, even Father Ogden at the pulpit, bomb shelters strong enough to withstand blasts of a certain degree, you'd need concrete walls, you'd need supplies and protective apparel for three to five days underground, there was a Mark I Kidde Kokoon shelter kit selling for $3,000 though others were available for less. An article titled "Yes, You Can Survive!" in the *Reader's Digest* emphasized optimism and positive thinking, for much of this *was* one's attitude, wasn't it?—even a person exposed to radiation who succumbed to radiation sickness had a fifty-fifty chance of recovering, a distinguished physician said. Also: nuclear fallout might cause mutations but mutations "frequently" work out to improve the species, a distinguished scientist said. On television Bishop Fulton Sheen in his magnificent finery led impassioned prayers for world peace but took a hard line on atheistic communism, Lyle Stevick couldn't trust himself to remain in the room when the Bishop came on, he and Hannah only ended up quarreling. Hannah was an adamant supporter of McCarthy's as well, convinced the army was hiding any number of Communists, but Lyle had learned not to be drawn into a discussion, he just ended up shouting at the silly woman, frightening and scandalizing his daughters, very likely the neighbors as well, nor was it good for his blood pressure! his heart! his peace of mind!

Thinking of such matters he sometimes felt the blood draining out of his hands and feet, then again his face might flush hot, his heartbeat erratically quickened or seemed perversely to slow in dread of all that was to come that must be endured. At Stevick's Furniture he caught himself standing ramrod straight staring in the direction of the basement stairs, fantasizing the rope he still kept hidden atop a beam though he hadn't the slightest intention of using it, he caught himself dreaming with his eyes open of the white-tiled underground room, *O let me not be mad, not mad, sweet heaven!* was Lear's desperate prayer and it was rapidly becoming Lyle Stevick's too.

He said nothing to Hannah but he sometimes wondered if perhaps he *had* been poisoned—during the war when he worked six days a week at Swale breathing in God knows what kind of toxic air, getting God knows what kind of toxic chemicals on his skin, the employees had been assured the job was absolutely safe, there was absolutely no danger unless you drank certain chemicals down: which asshole joke always drew hearty guffaws from the victims. Lyle Stevick had always blamed the premature loss of most of his hair on that damned place, it seemed to him in retrospect the blood pressure problem began there too, he'd started catching colds more easily, had trouble with his digestion. If only the money hadn't been so good!—that was the hell of it.

And all those years he'd been secretly gratified that he was doing so well while Felix was off fighting in the Pacific. Obscurely he thought being in the army fighting in the war would do Felix good—it might knock him down a peg or two if it didn't kill him.

What frightened Lyle Stevick now was, he'd been reading of some radiation laboratory workers out in California, research assistants who had to clean up after experiments, wash out sinks and test tubes, now some of them were coming down with leukemia and cancer of the thyroid gland, blaming the company. The company said the diseases had nothing to do with the laboratory work, it was all a coincidence; they had doctors to support them too but there it was. Goddamn bastards, Lyle thought.

He had the idea it was an old, old story.

These days when things were slow at the store and he'd had enough of watching the Army-McCarthy hearings on a Philco set very like the one he had at home he amused himself rereading *Lear, Macbeth, Othello,* old splendid leatherbound copies of the plays recently acquired with a household of secondhand goods and trash. He dipped into Cervantes too, Spinoza, Aristotle, though the philosophers were beginning to seem remote and abstract to him. He loved reading passages from *Gulliver's Travels* aloud, like the one in which the

Brobdingnagian king denounces Gulliver and his species: " 'I cannot but conclude the Bulk of your Natives to be the most pernicious Race of little odious Vermin that Nature ever suffered to crawl upon the Surface of the Earth.' " Wasn't it so! Wasn't it so!

But Jonathan Swift had paid for his wisdom by going mad, it was said, dying from the top down like an aged diseased tree, it was a fate that did not bear close contemplation.

Then in early June Lyle Stevick had a romantic adventure.

He was summoned to the Eaton Boulevard house of a woman named Mrs. Elvira French to appraise a number of items of furniture. The task in itself was routine, unexciting, but Eaton Boulevard meant money, very likely old money, not exactly Lyle Stevick's usual territory though in fact he had once lived there in a residential hotel with his mother and brother after the breakup of his parents' marriage, that shameful period of Lyle's life! that humiliating period of years, years! Mrs. French lived only two blocks from the building in which Lyle had once lived but he noted in passing with some relief that the old hotel had been tastefully transformed, a limestone façade, a stately portico, trim black shutters at every window, the place appeared now to be an apartment building of some distinction: his poor mother, so obsessed with appearances, reputation, social standing, would at least have been gratified. Mr. Stevick drove past the building slowly, grinning his half-conscious angry grin; he'd survived, by Christ, he'd survived, a pity the Eaton Arms hadn't been preserved in all its melancholy shabby-genteel pride, those old lives somehow preserved as well, mummified within. How far after all for his complaints and miseries he *had* come.

He had four fine children, hadn't he, of whom two were clearly special, his son and his youngest girl, it might be said they were all he had: but he had them.

Lyle Stevick's unhappy mother had died fairly young, in her late forties, slow to recover from a severe bout of the flu, then her heart gave out, he'd always thought she had died primarily from disappointment over the circumstances of her life. She had been so steadfastly *good,* so *moral,* so *pious!*—with such degrading results. Lyle had been twenty-four years old at the time of his mother's death but her final hissed words to him were an accusation that he'd broken something at her bedside, one or another of her silly spun-glass figurines, when of course he had broken nothing, no one could understand what

she meant, *"You* broke it, didn't you!"—in a tone of angry resignation. Broke what? Where? But in the next moment the poor woman
was dead.

Lyle's spirits lifted slightly when he came in view of Mrs. Elvira
French's house. It was one of those portentous mock-Tudors with
half-timbering like burnt gingerbread and stucco like soiled vanilla,
a number of narrow leaded windows, a slate roof in moderately good
repair. The grounds had been lavishly and rather pretentiously land-
scaped years ago and were now somewhat overgrown. A well-to-do
widow—a house crammed with excellent furniture—bargains for the
taking: hadn't Lyle Stevick hoped for a situation like this for years?

His first surprise was that the lady of the house and not a maid
answered the door, and that Mrs. French was not what he had expected—a much younger woman, younger in fact than he, a plump
pretty woman with a fair skin, rouged cheeks, wide startled china-blue
eyes, her hair silvery blond and arranged in careful curls on her
forehead like Mamie Eisenhower's. She wore an elaborately brocaded
silk dressing gown, kimono-style, and shoes with a smart two-inch
heel; her hands flashed with jewels. Mr. Stevick thought it puzzling
that she had answered the door herself, odder still that she appeared
to be both excited and intimidated by him; she asked nervously to see
his driver's license as verification of his identity, then apologized
profusely for having done so. "Not at all," he said joking to relax the
tension between them. "I wouldn't want a stranger impersonating *me*
after all."

He realized a split-second too late that his remark was not, strictly
speaking, a logical one. But Mrs. French laughed politely and invited
him in. She apologized for the fact that Mr. French was away on
business and that he was obliged to deal with her; she hoped he would
not be disappointed with what she had to offer. Mr. Stevick, led inside,
felt a curious stirring of excitement and anticipation as if he'd once
been to this house, or a house that very much resembled it, years ago,
and something marvelous had happened. Was it possible? he wondered. His heart responded illogically—it was not *impossible.*

The interior was dimly lit, rather cool, though the warm June sun
blazed outside; the rooms were surprisingly small given the dramatic
width of the house; there was an air of disuse. Still Lyle Stevick
admired the stateliness of Tudor architecture, its very tensions, old
money and old ambitions, an American hope of being mistaken for
being English. "This way, please," Mrs. French said. He caught sight
of marble fireplaces, crystal chandeliers, faded but elegant draperies,

Victorian and eighteenth-century furniture, antique styles he didn't know. Jesus he was out of his depth!—he'd make a fool of himself trying to bid on these things. Though Lyle Stevick had had to make a living out of trash for half his life, he could still recognize good furniture when he saw it.

"Mrs. French," he said embarrassed, "I'm afraid you have the wrong man. I really think—"

"Don't make your judgment too swiftly! Please!" Mrs. French said in a small hurt voice. A dozen or so pieces of furniture were crowded together in a parlor, she drew their covers off almost shyly, apologizing for the dust, the state of the house, evidently her maid had quit without warning a few days before and with Mr. French away life had become extremely difficult. She wanted to make this transaction as simple as possible, no third party need be involved. As she spoke Lyle Stevick stared gloomily at the furniture. It was all of high quality as he'd feared, a quality far beyond his means, a lovely Queen Anne table and chairs, what appeared to be a French provincial settee, for all he knew that might be a genuine Chippendale highboy, in itself worth many thousands of dollars. . . . Poor Mrs. Elvira French had telephoned a used furniture dealer when she had meant to telephone an antique dealer.

Again Lyle tried to explain that he wasn't the right man for the job, he hadn't the resources, but Mrs. French seemed scarcely to hear. She told him she was alone in the house, she'd been alone for days, life had become extremely difficult of late but she wasn't the sort of woman to complain to a man she scarcely knew. Would he like some sherry and biscuits while he was making his appraisal?—she was anxious that he not hurry, she had all the time in the world.

Mrs. French spoke so plaintively that Mr. Stevick had to say yes, yes he'd like some sherry, yes some biscuits, though the offer puzzled him: sherry wasn't a drink he knew, weren't biscuits something you served at dinner? Mrs. French seemed delighted, fussing over him self-conscious and girlish as if she and not her furniture were being appraised. She sat him down in a deep cushioned chair and offered him a hassock for his feet: "Please make yourself at home, Mr. Stevick! Please take your time!" The sherry turned out to be syrupy-sweet, the biscuits merely thin wafer-like cookies, but he found he had an appetite for both. He hadn't eaten since seven thirty that morning.

Mrs. Elvira French was a short woman, perhaps five feet two inches even in her high-heeled shoes, her bust was plump and full but not heavy, exuding a summery fragrance. As she spoke animatedly to

Mr. Stevick her face grew warmer and pinker, the jade-green brocaded kimono was open at the throat showing her warm flushed skin, she was nervous, excited, a rosebud of a woman Mr. Stevick thought, feeling a stirring of—was it desire? sexual desire?—he shifted uncomfortably in his seat scarcely able to take his eyes off her. Apart from rowdy half-drunk and insincere flirtations in one or another tavern or bowling alley Lyle Stevick had enjoyed no female interest in him in a good many years. Like the sweet sherry it was all going rapidly to his head!

Mrs. French talked, chattered, laughed rather gaily as if this were a social visit, she was a lonely woman it began to seem, mysteriously lonely, speaking of being estranged from her social circle, finding them all so dull and limited and without imagination or zest for life, she asked how long Mr. Stevick had lived in Port Oriskany, how long had he been in the furniture business, was he married, had he children, ah! he had *grandchildren!*—her blue eyes blazing up in coquettish surprise as if she meant to challenge his word. "Only imagine, a man of your comparative youth, with grandchildren!" she said eagerly. "You must have married very young, Mr. Stevick."

"Very young," Lyle Stevick said, smiling.

"But happily—?" Mrs. French asked.

He ran a hand rapidly over his head feeling the smooth exposed scalp; he hesitated only a moment before saying in a rather flat voice, "Yes of course."

Following this he set aside his glass of sherry, got to his feet to examine the furniture, his face was hot and his breath a little short, what *did* this woman want of him!—he felt suddenly anxious, impatient to be gone. He asked her what prices she expected for one or another item and she said in a vague trailing voice that she wanted merely a total sum, couldn't he just give her a total sum for everything to make the transaction as smooth and simple as possible?—after all, he was the professional, not she.

Mr. Stevick laughed, uneasily standing with his hands on his hips. Today was a Wednesday and he was wearing a fresh-ironed white shirt with a good starched collar, a decent necktie, his brown-checked suit fit him tight in the shoulders but still looked good, he felt both self-conscious and flattered by Mrs. French's feminine interest but could not puzzle her out. Was she mentally unbalanced? a solitary drinker?—but her eyes were clear, her manner charming, the flirtatious edge to her voice was perhaps only a social habit, the way women of her circle talked to men, meaning nothing of what they hinted. In a shadowy mirror in a sideboard against one of the parlor walls Mr. Stevick's figure appeared to some advantage, tall, straight, imposing, handsome. He *was* a handsome man though it had been years since he had thought so, though the crown of his head was bare, he had still a fine fringe of gray-red hair and sideburns, he had only to remember to lift his chin so that the flesh beneath didn't bunch.

Mrs. French called out breathlessly, gaily, "Five thousand dollars!"

Mr. Stevick turned to stare at her. "Five thousand—? For everything?"

Immediately she was contrite. "Four thousand, then? Thirty-five hundred? Why don't *you* tell *me,* please, Mr. Stevick!" She sat clasping her plump beringed hands in her lap, staring up at him in childish trepidation. "You have such an honest face, Mr. Stevick, such a good handsome decent American honest face," she said in a slightly slurred voice. *"You* tell *me."*

Mr. Stevick turned quickly away, pretending to be examining the furniture, rapidly he calculated how much cash he had for a down payment on the spot how much in the bank his checking account and the savings account he could borrow the remainder from Felix, so small a sum was nothing to Felix, he'd anticipated paying out maybe $150, $250 today but he could come up with $3500, haul the stuff away this afternoon, maybe sell it as quickly as tomorrow to an antique dealer downtown for God knows how much: $20,000? $50,000? God knows! But even as he stood there thinking such extravagant thoughts, he knew he hadn't the heart or the conscience for such a transaction, there was Mrs. French watching him with her strained smile and wide innocent injured eyes, Jesus, he just wasn't the man to do it. The silly woman was damned lucky she'd picked his name out of the telephone directory and not someone else's.

Annoyed, unsmiling, he said, "The furniture is worth much more than that, I don't even know how much more, you should call in a good antique dealer—two or three, to get estimates. I'm not even *in* the antique furniture business, Mrs. French, I buy and sell used furniture and there's a considerable difference."

Still she gazed at him, contrite, worried. She got slowly and not quite steadily to her feet and seemed for a moment about to reach out to take his hands. "But Mr. Stevick, as a *professional man—*"

He avoided her, edging toward the parlor door. "You're begging to be exploited, Mrs. French, but I'm not the man for you!"

"How dare you! 'Begging'—!"

Then the extraordinary thing happened, which Lyle Stevick was to contemplate with mingled dread and lust for many days, weeks, months to come.

Their voices had swiftly and alarmingly risen, suddenly Mr. Stevick was astonished to find himself in the midst of a quarrel very like a quarrel between lovers. So quickly! Leading him out into the corridor Mrs. French was so upset, fighting back tears, she somehow tripped on the carpet in her high heels and would have fallen heavily had he not caught her in his arms, once she was in his arms her plump perfumed little body so excited him he embraced her hard, even dared to brush his lips against her forehead: so quickly! With a breathless cry Mrs. French pushed him away.

"Mr. Stevick!" she whispered.

She smoothed back her hair, adjusted the throat of her kimono, then like any practiced hostess she led her guest to the front door to show him out. Lyle Stevick followed after her dazed and blinded, his heart plunging in incomprehension of what he had done. He tried to apologize but Mrs. French, trembling, not meeting his gaze, cut him off, saying in a near-inaudible voice, "It wasn't your fault. You couldn't help yourself. I chose your name out of the directory because 'Lyle Stevick' is a name I seem to know, then when I opened the door here and saw you on the stoop your face was a face I seemed to know, no one is to blame but we can't see each other again. Please leave."

"But—"

"Please, Mr. Stevick. *Please leave.*"

So he left, he fled, hurried down the walk climbed into his car slammed the door and drove away not daring to look back. The words *I alone have escaped to tell thee* ran crazily through his head.

There followed then a dizzying cascade of time, hours, days, eventually a full week, unique in Lyle Stevick's experience. Even at the height of his youthful infatuation for the Jewish furrier's beautiful daughter so many years before he had not felt quite like this: not only as if he were on the brink of madness but that madness was most tempting, ecstatic.

And he could tell no one his secret, he was entirely alone!

That evening before leaving the store he telephoned Mrs. French, thinking to apologize further, but her telephone went unanswered. Was he in love? At his age? Married, a grandfather? Had he really embraced the woman, kissed her?—yet so deftly and lightly he couldn't truly have frightened her. *You couldn't help yourself, no one is to blame;* her words rang in his ears. She had said too she'd chosen his name out of a directory, she claimed even to have recognized his face.

He knew it was preposterous, wildly improbable, yet he could think of nothing else.

Was he in love?

He had known immediately as soon as he'd stepped in the door. Mrs. Elvira French with her pale-blue lovely eyes, her fair skin, her plump perfumed bosom, her unmistakable attraction to *him:* no matter that she was a married woman, an Eaton Boulevard matron, of a social caste considerably higher than his.

No matter that he was a married man and a father, even a grandfather, his life was not quite played out!

He studied his face in a mirror, there was Lyle Stevick eager and hopeful, his skin rather coarsely flushed, the tiny speck of blood in his right eye glistening. Yet he feared there was something desperate about him too, something pathetic. *We can't see each other again* Mrs. French had said and surely that would be the wisest course.

Yet he dialed her number. And finally after three days the telephone was answered: there came Mrs. French's small sweet cautious voice that was like no voice he had ever heard before. Rather stiffly he identified himself, said he was sorry if he'd upset her, when she did not reply he went on to caution her against being exploited, she was too trusting and credulous a woman, she really must get estimates on the furniture as he had suggested. "Thank you, Mr. Stevick," she said quietly. And nothing more. Hurt, he supplied her with the names of several antique dealers whom he considered reliable. Again she thanked him, then paused and said, "But Mr. Stevick, I had chosen *you.*" And before he could reply she hung up.

And when he dialed her number again the telephone went unanswered.

What did she want of him, and why?—why at this late hour of his life?

Up at dawn to watch the nuclear explosion beamed in from the Pacific, the rest of his family asleep and the television turned down low, such events are history, why not be a fearless witness to history—he'd been awakened in any case from a dream of sweet Elvira French by a fit of coughing that left him shaken and breathless, unable to return to sleep.

There it goes!—a tiny ball of light rapidly enlarging atop a quivering column of pale smoke, the sky blasted away, the horizon gone, now the mushroom cloud gracefully shaping itself like a familiar figure in a child's cartoon. He stared affrighted yet unmoved, it was too much to absorb, the cloud of Death that was yet a living cloud trembling and rippling with its own unstoppable incalculable interior life. As an announcer spoke excitedly of winds, heat, billions of tons of dynamite, millions of human lives that might be extinguished, Lyle Stevick ran his fingers roughly over his unshaven jaw, telling himself it might be a mere studio trick like the special effects in science-fiction movies: a phenomenon no larger than the TV screen itself.

He switched off the set. He couldn't take any more.

Dear God it *was* too much to absorb, no one was absorbing it no one seemed to take especial notice among the people he knew, the soul went numb the throat tickled harshly with the need to cough out one's poisoned guts, he'd go back upstairs and use the bathroom and shave, he'd tell himself a happy little story in the bathroom mirror of a place of refuge underground built by Lyle Stevick's own hands for those he loved and for Elvira French herself if she would have him. If she would have him.

It was to Elvira French he told his silent story too of how one by one his children were slipping from him, eluding the bonds of his fatherly love, it was Time, it was Nature, how could a reasonable man protest? Yet he'd been upset, he had to admit, pretty goddamned upset, when Geraldine told them about this Neal O'Banan she loved she had to marry, Jesus God had to marry and as quickly as possible too. Mr. Stevick had come close to slapping his own daughter, calling her a whore a slut, he'd never forget poor Geraldine's frightened face when Daddy almost lost control: but Daddy hadn't lost control, had he. Daddy learned to swallow down his pride and his hurt, learned to shake hands with the young man who had impregnated his daughter, even to look him in the eye and smile at him, even eventually to like him, you swallowed down the poison and pretended it tasted good and why not! why not! it *was* only Time and Nature, how life was working itself out, whether you liked it or not. Now on Sundays two or three times a month visiting Gerry and Neal in their toy-cluttered mock-redwood "ranch" house in Lakeshore Meadows Lyle Stevick had to admit he felt most comfortable chatting with his son-in-law, he hadn't very much to say to his daughter apart from the usual talk of the grandchildren, the meal she'd prepared, things the O'Banans planned to buy—this season a Westinghouse refrigerator, last season a good-sized RCA television, next season perhaps a Starcraft speed-boat for Neal and the boys to haul up to Shoal Lake. Always there was automobile talk too: excited speculation about whether the O'Banans' next car should be a Dodge or a Plymouth or a Chevrolet, complaints about the present car, a Ford, which was always having engine trouble. Neal O'Banan politely solicited Mr. Stevick's opinion on such matters and Mr. Stevick was happy to give it: he hadn't a goddamned good word to say for any American car he'd ever owned.

"Daddy," Geraldine would say in a lightly reproving voice, as if she were scolding Neal Jr., "we have to drive *something,* don't we?"

Neal O'Banan's hairline was receding and he was putting on weight around his middle faster than his father-in-law, but that salesman's handshake and that salesman's white-toothed smile were as forceful as ever. You had to admire the kid, walking away from his old man's hardware store to take a job at AT&T, Mr. Stevick thought. Geraldine had been worried about Neal's move, Mrs. Stevick had been frankly frightened recalling Mr. Stevick's miscellany of jobs during the thirties, but what the hell it was good times now, the fifties weren't the thirties by a long shot, already Neal was in line for a promotion and Geraldine was crazy about the other wives. AT&T provided employees with insurance coverage of every kind and activities ranging from softball to bowling to amateur theatrics to puppet shows for the children, what more could you ask? Mr. Stevick didn't care to speculate on how Geraldine and her family regarded the old household at 118 East Clinton, the old decaying East Side neighborhood she'd managed to escape forever.

Lyle Stevick loved his daughter and his son-in-law, surely he loved his grandchildren, yet to Elvira French he might speak of the sense of melancholy and estrangement he often felt in their midst, his discomfort at baby smells and baby things and the damned television turned up high as if to drown out conversation. There was Neal Jr. about to start kindergarten, there was baby Andrew already two years old, now Geraldine was pregnant again, proud and excited and fully self-absorbed; the heat of fecundity was upon her, shining out of her eyes. In the children's presence she frequently called Mr. Stevick "Grandpa" which annoyed him more perhaps than it should, he didn't want to get touchy as he got older, become the butt of condescending jokes like his counterpart poor Grandpa O'Banan, that self-pitying boring old bastard.

So Geraldine was lost. And Warren: at the time of Enid's hospitalization Mr. Stevick and Warren had come close to quarreling, the precise reasons were mysterious but now Warren was always away, Warren planned on entering law school in Philadelphia, Warren telephoned perhaps once a month out of a sense of duty but no longer wrote and never came home to visit. And Lizzie had grown brash and common, she'd insisted on bleaching her hair a pale moony platinum-blond, wore heavy makeup and tight-fitting clothes, but what could you do?—nagging didn't help and shouting didn't help and threats didn't help, Lizzie was moving out to share an apartment with that tramp Nelia Pancoe and another girl, and Mr. Stevick didn't want to think too precisely what that meant. Still, Lizzie had managed to graduate from high school, she worked at Rexall's downtown and paid for singing and dancing lessons at a place called Henri's Music Studio, a second-floor walk-up on Main Street, she was a sweet good-hearted girl, just stubborn, wanting to go her own way, in and out of the house, unreliable, only eighteen years old but already Mr. Stevick guessed sexually experienced with a boyfriend in his late twenties named Eddy Carlisle who'd spent six months in prison for car theft, but Jesus what *could* you do, it was the way life worked itself out. Sometimes Lizzie hung on his shoulder, teased and cooed like she was his little girl again, just couldn't bear it if her daddy was angry; then again she was capable of telling him and her mother both to go to hell, telling them she didn't give a shit what they thought, she was going to do as she pleased and that was that. And that *was* that. The last time Lizzie and her parents had been close, caught up in something meaningful together, Jesus, it was back in October when Arthur Godfrey had humiliated poor Julius La Rosa by firing the singer over network TV: "Thank you, Julie, that was lovely," Godfrey had said to his boy, smiling his usual fatherly smile; then to the audience with a conspiratorial smirk, "And that, folks, was Julie's swan song," and there was a stunned silence; as the newspapers reported the next day, you could nearly feel it across the entire United States as the knowledge sunk in that Godfrey had fired his protégé Julius La Rosa in front of millions of viewers!—an event unprecedented in the history of radio or television. Lizzie burst into tears of hurt and indignation and Mrs. Stevick too was shaken, as if the baby-faced Italian singer were one of her own children. The two commiserated, talked of nothing else for hours: Lizzie said she hated Arthur Godfrey, she'd never forgive him, Mrs. Stevick was torn between sympathy for La Rosa and loyalty to Godfrey, Mr. Stevick joined in, strangely agitated himself though he'd never been able to stomach La Rosa's overripe style of singing.

But it was a hell of a thing, wasn't it, for Godfrey to publicly humiliate one of his own people over network television!

"That son of a bitch," Lizzie whispered, tears glaring in her eyes. "I'll never watch him again!"

"Lizzie!" Mrs. Stevick said.

"Lizzie, calm *down*," Mr. Stevick said. Though he hadn't at the moment felt very calm himself.

Then there was Enid.

She practiced piano most evenings before supper and Mr. Stevick was in the pleasurable habit of half listening to her as he read through the *Herald*, his attention wavering between the disquieting news and his daughter's skillful playing. It did surprise him—he had to admit it—that she could play piano as well as she did. Mr. Lesnovich hadn't wanted to take her on as a pupil because of her advanced age, fifteen at the time; now he felt otherwise, he seemed to think she had some talent for music generally, not just the piano but music itself, she was interested in going into teaching, she said, which was realistic and plausible: of course she'd never be a performer, how many pianists are concert pianists?—the life, Mr. Lesnovich said wryly, wasn't a very *accessible* one, as he himself well knew. But to have a small intelligent talent and to nurture it, to proceed slowly without pressure and without inflated illusions, that was a very different matter. With that he could sympathize.

"The secret is to scale one's ambitions precisely to fit one's talent," Mr. Lesnovich told Enid. His manner as always was grave, vaguely censorious. *"That* is the key to happiness."

Told of such matters by Enid, Lyle Stevick couldn't help but feel privileged, flattered; whatever degree of talent for music his surprising daughter had was not after all commonplace, it must spring from the genes, chromosomes, the tight little calcified buds of his own talent that had never been allowed to flower. She would justify him, she would redeem his failure, dear sweet lovely Enid who had almost died last year but who had *not* died. For there she was seated at the piano, tirelessly playing and replaying her increasingly difficult scales and arpeggios, her fingers were light, quick, pliant, her hair gleamed on her shoulders the very hue of chestnut-red his own had once been. Mr. Stevick scarcely minded the false starts and repetitions, he rather liked the exercise pieces, then there were the actual compositions Mr. Lesnovich assigned—an elementary rondo of Mozart's, several of the more accessible Chopin "Preludes," Bartók's "Ten Easy Pieces for Piano," Khachaturian's "Children's Album." Mr. Lesnovich was locally famous for rejecting the usual approach to piano instruction: he never assigned his pupils music he couldn't take pleasure in hearing numberless times.

Last June when Enid had been taken by ambulance to St. Joseph's and no one knew whether she might live or die, her father had humbled himself, turned himself inside out—"God, don't let my daughter die. God, if You exist, don't let my daughter die." How many times he'd murmured that prayer he couldn't have said, the hours there waiting outside the emergency room were collapsed into one eerily fluid dreamlike pocket of time that might have been days or might have been a very few minutes. The experience had been so profound Lyle Stevick was unable to recall it afterward; even before Enid was discharged from the hospital he had begun to forget the sequence of events, the terrible hours of waiting, of bargaining with a God he knew did not exist and Who if He had existed would not have given a damn for Lyle Stevick and his daughter anyway; like a woman living through the most excruciating labor pains, split open and washed clean by pain, he simply summoned all the strength of his soul to focus upon her recovery: for after all Enid's life was real, the near-death only a fiction.

And then, how nervously proud they all were of her, all the family—recovering swiftly as she had and in such good spirits, such a courageous determined girl, taking her high school examinations only a week late, scoring so high, then beginning piano lessons, though afterward it wasn't clear who had thought of them, maybe it was Enid herself, but maybe it was Lyle Stevick, yes, probably it had been Lyle Stevick wanting to give his daughter an extra reason to live, an extra margin of happiness, he'd come so close to losing her.

He recalled the time many years ago he had discovered Enid staring at a photograph in a news magazine, so absorbed she gave no indication of being aware of his presence. The photograph was of something hideous, heartbreaking—a young boy killed by Nazis, Mr. Stevick seemed to recall. He had closed the magazine and taken it from her, chiding her for looking at such things, but even then she hadn't responded normally, she sat stricken staring at nothing. Enid? Honey? Daddy's here to protect you from such things!

But Daddy had done a poor job of it, hadn't he.

Now she was sixteen years old ripening into a maturity he wouldn't be able to share. She loved him as she loved her mother but clearly they embarrassed her, gave her pain, she had her own life, caught up in friends and schoolwork and her piano lessons and the "activities" of an American high school girl of 1954. Her secrets! Her growing aloofness! She shrank from his touch, laughing nervously, dreading Daddy's fingers in her hair, claiming the smoke from his pipe left her breathless, made her eyes water. She no longer fell in with his loud flirty drunken banter and was suffused with shame if one or another of her girlfriends met Daddy in such a state. There were days when he didn't see her at all—he'd had his breakfast and was out of the house before she came downstairs, she didn't come back for supper and he'd gone to bed by the time she came home. Next day he'd confront her, trying to disguise his emotion. "Ah-hah! where were *you* last night?" he might ask, and Enid would face him openly, yet with an air of stiff disdain, her deep-set brown eyes lovely but shadowed. "At the library, Daddy," she would say, or "Out at the movies, Daddy." Hating himself he would rattle on. "Yes? Really? I can check on that!" and Enid's mouth would tighten in opposition to him, in dislike of poor Lyle Stevick who meant only well, smiling angrily at the last of his girls captive in his house. The old rapport between them seemed to be lost. Their old understandings in league against poor silly Hannah: now there were times, Mr. Stevick sensed to his chagrin, Enid preferred her mother to him!

God knew where her mind was, *he* didn't, only when she sat ramrod straight at the piano was he sure of her, playing and replaying her pieces with a curious fierce love, the piano's treble notes especially sharp, pellucid, powerful. Were he less grateful for the fact of her recovery, her life, he might have been jealous of her piano teacher, this eccentric Lesnovich who dared charge $15 an hour when no one in the family had ever heard of a music lesson for more than $5 an hour, he might have been jealous too of his brother Felix intervening to pay for the lessons and to buy the piano: but wasn't that just like Felix, Lyle Stevick thought, you can't predict which way he'll jump. Ignores the Stevicks for years then suddenly he's back in their lives. . . .

These things he meant to tell Elvira French one day soon, they weren't complaints exactly but puzzlements crowding his heart.

O let me not be mad, not mad, sweet heaven!

* * *

With each day spent in staying away from Eaton Boulevard, Lyle Stevick felt his desire grow. He was sleepless, he was racked with coughing, he had no appetite or, abruptly, too much appetite, eating himself into a stupor; a single glass of ale went to his head. Feverishly he rehearsed words, gestures, actions. He would take her hand, he would take both her hands, gently he would kiss her, speak her name. Was it possible? *Was* it possible? A man prepares for adultery, he discovered, as for battle, or death.

If he crossed the threshold into her house a second time—if she invited him in—they would become lovers. He knew! He knew! So he must go. But he was frightened to go. But he *must* go, it was his fate. Elvira French: his fate: at the age of fifty-three.

As for Hannah—he didn't give her a thought. She was there, she existed, she even slept her leaden sleep beside him, but he didn't give her a thought, for Elvira French moved freely and deliciously through his mind. Long ago he had stopped loving his wife and then he'd stopped making love to her as well; after having given birth to Enid she was terrified of becoming pregnant again, she wouldn't have allowed any form of birth control for birth control as the celibate priests taught was a mortal sin. You went to hell for not spilling your seed in the proper place! But it scarcely mattered because Lyle Stevick's sexual desire had sharply abated. He'd told himself for years he didn't care, his humor was bawdy, coarse, despairing, he *hadn't* cared until. . . .

Lyle Stevick would have telephoned Mrs. French to tell her he was coming, boldly and recklessly he was coming, but he feared her husband's answering the phone: what then! Or Elvira herself in her soft sweet frightened voice forbidding him, hadn't she warned that they must not see each other again? But it was their common fate, wasn't it, hadn't the dear woman said that too?

Then the following Wednesday at a quarter past twelve of a balmy hazy June day the romance ended, as abruptly and mysteriously as it began.

Lyle Stevick went to Mrs. French's house and was crudely rebuffed.

Lyle Stevick went to Mrs. French's house barbered and tastefully dressed (in his good navy-blue gaberdine suit, a fresh-ironed white shirt, handsome checked tie), all the courage of his manhood summoned forth, he rang the bell and waited trembling, his former life buzzing in his ears, and was confronted not by pretty Elvira French but by a most hostile female in a shapeless black dress who might have been an older relative of hers. "Yes? Who are you? What is your business with us?" the woman asked. With so severe and imperial a manner she could scarcely have been a servant, staring at him coldly, her pale-blue watery eyes slightly bulging as if she believed him a criminal or a madman about to force his way into the house. It was uncanny how closely she resembled Elvira French but Mr. Stevick dared not think this thought. Falteringly, trying to retain his air of gentlemanly composure, he explained that he was a "friendly acquaintance" of Elvira French's who wished to see her.

"She is unwell and seeing no one," the woman said curtly.

"Unwell? But what is wrong with her?" Mr. Stevick asked in alarm.

Now the woman regarded him with the mildest gram of pity and contempt. "That is for the medical community to determine," she said.

"But is it serious? Is she hospitalized?" Mr. Stevick asked.

"And she has no 'friendly acquaintances,'" the woman added.

She stood plump and triumphant in the doorway as if guarding the house against him. She was a short woman in her mid- or late fifties whose faded hair had been skimmed back flat and blunt on her rather small skull; her skin was creased and puckered; her stockings were wrinkled about her ankles. Mr. Stevick stared at her helpless and despairing, for she so closely resembled Elvira French, what was he to do?

"I'm sure that Mrs. French expects me," he said calmly. "If you would be so kind as to—"

"'Mrs. French' expects no one these days," the woman said. "She is unwell. She is incapacitated. She is in quarantine."

"But if you told her that Lyle Stevick is here—"

"She knows no 'Lyle Stevick,' I assure you."

"I was here last week examining some furniture of hers with the intention of—"

Suddenly the woman in the shapeless black dress lost patience with him and said, in dismissal, "The furniture has all been sold, sir, long ago, sir, and carted away. Goodbye."

And the door was closed against Lyle Stevick and he stood dazed on the stoop of the grand old Tudor house at 928 Eaton Boulevard, his folly washing almost visibly about him.

* * *

No: it would not bear thinking about. The mind just naturally and pragmatically shuts off.

McCarthy was finished, the swashbuckling senator gone down in a paroxysm of fierce angry glee, he'd been publicly humiliated with millions of American television viewers watching—at last! at last!— and Lyle Stevick alone in his store, his CLOSED sign in the window, joined in the applause that swelled and swelled in the Senate Caucus Room as if it might swell out of the television set itself, turning the air festive and radiant, purged. But it was summer 1954, that was the melancholy fact, years too late, years and years too late, the sons of bitches took away my country, Lyle Stevick thought, pouring himself another inch or two of Early Times.

Sure he'd predicted that McCarthy would hang himself if given enough rope and the assholes everywhere in the country had given him enough rope, years and years of it, unfortunately he'd hanged other people too, oh Christ had he hanged other people. Lyle Stevick saw in his mind's eye the rope hanging from the beam, the secret rope the secret beam, but he was too drunk to pursue it. Yes, the sons of bitches had won. It was June 1954 and very late.

In the days following he hadn't even the malicious energy to mock his wife for her continuing loyalty to McCarthy. Jesus, he could feel almost sorry for the woman, stunned and bewildered as McCarthy himself over the change in fortune. One hour America favored the senator, the next the senator was on the way out, an old story maybe but it was quite a riddle if you'd believed all that Hannah Stevick had believed. She would have liked to talk about it even with the risk of one of their arguments but Lyle Stevick hadn't the heart. That he could take no small bitter solace from McCarthy's defeat meant that his manhood was entirely gone.

"But he's still a senator," Mrs. Stevick said. "They can't take that away from him can they?"

Dr. Ritter's waiting room: amid young mothers with fretting babies and the dull stooped rheumy-eyed aged he did not dare contemplate, Lyle Stevick sat sucking at his unlit pipe (NO SMOKING PLEASE) waiting for his name to be called, glancing through old copies of *Time, Newsweek, Life, Collier's*. Of late he rarely read any articles all the way through, even fairly brief articles in the local papers, he'd stopped following the diplomatic moves and countermoves of the world powers as they were called, had been mildly but not seriously interested in the Supreme Court's decision back in May to "desegregate" the public schools, for after all Enid had only a year or two to go and East High was one quarter Negro anyway, wasn't it, who gave a damn. He flipped quickly past photographs of a sweating bull-necked shyly smiling Rocky Marciano, not wanting to have to think of his brother Felix, had Felix ever found out Lyle'd won $50 betting on Corvino that time?—the sort of thing Felix, smiling so warmly, laying a hand on Lyle's shoulder, stroking his flabby muscle, would never forget. He flipped too past photographs of Eisenhower looking fatigued, old, liver spots on his hands weren't they, his dumb cheery smile wasn't going to make the slightest bit of difference, and Lyle Stevick didn't want to know, in truth he was grateful Eisenhower had won and not Stevenson, the Russians would have pushed us into the sea by now that's the melancholy truth. A sequence of photographs of UFOs— flying saucers?—in Oregon, Colorado, Texas, Rio?—drew his attention for some minutes but finally upset him so much he had to turn the page. Yes that was plausible, that was very likely next, but he couldn't contemplate it, he hadn't the strength.

Then he came upon a photographic essay on bomb shelters. Ah yes: underground bomb shelters: something eerily snug, attractive about them, wasn't there. He saw the appeal suddenly. It was all quite insane and terrifying but he saw the appeal, he saw the romance, a man showed his love for his family, perhaps even for the greatness of America, by building a cozy place of refuge by lining the walls with concrete and storing up provisions for—some said a mere three to five days, others argued for weeks. The photographs of some of the shelters were quite impressive he had to admit, also the photograph of a tense smiling man of about his own age standing in his backyard in Iowa beside a great gaping hole in the earth, a mere pick and shovel at hand. He was studying an artist's sketch of a $2,350 shelter equipped to protect a family of five when Dr. Ritter's nurse called his name. The way the woman raised her voice, that slight sharp edge to her voice, Mr. Stevick halfway thought she was calling out his name for the second or third time.

10

Labor Day 1954 and there was Lizzie saying suddenly, vaguely, as if at this odd moment so many months later she'd only now remembered and wanted to set things straight, "Oh hey, Enid, y'know that time you got sick, y'know when the ambulance came and things were kind of confused? Well, Momma pushed in here and looked through your things, I don't know if she took anything if she found anything I mean I wasn't actually in the room all the time. . . ." Her husky voice trailed off into an awkward silence.

Lizzie stood feet apart dumping the contents of her underwear drawer into a half-filled cardboard box on her bed. She was excited, defiant, at last she was moving out of 118 East Clinton to a place of her own, let Momma bitch and Daddy call her a tramp, she had her apartment, she had her job, she had her plans for the future, Christ she was nineteen years old and it was about time. Lizzie and Enid had been nervous with each other all morning, Enid was determined not to cry because in fact she wanted Lizzie gone, she wanted privacy, she'd told herself that countless times. Now her sister's offhand remark surprised her, she had put the notebook out of her mind long ago, those pages in meticulous childish code, hadn't she done her best to forget so many childish things. She knew of course that someone had discovered it and taken it away and that that someone had very likely been Mrs. Stevick but now she flushed with shame and indignation, hardly able to speak. She was folding one of Lizzie's sweaters, refolding it patiently meaning to get the sleeves crossed just right though Lizzie would be unpacking it again within an hour or two. She said quietly, vaguely too, "That's all right, Lizzie, it was a long time ago."

Lizzie had grown into a striking young woman, fully mature for her age; even before she had dared bleach her hair to a glamorous ashen blond she'd been accustomed to being looked at in public, stared at, people were wondering was that girl maybe a professional singer at one of the downtown nightclubs? an exotic dancer maybe at one of the burlesque theaters? Her skin was generally clear but she never left the house without applying apricot-tinted makeup to her face, then powdering it a slightly lighter shade, she was fussy about plucking her eyebrows two or three times a week, took care to outline her soft wide fleshy lips with a tiny lipstick brush before filling them in lavishly in red. Her music coach Henri La Porte, who'd once studied with Fred Astaire in Hollywood or was it New York City, encouraged Lizzie in her inclination to dress conspicuously in snug-fitting slacks and spike-heeled shoes, sweaters or blouses with low necklines, if she wore stockings make sure they were stockings with a dark seam. The attention of strangers made her nervous when she wasn't in the company of her boyfriend, but it excited her too, she had to admit, it meant she was on the right path, she had a chance for a career. As Henri frequently said, you have to get people to *look* at you, then the bastards might *listen*.

Henri La Porte was a short slender fashionably dressed man of young middle age with slick black pomaded hair, a thin mustache, a voice that could be melodic or shrill depending upon his mood. Lizzie admired him enormously though as she reported to Enid he could be rather cruel at times, impatient, not so much with her—he seemed to like her!—as with some of the others. His pupils were all women and not all of them were young and promising like Lizzie. "He stresses the competition we'll have to face in auditions and that sort of thing," Lizzie said. "He says we might as well be realistic."

Lizzie had a job at Rexall Drugs she didn't much like, waiting on customers at the cosmetics counter; sometimes on Friday or Saturday evenings she substituted for a girlfriend who waited tables at the Gondola where the tips were good. Still she managed to take lessons at Henri's two hours a week and to practice as many hours as she could. Her course of instruction was what Henri called eclectic, an introduction to show business in general; Lizzie was hard at work learning tap dancing and ballroom dancing—fox-trots, waltzes, tangos, mambos—and how to develop her rich husky rather voluptuous alto voice by way of love ballads, blues numbers, even popular novelty songs like Johnnie Ray's "The Little White Cloud That Cried" and Patti Page's "Doggie in the Window." Sometimes Enid accompanied her on the piano downstairs if Mrs. Stevick wasn't in a mood to object, and it seemed to Enid that Lizzie had improved a good deal since the start of her lessons. Perhaps she did have talent: her voice was surer, her breathing controlled, she was cultivating a skillful set of mannerisms as she sang—smiling, licking her lips, moving her body suggestively, even stroking her arms and hips as if unconscious of what she did. Her most successful songs were slow and tremulous with feeling, almost vehement in yearning: "Ebb Tide," "Vaya Con Dios," "Blues in the Night." Enid felt her heart go out to her sister, wanting her to do well. For it was true as Mr. Stevick one evening said despite his disapproval of Lizzie's hopes for a career, his daughter was every bit as good as half the television performers he saw and damned prettier than many. "Oh, you're just saying that because you're my father," Lizzie said, blushing, and Mr. Stevick shot back passionately as if there'd never been any ill will between them, "I'm saying it because it's true."

Even so he couldn't resist adding, "Not that the truth has the slightest effect upon our lives."

When Lizzie started at Henri's Music Studio she was just slightly bitter about the fact that their Uncle Felix had done so much for Enid— Enid's piano lessons, Enid's new piano—while she, Lizzie, had to pay her own way. Maybe if she'd wound up in the emergency room at St. Joseph's she would be better treated?—though she never brought the subject up quite so tactlessly to Enid, she'd been rather reserved with Enid since the night of the ambulance and the subsequent disruption of their lives. But Enid was sensitive to Lizzie's tone and one afternoon mentioned the matter to Felix, who said at once, Why not? Why not pay for Lizzie too? as long as Lyle didn't take offense.

He wouldn't after all want his brother to think he was interfering in his family.

(Now that Felix's love affair with Enid had acquired a certain stability he assumed would be permanent until he chose to break it off, Felix worried less about being caught. Enid adored him, Enid would never expose him, he was growing careless about driving her around in his car, even walking on the street with her, the girl was his niece after all, there was a legitimate sense in which she could be said to be *his*. It wasn't a matter to which he'd given much conscious thought but he felt the logic of his impulses.)

Then what no one could have predicted happened: Felix learned the nature of Lizzie's music lessons and was outraged that any niece of his seriously planned a career in show business, he even made inquiries about "Henri La Porte" (a.k.a. Henry Hertzburg) and didn't like what he discovered, the bastard was practically a pimp! So he telephoned Mr. Stevick one evening incensed and indignant, telling him any asshole knew that a girl singing and dancing in public especially in a nightclub was one step up from a prostitute, couldn't Lyle control his own daughter, and he and Hannah had better not let Lizzie move out until she got married!

The household was disrupted for days. In tears Lizzie threatened to move out to live with anyone who would have her, saying for Christ's sake she was nineteen years old, she was self-employed, why should she put up with such bullshit!—and she wasn't going to mass any longer, she'd had enough of that too.

Enid apologized, told Lizzie she guessed she'd done more harm than good talking to Felix, and Lizzie said with a shrug, "Oh what the hell, Felix just knows too much." Looking at Enid quizzically she said, "What is it with you and Felix anyway these days, you're so hot for each other?"—the remark crude and casual merely tossed off to see its effect on Enid. But Enid said quickly, "Felix is just our uncle." Lizzie was watching her contemplatively, Lizzie didn't say anything for a long moment. "Oh yeah, that's it, is it?" she finally said.

Now the months of tension were over and Lizzie was moving out to live in an apartment above a Chinese laundry on South Olcott Street. She'd be sharing the rent with her old friend Nelia Pancoe, who worked on the assembly line at Chrysler, and a newer friend Thelma Price who was a cocktail waitress at the El Dorado nightclub and who like Lizzie hoped for a career in show business some day. Enid believed that Lizzie would be spending a good deal of time with her boyfriend Eddy Carlisle, at least when Eddy was available—it turned out that Eddy had been married years ago, even had a six-year-old son, and he and his young wife hadn't ever filed for divorce, they were wary of lawyers and of the courts and had just let things ride, an unfortunate situation but as Lizzie said, there wasn't a hell of a lot *she* could do, was there. Lizzie was in love with Eddy most of the time but she had her pride too and in any case other boyfriends, sometimes in a single week a half-dozen new men would call her, men even came up to her in Rexall's pretending to be looking at perfume to buy for gifts, they'd ask her was she married? did she have a boyfriend? would she like to go out sometime?—that sort of thing. So Lizzie wasn't going to eat her heart out like some tragic blues singer for Eddy Carlisle.

"Sure I want to get married some day, have kids," Lizzie said. "But I want my career first. *And I'm going to have it.*"

Still it was Eddy Carlisle parked out front to help Lizzie move to her new apartment. The Stevicks had forbidden him to enter the house, Mrs. Stevick threatened to call the police if he so much as set foot on her porch, so Eddy had mainly to wait patiently smoking cigarettes until Lizzie and Enid brought Lizzie's things downstairs, then he helped them load up the car. On this last morning of Lizzie's at 118 East Clinton, Mr. Stevick was at the store and Mrs. Stevick was lying down in her bedroom with a sick headache, she'd asked Lizzie not to disturb her, not to trouble saying goodbye, she was just too upset.

"Momma hates me," Lizzie said. For a moment she looked almost frightened.

Enid said quickly, "Oh, Momma's just crazy—you know that."

It was an odd disjointed nervous time, sorting through Lizzie's clothes, Enid had to swallow down wanting to cry, Lizzie made a show of being loud, silly, crude, snatching things off hangers and holding them up against her body modeling them in the mirror, Christ! how had she ever worn *this!* Half her clothes she was leaving for Enid. More than half her accumulation of shoes. A jacket with a fake fur collar, this pair of suede pants that had always been too tight in the crotch, here was an old red felt vest embroidered in white like some sort of weird Swiss little-girl thing Mrs. Stevick had sewed for her years ago: she tried the vest on but of course it no longer fit, too tight under the arms, wouldn't begin to close over her breasts. Lizzie tossed it over at Enid saying glibly it might fit *her.*

They joked, giggled, poked each other, they were no longer children but this was a room in which they'd been children, this was the last morning they'd share it together and Enid tried not to think of how things would be after Lizzie left. It wasn't a thought she could share with anyone except maybe Felix if he was in one of his quiet moods, not caring to talk himself but liking to listen, often he was curious about the Stevicks, about Enid's family life, how it was to have a brother and sisters you grew up with, to have a father still living, to have some religious beliefs even if they were bullshit. Sometimes sleepy and vague, Felix would go on to say he'd like a family of his own, yeah he'd like to have children, but he couldn't actually see himself married, that was the problem.

What is it with you and Felix, you're so hot for each other? Lizzie had said carelessly. Not meaning the words she'd uttered. No she hadn't meant them of course, she was just a little jealous but she had no idea. Enid decided to forget the remark. It wasn't one she was likely to pass on to her uncle.

Now Eddy Carlisle's car was loaded, Lizzie's half of the room was cleared out, the surprising thing was that the room looked smaller than before when you'd naturally have expected it to look larger.

Lizzie's bed was stripped to its mattress cover. She'd taken her pink quilted-satin bedspread and the half-dozen crimson throw pillows from Woolworth's Enid had been seeing for years, always thinking them too garish and distracting except now they were gone, tossed in the back of Eddy's car, she wouldn't be seeing them again.

Out front, at the curb, Eddy Carlisle gunning his motor, this was the panicked moment, this was the crisis, Enid couldn't keep back her tears any longer just trying to say she'd miss Lizzie, and Lizzie hugged her tight saying she'd miss her too, Lizzie's sobs were loud and hoarse Lizzie was smearing lipstick on Enid's cheek but hell look: she wasn't going to the moon or anything she was just going a few miles away, they'd see each other all the time wouldn't they?

Parallel with East Clinton Street an alley runs behind the row of houses and in the alley stands Mrs. Stevick burning something in a wire trash basket. It must be a weekday, nobody around. She is acting quickly and efficiently without sentiment, wanting only to destroy the evidence, tearing pages one by one out of a school notebook: her youngest daughter's sickness flaming up then turning to smoke to harmless ashes she'll sift through carefully with a stick.

11

He was superstitious, he said.

Which was why he owned a gun, in fact he owned two Smith & Wessons, a small nickel-plated .22 caliber automatic he sometimes carried in his coat pocket or kept locked in the glove compartment of his car and a heavier standard-issue .45 pistol he'd brought back from the war. He said that if he owned a gun he'd never have to use it. But if he didn't own a gun there would be a time, an hour, when he would have needed it badly.

Enid asked why did he need a gun at all.

Felix said, For protection.

Protection against what? Enid asked.

She was nervous pushing him, pressing him, she knew it might be a mistake but she couldn't stop. Her heart quickened in anticipation of his anger.

But Felix closed the drawer of the bedside table in which she'd found the big gun the way you might close a drawer to rebuke a child, scarcely taking note of the child. And as soon as the drawer was shut and the gun out of sight the issue became abstract. Felix was not a man who felt obliged to explain himself or even to consider himself, but he said now, speaking so slowly with such an air of abstraction Enid halfway thought he wasn't speaking to her at all—"You can always find something to be protected against."

12

It was November. Windy, rain-flecked, unsettled. Enid stood at a high curtainless window, her forehead pressed against the glass, looking out over Niagara Square eleven stories below. She felt only a mild tinge of vertigo though she did not look straight down into the street: that might be dangerous.

She was happy, she was in perfect equilibrium, her two selves perfectly balanced. Why then test herself by looking straight down into the street, at the sidewalk running flush against the building?

At this height the sky seemed to press in, riddled with cloud and harsh sunshine; the clouds were massive, clotted, heavy and ugly at first unless you saw how subtle was their texture, their convoluted shapes beautiful as if sculpted. There was a continuous restless displacement of shadow with light, light with shadow. Enid imagined high fierce winds, the gigantic clouds rather like mountains corroded by time. *God is a circle whose center is everywhere, circumference nowhere*— Mr. Stevick had once called her over that he might read this enigmatic sentence aloud to her out of one of his books. Yes, Enid thought. She hadn't understood, but yes. It was all she might salvage of God.

The November sky was so compelling she found it difficult to look away. But there was the city she'd never seen before from this position, suddenly a strange and intriguing spectacle, an uneven skyline of buildings along Main Street and Niagara she halfway recognized, church spires hazy in the uncertain light, the girders of the Niagara Street bridge, then to the east nearly invisible was the lake, dissolving featureless into the sky. Port Oriskany. Lake Oriskany. Knowing what your eyes took in had only to do with what you'd learned, but you wouldn't have the opportunity to see it if you stayed on the ground.

North of the lake the sky was so black it must have been raining; here the sun kept breaking through in blinding patches. That morning playing exercises in E minor for Mr. Lesnovich, formula patterns, triads, arpeggios, forced to play and replay perhaps six bars of a simple Mozart rondo her fingers couldn't grasp, Enid had heard rain pelting against the windows, she'd heard a distant crack of thunder and felt a childish pleasure in anticipation of a storm. But the storm never came and even the rain against Mr. Lesnovich's windows was merely imagined.

Mr. Lesnovich was in an irritable mood, unsmiling, unpraising; he reassigned her the complete lesson, even the exercises she'd played making no mistakes. On her way out he asked why was she so nervous, why so high-strung, so intense: it was only a music lesson. She reminded him of himself at her age, he said sourly. It was not a memory he cherished.

In the other room Felix was talking on the telephone, lying on the bed half dressed, cradling the receiver against his shoulder doing calculations on a note pad. He seemed to be laughing or was he impatient, asking questions in a rapid staccato voice. But Enid liked being alone: she liked having slipped out of the focus of her uncle's attention; still she was in his apartment where she'd never been before, still in his presence, protected. They had made love and her body was rapt, enthralled, the pleasure he'd given her was coursing slowly outward through her blood, having no longer anything to do with her, she was at peace, at rest. The view from his windows enthralled her too: the sky, the buildings, Niagara Square eleven stories below, a little island of green amid acres of pavement. She recalled a day she had sat there on one of the stone benches gazing up toward these windows. In yearning, in expectation. And now she was here.

It was late autumn and the square was wind-struck, most of the elms were leafless, dessicated. Here and there some oaks, maples, white birch, a scattering of colored foliage—pale yellow, slick dark red. From this height too the square was beautiful. Which bench had it been, so far below? And now she was here.

* * *

Is it always like this? Enid wanted to know.

Always, said Felix.

This was the season when Enid was in love with Felix but also in love with love. She loved what he did to her because she loved him, perhaps that was it. Consequently anything he did to her she would love. Was that it?

When he chose he fitted inside her like a hand in a silk glove. A foot in a silk slipper. He learned not to penetrate her too deeply, his penis high inside her yet in her imagined control as if it were a part of her, a completion of herself, an emptiness abruptly filled. She felt her eyes roll upward in her head in astonishment, gripping him tight, gripping and releasing in a quickening beat that began to anticipate and hurry his own; she saw a match raised to a scrap of cloth or paper, then the tiny flame took hold, flared violently upward, was not to be stopped. Now all veered away from her and she realized she controlled nothing surely not the tiny panicked muscles in spasms encircling him, her hands wild clutching at his back, his shoulders, his hair, she sobbed aloud crying his name O love love love love she was ravenous wanting it never to end begging him never to leave her. She knew then she could not draw a single breath without him, she was dead.

Afterward she lay exhausted, too weak to move. Her brain gone dark, tears darkening her face. Felix too could lie motionless without speaking, without seeming to think, for a very long time.

Do you love me? Enid always asked.

Sure I love you, Felix always said.

She might see him once a week, or twice a week; she might not hear from him for as long as fifteen days. He was in Chicago, Cleveland, Pittsburgh, Albany, New York City. He flew out to San Francisco in a private plane chartered by friends to see a boxing match and was gone a week. At home he spent days negotiating the purchase of rental units on the South Side, or vacant land beyond the Grand Street shopping plaza, or city-owned property along the canal, condemned warehouses on Kincross and Cadboro on land that might be extremely valuable one day depending on decisions made by the City Council. Some of these deals came through, others were postponed or dropped. Another of Felix's activities was betting and this kept him busy too.

So long as Enid knew she would be seeing him again she was all right. What mattered was the continuity, the promise. She had her own life—she was quite satisfied with her own life—held together by her love for Felix the way a pearl necklace is held together by something so simple and crude as mere string. You look and see the pearls, you never see the string: but without the string the pearls break and scatter.

She was in love and her love set her in a relationship with the world that was unexpected, potent, mysterious. Because of Felix she had the power to cultivate friendships where she wished, she had the power to cultivate her own quick restless analytic intelligence as if it were a factor distinct from her own personality. She gave herself up to hours of piano practice, grateful for the sensation of fatigue when she stopped—a head-swimming fatigue like that following love. Thinking of Felix, of when they'd last been together and when they would next meet, she felt her senses sharpened and dilated almost to the point of pain. Suddenly everything was vivid, piercing, tremulous with meaning: the faces of strangers in the street, the white-churning wake of a tugboat down in the canal, the rattling of boxcars across the railroad trestle, even the yeasty gritty taste of the air on certain mornings. Enid was terrified recalling how she had once wanted to die; how angry and desperate she had been to throw away the world, crumpling it like a piece of paper and casting it down. As if she had known anything of what she was discarding! Now what terrified her was the thought of dying—the thought of herself or Felix dead.

Enid spoke without thinking, in surprise and disappointment: "It looks as if no one lives here!"

"Does it?" Felix said genially. "That's almost right."

The apartment was not what Enid had anticipated. Blank white-plastered walls without pictures or mirrors, high windows without curtains, a parquet floor without a carpet—the living room looked like a furniture showroom incompletely furnished. There was a long low curved cushioned velvety brown sofa like something in a hotel lounge; a glamorous coffee table of dark smoked glass on brass legs; a few low-slung chairs, tables, lamps; that was all. Felix said he hadn't gotten around to having curtains put up or buying a rug, he'd only been living in the place six years.

It had to do with his retirement from boxing, he said. Before this he'd lived in a place a half mile from the gym, he'd been more comfortable there. Or so he seemed to recall. But it didn't matter really where you lived, did it. It wasn't going to help you all that much.

Felix was vigorously chewing a large wad of gum, five or six pieces of spearmint gum. He had given up smoking a few days ago, he'd been alarmed at his shortness of breath doing exercises and routines at the gym he'd done half his life. He had run a mere five miles along Lakeshore Drive and come back with a stabbing pain in his side.

At the doorway to Felix's bedroom Enid hesitated, faintly shocked. The room smelled airless, the bed was unmade, a tangle of bedclothes trailing on the floor. At one window a venetian blind was pulled tightly shut; at the other the blind was meagerly open allowing thin cracks of light through to fall slanted across the rumpled bedclothes, the bare white wall. It was like a tomb, Enid thought. A grave. Felix sensed her discomfort but said nothing. He embraced her from behind, breathing quickly, kissing her neck. She remembered he had been at a boxing match the night before and after such matches his lovemaking was always urgent and not to be postponed.

In the bedside table drawer she found the long-barreled revolver which had startled her but which in truth had not greatly surprised her. In the bathroom she happened to notice several hairpins fallen behind the toilet in a crack between the linoleum and the tile wall. The hairpins were an ordinary brown, lighter than the color of Enid's hair; seeing them did not greatly surprise Enid either though she would wish later she hadn't.

The bathroom was small but attractively designed with a tile wall of very dark glazed green to shoulder height, a shadowy sort of mirror. Enid moved in it headless, showing no injury. On the edge of Felix's white porcelain tub was a stack of dog-eared magazines—*Ring, Boxing News, Fortune, Time*. The *Time* cover story had to do with thirteen American "spies" being prosecuted by Red China; the new welterweight champion Johnny Saxton was on the cover of *Boxing News*.

One of the reasons Felix Stevick felt obliged to own a gun or two was because he frequently carried large sums of money. Kept large sums in the apartment overnight.

He had gradually developed a strong passion for betting in the past few years and he had a theory behind it: after a big win the temptation is to quit for a while, not to press your luck; also, after a big loss the temptation is to crawl away and lick your wounds; but the thing is you have to keep going, keep your hand in, otherwise you get rusty. It's like everything else in life, Felix said.

He had done well placing bets on boxers whose names Enid came to recognize though she knew nothing about them—Bobo Olson, Archie Moore, Carmen Basilio, Sandy Saddler. After he'd won a bet back in August on a welterweight named Kid Gavilan he had been in unusually expansive spirits, a little boastful, which encouraged Enid to ask bluntly how much money he had won. Guess, said Felix. Enid said she hadn't any idea: $500? $1,000? Felix just laughed so she said: $25,000? And he looked at her still smiling but with his eyes narrowed. "Maybe," he said. And that was the end of the conversation.

Felix was circumspect about his wins and losses both, but he seemed to like talking about the losses more than the wins, always something nagging there, maddening, like an aching tooth, like reliving the fight he'd lost. He had thrown away a fair amount of money years ago betting on old Joe Louis against Rocky Marciano because he couldn't tolerate the idea of Louis being defeated by so inept a boxer as Marciano, then again like an asshole he'd lost money in '52 betting on old Jersey Joe Walcott for the same reason, but this time he had figured it out shrewdly that Walcott was too intelligent and too clever to let himself get hit by Marciano after what had happened to Louis and for twelve rounds Felix had been absolutely right, the older man was winning, cutting Marciano pretty badly around the eyes, making him stagger; then the same goddamned thing happened again: Marciano got an opening, moved in, hit him with his right and knocked him out. And that was it, that was the end of Jersey Joe Walcott: the greatest fight Felix Stevick had ever seen but fuck it he'd had his money on the wrong man.

Marciano was twenty-nine at the time he became heavyweight champion—not young. But Walcott was thirty-eight.

It was said that Rocky Marciano's right punch was the most powerful ever thrown by any boxer in recorded history and Felix could well believe it. It was the kind of punch that would have taken off Felix's head if he ever had the misfortune to catch it. It was the kind of punch you had nightmares about, seeing it coming and trapped paralyzed unable to slip away. It was just deadly, beyond estimation, people liked to speculate how Marciano compared with Jack Dempsey and Jack Johnson in their primes, in any case there was nobody living in 1954 who could go against Marciano and expect to win. Felix had been appalled and fascinated studying the famous photograph of poor Jersey Joe taken at the split second the punch connected—his face scarcely resembled a human face any longer but something hideously distended, misshapen, about to shatter into pieces of flesh, bone, gristle. Felix had liked to make himself slightly ill contemplating the picture, imagining what Walcott had felt and knowing until that precise moment that Walcott had been a superb boxer performing beautifully, hardly even tiring, one of the great athletes of his time. And then. And then.

It allowed you to know, didn't it, Felix thought, that the sport wasn't a sport at all. It was just life speeded up.

Since that fight Felix had become a little crazy on the subject of Rocky Marciano. He didn't hate the man personally—he didn't know him. All he'd ever heard of Marciano from mutual acquaintances was good. But it was an insult to Felix Stevick himself that there was today a heavyweight champion who could not box!—clumsy on his feet, stocky, with so short a reach—a mere sixty-eight inches!—he couldn't even jab. (Joe Louis's reach was seventy-six inches, Dempsey's and Tunney's both seventy-seven, Felix's own reach was seventy-four.) Marciano's ring strategy as drilled into him by his trainer was no strategy at all, just to push inside and push forward, keep pressing forward taking punches and throwing punches knowing few of them would land, just slugging and waiting and slugging and waiting for an opening, waiting to connect with that one lucky punch that would bring an opponent down as if he'd been shot in the head with a bullet. Once that punch landed that was the fight, once Marciano connected you were dead.

Yes, it seemed to Felix Stevick morally wrong that so refined and difficult a sport as boxing was not constantly improving, that so crude a fighter could slug his way to the top: a Marciano supplanting Jersey Joe Walcott, Ezzard Charles, Joe Louis! It was unjust, it went against nature! Felix had a fantasy, he told friends, making them laugh because it sounded as if it were meant to be amusing, Felix Stevick did like to joke a good deal of the time, and one afternoon he told Enid: he was in the ring with Marciano, say he was in his prime yet not yet retired, maybe twenty-six years old. And he'd have to box. And he'd have to box his heart out. And he'd have to run but it was an error to back away because Marciano would just push forward. So he had to box. And the next round was the same. And the next. And the next. And he'd carry himself as light and quick as he could, moving out of the range of his opponent's wild swings until at last he'd begin to tire, he'd begin to wind down, it had to happen eventually because Marciano never tired Marciano was never going to stop and if Felix managed to hit him the punch counted for very little and soon Felix's own best shots were tiring him, it was his nightmare fight with Oscar Ellis once again, it was his nightmare fight with Gino Corvino but much worse, Marciano just pushed forward like a mountain or an avalanche or a gigantic wave waiting for that split-second opening, that moment of weakness, and all Felix Stevick had taught himself of discipline, of pacing himself, of controlling his fear and panic, even of swallowing down his own blood now went for nothing because sooner or later Marciano was going to nail him and he'd go down like a shot and he'd never get back up.

That's why he went to every match of Marciano's that came along, rare as they were, Felix said. He couldn't keep away from the bastard.

Enid listened fascinated, she halfway wondered was Felix insane?—or was this simply a man's fantasy, a masculine reading of the world so alien to her own she could barely comprehend it.

Felix had told her how wretched he'd always felt for days after a fight, even the many fights he had won, it wasn't just physical but mental, his thoughts racing like crazy, his heart fast, and in his sleep he'd relive the fight but this time wouldn't be able to defend himself: that was the crux of the nightmare—not being able to defend himself. Once he had seen a man killed in the ring, a young boxer named Jimmy Doyle knocked out by Ray Robinson defending his welterweight title back in 1947 and that memory lodged deep in him too.

Enid asked him a question she had wanted to ask for years: "But why fight?"

And Felix said coldly, "Why fuck?—it feels good."

Felix came out of the bedroom dressed, drawing a comb swiftly through his hair, and there Enid stood shivering, her arms tightly folded, leaning her forehead against the windowpane. He might have been startled. He might have seen that her face was damp with tears but he said nothing, it wasn't his style to indulge weakness.

"I'd better drive you home," he said. "It's after three."

The day had darkened, rain pelted hard and fast on the very edge of turning to sleet. Felix was obliged to drive no more than fifteen miles an hour even on wide windy Niagara with his headlights on and windshield wipers slapping.

On East Clinton Enid said, "Was it a special occasion today?"

"Why?"

"Taking me to your apartment."

Felix didn't reply at once as if giving the question serious thought. He had been on the telephone for the past forty-five minutes talking to several parties and his last conversation had been punctuated with laughter, so Enid supposed he'd been talking with a friend, not one of his business acquaintances. It meant he was in a breezy high-flying mood; his words at such a time flung carelessly out like gravel could sting.

Finally he said, "Sweetheart, it's always a special occasion."

He decided to take her right to 118 East Clinton, why make her walk through the rain. If anybody inside happened to be looking out, if they saw her climbing out of his car, she could tell them he'd run into her in a store downtown, even in the public library where Felix sometimes went to check out facts in the reference room. But nobody would be looking out the window. Nobody would ask.

13

Felix Stevick sat at ringside in a smoky South Side athletic club one night in December 1952 staring up at an eighteen-year-old amateur welterweight thinking, Love at first sight, is it possible?—even with his many faults the young boxer reminded Felix of himself at that age. But he had the idea that Jo-Jo Pearl was going to be much better than Felix Stevick had been even at the height of his career.

The occasion was an evening of amateur boxing sponsored by the Knights of Columbus, tickets $10 for all seats except ringside which were $12, the night was snowswept and very cold but Vince Mattiuzzio had talked Felix into coming out with him to see Jo-Jo. There was a good deal of interest in Jo-Jo among the Mattiuzzios and their friends: the boy had been a Golden Gloves lightweight champion at sixteen, he'd moved up into the welterweight division the following year and did equally well, now he was ripe to turn professional. He'd won all his amateur fights, eleven by knockouts, you could see what he might do with the proper training and guidance. And Christ he was hot as a pistol!

Jo-Jo Pearl looked younger than eighteen though he was a tall rangy broad-shouldered boy with well-developed calves and thighs. He had an open frank face now slick with perspiration, his damp hair was the color of sand and worn a little too long, his jaw was somewhat square, his neck not yet thickened with muscle. Felix liked it that he carried himself taut as a bow in the shrewd stance Joe Louis had made his trademark, body at an angle, chin tucked in, like Louis he tried for an absolutely deadpan expression, even his eyes narrowed and un-blinking, fierce with the desire to win; he was alert to his opponent's every movement and to the mood of the noisy crowd as well: a child who wanted to do injury and who wanted to please, the most deadly of fighters.

It was amazing, it was prodigious, the energy Jo-Jo Pearl had to squander!—tossed away negligently like the droplets of sweat that flew from his head when he took a lucky punch to the jaw. He seemed to understand he must absorb a certain amount of punishment in order to inflict his own, he'd trade punches standing flat-footed with his opponent, letting his gloves strike where they would, no matter if his own face was beginning to bleed. In the heat of motion, in the intense heat of battle he felt no pain, very likely took pleasure in showing his wounds to the crowd—his victory then would be justified! And when in the second round he suddenly dropped his opponent to the canvas with a wild inside right uppercut, he did not take advantage of the count of nine by standing quietly in a neutral corner; instead he danced about exuberant and gleeful, grinning out at his supporters. And when the other boy rose shakily to his feet Jo-Jo danced toward him with his gloves low, allowing him time to recover even further. Felix understood it to be a gesture of sheer naïve gallantry: Jo-Jo Pearl was a true amateur, a child wanting not merely to win his fight but to win the affection and approval of every onlooker.

Felix Stevick had hoped for that too, hadn't he?—a long time ago.

In the third round Jo-Jo tirelessly carried the fight to his opponent and the boy clinched with him, wrestled stubbornly with him, fearful of stepping away to risk being hit. Jo-Jo's opponent was swaying with fatigue but nearly as game as he, slapping at Jo-Jo's head and shoulders with his gloves, rabbit-punching him weakly in the neck. During one clinch he butted Jo-Jo in the forehead, opening a sudden cut, and Jo-Jo pushed him away before the referee could intervene. Jo-Jo was incensed, shocked, his deadpan expression melted away at once to a look of boyish chagrin and hurt. But now you can kill him, Felix thought. Now he's given you purpose.

So in the final round Jo-Jo tried for a knockout, panting and sweating and swaying on his feet, he tried every sort of punch, surely surprising himself—zipping left hooks, manic right crosses that connected with the other boy's jaw or missed as if by equal intention. He got no help from his corner, he appeared to have no trainer, only seconds who were young as himself, in any case he was in no condition to hear advice shouted to him from the audience, even Vince Mattiuzzio with his hands cupped to his mouth telling him to get inside, get inside, let the kid have it, now's the time! Felix too couldn't resist shouting out advice: Get inside! Use your right! Don't lower your guard! For Christ's sake come *on!* It seemed that Jo-Jo could box but he hadn't a powerful punch yet in either hand, he hadn't quite the strength for a knockout punch unless the situation was perfect, the timing and the leverage perfect, he was content to stand flat-footed to slug away with the other boy, trading punches as long as both could bear it. Half the crowd loved the brawling—the other half was calling out for the referee to stop the fight. Then Jo-Jo's opponent faltered, backed away, and Jo-Jo caught him suddenly with a left hook, knocking him sideways to the canvas, to his knees, forward onto his hands, blood running in a steady trickle down his face. The referee pushed Jo-Jo in the direction of a neutral corner and began his formal count but the boy was finished, too weak even to move, he'd had enough.

The crowd loved Jo-Jo, erupting in cheers. The young boxer and his seconds were jubilant and unrestrained as children, dancing about the ring. What did it matter that Jo-Jo's boyish face was cut up, that he might have a permanent scar from the butting, he was flying high in triumph, deserved triumph, nothing like it, maybe he even guessed who was sitting at ringside and how his future might move into gear after tonight, it was all good, it was all goddamned fucking good, nothing like it. Watching him Felix Stevick felt a stirring of both excitement and melancholy. He'd been this way before, hadn't he: yes, but this time it would be better.

Vince said, "Didn't I tell you the kid was hot, Felix?"

Felix said, "You told me."

So it happened that Jo-Jo Pearl signed on with the Mattiuzzios, turned professional, went into serious training. His official manager so far as the New York State Athletic Commission was concerned was a lawyer named Chris Delancy who had also managed Felix Stevick, his trainer was Felix's former trainer Dan Hickey; he continued working at the docks, reducing his schedule to two-thirds time, then to half-time, he'd quit altogether when he started making money. Within six months he fought three four-round matches against opponents his own age or a good deal older and he won each of the matches easily: he was on his way. It must have seemed to him that a mysterious yet benign machine had moved into place behind him now that he'd turned pro as in his innermost heart he had always known it would: wasn't he going to be the next Kid Gavilan! the next Ray Robinson! he'd get his weight up someday and take on Rocky Marciano! The machine was not quite visible to his eyes or perhaps to anybody else's but you hadn't any doubt it was there and it was immensely powerful, making telephone calls to distant cities, setting up matches, setting up deals, suddenly a preliminary four-rounder in Newark, New Jersey, where the headline match would feature ex-lightweight champion Paddy De Marco himself!—and suddenly too the surprise of having enough money for the first time in his life, small sums of cash advanced for a weekend, for a week, Mr. Delancy or Mr. Mattiuzzio or even Dan Hickey pressing $20 bills into his hand, upon occasion a $50 bill, Jo-Jo could take his father out for a steak dinner at De Marra's, buy him a few drinks to celebrate, the season of Jo-Jo's happiness had begun.

Felix frequently watched Jo-Jo work out in the gym mornings, a sweaty glittering nimbus surrounding his body as if his soul in ecstasy were pushing through his straining flesh. Tell him what to do and he'd do it, he'd do it a dozen times over, he was ravenous for affection, starving for approval, his eyes filmed over with tears of excitement, then suddenly he'd be at the speed bag making the bag into a noisy blur his fists punching faster and faster hypnotizing himself he'd be grinning and laughing, talking, teasing, it was the speed bag to which he spoke in his ecstasy, an imagined opponent or a friend or a lover, yes somebody he was crazy to love, climb all over and beat into perfect submission. It was ecstasy, it was oblivion, the joy of the body as Felix Stevick had once known it before he'd been made to realize he was going to die.

Vince Mattiuzzio said to Felix, "Let's hope he doesn't get hurt too soon."

* * *

Jo-Jo had learned to box at the age of fourteen at a state juvenile detention home in Red Bank, a rural facility south of the city. His sentence was six to eight months for attempted car theft, breaking and entering various stores in his neighborhood off Lloyd Street; like most boys on the East Side he ran with a gang, but it was his vehement story that he'd been suckered along by older kids, he hadn't ever actually done anything himself or gotten more than a few dollars out of what he did. At Red Bank he'd known he could be a boxer, he'd beaten the shit out of everybody, even guys who outweighed him by twenty, thirty pounds. The athletic director at the facility said Jo-Jo could be another Manuel Ortiz or Willie Pep but that was before Jo-Jo began to put on weight. Now Johnny Saxton was his hero.

He was greatly admiring of Felix Stevick though he hadn't ever seen Felix box. He sort of remembered his father talking about Felix, maybe, some articles in the newspaper maybe, when he was a young kid.

As Jo-Jo began to win matches locally and elsewhere in the state the sports editors of the Port Oriskany newspapers naturally took an interest in his career. Chris Delancy carefully coached him before he was interviewed, monitored all his conversations with media people, they were trying for a nice clean image for Jo-Jo that went along with his looks and with his actual personality; as Jo-Jo said, he hadn't run with any gang in years, he worked damned hard at the dock, gave half his paycheck to his mother, he was through forever with any kind of shit like stealing cars, he just wanted to box, he wanted to prove himself, how far he could go. Only when he got to the top, like Rocky Graziano, Jake LaMotta, guys like that, would his background come out that he'd been in a reform school and learned boxing there but then it wouldn't matter: he'd be at the top.

It was one of the subjects he talked about repeatedly with Felix, in the gym, in the locker room, at a nearby diner where Felix sometimes took him for lunch: if he got to the top, if he was a world champion, that meant everything in his life was okay after all, didn't it?—everything in his family's life too? "All the sad asshole kinds of things that happen to you, dumb things you'd like to forget," Jo-Jo said earnestly, "also big things like my father getting shot up in the war, my mother so mad at us kids like she mostly is, you know? You know what I mean? They just fall into place, right?—if you're a world champion? Like Joe Louis, right? That he was fighting at first to get food stamps or some goddamn thing for his family? That he had to get called a nigger? Like that? So any bastard sticks his nose in your business can't say one fucking thing about you that was a mistake, or he's better than you, right? You know what I mean? It all falls into place if you get to the top."

Felix always said, That's right.

He didn't know if it was true, he'd never gotten anywhere near the top himself, but it sounded good. And it always relaxed that look of strain around Jo-Jo Pearl's eyes.

Jo-Jo himself quickly fell into place in Felix's life as Enid had fallen into place. Felix wasn't a reflective man—he didn't give a good deal of conscious thought to anything, just trusted his instincts—but he understood they were valuable to him, sometimes Enid more than Jo-Jo, who could be cocky and arrogant, sometimes Jo-Jo more than Enid, who would have to be given up soon in any case, it seemed crucial to him that they never meet. Enid kept asking and Felix said no it wasn't the right time. Enid said, My father could come along couldn't he?—to see Jo-Jo box here in town?—and Felix felt a sudden violent dislike of Enid that she could imagine herself capable of manipulating Felix Stevick even in so trivial a matter, getting him to do something his instinct warned him against. "Get your old man to buy you both tickets, why do I have to be involved?" he said.

Felix wasn't any fool, he didn't want Jo-Jo Pearl meeting a girl attractive as Enid who was also Felix Stevick's niece: putting himself in Jo-Jo's place with Jo-Jo's head getting slightly swollen from his early successes, the usual crap in the newspapers and people talking him up in town, he could see how this might shape up. Jo-Jo had girlfriends, Jo-Jo was hot stuff these days down on Lloyd Street, but no matter. Felix remembered how Enid had struck him at Shoal Lake, how he'd been looking at her without exactly knowing it, watching her not even thinking any particular thoughts, the way she'd gone after him and wouldn't let it rest. Also he needed Enid set off in some private space he could enter when he wanted, it was a compartment in his mind like memory, like going along a corridor and opening doors in his father's old house, suddenly seeing what was inside before he could have remembered it, on the very brink of sleep—he needed Enid there, alone, just there, he'd find himself thinking of her, getting excited, aroused, he was crazy for her so why not follow it through: he guessed nobody was going to get hurt. He'd stopped worrying she might try to kill herself again, or get pregnant, or bother him on the telephone, it wasn't likely she'd tell anybody after so long: who would it be? Not that loud-mouthed asshole father of hers, not her mother she said never talked to her. Felix Stevick himself was her closest relative.

Come meet my father, Jo-Jo kept saying. Come over to the place he's staying at and have a drink, he just wants to shake your hand: he used to watch you box.

So Felix went against the grain of his instinct and said yes. And it was a mistake, as any asshole might have foreseen.

Jo-Jo's father Leroy Pearl was estranged from his family and living in a rundown boardinghouse on South Union Street near the Ingersoll-Rand factory. Jo-Jo was bitter about him, said he'd been an air force bombardier wounded in Italy, shrapnel in his legs and skull, and the U.S. government gave him two Purple Hearts and a permanent disability pension that didn't add up to shit. Also he had some sort of sclerosis of the spine the doctors claimed wasn't the government's fault.

Sometimes he went on a drinking binge too, Jo-Jo said. Which was the main reason Jo-Jo's mother had kicked him out.

On their way to South Union Street Jo-Jo confided in Felix that he was going to bail out his old man as soon as he started making real money. Find him a better place to live. Get him some good doctors, not the sons of bitches at the VA hospital that wouldn't give him the time of day. He didn't know why the Mattiuzzios weren't bringing him along faster if they thought he had talent, Jo-Jo said. He wasn't complaining, he wasn't second-guessing anybody, just telling Felix how he felt. For instance he'd heard that Joe Louis had gotten a top match only five months after he turned pro when he was Jo-Jo's age, and that his manager had let him fight every week if they could find somebody to fight him: every fucking week! While Jo-Jo was being held back, treated like he was still an amateur. He knew he was ready to fight in eight- or even ten-round matches, he was ready to take on guys older than he was, some of the welterweight contenders people thought were hot shit, if he'd just be allowed the chance to prove himself.

Felix interrupted to say that Jo-Jo was being brought along no slower than anybody else in his position, it was dangerous to be pushed too fast, and there wasn't much point in comparing himself to Joe Louis at any age because he wasn't Joe Louis, was he. And Jo-Jo said quietly, "Put me in the right place at the right time I'll surprise everybody with who I am."

This would turn out to be the primary theme of Leroy Pearl's conversation too though Pearl began by greeting Felix lavishly, shaking his hand and flattering him in a rummy's marveling grating half-mocking voice: Christ he remembered what a beautiful boxer Felix Stevick had been, he'd caught some of his local fights and always thought Felix would go right to the top, seems just like yesterday doesn't it?—winning a TKO from some luckless bastard named Willie, Wylie, name like that, a white guy hadn't a chance against Felix Stevick's superior boxing skills, Felix Stevick could manipulate his opponent like Billy Conn himself in his heyday. He wasn't clear just how Felix's career had turned out, Leroy Pearl said, but he understood he'd retired, Christ it was a shame Jo-Jo hadn't ever gotten to see him box, the kid might learn a thing or two. Well, it was an honor! It certainly was an honor! It was an honor that didn't happen every day in Leroy Pearl's life!—as maybe you could judge by this hole of a room.

The place was so narrow, so cramped, there was hardly room to breathe, and there stood Leroy Pearl quivering with a drunkard's excitement, clasping Felix's hand in both his hands not wanting to let go. He was in his stocking feet, an inch or two shorter than Felix, perhaps in his mid-forties, no older, with a broad puffy vein-threaded face, a swollen porous nose, stained mismatched teeth in a wet smile. His rheumy eyes were wide with sincerity and pleasure. As Felix drew coldly away Pearl spoke again of the honor of the occasion, the solemnity of the occasion, would they all like a drink to celebrate?—he'd sent a pal to buy a fifth of Jack Daniel's that morning, not his usual taste in whiskey.

"Not me, Pa," Jo-Jo said, annoyed. "You know I'm in training."

Leroy Pearl offered Felix the only chair in the room, a low-slung easy chair with filth-encrusted cushions and stuffing leaking out of its seat. Pearl sank back slowly onto his bed wincing with pain, he caressed his knees surreptitiously, mumbling, "No drink for Jo-Jo of course, Jo-Jo is in training, no liquor no tobacco no women, 'course I know." He poured Felix a drink in a cloudy glass, his hands trembling, then poured himself a drink and ceremoniously raised his glass to touch Felix's. Mumbling again of honor, of how proud he was, his son in his new grand career, his son on his way, owed it all to Felix Stevick and to Felix Stevick's friends. His eyes blazed up in tears, his hand shook as he raised his glass.

Felix set his own glass on the floor, not taking so much as a sip. He was furious with Jo-Jo for bringing him here, why hadn't the kid known his father would be drunk, what an insult to Felix Stevick, what a shithole to stumble into! Jo-Jo moved restlessly about as his father babbled, not wanting to sit on the lumpy bed, casting despairing sidelong glances at Felix. But Felix wouldn't look at him. Felix was rigid with contempt, staring at Leroy Pearl: a man who'd let himself go in the worst way, caved in on himself, gone to fat in the face and gut, stinking of whiskey of unwashed flesh of dried urine dried vomit bedclothes that hadn't been changed in weeks, punchy as if he'd been slugged in the head one too many times. And that wet half-mocking grin. And that insidious singsong voice. War veteran or not, Leroy Pearl was the kind of human being who filled Felix with absolute revulsion . . . as if he'd opened the wrong door to see something he'd never forget.

Yes, Leroy Pearl would be better off dead: like those derelicts who slept in doorways and lined up at the Mission for food, straggling along the street, sometimes urinating where they stood. Running in the early morning in the lakeside park, then cutting back through Kilbirnie, then through Niagara Square, Felix frequently saw men who were hardly more than clumps of rags lying comatose in alleys, in doorways, on park benches or even beneath park benches, rummies in the last stages of alcoholic degeneration. Sometimes one of the men stirred, agape and imbecilic, to look up at Felix sprinting by. Felix tried not to look, he didn't want to see, his soul filled with loathing that left him trembling and breathless.

Jo-Jo's father took note of the fact that Felix wasn't drinking; he smirked, shrugged, scratched at his crotch, poured himself a second drink this time nearly to the rim of his glass. His hands shook, the whiskey spilled onto the floor. In his intimate too-familiar voice he was trying to query Felix about Jo-Jo's prospects, whether Jo-Jo's manager wasn't "holding him back," maybe they had the next Joe Louis here, Kid Gavilan, Sugar Ray, look how Jo-Jo'd done in the Golden Gloves look how he'd won his first fights wasn't he on his way?—but the next match was just another four-rounder preliminary, the kid wouldn't make more than $250 if he was lucky. Felix said very little, staring coldly at Pearl until Pearl had to look away, licking his lips, grinning foolishly. Christ he was only about forty-five years old, you could see he'd been good-looking like Jo-Jo, that square jaw, broad cheekbones, pale eyes, hairline badly receded but the hair was the same stony sandy shade as Jo-Jo's. And the nose would have been Jo-Jo's too except for the swollen cracked veins and a dent at the bridge as if it had been broken long ago. In a street fight maybe: if Leroy Pearl had done any boxing he would have boasted of it by now.

Felix was ready to leave, Felix was looking at his watch, Leroy Pearl began to speak more rapidly, all but laying a hand on Felix's arm, asking now if Jo-Jo could trust his manager, could he trust the Mattiuzzios, you hear all the time of rising young athletes defrauded by businessmen if not outright racketeers, remember the Kefauver committee, who was it confessed he'd thrown a fight a few years back was it Jake LaMotta who'd actually gone on to be a world champion?—in the hire of some New York racketeer named Palermo. And another one was Frankie Carbo, wasn't he right in solid with the boxing promoters and managers: had Felix ever heard of Frankie Carbo?

But Felix had had enough. He got to his feet saying lightly, "Who? How do you spell the name?"

"I don't know how to spell it! Anybody can spell it!" Leroy Pearl said loudly. He too made an effort to stand but without success, glaring up at Felix in idiotic rancor. Now his manner had changed totally—he stretched his lips in a mocking malicious smile, showed the tip of his tongue, made his eyes bulge, his hand dropped to his crotch, rubbing vigorously as he said, "What about Giulio Rimi, you know anything about him, *I* know all about him, you know anything about him, Mr. Stevick? Felix?"

Jo-Jo said miserably, "Pa, what the hell—?"

"I'm asking him!" Leroy Pearl said. "I'm asking! I got a right to ask! He's here, I'm here, we're having a drink, you don't want me at the gym and you don't want me talking to no lawyer, now your bigshot friend's here so I'm asking! I signed some papers 'cause you're a minor but I don't remember what they were so I got a right to ask, I got a right to know if anybody's going to take financial advantage of my son!"

Jo-Jo tried to intervene, saying, "It's just something he got out of the newspaper, he don't mean it," but Leroy Pearl gave him a vicious swipe with the edge of his hand and told him to shut up.

"I'm asking: what kind of life insurance is there? Accident insurance? Personal injury?" he said loudly. "Look at me—look how they left me! I know what I'm talking about! I take the goddamned fucking bus up to the hospital, have to transfer at Union, then I get there and they look at me like I was some kind of filth crawled out from under a rock, they look at me saying there's nothing they can do, go slit your throat, right?—go jump in the lake, right? Were you in the war? What the hell did you do? Where'd they send you? I saw that car you drove up in from where I'm sitting, parked the fucking thing at the curb and locked it, how much does a car like that cost, huh? You listening? You think you're pretty good don't you? Felix the Cat—I remember you—the newspapers making you out such hot shit till you landed on your ass like everybody else."

Afterward Felix was pleased how he'd behaved, enduring that son of a bitch's outburst, he'd wanted badly to slug Pearl squarely in the face, Jesus he'd been hot to give it to him, sickened and excited by his half-crazy smirk and the way he was going at himself between his legs like nobody could see. Felix could have given him a right uppercut that would have driven his lower teeth up through his palate and unhinged his jaw or a stiff right cross of the kind he'd hit a man with years ago in a preliminary match in Cleveland—or had it been Chicago, a big drafty smoky beery auditorium—Felix had slipped inside his opponent's guard and hit him with a right that shattered his nose and cracked the cheekbone, he'd felt the bone break and give way unresisting as broken crockery, the sensation through the thin leather of the glove communicating itself instantaneously through all the parts of his body!—then a torrent of blood flowed out onto both Felix and the other boxer as the man grasped at him, clutching and clinching, terrified of letting go. Felix had loved landing the blow because it ended the fight on a spectacular note but he hadn't liked disfiguring the other boxer, who was a boxer he respected in the ring, but in the case of Leroy Pearl, this loud-mouthed insulting bastard, he would surely have enjoyed disfiguring him, making his ugly face uglier, how dare he talk like that to Felix Stevick? insult Felix Stevick in front of a third party? except of course Felix would never strike a man in his condition who couldn't defend himself. He would never strike a man who had not in fact struck the first blow: it was a promise he'd made to himself a long time back.

So he simply eased away from Leroy Pearl, out of reach of the man's flailing hands. "Sorry," he said. "I'm leaving."

Jo-Jo said in a boy's raw hurt voice, "Pa, for Christ's sake you're *drunk*. So shut *up*. Just shut *up*. Why are you doing this to me? *Shut up*."

Felix left the house, waited for Jo-Jo behind the wheel of his car. He'd had enough of Leroy Pearl, he was proud of himself for the way he'd behaved, his head ringing to do injury against an enemy, his groin hot with it, but still he'd had enough, in truth he was sickened to the very depths of his soul and he wouldn't recover for hours, very likely for days, but when Jo-Jo joined him, shamed and anxious to apologize, Felix said in a blunt cold furious voice, "Forget it."

And the subject of Leroy Pearl was never again raised between the two men.

Sparring with Jo-Jo once or twice a week when he felt up to it Felix imagined time looping luxuriantly back upon itself, he was a kid twenty years old again dreaming all his life to come, his head ringing with those promises and predictions he hadn't understood were lavishly made to any young talented boxer: the sport was so fierce and cruel lies were needed to make any of it possible. Sometimes if he was lucky, if his legs held out, if he'd slept well the night before, he was able to give Jo-Jo a real workout, sending him back into the ropes, leaving him panting and dazed smiling that thin curly smile of his that didn't mean mirth or affection or even at times simple recognition. Then Felix felt a thrill of sheer gloating happiness, half hearing the response of the crowd: wasn't this proof that nothing had changed?

He could still hit hard with either hand, he was dangerous once he got into stride, those rapid-fire combinations patterned on Joe Louis's he'd put together and memorized years ago, performing at times like a robot or a zombie, two thirds of his vision gone because his eye was swollen and pain impacted in his ear because his eardrum had been broken. On the best mornings he could feel power snaking down from his shoulders into his chest, a sensation that mesmerized him, illuminated him as if with the holy fire of God; they said a boxer's best punches were the last things to go and Felix wanted to believe. He was teaching Jo-Jo a punch he'd developed to perfection under Dan Hickey's tutelage, part left hook and part left uppercut to the upper part of your opponent's abdomen where the muscles can't be adequately strengthened. It gave him pleasure to see Jo-Jo take it up like a child with a toy, greedy to learn all Felix had to offer. Jo-Jo's going to be your pup, Vince said, teasing, and Felix laughed, saying, Why not?—he's got nobody better around here.

But here was a stark new truth lodged deep in him as an eye in a socket: outside the ring he was a young man in perfect physical condition, thirty-one years old, thirty-two years old; inside the ring he began to feel the strain within a single round, the slowness in his legs, the mysterious shortness of breath, was it possible?—your brain knows what to do but your body can't deliver. A beautiful opening to Jo-Jo's blunt chin for instance, but Felix's legs can't get him there in time. Or he sees a left hook coming and can't get away in time. And always there's Jo-Jo nipping and biting, pushing, jabbing, feinting low blows and sometimes even delivering in a pup's brash innocence, knowing he'll be forgiven: Jo-Jo wearing him down until his chest is heaving and his legs have never felt so exhausted, though once he'd danced his way through ten three-minute rounds inwardly calculating how it would feel to go fifteen. Afterward in the shower he'd be grateful for this very fatigue, even the buzzing and ringing in his ears. He tried to imagine what it had meant, Jersey Joe Walcott winning the heavyweight title at the age of thirty-seven from Ezzard Charles seven years younger, but he really couldn't imagine. It was as if he'd never boxed at all. He didn't know anything at all. He hadn't yet begun. He was through.

One night at De Marra's where some of them had gone for steaks, Felix was seated next to Jo-Jo drinking scotch while Jo-Jo drank his usual ginger ale, three, four, maybe five bottles of Vernor's, and Felix found himself confessing to Jo-Jo how nervous how frightened he'd been before his fights, even his so-called easy fights, never told anyone he'd been so ashamed of himself. Yes he wanted to fight—he was starving to get to that time, to fight, nothing he wanted so much—but there was this taste of something black in his mouth, all nerves strung out in his guts and chest, the feeling got worse so that he couldn't sleep, lost weight he couldn't afford to lose, then the day of the fight the hours leading up to the fight he'd be almost shaking he was so nervous until the moment he actually stepped into the ring and saw his opponent in the opposite corner looking at him: then the fear dropped away. Then he wanted to get going. Then he was wild to get in there, get started, he was all right.

He told Jo-Jo he shouldn't be afraid of getting hit—the classiest fighters are going to get hit, seriously hit, sooner or later. You just pick yourself up if you can and keep going.

Jo-Jo was nodding, listening, that thin curly smile, the thick-lashed pale eyes downturned as if he didn't know what to make of Felix Stevick saying such things to him, was Felix maybe a little drunk?—saying things the other men might overhear. In any case Jo-Jo Pearl was on a winning streak, fighting every few weeks and winning by knockouts sometimes, developing a real style, the newspapers were saying, the hottest young local talent in many years. Jo-Jo hadn't yet been hit in the way Felix meant and couldn't believe he ever would be, knocked down a half-dozen times in his entire career not counting brawls at Red Bank, always Jo-Jo jumped back up, his legs like elastic, too proud to take a count of nine or even a count of six, five, grinning to show the admiring crowd he scorned taking a rest, he wasn't hurt in the least, maybe he hadn't been knocked down at all, just lost his balance for a moment and slipped. Which was why he shifted uncomfortably in his chair listening to Felix confide in him things he didn't much want to hear, things that might make him think less of Felix Stevick, who'd always intimidated him, a classy boxer himself people were always saying Felix had been, but look how his career turned out: the hint that maybe he'd quit too soon, got scared and quit too soon, he'd lost his nerve for fighting which was a way of saying wasn't it he'd lost his courage. But none of this applied to Jo-Jo Pearl.

So finally Jo-Jo said, smiling and impatient, hardly troubling to keep down his voice so the other men wouldn't hear, "Hey you know I'm not like that. I mean, what you're talking about, I can see it, I get it, but actually I'm one of those guys, you know, you hear about, that could almost fall asleep in the dressing room, you hear about them sometimes—like Marciano? somebody was saying? Or drink a bottle of beer then go out and fight? I don't see no need to think about it that much. I mean—it's got to be done. I'm going to do it. Like I tell myself, Felix," he was saying now, excitedly, "it's all over with, the fight, it's over with and I won easy, I can sort of see it in the newspaper, you know? ahead of time? like a headline? You know what I mean? Then I go out and do it."

So Felix was rebuffed by the cocky little bastard. As he supposed he deserved.

I'm not like that. I don't see no need to think about it that much. You know what I mean?—I go out and do it. Shaving in the mornings Felix heard again these words that were not even boastful, just straightforward, sincere. He shaved carefully, controlling his emotion, studying his face in the mirror, always the thin white scar drew his attention—the cut had required twenty-eight stitches so you could say it had healed pretty well.

Already Jo-Jo Pearl was accumulating hairline scars above his eyebrows, tiny half-moons in the flesh, almost invisible. But they were there. And he let his left drop so frequently after using it his nose was beginning to look puffy: if he wasn't careful it would be broken before he fought in his first semifinal match.

Cocky little bastard, Felix thought.

Let him come to me next time, Felix thought.

* * *

So Felix in his pride made it a point to keep a certain distance from
Jo-Jo Pearl. He had his own life after all; he had at times more than
he could readily handle. And though watching the young boxer perform in the ring was one of the true pleasures of his life he didn't
always attend Jo-Jo's matches, even those in town—taking another
kind of pleasure in guessing that Jo-Jo would wonder at his absence
and inquire after him.

As he did, sometimes.

Or so it was reported to Felix.

But Felix Stevick did have his own career—attorneys, accountants, real estate agents, bank and loan company officials, Al Sansom,
lunches lasting until 3:30 P.M. and dinners lasting beyond midnight.
Some of the business deals were complex and required more energy
than Felix was willing to give them, he'd play hunches, move in the
direction his intuition nudged, if he lost money one month he might
make money the next and, as Al Sansom liked to say, the future was
"up in the air." Sansom & Stevick, Inc., endured some rocky weeks
in early June 1954 when it appeared the Villa Rideau might go under,
then a sizable loan came through, business in the Adirondacks picked
up, Al Sansom boasted afterward that he hadn't really been worried—
had Felix?

Felix shrugged, Felix too liked to keep the tone light, casual. He
said, "Once I start worrying in this game I'm finished."

(For what was business but a game?—not a sport but a game: you
wanted merely to win, it went no deeper.)

Apart from Sansom & Stevick, Inc., and perhaps contrary to the
interests of that partnership, Felix frequently explored other courses
he might take, ways of investing his own money. A sizable bet was
an investment after all and winnings came in cash, no "earned income" to report even to his tax accountant. Felix knew it was necessary to keep in motion through the daylight hours: he saw himself as
a racing cyclist in an indoor arena, pedaling swiftly around a steep-
banked track. Staying high on the track against the tug of gravity
was a matter of speed, and nothing was more exhilarating than
speeding close to the edge. He had Enid but he also had money. If
he lost $12,000 on Tuesday he might win $15,000 on Friday. If he
won $20,000 early in the month it might mean he was fated to lose
$25,000 later in the month, but that was a risk Felix Stevick was
willing to take.

There was his investment too in Jo-Jo Pearl which might one day pay off handsomely. And he'd be betting on Jo-Jo too when the stakes got higher.

Unless, as Vince said, the boy got hurt too soon.

Jo-Jo's first semifinal match, eight rounds, was fought in Yonkers, New York, early February 1955, against a boxer named Byron McCord who had a reputation for being unreliable if not professionally unstable. Some years ago McCord had been a serious contender for the lightweight title until the champion-to-be Ike Williams stopped him; then he retired for a year or two; then in 1953 he returned as a welterweight, winning some matches, losing others, his official age was thirty-four but it was generally known he might be as much as three years older. Felix had seen him box a few years before in a preliminary match in Madison Square Garden and already the poor bastard was slipping, he'd stayed gamely in the fight, going the distance of eight punishing rounds, getting his face chopped up, then he'd lost the decision as everybody knew he would to a kid ten years younger on his way up. Still, Byron McCord had a reputation and his name meant something: managers understood he was worth beating.

Vince said it would look good on Jo-Jo's record, a win against McCord. He'd get some national attention—*Ring, Boxing News, Sports Illustrated.* Vince argued that McCord was one of those boxers like Jack Sharkey—on a lower level—unpredictable, wild, gifted, capable of doing astonishing things in the ring, then tossing it all down the drain, a born loser. People were drawn to McCord, liked to see him lose. He only fought for money now and he didn't care who he fought, his manager too calculated that time was fast running out so why not a match every month as long as McCord could deliver: Albuquerque, Seattle, St. Louis, Tampa, Pittsburgh, Yonkers against a twenty-one-year-old kid with a 12–0 record. What did it matter?

When they told Jo-Jo of the match his first response was intense excitement: he'd seen McCord fight once as a lightweight, the man could *punch.* His later response was more puzzled: wasn't Byron McCord actually *retired?* weren't his brains *scrambled?*—those were the kinds of things you picked up.

They told Jo-Jo McCord was the right opponent for him at the present time. A year from now, no, probably not. But now Byron McCord was just fine.

On February 9 Felix drove down to Yonkers to see Jo-Jo in his first eight-round match, he'd bought a new 1955 Cadillac the week before and wanted to test it on the Thruway. To keep him company Vince Mattiuzzio rode with him instead of taking the train with the others. Was there anything he should know about the fight? Felix asked Vince at one point, and Vince said without hesitation there was not. Felix was betting Vince $1,000 that Jo-Jo would win by a knockout maybe in the first or second round, Vince was betting that Jo-Jo would win by a decision.

In the early minutes of the fight Felix felt an involuntary tug of sympathy for Byron McCord—not only was Jo-Jo Pearl outboxing him, a boy who looked young enough to be his son, the atmosphere in the auditorium was unusually raucous and derisive. Though Jo-Jo was unknown in this part of the state there were immediate cheers when he connected with the most harmless of blows; when McCord crouched and held his gloves to his face or wrestled his opponent into a clinch, there were shouts for him to move his ass. To get through eight rounds the older boxer knew he had to conserve his strength, and the crowd was on to his game from the start.

Also there was a good deal of movement in the aisles and at ringside: a ceaseless filing of spectators to their seats. They were coming in for the main bout of the evening, a non-title match of Archie Moore's to follow this match, and the fortunes of aging Byron McCord and young Jo-Jo Pearl were of only marginal interest to them.

Seated at ringside Felix Stevick watched with great intensity, hardly allowing himself to breathe when the fighters exchanged blows. He hadn't seen Jo-Jo fight for nearly two months so it was a relief to note that the boy was at the top of his form: less brash than Felix remembered but still belligerent, pushy, circling his opponent and rushing him with brief volleys that seemed spurred in part by the audience's impatience. In the stark bright overhead lights Jo-Jo's handsome face was carefully without expression, his body quick, urgent, lithe. He was taller than McCord by perhaps two inches and lighter by six pounds though his torso was now well developed with muscle, his neck somewhat thick. By contrast McCord looked punchy and uncoordinated, swinging crudely, not minding that he missed his target, standing flat-footed and swinging again, head ducked down, knees bent, showing Jo-Jo a dull dogged beady-eyed look of malice. Suety flesh rippled above the waistband of his black trunks, his thigh muscles quivered sickly white. His nose was more flattened than Felix recalled and his chest oddly hairless. The only solid punch he landed in the first two rounds was a mean low blow to Jo-Jo's groin, called by the referee and booed loudly by the crowd. This was the man who'd been number-two or number-three contender for the lightweight title when Felix himself had been in mid-career. . . .

Jo-Jo Pearl was not yet the most consistently agile of boxers but he danced around Byron McCord with the spirited ferocity of a predatory bird, jabbing and poking, prodding, opening a cut or two in McCord's forehead, then in the third round landing a swift left hook to McCord's chin that hadn't looked especially powerful to Felix's eye but sent the older boxer heavily to the canvas. McCord sat stunned, his gloves pressed against the canvas as if to keep him upright and his knees awkwardly raised. The crowd was shouting, Felix hoped the fight was over—he would have won his bet, Jo-Jo wouldn't yet be hurt—but as the referee counted eight the panting bleeding McCord began the muscular effort of hoisting himself to his feet.

Between rounds Jo-Jo's corner instructed him: Keep it up, just keep it up, don't risk trying for a knockout just keep it up, the old fellow's legs are gone, stay out of his way and he can't last.

With the next round however McCord changed his strategy: he must have gauged that Jo-Jo hadn't that strong a punch in either hand so why not try for a lucky punch of his own, it was the only chance he had to win the fight—swinging with a cynical sort of desperation and ignoring the crowd's jeers. His torso quivered with loose flesh but his biceps were still hard, his neck powerfully thick, with the cuts in his forehead newly opened and bleeding he looked savage and indignant yet oddly unhurt, intractable. With surprising agility he ducked one of Jo-Jo's reckless right crosses and rose up with one of his own, followed swiftly by a left hook, and there suddenly was Jo-Jo staggering back into the ropes unable to fall and McCord hammering away at him to the heart to the gut to the head slicing him open around the eyes and mouth in a matter of seconds as if he'd taken a razor to the flesh, so very quick and deft, so sinister in his sudden aroused efficiency, the crowd was on its feet sensing the end. And Felix Stevick sat rigid, staring, his heart torn out of him. He couldn't believe what he was seeing.

But Jo-Jo slipped away under McCord's arm, dazed and dripping blood. And McCord like a drunk capable of only a minute's frenzy let him escape.

Between rounds Felix hung over the ropes in Jo-Jo's corner to speak to him but Jo-Jo didn't seem to hear. The seconds were sponging him liberally with cold water, wiping away the blood; Dan

Hickey's practiced fingers squeezed the lacerated flesh together and smeared on Vaseline. Felix felt sick and aroused, smelling the liquid adrenaline, the ammonia fumes. He spoke to Jo-Jo, massaging the boy's tense neck muscles. Jo-Jo grimaced in pain as Hickey worked on his face oblivious to Felix, murmuring Yeah, okay, okay, got it, then leaned over to spit out a gob of mucus and blood into the bucket. Across the way sat McCord with legs extended, his own head tilted back as his seconds worked feverishly on his bleeding face. Felix was reluctant to leave, drawing a hand slowly across Jo-Jo's damp shoulders and squeezing the muscles familiarly, half angrily, as if they were his own and were failing him. To Dan Hickey he said in a low aggrieved voice, "Fuck it. We're in for it now."

Now he had hurt his cocky young opponent Byron McCord pushed forward zestful and exhilarated, crouched to a height of perhaps four feet, head lowered, gloves to his face, it was the legendary Dempsey stance and McCord used it with a comical sort of exuberance, bobbing and weaving cobra-like, feinting punches then throwing them as his amazed opponent backpedaled. Jo-Jo had never encountered a situation like this, none of his sparring partners had prepared him for this, he simply couldn't think, he couldn't reason there in the ring with punches flying at him too light to hurt but dazzling in their very profusion. McCord struck low again to the groin then grabbed Jo-Jo in a clinch, wrestling him off-balance, grinding the laces of his gloves into Jo-Jo's reopened cuts then into his unprotected left eye before the referee broke them up. The crowd was shouting in excitement, this was the old reckless Byron McCord, the son of a bitch in top dirty form.

But Jo-Jo managed to stay on his feet, landing a punch now and then as if by accident or rote, he was bleeding badly from both eyes, his nose, his mouth, McCord was bleeding too, they clinched together repeatedly, staggering into the ropes like two exhausted drunks unable to get free of each other. At one point McCord butted Jo-Jo in the forehead by accident as his left knee buckled and he seemed about to fall, held in place by Jo-Jo's stricken arms. Again the referee tugged the men apart, his face flushed plumply with heat and annoyance. Isolated catcalls echoed through the gallery but the boxers were aware of nothing except each other, though in the final seconds of the round neither had strength enough to lift his gloves, still less to fight.

The end of the fourth round.

Felix thought: He's finished.

But Jo-Jo answered the bell for the fifth, Jo-Jo was to answer the bell for the sixth, he was young he was strong he could recover with amazing swiftness and his corner had worked a miracle on his chopped-up face getting the blood to coagulate into Vaseline-smeared crusts. The problem was his left eye, swelling to the size of a peach or an apple or maybe a small melon, bruised and fearful in its colors which were not the ordinary colors of human flesh exposed to the air. But Jo-Jo came out for the fifth and landed some telling punches, Jo-Jo made his opponent stagger; he came out for the sixth groggy, blinking, very likely not knowing which round it was precisely or what he was obliged to do, but his legs were holding up beautifully: after all he was twenty-one years old. His opponent was perhaps fifteen years older and his legs were gone so there Byron McCord stood in the center of the ring, flat-footed, taunting in his Dempsey's killer crouch waiting for Jo-Jo to try a lead. Jo-Jo circled him cautious, staring. But it must have been through a dazzling rosy haze Jo-Jo saw the other boxer or the shape of the other boxer because Jo-Jo's left eye was useless and his right was swollen too, then the crowd's shouts of impatience spurred him to try some jabs, a wild left hook, then his left dropped in that old bad habit of his and Felix steeled himself for McCord's right smash but McCord was too cautious, crouched to a height of scarcely more than four feet, his head lowered so that his pale scalp shone through quills of wet plastered-down hair. Jo-Jo continued to circle him bouncing on his toes and feinting as if his body performed by rote while his head rang, aglow with pain so intense it had no name. Move! Fight! Get in there! came isolated shouts. Spectators drifting down the ramped aisles to their seats were pausing to watch, blocking one another and jamming the passageways; the atmosphere in the auditorium was highly charged, half the crowd for the kid Jo-Jo Pearl who was putting on such a valiant fight in his first eight-rounder as the newspapers would report next morning in the single brief paragraphs of newsprint allotted to the McCord-Pearl fight, but the other half in its fickle exuberance was for Byron McCord, chanting his name hoping for some frenzied action, he'd surprised them all once and he could surprise them all again.

In the next exchange McCord went savagely for Jo-Jo's eye, gouging with the thumb of his glove, he pushed in trying for a blow to the kidneys, clinching and raining rabbit punches against Jo-Jo's neck; stepping back from the clinch as the referee pushed him McCord shot a sudden clumsy right uppercut to the point of Jo-Jo's chin that brought him down. Only a few yards above Felix and Vince, Jo-Jo lay stunned on his back; his elbows, his legs were working as if he believed himself standing but couldn't for some reason get a foothold on the floor. His face was unrecognizable, a mask of incredulity and despair as his brain tried to comprehend what had happened and what he must do next. The fight was over, Felix thought, he couldn't believe Jo-Jo would get up, he cupped his hands calling for him to stay down, still Jo-Jo managed to rouse himself, preparing to stand as he'd been trained, against all expectations he was on his knees by the count of eight, already by the count of nine he was on his feet, swaying, his gloves raised to defend himself against his opponent's finishing blows. Felix would remember this sight for the rest of his life, always with a pang of nausea at the knowledge that he'd given himself, his youth and manhood, to such madness—a young boxer struggling to his feet his left eye streaming blood his entire face chopped and swollen, to the shouts of the crowd he got to his feet preparing himself to fight though what he could see of his opponent must have been little more than a shadowy blur.

Felix called out, "Jo-Jo! Don't!"

He stood watching. There was nothing to be done. He was gripped by a despair so violent he feared it could not be contained but of course it was contained, he simply stood watching with the thousands of other spectators in the Yonkers Civic Memorial Auditorium amid the smoky air as Byron McCord pushed forward, hammering at Jo-Jo's head then at his body, trying for a knockout before his own strength failed him and the round ended. For after this round there would be another, and another. The fight was infinite unless it was stopped! Felix blinked up into the lights recalling the fight he'd stumbled through with the black man Oscar Ellis, who had absorbed his most powerful desperate blows without flinching, he recalled that sense of absolute profound unmitigated despair that comes with the knowledge you've done your best you've given your last strength but it hasn't been enough you're finished you're defeated to the jeers of the crowd, but Felix had in fact won his fight with Ellis by way of a controversial decision while there was Jo-Jo still mixing it up with Byron McCord trying to trade punches as if believing what they'd told him at the gym, or was it Felix Stevick who'd told him in one of Stevick's extravagant moods—a boxer can't be knocked out if his will is strong, he can't be knocked out unless he surrenders, then of course he deserves to be knocked out, he deserves whatever happens to him.

The round was in its final minute but the men were gamely trading punches, Jo-Jo with his battered head lowered and his shoulders hunched, McCord out of his deep crouch knees bent and visibly trembling. Their chests heaved and glistened with blood, blood showed shockingly on Jo-Jo's white shorts, the canvas was spotted, smeared underfoot, still the men slugged at each other in a frenzy to knock each other out and the auditorium rang with shouts of encouragement. At last something gave way—McCord connected with a wild left hook, striking Jo-Jo's face high on the swollen cheekbone and Jo-Jo staggered backward astonished as if he'd been hit for the first time in his life. As he fell McCord swung again, this time a clumsy right cross, swung and missed by inches, somehow McCord tangled himself in Jo-Jo's legs and fell to the canvas as heavily as he, his fatty shoulders and thighs quivering as if with indignation to spasmodic outbursts of applause and laughter. Jo-Jo lay unable to move but McCord crawled to the ring apron to hoist himself up on the ropes, his head tilted sharply backward so that he could breathe. He looked savage in victory—one of his eyes puffed closed and his swollen lips drawn back from his mouthpiece caked with blood. He appeared to be shaking his fist at someone high up in the gallery or was it in mid-air?—while the perspiring referee squatted beside Jo-Jo not troubling to raise his hand for the count. The fight was over, end of the sixth round, Byron McCord by a technical knockout.

In the ambulance en route to a local hospital Jo-Jo partly revived and began to speak incoherently. Felix was riding with him, seated on a jump seat close beside him, but Jo-Jo's eyes were swollen shut and in any case Jo-Jo seemed not to recognize his voice. "You'll be all right, Jo-Jo," Felix said. He spoke slowly and calmly hearing the siren above his voice surrounding them and bearing them rapidly onward. He repeated himself several times. "You hear?—you'll be all right." The boxing gloves had been removed from Jo-Jo's hands back in the ring but his hands were still tightly bound with tape and gauze and Felix occupied himself by peeling it off in long curling strips, letting the strips fall to the floor. Jo-Jo stank of Vaseline, ammonia, sweat, odors that washed about Felix like a familiar drug, he had only to shut his eyes to recall his own emergency trip to the hospital years ago in another city, Felix Stevick encased in pain neither conscious nor unconscious yet grateful that whatever happened to him from that point onward would not be his fault. His body had passed into the responsibility of others, his soul was reduced, shrunken, to a tiny flamelike pulse barely his own. Yes he'd had a concussion but the electroencephalographic tracing hadn't shown any severe hemorrhage, he'd only required stitches on his face, was that really so bad? He guessed that Jo-Jo would not be so fortunate.

Jo-Jo's lips were badly torn, caked with blood. In a childish sleepy voice he asked what time was it. Where was he supposed to go. He didn't want to miss his fight, he said. After several misses he managed to twine his fingers around Felix's wrist not knowing who Felix was or seeming to care but eager to know where he was being taken, he could feel something moving beneath him, what time was it. He didn't want to miss his fight, he said. He'd come a long way for it. He said they'd brought him down on the train.

14

Felix said to Vince Mattiuzzio, bitter and amused and half taunting since the men had been friends for so long, I know you'd never lie to me so what was the deal on that fight in Yonkers: just tell me was McCord supposed to go down?

And Vince Mattiuzzio always insisted sometimes in a hurt belligerent voice that the fight had been a goddamned absolutely fair one from start to finish, hadn't Felix seen it?

Felix said he knew what he saw, what he was asking Vince was was he supposed to have seen it.

Felix Stevick and Vince Mattiuzzio had been friends since eighth grade at St. Ignatius Loyola over on the West Side, the fall of 1935, which meant they'd known each other for twenty years: more than half their lives now. Vince was less temperamental than Felix, at least in public, less attractive, thick-chested, arms rather stumpy, he'd built up his body lifting weights and was vain and anxious about keeping to his regimen because muscles turn to fat and were in truth already turning to fat and Vince was only thirty-three years old. His skin was swarthy, his eyes dark and watchful, he wore his thick black hair combed straight back from his forehead as young men did in those days.

Vince had three brothers with whom he'd always vied for the favor of their father so in time he had grown to hate and distrust his brothers. Felix was brotherly to him in a way, yet not in a way that seriously counted. Vince would never have to compete with Felix Stevick for his father's love.

Between Felix and Vince was the fiction that the Mattiuzzios were legitimate Port Oriskany businessmen with their primary interest the gym, local boxing promotion, now and then the training and management of a boxer, also the fiction that Felix Stevick had repudiated his boxing career too soon he'd had the talent to go right to the top, a rematch with Corvino and he would have had Corvino down cold, he could have studied a film of the fight he could have seen how that fucker had dealt him any number of dirty blows, Felix had had some bad luck in the fight but his friends and investors in the city had still had faith in him et cetera. Tactful and rarely ironic about the first of these fictions—for how men made their money meant absolutely nothing to Felix—he had become inclined with the passage of years to be impatient with the second. Now if Vince made an allusion to Felix's aborted career Felix might turn away embarrassed, saying, Let it go, will you? Just let it go.

The men would have been deeply ashamed to speak to each other of their more private feelings and of their personal affairs. Felix was godfather to Vince's seven-year-old son, Vince had lent Felix approximately $35,000 when he'd started out as Al Sansom's partner, but Felix would never have spoken to him of his relationship with Enid or with other women, and Vince would never have spoken to Felix of his relationship with his wife, his family, his business associates. Their friendship was not very different in kind from what it had been in 1935 when they were thirteen years old and in opposition to their rigorous Jesuit teachers at St. Ignatius Loyola, except now as adults they spent less time in each other's company.

After Jo-Jo Pearl's death as a consequence of severe subarachnoid hemorrhaging a certain degree of awkwardness developed between the two men. The death itself was enough of a shock after a protracted three-week coma in the Yonkers hospital but Felix had been particularly struck by the fact that, had Jo-Jo recovered, had he ever returned to normal consciousness, he would have been totally blind in his left eye: the thumb gouging and the repeated blows had left the retina permanently damaged. Shortly following the fight word got back to Felix that Byron McCord's manager had owed a favor of some undisclosed kind to Leonardo Mattiuzzio, so what had gone wrong? At first Vince told Felix this was a lie, then he'd admitted possibly McCord's manager had told him to go easy on Jo-Jo, secretly thinking McCord couldn't get through the first round in the shape he seemed to be in, then evidently McCord got excited tasting blood and never listened to him after that. These were chances you took with the most carefully matched of fights.

Still, said Vince, Jo-Jo had fought a good fight, hadn't he, despite his lack of experience.

III

SHELTER

March 1955–
March 1956

1

If you would fill me with your life. Your warm coursing blood. O then I would never die: never! Your strong hard bones a tree of veins inside your flesh I am safe inside your skin looking out through your eyes and the world is harsh and vigorous all angles bright hard dazzling sun-lit colors.

2

Now he was often angry, she couldn't anticipate his moods.

He was grieving for the young boxer who had died, Enid knew, Enid knew but hesitated to inquire.

(Both Port Oriskany newspapers gave generous coverage to the death, ran photographs of Jo-Jo Pearl on their front pages as well as in their sports sections. An editorial appeared in the *News Transcript* denouncing boxing as a primitive blood sport, an editorial appeared in the *Evening Herald* lamenting the death of Jo-Jo Pearl but in praise of boxing itself, perhaps the noblest and certainly the most challenging of all manly sports.)

Enid didn't see Felix for twelve days after Jo-Jo's funeral. He might have been out of town, he might have been at Niagara Square not answering his telephone, she tried only a few times half in dread of his voice—he never liked her calling him. He didn't approve, he said, of women calling men. And when they met she made the error almost immediately of speaking of Jo-Jo Pearl. She heard her faltering voice, her inadequate idiotic words, what right had she to offer sympathy to Felix Stevick!—saying too without really knowing what she meant that she was sorry she'd never met Jo-Jo. And now it was too late.

Felix stared at her without speaking. He was so furious the blood drained out of his face; even his lips were ashen. For what right had *she* to offer sympathy to *him*. What right had *she* to intrude upon *him*. Yet she heard herself continuing, blundering, as if her pretty childlike manner would carry her through, make everything all right—"I'm sorry I never met him, you liked him so much, I know I would have liked him too"—until Felix said, "But why?—we're better off not knowing dead people aren't we?" He ran a hand slowly through his hair, he was smiling a queer hard smile, swallowing down his emotion, so that Enid standing a few feet away had no need really to know how he felt. How his hands trembled, how rage coursed through him. How Jo-Jo's death had ravaged him and maybe he wanted to take hold of her to shut her up, to erase that look from her face—big-eyed, silly, blinking. Enid was pretty and she knew she was pretty but pretty wasn't going to help, was it. So she knew never to mention Jo-Jo Pearl to him again.

It was true he was often angry now, but he was often kind too.

Bought her an RCA phonograph one Saturday so that she could listen to classical music at home, took her down to Weissman's Music Store to buy $100 worth of records. If Enid's parents were suspicious, she'd tell them—what? Loving Felix she'd acquired from him a certain arrogance, telling so many lies she'd acquired a zest for lies and quite preferred them to the truth. For a lie had to be invented, "truth" was common property.

Enid told her parents that Felix was her uncle after all: he wasn't married, hadn't any children of his own; he was naturally generous and had money to spend, and maybe too he felt a little sorry for her. (If ever Enid alluded to her "accident" of June 1953, however innocently and obliquely, both her mother and father went silent. They had nothing to say. They were so without thoughts on the subject it might very well have been that they had forgotten it.)

Most of the records Enid bought at Weissman's were of piano music—Mozart, Beethoven, Chopin, Liszt, Debussy, Ravel. The pianists were Artur Rubinstein, Artur Schnabel, Robert Casadesus, Vladimir Horowitz, Alexander Brailowsky, a young Hungarian named Tamàs Vàsàry whose work with Chopin Mr. Lesnovich admired. Her piano teacher sent her too to buy re-releases of Rachmaninoff playing his own work and Josef Hofmann playing Chopin, Schumann, Strauss. He halfway envied her he said for all that she didn't know—all she had yet to discover. "You are like myself so very long ago I cannot even recall," he said.

Enid smarted inwardly at the remark, knowing it an insult yet knowing it true. Mr. Lesnovich was right to scorn her even as he patronized her. He would have protested, smiling his thin-lipped smile, that he meant no harm—he liked Enid Stevick very much!

She did not always like him in return, she rather resented his attitude, his demeanor, the sharp knobby face, the long nose, the gray hair in a feathery fringe around his head, the high round belly straining against his vest, the nervous gestures of his fingers as she played her lesson. He was a delicate frail-boned aging man, yet unpredictable, waspish: he could sting. So she longed for his approval, for his mildest praise, anxious to read in his every facial expression a clear sign of her own fate. Should she give up? Should she continue? The music teacher at her high school had suggested she enroll in an evening class in music theory at the local college—what did Mr. Lesnovich advise? He was contemptuous of the music courses taught in the city and of the college in general—it was "third-rate," a mere state teachers' college—still Enid worried that the material would be too difficult. She understood that she was passing into a sphere in which her easy A's and A+'s in school had no significance.

Set beside Mr. Lesnovich's other pupils, most of whom came from well-to-do families who lived on Lakeshore Drive or in the Eaton

Boulevard–Prudhoe Park area, she knew herself profoundly ignorant, disadvantaged. These were people, she gathered, who routinely attended chamber music concerts and symphonies; they traveled to New York City to the Metropolitan Opera; they inhabited a world in which music was a common and even casual pursuit. How unlike her own!—even Enid's father with his claim of loving classical music clearly preferred the popular jingly tunes he whistled or hummed under his breath. When the phonograph was new to the house he came into Enid's room to listen to records with her—Rubinstein playing Liszt, Chopin; Schnabel playing the Beethoven sonatas—and though he declared himself greatly moved by such beauty he seemed in no hurry to return for more. Enid's mother showed no interest at all. It gratified her, Enid sensed, that Felix Stevick was doing something for one of her children, she was pleased partly because Enid's father was thereby chastised, lessened, yet she showed no interest at all in the music and rarely commented on Enid's own piano playing. It is as if I don't exist, Enid thought. She told herself she didn't give a damn.

Why should she?—they knew only Enid Maria, they didn't know *her*.

She lay on her bed alone in the room she'd shared with Lizzie for so long listening to the phonograph late into the night, the volume turned low. Sometimes she followed the music if she had it—she was particularly interested in Chopin's Preludes and Second Sonata. At such times she was absolved from thinking of Felix though she might have been with him—at his apartment; they only went to his apartment now—that very day: her body still slightly heated, slightly smarting, chafed, from what he'd done to her. She listened intently to Rachmaninoff playing the Second Sonata—the "Funeral March" as it was popularly called—allowing the phonograph to repeat the record if the mechanism failed to switch off properly. Again and again, again: it was not the familiar "Funeral March" that most excited Enid but the final movement, those rapid glimmering uninflected triplets played in bare octaves, no melody no harmony no emphasis no resolution only *presto*, only *sotto voce e legato*, only a single powerful chord at the end. Enid was never quite prepared for it—hadn't the music suggested eternity, infinity, the irresolution of waves breaking on shore or wind blowing through grasses? But the mysterious sonata concluded with a single rather harsh chord. Then silence. There was always the shock, the hurt—that silence.

She had been told her heart stopped in the emergency room, which meant she had in fact died. June 7, 1953. Now she wondered was this music of Chopin's the secret murmurous call of Death she could remember only faintly . . . lying on her bed drugged and ecstatic, her eyes open, listening to a pianist now dead play music by a composer dead for more than a century. What did it mean! Could she bear its meaning? Drifting by degrees into sleep she began to think of Felix. Or had she been thinking of Felix all along? Stroking her shoulders, her breasts, her belly, between her thighs, entering her enormous and impatient with life. For this too she was always unprepared, steeling herself against the pain even as she moved toward it meaning to envelop it with her flesh.

One day impulsively she told her piano teacher she so admired the Chopin sonata she would never be unhappy again in her life, she'd never fear or be dismayed by anything in her life or in death itself, if she could learn to play such music as it was meant to be played: Enid Stevick with her bright defiant eyes, that air of surprise she heard so frequently in her voice when she didn't expect it. But Mr. Lesnovich was in no mood that morning to indulge such fantastical thinking in a sixteen-year-old of no more than modest gifts. He bared his discolored teeth in a melancholy smile, cruelly he informed her it was "highly unlikely" she could ever play that particular work of Chopin's as it was meant to be played, and in any case she was deluded—like so many young musicians—as to the power of such a feat to alter one's life.

Enid shrank from his quiet reasonable pedantic tone as from the familiar smell of his ill-laundered clothes and his slightly stale breath. "For after all," he was saying, spreading his fingers, "you see before you a 'young pianist' who once played that piece quite satisfactorily— and what difference has it made in my life? What lasting difference? And you might consider poor Chopin himself, his predecessor John Field, surely Mozart, and Schumann, and Schubert, and many another—their music did not spare them unhappiness. Music is only itself, you see, it carries you out of yourself but then you must return. Do you understand?"

Enid did not answer at first. Then she said yes in a near-inaudible voice.

"Well—it's a popular delusion, I suppose," Mr. Lesnovich said slowly. He seemed reluctant to allow the subject to drop though Enid was standing silent before him, clearly smarting with hurt. "Maybe even harmless up to a point. Am I wrong to speak so frankly? So directly? After all, it is not the sort of instruction for which my pupils' fathers pay their weekly fees."

Now he meant to be kindly, amusing. Flexing his fingers nervously. But Enid resisted, despising him. Lightly mocking she said, "My father doesn't pay for these lessons, Mr. Lesnovich—my uncle does."

It was a remark of such baffling irrelevance Mr. Lesnovich simply blinked at her as if he hadn't heard. He was watching her closely, curiously, as if to gauge the depth of his injury to her. Perhaps he had only meant well all along; he seemed genuinely fond of her. "Still," he persisted, "it is healthy to recognize certain delusions at the start, isn't it?—so that their grip on us is weakened. Do you understand?"

"Yes," said Enid mockingly, sullenly.

Meaning no: she didn't understand and she didn't believe.

The music was a secret consolation like her love for Felix, telling her that the long oblivion before her birth had no power to terrify, why should the long oblivion to follow her death have that power?

Drifting into sleep she knew herself protected. Her lover close beside her—his warm damp breath against her neck, his weight against her side, one leg maybe flung over her legs. A close rank smell of sweat and menstrual blood. The damp sheets. The towel bunched up beneath her sticky with her blood. And what time was it?—she wanted to know because it was important to know, then she lost interest suddenly, her eyelids too heavy to open.

It was the first time in all these months Felix had made love to her during her period. Always in the past he'd allowed her a measure of privacy, he'd put no pressure on her, Enid saying stricken with embarrassment that she didn't feel well she had a headache and stomach cramps please she just didn't want to today; but this time Felix said teasing, Yes you know you do.

He told her she couldn't get pregnant, the bleeding washes it all away, it was the perfect time for fucking and women were hot at such times, really she wanted it as much as he did. Also he wouldn't have to fit a Trojan on himself: he'd come to hate the paraphernalia of contraception, laughing, impatient, irritated, as if the fault lay with Enid herself, this terrible risk of getting pregnant.

What is there to be afraid of or ashamed of, Felix said, didn't she know he loved everything about her?

He spread the bath towel for her to lie on. And if the sheets were afterward stained with blood it didn't matter in the slightest, he'd tear them off the bed and stuff them in the laundry hamper for his housekeeper to wash, he hired a woman to come in twice a week. Making love with Enid he was likely to be cheerful, practical, he felt so goddamned good with her he said he could fuck and fuck and didn't she feel the same way.

Yes she knew she did.

The month before, Felix had traded in his 1954 De Soto Deluxe on a 1955 Cadillac Eldorado Brougham, a four-door sedan with white-walled tires, wire wheels, and a creamy finish so elegant so gleaming glittering with chrome that people stared after it in the street. That lacquered creaminess was very nearly communicated to one's tongue!—the car was grand as a yacht. It had soaring fender fins, a wide graceful grille, wide graceful front and rear bumpers, a teak dash and instrument panel, ruby-red leather interior smelling tart as wine.

Enid was delighted as if the car were for *her,* a present of a sort for *her,* she breathed in deeply that odor of newness feeling slightly intoxicated. For the hell of it, Felix said, he'd give her a few driving lessons, why not, she should learn to drive she'd learn eventually so why not now. It didn't look, Felix said, as if Lyle was in any hurry to teach her.

Enid said doubtfully that she could take driver's education at school and wouldn't that be safer?

Felix said no it wouldn't be safer, he'd teach her himself.

When Lyle Stevick heard—not from Enid, from one of the Pauleys—that his brother had bought a Cadillac Eldorado the first thing he did was telephone a dealer to determine the probable price of such a car. He came away dazed and resentful with the figure of $16,000.

Was it possible!—$16,000 for a car!—while the rusted old rattle-trap 1948 Ford Lyle Stevick drove was worth perhaps $200, should anybody be fool enough to buy it from him.

No, he didn't like the idea that Enid was taking driving lessons from her uncle, how odd that was, how odd that would appear, and what if she had an accident with the car?—would Felix's insurance cover it?

Lyle said he knew how Felix's mind operated. Felix might very well end up angry with *him.*

Mrs. Stevick couldn't agree. She thought it was very kind of Felix, very generous, she only wished she had been taught to drive a car when she was young enough; now she was fifty-three years old and it was too late.

"Yes, but you didn't want to drive," Mr. Stevick pointed out.

"I wanted to drive," Mrs. Stevick said at once, "but you didn't want me to."

"Hannah, that isn't true. You know that isn't true."

"You said I'd be better off taking the bus. Or you'd drive me—that's what you said. You didn't see any reason for women learning to drive, you said, don't tell me you don't remember."

"I certainly do not remember," Lyle said patiently. "You're confusing me with your father—it was your own father, Hannah, who said women weren't capable of operating machinery."

Now Hannah lost her temper, slamming something down on the kitchen counter. "Don't tell me you don't remember! I remember!" she said. "I was pregnant with Lizzie when I asked was it too late for me to learn to drive a car?—and you said yes it was too late. You said you didn't have time to teach me. You said I could take a bus anywhere I wanted to go in the city, couldn't I, you'd drive me anywhere I wanted to go—*don't tell me you don't remember.*"

(In the other room Enid sat stiff at the piano running her fingers swiftly and mechanically over the keys: she wasn't listening but she heard; her parents heated and vehement, misremembering their common past and speaking rather loudly as if to appeal to her?—or to their other children no longer living at home. She was amused, perhaps a little upset, but why, why be upset after so many years? As Warren said, it was their way of talking to each other maybe, a way of connecting, the years they'd lived together snarled and confusing as the inside of the television set where wires, tubes, screws, tiny plastic knobs were bound together in an incomprehensible logic.)

She would have supposed the March morning too damply cold and gusty yet there were two neighborhood mongrels barking, whining, copulating in the alley just off Decker, so Enid quickly decided to cut through someone's yard to avoid them, ducking under laundry flapping in the wind. It was early, only 8:25 A.M., and she was unobserved, yet her face burned as if with insult as if a crowd of neighborhood boys had gathered to jeer at her, Enid Maria, Enid Maria, Enid Maria! you aren't seeing something you haven't seen before! And it was true of course, how could it not be true, the male dog's penis so luridly pink and erect, the female crouched in submission barking and whimpering and slavering, her eyes rolling white, you could say it was a perfectly ordinary insignificant sight or you could say it was repulsive and obscene; whichever, it was wisest to duck through a stranger's yard to escape. The dogs were so desperate locked together and nipping at each other Enid could imagine them attacking her for coming too near. For violating their privacy. She remembered some years ago Mrs. Stevick complaining of two neighborhood dogs stuck together most of the day out on the front lawn, she'd been furious and disgusted saying the police should be called, wasn't it a disturbance of the peace, a public nuisance, shouldn't the dog owners be fined.

President Eisenhower appeared on the 6:00 P.M. news, his familiar face creased with frowning smiles, smiling frowns, his voice direct and earnest as always, *Our government makes no sense unless it is founded in a deeply felt religious faith and I don't care what it is!* Enid waited for her father to snort in derision but the moment passed, he said nothing, he was sitting slumped in his easy chair staring at the television screen, a glass in one hand and a bottle of Molson's ale in the other, the smooth crown of his head gleamed, his throat bunched fatly beneath his chin. Any television appearance of his old enemy Joe McCarthy (now looking ravaged, sickly) still had the power to rouse him to scorn and indignation, also to a lesser degree John Foster Dulles, Syngman Rhee, Chiang Kai-shek, but the news that most agitated him of late had to do with atomic weapons, particularly the H-bomb; that had become his great fascination. One evening he'd shown Enid surprisingly elaborate plans he'd drawn up for an underground bomb shelter he hoped to construct in the basement, the plans looked to Enid's inexperienced eye like real architect's plans, in blue ink on tissuelike paper, everything drawn carefully to scale, she'd been unable to respond as perhaps he had wanted her to—with excitement, interest, admiration?—a shared absorption in the project?—and he had been disappointed, folding the papers up and taking them away. He said, scolding yet still with his old mocking humor, that even if you believed in Heaven (and Hell) the H-bomb was more important because as the fool priests (and the fool ministers and rabbis) failed to acknowledge, the very purpose of the afterlife would vanish if this life vanished, which is to say *this world the third planet from the sun.*

Enid's mother allowed that maybe there was some purpose to bomb shelters, yes she'd been hearing about them too, seeing picture layouts in the magazines; still she dismissed her husband's plans as nonsense—how could they afford a bomb shelter (the estimated cost was $4,300 if it was done right and Lyle Stevick meant to do it right) when they could barely afford household expenses right now? and they didn't own their house they only rented it, why should Lyle Stevick slave away building a bomb shelter for their landlord?— wouldn't that be just like him, investing time and money and energy and hope in something for another man.

Also she didn't think the H-bomb was going to be dropped on Port Oriskany next week. She just didn't think that, she said.

In a voice heavy with sarcasm Mr. Stevick said that that was precisely what could happen: an H-bomb dropped on Port Oriskany next week.

Well, Mrs. Stevick said. She just didn't think it would happen.

And how did *she* know? Mr. Stevick asked.

She didn't know, she just had a feeling.

A nuclear holocaust was no silly fancy like science-fiction movies, like *The Thing* and *Destination Moon,* Mr. Stevick said; yes it was real, the danger was imminent, it could happen next week and where would they be?—118 East Clinton maybe blown away by a blast out in the area of GM and the chemical plants, five megatons let's say (five million tons of TNT!), in any case there'd be winds, fires, radioactive fallout, just where did Hannah think they'd be when all this took place?

His blustery bullying tone offended her, she retreated into the kitchen where she had work to do. Why didn't Lyle write another of his letters to the newspaper, she said.

Enid got her learner's permit in mid-March and by the first of April Felix had taken her out a half-dozen times to give her driving lessons in his new car, it was the stuff of family legend told with zest by Hannah Stevick and repeated with envy and resentment by other relatives. In suburban neighborhoods where traffic was light Felix taught her to steer the heavy car properly, to accelerate and brake and shift gears, he taught her to back up slowly, glancing from the rearview mirror above the dashboard to the rearview mirror on the outside of the car; one day he even taught her to parallel park, insisting she keep trying when she wanted half in tears to give up. "If you're going to do anything at all do it right," Felix said coolly. He rarely touched her when she was behind the wheel except perhaps to squeeze her thigh when she executed a difficult maneuver successfully. They might have been niece and uncle—they might have been strangers—fully absorbed in a common task.

On good days it greatly excited Enid to sit behind the wheel of the gorgeous cream-colored automobile, to be driving in traffic like an adult among adults—so this was life! *this!* Felix gave her instructions in a matter-of-fact voice if she required them: "Use your brake. Use your horn. Signal to change lanes—come on, don't hang back. You can make the traffic light easy, come *on.*" He encouraged her to pass cars as if for the sport of it; several times he got her caught in an intersection trying to make a left-hand turn after the light had changed to red and traffic was moving against her. "Just stay where you are," Felix might say. "You're all right. You're doing fine. Why are you so nervous?" She cast a sidelong look at him, seeing that he was smiling, amused. He loved her, she thought. And her heart beat in a drunken sort of elation: this was life!

On other days—they might have been windy, overcast, or merely colored by Felix's wayward moods—she was uneasy driving with her uncle so very uncharacteristically beside her in the passenger's seat, his hands idle on his knees. He might lapse into silence as if his thoughts were drifting elsewhere, he had business worries maybe, he wasn't getting along with his partner maybe, he was plotting or calculating or rehearsing or remembering something that hadn't gone as he had wished, and Enid felt a lick of terror, knowing herself unobserved and therefore rudderless. She must drive and drive and drive until Felix became aware of her again, took pity on her worry and confusion, she tasted ashes, anxiously alert yet seeing no danger until it was upon her—"Watch it!" Felix would say sharply, waking from his trance, and Enid would jam on the brakes, throwing them both forward, groping for the horn with the heel of her hand and not finding it—now that it was almost too late seeing a delivery van backing defiantly out of a driveway into her path, a kid with a greased DA haircut in a souped-up fenderless jalopy speeding through an intersection, not giving a damn if Enid hit him. "Son of a bitch," Felix whispered in Enid's place. But Enid felt no anger, only panic sweeping through her powerful as the old Death-panic she had nearly forgotten—how close she'd come to disaster.

She could hear her father's gloating words: He'll kill you if you smash up that fancy car of his, I know Felix. *No matter what he says.*

Felix was saying irritably, "You're all right, just keep going," as Enid pulled the car to the curb to recover from her fright. "Why don't you drive now," she might say weakly, not even trying to smile. "I'm tired." But Felix would say, "No, you're not tired or anything else, just keep going." He might think to give her shoulder or knee an absentminded squeeze as one would comfort an anxious child. "You've only begun."

One chilly sunny day for the hell of it Felix gave her a shooting lesson as well: miles out into the scrubby countryside on the potholed West Clinton Extension where he'd instructed her to drive at a steady speed. Where are we going? Enid asked, and Felix said, You'll see when we get there. She laughed, seeing him take a gun—it *was* a gun—out of the glove compartment. His trim little .22-caliber nickel-plated revolver, Felix said. He wondered if it was still in firing condition, he hadn't used it in years.

You don't get much use for a gun really, Felix said.

Enid laughed breathlessly, hardly able to keep her eyes on the road. She'd known from a casual remark of Felix's that he kept a pistol locked in his car but she'd never seen it.

Felix was in a genial celebratory mood since he had made some money on the Saxton-De Marco title match just the other day, poor Johnny Saxton out on his ass and Tony De Marco in: twenty-three years old, world welterweight champion. The odds were 4 to 1 Saxton but Felix had had a hunch De Marco was hot enough to take him. His friend Vince Mattiuzzio had lost money on Saxton. So Felix felt good. Might as well celebrate. Just for the hell of it he'd give her a shooting lesson, had she ever shot a gun before?—no?

Nothing to it, Felix said.

She didn't think she wanted to, Enid said.

Nobody's going to hear us out in the sticks, Felix said.

He locked up the car and they followed a lane into a grove of trees. Smooth-bark beech trees, clumps of thin reedy birches. It was the second week of April but still late winter and the trees were leafless, the swollen buds a vague fuzzy dreamy green that seemed to exude light. The sky was cloudless, a hard ceramic blue, but the air smelled of snow.

The only thing that was likely to be upsetting was the noise, Felix said. But you get used to it fast. He hadn't fired a gun or a rifle until the army, until boot camp down in Texas, then in a few days it seemed as if he'd been firing guns all his life.

Enid said again she didn't think she wanted a shooting lesson.

She was afraid of guns, she said.

She didn't know anything about guns, did she, Felix said. But one day she might have to protect herself.

In the war all those years, Felix was saying absentmindedly as he checked the bullets in the chamber, what he'd had to do didn't seem right to him but he'd had to do it. Using a high-powered rifle trying to kill men at a distance, machine guns, hand grenades, killing men you didn't know whose faces you couldn't even see most of the time—that wasn't his idea of fighting but he'd had to do it.

Enid asked nervously did he have a permit for the gun.

Felix said sure.

Felix said they were perfectly safe out here.

He walked off a few yards to fire the pistol raising it slowly in both hands and sighting something in the near distance. He didn't mean to frighten her, Enid thought. He couldn't know how she felt. His color was up, his expression more animated than it had been in weeks.

Enid steeled herself as he pulled the trigger: the retort was quick and sharp and thinly earsplitting as a crack of thunder. Felix must have hit what he'd intended, he seemed pleased. Now it was over Enid rubbed her ears, blinking and resentful. He bullied her, he gave her no choice. But she rather liked the harsh acrid odor of gunpowder—she'd never smelled it before.

Felix gave her a sidelong smile. Insisted she give the gun a try just once. There couldn't be any danger so long as she kept the barrel pointed away from both of them—right?

Enid took the gun from him reluctantly. She beat down a lick of panic—it rose and fell in a single instant. Felix stood behind her, his arms around her, carefully positioning her hands on the gun and raising it to eye level. Then he stepped back. Go on, he said. Aim for something. There's that dead branch in that tree—see it?—there? Go on and try.

Enid held the gun unsteadily in both hands, sighting along the barrel, one eye closed. Felix told her to use both eyes. She was trembling, fighting down laughter, in truth she felt suddenly giddy thinking how like Enid Maria to make too much of things, to take herself so very seriously: it was only a shooting lesson after all.

She pulled the trigger, shutting her eyes. She'd missed her target, Felix said, by two or three feet.

He told her to try again. Just hold the gun steady, take her time, don't make such a big deal of it, and pull the trigger as she inhaled. Got it?

So Enid tried a second time. And after that a third. And a fourth.

She was stiff, self-conscious, resentful, fighting down the impulse to laugh.

Just keep trying until the bullets run out, Felix said.

Felix drove back to the city not speaking for several miles, then he asked suddenly if Enid thought she could ever shoot another person.

Enid said no.

"I mean if you had to," Felix said.

"No."

"To save your own life."

Enid said uncomfortably, "I don't know. I don't want to think about it."

"Why not?" Felix said.

"I don't want to think about it."

"To save your own life, or somebody else's," Felix said slowly.

They drove in silence past small farms, shantylike houses, ragged fields and meadows, peeling billboards advertising Port Oriskany merchants. The sun was slanted and the entire western sky was overcast with thin smudged clouds. Enid's head had begun to ache—she could hear the faint jeering echo of the gunshots in her skull.

"What would it take," Felix asked, "to shoot me?"

"That's a terrible thing to say!" Enid said.

She looked at him shocked and saw he was smiling, teasing. His tinted sunglasses gave him a mocking expression.

"Why do you say things like that?" Enid asked angrily. "I don't like you when you're like that."

"Like what?—I'm just asking," Felix said.

Enid didn't reply. Felix said in his playful mild voice, "If you knew I went out with other women?"

"No."

"Look at me."

"*No.*"

There was a quickening of the air between them. Enid stared out the window at the passing fields feeling sick, ashamed, suddenly desperate to be home. She did dislike him, she thought. She hated him.

"A woman tried to kill me once with a gun," Felix said, as if he only now remembered the incident. "She had her chance, then I had mine." He paused. He glanced at Enid. "What would it take? If you knew I was fucking somebody else?—but you must know that."

His last words were murmured, incidental, Enid wasn't really required to have heard.

Still she said, "I hate you."

She said, "I hate you, Felix."

She laughed, wiped at her mouth with the back of her hand, half lay with her head against the car window staring out at the dull passing fields. Farmhouses, barns, then suburban houses with asphalt siding meant to suggest brick. More billboards. Gas stations. A Tastee-Freez not yet open for the season. Suddenly she realized they were driving on West Clinton, the very street on which she lived on the other side of the city, but she might have told herself she'd never been on this street before. She saw nothing she recognized.

Felix would say nothing further so she was safe, protected. He had switched on the car radio to Vic Damone singing a love ballad, or was it Perry Como. Enid's hands were freezing so she slid them inside her unbuttoned coat, sliding them tight under her arms in her armpits, hugging herself in secret. He loved her, he would never hurt her, she understood that.

Locked away in the Cadillac's glove compartment was the nickel-plated pistol, now harmless, emptied of its bullets. She'd emptied it firing at nothing.

3

There was a dog-eared wrinkled snapshot in black and white of Warren and his baby sister Enid, Warren a husky child of seven in short pants standing in the backyard at 118 East Clinton with Enid cradled in his arms, Enid hardly more than a year old, tiny face blurred, arms flailing and blurred, stubby legs kicking. Though the snapshot had been overexposed and sunlight poured in a fiery flood from above, you could see the little boy *was* Warren Stevick, the eyes, the curiously adult set of the mouth, that look of pride and worry and strain. It must have meant something, they'd trusted him not to drop the baby on the ground. They'd always trusted him.

Something comical about the snapshot: the latticework of the porch directly behind Warren's head was vivid in its detail, also the chopped-looking grass at Warren's feet, but the children themselves were bleached, ghostly in so much light. They might have been about to fade away into nothing. Who had taken the picture? Enid wondered. Well, it must have been Mr. Stevick—there was a gnomish hunched shadow on the grass that must have been his. He would have taken pictures on a Sunday morning after ten-thirty mass, making a game of it, teasing, pretending to scold, giving them all commands— stand still!—stop smirking!—*smile!*—one, two, *three!*—though sometimes he lost his patience and scolded in earnest. He would have been using his old Kodak Brownie box camera with the fake kidskin covering that smelled so sharply inside—leathery and oiled and dark, mysterious. (Though the children were forbidden of course to play with Mr. Stevick's camera, even to touch it. Particularly to pry the rear open to examine the dark red paper looped and wound about tightly on its rollers.)

Enid stole the snapshot out of Mrs. Stevick's broken-backed album where most of the older snapshots dating back to the early years of the Stevicks' marriage had long since come unglued, she hid it away in her desk to contemplate when she wished. "WARREN & BABY ENID MAY 1939" someone had penciled in in careful block letters on its reverse side but the snapshot was no one's favorite—no one would miss it. Seeing Warren such a little boy but so oddly confident, adult in his pose, trying to smile under the strain of the squirming weight in his arms made Enid want to laugh aloud: yes that *was* Warren, even aged seven. That was always Warren. He'd always adored his baby sister, hadn't he. Protected her. Made more of her than she deserved.

Are you happy, Enid, he asked in his new guarded voice, telephoning home from Philadelphia. Are you all right now, Enid?—You can tell me.

Except of course she couldn't.

Enid had read that people are incapable of truly recalling themselves as small children. Memory is a hoax: the visual memories we claim of ourselves are in fact merely memories derived from family snapshots.

So it should not have puzzled her that she remembered nothing of that moment, that day, that time in what was said to be "her" life, BABY ENID who might have been anyone's baby held aloft in Warren Stevick's arms wearing a pretty white dress or was it maybe a nightgown, white ankle socks, tiny white shoes. Tiny hands and feet too and that head looking so small and delicate as an eggshell beside Warren's. The closer you peered at the snapshot the less you saw of Enid, and even Warren's look of smiling brotherly pride began to fade. That moment, that day. That time in their lives. Maybe Warren had not really wanted to hold his baby sister for Mr. Stevick, maybe he'd been frightened of dropping her, the very pose stiff and fabricated, unnatural. But the shadow hunched in the grass was prepared to glance up, annoyed, issuing its commands which must be obeyed: Stand still. Smile.

Enid stared at the snapshot, wiping her eyes, trying to understand her feelings. Sitting here late at night—it was past midnight, the others were asleep—peering into a lost sun-splotched instant of May 1939. Did she in fact feel anything? Did she want to cry?—or was it only a nervous muscular spasm, not wanting to laugh at how sad and lonely it all was. Being here. Being alive. If Enid could not remember that moment in Warren's arms then perhaps the moment had never occurred. You could argue that. You could make a case for that. "Baby Enid" had no connection with the Enid of April 1955, just turned seventeen years old. "Baby Enid" had scarcely existed, for to exist without memory isn't human, is it.

Felix once said it was better for a boxer to die in the ring than to survive with brain damage.

Enid pushed the snapshot away beneath a pile of papers on her desk. To settle her nerves she was copying vocabulary words from one column to another on a sheet of scrap paper—*chthonic, rhizome, palimpsest, obloquy, oneiric, strappado, abulia.* They were exotic words of her own discovery out of the dictionary, very likely in excess of the words she'd be required to know for the New York State Regents examination in the spring of her senior year of high school; still, she had collected sheets and sheets of such words; she prized them, perhaps for their uselessness. *Refulgent, inanition, kickshaw.* Like listening to piano music beyond her ability to play or even to contemplate playing: beauty that existed for its own sake and for no narrow human purpose.

Yesterday she'd driven with Felix out into the country and this morning, Sunday, she'd gone to early mass at 8:30 A.M. with her mother, had to go to communion beside her mother, the two of them kneeling side by side at the communion railing: and there came old Father Ogden mumbling his singsong Latin, his hands smelling of nicotine and harsh gritty soap: then the papery wafer melting in slow clots in Enid's mouth. It was just a gesture, she knew, a token, a ritual cannibalism she'd read somewhere, it had not the power to hurt but it had the power to embarrass. She was ashamed of herself for her weakness in acquiescing in going to mass Sunday after Sunday with her mother when she didn't believe: wait until you move out, Lizzie counseled her, Jesus don't provoke her *now*. Though Lizzie still believed in the church, sort of. She just didn't go to confession any more and she didn't go to communion so why go to mass, people would just wonder. But Enid was doubly cowardly, she did not believe and she continued to take communion in a perpetual state of mortal sin in which she didn't believe either. Don't cause trouble, Felix too advised. Don't call attention to yourself right now.

And tonight Warren had telephoned the Stevicks from Philadelphia as he was in the habit of telephoning every third or fourth Sunday in the evening. Warren was a good son, a dutiful son still, though he kept his distance now, living in a city hundreds of miles away on a street and in a house none of them would ever see. No time to write letters any longer, so caught up in his first-year law courses, in his headachey relentless cramming of dead facts as he called them in criminal law, property, torts, contracts. He was careful to tell them he wasn't disappointed in law school, he'd simply have to work twice as hard as those classmates of his who seemed to take to it naturally, whetted by the competition. If Warren Stevick wanted a career in government or in public defense, advocacy, maybe even in politics, he hadn't any choice. You can't bring about change in American society without operating from a base of law and within a sphere of power. . . . So Warren said.

He didn't have to be any kind of lawyer, Mrs. Stevick would point out, as if they'd been debating the subject for years. Why didn't he come home and get some other job, what about sales, sales and promotion, like Neal O'Banan at AT&T?

Why didn't he come home and get married?—it was time.

When Warren telephoned he always spoke with Mrs. Stevick first, then with Mr. Stevick if he was home (tonight he wasn't: went where?), then with Enid, who would have been waiting tense and expectant, steeling herself for her brother's familiar voice that was so warm and friendly with its slight stammer, yet so guarded. Pressing her forehead against the doorframe Enid halfclosed her eyes knowing Warren saw her in the hospital bed, her eyes bruised and bloodshot, her skin bled white, tubes stuck in her nostrils and veins, the kind of quick nightmare vision talking over the telephone evoked. She had lied to him then, hadn't she?—and he knew she lied and she knew he knew et cetera so he'd be a fool to trust her again, her soul was sick with lying, he would never love her again and Enid worried there might be a time when she needed his love badly.

Still he was Warren Stevick, wasn't he, to whom God had spoken somewhere in the countryside of Korea?—which meant he was bound to love all of humanity and had an obligation to all of humanity not excluding his youngest sister whom he feared and disliked.

Tonight when it was Enid's turn to speak with Warren she asked him quickly how he was before he could ask her his usual questions, she maneuvered him into talking for a few minutes about his law courses and his political activities—he was helping organize a pacifist group on the Penn campus, a chapter of the Society for Non-Violent Action—and what of his personal life, was *he* happy? Warren spoke hesitantly in the manner of a naturally shy person who has considered himself so infrequently he doesn't in fact know what he thinks and must invent, improvise, on the spot. Words seemed to come to Warren with some mysterious difficulty, it wasn't just the stammer, Enid thought, but something else, she wondered how he could hope to be a lawyer, a public person of some kind, but he'd told her once that one of his heroes the great Mohandas Gandhi himself as a young untried lawyer had been so stricken with shyness he had had to rush out of the courtroom one day, he had had to pay another lawyer to defend his client. And this was Gandhi the future leader of India, one of the political geniuses of all time!—so perhaps the prospect was not absolutely forbidding. Perhaps you learned to overcome your failings under duress.

Warren paused, then said impulsively that he might have some news soon. Something to tell them soon. But he didn't know—he couldn't say anything further.

Enid leaped in, elated like any sister: News about what?—was he in love? Was he going to get married?

But Warren wouldn't say anything more.

Enid tried to tease him, cajole him, she promised she wouldn't tell anyone, certainly she wouldn't tell Momma, didn't he know he could trust *her?* "Are you in love? Is that it?" Enid asked. "Are you thinking of getting married?"

"Enid, let's drop the subject," Warren said.

"But are you in love?" Enid persisted. "Tell me yes or no."

"No."

"No you're not in love, or no you won't tell."

"No I won't tell," Warren said, annoyed. "Let's drop it, all right?"

"Just—yes or no?" Enid said.

He said nothing. She knew he was angry, offended, he'd be regretting he had ever said a word, but still she kept up the pretense of a sisterly enthusiasm, teasing as if they were both children: "Silence under the law means assent—didn't you tell me that? So if you refuse to answer—"

But Warren just laughed, he refused to be drawn out. He'd had enough of the subject.

Now he asked Enid about herself, her birthday the other day: sorry he'd forgotten, he'd meant to send a card, then suddenly it was too late and he thought he'd just telephone. How have things been? he asked casually and Enid tried to reply despite the wave of sick cold dread now washing over her, for what if Warren was really in love, what if Warren hoped to marry, she didn't want that to happen. There was no one worthy of him after all.

4

Lyle Stevick called Felix Stevick and asked could they have a drink together, he wanted to talk with Felix about something.

"About what?" Felix asked.

"A personal matter," Lyle said.

So they arranged to meet at the Rainbow Lounge out on Van Buren Boulevard. A fifteen-minute drive from the furniture store but Lyle was in no position to complain: he'd have to be grateful, he supposed, that Felix with his business deals and out-of-town trips had time to spare for him.

And in any case Lyle Stevick would have been embarrassed to meet his brother at one of his usual hangouts on the East Side where everybody knew him and took him for granted—the Cadboro, for instance, which seemed to be attracting a low-life kind of customer these days, loud rough younger guys, now that a pool hall was opened where the dining room had been. The Rainbow Lounge was one of those massive supper club places on the boulevard, just an ugly windowless concrete block by day, then by night aglow with neon tubing, parking lot paved in blacktop and big as a lot for an A&P. Who patronized these places? Lyle Stevick wondered. He wasn't even envious. He felt like Gulliver in the world of the Lilliputians or was he Gulliver in the world of the Brobdingnagians, his sanity askew, seeing human beings so greatly magnified they were monstrous, comical— the fairest complexions revealed as coarse and pitted, beauty a mere optical illusion. There was poor blushing Gulliver prankishly placed upon the erect nipple of an enormous breast belonging to an enormous female considered lovely and desirable in her own dimension and here was Lyle Stevick blushing stupidly like a country yokel exchanging greetings with a pretty hat-check girl (who knew damned well she was pretty) smiling at him—a stranger!—as if they were old flirty pals and she had the right to josh him for not having a hat (or a coat or an umbrella or a briefcase) to check with her. He wondered confused if he was expected to give her a tip anyway, maybe a dollar? Just fold it over discreetly and slip it into her hand, was this what you did? Were other men doing it? But the girl was so pretty with her strawberry blond hair curled under, her wide bright eyes, her crimson mouth, her breasts part-exposed in a sort of satiny ruffled bodice like something out of an Edwardian picture given a risqué touch, she seemed so quick-witted too he was worried he might offend her, that wide moist smile would fade. Then other men were coming in, customers she knew by name, Lyle Stevick's turn was over but he managed cleverly—the old goat!—to get a seat in a booth facing the door allowing him to watch the girl at his leisure, damned glad he'd come ten minutes early, thinking he'd like to arrive before Felix to rehearse what he had to say to Felix. But Jesus he'd been desperate to close up the store, get the hell out of the store and get a drink, no real reason, he'd made $75 clear profit that day which wasn't all that bad though it wasn't much good either: $75 profit and he owed the bank, and the car needed repairs again and the rent was due—when? first of May, must be next week sometime. It just went on and on, relentless, the cycle, Nietzsche had spoken grandiloquently of Eternal Recurrence but the mad son of a bitch hadn't had in mind the eternally recurring first of the month, had he, or grocery shopping at the A&P, or going to the doctor. That son of a bitch: how Lyle Stevick had adored him, in his youth.

Lyle ordered a scotch-and-water from a cocktail waitress nearly as pretty—but wasn't sexy the word?—as the hat-check girl, sat to nurse it, lit his pipe content to foul the air with his familiar stink, it

surely was *his;* when there'd been four females in his household they'd
ganged up against him, driven him out into the alley sometimes to
smoke in peace. The scotch went down smoothly. It wasn't Lyle
Stevick's usual drink but the Rainbow Lounge with its bluish-white
statues in the foyer and its fake potted trees or were they real trees
wasn't his usual place. If Hannah knew where he was!—frankly eyeing
a hat-check girl his daughter Geraldine's age, noting her legs in black
patterned stockings, her feet in black stiletto-heeled shoes, feeling the
first dim stirrings of desire so faint and so sad it was like hearing a
telephone ringing and ringing in a distant room you couldn't hope to
get to and if you did the call wouldn't be for you.

Lyle Stevick nursed his scotch, smoked his pipe, loving the taste
and able to fight down that tickle in his throat, his soul expanded in
contentment being here alone, solitary, waiting for someone to arrive
and it might be a beautiful woman, you couldn't tell. He was a good-
looking man yet, despite his shiny head and pouched eyes, that bunch
of flesh under his chin; the lapels of his brown-checked sports coat
were wide enough to be fashionable again, he carried his weight well,
remembered to keep his shoulders back in a posture that might have
been learned in the military. Yes, he was content here where no one
knew him. Not minding the fact that Felix was late as Felix invariably
was, since after all their conversation might be awkward, Lyle Stevick's side of it at least. To appeal to someone you disliked was always
degrading.

Surprising how much he liked the Rainbow Lounge and it wasn't
just because of the hat-check girl, the waitresses in their skimpy costumes. He seemed to recall the place was owned by a man named
Farolino whom Felix probably knew, very likely mob-connected,
which accounted for the lavish decor, black-cushioned leather booths
and flashy red tiles on the floor, bronzed mirrors, the nude "classical"
statuary and across in the dining room Englishy pretensions of crossed
swords and lances, brass shields, maces, you had to hand it to the
Italians, flamboyant and reveling in such vulgarity and actually bringing it off. Now they operated like regular businessmen, Lyle had read
recently—maybe the *Reader's Digest,* some piece on J. Edgar
Hoover—they had lawyers, tax accountants, lobbyists in Washington,
high-placed connections with WASP last names who were bankers
and judges maybe even the DA, who knows?—Lyle Stevick surely
didn't. You only became aware of the mob or the syndicate as it was
called when internal fractures occurred, somebody machine-guns
somebody else and it's in the newspapers, maybe when old Giulio

Rimi died trouble would start up again, which meant the Mattiuzzios too, but really Lyle Stevick knew nothing about it. A long time ago he'd asked Felix point-blank about the mob but Felix cut him short, saying he only knew what he read in the newspapers and he didn't believe half of what he read in the newspapers.

Jesus he almost winced looking at the hat-check girl's shoes when she stepped out from behind her little swinging counter: spike heels and then the toe so pointed, how could the poor thing bear the pain?—for there must have been pain. Though you wouldn't know it from her laughing flirty manner with her male customers. Accepting a kiss on the cheek, giving a kiss on the cheek, what did it all mean? Women wore shoes like that, crunching their tender toes together so that their rear ends were uplifted, sort of, and the calf of the leg tightened. Lizzie too, the last time he'd seen her. The hat-check girl wore her hair in a schoolgirl pageboy so you were meant maybe to think of Dorothy Collins—all innocence, wide-eyed and breathless— but this was mock-innocence and she knew her business, a narrow waist and shapely hips, lovely full breasts thrust out and upward inside the black satin bodice probably by one of those wired contraptions Howard Hughes had allegedly invented, the strapless brassiere a marvel of American know-how defying gravity, invented for that busty film actress Jane Russell who was probably one of his mistresses. A thing like that must hurt as much as the high-heeled pointy-toed shoes, Lyle Stevick thought, worse than the corsets poor Hannah wore, sighing and lacing herself up as if the flesh was something you had to carry around with you, not exactly you but your burden and responsibility. But Jesus that Jane Russell: enormous breasts on the posters, billboards, must fill up the entire movie screen, terrifying close up, probably, a man would be reduced to Lemuel Gulliver sweating and blushing in dread of being exposed as inadequate. What would a man, an average normal man, do with a woman like that? Lyle Stevick thought, staring sadly into space.

But wasn't everything terrifying close up?—the wisdom of the ages.

When Felix finally arrived fifteen minutes late Lyle noted with interest how the hat-check girl welcomed him—and he had a trench coat to hand over to her, stylish-looking, khaki-colored—probably address- ing him by name and smiling, teasing, tilting her head, making sure the little counter swung open so that Felix could see her rear as she went to hang up the coat, her legs, those stiletto shoes, but Felix wasn't watching, he was shaking hands vigorously with a man who'd come up to him like an old friend, beefy swarthy guy Lyle's own age, a woman with him greeting Felix too warmly, happily, her hand on his arm, leaning forward to kiss his cheek as if they were old, old friends—Jesus, Lyle thought, like something on television. What did it mean? Did it mean anything? This woman was a blonde nearly as tall as Felix, spike heels too and an orangey-brown jersey dress clinging to bust, hips, a good-looking woman and she knew it, diamonds sparkling dangling at her ears, a diamond on her hand Lyle Stevick could see flashing at this distance. What did it mean? Felix smiling his easy smile, Felix relaxed and springy just as he'd basked in the admiration of the rowdy arena audiences while never exactly looking in their direction, that wasn't his style, that superficial charm he'd cultivated long ago which meant, Lyle Stevick knew from past experience, absolutely nothing. Felix wore a beige sports coat, dark trousers, a dark shirt without a tie, his hair was neatly brushed, looking damp, dark, oiled, perhaps beginning to recede just perceptibly at his temples?—or was Lyle imagining it. He had to admit the first thing he looked for in Felix was signs of decay.

Karl Stevick's youngest son, wasn't he. His best-loved son.

Still, Felix hadn't had his father for very long. He wouldn't really have known him as Lyle and Domenic did: fatherless for most of his life, in fact.

(There was a family tale that when the eight-year-old Felix saw old Karl in the satin-lined casket at the funeral home he hadn't recognized him. The hearty pancake makeup, the rouged cheeks and lips, that expression of absolute peace and repose though the man had been dying ravaged by cancer for months—Felix had recoiled dry-eyed: "That isn't him!")

The first ten minutes or so of their conversation was taken up with family news of one kind or another, all Lyle's news of course. They had greeted each other warmly enough, shaken hands warmly enough, yet Lyle thought his brother was just slightly uneasy wondering why Lyle had set up this date and maybe even guessing the drift their conversation would take. Felix ordered a martini, Lyle a second scotch, messing around too with his pipe which always gave his hands something to do, he'd noticed that Felix no longer smoked but had no intention of bringing up the subject. Just hoped to Christ he wouldn't start coughing.

So Lyle did most of the talking. Amiable, garrulous, wanting to put his brother at ease. Now that they were seated in the booth together he could see that Felix did look a little drawn, tired, wearing away at the edges maybe with all his deals and contacts, God knows what kind of hours he slept, what kind of food he ate, living alone the way he did, never even visiting his mother. There was a nick or a dent in Felix's chin Lyle didn't recall. His skin tone was slightly sallow from the long winter maybe, he seemed to have a cold too—nostrils red-rimmed, eyes watery. The knuckles of his right hand were swollen and bruised and Lyle asked, joking, had he been in a fight and Felix said, smiling, no, he'd had an accident. What kind of an accident, Lyle asked curiously, keeping it all frank, open, brotherly. Just an accident, Felix said. A car door slammed on my hand.

The hell it did, Lyle thought.

But he didn't pursue the subject. The secret about Felix Stevick which no one knew except Lyle and maybe Domenic was that the man didn't trust you: that was the bottom line. No matter how warm and congenial and even affectionate Felix might be, fundamentally he didn't trust you. That was his instinct and his training both. The oldest ring strategy they'd drummed into his head as a kid of eleven or twelve, maybe it was the wisdom of the race, Christ knows: keep your guard up, protect yourself at all times.

As the referees always said, Now fight a nice clean fight, boys. And remember to protect yourself at all times.

Lyle chatted briefly of "Father" Domenic out in Foxboro. It was a way of immediately establishing kinship with Felix since both he and Felix were normal men, manly men, that little thrill of superiority edged maybe with some resentment and unease—Domenic was after all a "man of God," a "man of the cloth," didn't that mean he had some advantage over them?—hadn't in any case put himself like Lyle into harness, marrying and raising four children. The only real news Lyle had of his brother was that Domenic had had root canal work done on his mouth, damned nasty stuff, the kind of thing to test your faith in God, he guessed, but Felix just nodded vaguely, smiling, sipping nervously at his drink, probably not even knowing what root canal work was: he wasn't more than thirty-four years old after all. Yet he seemed interested. Asked a few questions. Asked about Hannah too as he always did, a queer intensity to his voice sometimes, was it possible Felix halfway envied Lyle his domestic life? wondered at its secrets, its special revelations? From where Felix stood, unmarried and unattached, maybe Lyle Stevick's predicament appeared enviable, even exotic. The Catholic Church had a shrewd ad campaign going— *The family that prays together stays together*—and though there was absolutely no truth to the childish little jingle, it caught your eye on the billboards around town, probably made single men and women feel a pang of loneliness if not actual grief for what they might be missing. The bishops weren't fools like your average parish priest, they knew how to operate, how to manipulate the flock, didn't stint paying Madison Avenue to drum up a juicy slogan; "prays together/stays together" was worth millions probably, like "single blessedness" in an earlier decade. "Single blessedness"! Now in the fifties everybody was hot to have babies, kids marrying younger all the time having as many as God sends, as the expression went. Like Neal O'Banan with his big wide sweet smile saying he liked large families he was from a large family himself ready to rear five or six or Christ knows how many children as long as Gerry's health held, you never had to worry about being *lonely,* Neal said, and that was surely the truth.

So Lyle tempered his sarcasm chatting with Felix, kept it all casual, brotherly, giving not the slightest hint of the bitterness he gnawed, like gnawing his own black heart, though he couldn't help exploding with laughter telling Felix about the most recent upset in poor Hannah's life: It seemed she and Ingrid embroidered any number of towels for the St. James's Ladies Sodality annual sale and did such a professional job the towels were nearly all missing the first morning of the sale, meaning the sodality officers must have helped themselves and Hannah and Ingrid were mortified. God, they were speechless for once. Crushed. Not knowing whom to accuse or maybe afraid to accuse anyone at all for fear they'd get snubbed, eased off the committee or whatever they were on. Hannah got around part of the problem by going to confession to Father Ogden saying she was eaten up with anger because of the incident, actually breaking into tears in the confessional, but all Ogden would do was treat it like a sin of Hannah's, brush it off, probably not giving it a second thought, just a lot of silly women squabbling. Towels, tea cozies, potholders, some of them knitted little baby sweaters and booties. "God, that's sad," Felix said. "That's so sad," he said, staring at Lyle as if through Lyle he could see poor Hannah, her face drawn and creased with disappointment. Felix seemed so sincere, Lyle was slightly ashamed at his own laughter.

"It's sad all right," he said, knocking pipe ashes into an ashtray. "If you lived with Hannah you'd know how sad."

Lyle glanced at Felix feeling a stab of elation. Maybe the two of them should get drunk together, for once?—that might help.

After a pause Felix said casually, "What's it like being a father?

I mean having your children," he went on embarrassed. He was sipping at his martini, watching Lyle closely with that queer intense calculating look of his, absolutely deadpan.

What's it like being a father!—Lyle stared at Felix incredulously.

"I mean—do you think about it all the time?" Felix asked. "Is it something always on your mind?"

Lyle's first instinct was to make a nervous joke, but he tried to take it seriously, soberly, he didn't want to offend his brother now of all times. He said, "It depends. Sometimes it does seem to me I'm thinking about them constantly, obsessively, even when I'm not exactly aware of it. Other times I guess I'm capable of forgetting." Conscious of sounding lame, inadequate, he said apologetically, "When the children were little what I mainly felt was worry. I mean after love, of course! After love. Then I felt worry. Maybe it was worse than worry—some kind of sick sensation in the gut. I'd go to sleep with it and wake up with it. Especially when there was a baby in the house, you know? Not just because of money though Christ knows I never had enough," he said more rapidly, fussing with his pipe, "but because of how things are. The world, accidents, sickness, that sort of thing. What would happen to them if something happened to me like when I was working at Swale, you know?—breathing in poison or actual nerve gas, the kind of work I did. Or if I got sick, had a heart attack, you know?" Felix was staring at him so intently he felt his face grow warm. He went on, vaguely embarrassed, "I suppose it's the crucial thing in my life. All Hannah and I have really done, you know? Because, well, what else *is* there . . . ?" His voice trailed off vaguely. He finished his drink, feeling again that tug of wild elation on the way to getting drunk.

Half mocking, he said, "Why do you ask, Felix? Are you thinking of getting married?—having children?" He grinned, laughed, the moment was sheerly brotherly. "Better late than never."

Felix shrugged, finished his martini, and signaled to the waitress: two more drinks. His narrow but rather muscular shoulders were hunched as if he were straining against the table; the cords of his neck looked taut. All the exercises he'd done all those years, Lyle thought half in contempt, building his body up to withstand blows, absorb pain, while he, Lyle Stevick, had gone about the world exposed! From time to time without knowing what he did Felix brought his bruised knuckles to his mouth to breathe on them lightly and soothingly— there was something childish in the gesture.

"Being a father, a parent," Lyle went on, hearing his words slur as if in urgency, confidentiality, "the hell of it is you think you should *know* but you don't *know*. You don't know a goddamned thing except you're worse off than before! Before I got married it was just myself, you know?—nobody else to think about. Then, well, Hannah got pregnant, you know, then we got married, got started, and Christ it hasn't let up for a day!—like getting on a roller coaster all innocent and set for a good time, then the roller coaster keeps on going, keeps on going, scaring the hell out of you and wearing you out and the only way you can escape is by jumping off the goddamned thing and breaking your neck. When there was a baby in the house things were always edgy, worrisome, Hannah had some kind of psychic thread connecting her and the babies their first twelve months or so, she wasn't even there when I'd talk to her, also her health went bad but I won't go into it, it's nobody's fault. Now the babies are grown up but I still have that sick kind of worry, you know?—like something you see in the corner of your eye but when you turn your head it's gone. Jesus, I think about them, though. Like at night. Or at the store when business is slow. Warren I worry about, he's so goddamned unrealistic. Then there's Enid and Lizzie. Enid scaring us like she did—two years ago, was it—something so closed off and secretive about her, not my little girl like she used to be though the doctor says she's in fine health and she seems happy, I mean she always seemed happy, what can you know about other people?—but then there's Lizzie. Down on South Olcott running around with men including some son of a bitch who they say is married, even has a kid, she's taking these singing lessons or whatever they are, dance lessons, Hannah telephones and one of Lizzie's roommates picks up the phone says Lizzie isn't there and Hannah swears she can hear giggling, Hannah just knows Lizzie is standing right there refusing to speak with her own mother, what can you do? If you're a parent, if you have daughters in this day and age, what can you do?—knowing the kinds of men they're basically going to meet. Bastards, right? Shits! Christ, it makes you sick and dizzy thinking about it, you want them to be happy, to be safe, but you can't control them, and you can't control a goddamned thing that happens to them, that's the lesson drummed into you if you're a father. That's the lesson, Felix." He paused dramatically. He did feel mildly sick, a wave of dizziness rising from his bowels; he blinked and wiped at his mouth, and there was Felix on the other side of the booth staring at him, his eyes dark and dilated, the scar in his eyebrow prominent like some exposed humiliation of his own, Felix Stevick staring expressionless, sucking at his swollen knuckles like a small child. Lyle was ashamed, trembling on the brink of tears, he hadn't meant to say such things and he hadn't meant to go on at such length, opening himself up to Felix of all people.

The waitress brought them their drinks and the spell was broken.

Lyle said with a hearty mean laugh, *"Are* you thinking of getting married?"

"No," Felix said curtly.

"Well—" Lyle tried to think of a reply. He was feeling shaky, resentful. He cleared his throat, mumbling, "You're a man who follows his hunches, right?—you follow where they lead."

Felix said, "Hunches can play out."

"What? What's that mean?" Lyle asked, staring.

Felix shrugged. Fumbling in his pocket for a Kleenex, blowing his nose. Odd, Lyle thought, to see his brother with a cold—gratifying in a way.

They fell silent. The air between them was almost palpably tense and Lyle had gone warm inside his clothes. His eye strayed to the strawberry blond hat-check girl but the foyer was jammed with people, men and women both, he could barely get a glimpse of her. Teetering in her high-heeled shoes, breasts half exposed. What did it mean? Did it mean anything? He swallowed a generous mouthful of scotch that both seared and comforted his throat—Jesus, it felt good—drew a ponderous breath, and said, "Well, I suppose you're wondering why I asked you to meet me?"

"Sure," said Felix amiably. But his eyes were narrowed as if he was steeling himself for something ugly.

"Felix, it's this: I'm in a quandary and I need money and I'd like to borrow it from you and I don't know when I'll be able to repay it." The terrible words came out in a rush, Lyle's face burned. Seeing that Felix's expression hardly changed, he went on speaking quickly, gesturing with his pipe, the pent-up words tumbling about them: He needed $4,300 for the purpose of constructing an underground bomb shelter with at least four feet of earth between the roof of the shelter and the air as the Civil Defense people were now advocating, the latest disclosures were that an ordinary shelter in an ordinary basement would be all but useless given a saturation attack by the enemy. He'd be willing to pay whatever interest Felix wanted, he said. But he had to have the money soon. He'd been waiting too long, he simply couldn't wait any longer.

Felix was staring at him as if he wasn't sure he'd heard correctly.

"It's money you want?—for a bomb shelter?" Felix asked.

"Money with interest," Lyle said quickly, shamefully. "I mean—I want to pay you interest. Whatever you say. But I need the forty-three hundred as quickly as possible, I've already waited too long, I simply can't wait any longer. The earth is thawed now, or anyway thawing—we can begin to dig."

While Felix listened, staring, Lyle spoke rapidly, just slightly impatiently, he'd argued with Hannah so many times, after all, he'd argued with acquaintances and strangers at the Cadboro and elsewhere, sometimes fell into animated discussions with customers, they were heartily on his side or vehemently against, in most cases it turned out they were in possession of very few hard facts and easily refuted, easily nonplussed by Lyle Stevick's superior knowledge. Within a few minutes you knew you were in the presence of a man who knew what he was talking about, and what he was talking about was a matter of life and death—the survival of the species. "It isn't even political, Felix," Lyle said, swallowing a large mouthful of his scotch. "American imperialism, Russian imperialism—Bulganin, Eisenhower, Secretary of Defense Wilson, Anthony Eden, Konrad Adenauer—what do we care about *them*. This transcends all politics, it's a matter of *destiny*."

He'd brought along a copy of the most recent CD pamphlet if Felix was interested. There was no glossing over the fact that nuclear war was imminent, the politicians on both sides knew it was imminent, the churchmen like Billy Graham, Fulton Sheen; you can't compromise with the devil, they were saying, and the meaning was clear. Lyle had facts, Lyle had statistics!—if for instance there was a nuclear attack consisting of 263 weapons ranging in size from 1 to 10 megatons totaling 1,446 megatons scattered across the U.S. (specifically, in relation to "strategic" and "population" targets) you'd have a situation in which there was virtually no place in the country more than fifty miles from a bomb detonation. *No place more than fifty miles!* First the bomb then the firestorm then the fallout radiation, inescapable, the sequence was inescapable, all a man had in his control was whether he could protect himself intelligently or not. All that was left of free will, Lyle said passionately, lowering his voice in anger, was whether he could save himself and his family from nuclear death.

He'd brought along too to show Felix a printout of the CD Sloan Report showing tables of intensities of radiation at various times after detonation corresponding to 1 kiloton of fission products per square mile—experiments done by the Naval Radiological Defense Laboratory—absolutely up to date and absolutely reliable, Lyle was sure.

According to the tables the initial level of radiation (after the first hour following detonation) would be 3,629 roentgens per hour for 1 kiloton of fission per square mile, and with 4 kilotons per square mile you'd have approximately 14,500 roentgens per hour as the *average* level of radiation!

According to scientists a whole-body radiation dose of 200 roentgens would cause radiation sickness and a dose of 500 would be lethal in maybe half the cases and a dose of 1,000 would be lethal in all cases without exception. (And who knows what "radiation sickness" really is?) A person in the open exposed to ordinary radiation would die in less than five minutes; in a basement he'd die in maybe an hour; in a low-cost backyard or basement fallout shelter he could live for maybe two months; but in a deep shelter with four feet between him and the radiation—assuming absolutely no contamination or leakage—he'd be safe for months, a year. The plan being advanced was that a family would stay locked up inside their shelter after the detonation for the first two weeks, then a cautious schedule of one hour a week outside which would be gradually accelerated according to CD guidelines. They were aiming for a dose of 100 roentgens spread over half a year—which shouldn't be serious except for the very young or the very old or the infirm.

And eventually—of course—survivors would be able to leave their shelters permanently, following CD guidelines.

As Lyle spoke excitedly he was conscious of Felix listening but did Felix truly *hear:* that deadpan respectful yet resistant look Lyle Stevick had seen in so many faces, so many fools' faces, when he spoke on this subject. No matter that the holocaust *was* imminent!—they simply didn't want to know. Eyes glazing over, twitches about the mouth. The ones who said not a word in disagreement were more insidious than those who did—you were wasting precious breath on them but hadn't any way of establishing the fact.

So Lyle quickly outlined the plans he meant to follow, itemized for Felix the major expenses, he'd be doing most of the labor himself of course, but he'd need help with the excavation and the concrete, now spring was here he wanted to begin as soon as possible and yes he'd gotten permission from his landlord though he'd have to pay the shrewd son of a bitch rent for the shelter too starting as soon as the excavation was dug: imagine that, *rent* for something Lyle Stevick was building himself, paying for out of his own goddamned pocket! An extra $15 a month tacked onto their bill—that son of a bitch!

"But of course it's worth it," Lyle said. He was excited, panting. "You can't argue with destiny."

He would have continued briskly itemizing other expenses but Felix interrupted. Sure he'd be happy to lend him the money only he didn't have $4,300 in his wallet. He'd write out a check for Lyle, he said. Mail it in the morning.

As if his victory had been granted too easily Lyle said, frowning, "But I intend to pay you interest, I don't want charity. I insist upon paying interest."

Felix made a gesture of embarrassment, annoyance. "You're not going to pay me interest," he said. "Forget it."

"But I insist," Lyle said boldly. "How about three percent? four percent?"

"I'll just lend you the money, pay it back when you can," Felix said. Clearly he was restless, eager to escape—he'd finished his drink and had shoved the glass aside. "No hurry. Take your time."

"Felix, I don't want charity," Lyle said. "You know me better than that. You know how our father would feel."

"Do I?"

"Don't you?"

Felix said impatiently, "He's been dead a long time—what the hell difference does it make?"

"He had his pride, his integrity," Lyle persisted. "He'd want his sons to have theirs."

Felix glanced at his watch. Lyle wondered if he'd upset him by talking of the holocaust—it was the one thing people didn't want to hear about. Or had he insulted him by forgetting to say that of course Felix was welcome in the shelter too if he could get there in time.

"We're both businessmen," Lyle pointed out stubbornly. "This is business."

"All right," Felix said.

"It's a deal?"

Felix laughed, suddenly he was cheerful, indifferent. "Pay whatever fucking interest you want, Lyle," he said.

So the brothers shook hands and it was a deal, completed. Felix said he'd mail the check in the morning, then he excused himself saying he had to leave he had a date he'd enjoyed talking with Lyle et cetera and Lyle should say hello to Hannah for him. And Lyle remained behind in the booth with the intention of having another scotch-and-water to celebrate—it was still early.

Why not? he thought. You don't live forever.

He signaled the waitress, prepared a fresh pipe, sat smoking, brooding, trembling and elated. His fingers tingled from Felix's quick hard grip, Christ the bastard was strong, couldn't help showing off his strength even when he wasn't conscious of what he did!—but this wasn't a time to nurse a grudge against Felix, Felix had come through wonderfully as Lyle had somehow guessed he would. The check would arrive day after tomorrow he didn't doubt, which meant he'd be safe telephoning a contractor in the morning to get things started. If the madmen running the world held off with their bombs for another two or three months maybe the Stevicks would have a chance.

So pleased was Lyle Stevick with the way the meeting had gone, he stayed in the Rainbow Lounge another hour celebrating, smoking his pipe and nursing his drink; he scarcely cared that he was alone, in truth he liked being alone, it cleared his head. Why not, he thought, as if addressing Hannah. You don't live forever.

But Lyle Stevick's good fortune continued.

For that night unexpectedly Felix telephoned him saying he'd been thinking it over and he had an idea, see what Lyle thought. Sure he'd lend Lyle the money as they agreed but throw in another $1,500 maybe and with that $1,500 free and clear Lyle could place a bet on a hot young welterweight named Carmen Basilio who was scheduled to fight Tony De Marco next month for the championship. The odds would be in favor of De Marco but Felix had a hunch Basilio was going to take him, he'd seen Basilio fight in Syracuse and the man was mean and sharp and quick with a vicious left hook, so why didn't Lyle take the extra $1,500 and make an intelligent bet where he could get the best odds, the fight was scheduled June 11 and if Lyle won the money would be his free and clear, right?

Lyle said hesitantly he'd think about it.

He didn't really approve of betting, he said. But he'd think about it.

You do that, Felix said.

That night he could scarcely sleep, his thoughts crowding one another and his pulses racing with excitement—his most profound wish so readily granted, his fortune turned for the better so mysteriously!—as if his life were a kind of fairy tale after all, one of those benign fairy tales where wishes come true, not a protracted tragedy as he'd always supposed. Or was it like that wildly popular new television show, the quiz show "The $64,000 Question" Hannah and her sister Ingrid

were so crazy for, where riches fell in your lap if you were quick and
sharp enough and knew the right answers to those lunatic questions.

5

Warren Stevick's love affair with Miriam Brancher began without
warning one afternoon in late March.

Always Warren would remember it as the most unlikely of meetings: he'd come home from the law library to his rooming house to
find the young woman, coatless, barefoot, in a sweater and blue jeans,
out on the roof perhaps fifteen feet beyond the window of the stairway
landing on the second floor.

On the roof? In this weather? What was happening . . . ?

On his way upstairs he had known something must be wrong
because the window at the landing had been raised to half its height
and cold air was streaming in. But he hadn't been prepared to see
anyone outside.

"What is it? What's wrong?" he called.

He stood amazed, staring: it was the young woman with the long
blond hair, Miriam Brancher, whom he knew only by name—an
artist's model one of the other tenants had told him—beautiful hard-
faced Miriam Brancher who smoked cigarettes on the street, wore
men's shirts, blue jeans, boots, though sometimes provocative whor-
ish clothes and absurd spike-heeled shoes—a drinker and a brawler,
people said of her, though Warren had always been attracted to her,
looking after her when she passed him on the stairs or in the corridor.
Now Miriam Brancher was sitting most improbably out on the roof
in the chilly March air, a bottle of wine in one hand, a cigarette
burning in the other. Warren leaned out the window, embarrassed for
her. Asking again what was wrong. Did she need help? In the confusion of the moment he hadn't any coherent idea of what he thought
she might be about to do—jump? lose her balance and fall? The pitch
of the roof was steep, the shingles damp, but the young woman was
half-sitting half-lying slack and motionless, her legs spread, her blond

head tilted back. Except for the overcast sky she might have been brazenly sunning herself.

She heard him at the window but didn't turn at first. He spoke to her, stammering, agitated. "Be careful. Don't move. I'll help you back in. . . ." Finally she looked at him, making a gesture of dismissal, mumbling words he couldn't make out. Telling him to go to hell? To leave her alone? Warren was thinking he'd never seen an adult in any place so unexpected and disorienting: a human figure where one shouldn't be. It seemed not to have occurred to him that he might have gone upstairs to his room and shut the door and forgotten her.

"Look, somebody will call the police if they see you," he said. "Do you want the police here? The fire company? If Mr. Novick hears about it—" Novick was the apartment house superintendent, as he called himself, a fat-faced irascible man in his fifties who lived in a ground-floor apartment and rarely had a kind word to say to the tenants. "Why don't you let me help you back in? It isn't very pleasant out there, is it?"

She was inching away from him, recklessly sliding her buttocks along the roof. Drunk, sullen, muttering to herself. Her bare feet were shocking in their whiteness—Warren was touched by the sight of them, so exposed, so intimate; he felt a pang of pity and tenderness and impatience. "Don't! Stop! Stay where you are!" he said. The cigarette fell from her hand and rolled down the roof, then the bottle of Gallo wine—she gave a shriek, reached after it, nearly slipped. The bottle rolled noisily down the roof and bounced off the rain gutter and fell to the pavement two floors below: they could hear it break.

She shouted something at him, blaming him maybe for the loss of the bottle. Bitter mouth, pale triangular face, unwashed hair in a blond tangle blowing across her eyes. Warren recalled the last time he'd seen Miriam Brancher—several nights before, climbing the stairs in the company of a man he had seen her with recently, good-looking, early forties, camel's-hair overcoat and a tan fedora tilted back on his head, pretty Miriam Brancher and her boyfriend pleasantly drunk, their arms around each other's waists, laughing and stumbling up the poorly lit staircase. Warren stepped back against the wall to let them pass. He had never exchanged any words with Miriam Brancher, though he knew her name from the occasional letters she received scattered on a table in the vestibule; yes, Warren had stared at the letters, puzzled over them without touching them, wondering who wrote to her: what her life was. She was the sort of girl he never met, wouldn't have known how to approach and wouldn't perhaps have wanted to approach—just someone to stare at in the street, admire in passing. She had the brash funny swinging gait of his own sister Lizzie when Lizzie was in a good mood but she was much prettier than Lizzie. He knew about her from stray remarks made by the other tenants and by Novick, she was an artist's model for one thing—which meant nude modeling—though she might have had a regular job as well—secretarial work? waitressing?—certainly she had a good many boyfriends of varying ages and dispositions but she never annoyed the other tenants in the house to the point where anyone seriously complained. On the stairs that evening Miriam smiled happily at Warren, running her eyes over him in childlike high spirits as women sometimes do in the company of their lovers, feeling rich, careless, bountiful in their beauty and sexuality—"Hello, how are *you!*" she'd murmured as if Warren were an old friend, someone slightly foolish, an object of fond but condescending humor. But before Warren could reply or even demonstrate by a certain surprised irritation how he felt, Miriam and her boyfriend pushed past him and were gone. In their noisy wake Warren smelled perfume, hair lotion, alcohol.

He'd thought of the incident afterward. For some time afterward. Miriam Brancher's wide green eyes and her delicate snub nose and that lovely mouth with the short upper lip—her drunken vivacity that promised so much! She was older than he by a few years, he judged. Much older in experience. But the next time Warren saw her she passed him on the street swinging along in a cheaply glamorous suede coat without giving him a sign of recognition. She'd looked right through him: he hadn't existed.

Now she was watching him, hunched over hugging her knees like a frightened child, as he made his way cautiously toward her across the fifteen feet of wet shingled roof, Warren swallowing down his panic as he inched along—God the shingles were wet, slippery, the roof was steeper than he had thought—"Stay where you are, please don't move any farther"—his voice forceful and his stammer miraculously gone. He knew that at any moment he might lose his precarious footing, lose his grip on the peak of the roof, he could slip and fall and crack his skull on the pavement below; still he kept going, his breath faintly steaming and his sides trickling with perspiration. A wind out of the northeast blew thinly, making a whistling noise through the partly crumpled bricks of a chimney close by; on the other side of the roof pigeons or mourning doves cooed undisturbed; down on the street the familiar noise of traffic, truck gears grinding. Warren tried to speak lightly to Miriam Brancher, saying they'd both be back inside safe in another five minutes, why didn't she put out her hand?—lean this way and put out her hand?—he wouldn't hurt her. But she didn't move. Didn't budge. Hugging her knees, sick-faced, sullen, maybe now the wine was getting to her, the partying was over. She watched Warren without expression as if from a distance. An asshole, she was probably thinking: a goddamned fool sticking his nose into her business. Only because she was weak, at a disadvantage, she'd made an error of judgment climbing out onto a roof as if it were summer and the sun hospitable and the roof itself flat enough to keep her upright. "Please—can't you lean this way a little?" Warren asked.

He didn't want to show the desperation he felt. But he had seriously underestimated the danger, the slope of the roof, the treacherous shingles, the soles of his shoes were worn smooth and kept slipping—he'd have been better off barefoot clambering along like a monkey!—it was like crawling across unprotected terrain waiting for enemy fire to begin. That dawn on the Imjin River. One thousand casualties, they'd suffered. "Casualties"—what a word! Being exposed to the terrible openness of the sky from which mortar might fall raining fire and death. Without knowing it Warren was steeling himself, waiting for an explosion so deafening he wouldn't be able to hear it.

From the street the grand shabby old 1920s frame-and-stucco house with its numerous sloping roofs, dormer windows, steep pinnacles and arches and tiny ornamental porches gave an impression of crazed exuberance, an architect's fancy, but from Warren's new perspective it was a region of nightmare angles, sudden drops, fierce gusts of wind—a child's playground turned horrific. Why had he climbed outside so readily? why hadn't he telephoned the police or the fire department? Now he was sweating inside his clothes, now his glasses were misting over with a desperation he found increasingly difficult to hide. What disoriented him most was the persistent tug of gravity—his left foot and ankle supporting virtually all his weight at a sharp downward angle. If his ankle gave way, buckled suddenly—! He shut his eyes, remembering the time he'd climbed the roof of a boarded-up warehouse behind his father's Lock Street store, climbing higher and higher in terror of not knowing how to turn back, how to retrace his steps, yes he'd been terrified too of simply looking down, a child of nine or ten, panicked, trembling, bird lime on his hands and trousers, the stink of tar, a pitiless beating summer sun—

How he'd finally climbed back down, he couldn't remember. Now he was holding his hand out to Miriam Brancher, urging her to take it. Yes? Now? But be careful! She eyed him bitterly but gave in, they clasped hands, her fingers surprisingly strong—cold, dry, firm, capable. In his elated nervousness Warren made a joke of it: "We've never been introduced, have we—I'm Warren Stevick—" but Miriam made no reply. He saw she was crying, her cheeks shining with tears.

At this time Warren was in his first year of law school, completing a difficult spring term; he worked part-time—up to twenty hours a week—in the law library, for $1.50 an hour (before taxes); but his fullest energies went into helping recruit members for the Philadelphia chapter of the Society for Non-Violent Action, a pacifist group with a particular commitment to mounting demonstrations against nuclear warfare, nuclear bomb tests and research. The group was international, with headquarters in London and New York City: it was supposed to have some two thousand members. (The local chapter had only about twenty who might have been said to be reliable.) Warren was devoted to the organization but determined not to neglect his studies and his health, as he had during the Stevenson campaign: the law is a weapon, after all, a weapon to be used against weaponry—he wanted his degree for purely utilitarian purposes. He intended to go into public service law, public defense or civil liberties work, in a few years run for office on a peace ticket, perhaps out of the very congressional district in which he now lived. Though he was reluctant to tell his parents, he had no plans ever to return to Port Oriskany: he had no future there.

Indeed he never thought of Port Oriskany without a sensation of panic, alarm, though he couldn't have said why. He'd had a happy childhood there, he seemed to remember.

Despite its low membership SNVA, as it was coming to be called, had been active locally and had drawn a fair amount of attention—the group had marched on the Penn campus and in the city the previous fall in protest against the Eisenhower Administration's policy on nuclear arms; they had drawn up a petition addressed to Eisenhower and Soviet Premier Bulganin both, calling for arms negotiations, and sent it off to Washington with several hundred signatures; they had sponsored the showing of a controversial documentary film about the Japanese fishermen aboard the luckless ship *Fortunate Dragon* who were stricken with radiation poisoning following a U.S. H-bomb test in the Pacific in March 1954; they were tentatively planning to picket ROTC headquarters at Penn sometime in the spring. Local sentiment was generally hostile to the group, but Warren and the others spent hours each week passing out mimeographed leaflets; and Warren volunteered to explain the society's beliefs and intentions to local organizations—the Young Democrats, the St. Thomas More Society, the Law Students League, various honorary fraternities and religious groups. Despite his intermittent stammer he had developed into a quite personable speaker, he was nervous but enthusiastic, even rather admired in certain quarters—a tall broad-shouldered earnest young man with a roughened, flushed complexion, close-cropped brown hair, tortoiseshell glasses—something wrong with his left eye, it seemed, the left lens of his glasses was greatly magnified. He was known to be a Korean veteran with two Purple Hearts but he always introduced himself as a representative American citizen of his generation. His clothes were frequently shabby or rumpled but he always wore, for public occasions, a white shirt, necktie, sports coat—Warren Stevick and his compatriots in SNVA were no beatniks of the type being luridly publicized by *Life* and *Time,* their rebellion was of quite another quality.

Still he drew a sobering amount of abuse, appearing before local organizations, daring to take the platform to speak of civil disobedience and Gandhi's *satyagraha,* or nonviolent protest, in terms of resistance to the U.S. government's defense policy. Repeatedly the question was put to him: If the United States is engaged in a struggle for world domination with the U.S.S.R. and if American citizens advocate noncooperation with the government aren't their actions treasonous?—traitorous?

Warren's fellow law students were the most contemptuous, speaking of anarchy, chaos, sheer insanity, if every individual "took the law into his own hands" et cetera, but Warren stood his ground, Warren was fully prepared for the most vicious attacks. Always he made an effort to speak informally, even intimately, as if addressing several individuals instead of a larger group; in atmospheres grown rowdy and ugly he continued undisturbed, only slightly embarrassed, rarely raising his voice to be heard over the shouts that assailed him. He was in control! He was himself! And this was life—public life! The principle that guided his own behavior, he said, was that of action dictated by conscience: a purely nonviolent noncoercive action of the kind exemplified by Henry David Thoreau in refusing to pay his $1.50 tax to the State of Massachusetts in 1846 out of moral revulsion at slavery in the South and the American war with Mexico, and by Mohandas Gandhi in his long campaign of *satyagraha* against British rule in India. He made an effort to disarm his opponents by speaking of action dictated by conscience in transgression of the law in Nazi Germany, in the English and Spanish colonies in America, in the Roman empire at the time of the Christian martyrs. The Roman world fell after all as a consequence of Christian disobedience in terms of a higher law—could the fact be denied?

No matter if Warren's own talks were picketed, no matter how he was called names—"Commie," "traitor," "jerk," "asshole"—he retained his stubborn good nature, he was congenial, unassuming, articulate, respectful of his opponents' arguments. Gandhi had been jailed numerous times, might well have been killed at any time, these verbal insults were nothing to Warren Stevick. Only upon occasion was his pride—his manly vanity, it might be called—injured: but that was nothing too.

As he was to try to explain to Miriam Brancher, one's opponents are not evil in themselves though their beliefs may be evil. That was Gandhi's understanding, of course: the aim of *satyagraha* is not victory over an opponent, certainly not the defeat of an opponent, but compromise in the establishment of objective truth—after which, as Gandhi proved, justice will follow.

After truth, justice.

A principle of the universe, perhaps.

She was frightened of returning to her own room, Miriam Brancher told Warren. She didn't want to be alone, she said, so Warren brought her swaying on her feet and stumbling into his own room where she lay on the bed white-faced and dazed, all resistance gone. It seemed to Warren the most natural thing in the world—the way this woman sank onto his bed, drawing her knees up to her chest, her feet so very white, tender, even the dirty soles gleaming white beneath, a sight that struck him to the heart. She hardly knew him but she trusted him, subdued now, telling him she was sorry, she was so ashamed, grateful for what he'd done, saving her from killing herself maybe, or the police or the firemen making of her a neighborhood spectacle, she knew it was a mistake to drink alone but once she'd taken that first drink it was too late. Warren covered her with a quilt, brought a washcloth soaked in cold water to press against her face; her fingers gripped his as she pressed it hard against her eyes. There was this man, she said, he hadn't treated her very nicely, that was the size of it, promised certain things, then it was another story, but God she didn't want to bore Warren with her troubles, the story of her luckless life bouncing around from one man to another. The real thing was, she said, her soul was hundreds of miles away with her little boy. Nobody in the house knew she had a little boy, did they?—Mikey was five years old. He lived with her mother and her soul was with him but her life was here and she couldn't bring the two together.

"I was married, though," Miriam said. "When I had him. Mikey. It isn't maybe what you think." She spoke bitterly, sleepily. Warren told her to sleep if she could, he wouldn't bother her; then he sat for a long time in a trance of astonishment and love staring at her as she slept, the grainy skin, strands of greasy dull-blond hair, a fading bruise on her forehead and the flesh about her eyes discolored in fatigue— still she was beautiful to him: he'd never seen anyone so beautiful. Delicate features but there was something powerful in the shape of her head, the strength of her jaw, her neck, her shoulders. She reminded him of Rodin's Eve, that lovely female figure with the tense muscular strength of the body, the lower body in particular, perfectly formed thighs and buttocks. Yes, Warren thought, Rodin's Eve: not the idea of a woman but the woman herself.

Miriam Brancher slept nearly fifteen hours uninterrupted in Warren's bed.

It was a cotlike bed, narrow, with a lumpy mattress, pushed into a corner of the room Warren rented for $45 a month on the third floor of the house at 4722 Hickory Street. The house in its decaying grandeur had been crudely partitioned into some fifteen "apartments" of varying sizes and rents; it was one of the first places Warren Stevick looked at when he came to Philadelphia in September of the previous year. His demands were modest, his resources limited. He liked the seclusion of his long narrow room under a sloping side roof with a single dormer window facing a neighboring house some twelve feet away; a mysterious smell of wet ashes stirred at times by rain and wind awoke in him powerful memories, similarly mysterious, infinitely evocative, of boyhood places. Sunlight entered the room aslant only in late morning, if at all; the remainder of the time the room was twilit, shadowy, requiring a lamp if Warren wanted to work. But he liked it here, he'd felt immediately at home.

The room was sparsely furnished: the bed, a table used for both meals and studying, a desk chair, bookshelves made of raw boards and bricks, a shabby wing chair bought for $10 from the Salvation Army store on Thirteenth Street. He might have been living, Warren thought, in Lyle Stevick's very place of business. In a cramped alcove was a Pullman kitchen, so-called—midget refrigerator, two-burner stove, badly stained sink; beside the kitchen was a bathroom with an old-fashioned tub, also badly stained, rather stately, resting on clawed feet. The tub was eerily like the one at 118 East Clinton in Port Oriskany—sometimes while bathing Warren dozed off, woke to tepid water and a sense of inexplicable loss, not knowing the year, the time, his own age.

The few visitors to Warren's room were invariably struck by the items taped to the wall beside his desk—a portrait of the young bearded hollow-eyed Henry David Thoreau; a photograph of Mohandas Gandhi in his loincloth, at prayer; an elaborate calendar of the year 1955 with many dates blackened out and others outlined in red; a sign on white construction paper hand-lettered in India ink—

WAR IS OUTMODED. ITS THREAT
MUST BE ABOLISHED IF
THE WORLD IS TO GO ON.
                                   —*General Douglas MacArthur*

("MacArthur? That madman?" one of Warren's acquaintances said when he saw the sign. "He wasn't a madman, he was a soldier," Warren said stiffly. "It was the war that was mad.")

That night while Miriam Brancher slept in his bed Warren managed to sleep, partly undressed, in the wing chair with its sagging cushion and its smell of dust and mildew, familiar cozy smells again reminding him of home. His sleep was light and intermittent very much aroused by the woman's presence, the scent of her hair, her body, her winey breath; desire stimulated him, forcing him into awkward positions, the beat of blood in his groin pleasurable at first then rather daunting. He would have believed he hadn't been asleep but then he was being awakened by Miriam Brancher's faint snoring breath or by a small exclamation in her sleep—or was it in his own sleep?—until at last he was fully awakened, hearing the noise of the shower in the bathroom, seeing the empty disheveled bed and the bedside clock, its radium numerals glowing at five minutes to seven. Incredibly, it was morning: they'd shared the night.

Warren got to his feet, put on his glasses, waited trembling for Miriam's return. He'd awakened aroused and his sexual desire was the more provoked by the sound of the shower, the very look of the bedsheets—he rearranged them, straightened them, brisk and efficient as if making up his barracks bed. He breathed in the heady rank odor of Miriam's hair on the pillow. Seven o'clock in the morning of March 26, 1955: a day unmarked on his calendar.

After some minutes Miriam entered the room releasing a cloud of steamy fragrant air; she wore Warren's white terry-cloth robe many sizes too large for her, hair carelessly wrapped in a towel; she was barefoot, transformed and springy, smiling, confident as if knowing well the strength of his desire. How sleep had restored her!—even the bruise on her forehead seemed to have vanished. Good morning, she said, and Warren staring was hardly able to reply. She sat on the edge of his bed. The most natural thing in the world. Toweled her hair dry slowly, wriggling her toes in pleasure. Asked him did he have a cigarette?—no? Asked him did he have to be anywhere soon that morning? Her skin was lightly flushed from the shower, her eyes were green flecked with hazel or gold, her mouth fleshy, lovely. Warren heard pigeons on the roof, something scrambling under the eaves. Footsteps overhead. A dull throbbing in the radiator like the pulse of his own blood rushing into his groin. Smiling at Warren she asked him his name again—Warren *what?*—and in a trance of desire Warren went to her and would have stooped to kiss her but she embraced his thighs suddenly, hard, pressing her face against his groin. Warren was stricken sharp and keen as if a knife blade had entered his flesh—now he'd never let go.

So it began. The first love affair of Warren Stevick's life.

Miriam would never forget, she said, how kind Warren had been to her. How he'd "saved" her. (Though had she been in any danger really?—bringing up the subject of the roof from time to time she said speculatively that probably she wouldn't have fallen, she had fool's luck, if Warren hadn't noticed her she would have crawled back inside in a few minutes. Or so she thought.) She was childlike in her gratitude, however; told him he resembled her older brother whom she'd lost; he was nothing at all like her husband—the very antithesis of Bob Brancher, she said, if "antithesis" was the word she wanted.

Her husband? Was she married?

Not exactly, Miriam said.

She'd gotten drunk and crawled out on the roof to clear her head because of her boyfriend (Curt: the one with the camel's-hair coat, the stylish fedora) who'd told her yes he loved her he was crazy about her but not enough to change his life for her. The son of a bitch! It might be amusing, Miriam said, if it wasn't so goddamned tragic.

"Really he got frightened because of Mikey," she added.

Precisely, clinically, Warren Stevick had not been a virgin when he first made love to Miriam Brancher but he'd never had sexual relations with any woman more than a single time; he'd had very few sexual relations at all. Out of shame he tried not to recall the various incidents. His memory misted over, distorting boyhood fantasies into fact, fact into erotic fantasies; though he was now fully adult and years removed from the familiar Roman Catholic cycle of sinful thoughts and deeds and confession and absolution and communion and sinful thoughts and deeds and again confession and again absolution and communion, he could not overcome the conviction that sex was very likely sinful or in any case demeaning to both men and women. His body was ungainly and still an embarrassment to him. The drift of his thoughts. He had never been in love with any girl or woman though he'd hoped from time to time to fall in love, seriously in love—life was too lonely otherwise! But his romances (in high school, at Cornell) were promising and exhilarating at first, then turned clumsy, talky, self-conscious. At Cornell the young women he'd known were obsessed with marriage, even those who disapproved of their parents' narrow lives; they were fearful of losing their virginity beforehand—"losing," an expression Warren could understand, like losing a game, losing money, losing your best chance, the bargaining power of virginity with its equivalence perhaps—who knew?—in actual cash. He couldn't blame them, this was an era of fiercely defined morals for women; you knew what was right, what was wrong, an entire life might be thrown away mistaking one for the other.

And when Warren thought of his sisters he felt an immediate sense of vulnerability, risk. Lizzie in particular: he dreaded the Sunday evening he called home and his mother would tell him Lizzie was in trouble at last—"in trouble" at last—and would the man marry her or wouldn't he. He could very nearly hear his mother's voice swallowing down her grief and outrage, that flat resigned embittered voice he knew so well. Lizzie the slut, the tramp. Lizzie with her dirty mouth.

As for Enid: he worried she would try to kill herself again someday and this time she might succeed, slip away from them forever, giving no reason. A crude or unfortunate sexual experience might do it but who could protect her? keep her from being defiled? Warren was certain Enid was still a virgin, she was still a "good" girl in spite of the terrible school she attended, East High, now worse Warren had heard than when he'd gone there. Unthinkable that Enid was anything but a virgin but still: who knew. Trying to kill herself as she had was like losing her virginity, wasn't it. . . .

Warren had believed love was a matter of infinitely subtle moves and countermoves as in a game of chess, feints, delays, demands, subterfuge, and here in the early days and weeks of his love for Miriam Brancher he and Miriam saw each other when they could and made love when they could, sometimes they had supper together and she stayed with him all night, waking him in the morning, straddling him, her hair hanging in both their faces, her breath short and quick and her sleep-encrusted eyes shut tight in muscular exertion. She was funny, sweet, vigorous, bawdy, like no woman Warren Stevick could have imagined: making love was something you did because you wanted to, as simple as that. Miriam gripped him with her knees, her arms beneath his neck, Warren laughed, astonished, feeling himself dwarfed by her slender body, even his penis that seemed so enormous and blood-engorged overcome finally by her springy audacity—the swift skillful movements of her pelvis and hips bringing them both to orgasm. The cords of Miriam's beautiful neck were taut, her face shining and triumphant. In the ecstasy of these long moments Warren could feel the rapid contractions of her vagina, thrust up deep inside her as he was, ring upon ring of spasmodic contractions exciting him to an intense pleasure of his own. Oh Jesus it's so good, isn't it, Miriam would say, sobbing, when she could speak.

Sometimes burying her face in his neck she said, Oh Jesus I love you.

And Warren in a trance of happiness said, I love *you.*

That first day they didn't leave Warren's room at all. Ate a lazy late breakfast of oranges, toast, a single slightly stale doughnut covered in powdered sugar, two tall jam glasses filled to the brim with milk. Warren drank a quart of milk a day: he'd drunk that much since the age of fourteen. The sharp smell of the oranges—fruit, skin—stayed with Warren as if lodged beneath his fingernails—he'd ceremoniously peeled the oranges for them both—mixed with his infatuation for Miriam Brancher sitting there so calmly in his old terry-cloth robe he wished was cleaner, hair brushed back from her face. This is the way it will be, Warren thought. After we're married.

Miriam studied the photographs taped to the wall: Gandhi the leader of all India sitting cross-legged at prayer, a frail bald elderly man with wire-rimmed glasses; the melancholy staring portrait of Henry David Thoreau. She asked about them both. Who were they?

What had they done? Why was Warren interested in them? Thoreau's name was familiar, she thought, they'd studied him in high school—something about a pond? in the woods? a man living alone by a pond in the woods? They hadn't read an entire book, just excerpts, Miriam had always wanted to go to the library and read more. There'd been so much she had wanted to do in those days!—but she and Bob Brancher this guy from her home town Litchfield got married fast, he was twenty-five, enlisted in the army, she was eighteen and had to drop out of school a month before graduation. "One thing that always worried me," she said slowly, smiling at Warren, "there is so much in the world to read, so much to learn, if you once got seriously started how could you *stop?*"

Her attention was drawn too to a glass paperweight set atop one of Warren's bookshelves, a birthday present from Enid long ago, one of those small transparent globes that when turned upside-down releases a miniature snowstorm. The paperweight was a souvenir of Shoal Lake; the words *Shoal Lake, N.Y.* were embossed on its base. Miriam held it to the light from the window, turning it slowly in her hand. The swirl of mock snow, tiny uniform white chips in an element denser and more mysterious than air: these things are so pretty, Miriam said, so ingenious, aren't they?—she'd never been able to figure out how they worked. Inside the globe was a chunk of glittering quartz meant perhaps to be a mountain lifting out of a cobalt-blue lake. Her grandmother had had one of these, Miriam said, in the front parlor of her house. But as a child she hadn't been allowed to touch it. A scene like a little village, some tiny houses and a church, then the snow.

Warren had been carrying the paperweight around with him for years, always packing it with his books, a sentimental gesture solely, he had no use for the thing. He couldn't remember how old he'd been when Enid gave it to him—maybe thirteen. "Mikey likes things like this too," Miriam said. "Except he breaks them."

Warren hesitated. "Tell me about Mikey."

"You don't want to know," Miriam said.

"What do you mean?—of course I do."

"I'll tell you sometime," Miriam said.

But as the weeks passed they saw each other far less frequently than Warren had anticipated. She'd asked him not to come to her room out of embarrassment she said for its condition (and it *was* astonishingly messy) and the partitioned walls were so goddamned thin on her floor her next-door neighbor could hear everything. She came to him when she wanted, she rose from lovemaking refreshed and forgetful while Warren, poor lovesick Warren, would think of her for hours, his body still heated from her and blood flowing downward into his groin. He'd spoken of marrying her almost from the start, keeping the subject casual, provisional, he believed his advantage over her other male friends was that he *would* marry her; he would adopt her son too. But Miriam invariably said he didn't mean it. He was so sweet, so kind, but he didn't know the circumstances, he didn't know her. Often he couldn't extract from her a clear promise of when they would see each other again. The next day? The next night? Miriam would kiss him saying apologetically she didn't know, she had a modeling session all afternoon at the Pennsylvania Academy of the Fine Arts—a big figure-drawing class, forty-five students—then she was meeting some friends on Sansom Street downtown, she didn't know when she'd be back. (No, she wasn't meeting Curt any longer, they were finished. The son of a bitch had been coming around but she'd told him to go to hell.) Warren hid his disappointment, kissing her lightly as she kissed him, kisses like moths or butterflies, fondling her as she tried to dress, the two of them stumbling and laughing breathlessly together. In Miriam Brancher's presence Warren Stevick was like no person he'd ever known—playful, boyish, his ungainly body free for a spell of its various aches and memories, he dreaded the mirror less since Miriam assured him he looked perfectly fine— and if people noticed anything they would know immediately he'd been wounded, he'd had surgery, so what? He was a handsome man, she insisted. He just had to see himself right.

Warren loved Miriam's body, mesmerized at times by the extremity of the pleasure it could give him, he loved her breasts, the bluish-milky fullness, the brown nipples like blossoms, her slightly rounded belly with its old stretch marks faded nearly invisible. She asked him one night after they made love would he know she was a mother?—she'd had a twenty-hour labor? and Warren was embarrassed not knowing how to reply. "You're a beautiful woman," he said, as if that were an answer.

"Yes but would you *know* . . . ?" Miriam asked with a curious intensity.

Though she looked Warren's age or even younger Miriam would be twenty-seven in October. She was self-conscious about her beauty, perhaps a little anxious: in any case as she said being an artist's model cured you of certain illusions. You lost faith damned fast in what you'd always been told were your good looks.

The photographers tried to make you look good but the student artists equated ugliness with art. Sagging breasts and belly, wattled ass—meaning *art.* Miriam Brancher posing for them was only the pretext.

Warren didn't like it that she was an artist's model so he asked her very little about the sessions, he knew he couldn't have kept the disapproval, the repugnance, out of his voice. Miriam too seemed to hate the work, then again she rather liked it, it was so easy, she'd had to take a lot of crap working as a waitress, one of the places she'd worked downtown some of the other waitresses were turning tricks between shifts and certain male customers naturally expected Miriam was too, then the sons of bitches had the audacity to get angry at *her,* to leave dime tips for *her.* So she did the modeling, she was friendly with the art instructors at the Academy and in the art department at Penn, a strain sitting in one position for so long but she could make her mind go blank, she could sort of hypnotize herself, sometimes that worked really well.

But it was sobering to see what the students made of her. How they saw her. If they saw her at all. Lately she'd stopped looking, even for laughs she'd stopped. It was depressing. What it said of human nature, people seeing things so wrong, so crazy, different from one another—how could they agree on anything? She teased Warren about his political hopes, the peace movement, SNVA, of which he'd told her a good deal; he wanted to change how people thought but he'd have to change how they saw things first. "It must be always like beginning at zero," she said, shaking her head. As if the very thought of it wearied her. "Going back again and beginning at zero."

Warren seemed to agree though really he didn't quite know what Miriam meant.

In early May she told him about Mikey: five years old, living with Miriam's mother in Litchfield, Pennsylvania, up by the New York State border. Showed him a pile of snapshots. "Here. Look. Take your time," she said.

Eagerly Warren picked up the snapshots thinking he would see at last the child who would be his son—*his* son.

But what to make of Mikey!—this subtly misshapen child with his small marble-shiny unfocused eyes, fat lips, brutal snub nose—a child so ugly Warren felt a kick of grief looking through the snapshots, seeking the one that might refute the others. Warren had thought all small children were beautiful or in any case attractive but what were the words he could say to Miriam about this crouched wizened child with bright dead eyes staring up at the camera?—thin pale hair the color of Miriam's combed wetly back from his low forehead, fat lips drawn back from his teeth in a semblance of a smile. In the background was an incongruously lush Christmas tree trimmed with gaudy ornaments, loops of silvery tinsel, dime-store colored lights glowing red, yellow, blue, green, an angel with a flat Slavic face and spun-glass hair like an old Christmas angel of Mrs. Stevick's. In one of the snapshots Mikey sat amid a pile of wrapping paper as if he'd exhausted himself in a fit of tearing and ripping. One of his eyes had shifted inward, his mouth was wet with saliva.

Warren said in a faltering stupid voice, "He doesn't seem to resemble you." Miriam said, "Yes he does," taking the snapshots from Warren's hands.

Mikey's "condition" she said was permanent. It wasn't any kind of illness and it wasn't genetic, he'd suffered brain damage at birth—hadn't had enough oxygen and by the time the obstetrician and the rest of them in the delivery room noticed, it was too late. Miriam was on the delivery table knocked out—she'd had a hell of a time in labor, lost a lot of blood. An army base hospital in Fort Worth, Texas, where Bob Brancher was stationed at the time. Back in Litchfield nobody had a clue to Bob Brancher but once you saw him in the army you knew who the man was and that was enough. A classic army type, Miriam said mockingly: taking orders, giving orders; swallowing down insults, giving out insults. He got his ass kicked a lot and kicked other people's asses a lot. Simple as that. Having Mikey the way he was and knowing how he'd grow up just wiped Bob out, he said, he couldn't deal with it, had a savage temper as it was, then things got worse, even when he was sober Miriam could see how he hated them both, wouldn't have minded if they died.

So Miriam couldn't take it, why the hell should she take it?—getting knocked around when her husband felt like it, the baby in danger; when he got in one of his moods, his tantrums, Bob would shake him so you thought his head might fly off. There wasn't even any other man though she'd had a lot of opportunities, she just left, walked out, took a Greyhound bus back east, her and Mikey. Now Brancher was stationed in Germany, they hadn't spoken in three years, the hell with it all.

But were they divorced, Warren asked.

Oh sure, Miriam said wearily. I've had enough of that shit.

Are you in love, Warren? Enid asked. Are you going to get married?—a curious edge to her voice, fear or was it actual malice beneath the schoolgirl excitement.

Didn't know. Couldn't say. Damn him for having brought it up, even hinted.

Sometimes if Miriam stayed the night they showered together in the morning, then Miriam played at helping Warren shave, lathered his jaws, then stood with her arms around his waist, peeking over his shoulder, watching him in the mirror. "I want to be your odalisque," she said. "Hey, do you know what an odalisque is?" Warren laughed but felt keenly at such times how much of a game this was, how easily Miriam did it. He said, "Of course I don't want you to be my odalisque—do *you* know what it means?"

He told her it made no difference about Mikey.

Yes it does, Miriam said.

Some difference but not much, Warren said.

He thought it over: No, he said. No difference at all.

Miriam kissed the scarred and serrated flesh of Warren's face, his chest, his back, his belly. Asked him if he still felt pain, did he still feel afraid, he wasn't like other veterans she knew, didn't like to talk much about himself. "I've never known anybody like you," she said.

Sometimes she ran the shower, leaving the bathroom door open to fill both rooms with steam. Straddling Warren's thighs she massaged him expertly as he lay on his stomach. In a trance of her own pleasure in giving pleasure, she stroked and caressed, spoke to him, saying she loved him, loved his body, loved being with him he was so kind so good, he just didn't know how good he was. Kneading the small of his back, his buttocks and thighs. Her fingers were slow, reverent, strong, curiously impersonal. When Warren turned over in the bed wanting to embrace her she held him off, insisting she continue to massage him, his shoulders, his chest where so much tightness was, his abdomen, belly, she was grave, taking at last his stiff hard penis in her hands and stroking slowly, insistently, watching Warren's face until unable to bear the sensation any longer he came to climax —an intensity of pleasure so extreme Warren thought it hardly his own, a property of his own.

* * *

Still she wasn't his fiancée exactly, she loved him she said but there were difficulties. Such as? Warren asked. She needed to see other people, she said. Not just other men but other people, people she'd known before she met him, did he understand?—mainly she didn't feel comfortable knowing somebody was thinking about her all the time expecting something of her she maybe couldn't give. Did Warren understand, she asked, and Warren said, smiling, yes he did.

As if he had any choice.

Then one day, unexpectedly—it was in mid-June—she surprised him by wanting to see a special showing of the documentary *Hiroshima* the Society for Non-Violent Action had arranged on the Penn campus: but during the sequences involving maimed and disfigured and dying children she whispered she felt faint, sick, couldn't take it—she'd have to wait for him out front. But a few days later she surprised him again, going with him to a meeting of SNVA where Gandhi's *satyagraha* strategy was discussed at exhaustive length; also his principle of *ahimsa,* or active goodwill; and his disapproval of *dhurna,* or willful obstruction. (There were participants in the peace movement who wanted to take fairly vigorous action one day soon: disrupt work on missile sites out west by blocking roads, station themselves close to testing grounds, that sort of thing.) Miriam went to a talk of Warren's sponsored by a local Presbyterian church—"A Pacifist Speaks Out Against War"—and was shocked at the hostile atmosphere he aroused. Warren had warned her but she hadn't believed him and for days afterward she spoke of the episode, marveling at his composure as he was interrupted, contradicted, heckled, even called names—*she'd* have been furious, telling those mouthy bastards what to do with themselves. But Warren had been so calm, so matter-of-fact, how was it possible? Warren said it was just part of his job.

After all, he told her, she did things he couldn't bring himself to do.

Such as? Miriam asked.

Modeling. Exhibiting her body.

Oh, *that,* Miriam said.

It was something, Warren said, choosing his words carefully, he couldn't do.

Yes he could, Miriam said. If he had to.

She puzzled over the idea of unilateral disarmament. Saying the words aloud as if testing their validity: "unilateral disarmament."

She meant to quarrel with Warren though she shied away from

quarreling with his friends. Stop manufacturing weapons and get rid of the ones we have—how was that going to work? With the Russians crazy as they were?

Warren was in no mood to quarrel, he wanted love.

He told her it was a little more complicated than that.

But Miriam was working herself up to being incensed. It was fascinating to watch her. "After Hitler for Christ's sake! After the Germans! Pearl Harbor! Those Nazi death camps! Guadalcanal where my brother Jackie got killed!"

She said, "You've got to be crazy taking something like that seriously for more than five minutes. I mean—in the year 1955! Letting whatever happens happen without defending yourself!"

Warren said, "Whatever happens is going to happen anyway."

She stared at him as if she'd never seen him before.

"I hate that kind of thinking," she said.

"I do too," Warren said quietly. "But there you are."

One hot July day Warren took Miriam to the Rodin Museum off the Parkway. She'd heard of Rodin, she said, he was a great sculptor wasn't he?—she knew about the museum too and had always wanted to see it.

Of the numerous works of art Warren had seen since moving to Philadelphia it was the bronze of Rodin's Balzac that most excited him—just to stand gazing at that bloated swaddled impossible figure was a deeply moving experience. How bizarre, the misshapen head! the misshapen face! In Rodin's Balzac's ungainly presence Warren Stevick was filled with an inexplicable passion and an inexplicable consolation.

He was anxious that Miriam feel something of what he felt and she did not disappoint him. Or disappointed him only slightly: staring at the Balzac, that short fat grotesque man in what appeared to be a dressing gown, the face but part human, the eyes empty, staring for a long moment with her white-rimmed sunglasses pushed atop her head, mouth working as if she wanted to smile but didn't dare—is this piece of sculpture meant to be so strange?—so ugly?—funny?—some kind of a peculiar joke?—housed in a stately mausoleum of granite, marble, polished floors, staid high ceilings. Museum guards looking impassively on. Visitors murmuring in hushed voices. Miriam was very pretty if rather slapdash today with her ashy blond hair in a ponytail falling halfway down her back, bangs combed to her eyebrows, blue pedal pushers and a snugly fitting polo shirt, lime green, and high-heeled straw sandals that made walking a little difficult. Her bare legs were lightly tanned, the calf muscles smooth and shiny. Straw purse slung negligently over her shoulder, hands on her hips. Miriam Brancher stood in front of Rodin's Balzac passing judgment.

Sighing, baffled, she said at last, "God, he really was something, wasn't he. . . ."

"Do you mean Rodin or Balzac?" Warren asked.

Miriam glanced around to see her lover watching her with his perpetual smile. That look of love, anxiety. Was he disappointed in her? One of his eyes sharply in focus, the other vague and magnified, dreamy, behind its thick lens. Miriam colored slightly; put on her glamorous sunglasses; said as if making a joke, " 'Rodin or Balzac'— they're the same to me—just names to me. Honey, how would I know?"

Miriam seemed eager to leave the museum—it was airless, not very cool—though afterward she told Warren she'd been very impressed; maybe they could go back again sometime. So that was Rodin: statues like "The Thinker" she'd known about for years, seen reproduced all over. They stopped for beer in a tavern on Sansom Street where the bartender knew Miriam, waved hello, stared unsmiling at Warren. Above the bar was a small television set turned to a quiz show. Miriam and Warren sat in a booth and Warren spoke excitedly of Rodin, of what Rodin's work seemed to mean, to him at least—striking so deep—yet it was immediately appealing too—on the surface—disturbing to the eye. He told her what he knew of Rodin's aesthetics. " 'Every form thrusting outward at its point of maximum tension.' " Most of Rodin's pieces, Warren said, had originally been much smaller, the mere stretch of the sculptor's hand: wasn't that remarkable? Miriam sipped her beer, watching Warren's face closely. In the dim beery fan-cooled air of the bar she looked refreshed, restored to confidence. Now her sunglasses lay on the table beside her pack of Chesterfields.

She said yes she'd liked the museum, it had given her something to think about except the damned police watching made her nervous, staring at her as if she didn't belong there, as if they were waiting for her to break something. Warren said, surprised, they weren't police, they were museum guards. "Sure," said Miriam. "But they acted like police."

A little later she said with a vehemence that surprised Warren too that people had to make something out of one another, didn't they? —or out of statues, paintings. "What do you mean?" Warren said. "I don't know what I *mean,*" Miriam said impatiently. "It's what I *said.*"

She had another beer. And another. Looking distracted, irritable. Her eyes drifting in the direction of the bar, the bartender, the noisy TV. Warren took her hand, hesitantly linking her fingers with his, and she didn't respond for a moment, as if she'd forgotten who they were, who they were supposed to be. He had invited her up to Port Oriskany to be introduced to his family but she'd said it wasn't the right time, she thought it might be better—wouldn't it?—for Warren to come with her to Litchfield first to meet Mikey. Then he'd know, she said. Then they'd both know. "But I know now, honey," Warren said, smiling. "Why do you doubt me?"

Now he brought up the subject again but Miriam didn't reply.

He said suddenly, "Look—if you and Brancher aren't legally divorced I can help you."

Miriam said evasively, "We *are* divorced, I told you. It's all settled."

"Do you have the papers?"

"Sure I have the papers."

"Can I see them sometime?"

"Sure, honey. Sometime," Miriam said.

6

The little bitch. He saw her there on the sidewalk with the others but he wanted to be sure. Maybe it wasn't Enid.

Early October, sunny blazing noon, Felix Stevick had an appointment in a half hour to look at property along the canal above Railroad Street, a derelict old building formerly a cannery warehouse he could buy up cheap, no mortgage—driving east along Nine Mile Road in no hurry, his car radio turned up high to Fats Domino, the window beside him rolled down despite the traffic stink. Felix was feeling fairly good if a little hung over from the night before, he'd had maybe five hours' sleep which wasn't bad, eyes just slightly bloodshot, puffy, he'd have to wear his dark-tinted glasses in any case because of the sun. Still he felt fairly good, he felt all right, a serious problem might be developing with his partner Sansom but it wouldn't be wise to think of that right now, he'd had only two cups of black coffee for breakfast, he was edgy, high-keyed, why upset himself thinking of Sansom's mysterious ways considering the day was so sky-blue and bright, a day when anything could happen. The boarded-up condemned old warehouse and the frontage on the canal along the stretch beyond Tuscarora looked so bombed-out even the Negroes wouldn't live there—five hundred yards of frontage on the canal or was it six hundred—all going for $25,000 cash plus the $5,000 and the $1,500 extras that wouldn't show on the contract filed downtown or in anybody's books: yes, it looked good, it was a sweet deal Felix couldn't afford to pass by.

His luck was erratic these days, he couldn't afford to play things safe.

Told himself that Al Sansom had his own deals, didn't he, his own secrets. Felix wasn't stealing Sansom's money. It wasn't Felix Stevick's fault either that people liked him without exactly knowing him and that he had contacts in the city going back in a sense before his birth—almost a quarter of a century after Karl Stevick had blown out his brains men still remembered him, spoke of him with a curious fondness. Now that he was long dead! During his lifetime Karl Stevick had had plenty of enemies.

In any case why the hell should Felix worry about Al Sansom? They were partners but they hadn't seen each other in almost two weeks: Sansom was in Miami Beach, Claudette said.

Love at first sight, Sansom had said once, eyeing Felix with his moist mock-wistful look. But that had been a long time ago too.

Driving along Nine Mile Road, Felix wasn't going to think of these things, he was feeling good, he'd had the Cadillac washed and polished the day before, now at noon sunshine flooded down brilliant and almost blinding off the hood and Felix noted people glancing in his direction, drivers in other cars he passed at his effortless speed five miles above the limit; then he happened to see two girls and some boys—high school students probably, East High was only a block or two away on Decker—and one of them looked like Enid: the chestnut-red hair falling past her shoulders, the slender narrow-hipped figure. Felix stared at the girl, narrowing his eyes, seeing her with her friends, classmates, laughing together, crowding one another on the sidewalk, very much together in their tight little knot. A flame ran over his brain, he couldn't bear it.

Felix slowed his car at once. In all the time they'd been lovers he had never happened to see Enid like this. By chance. On the street. Unaware of him. In a world that excluded him. Once or twice he'd seen her crossing Niagara Square in the direction of his apartment building, recognizing her coat or her hair or the way she walked, and he'd watched her hurrying with a half-resentful pleasure he couldn't have explained, knowing that that girl was coming to *him* she belonged to *him* he could do with her virtually anything he wanted because she understood that Felix Stevick was the only person in the world who really loved her. She was crazy for him, said she'd die for him, she'd die if he didn't love her, her sweet tight cunt opening only to him, her Uncle Felix she adored. And the rest of her life didn't exist. Wasn't important. If he'd been asked, Felix would have said she was seventeen years old, his pretty niece Enid, and a high school senior with friends probably, classmates, interests he couldn't guess, but none of that was real to him, it had no significance.

He stared. Drew up close behind them. It *was* Enid—the little bitch—in plain daylight like that on Nine Mile Road swinging her ass in a black pleated skirt that fell to mid-calf and a fleshy-pink cardigan sweater worn backward and buttoned up tight to the nape of the neck in the silly teenage style of the day, white socks like they all wore, loafers. Felix saw with loathing those three boys, one of them hanging over Enid, six feet tall, sandy hair in a crew cut, but would the bastard dare touch her with Felix watching?—all of them talking together, laughing, the ease of it was intolerable, Enid Stevick with her friends whom Felix Stevick didn't know, as strange to him as if he'd never seen her before.

The smart thing to do was let it go, just let it go for Christ's sake, Felix: after all he had an appointment on the other side of the canal, a twenty-minute drive. But his heart was beating powerfully, the blood was hot in his face.

The sky-blue day opening up like a fracture in Felix Stevick's skull, letting in too much light.

He braked at the curb and tapped the horn impatiently, calling out her name, and all of them looked around at once startled—the first thing they saw was the car, and the car was enormous, gleaming, it looked good so creamy-pale and polished, like a million dollars—then Enid recognized him and came over breathless to lean in the window, trying to smile, trying not to show the apprehension she felt. Felix told her to get in the car.

"Get in? Now? But I can't," Enid said.

"I said get in," Felix said.

"I don't have time. It's my lunch hour. I only have until a quarter to one, we were going up the street to this place—"

"I'll take you to lunch, Enid," Felix said. "Just get in the car."

Still she leaned in the window staring at him, trying to smile at him, the whites of her eyes unnaturally white, Felix thought—maybe with knowledge of him. Maybe she saw something in his face he didn't know was there.

"I can't," she whispered, frightened. "Please. Really. I can't right now."

"Just get in," Felix said. He switched off the radio so they wouldn't misunderstand each other. "I'll take you to lunch. I'll get you back to school on time. Tell your friends to go on without you."

Enid's classmates were standing a short distance away staring at them. Not knowing what to make of it probably: Enid Stevick leaning in the window of a big cream-colored Cadillac Eldorado talking with a youngish man in sunglasses.

"I said—tell them to go on without you," Felix repeated.

Enid froze for another precarious moment risking Felix's anger, then she turned to wave them on. She was all right, she called out, it was just her uncle, she said lightly, she'd see them back at school. The tall boy with the crew cut called out something Felix couldn't hear and Enid said again she was all right, she was going to go to lunch with her uncle. Felix thought how beautiful it would be to smash in the boy's face, break the nose in one clean blow. Enid slid into the car beside him and slammed the door, a little out of breath, smelling, Felix thought, of something sweet and panicky. She'd be sweating inside her clothes just as he was.

But she looked good, Felix thought. And she knew it.

Leaning over to kiss him lightly on the cheek—a niece's kiss chaste and hurried. She was self-conscious, rattled. The pupils of her eyes dilated, the whites bluish-white. Licking her lips. That girlish pleated skirt but the sweater buttoned up the back provocative and a little sluttish showing her small hard breasts no bigger than her own clenched fist. Felix pressed his foot down hard on the gas pedal, the Caddie's tires squealed faintly as he pulled away from the curb. In the rearview mirror Enid's friends stared after them, left behind on the sidewalk, and Felix told himself he wasn't going to be upset thinking of them, why the hell should he.

"Surprised to see me?" Felix asked with his easy smile.

"Yes," Enid said. "I mean no. I mean—yes."

"Nice day, isn't it?"

Enid laughed breathlessly, settling in beside him, squinting out at the sky as if to check: was he teasing or not.

"It was a little cold this morning," she said, smoothing some pleats across her knee. He saw that her fingernails were polished—a pink so light and translucent it was almost invisible. "Then it got warmer. It could almost be like summer again," she said in a nervous little rush as if she sensed Felix wasn't paying attention to her words.

East along Nine Mile in the direction of the Lakeshore Drive and Kilbirnie Park and Felix was driving no more than ten miles above the speed limit, snaking his way in and out of traffic, changing lanes as he approached the busy intersection at Stupp Boulevard where traffic grew dense, combative. He changed lanes often, adroitly switching from left to right, right to left, outside lane, middle lane, inner lane for a few hundred feet, then swiftly into the middle lane and out again, using his horn when he was forced to and swinging out not quite impatiently behind slow-moving vehicles, he wasn't impatient and he wasn't angry, just the slightest edge to his nerves but really he liked that edge when he was driving in serious traffic, you needed it to make your brain work faster than the next guy's. Felix was a good driver when he was in a good mood and wasn't he in a good mood now?—trusting to instinct to tell him where he was going, what he was going to do.

"Sorry to miss lunch with your friends?" Felix asked.

"No." Enid paused, considering. "I see them all the time."

She settled in beside him as if nothing was wrong, even turned on the radio not too loud—Kitty Kallen singing "Little Things Mean a Lot"—and nothing *was* wrong so far as Felix was concerned. The strain between them was mainly surprise, excitement, as if it might be years ago and Felix had just happened to stop to take her with him maybe out of the city north of the city along the lake to one or another of those motels where he'd been so crazy about her and being alone with her was terrifying because he always thought he might injure her, what if she began hemorrhaging and couldn't stop, then afterward the shame, the public exposure, his pride in his life crumpled like one of those cheap lightweight aluminum beer cans crumpled when you step down on it hard. At a traffic light he glanced at her, seeing she was wearing pierced earrings but not ones he remembered having bought her—ceramic in design, dusky pink like seashells mimicking the delicate pink whorls of her ear. (Back in June in a splurge of loving good feeling after one of their driving lessons and after Felix had cleaned up on the Basilio-De Marco fight he'd taken her to Renwick's Jewelers downtown and paid for her to have her ears pierced properly and bought her a dozen pairs of earrings—Enid had asked how she could safely explain all this to her parents and Felix had said indifferently, Tell them anything you want.) But the earrings were attractive. Her exposed ears attractive. Those long dark lashes, the curve of her eyebrows, down on her upper lip, soft near-invisible down on her cheeks. . . . Sure she looked good and she must know it, high school kids hanging over her, probably men staring after her in the street and she'd watch them shyly slantwise as she watched Felix, as if even now, after so much time, she couldn't quite bear to look at him head-on.

"Is something wrong?" Felix asked.

"Nothing," said Enid. "Nothing's wrong."

"You don't seem to want to look at me."

She laughed breathlessly, baring her teeth. Her skin warm, flushed. Still she sat looking rather stiffly ahead so in a playful gesture Felix gripped her chin between his thumb and forefinger and turned her head toward him and still she smiled, retained her smile, though he could see she was frightened. "That hurts," she said. "Don't."

"Don't provoke me."

"I'm not provoking you."

"I'm the judge of that, aren't I," Felix said.

The traffic light changed to green; he drove on, his blood beating, pleasantly heated.

Now north along wide windy dirty Stubb Boulevard then eastward again along a residential street opening onto Lakeshore Drive: so that was where Felix was headed.

What did Enid see, what did she ever see, looking at him in love? Felix wondered. Christ, he'd wondered often enough, in the beginning especially: those wide-spaced beautiful eyes, dark, luminous, watchful, with a dampness to them, a look of hurt. Brimming he could see with love but love for what purpose? for whom? Sometimes it came upon him with an almost visceral force, a terrible hunger—to see himself by way of her. Seeing Felix Stevick through her he might understand the secret of his life otherwise hidden from him, like the surprise of glancing up in Vince's office to see a framed photograph of himself taken years ago, Felix good-looking and boyish in his boxing trunks, his gloved hands raised, vain self-conscious smile, not a crease or a wrinkle in his forehead and no facial scars either. But it had to happen by chance, he had to be surprised, unprepared. Maybe it was like the way they said Karl Stevick had studied his thinning face in a hand mirror those final weeks in the hospital, a dying man staring at himself without any special bitterness, just interest: so this is it? But what *is* it?

Now they were on Lakeshore Drive headed north and the immense lake to their right opened out, a splendid enamel blue just slightly cracked, frothy with little gusts of wind. The sky was unusually clear. The October sunshine gave a hard sharp edge to things. Close in on the lake were several sailboats and in the distance two freighters moved slowly toward each other as if on a collision course, their gray-white smoke rising lazily, hooking into the air, then dissolving. Felix felt drawn to the lake today though the whitish sunshine hurt his eyes. To his annoyance Enid was turning the radio dial restlessly: a snatch of news—Ike continues to recover "steadily" from his heart attack, Khrushchev in Warsaw believed on a "secret" mission—then a deep masculine voice intoning gravelly singsong repetitive words— *Oh, happy day, oh, happy day-ay*—and Felix said, "Turn that damn thing off, will you?"

Enid quickly switched off the dial. It was a song that grated against her nerves too.

After a moment she went on to say in a slow deliberate voice that she was happy to see him, she'd missed him pretty badly, only she'd been surprised back there on Nine Mile and she *was* worried about getting back to school on time. . . . She had a chemistry quiz fifth period and for a project in English class she had assembled a play for voices out of some poems of Robert Frost's and her teacher Mr. Tate who was also the drama coach thought maybe they could use it for a real production later in the year and Enid was involved and they were getting together during her sixth-period study hall. . . . And today was Wednesday, she had to go with Valerie and Marsha and some others to that children's home on Kincross, had she told Felix about it?—she thought she had but probably he didn't remember. . . .

Her voice trailed off. Felix said nothing. He was aware of her shallow quickened breath, her hand small and motionless on the seat close beside his knee should he want to give it a belated squeeze in greeting, but Felix didn't appear to be interested, he hadn't telephoned her since sometime in mid-September because he'd been too busy, his life becoming ever more complicated and demanding, exciting at times and at other times vomit-weary like the moments he'd had in a number of his fights where he was too exhausted to lift his gloves, too exhausted to take advantage of his opponent's exhaustion and his vision spun and blurred with the knowledge he had a long way to go, he'd come an excruciating distance and he had a long way to go and maybe wouldn't make it. But there was an old unresolved disagreement between them too, primarily on Felix's part, and he liked nursing it, he liked being just a little angry with Enid, it made him feel less guilty fucking her: what he might do might be part of her punishment.

The disagreement went back to midsummer when Enid's mother suddenly changed her mind about letting Enid work up at the lake at the Villa Rideau where Felix had arranged for her to be a waitress in the big elegant dining room with the French doors overlooking the lake; out of nowhere Hannah said she didn't want Enid away from home for so long and she didn't want her mingling with who knows what kinds of people. Enid protested bitterly and Felix himself dropped by at the Stevicks' to explain to Hannah that most of the waitresses at the hotel—in fact at Shoal Lake generally—were high school and college girls, they lived together in dormitories but if Enid didn't want to live in a dormitory Felix could certainly find other accommodations for her. He'd be in and out of Shoal Lake over the summer, he could keep an eye on her, also the O'Banans would be there in August; yes, Hannah said slowly, seeming to agree, maybe flattered by Felix's presence, but as soon as he left she reverted stubbornly to saying she didn't want Enid away for so many weeks, she didn't want her turning out like Lizzie. And Lizzie hadn't even been *away* until she moved out!

So Felix thought the hell with it, why should he give a damn, he cut off Enid's explanations, wouldn't listen to her tearful apologies, knowing it was hardly her fault but blaming her anyway for Hannah's stubbornness or maybe it was Hannah's peasant shrewdness; Lyle went along with the plans but Hannah stood her ground and that was that. And secretly Felix felt some relief because having Enid at the lake and being responsible for her, having to deal with other people observing them, wasn't maybe such a good idea after all.

Still, he seemed to blame Enid for the situation and she seemed to accept the blame and there was a certain stiffness between them even after the passage of months.

As if he only now thought of it Felix asked casually, "Who were they?—those boys."

"Just boys from school," Enid said.

"You were all getting along pretty well," Felix said.

He was speaking quietly but Enid said, "—Just boys in my class."

"That one with the crew cut—what's his name?"

"Who? Peter?"

"Peter what?"

"It doesn't matter what his name is."

"You know his name, don't you?"

"Of course I know his name, I've gone to school with him since sixth grade," Enid said. "It's Venner."

"Peter Venner," Felix said as if testing the syllables. "Is he somebody you like? I mean—you like especially?"

"No. We're just friends."

"What would you be, then, if you weren't just friends?"

Enid laughed angrily. But she was frightened: Felix could tell.

"I don't understand that question, Felix," she said.

"I'm asking—what would you and that kid be if you weren't 'just friends'? You were the one who said it that way—'just friends,' " Felix said. Suddenly his head had begun to ache behind his eyes, the hot harsh light reflected off the Caddie's hood pierced him like a blade. "You were the one to say it, sweetheart. Not me."

Enid was smoothing out the pleats in her skirt again, hunched a little against him. When she didn't reply he repeated, keeping his voice steady, "You were the one to put it that way—'just friends.' But the two of you looked like more than friends to me."

Enid said faintly, "No."

"What?"

"*No.*"

Felix was headed up the drive keeping a good steady speed of 40 miles an hour though the speed limit was 25, weaving in and out of slower-moving traffic, handling his big car effortlessly as in a dream. He wasn't angry at Enid but he wasn't feeling quite himself—the black coffee thrumming his nerves, leftover sensations from the night before when he'd had too many martinis—losing $600 playing poker with Vince and Freddy and the others but Felix was an amiable loser, he'd always been a sweet loser in small things, his friends loved him for keeping his rage swallowed down—now he was feeling elated and annoyed both but still he could play it as a joke if Enid would fall in with it, if she didn't try to lie to him, sitting on the far side of the seat from him looking out the window. He smelled her panic, that special heady sweetness, her hair, her underarms, the moist kinky curly hair between her legs. It was as if a part of Felix Stevick himself was pulling off from him trying to deceive him, he couldn't bear it. "What about the others?" he heard himself asking. "You all looked like a lot more than friends to me."

"That was Valerie, the girl was Valerie Sherman my friend Valerie," Enid said quickly. "She's my closest friend now . . . she takes piano lessons too but not from Mr. Lesnovich."

"Is that kid your boyfriend? Peter Venner?" Felix said.

"No."

"Do you go out with him?"

"No."

"Do you see him after school? Around school? Or when?" Felix asked. He was looking straight ahead, guiding the car effortlessly. Passing the intersection with Twelve Mile Road, the traffic light changing from red to green as he sped through. "Do you go out with any of the others? What do you do with them? Things I taught you? Do you? Is that what you do? Is that why they like you, those little bastards? Are you fucking around with them?"

Enid laughed nervously. "No. You know that."

"I know it," Felix said. "But I'm asking you."

Enid didn't reply.

"I know it," Felix said. "And you'd better know it too. I'll kill anybody who fucks around with you."

Again Enid laughed nervously. She made a motion as if to touch him but thought better of it.

No, they weren't headed for Kilbirnie Park which was south on the drive, they were headed maybe for Roosevelt Park, the acres of woodland along the lake stretching from the Port Oriskany city limits up into the suburb of Deerfield. Felix said, "I'm not angry, Enid, but I don't like it." He said, "You know I love you, honey, don't you?—I just don't like it." After a pause he went on, still speaking in a low reasonable voice, "If I catch you fucking around with anybody I'll kill whoever it is—you think I won't?—I love you, Enid, and I'm not going to share you with any high school punks and fuck-offs like a piece of meat, is that what you want to be?—look at me, is that what you want to be?"

Enid had begun to cry.

"I'll kill whoever it is," Felix said. "I'll kill you both."

He didn't mean it but he said it, the words came unbidden, easy, he wasn't really angry but it infuriated him that Enid held herself so stiff, so frightened, unwilling even to look at him, why didn't she settle in beside him, lean her head against his shoulder, why didn't she stroke his hair and kiss him and be his sweetheart as she'd done many times, she could bury her damp face in his neck, he'd have to get her a little drunk sometime soon he missed her twining her arms around

him silly and giggly whispering I love you I love love love you, what
he wanted to do was sit her on his lap her thighs open to him gripping
him at the waist he was crazy to fuck her in that position he could
knead her ass he could thrust himself far up inside her the sweetest
kind of loving they did sometimes in the car then at a certain point
neither could move they held themselves still fearful of moving of
ending it so abruptly Felix's mind gone everything gone into sensation
thrumming his nerves like being punched really hard on the point of
the chin so you're beyond pain there isn't any pain it's all nerves the
nerve in the chin paralyzed and the nerves running down that side of
the body paralyzed everything pins and needles the knee, the foot,
everything gone dead but it felt sweet it didn't feel like pain you
couldn't even remember what pain was.

Enid whispered, "I hate you. I *hate* you."

Though afterward Felix would remember clearly seeing her hand
on the door handle, half seeing it in the corner of his eye, what she
did took him completely by surprise—when he stopped at a red light
she opened the door, swung the heavy door open, and got out before
he could grab hold of her; she ran blind and blundering through two
lanes of cars to the sidewalk. And Felix Stevick in his astonishment had
a choice of driving on ahead and maneuvering his car to the curb or
leaving his car where it was in the middle of the street and running
after her, but already he'd made his decision, he switched off the
ignition and took the keys and ran after her, catching her halfway
down the block—as if she could outrun him!—slinging his arm around
her, catching her hard across the midriff as she struggled with him,
swearing and sobbing she hated him he was crazy she hated hated him,
and Felix told her he'd kill her if she ever tried a trick like that again,
the two of them breathless on the sidewalk in what appeared to be a
residential neighborhood—yes, it was Deerfield, large brick houses
set back from the street, well-tended lawns, graveled driveways, the
whitish October sun giving a hard edge to the trees, the shrubbery—
Felix's head was pounding now he saw where Enid had been going
a bus stop halfway down the block where a bus was easing away from
the curb, and Felix gripped Enid tight, waiting, and sure enough the
driver braked the bus to a stop, opened his door, and called out,
"What's going on there? What's happening?" and at each of the
windows a face strangers' faces all those eyes turned upon Felix Stevick and the sobbing girl still struggling weakly against him, trying to
push him away with her elbows. Felix shouted back, "Mind your own
business!" The driver left his seat and leaned out the door trying to

look courageous—fat gut inside the uniform, beefy jowls, frightened eyes he was maybe fifty years old and Felix could kill him and they both knew it—"Miss? Do you need help?" he asked and Enid shook her head no, she said no she was all right, hiding her face, she was all right, she said, and the bus driver hadn't any choice but to believe her, staring out at the two of them as the bus passengers were staring, and Felix had to hold down his rage walking Enid back to his car where he'd left it goddamn it in the middle of Lakeshore Drive, Enid was going to pay for this Enid was going to pay for this for a long time though she was saying in a childlike voice she was sorry, she was sorry, she loved him, why did he want to hurt her? and Felix said, surprised, "Honey, I'd never hurt *you*."

So he drove up to Roosevelt Park where at the end of a service drive in the woods beyond the deserted playing fields they made love in the front seat of Felix's car exactly as he'd wanted, there wasn't much time but then it was so sweet they lost track of time and Enid did grip him hard as he'd wanted Enid did clutch at him her arms around his neck kissing him in a trance of pleasure I love you Felix I love love love you till he couldn't bear it.

7

Early in the summer a two-man construction crew came with a bull-dozer to tear out the rotted old backyard fence by the alley behind 118 East Clinton and with half the neighborhood looking on dug an enormous hole in the yard close by the Stevicks' back porch!—chil-dren ran wild with excitement dangerously close to the bulldozer, neighbors on both sides watched impassively. There was Lyle Stevick himself in clean white shirt and necktie, the bald dome of his skull gleaming a deep embarrassed pink, supervising the initial step in the construction of the first underground bomb shelter on East Clinton Street, curtly answering questions about the shelter which was to be of course a private shelter for himself and his family to contain supplies and provisions for nine persons (six adults, three children) for a sixty-day period, and yes it was to be built according to the most recent CD guidelines, yes he'd applied for the proper building permit from City Hall he had it right here in his pocket should anyone be curious. No he didn't really care to disclose the estimated price of the shelter though it was not, he said quietly, going to be one of those "bargain" $2,350 shelter kits advertised in the newspapers that, when the bomb is dropped, would turn into an oven and roast all occupants the way people had been roasted during the firebombing of Dresden hiding out in their tragically inadequate cellars and shelters.

No he certainly didn't want to predict any atomic war with the Russians no matter what Dulles was saying these days, and J. Edgar Hoover!—he wasn't by temperament a doomsayer, he just believed it wisest to prepare for the worst while hoping it would never come about.

Yes the shelter would be locked of course. Yes he had the key.

Yes it would be private: private property.

Private property the way a man's house and car are his private property.

Did he intend to stock firearms in the shelter to keep people from breaking in in time of emergency?—like that retired investment broker interviewed in *Life* with a .22 rifle issued to each member of his family and that schoolteacher the other night so riled up on the Jack Parr Show saying he'd been denied a permit for a machine gun for his shelter. This was a tricky question, Lyle Stevick understood, so first he said "No," then he said "Yes—perhaps," then he said "Hannah and I haven't yet decided." To neighbors with whom he was on fairly amiable speaking terms he confessed that he disliked firearms, he wasn't by nature a bellicose man, still he was hardly in sympathy with pacifism—how would those fool pacifists have fared against Hitler? So he hadn't decided. He didn't know. Maybe just having a key and a strong lock would be enough. He'd have a periscope too. He was looking on the bright side of things generally. He *wasn't* a doomsayer, no salesman is a doomsayer!

Still: that theologian for the Catholic Church, what's his name, written up in *Time* the other week—"bomb shelter ethics"—a Jesuit saying that a man's first duty is to protect his family, so just as he would have to shoot someone trying to break into his house he'd have to shoot someone trying to break into his bomb shelter, wouldn't he?

Then there was the news these days worsening all the time: Secretary of State Dulles issuing his warnings about U.S. military preparation vis-à-vis the Soviets' and Defense Secretary Wilson demanding $35.5 billion for the Pentagon for 1957, the big project being the production of guided missiles, what they were calling the "ultimate weapon," an intercontinental ballistic missile with a nuclear bomb as a warhead!—diabolical.

"There you are. The way the world is. A man has to be realistic," Lyle Stevick said.

By 6 P.M. the men from Poole's Construction had finished digging the hole and had carried away in a dump truck what looked like tons of moist clayey earth so neighborhood interest in the Stevicks' back yard rapidly diminished. Mr. Stevick chased off the last of the rowdy children and went inside to get an ale. Mrs. Stevick was preparing supper in the kitchen: she'd watched out the window for a while but hadn't cared to come outside, she disliked so many nosey neighbors, she said, but primarily her attitude toward the shelter was unsettled—she resented Lyle's spending so much when they could use the money elsewhere and now this meant they were stuck at 118 East Clinton forever, didn't it?—with the neighborhood going downhill around them, a colored family moving into a duplex right on the corner of Packer.

Lyle Stevick felt both weary and exhilarated. He said, "Christ, they're already asking if we intend to keep guns in the shelter!" Mrs. Stevick looked at him blankly. "You know—to keep out intruders," he said. "In time of war." Mrs. Stevick went on with her work, frying chopped-up onions in a big iron skillet, stirring them patiently with a fork. "I told them I didn't know," Mr. Stevick said uneasily. "I told them I'd talk it over with my family. . . . It isn't anything I want to do."

"No," Mrs. Stevick said in a voice so flat and bemused as to be beyond irony. "But you will."

For much of the summer of 1955 Lyle Stevick's sole occupation apart from his furniture store was the construction of the bomb shelter following the precise requirements of his plans: no false economies here, no bargain-rate supplies. With the help of an old friend who worked at Ingersoll-Rand he poured the concrete floor and walls, insisting that the walls be no less than two feet thick though they were to be protected by solid earth on all sides. With the help of another old friend who had a modest carpentry shop in the neighborhood he put in various installations—the generator, the chemical toilet, the water tank, the storage shelves, the three pairs of bunk beds—and constructed the roof/ceiling which was of course heavily insulated and would be covered with four feet of earth when set permanently in place. (The ceiling was made of layers of asbestos siding that glittered a faint iridescent-gray like starlight seen through a scrim of mist.)

From a bomb shelter supply company in Albany came a Sterno stove, a first-aid kit, a three-way portable radio, a radiation detector and radiation charts, "protective apparel" suits for both adults and children looking hardly more exotic than undersea diving suits. From Stevick's Furniture a few household items—Formica-topped kitchen table and chairs, two lamps, a woolly lime-green afghan carpet. A pick and shovel for digging out after a blast if the shelter happened to be covered with rubble and debris. And various supplies of a domestic sort—canned goods, chinaware, cutlery, cooking utensils, soap, blankets, towels, board games (Monopoly, Parcheesi, checkers), a random selection of Mr. Stevick's books including the tragedies of Shakespeare, *Don Quixote,* Thucydides, Aristotle, *Gulliver's Travels,* and the Durants' *Story of Philosophy.* Mr. Stevick did all the work himself since neither Hannah nor Enid took much interest in the shelter but he supposed this was all for the best—he could then be absolutely certain things had been done right. After the bomb fell there would be no time to rectify careless mistakes.

The most ingenious feature of the shelter, he thought, was its hatchway, which resembled that of a submarine and which was equipped with a ladder that opened to a length of five feet. Also its periscope: he'd never had the curious experience of looking through a periscope before. After the roof was set in place and covered with soil Mr. Stevick often went down into the shelter to experiment with the periscope, turning it slowly around, fascinated by the way the wire-protected lens picked up familiar sights—the back porch and windows of the house, Mrs. Stevick's drooping clothesline—and distorted them so that they were hardly recognizable. There was an air of eerie dreamlike beauty to these fugitive visions pressed close against his eye so that he did not always find it a melancholy prospect to imagine that the bomb had already fallen and that he was safely underground, the hatch shut tight and locked, and all the world beyond contaminated with radiation poisoning.

Because the 20- by 15-foot shelter was so jammed with things, little wall space remained open but what there was Mr. Stevick gradually covered with strips of shiny pale paper. First some Masonite over the rough concrete, then the paper—aluminum foil found around the house or even on the sidewalk or in the gutter, a sheet of used Christmas wrapping paper from Mrs. Stevick's supply. He didn't know why he was decorating the shelter in so haphazard and eccentric a fashion but he liked the quiet luminous effect—it was festive yet it soothed his nerves when his nerves needed soothing, reminded him of something but he couldn't remember what except to know it wasn't terrifying any longer, the white-glaring walls now contained and snug beneath the protective layer of earth.

It was Mr. Stevick's practice to check out the shelter every day before supper. Sometimes he lay on one of the lower bunks with only a single 100-watt light burning, his arms behind his head, his eyes half closed, seeing the silver-papered walls as if they weren't walls at all but a mysterious part of his own soul. He had done it!—he was here. If he played the three-way radio and lay listening to it not even the most startling news could upset him any longer. Once he was awakened not knowing he had been asleep—he couldn't have been down in the shelter for more than ten minutes—to hear the brisk vehement voice of J. Edgar Hoover himself filling the space. Where once Mr. Stevick would have been moved to anger or grief or even despair he was now only mildly amused: that day Hoover had delivered a speech charging that Communists in the United States had launched a new "campaign of vituperation" to deprive law enforcement officers of much of their power. Reds do their most destructive work through pseudo-liberals, Hoover said.

But Lyle Stevick just smiled a small weary smile. He wasn't a pseudo-liberal any longer. He wasn't anything J. Edgar Hoover of the Federal Bureau of Investigation could have named.

Some weeks ago Senator Joseph McCarthy, his old enemy, had been formally "censured" by his fellow senators but Mr. Stevick had not greatly cared about that either. It was too late, wasn't it—too late to undo the damage McCarthy had done. And now Hoover meant to begin it all again! Still, Mr. Stevick couldn't feel much genuine anger. *He* was safe.

When at last Enid agreed to visit the shelter in her father's company it was the silver-papered walls she remarked on—*"That's* pretty, Daddy, what is it?—not regular wallpaper?"—in a light nervous voice as if she couldn't think of a single other thing to say. Except for Neal O'Banan and his rowdy little boys no one in the family was eager to visit the shelter: not Mrs. Stevick, who worried that the ladder was "too steep," not Geraldine, who was pregnant again and having a hard time with the heat of August and much of September, not Lizzie, who kept promising and promising to drop by soon maybe for Sunday dinner—but then her visits were always canceled at the last minute for reasons never satisfactorily explained.

But Enid came. Enid obliged her father. One day after school, still in her pretty tartan skirt and high-collared white cotton blouse, a tiny gold pendant on a chain around her neck, tiny gold studs in her ears. Climbing down carefully into the underground space Enid blinked at the brightness of the lights (Mr. Stevick had switched them all on) as if she had expected something quite different. While her father spoke at length, explaining various aspects of the shelter, Enid stood stiffly crouched, her forehead furrowed, sniffing the musty air as if she thought it might be poisoned and frowning into the corners of the room as if she feared spiders or mice. Mr. Stevick tried not to be annoyed. He was annoyed by Enid so often lately. Now seventeen years old and a senior in high school, the last of his children—so he calmly considered her—making plans for the future that excluded him, she'd become touchy and distant and superior, staring without comment, even now as in his pride he pointed out certain things—the radiation detector, the fold-out radiation chart with its elaborate up-to-the-minute graphs and data, the three-way radio with its special equipment. To demonstrate the radio Mr. Stevick switched it on. There was an outburst of static followed by a loud percussive downbeat—Bill Haley and the Comets launching into their big hit "Rock Around the Clock"—and Mr. Stevick angrily cut the racket dead. In time of emergency, he told Enid, only the Port Oriskany civil defense station would be operating.

Enid laughed nervously but what was the joke? Smoothing down the hairs on her arms as if she had goose pimples.

She admired the wallpaper. And was happy to see, she said, the shelf of Mr. Stevick's books. And the games—it would be good to have games to play, if they were stuck down here for very long. But her voice was lame, faint. She looked frightened. Kept swallowing and brushing her hair out of her eyes in the way she'd done for months but her father wasn't going to lose his temper with her if he could help it.

With just a little difficulty he opened the metal door of the chemical toilet and Enid stared inside without comment. He opened the door to the storage closet, pointing out the shelves of Campbell's soups, all the children's favorites—alphabet vegetable, chicken noodle, cream of tomato, beef barley; how cheerily familiar, how comforting, the red and white labels in this strange space!—the tight-stacked rows of canned tunafish, salmon, mackerel, deviled ham. Also canned vegetables of every kind. Jams, jellies. Bottles of fruit juice. The shelves were three feet deep reaching back into the darkness as if into the earth itself. "We're prepared for at least sixty days," Mr. Stevick said. On the bottom shelf were three dozen gallons of fresh spring water, two dozen twelve-ounce bottles of Coca-Cola, giant economy-size boxes of potato chips. And several cans of Planter's peanuts—one of Mr. Stevick's favorite snacks. Enid laughed again. "It's like a picnic!" she said.

"It won't be a picnic," Mr. Stevick said, reproving, "but it doesn't have to be grim either. In fact it can be anything we make it."

He went on to lecture her in specifics—things he'd maybe already told her and Hannah at mealtimes but it was good for her to be told again. This particular model of family shelter promised a protection factor of 1,000; did Enid know what 1,000 meant?—no? —it meant that for individuals remaining inside constantly for a sixty-day period the radiation dosage would be only 45 roentgens—a negligible amount—assuming a nuclear explosion of approximately 200 megatons in the northeastern United States. And if a *full year* of constant occupancy was required the dosage would only increase to 50 roentgens. "I hope you can appreciate how remarkable that is," Mr. Stevick said.

Enid didn't answer at first. She was crouched examining the radiation detector.

"Yes," she said finally. "It's remarkable."

He saw that she wasn't going to argue with him any longer, thank God, she'd gotten past that stage: tension between them, and Hannah staying clear, and several times that summer they'd quarreled at mealtimes and Enid had rushed from the table hot-eyed and sullen having been lambasted by her father for her ignorance and for daring to challenge him in his area of expertise. How could she offer any opinion about the bomb shelter when she knew so little?—when she hadn't any facts with which to counter his? She had asked impertinently one evening how any sane person could stay for six days underground let alone sixty when there'd be nothing to live for afterward! and what about going crazy down there jammed in with other people it didn't matter if it was your own family or whatever, *she'd* go crazy just thinking about it!—and Mr. Stevick had calmly commanded her to leave the table, just to get out of his sight.

For years he hadn't struck any of his children, of course. But at such times he came dangerously close to striking his youngest daughter.

Much of the summer Enid hadn't been on comfortable terms with either of the Stevicks. Short-tempered, ironic, with but the merest pretense of being her usual sweet agreeable self, quick to burst into tears at the slightest provocation—Hannah's sister Ingrid kept saying that Enid was "going through a phase" but Mr. Stevick wondered if it might not be something more permanent. First there was the drawn-out bitter quarrel about the job at the Villa Rideau Felix had arranged for her she'd wanted so badly, she threatened to leave home to go up to Shoal Lake by herself to ask Felix if she could live with him, then she'd changed her mind abruptly and got a job with one of her girlfriends at the Tastee-Freez on West Grand but both girls were forced to quit by August first, the working conditions were so awful, some of the male customers so insulting, and worst of all the manager was too familiar with his girl employees. Lately too her lessons with Mr. Lesnovich seemed to give her anguish, she loved the piano, she said, but sometimes in Mr. Stevick's opinion just going to the piano seemed to frighten her, why were things so important for her—as they'd been for Warren?—and not for the other children so far as he knew. Hour after hour working on a little rondo of Mozart's that wouldn't take five minutes to play for Mr. Lesnovich but poor Enid couldn't get it right or maybe she wanted to get it perfect and her father was there to tell her she never would: that was the human lot. He felt sorry for her but he was damned annoyed too. Enid sitting stone-still at the piano not even playing sometimes just sitting there staring at the much-annotated sheet of music in front of her, tears welling in her eyes, and Hannah was beginning to threaten her, saying maybe those piano lessons should stop if they were making Enid so unhappy. What was the point of them anyway: did she really think she was good enough to go to the Westcott School in Rochester?—did she really think she was good enough to teach piano, like Mr. Lesnovich himself?

"She'll only get married anyway," Mrs. Stevick said in so neutral a voice it was impossible to determine whether she thought this a good thing or a bad thing; or maybe it *was* neutral.

Still, Enid was planning to apply to various colleges and universities in the state and of course to the teachers' college in the city—if she won a New York State Regents scholarship as her teachers seemed to think she should, a number of the schools would match the scholarship or even complement her tuition and Felix had told Lyle he'd be happy to help them out if they needed help. But Mr. Stevick hadn't said yes or no. He was ambivalent about Enid's leaving home. Maybe the local college would be all right (though it was only mediocre academically), at least Enid could continue living at home—she'd be his girl his Enid Maria for a while longer. Even so he didn't really want his brother helping out financially because Felix had already lent or given them so much money it was embarrassing, Lyle Stevick had his pride, after all *he* was a breadwinner too. (He had placed that secret bet on Carmen Basilio back in June as Felix had suggested, going to a bookmaker who operated out of a tobacco shop on Union Street, and by Jesus he'd made a cool $4,500 on a $1,500 investment!—but he was too prudent to try again, he knew not to press his luck further. According to family rumor Felix had made maybe $25,000 on that fight but then he'd lost as much or more on another fight shortly afterward—he'd bet on the twenty-six-year-old Bobo Olson to win over the light-heavyweight champion Archie Moore, who was an astounding thirty-eight years old and still going strong. Somehow Moore had knocked out Olson in three rounds! Felix had told Lyle to bet on Olson since the odds were good and Lyle craftily hadn't bet a dime, then afterward Felix telephoned to apologize for giving him a poor tip and Lyle Stevick said only, rather coolly, "We all make mistakes sometimes, Felix.")

"Enid, is something wrong?" Mr. Stevick asked sharply.

She hadn't been paying attention. He could tell. Standing leaning her forehead against one of the ladder's rungs as if she felt faint or dizzy. She was breathing in what fresh air wafted thinly down from the open hatchway and the pale glimmering sky above and at first he didn't think she had heard. Then she said, "Nothing is wrong," in a small voice. Then without looking at him she said, "Daddy, I don't think I can make it."

"What do you mean?"

She just stood there turned from him, holding the ladder with both hands and pressing her forehead against one of the rungs, and for a long painful moment neither spoke. Lyle Stevick felt a touch of fear. Didn't think she could make it! What kind of extravagant talk was that?

"Honey, what do you mean?" he asked gently. He was making an effort to stay patient, even lay a hand tentatively on Enid's shoulder, knowing she might flinch just slightly at his touch—as she did. "Are you worried about an atomic war? Is that it? But the point of this is

329

that we'd be ready, don't you see, honey? Your old man will take care of you as he always has—right?"

Was she crying?—still turned away from him risking his anger. He could hear her quick shallow breath, he could smell something sweet and despairing loosed from her hair, poor girl, poor Enid Maria, he was frightened for her but he didn't want to risk turning her around to face him, didn't want her weeping suddenly in his arms, that would make too much of the moment, give the scene a melodramatic quality like something in a Hollywood film. Christ he didn't want *that*, he was feeling shaky enough himself—the prospect of an atomic war and the end of civilization as he'd known it for fifty-four years was no laughing matter.

"Your old man will take care of you as he always has, you know that," he repeated. His tone was robust, half teasing.

"Yes, Daddy," Enid said.

For all he knew she wasn't even thinking of atomic war. Of the grim world's future. She was seventeen years old, she might be thinking of something else something private and immediate and Lyle Stevick wasn't the person to learn what it was: that would be Hannah's job.

So the awkward moment passed. They climbed back up into daylight, Enid first, her daddy second; as always when he left the tight snug space of the shelter Lyle Stevick felt a moment's vertigo, knowing he was now exposed and vulnerable standing on the surface of the earth with only a thin membrane of skin and flesh to protect him. A fireball *could* leap from the sky. . . . "Now that wasn't so bad, was it!" Mr. Stevick said. And Enid murmured "No," or what sounded like "No." She eased away, leaving him to close the hatch with a grunt and lock it, and that was the end of the visit: she never came back again.

That autumn Lyle Stevick examined his conscience, should he get a rifle for the shelter, should he be prepared to defend himself and his family in case of attack. Neal O'Banan said yes: a man would be a fool not to.

Neal O'Banan said he sure as hell was going to bring *his* .22—if he got to the shelter in time.

Puffing on his pipe, strolling about the backyard contemplating the uneven swell of the ground above the shelter, Mr. Stevick frightened himself with nightmare visions of his neighbors—Art Flagler up the street, for instance, weighing two hundred seventy pounds; old

Schultz next door, drunk and belligerent; some of the women!—Jesus there were tough women in the neighborhood!—storming the shelter, trying to wrest it away from the Stevicks. In time of atomic attack there'd most likely be the declaration of military law in the city, which meant: lawbreakers shot on sight?

Mr. Stevick pondered the issue, thinking now yes, now no, he feared if it came right down to it he wouldn't be capable of pulling a trigger against his fellow man, let alone his neighbors, but perhaps the mere fact of the rifle, the fact he was armed, would be a deterrent.

Weeks passed, he did nothing. Without quite knowing it he'd become more religious. Saying little prayers—sometimes just *Jesus, Mary, and Joseph!* under his breath as he'd been taught so long ago, in times of temptation especially, to ward off evil or unclean thoughts; sometimes, lying on "his" bunk, only a single light bulb burning in the shelter and the silvery walls luminous and seemingly distant, he'd lose track of time, was it night, was it day, and a prayer would run through his mind *Hail Mary full of grace the Lord is with Thee* graceful and effortless as a school of minnows darting and flashing through turgid waters. He was half embarrassed to catch himself praying, Lyle Stevick of all people, but *why:* nobody knew!

A few days before Thanksgiving it was reported that Pope Pius XII while gravely ill saw a vision of Jesus Christ, who appeared to him to indicate that his time had not yet come: he wasn't to die. And immediately afterward the Pope began to recover from his illness!— "miraculously," in the opinion of Vatican physicians.

The story was widely reported. Cardinal Spellman interviewed on television, a local priest on the Port Oriskany station, the 6 P.M. news, was this an authentic miracle? Well, that depended upon the definition of "miracle" but very likely yes: Jesus Christ appeared to the Pope to tell him his time had not yet come, he was to remain on earth for a while longer.

A few months ago Lyle Stevick might have sneered at such a tale, ridiculing Hannah and her sister Ingrid as they spoke of it, now he wasn't so sure; clearly these were unusual times. Maybe it wasn't a mistake to pray now and then.

He asked of God—if there was a God—should he buy a .22 rifle. Or should he depend upon Neal O'Banan's.

There was the possibility too of a handgun. A .45-caliber pistol maybe.

For the past few years Mr. Stevick had wondered should he get a permit for a handgun of some kind to protect himself at the store.

HORIZON SEWEROOTER burglarized last spring, a salesclerk held up at gunpoint (by two young Negro men) at DE SANTIS POWER TOOLS over on Canal Street, what if armed robbers forced their way into STEVICK'S BARGAIN & UNPAINTED FURNITURE with the intention of taking Lyle Stevick's money and ended up taking his life! Lately he was thinking of such things more and more frequently, even closing up his store on dull dark malevolent days, and now that winter was imminent he planned to close at dusk no matter the time though he probably would not come directly home—he didn't want Hannah monitoring his every move. He'd contemplated buying a pistol for the store but hadn't gone any further than just thinking about it. Maybe the prospect of owning a gun scared him in a way that keeping that length of rope down in the cellar didn't scare him: the rope was so old, grimy, familiar.

8

One windy sleeting night in mid-December Felix Stevick nearly got killed driving home from the Armory: had an accident on the Union Street bridge where the pavement had begun to freeze over in patches, another car approached him going too fast, sliding head-on, and Felix hadn't time even to use his horn—though what good would his horn have done him?—turning his wheel in a desperate reflex as the cars collided with a terrific noise. He would recall afterward he hadn't been afraid of dying maybe because it was so familiar—going out, going down, why not now if it was going to be later?—a reasonable proposition flashing through his brain. He'd been drinking a little but only beer at the Armory while watching the boxing matches, he wasn't drunk but the driver of the other car was "intoxicated" as the newspapers would report, so it was only just that the bastard was the more seriously injured of the two: skull fracture, broken ribs, lacerations, two quarts of blood lost and his 1953 Mercury sedan totaled. Felix's luck held though his car too was smashed beyond repair: got away with a sprained left wrist and a dozen shallow cuts on his face from the windshield and some bruises on his body but that was the extent of it. He liked to think afterward that his reflexes saved him. He liked to think he'd acted on instinct, slipping the punch: you can't be knocked out if you see the punch coming, he'd always believed, and this flashed through his head even as the other car's headlights blinded him and he gritted his teeth, not wanting them to be knocked out.

Taken by ambulance to St. Joseph's, walked out of the emergency room at 2:20 A.M. with his face neatly stitched, wrist bandaged, he'd refused to stay overnight for observation knowing he wasn't hurt. He took the accident in stride. He didn't mind accidents. He'd wanted a new car anyway—bought a 1956 Lincoln Continental the next day, gleaming metallic-black four-door sedan with maroon plush upholstery, kidskin lining the color of fresh cream. It was in this car the very first time Felix drove her in it that Enid told him she was pregnant. Felix countered, "You mean you think you're pregnant."

9

The glass paperweight was missing from Warren's desk. Not on the windowsill either, or on a shelf. Warren wondered had Miriam taken it?—slipped it into her pocket and walked off with it that final time?

Which he hadn't known was the final time.

That summer, he'd been telephoning the Stevicks less frequently; postponing a call for days, weeks—until finally Mr. Stevick or Enid called him. In love with Miriam he was reluctant to tell his family about her, still less about being engaged, planning to be married. (But when? After he finished law school? Next year? Next month?) Nor could he bring himself to tell them about his disappointing grades in law school: Warren Stevick stood eighty-ninth in a class of two hundred fourteen.

(He'd never performed so poorly in any academic situation. And he *had* studied, that was the shame of it.)

It was painful these days, too, to talk with Mr. Stevick. Though father and son would appear to be on the same side regarding the imminence of atomic war they inevitably ended up quarreling. Warren believed that any and all bomb shelters were immoral because they invited war; Mr. Stevick believed that pacifism, as a political strategy, invited war. "As a fledgling lawyer you should know better," Mr. Stevick chided. "As a fledgling lawyer I suspect you *do* know better but don't want to admit it."

To please Warren, or to keep him company, Miriam joined SNVA and spent several long summer afternoons on the Penn campus passing out leaflets and poetry broadsides condemning war; participated along with thirty-odd other members in a protest against ROTC headquarters on the Penn campus—pickets carried hand-lettered signs reading PEACE NOW & FOREVER; LET U.S. DISARM NOW; NO MORE WAR; NO! TO ATOMIC DEATH. The picketing drew a considerable amount of local attention, most of it neutral or indifferent, some of it hostile—the usual taunts of "Commies," "Reds," "traitors," even "pinko-Jews," crude remarks made against the women—but the pickets comported themselves with dignity and patience, making their slow stubborn march back and forth, back and forth, in front of the ROTC building. Warren was doubtful of the group's effectiveness: people stared but did they *see?* they read picket signs but did they *think?* The irony of public protest is, you mean to proclaim a sacred abstract truth and you wind up seeming to represent only yourself in a certain costume. Denying the self in submission to a higher law, you wind up theatrically exhibiting the self!

Miriam found the experience grating, frustrating, invigorating. As bad, she said, as nude modeling. "Except the bastards don't have to pay for the privilege of insulting you."

At meetings of the Society for Non-Violent Action, Miriam rarely participated in the discussions, though she listened with an attentiveness that pleased Warren. There was much in the news in those days of the possibility of a weapons truce between the U.S. and the U.S.S.R., much of the Atoms-for-Peace Conference scheduled for August in Geneva, Switzerland. Warren thought it an exciting time in which to live when "radical moral change" might be effected within the next few weeks or months—in his public speeches he always concluded by saying that he didn't doubt that public sentiment would swing to the side of the peace movement once Americans really understood the issues. "It's only common sense, after all."

To commemorate the tenth anniversary of the dropping of the atomic bomb on Hiroshima in 1945 SNVA held an all-night vigil beginning at dusk on August 6 in Independence Mall—its most ambitious project yet. (Unfortunately the gesture was undermined by the announcement, on August 4, that the U.S.S.R. was resuming nuclear bomb testing.) Many hostile onlookers gathered to challenge the seventy-five peace demonstrators, among them a number of men who identified themselves as World War II army veterans who "owed their lives" to the atomic bomb. (Like Felix, they'd been aboard a carrier ship bound for Japan when the bomb was dropped.) There were jeers, taunts, threats, scuffles, a few incidents of attempted assault. But the Philadelphia police were on hand and no one was seriously injured; within its limits the vigil was a success. (The *Philadelphia Inquirer,* for instance, published a feature article expressing some intelligent sympathy, if a good deal of reserve, for the Society's aims. And other news coverage was generally respectful.)

Miriam was the angriest of the demonstrators, incapable of not responding when provoked, shouting back curses, imperatives—"Go to hell, you!" "Go fuck yourself, you!" Warren tried to calm her, comfort her: the wisest strategy, he said, was to consider what she did as history—"impersonal, selfless history"—they were doing things that required being done, not things they wanted to do as individuals. Miriam said sullenly that she didn't understand and didn't want to understand. " 'History'—what's that? This is here, this is now—we're living right now. And we won't get another chance."

Warren rather feared her at such times—her rage, her tears. But he adored her too. And when, afterward, in his room, they made love, Miriam wept helplessly and said he was right, of course he was right, she knew he was right they were all right and she was wrong, she'd try to be wiser.

In October the pacifist hero Elias Bond spoke in a Unitarian church in downtown Philadelphia and Warren Stevick had the honor of introducing him. Bond was in his mid-eighties, a former biologist now wholly committed to the international peace movement: born in Manchester, England, emigrated to the United States at the age of seventeen, then during World War I he refused to be inducted into the army, was sentenced to death but refused to recant, and eventually his sentence was commuted to twelve years in Leavenworth and after his release he returned to school and distinguished himself in biology; but he had not neglected his work in the cause of peace in an atmosphere of indifference and hostility—he embraced the Quaker faith, opposed the entry of the United States into World War II, and in 1950 publicly refused to pay his taxes in protest of the Korean "police action" and once again was threatened with prison, and since that time the federal government was illegally defrauding him of his Social Security pension and had made numerous underhanded attempts to have him declared *non compos mentis* and sent to a state mental institution, but each federal justice Bond appeared before dismissed the case, ruling in favor of Bond's sanity once he was allowed to speak in his own defense. . . . Warren had not intended his introduction to be quite so emotional but when he was finished the applause was prolonged and Elias Bond himself seemed deeply moved. "Thank you, my son, my dear boy—thank you," Bond said. He gripped Warren's hand in both his hands and stared up at Warren as if about to embrace him. "You are"—he searched for the right, the perfect, words—"a generous, noble soul."

Warren took a seat behind Bond, his face burning. He could see Miriam in the audience a few rows from the front, her expression grave, expectant, slightly quizzical. She knew a little about Elias Bond, had read a part of his memoir *A Small Utopia,* had shared to a degree in Warren's excitement about his visit. She'd applauded energetically, smiling at Warren, but she might have been at that moment a stranger to him—her attention focused upon Bond at the pulpit, frail and white-haired, stoop-shouldered. Bond's subject was "The Corruption of Science" and in a sharp, high, only occasionally faltering voice he spoke for more than an hour, leaning over the podium, regarding his audience with quick-darting intense eyes. He used no notes, yet his talk, or lecture, was carefully orchestrated. Warren could see the palsied tremor of Bond's hands but the man himself seemed tireless, remarkable—drawing strength and confidence from the packed church even as he shocked some of his listeners, clearly dismayed them, frightened them. He knew so much—so irrefutably much!

He spoke of the corruption of science in the twentieth century, the pact with the devil ("By the devil I mean DESTRUCTION") made by even well-intentioned scientists like Einstein, then he summarized in some detail what he knew of postwar Army Chemical Corps classified research into chemical-biological warfare—the crisis of conscience of numerous young scientists, of whom his own nephew was one. He spoke of the history of atomic bomb research since the closing days of World War II—the "successful experiments," so-called, of Hiroshima and Nagasaki. Did his audience know that a 100-megaton bomb of the kind currently being developed by American and Russian scientists if detonated at the height of a few miles would set fire to everything combustible in an area the size of Ohio—and kill virtually everyone in that space, either immediately or within a few days? Did they know that if nuclear testing continued the radiation fallout and the strontium element would cause in time the genetic deterioration of the race and its ultimate extinction?—*if no nuclear war is waged at all.*

Did they know that, contrary to the government's reiterated claims, it would be impossible to evacuate Americans from lethal zones in time of war *or* in time of accidental explosions occurring in domestic atomic piles now in use? Did they know that the Civil Defense Bureau had recently reissued its notorious and utterly worthless pamphlet ("How to Survive Nuclear War") in a printing of twenty-five million copies? ("This pamphlet is a scandal to all scientists for its false, one might even say its cynical, optimism—suggesting as it does that ordinary homeowners can build bomb shelters in their backyards capable of 'saving' themselves and their families from nuclear death: equating, in a sense, preparation for atomic war with patriotism.") Did they know that nuclear war would be like no other kind of war because nuclear weapons are like no other weapons?— that their destructive capacity is so enormous that *there is no practical physical means of defense against them* and this is something so new in the history of civilization its true significance has yet to be grasped?

Did they know that each time one of these weapons is tested *there is an incalculable addition to the pollution of the earth's surface and atmosphere?*

He doubted, Elias Bond said dryly, that anyone in the room really comprehended these statements—including himself.

Bond concluded his address with a brief history of the peace movement since World War I and with an impassioned appeal for unilateral disarmament, "the only realistic strategy now open to mankind." Critics of disarmament dismissed it without understanding its principles, without wanting to acknowledge that atomic war is suicide war, pure and simple, irrefutably: suicide. Whereas unilateral disarmament is war against the very concept of war itself.

"My friends, thank you for your kindness tonight in hearing me out, and God bless you. God bless us all in our united hope that we might set the earth's axis aright. The twentieth century thus far has been a half century of unmitigated horror, a waking nightmare. The Great War, the Holocaust, the unleashing of the atomic bomb on Hiroshima and Nagasaki—these three events have been the touchstones until now of our humanity. In the last fifty years of our century the earth has been tilted on its axis, morally and spiritually, and it remains for us now, in the brief space of time allotted to us, to restore balance.

"My friends, let me say good night. God bless us and have pity on us all."

With enormous enthusiasm the audience began to applaud—applauded and applauded for many minutes. Though the interior of the building was overwarm and the air rather close, no one appeared to be in a hurry to leave.

A number of pews, including the one Miriam was in, gave Bond a standing ovation. Such emotion! such love! One could very nearly feel it in the air.

Before the applause had completely subsided Elias Bond turned toward Warren, extending a hand. For a puzzled moment Warren thought Bond wanted him to join him; then it became clear that Bond simply needed help in getting down from the pulpit and down from the stage—he'd exhausted himself giving his address.

"I'm an old, old man," he told Warren, smiling, gripping his arm hard. "Your generation will have to do better."

The previous day Warren had signed out from his job in the law library with the excuse of feeling sick to his stomach, and it was true he'd felt mildly sick for days, perhaps it was the unnaturally warm, balmy autumn weather, perhaps it was certain obsessive thoughts; he'd run most of the two and a half miles to meet Miriam at the Academy where she was posing for a figure-drawing class. Naked, exhibiting herself. "Nude." The woman's brown-nippled breasts, the smooth swell of her belly. Light brown pubic hair in a triangular bush. Shoulders, thighs, ankles, feet: those bare feet so white so startling on the roof he'd never seen anything like it, stopped dead in his tracks. He waited for her to dress and she took her time, then appeared smiling a careless gorgeous smile, teasing, "Are you spying on me, Warren?"—embarrassing him before a knot of students who overheard. But she introduced Warren to them as her fiancé. Warren Stevick, my fiancé. The word sounded exotic in her mouth, as if it must have an odd taste.

Now, on their way home from Bond's talk, he watched her slantwise, rather jealously. She'd been shaken by the elderly man's words though much of what he said must have been familiar to her. Slipped her arm through his by force of habit. She was unnaturally quiet, distracted.

Though the substance of Bond's talk was familiar to Warren too he'd been powerfully moved by it; had begun sweating inside his clothes. It was said that you could not contemplate the possibility of nuclear holocaust for more than a few minutes—if that long. Like contemplating infinity, or your own death. Can't be done. But still Warren could frighten himself with the possibility—could recall how, in Korea, in that old life, he'd been overcome, annihilated, by flames erupting from the sky. *And it can happen again. At any moment.*

It was an unusually warm evening. Warren wiped his face on his sleeve, felt a constriction in his chest as if an invisible adversary were pressing him back even as he pressed forward. This was his summer feeling—a sense of constriction, suffocation. Since childhood he'd preferred winters, freezing air a tonic to the skin, razorlike, slicing the lungs to wakefulness, not a trance of heat, flesh encased drowsily in heat. Walking beside Miriam, who held herself stiffly and seemed in no hurry to break the silence between them, Warren allowed his thoughts to drift—thinking suddenly of the East Clinton bus rattling along with windows open to blasts of sun-heated air, the stink of exhaust, leather seats burning his skin. Outside, the city stretched away forever—streets and sidewalks radiating heat palpable as fire. Then at Kilbirnie Park when they were children the cement burning too beneath his bare feet, the lapping agitated water of the children's swimming pool, so many frantic bodies, so much screaming and pummeling and splashing, boys throwing themselves in the water shrieking *Bombs away Toyko! Bombs away Tokyo!* and there'd been a kind of wild excitement in the air, a tug at Warren Stevick's own heart, something in him that thrilled to noise, frenzy, brainless destruction. *Bombs away!*

But he'd withdrawn, always he'd withdrawn. The shy boy. Big, but shy. A pushover. Lizzie had more spunk and even Enid, years younger, was possessed of a stronger, more stubborn will.

Miriam lit a cigarette and tossed the match away—a profane gesture after the solemnity of Bond's talk. Screwing up half her face against the smoke. Eyes damp, evasive. Yes, she'd been frightened of what Bond had to say as they all were, she was thinking perhaps of her little boy?—of the future?

Warren was in the habit, these days, of quizzing himself. Should he feel guilt for the change in this woman?

For she *had* changed. Didn't wear a ring but still she was his fiancée, would be Mrs. Warren Stevick sometime after the first of the year. In recent months she'd become more thoughtful, more mature;

didn't drink as much, or as compulsively. She was still Miriam Brancher but not the woman he'd seen on the roof of the apartment house, whom he'd rescued against her will.

Warren said hesitantly, almost apologetically, "Bond is right, of course. 'Setting the earth back on its axis'—that's right. And we can do it, if enough of us work together." When Miriam made no reply he slipped his arm around her shoulders and said with more enthusiasm than he felt, "Miriam, don't be so sad. It isn't too late—it *can't* be."

Miriam was smoking her cigarette in quick short puffs. Beneath her grainy powder her skin too was damp, the wings of her nose oily. She was there beside him, an incalculable distance away. "Warren, what?—sorry, I didn't hear," she said.

———————

For a very long time they'd been talking of going to Litchfield together so that Warren could meet Mikey and Miriam's mother, but something always came up to alter their plans. Now Miriam was saying she thought it would be better for her to go alone to prepare her little boy for meeting Warren. "I'm just worried it would be too sudden for him, honey, the two of us together, he'd maybe confuse you with Bob," she said. She looked at Warren frankly. "That's the one thing I dread—Mikey confusing you with Bob."

"Do we look so much alike?" Warren asked.

"That isn't the point and you know it."

"But I have to meet him sometime."

"Bob traumatized him—hitting him the way he did. Him and me both. So much shouting, self-dramatizing—"

"Yes, I know," Warren said. "You've told me."

"I've told you but you don't *know,*" Miriam said, hurt. "You can't understand it from the perspective of a child in Mikey's condition." She paused, still regarding him frankly, speculatively. "I'm worried about him and I'm worried about you."

"Don't worry about me, Miriam," Warren said.

If she wanted to get away from Philadelphia and from him for a few days why not say so?—why the subterfuge? The several times Warren had suggested they might visit Port Oriskany so that she could meet his family she demurred, saying it wasn't the right time yet. Then she said she was frightened of meeting them, worrying they'd dislike her—wouldn't approve. Aren't they expecting you to marry a good Catholic girl? she asked.

"I do worry about you," Miriam said. There was a prim edge to her voice as if they'd been quarreling though in fact they were speaking quietly and earnestly, sitting side by side naked on Warren's bed. Now Miriam let her long hair fall forward, releasing a scent of perspiration, heat. She said softly, "I worry that you're making a mistake, honey."

"Because I love you?"

"Because—"

She stared at her bare wriggling toes for a long luxurious moment. Her mouth worked, twitched; she might have been a small child trying to calculate. "Because you don't love me enough," she whispered, teasing. And the mood was broken, the tension gone; Miriam turned playful, sly, coy, slinging her arms around her lover's neck as if she meant to wrestle him down and she was—almost—strong enough to do it.

Afterward Warren thought, stunned, not yet bitter: But that was it. The end.

He hadn't known of course and wondered if she had. Overcome by desire or by something yearning and frantic he'd mistaken for desire, his backbone seized with pain, old pain in his eye, still he'd been able to make love to Miriam Brancher another time to bring the woman weeping to orgasm another time but still that was the end, that hour.

"You're so good to me," she said. "Oh Christ it's so good."

Could she borrow maybe $150 from him?—for the trip to Litchfield. The Greyhound bus, things for Mikey, something for her mother, et cetera. Shamed, Warren had to admit he didn't have that much money right now. Would $80 help? $95?

Sure, said Miriam. Anything at all would *help*.

In all she would have borrowed a little in excess of $350, always insistent she was "borrowing" the money and would be "repaying" it though Warren insisted on his part that that was hardly necessary. Since they were going to get married after all. Weren't they?

So she left Philadelphia, went to Litchfield. Or at any rate left Philadelphia. She promised to telephone Warren the following night but no call came and another day and another night passed and no call so Warren tried to dial the number she'd given him in Litchfield and an operator came on the line informing him there was no such number. Please check again, sir, she said.

* * *

So she'd left. Without, as the cliché would have it, saying goodbye.

Though it seemed she'd taken the glass paperweight with her. Souvenir of Shoal Lake, Enid's old gift. That miniature snowstorm, fake snow chips she'd admired or pretended to admire and in any case if she'd stolen it from him in a sentimental moment she would surely mislay it, or toss it away, in time. What's this thing? her new lover would ask, holding the heavy little object in his hand, and Miriam would say, Oh—just something.

Oh—nothing.

Warren learned by way of Novick—hearty, malicious Novick!—that Miriam Brancher returned to the house one afternoon toward the end of November when Warren was out—Miriam, "looking herself" and in the company of a "male friend"—and cleared her room of her things, handed in her key. She was weeks behind in rent and promised to send a check—"But we know what *that* means, don't we!"

Warren didn't ask if Miriam had left any forwarding address. Too much pride. Too highly developed a sense of futility.

Nor did he mention his disappointment—would you call it heartbreak?—to his parents. To what purpose? When Enid tried to tease him in her schoolgirl manner he cut her off sharply. "It's all over, Enid. So drop it."

And Enid, chastened, did.

Very little in Warren Stevick's outward life changed except of course he had more time—a good deal more time.

Worked very hard at his studies, dreaming sometimes with his eyes open, moving like a somnambulist through his life, the tightly plotted schedule of a law student's existence. Day blurring into night and night into day: lectures, notes, books, memorization. He told himself sternly that this too was impersonal from a certain vantage point. (If you were to be, in time, Thoreau. Gandhi. Elias Bond.) His impersonation of "Warren Stevick" opening like a multifoliate flower of a species unknown to him, opening slowly by degrees, unfolding petal by petal until he saw that the flower *was* himself. He had only to submit.

A night, late, in December. Warren Stevick at his desk hunched over one of his law books utterly absorbed in reading and memorizing, underlining with his pen, not distracted by the cooing of pigeons on the roof or raised voices from a downstairs apartment or the hope, or dread, of hearing footsteps approaching his door followed by Miriam's hesitant knock, her guilty voice, "Warren . . . ?" as he'd heard, or seemed to hear, so many times. So many late nights, weeks. But now, nothing. He was utterly absorbed in his work which he detested, recalling his father's smiling shrug, defining work as what goes against the grain of your soul but you've got to do it, you poor s.o.b., 'cause what's the alternative. Mr. Stevick's voice rising through the floorboards as Warren guessed it would for the rest of Warren's life.

But better to light a single candle than curse the darkness—right?

His pen slipped from his fingers, he must have been dozing off. An exam in the morning and he was cramming at the eleventh hour, stuffing his head, it very nearly seemed, brain aching, vision blurring, and when, awkwardly, he got down on his hands and knees to look for the pen he discovered to his surprise—his shock, actually—the glass paperweight on the floor behind one of the bookshelves.

So she hadn't taken it after all.

The little globe was covered with a film of dust. Warren wiped it clean. Turned it slowly in his hand. Immediately the miniature snowstorm began, tiny white chips like snow falling in a dream or in an old memory that should have been outgrown long ago. *Shoal Lake, N.Y.* in fake-gilt embossed letters.

Still, Warren was happy to have found it. Squatting on his heels he pressed the glass against his face, against his left eye, he was grateful for its coolness, it was cooler and seemingly of a texture different from that of the surrounding air. It might bring him, mightn't it, some relief.

10

Momma, don't be angry, I have something to tell you.

Momma?—please don't hate me.

Upstairs in Mrs. Stevick's sewing room—Warren's old room—a bright windy morning, the last Saturday of November, kneeling on the carpet helping her mother and her Aunt Ingrid lay out the delicate tissue-thin Butterick patterns on the outspread cloth—yards and yards of fine-spun pale yellow wool—expensive material for a full-skirted dress in a modified A-line Dior style the sisters were sewing for a well-to-do woman in St. James's parish: there Enid rehearsed compulsively words she knew she would never say. *Momma can you help me?—I'm in trouble.*

She had wondered since starting to count the days—faint pencil marks on her calendar: October 11 the onset of her last menstrual period which meant November 8 to begin worrying and each subsequent day to worry more seriously, telling herself *It can't be: don't think it!*—she'd wondered how many young girls on East Clinton Street, how many girls in her school had gone to their mothers over the years in desperation saying *Momma, I'm in trouble*— the oldest story.

And their mothers looked at them appalled and unsurprised, saying—what? Enid couldn't imagine the words.

Make sure you're not bunching up the cloth beneath the patterns, Enid's mother cautioned her fussily—are you doing it right? Enid's task was to secure the tissue paper to the cloth with straight pins, working slowly and fastidiously hunched over the carpet—the older women weren't so supple as Enid, couldn't get down on the floor and expect to get back up again—then to cut out the patterns with a dressmaker's scissors. Snip snip snipping as she'd like to snip out something juicy and hidden deep inside her—that part of her not known to her, the anatomical drawings (Jesus how often she'd been studying such drawings lately) called the "womb." It wasn't her but it was lodged deep inside her, deep as her very soul.

Anosognosia was one of her new vocabulary words. Also *macerate. Obbligato. Harlequinade.*

In September, Mrs. Stevick and Enid's Aunt Ingrid had decided to become professional dressmakers: this yellow wool dress for a customer named Mrs. Brooks was their third assignment. The idea had been Aunt Ingrid's originally: everybody was always telling the sisters they sewed beautifully, their things were always praised, they were always being asked to volunteer their services so why not—why not!—set themselves up as "dressmakers" with a notice in the *East End Weekly Observer* as a few other neighborhood women had done, women whom Ingrid knew—and knew they weren't so capable as Hannah and her, not by a long shot. At first Hannah said no, she'd be embarrassed, ashamed, and Ingrid said, Embarrassed of what? and Hannah said she didn't know. Ingrid said, Ashamed of what?—and Hannah had to admit she didn't know. So the sisters made their plans in secret and didn't break the astonishing news to the family until the first notice appeared in the *Observer*.

DRESSMAKERS À LA MODE

Ladies & Girls Fine Apparel
Our Specialty

tel. CLinton 8-3827

They had run the ad three times at a cost of $15 each time and thus far no one had telephoned—their customers were all acquaintances, their merit would spread by "word of mouth" if at all—but Mrs. Stevick and Aunt Ingrid thought the notice well worth it. There it was—a public declaration! "Dressmakers à la Mode."

Enid volunteered to run errands for them—quick trips to the Kresge's on Union Street to get thread, extra straight pins—she was eager to help out, smiling and excited, hoping to distract herself from her worry—she calculated she was five weeks pregnant but she hadn't yet told Felix, hadn't yet even rehearsed the words she might use to tell him, perhaps she was waiting but what, for Christ's sake, was she waiting for?—something to happen. The bleeding to start. That pain deep in the belly, the unmistakable onset of cramps, faintness. Counting days, an ignoble task, counting and recounting, *you poor sad stupid cunt,* a nightmare that shaded gradually into numbness, silence. She could sit through a meal without speaking to her parents, without hearing a word either of them said, smiling, clear-eyed, and seeming to agree, even to be impressed with Daddy's comments on this, that, the other. Where Enid had wept easily in the past, imagining herself pregnant (yes, Felix had given her numerous opportunities, he'd become careless this year) or for no reason at all, these days she rarely wept even in the privacy of her room. Oh God she was terrified of losing control, burying herself in her mother's arms, pressing herself against her mother's big warm breasts, *Oh Momma can you help me, can you help me.* It was degrading, it was mad, no Enid she could recognize—*Oh Momma help me!*

As if she would ever allow herself to break down.

But this morning she'd offered to help her mother and Aunt Ingrid instead of going downtown to her piano lesson—she told them Mr. Lesnovich had canceled the lesson for today, he had to be out of town, and on the phone she told Mr. Lesnovich her mother wasn't well and she had to stay home with her. Mr. Lesnovich seemed genuinely concerned, said he was sorry to hear it, he hoped it wasn't anything serious, and Enid said softly, swallowing down her grief, "Yes, it might be serious—we don't know yet."

Even as she spoke, nervously attentive to her body, waiting—so many days, weeks, of waiting!—for that first seeping of blood in the loins. And of course there was none. There was going to be none.

You poor stupid cunt, you asshole—the voice of that other Enid rose bitterly—*letting him fuck you like that. Letting him do whatever he wanted!*

The irony did not escape Enid—these days no irony escaped her—that Mrs. Stevick was in excellent health, supremely high spirits, now her talk was all of her dressmaking—and she used the word "dressmaking" conspicuously often—her customers, the various prices of various kinds of material, Butterick and Vogue and Simplicity patterns, how much she and Ingrid might hope to charge for this fancy woolen dress with the flaring skirt, cloth-covered belt, batwing sleeves, fine muslin lining. Mrs. Brooks wanted it for Christmas and they'd promised it for Christmas and they were going to get it done for Christmas—that was the challenge! The first fitting was already scheduled, penciled in on Mrs. Stevick's kitchen calendar.

Enid was surprised, perhaps like others in the family a little disconcerted, by the change in her mother but happy too—of course she was happy—she'd be a selfish bitch otherwise. Hannah Stevick with her hair newly permed, so fair a graying brown it might almost have been blond, her eyes bright if still rather sunken, her skin ruddy, taking pains now with her own appearance—a new black felt hat to wear to mass, a new pair of gloves, new shoes. She was markedly less irritable around the house, perhaps because she had less time. At mealtimes at first her manner had been slightly defensive, just slightly combative as if she feared her husband's ridicule, but that phase was seemingly past. For a while Mr. Stevick had indeed been lightly mocking, teasing, incredulous, then overnight his attitude changed —he had to be impressed with the fact that his wife and his sister-in-law were making money. Not much money but damned better than nothing, he said. "Now you're in business, Mrs. Stevick," he told Hannah with his cheerily bitter smile, "you can support *me* for the next thirty years."

So Enid was happy for her mother. Yet felt a little rebuffed by her—her busyness, her work upstairs with Ingrid. The furious pedaling of the sewing machine. She wondered was the change in her mother somehow related to the change in herself.

*   *   *

Now the Death-panic began to assert itself. Or had it been there all along.

Not giving a damn, making love with him in the car, in the park that day, she was desperate to believe he still loved her, he was still crazy for her though he was so frequently angry with her or with someone or something, he didn't always take care not to hurt her and Enid herself scarcely cared—whatever happened she deserved. She knew she deserved it because it happened.

Once they'd showered together in Felix's bathroom, Enid's long hair wrapped clumsily in a towel because she couldn't get it wet: what would Mrs. Stevick say?—coming home from her piano lesson, from the library, with her hair damp. Felix was in a sweet mood in the aftermath of passion, soaping and lathering his girl, his little girl, his beautiful little girl he adored, kissing her, sucking at her breasts, bent over her stumbling and playful the two of them giddy as the warm water streamed over them and Felix wanted to make love again, Felix's penis was hard again, probing and poking against her wet belly, he tried clumsily to enter her but failed, tried again, grappling, impatient, straining against her, not caring that the tile wall was hard against her back. Enid felt a sudden rush of fear and repugnance for him and for the urgency of his need; she stiffened, no longer having the strength to embrace him, letting her arms drop to her sides as if she'd suddenly lost all will, even consciousness, knowing he wasn't going to stop because he couldn't: all that was him, his life, his being, his love for her, concentrated in that hard frenzied thrusting against her. And he must have known. And he must not have cared. He'd have liked her to take his cock in her mouth as he was always urging, teasing her to do, making a joke of it—It won't kill you, honey: what are you afraid of?—but she caught the undercurrent of resentment, hurt pride; there was no part of Enid's body after all he didn't adore, but Enid couldn't bring herself to do that for him, her instinct was always to wrench herself away gagging and panicked, why should she suck Felix off?—she knew the expression well, saw it written on walls, sidewalks, heard the boys use it frequently at school—when she didn't want to. But now Felix gripped her shoulders pushing her frankly down, almost without knowing what he did he gripped her head, pushing it down, Enid tried to squirm away protesting, C'mon honey, sweetheart, c'mon Enid, Felix was saying, and she felt the panic of death rising in her—to give in to him now would be to die.

She dug her nails into Felix's hands and he relented. He was enormously excited but he relented, eased up, turned her around in the shower trying to be reasonably patient and gentle fitting his cock between the cheeks of her buttocks then lifting her in his arms, his arms tight and crushing around her rib cage so that she could hardly breathe but she shut her eyes tight swallowing down the pain, the surprise of the pain, Felix thrusting and groaning against her convulsed at the moment of orgasm and then it was over.

Felix told Enid afterward it was safe enough, what they'd done— the shower would have washed everything away.

Still, he seemed repentant. Telling her he was sorry; the towel had loosened, slipping from her head, and her hair had gotten wet after all.

In truth Enid rarely worried about becoming pregnant or of the recklessness of what they did when they did it, she tried not to think of such things at all. Only afterward alone, usually in her bed, she'd feel a feathery touch of fear, panic, excitement—*what if?—what if?*— turning like a precious jewel in her fingers as she drifted off into sleep.

It hadn't been that time but the time in October when he'd picked her up on Nine Mile Road and driven her out to Roosevelt Park: Enid knew. She was to count the days frequently enough afterward, counting and calculating, looking up facts already knew in the *Family Medical Encyclopedia.* Menstruation—ovulation—conception—fertilization: the microscopic egg cell implants itself in the lining of the uterus. And so it begins.

Momma I have to talk to you.

Momma don't hate me!

Still she couldn't quite believe it even as she marked off the days on her calendar, careful to use a light pencil in case Mrs. Stevick was ever to see. Imagining with a pang of hope she felt the first seeping of blood then checking her panties, checking with her finger, seeing nothing. Then in a sudden despairing rage pounding her belly with a fist, she'd make herself bleed! she'd make something happen! but there was nothing.

Momma I think I'm in trouble.

But that day in Roosevelt Park she hadn't cared. Anything Felix had wanted her to do she would have done. She was crazy for him, she couldn't bear his anger, if he stopped loving her she would die, it was death she was terrified of and not Felix Stevick, who would never have hurt her. If he would fill her with his life!—but their loving always had to end.

Then they were two people. Sitting apart. Sometimes resentful, sullen, Enid couldn't have said why, her lower lip swollen with hurt, God damn you, fuck you, she'd thought, bringing her back to the fucking high school after 1:30 P.M. and she'd told him about the chemistry quiz, she expected him to remember, what a bastard he was, goddamn son of a bitch, hot to screw her out in the open where somebody might see where a cop might have seen and then what!—she was so furious with him she slammed the car door behind her, ran up the school walk without looking back, didn't glance over her shoulder as he drove away, fuck him she was late! faint with hunger too because he'd never bought her lunch. In the corridor outside her chemistry class she stood staring into the room watching her teacher Mr. Sorenson at the blackboard, thinking how foolish human beings looked when you couldn't hear what they were saying, you could only see their movements, their facial expressions, and what the fuck did it all add up to? Daddy'd joked about some Greek philosopher saying it was sweetest never to have been born but sweet enough to die young but how then would you know if you were dead? Her lips were dry and chafed from Felix's kisses. The insides of her thighs rubbed raw. Christ, she could feel his semen leaking down inside her, soaking her panties, the feel of it transfixed her. Oh Christ, she thought, I don't care what happens.

Then to her embarrassment Mr. Sorenson caught sight of her. Came out into the corridor to speak with her. "Enid, is something wrong? Enid, why weren't you in class?"—staring at her, surely wondering at her dazed disheveled appearance, her rumpled clothing, pink sweater damp with perspiration and the pupils of her eyes dilated: Enid Stevick his A+ student, about whom the school rumor was she'd tried to kill herself a few years ago. Mr. Sorenson was a youngish man of moderate height, thinning fair hair, tortoiseshell glasses, severe in his grading and much disliked by some students but popular with others for his frank smiling no-nonsense manner—he'd befriended Enid back in September, giving her advice about colleges, urging her to go somewhere other than the local teachers' college; now he stared at her concerned and puzzled, persisting, "Enid—did something happen to you?" while Enid backed away, shaking her head, shy and sullen. In a nearly inaudible voice she told him she was sorry to have missed class could she make up the quiz she seemed to have something wrong with her insides she'd been in the lavatory for a half hour but still didn't feel well please could she make up the quiz another time?—lifting her eyes to him as she retreated, seeing he didn't know what to believe, yes very likely he could smell Felix on her but what was he to say or do he didn't after all know what to believe, Enid had become so practiced and convincing a liar.

He peered at her through his glasses. Told her she could make up the quiz—of course. Seemed about to say something more, then thought better of it and let her go.

The remainder of the day passed like a dream. She might have been a swimmer making her way through an element that resisted her slightly but could not contain her. That evening at supper, scarcely listening to her father's talk of politics, hearing instead her lover's voice, *I'll kill you, I'll kill you both;* she'd examined herself, taking a bath before supper, seeing her buttocks bruised, vague yellow-purplish discolorations in the flesh, *I'll kill you* Felix had said but of course he didn't mean it look how he'd loved her: crazy for her as he'd always been. His sweetheart, his little girl. His niece he'd never harm.

That night the telephone rang. It was late, past eleven o'clock, Enid stood in the doorway of her room listening to her father on the phone—a wrong number?—but she seemed to know it was Felix so after her parents went to bed she went downstairs and dialed his number. He said, "Enid?—I'd like to see you for a few minutes." Enid said in a low frightened voice, "Tonight? Now?" He said, "Enid honey I'd like to see you just for a few minutes," he sounded a little drunk or maybe it was just the urgency of his voice. "I'll drive up there and park at the corner and you come out, all right?—I just want to see you for a few minutes, honey." Enid said, "If they catch me—" Felix said, "They aren't going to catch you, just be quiet leaving the house." Enid said desperately, "But it's late, it's almost midnight. I'm going to bed." Felix said, "We'll just drive around a little, then I'll take you back." Enid said, swallowing down her panic, "Couldn't I see you tomorrow?—at noon?" Felix said, "I want to see you now, I said some things today I didn't mean—I did some things I didn't mean—I just want to make it up to you, honey, you know I love you don't you?" and Enid said softly, "Yes," so softly she had to repeat it, and in the end she agreed to meet Felix as he wanted, she hadn't any choice.

And now she was pregnant, five weeks by her calculation, kneeling in her mother's sewing room on the carpet like the good little girl she'd always been, her mother's and her aunt's chatter washing harmlessly about her head. Minutes were passing, a full hour gone, *Momma I hate to be telling you bad news at such a time,* teasing herself with words she'd never dare say, the way she used to tease herself with the possibility of sin by running her rosary swiftly through her fingers, glass bead after glass bead a prayer she wouldn't say, let God see how she defied Him.

It surprised her that she could manage the tiny straight pins and the dressmaker's scissors as skillfully as she did. Her fingers were clumsy these days, slightly swollen like her breasts, the tips sensitive like her nipples. Anguish to practice piano now when she was always striking wrong notes or hesitating so that her timing was off, Mr. Lesnovich lost patience with her, saying in a cutting voice her mind was on other things, clearly: why bother then to come to her lesson? Without her piano practice Enid's life would have been unendurable but now it seemed to her humiliating, shameful, to mangle her pieces—Mozart, Bach, Chopin—how did she dare!—even playing her familiar scales and arpeggios she was tense, anticipating the first mistake and yes, goddamn it, it invariably came no matter how careful she was, how alert and attentive, her very soul primed to acquit herself to perfection.

But she'd cut out the patterns in the cloth perfectly.

Mrs. Stevick with her critical eye could find nothing wrong: "Thank you, Enid." And Aunt Ingrid said, "Thank you, Enid, aren't you sweet!"—smiling happily at her as if she were perhaps eleven years old.

So Enid's task was over for the morning. She couldn't remain in her mother's sewing room much longer without evoking suspicion, moist-eyed and scared, smiling her sick little smile like death warmed over, she hadn't slept more than three hours the night before, she hadn't been able to eat breakfast, nauseated by food and by the smell of food and sometimes by the mere thought of food. Of course she was pregnant—but she couldn't believe it. She couldn't believe it but she knew. She knew the symptoms. Still a voice kept saying maybe there's a mistake—though there wasn't any mistake and she knew it. So stupefied so frightened of what was going to happen, what Felix would say or do, she was turning into somebody crazy like that poor woman in *The Snake Pit*—God, that movie had scared Enid and Lizzie both, Geraldine too—Gerry'd taken them to see it on the sly—she'd be like poor Molly Deal in eighth grade five months pregnant and still going to school until Miss Holland called her into her office and Molly wouldn't admit it, Molly denied everything, the story went around she insisted she wasn't pregnant she couldn't be pregnant she didn't even cry or get hysterical with Miss Holland, just denied everything flatly and maybe she *was* crazy, so scared. Miss Holland wouldn't talk about it afterward. And the Buehl girl, where people were saying it was her own father who'd gotten her into trouble! then her mother who tried to get rid of it using a clothes hanger or an ice pick, oh Jesus Christ in one version of the story she bled to death. And Enid never learned the truth.

"Enid," Mrs. Stevick said absentmindedly, "is something wrong?"

"What? No."

"Why are you just standing there? You're blocking my light."

Mrs. Stevick wore bifocals now that gave her eyes a curious slitted look. The frames were clear plastic, pink, smartly styled. She'd become an attractive woman, Enid thought, with her short permed hair, her energetic manner—a saleslady at Sibley's maybe in one of the better departments. Aunt Ingrid too at the age of fifty-seven—plump, round-faced, nervous—had taken on a new air of assurance. "Why don't you go downstairs and play the piano, Enid?" Mrs. Stevick said. "There's nothing more you can help us with right now."

Enid went downstairs but not to the piano. Stood for a while at a kitchen window staring into the backyard, her eyes welling with tears. It was all so damned degrading anyway—even to contemplate telling her mother. *Momma I'm so afraid. Momma what will happen to me. Momma please don't hate me.* And if she'd broken down and begun to cry, what then? Felix once told her of soldiers in the hospital with him in Australia, kids his own age brought into an open ward to die, so badly wounded sometimes their faces were half gone, their arms, legs gone, when the morphine wore off they cried like children, like babies screaming for their mothers, the most terrible sound he'd heard in his life, Felix said. Eighteen, nineteen, twenty years old and crying for their mothers, out of their heads with pain and terror, but the worst part of it was the rest of the ward got fed up with their noise, yelled at them to be quiet, to die for Christ's sake if they were going to die but to be fucking *quiet!* Enid put her hands over her ears, saying, Don't tell me things like that, and Felix said, Why not? Who else is going to tell you?

11

About Al, she said.

What about Al? Felix asked quickly.

There's some trouble, she said.

He was dressed, ready to leave the hotel, anticipating with pleasure the long nighttime drive back to Port Oriskany alone in his car, but there she was sitting unhappy and stubborn on the edge of the bed, starting to cry, he hadn't any choice but to comfort her, had he. And then she told him something he wished he'd never been told.

Sitting quietly crying on the unmade bed, the satin coverlet twisted beneath her. Slope-shouldered in her lacy white slip, breasts tightly cupped in lace, the cleavage between them deep and perfumy. She had been dressing with unusual slowness as if reluctant or disoriented: one silk stocking on and one leg still bare, shapely and a little plump above the knee, bare toes like a child's toes digging nervously into the carpet. Even with the ends of her honey-tinted hair gone limp, mascara smudged beneath her eyes, mouth contorted with the effort not to cry harder she was beautiful, her skin looked hot, smooth and hot, the blood beating close beneath the surface, he felt some tenderness for her but Christ it was difficult to take her tears seriously. Felix asked what was the trouble this time, he kept his tone light hoping to nudge her out of her mood, being involved with a married woman no matter who the woman was—no matter who her husband was—was always a risky proposition, one day you suddenly heard the small sad despairing angry undercurrent: *Love me, help me, save me.*

The first time they'd made love two years before, Claudette had wept dramatically claiming she loved Al Sansom, she owed Al Sansom so much, she'd rather die than betray him or hurt him, there had to be an understanding between her and Felix that she would never break up her marriage for Felix, did he agree?—and Felix whose mind at that time had in fact been on other things said sure, he'd never be disloyal to Al Sansom either. They weren't able to see each other regularly but when they did—often here in Syracuse, in the grand old Hotel De Witt—Claudette usually cried for a spell at about this time, stricken with guilt, remorse, the aftermath of passion, then she recovered swiftly enough, smiling her wide white sunny glamour-girl smile by the time they said goodbye in the hotel's parking lot up the street.

Why not smile?—Mrs. Al Sansom had a six-bedroom "Tudor" house in a wealthy suburb of Albany and a sable fur coat and an ermine jacket and a mink cape and a good many jewels and a sporty new canary-yellow Buick convertible, two-door, a gift from her husband on the occasion of their fifth wedding anniversary.

When Felix was away from Claudette he tended to forget her; when he was with her, physically close to her, he felt a quickening of hope that was like desire. He'd wanted to fall in love with Claudette Sansom, hadn't he, at the start, as a way of saving himself from the other, but for some reason it hadn't worked out.

Claudette was turned slightly away from Felix, shielding her damp face from him, she hated anyone to see her weeping, ugly. She had a horror she often said of losing control. Downstairs in the lounge where they'd met before registering at the front desk as Mr. and Mrs. Felix Stevick, Claudette had ordered two sloe gin fizzes instead of her usual one and she'd talked rather compulsively of things in which Felix had no interest: the impending holidays, how melancholy Christmas made her feel, a January trip she and Al were tentatively planning to the Virgin Islands where Al wanted to invest in some real estate.

Did she want to make him jealous, Felix wondered.

Now Felix stroked her warm bare shoulder urging her to tell him what was wrong, he hoped to Christ it wasn't more of Al Sansom's disappearances, Al Sansom's drunken crying jags, Al Sansom's talk of flying saucers, that desperate undercurrent *love me, help me, save me* he wasn't going to hear. Hadn't their understanding been that Felix wasn't there to extricate her from her marriage?—yet now Claudette was behaving strangely, extravagant in her emotions, making love with Felix this afternoon she'd pretended a passion Felix doubted, much of it display, drama. Something in her was cinematic, her ecstasy meant to flatter him and arouse him, it was like women faking orgasms in porno films, at a certain point you didn't give a damn what was real and what was fake, maybe the fakery was more exciting, less danger to it. Felix soothed her, called her sweetheart, honey, did she want another drink?—he'd brought a bottle of bourbon up to the room, still a quarter full. Once their lovemaking was over he began to get restless, thinking of escape, of the two-hundred-mile drive back east to Port Oriskany in the dark—it was December second, daylight ended now by four thirty in the afternoon—thinking he wouldn't even turn on the car radio, sometimes the radio jangled his nerves, the only music he liked was jazz, Miles Davis, Erroll Garner, Count Basie, but nothing loud or fast or with too much drum solo, no Dixieland, that made his heartbeat accelerate unpleasantly, but he couldn't hope to get jazz on these local hick stations. Behind the wheel of his car he could lose himself in silence, freed from having to think of anyone or anything. He could lose himself in speed as he'd once lost himself in violent physical exertion. The car's headlights would illuminate the rushing highway and give to the swirling powdery snow fantastical dream shapes dancing in the corner of his eye. There was the danger of being hypnotized, falling asleep at the wheel, but it hadn't happened yet.

Claudette said rather sharply she didn't want another drink, said she was half drunk now. Then she changed her mind, yes maybe she did want a drink—and a cigarette too. So Felix poured her an inch or so of bourbon, tossed her her Chesterfields, she was shaky lighting up a cigarette, holding Felix's hand, cupping her slender fingers around the lighter. Claudette's perfectly filed red-polished nails, the sad glitter of her big diamond ring. Thirty-three years old, wanting a baby so badly she rarely spoke of it any longer to Felix. He wondered did she dare bring up the subject any longer to Al Sansom? Did she contemplate some other man, some other lover, who might help her where Felix Stevick would not?

At first Felix thought Claudette was going to tell him things he already knew: Al Sansom's secrecy about money, his half-dozen bank accounts or were there more, Al Sansom disappearing from Albany then telephoning poor Claudette from another city, Chicago, Tampa, New Orleans, Los Angeles, never explaining why he was there, sometimes sounding angry and incoherent, telling Claudette he was being spied on, he was being betrayed by certain of his associates—not Felix Stevick, whom he loved and trusted like a son—not Felix Stevick but others, unnamed, former friends of his, business contacts, men who hated his guts who were jealous of him who wouldn't mind seeing him dead. Felix was uneasy, knowing Claudette wanted some response but he hadn't any response to give, *You married him, didn't you? You spend his money, don't you?* He buried his face in Claudette's hair, inhaling the woman's warm yeasty familiar smell; it came back to him powerfully at such times what a solace a woman was, a woman's body; he recalled occasions when he'd felt so broken down so fucking rotten having been exposed and humiliated sick with rage at himself for having performed poorly in the ring, or though he'd won his fight having won it without having done as well as he knew he could do and as others knew he could do—others always knew, they were always watching, that was what the ring and the lights meant—and he'd wanted desperately to get away to where nobody knew him, nobody staring and shouting insults at him, jeering at his bleeding face, he'd wanted only to bury himself in a woman, find a woman who loved him and bury himself in her deep, deep, it wasn't even fucking that mattered though fucking had to be the way in, impossible otherwise.

Claudette was saying softly she didn't know what was happening exactly to Al but she knew she couldn't continue to live with him if things kept on as they were. It wasn't even that he was jealous of her, that he suspected her of seeing another man, in a way it was worse, he didn't seem to have any particular awareness of her at all, of her as a person, he'd be out until two or three in the morning, then up at six already in his study making telephone calls with the door locked against Claudette, some days he stayed home drinking didn't even get dressed, in his pajamas and bathrobe waiting for the telephone to ring, and when it didn't ring he'd get more and more nervous, excited, even sweating, talking fast and loud making jokes to Claudette that weren't funny, that in some cases she couldn't even understand. His temper was terrible now, unpredictable, of course he was basically sweet as always and she knew her Al would come back, she didn't doubt him basically, but sometimes he'd get angry claiming she was spying on him going through his mail or papers, things in his safe, but she didn't have the combination to the safe and he knew it but he wouldn't listen to reason. She was afraid of him when he was drinking he'd actually slapped her a few times recently, of course he was always apologetic and repentant deeply sorry afterward saying he was under a lot of pressure right now, please would she forgive him, he couldn't live without her he loved her so much, and Claudette believed him, Claudette understood that if she left Al he'd crack, he simply wasn't the man he'd been a few years ago, so in control of his life, surely Felix felt the same way, wasn't that why Felix avoided Al?—also, Al's financial situation was a mystery to his own wife, Claudette had heard a rumor in Albany that he was paying fees and penalties to the IRS for back taxes and did Felix know anything about that?—no? Well, the worst of it was—and here Claudette's voice dropped, frightened, she began to speak rapidly as if knowing she shouldn't be telling Felix such information—the worst of it was she had reason to suspect, actually she had reason to be fairly certain, she'd overheard some of his conversations with his lawyer, the crisis had to do with Al Sansom having been served a subpoena by a state grand jury investigating what they called "racketeering" in upstate New York and Al was

maybe going to be granted immunity in exchange for testifying and
did Felix know—

"Claudette for Christ's sake—don't say another word!" Felix
interrupted.

He shoved her roughly from him without knowing what he did.

Claudette recoiled in hurt and surprise. "Felix—"

"Don't say another word!"

He was on his feet moving blindly toward the windows, moving
out of striking range. He didn't want to hurt her. He didn't know
what he might do. In an instant sweat broke out of his every pore, an
explosion of radiant physical heat, his heart beating so rapidly he
could hardly breathe. The bitch! The cunt! What did she mean! What
the fuck was her game?

Claudette remained sitting on the bed where he'd left her, too
astonished even to cry. Felix kept his distance from her, wouldn't even
risk looking back at her, it was one of those moments he'd remember
all his life—a weight overturning upon him out of the air, a punch he
hadn't seen coming that caught him on the point of the chin. Or had
he seen it coming.

The previous year he'd taken the Sansoms to see Sandy Saddler box
in a non-title match in Port Oriskany. When the Sansoms were in town
the three of them often went out together.

Al Sansom had been saying he'd like to see the famous featherweight champion in action, he'd heard so much about Saddler—the
nigger who'd won out over Willie Pep, wasn't he?—also frankly he
was curious about what there was in boxing that so fascinated Felix.
"Hard to look at you now," Al would say, "and think you were ever
a boxer."

"Meaning what?" Felix asked amiably.

"Meaning—I don't know," Al would say, smiling and backing
off. "You don't look like a boxer."

Claudette explained to Felix that Al didn't mean anything by such
remarks, sly fond-familiar remarks, laying his hand on Felix's arm and
smiling his mysterious smile, it was just that he thought of Felix as
friendly and good-natured and so forth, Felix shouldn't take offense.

Felix smiled, still amiable. "What makes you think I'm
offended?" he said.

He arranged for fourth-row seats. As it turned out Al Sansom
knew very little about boxing, he'd seen maybe some televised fights;
Claudette knew nothing except what she'd seen in Hollywood mov-

ies, the fourth row was maybe too close. They came in near the end of a preliminary match between two local middleweights, both black, one with a shaved head in the style of old Jack Johnson, both men hard mean punchers with nothing fancy about them, almost at once Al Sansom began making nervous wisecracks and Claudette sat very still in her seat not wanting to take off her sable coat despite the heat, poor Claudette sitting staring at the muscular half-naked sweating black men in the ring beneath the bright lights as if she'd never seen anything like it in her life—though when Felix asked her would she like him to change their seats to farther back she said no she was fine and even tried to smile. Early in the main bout, however, when the men first began trading blows seriously and Saddler's opponent—a twenty-eight-year-old from Philadelphia named Greza—was trapped in the ropes close by, streaming blood from his eye as the bell rang, Claudette said she didn't feel well she thought she'd better go up to the ladies' room, and Felix said quickly they could leave if she wanted to leave, and Al said no goddamn it they were staying, they were here and they were staying, it was only a little blood after all—did Claudette think boxers minded blood? He looked shaken himself, wiping his mouth with a handkerchief.

Felix escorted Claudette up the crowded aisle, gripping her arm above the elbow, caressing the silky fur, he told her it was probably a mistake for her to come, he guessed Saddler's strategy would be to carry Greza for another few rounds, then knock him out so maybe Claudette hadn't better watch if she felt a little faint now; it was going to get worse. He'd take her back to the hotel if she wanted to go back, Felix said, and the hell with Al, and Claudette said in a childish angry voice she couldn't do that—why did he even suggest it! "You can do anything you want, Claudette," Felix said. "No I can't," Claudette said bitterly. "Not and live with him."

White-faced, Claudette spent the remainder of the fight in the ladies' room holding damp towels against her forehead as she told Felix afterward, Felix returned to his seat to Al Sansom with his fedora tilted back on his head his face caught in an expression of droll disdain. "That nigger's good isn't he?" Al said grudgingly to Felix and Felix didn't trouble to reply or even to look at him. It turned out that the featherweight champion wasn't in the peak of condition and the near-unknown Greza was wired for a while so the fight wasn't as one-sided as Felix had anticipated though of course Greza couldn't win—hadn't a chance. But by the time the fight ended in the seventh round, Greza counted out at last, flat on his back, his arms shielding his battered face, Saddler himself breathless, looking punched out, Felix discovered himself caught up in the action, Christ he was excited, wrung dry, he identified now with losers like Greza fighting their frenzied doomed fights, knocked repeatedly to the canvas as the crowd erupts in screams, getting to their feet swaying and dazed, dripping blood, prepared for more, more punishment, showing they could take it. Felix knew the madness in their heads: *It isn't over yet, keep going, try for a knockout of your own.* Blows to the face Felix could very nearly feel, blows to the head that were even crueler, to the kidneys, to the liver, low in the abdomen, and the referee doesn't seem to notice or give a damn, near the end of the seventh Saddler's hard straight right to Greza's unprotected head and his glove deliberately open, the thumb gouging deep, yet still the poor bastard kept going, didn't fall for another several seconds, you had to wonder what the fuck was keeping him up, or why.

Then after it was over and they were headed up the aisle amid the crowd Felix suddenly remembered Jo-Jo and felt a wave of belated panic, tasted something black and gummy in his mouth. His partner Al Sansom looked resentful, wiping his plump damp face with a handkerchief, trying to joke, saying he was damned glad Felix hadn't gotten them first-row seats—the ring apron in the corner nearest them was splattered with Greza's blood, the camel's-hair topcoat of a man seated in the first row was luridly stained—"This is all very animal isn't it?" Al said and Felix said coldly, "No more animal than you, Al, what did you expect?"

Felix had never felt comfortable around Al Sansom, hadn't ever really trusted him, and since midsummer the two men were more or less estranged—still, Felix didn't want him dead.

Near midnight of the day they'd been together at the Hotel De Witt in Syracuse Claudette telephoned Felix in tears asking why, why had he been so angry with her, who the hell did he think he was, pushing her around, treating her like shit. She was drunk; Felix let her talk. The next morning she telephoned him again. What did I say? she wanted to know. What did I do wrong? Nothing, Felix said. He was going to relent but somehow he didn't, couldn't. Claudette said, beginning to cry again, I just told you something I thought you'd want to know, you're Al's partner, aren't you? and Felix said, rubbing his eyes, Honey, just forget it, will you?—forget you ever told me.

Claudette asked what did that mean.

Felix said it meant what it meant.

That evening unlocking the door of his darkened apartment he heard the telephone ringing, the sound echoing in the uncarpeted living room; he let it ring, locking the door behind him, going into his bedroom which smelled airless, stale; he switched on a light, listening to the phone ring, angry beforehand at the sound of Claudette's hurt husky voice, but when he picked up the receiver it wasn't Claudette after all, it was Vince Mattiuzzio. Hello, the men said, how are you?—falling by instinct into the cadences of warmth, friendship, boyhood camaraderie. Though since Jo-Jo Pearl's death Felix seemed to be withdrawing from Vince's world. Though Felix had a fairly good idea why Vince was telephoning. Vince asked Felix why hadn't he seen him for so long and Felix said he'd been out of town on business, then Felix asked Vince how things were and the men talked for a few minutes casually enough—Vince's father, Leonardo, was in the hospital but it wasn't anything serious and if Felix heard rumors he should discount them—then they speculated on the upcoming big fight in Chicago, Sugar Ray Robinson coming out of retirement trying to get back the middleweight title from Bobo Olson and if Robinson could do it he'd be the first ex-champion to come back but Vince didn't think he'd make it, Vince had a grudge against Robinson dating back to some contractual squabble when they'd promoted one of Robinson's fights, Vince was placing his money on Bobo. And Felix said he wasn't even going to bet this one, he'd lost enough on that asshole Bobo last time but he couldn't really see Robinson winning either after he'd been out for so long, beautiful boxer as he was, wasn't he thirty-six years old now? Then the men fell silent. Then Vince asked Felix still in a casual voice did he have any news about Al Sansom, when was the last time he'd spoken with Al Sansom, and Felix said he hadn't seen Sansom in a few weeks and he hadn't heard any news of any particular interest.

"No news?" said Vince.

"No," said Felix.

"No?" said Vince.

"No," said Felix.

"Nothing?" said Vince.

"Nothing," said Felix.

Vince paused and Felix knew he'd be expected now to ask what this was all about, what was Sansom up to, and so on and so forth playing dumb but Felix felt too much contempt to play dumb, let Vince sit there stewing, thinking, his eyes widening and narrowing as they did when he concentrated hard, something mean in his bones beginning to push out through his fleshy face. Finally Vince said, "He could get us all into trouble. If he wanted to."

Felix said, "Who knows?"

Before he hung up, Vince said as if embarrassed, "About Claudette Sansom—you're seeing her?"

Felix hesitated. "No," he said.

Not that time but another time, a few days later after another conversation with Vince—could they meet? have a drink? there were things Vince didn't want to discuss on the telephone—Felix opened the drawer of his bedside table, there was the .45 inside which he liked seeing there but which he didn't touch. He remembered amused how startled Enid had been seeing it, how shy of it and of him, why not open a drawer out of girlish curiosity and see something you're not supposed to see, like following your own uncle upstairs in a boarded-up hotel knowing he's hot to fuck you and you're curious if he will. He liked seeing the gun, there's always solace in owning a gun, having the power to pull the trigger if you want, not pulling it if you don't want, he recalled a friend of his of some years ago another young boxer who'd been cut up terribly in his third or fourth pro fight looking as if somebody had clubbed him with a baseball bat or brass knuckles, nose broken, jaw broken, eyes swollen shut, a dozen big cuts, but the main thing was his eyes, a tear in the iris of his left eye so he'd never fight again even if he could bring himself to fight again—that was it. Later it turned out that the other boxer or the other boxer's trainer had sliced his gloves. Taken out some of the padding so that Felix's friend was being hit with taped knuckles, not eight-ounce gloves. And after that Felix's friend dropped out of sight and a few years later Felix heard he'd killed himself—shot himself in the head with a .22-caliber rifle in the basement of his father's house—and Felix had been angry, disgusted, incredulous, why the fuck shoot yourself if you can shoot somebody else? But now he was coming around to seeing his friend's position. You rid yourself of yourself and you rid yourself of every problem, past present future.

And of Enid. What of Enid.

He knew about Al Sansom, more or less—what would probably happen. But he didn't know about Enid.

He loved her, he'd never hurt her. Even if she provoked him. Still he resented her—he resented the energy spent on thinking about her—since that day he'd happened to see her walking on Nine Mile

Road with a boyfriend or boyfriends, whoever the bastards were. He found himself angry with Enid much of the time except when he was actually with her, making love with her, then he could be certain of her, there were things she couldn't fake. With one part of his mind he understood she was faithful to him, she'd never lie to him, in all the world she really had no one but him—he understood that. It was a story of a kind he told himself often now that he'd run out of other stories to tell himself. But still he knew she'd never betray him, he knew he could trust her, he'd be the one to break it off when it was time to break it off and that time was coming soon.

Yes she vowed she loved him, pressing herself in his arms, urgent and frightened he might stop loving her, she didn't think she could live without him she'd said many times, and Felix couldn't know if it was true, how could he know until they tried it. In any case she was going away to college next year. So that would be that. He wanted her gone, out of the city and out of his life, he resented thinking so much about her and he resented too the underground stream trickling through his soul, accumulating suspicions, jealousies, small stinging humiliating hurts when he was superior to such things, a man in full control of his emotions.

Still: he couldn't help but think she frequently lied to him. He couldn't help but think she must be attracted to other men, to mere boys, those pimply-faced sons of bitches, in all fairness and reasonableness that was only natural, wasn't it, he knew it but couldn't accept it but in his innermost heart he *did* accept it, he was superior to such wayward moods. As proof he wasn't going to telephone her for a long time. And when he telephoned her and when he saw her he wasn't going to accuse her of anything—let her be the one to show hurt and surprise, jealousy too, the little bitch planning her life without him. He wasn't going to think of her—she was his niece after all—he wanted to concentrate on thinking of Al Sansom and of Claudette, of what he must do if he was going to do anything, and when he'd have to do it before it was too late. Which was why he liked looking at the pistol for long minutes at a time but didn't want to touch it, that might be too physical. He'd gone through a part of his life when everything was quick, direct, physical—a matter of touch, of feeling things resisting him and being excited by resistance, needing to be hit in order to be released into hitting—now maybe he'd be suspended, just thinking, staring. That way he could do no harm.

* * *

These were new stories Felix Stevick told himself. Maybe since Jo-Jo's death. Since Enid had begun to mean more to him than he knew she should mean.

Why think of Jo-Jo, what was the point, he was dead. What point in thinking of the dead. Like thinking of Karl Stevick who was long dead and Ursula a widow again last year but now planning to marry a retired stockbroker, wealthy, seventy-two years old, a widower himself—Aren't you happy for me, Felix? Ursula asked ironically over the telephone and Felix's response was, Sure. But what was the point.

They said that Leroy Pearl dropped by the gym from time to time demanding to see the men "responsible" for his son's death—Felix Stevick, Vince Mattiuzzio, Dan Hickey, Chris Delancy. Though the son of a bitch had been paid off. To a degree paid off. Swaying drunk and noisy in the street outside, stopping people to tell them how his boy'd been taken from him and mishandled and killed, the fucking bastards might as well have dropped his body in the lake, tossed it out of a car, bastards taking advantage of a young sweet gifted kid who didn't know any better than to sign his life away. Instead of bringing him along slow and cautious they'd pushed him like he was some white-boy Joe Louis, fighting a fight every month or was it every week, not giving a damn for him or for his old man who was crippled, you could see he was crippled, sclerosis of the spine he could hardly walk he'd been shot up by the Japs and left to rot by the U.S. Government, the fucking hypocrites at the VA Hospital and in Washington, what did they care about a man's livelihood let alone his life and his pride?—then two or three men from the gym would come out and deal with him, get him out of the neighborhood. Vince didn't want him hurt but he thought it might come to that eventually. Felix said, He's asking for it isn't he. You can always tell when somebody is asking for it.

The last time Felix saw Al Sansom alive was to be the evening of December 12, 1955.

Al telephoned Felix the night of the eleventh, his voice slurred and uneven, apologizing for having been out of touch for so long. He'd been traveling, he said, exploring investment possibilities for Sansom & Stevick, had a few prospects to put to Felix before he and Claudette left for the Virgin Islands. He knew he owed Felix an explanation but it would all come out in due course. So why not meet for drinks tomorrow, Al said. Some quiet place, nothing downtown or fancy. Some neighborhood place.

Felix suggested a tavern on the West Side down the street from

St. Anne's Church, he got there at nine o'clock and waited twenty minutes, then the bartender came to his booth saying there was a telephone call for him if his name was Stevick. So he went to take the call and Al Sansom was on the other end saying in a low guarded voice that his plans had been altered, could Felix meet him at Olcott's Bowling Lanes on South Olcott Street in ten minutes. So Felix drove down to Olcott's Bowling Lanes and when he turned into the parking lot Al Sansom hurried out from his parked car signaling for him to stop. "I don't like this place after all," Al told Felix. "Let's go somewhere else."

Al didn't look quite as bad as Claudette had described him but the man had certainly lost weight, his skin was parchment-colored, lips thin and nervously ironic but in a new way Felix couldn't gauge, he gave off an odor of excitement and fear that Felix wasn't going to contest. "Sure," he said. "Where?" He'd thought Al would follow him in his car but no: Al said his car motor wasn't working right, he didn't trust it. So Al rode beside Felix in Felix's car along Olcott down to busy Grand Street then east to Decker, looking for a suitable place to stop for a drink, Felix could smell whiskey on him, he could see a gummy-looking white stain on the sleeve of his black cashmere topcoat. It wasn't like sporty Al Sansom either, to sit so slump-shouldered, like a little old man whose bones were curving in.

To humor him Felix drove for ten minutes, passing one place after another until Al gripped his arm, saying, "Here—this looks safe": an ordinary neighborhood tavern with a red neon *Schlitz* in the window. He asked Felix was anybody likely to recognize him here; Felix said no he didn't think so; fine, said Al, this is it. Inside the tavern, seated in a booth with his back to the crowded barroom, Al ordered a double scotch and lit up a cigarette using an ivory cigarette holder Felix hadn't seen before, he leaned forward to speak confidentially to Felix, smiling and grinning, seeming to make a point of not glancing around at the other customers even when wild waves of laughter broke out among them. The tavern was close by the GM radiator plant, the men were factory workers, Felix supposed, spread out in loud friendly clusters along the bar, everybody knowing everybody else since grade school.

Al Sansom was keyed up, nervy, trying almost visibly to relax. The tricky thing about being summoned to testify before a grand jury and being granted immunity, Felix thought, was you couldn't plead the Fifth Amendment: you *were* granted immunity, were in no legal danger of incriminating yourself. So if you refused to testify or if you lied you'd be cited for contempt and each contempt citation carried with it how many years—five? It had once been explained to Felix and he'd marveled at the ingenuity of the thing. The prosecutors, if they got you just right, really got you. But it was likely to be your friends who finished you off.

Al was saying in a hushed rapid voice he'd been in seclusion. And traveling. In seclusion *and* traveling. Gazing into the depths of his soul and by Christ he'd discovered he did have a soul!—something there after all. Only maybe a few grains like sand or grit, he said, grinning. D'you know what I mean, Felix?

Felix let him talk. He didn't intend to fall in with his mood, nerved-up people filled him with contempt. Like listening to loud fast music—your heart speeds up to no purpose.

But mainly, Al said, he'd been traveling. On business. Florida, the Caribbean: the world of the future, and Sansom & Stevick could do worse than invest in the future—right? He'd begun to feel constrained in this part of the world, even the Adirondacks, granted the mountains are beautiful, the lakes et cetera, so many thousands of acres up there to be developed and sold off but maybe they should put the Villa Rideau on the market and invest in some winter resorts maybe in south Florida, the Keys, Jamaica, the Virgin Islands, even Haiti where everything's for sale. Al had some good contacts down there, fresh talent, he'd introduce Felix to them someday. "Christ it's beautiful down there, those islands," Al said, blinking as if the sun were shining into his face; he groped for his drink, smiled a vague twitchy smile that made Felix uneasy since it wasn't any smile of Al Sansom's he'd ever seen before.

The other evening Vince Mattiuzzio had dropped by uninvited to have a drink with Felix to suggest that if he heard from Al Sansom why didn't he give Vince a call. Felix said coldly he doubted he'd be hearing from Al, they were out of touch, they weren't friends. Yes but you're business partners, Vince said. Felix shrugged. Will you do that for me, Felix?—one telephone call, Vince said. When Felix didn't reply a second time Vince said contemptuously, You don't have to have any part in it beyond that. Sure, said Felix. I know all about that.

People were saying things about him, Al said, speculating all sorts of things based on no evidence at all. Because he'd been out of sight for a while. Which was why Felix hadn't heard from him in a while and there was a little trouble about cash flow, taxes, actually they were back taxes, also fees and penalties for 1953 and going into 1954 but it was about to be straightened out, you have to fight the IRS with its own ammunition. Claudette worried about him too much, people told her things and she seemed to want to believe the worst, that son of a bitch her first husband had treated her like shit, did Felix know?—now her outlook on life was naturally a little distorted. "Once we get away to the islands things will be all right," Al said vaguely. "It's paradise there—I mean *paradise.*" He paused. He swallowed down a large mouthful of his scotch. "If you avoid the other parts," he said.

A tavern called Davy's on the corner of West Aiken and Belvedere, from approximately 10 P.M. until around 11 P.M. of the night of December 12, 1955, the last time Felix Stevick would be having a conversation with his business partner Al Sansom, and possibly Felix guessed that might be the case. Still his thoughts drifted free of Al and Al's nervous pushy voice. Al talking of real estate in warm lazy tropical places with names like Montego Bay, Port-au-Prince, Santo Domingo, San Juan; Felix thinking of the Adirondacks and of the cold, snow falling up at Shoal Lake, l'Isle-Verte very likely deserted at this time of year, the summer places shut down. Felix had never been there in the winter, why was he thinking of it now?—thinking for some reason of his father's old house on the water—those airy high-ceilinged rooms, the flagstone terrace, fancy brown shingleboard that rotted easily and fancy white trim along the roof's edge, old-fashioned lightning rods on the roof. Somebody had asked him why hadn't he ever gone back to visit the house and he'd said why should he. He remembered his father's sailboat which he'd never really learned to sail. His father shouting at him that time—or another time. Maybe it was all the same time. He'd been a small boy then but already he was disappointing people. The story of Felix Stevick's life. He hadn't liked the mountains, space and solitude and "beauty" bored him shitless, he was himself only in the city. He needed his friends, he needed some action. One day in Felix's hearing Ursula had said to his father, He's yours, her voice flat and bemused, and he'd wondered what she meant. He's yours? and not mine? But Felix and Ursula had always resembled each other. In looks, in temperament. His mother's vanity that he shouldn't get his face injured—the main thing she'd worried about when he started boxing.

Oh go to hell, he'd told her. Just go to hell, will you.

Go down to Miami Beach and get married again. You're past the age for fucking, just get them to marry you, get the will in your favor.

As Al Sansom got drunker his skin got softer, pulpier, like whitish dough now so when he leaned his head on his hand the fingers left shallow indentations in his cheek. He's getting crazy, Claudette had said. But still he spoke coherently. Though moving from subject to subject—real estate to local politics to Claudette herself ("I love that girl—I'd die for her") to his favorite topic of Unidentified Flying Objects: flying saucers as the media vulgarly called them. Had Felix seen the big feature in *Collier's*—how UFOs were being explained away by the Eisenhower Administration as aerial balloons or weather phenomena or stars or meteorites or clouds or mere air pollution! But it was a historical fact that UFOs—whatever they were, wherever they were from—had been sighted by mankind for centuries, particularly in the past decade, the month of May 1953 had been a high point of sorts with sightings in Oregon, Colorado, Texas, California, New York, in Brazil, over in Scandinavia, Japan—Eisenhower and the Civil Aeronautics Board couldn't continue to suppress the truth, whatever the truth was. Did Felix know there was an actual Censorship Department in the Pentagon? Al asked. It was responsible for obscuring reports of UFOs and casting derision on citizens who claimed to see them, of course some of these citizens were cranks and maniacs and sensation mongers, but Al wasn't talking about them. "I'd dismiss it all myself," Al said, "if I hadn't seen such convincing photographs. One taken in Texas last month—a thing like a metal dirigible, glowing white, pulsing—witnesses said it shot upward directly vertical and disappeared in a matter of seconds. Some of them are flat, some are cigar-shaped, some are saucer-shaped, they're always extremely big though nobody knows their dimensions. In the photographs—I should have brought some of the magazines along to show you, Felix—the trouble is you can't judge how big they are, or how small. The thing might be the size of a pinwheel or the size of a barn! The most famous instance—you might know about this already—took place on July first, 1954, when a pilot and his radarman in an F-Ninety-four fighter plane followed a huge 'saucer' that was giving off blinding light—somewhere above Griffith Air Force Base—then suddenly according to the men's testimony the jet's engine cut off—no warning—the cockpit of the plane got very hot—like a blast from a blowtorch, the pilot said—so both men bailed out, the UFO vanished straight up, the fighter plane crashed in the mountains, and before the military could censor them the pilot and the other man spoke with civilians, told them everything that had happened so it's all on record, it's historic, it can't be denied." By degrees Al had begun to speak more rapidly and excitedly, gesturing at Felix with his ivory cigarette holder. "I should have explained," he said, faltering. "Griffith Air Force Base is up by Walesville. D'you know where Walesville is?"

Felix was getting impatient having to listen to all this, Al Sansom's voice so pleading, what was the poor bastard thinking underneath if he was capable of thinking anything at all? Wide dark nostrils more prominent than usual, waxen sheen to the nose, a light coating of sweat on his forehead and Felix supposed he was tasting fear like scum in the mouth—Felix knew just how that tasted. He interrupted Al, saying abruptly, "Did you want us to get together to talk about that shit?" and while Al stared hurt he felt the impulse to laugh, adding, "or some other kind of shit?"

There must have been a moment, a hair's-breadth of a moment, when Al was going to tell Felix all that was happening: he had the look, Felix afterward thought, of a man in a rapidly falling elevator. But then he thought better of it. Jowls shivering, nostrils contracting in disdain. He stubbed out his cigarette in the ashtray pretending not to have heard Felix's words, though he caught the drift, you could say, of Felix's intent. "I want to go back to the hotel," he said in his old haughty voice. "I'm tired. I have an early day tomorrow. I don't even know who you are."

He stood up awkwardly in the booth, swayed, clutched at his head, but when Felix tried to help him he waved Felix irritably away. Had to go to the john, he said. So he went walking carefully, threading his way through the tables, the smoky drifting air, millionaire investor and real estate speculator Al Sansom in a custom-made dark flannel suit now baggy in the rear, rumpled across the shoulders. Felix watched him more in disgust than pity, his heart was hardened against pity, this was a man who could do injury to him if he wished or even if he didn't wish, if others coerced him into it. All right, you fucker, Felix thought.

Felix paid for both their drinks and waited for Al up front and eventually Al appeared looking as if he'd washed his face and hadn't quite dried it, he'd combed his hair back wetly from his forehead and made an effort to adjust his clothes, walking slowly, self-consciously, his left foot dragging. He cast a damp pleading look at Felix meaning he wanted to be forgiven but couldn't remember what he'd done to be forgiven. "Felix—wait," he said. He needed help leaving the tavern, actually getting out the door and into the cold. Leaning on Felix's arm panting his whiskey breath and Felix could feel his eyes darting rapidly from side to side. This is it, Felix thought, now they were exposed. There was a hard stiff wind from the lake tasting of cold, of snow, an underlying chemical smell from somewhere close by. Al Sansom shivered inside his expensive coat, leaning heavily against Felix, asking where was his car?—telling Felix please to wait, not to drive off without him. Felix was mystified how much shorter Al had become than he and Felix Stevick wasn't a particularly tall man, just six feet, which was tall for a middleweight but otherwise not. Felix told Al he'd left his car back at Olcott's—the bowling lanes, didn't he remember?—now Felix would drive him back.

Crossing the snowy cindery lot to his car Felix stiffened waiting for something to happen even before the headlights of a car close by switched on blinding them both. This is it, he thought for a second time, oddly calmly staring into the lights while Al stumbled against his legs. But it was just another customer driving out of the lot.

Since Al Sansom was in no shape to operate a car Felix decided to take him directly back to his hotel. It was the Onondaga, downtown, Felix stopped at the curb by the bright-lit front entrance but for a long moment Al just sat beside him breathing hoarsely, staring at his hands in his lap. Felix's eye was drawn to the gold wedding band, the tiny glitter of its diamond. That gummy stain on Al's coat sleeve.

When Felix was about to ask him did he need help getting into the hotel, Al roused himself and opened the door. He thanked Felix for the ride; shook hands with him saying he knew he had a lot of explaining to do, Jesus he was sorry but this just wasn't his night. He shook Felix's hand again as if not wanting to release it. His voice was vague, bewildered. "I wish I knew what I could do for you . . ." he said.

Felix laughed. "Do you?" he said.

Al heaved himself out of the car, managed to get the heavy door shut tight, walked off swaying in the direction of the hotel's revolving doors, but Felix didn't wait around to see if he made it.

12

Swiftly and cleanly the needle entered her flesh, the tender skin of the inside of her arm just below the elbow. *Don't move,* the nurse warned her—as if she required being warned.

* * *

Around her head a flaming nimbus appeared. There was a dove whose feathers were afire. Enid was the dove but she was also watching the dove flying upward in wild widening fiery circles out of her vision.

When she awoke the air smelled scorched, her hair was singed, the pupils of her eyes contracted to pinpricks. A woman in a nurse's uniform was asking her where she was. On the operating table, Enid said faintly. No said the woman, not now. It was all over.

Those long weeks Enid nursed her secret she'd carried herself numb and cold as if anesthetized, or dead. A dreamy deadness where you keep going with no heartbeat and nothing there behind the eyes, just the usual smile and people smiling back or not smiling back. She wasn't afraid and she wasn't angry, telling herself pointless exclamatory words she couldn't have interpreted except they seemed to give her solace. *Sure. Why not. Watch me. Like this. Okay.* Then in Felix's presence in Felix's big beautiful new car she began screaming, crying, she'd have liked to rake his astonished face with her nails, *You did this on purpose didn't you, I know, I knew at the time, didn't you, you bastard, I hope I die, I hope it kills me, I never want to see you or think of you or hear anything of you again.*

Her skin was feverish, hot to the touch. She calculated she was nine weeks pregnant. Her small breasts beginning to swell and thicken, a sensation of swelling in her belly, spells of terrible heart-stopping drowsiness during the day—she told Felix she'd fallen asleep on the Clinton Street bus and gone all the way to Van Buren Boulevard before someone woke her. Sometimes helping her mother prepare supper she got violently sick and ran away to vomit upstairs, other times she was ravenously hungry and ate so much both her parents took note, amused, or puzzled. The person she had to avoid was Geraldine—one look at Enid and Geraldine would know.

Felix asked why hadn't she told him for so many weeks.

Enid said she didn't know.

Had she thought it might go away? he asked.

She didn't know.

In his arms she wept bitterly, furiously. He'd done it on purpose, hadn't he. No, Felix said, pained, of course not, his voice was anguished and guilty; why would I do such a thing? I don't know, Enid said. Why did you. Being pregnant was a kind of dream in which Enid both was and was not merely Enid, another person seemed to be pushing forward, reckless, happy, all flesh and heat, urging mad thoughts upon her—why couldn't she have the baby! why not! it was wrong to want to kill it, it was murder, the gravest of all sins, she could run away to a Catholic home somewhere wasn't there a home for unwed mothers somewhere near, week after week a notice in the *Catholic Home Messenger* asking for donations, though maybe Felix would want to take care of her and they could live together—not in Port Oriskany but in another place—then it wouldn't be murder, neither would be to blame.

But she seemed to know Felix would never touch her again—not after this. Nor would she want him to.

One day shortly before she decided to tell him, on an errand for her mother downtown, she'd started suddenly to run to fight off a sensation of terrible drowsiness, didn't give a damn for the traffic on Main Street or the icy sidewalks she felt the pull of something vast and dark and sweet she couldn't have given a name to, running along in her smooth-soled boots that made her slip and plunge, her head bare because her scarf had blown off, hair wild in the wind and eyes probably glittering like a madwoman's—the secret of the mad, Enid thought, must be they were *happy,* they'd *escaped*—and she saw in the corner of her eye a truck speeding toward the intersection ahead and her legs carried her forward in a delirium of excitement but she wasn't fast enough, the truck rushed by leaving her standing panting and baffled at the curb. And it was a measure of her craziness at this time that having failed to throw herself under the wheels of that particular truck—and a lovely heavy truck it had been, carrying a cement mixer behind—she lost her strength, her resolve, her very soul filled with self-loathing knowing she hadn't any longer the courage to kill herself. Somebody else would have to do it for her or it wouldn't be done at all.

That day, in Sibley's, buying several spools of silk thread and a half-dozen yards of unbleached muslin, Enid happened to see her old junior high school teacher Miss Holland in another aisle, saw her and immediately turned away avoiding her, that eagle eye of Miss Holland the girls had all feared. From time to time since leaving De Witt Clinton Enid had encountered Miss Holland downtown and generally avoided the woman out of shyness rather than dislike, though maybe there was dislike too, anticipation of Miss Holland's mysterious mocking smile, something disappointed and blaming in her jauntiness,

How are you, Enid?—surprised I remember you, Enid?—when you've changed so much!—that sort of thing, leaving Enid smiling and tongue-tied wishing she could escape.

Holland's queer for you, Angel-face!—so the girls had teased. Long ago. And it made her slightly sick to be reminded.

She left Sibley's hurriedly without glancing again in Miss Holland's direction—if the woman had sighted her, too bad, she didn't give a damn about being rude. But on the bus home she fell into a dreamy state seeming to see herself as she'd been years ago, wiry little monkey-nimble Enid Stevick amazing everyone with her stunts on the mats and the trampoline. She didn't doubt she'd been good and now she inhabited her body as if it belonged to someone else, she had lost forever the sweaty childish excitement, throwing herself high into the air, allowing herself to plunge down flat on her chest and belly on the coarse canvas of the trampoline, arms extended like wings. What had she cared that she might damage her breasts—the flesh there is very tender, Miss Holland had scolded—Enid Stevick hadn't wanted breasts had she! Like her mother's and her aunt's, heavy and pendulous, caught up in brassieres like harnesses, ugly straps and wires and hooks. Now the trampoline itself was banned from Port Oriskany public schools because a boy at Central High had broken his back performing on one the previous spring.

Enid recalled the day Miss Holland called her into her little cubicle of an office (a plate-glass window on one side looking into the entrance to the girls' locker room, a plate-glass window on the other looking into the gymnasium itself) that smelled of Vaseline, perspiration, rubber-soled shoes, spearmint chewing gum. There was Miss Holland frowning over her little much-thumbed class book asking Enid if she was well—if she'd been examined by a doctor recently—according to her records Enid had asked to be excused from class just two weeks ago because of menstruation and cramps and now she'd given that excuse today and the records showed she was having her periods alarmingly frequently was it every nineteen days sometimes? sixteen days?—there was supposed to be danger of anemia, Miss Holland said quietly, if the periods came more often than twenty-one days, she didn't want to frighten Enid but she thought Enid should know if her mother wasn't aware of the situation, if in fact the excuses she was giving were legitimate. "I have to take these things on faith," Miss Holland said, fixing Enid with her sad calm accusing gaze. And that tight little smile of hers, so grudging.

I have to take these things on faith!—so absurd and preposterous a remark Enid knew she'd remember it all her life, she'd remember too her choked-down rage, her humiliation, sitting there staring at the floor trying to sort out what was the accusation being made against her, how could she reply, what was happening, *she's queer for you, Angel-face* the girls would afterward snicker but Enid sat wordless and blinking, her mind gone blank. The impulse came to her to stick a finger into herself to show Miss Holland the blood, that would do it, but Enid Maria wouldn't dare such a gesture. She sat blushing while Miss Holland went on to talk of health, puberty, "maturation," did Enid understand how it was dangerous to be intimate with a boy, had her mother or anyone in her family explained how dangerous it was, had she ever read anything on the subject, and Enid murmured yes, a vague confused yes, sitting there staring at the floor waiting for it to end. "Do you know what is meant by 'intimate'?" Miss Holland asked quietly, half chidingly, as if she were speaking to a recalcitrant child. "You'd be surprised the girls your age—and older—who don't know and who allow boys to take advantage of them. Then of course they get into trouble." After some minutes of Miss Holland's catechism Enid was allowed to leave; she had another class to get to. Sure she knew about "intimate" and she knew about "trouble" but what good would her knowledge do her, she was already in love with Felix Stevick though she hadn't quite realized it at the time.

Felix took her to a doctor in the suburb of Lakeshore Heights the day after she told him her news. She had only to trust him, he said, if she was really nine weeks pregnant they hadn't any time to waste. "This doctor," Enid said skeptically, "what's his name?" "It doesn't matter what his name is," said Felix. "How do you know about him?" Enid asked. "I know about him," said Felix. "Because you've brought other girlfriends of yours to him," Enid said, mocking. "Isn't that it?"

Enid had heard many tales of girls and women in the neighborhood who had had abortions—"real" abortions done by doctors, or men who claimed to be doctors—she knew of a half-dozen cases involving hemorrhaging, infection, sepsis. Once she'd been sickened overhearing her mother and one of her mother's friends talking of a mutual acquaintance, a woman of thirty-nine who had five or six or seven children and got pregnant and arranged to have an abortion, and whoever did the "abortion" didn't know what he was doing and she went home bleeding, then began hemorrhaging and finally called a cab to take her to the emergency room at St. Joseph's but at St. Joseph's they wouldn't accept her as a patient because she'd been a party to a criminal act, a mortal sin, so she'd had to go away again and—this was the nastiest part of the story, recounted by Enid's mother with particular relish—she couldn't get any taxi driver to take her as a passenger because by now she was bleeding badly, her clothing was all stained, she tried to walk home and collapsed on the sidewalk and was finally taken by ambulance to Port Oriskany General on the other side of town where they saved her life—barely—but "of course" the woman would never be quite right again, not physically or mentally, that was what came of trying to have an abortion, Mrs. Stevick said, going against God's will.

Enid told Felix these things, some of them, on the drive out to Lakeshore Heights. She even imitated her mother's voice. Felix said with a pained expression, "Honey—why don't you stop."

She'd never had a complete pelvic examination before, she'd never been required to remove her clothes and put on a coarse white paper smock and lie atop a table with her bare feet in metal stirrups and her knees spread trembling and wide so that someone might probe deep inside her with an instrument that was sharp, excruciating, unbearable—but she was going to have to bear it, that was why Felix had brought her here. Next the doctor brisk and matter-of-fact examined her internally with his rubber-gloved fingers, her vagina, her anus, Enid lay frozen, her hands closed into fists and her nails digging into her palms, thinking, This is only the beginning. Thinking ironically, This is life! And how remote, how unlikely it now seemed, her lovemaking with Felix, her long infatuation with Felix, sitting now in the waiting room one leg crossed over the other, his eyes shadowy and hooded as if in sleep, a faint cloud of bluish smoke about his head because he'd begun smoking cigarettes again because he was as frightened as Enid but wasn't going to show it.

The doctor hadn't any name Enid was ever to learn. Surely Felix knew it but Enid quickly lost her curiosity. He was a man of her father's age probably, hair gone thin, small creases and tucks in his face, a small pursed closed-in mouth she wanted to be kind but saw was merely indifferent, perfunctory—he asked her none of the questions she had feared ("Who is the father?" for instance), only a few quick questions about her health and her medical history and her menstrual periods, the date of her last period, and so on and so forth, he told her they needed a urine sample to be absolutely certain but by his estimate he guessed she was nine or ten weeks pregnant, didn't that tally with her own estimate, now a glimmer of impatience in his expression as she began to sob, sitting with her arms tightly crossed and her head bowed, hair in her face, raw and dazed and throbbing with pain between her legs. This is life! he maybe wanted to tell her. Didn't you want it?

He let her cry, he lit up a cigarette, sighing and expelling smoke, going on to explain the procedure—it was always a "procedure" never an "abortion"—which if she wanted could be scheduled fairly soon, between Christmas and New Year's was a good time, a slack time, probably they could work something out once the urine sample came back. There would be a general anesthetic which was of course a serious measure but the actual surgery involved—the scraping of the inside of the uterus, the removal of the fetus—was not major surgery, did she understand. And there was nothing humanly or morally wrong with what they were going to do but since the procedure was outlawed in the United States except for therapeutic reasons it had to be done in absolute secrecy, did she understand.

Enid stopped crying, wiped her face roughly with a tissue. "I understand," she said. "Isn't that why I'm here."

It was all so routine, so perfunctory—how many sobbing girls and women had sat here listening to the doctor's little speech—she realized it was pointless to feel shame, sorrow, despair; all the transaction really required was money.

("How much is it going to cost?" Enid asked Felix but Felix refused to say. "A thousand dollars? two thousand? five thousand?—I have a right to know." But Felix refused to say, staring at her vaguely shocked it seemed by her tone, her mood, something brittle and nervously electric about her; if he tried to touch her she pushed his hand away, if he tried to comfort her she laughed, saying it was too late for that. "How much is it going to cost?" she asked. "Getting rid of the 'fetus'—is it expensive?")

Enid knew she was pregnant and she knew she'd have the abortion—why not sometime between Christmas and New Year's, surely it was a "slack time"—still, when Felix telephoned to say the urine test had come back positive, he'd gone ahead and made arrangements, telling her the day, the time, she was overcome with a sensation of light-headedness, dropped the phone receiver to the floor, her heart beat wildly as if it were another's heart inside her, maddened with terror of its life being extinguished.

For surely it was murder, what they meant to do: she knew, she knew.

But they were going to do it.

Her stage name was "Lizabeth Somers" which wasn't quite so exotic as Henri La Porte had wanted but which suited Lizzie fine, she'd always been embarrassed by a name like Stevick because hearing it people automatically put you into a category, names like Nicolaou, Ziegler, Kroetz, Rossky, Esposito, Weir, embarrassing names like that, she wanted an American name so she'd gone through the telephone directory taking her time and experimenting, pronouncing names aloud until she happened upon the right one: it must be like choosing your baby's name, she said, you've got to get it just right. "Half the history of show business," Lizzie told Enid, "Henri says, is finding the right name to express your talent."

Mrs. Stevick still disapproved of Lizzie's singing career but a few days before Christmas the Stevicks went by invitation to hear Lizzie sing at the Cloverleaf Club downtown—Mr. and Mrs. Stevick, Enid, Geraldine and Neal O'Banan—Lizzie's mentor Henri La Porte insisted upon treating them to a late supper and drinks, saying it was Christmas week after all, the season to celebrate, he was damned proud of Lizzie and thought her family should be too. In some excitement he told them he believed Lizzie was at the start of a brilliant career—if she was properly managed. "Talent can get you only halfway," he said. "The rest is brains." Enid thought the handsome little man with his very black slicked-down hair, tiny black mustache, and black button-shiny eyes fatuous and overbearing, kissing the women's hands, murmuring *"Enchanté"!*—busily playing host at the Cloverleaf—but she could see why Lizzie might be drawn to him, appeared in fact infatuated with him, his personality so intense, so authoritative, every utterance exclamatory and every gesture charged with drama. There was something attractive about his very cunning—the way he played up to Mr. Stevick knowing Mr. Stevick disliked him, the exaggerated court he paid to Mrs. Stevick which left her embarrassed and flattered. And who knew?—maybe Henri La Porte was right about Lizzie's talent and what he called Lizzie's "future." You wanted to believe, in any case.

The Cloverleaf Club, recently refurbished, was in an old brick building on South Main Street close by the notorious Bijou Burlesque and the ancient Tiffany Theater, where movies of a questionable quality were now shown. Inside, however, the nightclub had been decorated for Christmas and its frantic festive atmosphere seemed in a way consoling— "Lizabeth Somers" was only one of several performers scheduled for that evening, not the main attraction, the nightclub crowd was noisy but sporadically effusive with its applause and Enid wasn't so nervous for her sister as she would have been in a starker setting. How could anything matter here at the Cloverleaf!— amid jammed-in tables and hilarious drunken patrons and lewd red-winking Christmas bulbs overhead. And Henri La Porte had coached his protégée well: Lizzie sang with professional competence, her voice straining only on the highest notes and wavering only now and then when she found herself out of rhythm with the three-man ensemble that accompanied her. She looked glamorous, even startling, in an electric-blue strapless gown with a very tight bodice, a shirred waist, and a stylish full-circle skirt that fell to mid-calf; her platinum-blond hair was lavishly upswept and fastened with rhinestone-studded combs; her voice was husky, suggestive, ingratiating, intense, and dramatic by turns. The bright spotlight seemed to fall upon her rudely, yet she appeared in Enid's eyes oddly healthy, even wholesome, the wide generous contours of her face exposed through the thick pancake makeup, the Stevick cheekbones and nose, her prettiness given a translucence and even an innocence hardly evident in ordinary light. As she sang she used her arms skillfully if rather mechanically and her eyes shone with moisture that might have been genuine emotion aroused by her songs—"Crying in the Chapel," "Body and Soul," "I'm Dreaming of a White Christmas." Henri La Porte must have counseled Lizzie to pay not the slightest heed to rude customers—Lizabeth Somers had too much talent for *that*—and to smile happily, and bow from the waist, and blow dimpled airy kisses out into the crowd no matter how few people actually applauded at any particular time.

Since late October Enid had been dropping by the apartment Lizzie shared with Nelia Pancoe and Thelma Price, taking solace of a kind from the slapdash atmosphere there and the hint of slapdash lives—the girls were always "in and out" of the place as Lizzie vaguely explained, staying away overnight or for days in a row with one or another of their boyfriends. (Even Nelia Pancoe, coarse-faced, chunky, with a loud boisterous laugh, had a boyfriend of sorts— though "boy" was perhaps not the appropriate term since he must have been twice Nelia's age.) How different South Olcott Street was from East Clinton, where Enid hid herself away in her room thinking her trapped desperate thoughts—she must be pregnant, she couldn't be pregnant!—not wanting even to practice the piano any longer for fear her playing would expose her. At Lizzie's apartment people were always stopping by, the telephone was always ringing, the radio or the record player was always turned up full blast playing Chuck Berry, Bill Haley and the Comets, The Drifters, The Orioles, The Fontane Sisters. Quarrels among Lizzie and Nelia and Thelma flared up but were forgotten within minutes. You got the impression, Enid thought, that nothing much mattered beyond the next hour.

Once when Enid visited the apartment after school Rose Ann Esposito was already there visiting with her year-old daughter, Mrs. Mick Hamill she was now, still pretty in a sour smirking way though her hair hadn't been washed in days and she'd gained maybe twenty pounds since her pregnancy and her secret was things weren't "too hot" between her and Mick and yes she was pregnant again—three months and already she was starting to show, she'd blow up like a balloon this time. The girls squealed and congratulated her, even Enid congratulated her, but Rose Ann said indifferently, "There's lots more where this comes from." Lizzie and Nelia and Thelma and Rose Ann had been drinking beer before Enid arrived, eating cold sloppy slices of pizza, they were in high spirits welcoming Enid—"Hey, it's Angel-face"—"D'you remember Angel-face?"—and after two or three beers of her own Enid had the sudden impulse to tell them her secret, to share it with them. She was as frightened at the time of telling Felix as of the pregnancy itself: she knew once Felix was told he'd never be able to love her again.

But she said nothing. Sat there smiling and blushing on the floor by Lizzie's feet half listening to the coarse rowdy riotous talk that swirled about her, thinking how little anything in her life had to do with her any longer, how little it touched on *her*. Rose Ann was complaining of Mick, and Nelia was joking about her boyfriend Mitch, and Thelma was telling a convoluted giggly tale about an ex-boyfriend of hers, then Lizzie spoke of Henri La Porte, of how he intended to give her a ring soon, in fact they had a diamond picked out, and Nelia snorted with laughter, saying, Hell isn't that guy already married? and Lizzie countered aggressively saying, So what?— Henri loves me, he's the first man who ever gave a damn for me and my future. Then they teased Enid about having a boyfriend or didn't she have a boyfriend, what was wrong with her not having a boyfriend, arguing back and forth about young men they could fix her up with, shouting names, laughing, Enid sat at Lizzie's feet smiling her vague sweet smile pretending to listen knowing they meant well they liked her or the person they believed her to be—*was* she Angel-face maybe, all these years! She thought how coarse was the connection between men and women, you started out thinking love and wound up thinking sex, everything reduced to jokes that were vulgar, flippant, sometimes even funny, Felix himself used the expression *fuck* a good deal as if intent upon showing her how little it all meant really, how little she could count upon it, *fuck* like *shit* and *piss,* something your body did with no sentiment attached. At the start Felix had said it wasn't love it was just something they needed to do, and though so very long a time had passed—it might have been her entire life—Enid didn't know even now whether she loved him or he loved her or whether their feeling for each other was a sickness lodged deep inside them that others would see at once was a sickness and recoil from in disgust.

Dreamily she thought, He might kill me.

She thought, He might kill himself and me both, he could use one of his guns, he could park somewhere in the country or by the lake, by night, it would have to happen at night, he could run a length of hose through a window of his car from the exhaust pipe. . . .

The girls saw her staring into space, lost in a trance that might have been melancholy or deep pleasure, they teased her, calling her Angel-face, asking what was wrong? why so unhappy? but Enid didn't respond, suddenly she wanted to be gone. What did she care really for Nelia, Rose Ann, her own sister Lizzie: they knew nothing of her.

Still she was shrewd enough to ask Lizzie could she come stay overnight sometime just for fun to get away from home. And Lizzie said, Sure, I'd love that, sweetie; Lizzie kissed her and said, Sure, if Momma doesn't object. Momma's got her suspicions these days about *me.*

So at the Cloverleaf Club that evening when Lizzie alight with triumph and excitement joined their table—she'd finished her first performance of the night and had been well received, Henri La Porte had ordered a bottle of French champagne in celebration, Henri had dared kiss "Lizabeth Somers" dramatically on the lips in full view of her family!—Enid waited for things to quiet down a bit, then asked Lizzie carefully could she spend a few days with her over Christmas vacation, maybe go with her to Henri's studio to hear her rehearse, and of course Lizzie said yes. The tricky thing—so Enid and Felix thought—was that Mrs. Stevick should hear Enid ask and should hear Lizzie's answer, that way it seemed spontaneous and impulsive, not at all calculated; naturally Lizzie would say yes, Mrs. Stevick might not even object under the circumstances. (Enid's mother was sitting slightly dazed as if not knowing what to think of Lizzie's public performance—stared and stared at her with a look that might have been of pride or exhilaration or simple perplexity.) There would be time later, Enid thought, to tell Lizzie a part of the truth.

Which was: Enid wanted to spend two nights with a friend but give her parents the excuse she was staying with Lizzie.

" 'A friend'?" Lizzie asked, staring. *"You?*—what's going on?"

"It doesn't matter," Enid said. She looked at her sister unflinching. "I'm just asking you to do a favor."

Lizzie seemed shocked, puzzled. Eyeing Enid as if she'd never quite seen her before. "You mean you want to stay with—who?—a man?—a boyfriend?—and want me to cover for you."

"I'm just asking you for a favor," Enid said. "And it isn't much of a favor, is it."

"Who is he? What's going on?" Lizzie asked.

"That's my business," Enid said.

"The hell it is!" Lizzie said excitedly. "I don't want you—you know—to get into trouble. If I'm responsible for you I sure as hell don't want you to—"

"You're not responsible for me, Lizzie," Enid said calmly.

"But if you stay with me here—"

"I'm not going to stay with you."

"But if you say you're going to stay with me—"

Enid remained calm, explaining that Lizzie would have nothing to do except say Enid was staying with her if their mother checked which she probably wouldn't do—she was so busy with her dressmaking these days—but if anybody from home telephoned whoever answered the phone might say that yes Enid was there in the apartment but couldn't come to the phone right now or Enid had gone out to the movies—was that too much to ask?

Lizzie was staring at Enid, smiling, baffled, a little hurt. She kept shaking her head as if she couldn't believe it. "Is he anybody I know?" she asked.

"No," said Enid.

"You're sure?"

"Yes."

"But it's a boyfriend you're going to be staying with?"

Enid had prepared beforehand most of what she was saying but now with her sister standing so close, watching her so closely, she began to falter. She feared Lizzie could peer into her head, read her thoughts. Her very fingertips had gone cold! In a rapid voice she said, "I'm going to be away from home next Thursday from six o'clock on and all of Friday and I'm not sure about Saturday—maybe I'll go home on Saturday afternoon. Lizzie, I'm going to do it whether you help me or not," she said, raising her eyes to Lizzie's, seeing that her sister maybe knew, maybe guessed, wasn't it all so transparent, Enid Maria in trouble for the first time in her life? "I'm going to do it," she said, her voice faltering, "whether you help me or not."

"Oh Christ, honey," Lizzie said softly.

She sat on the arm of a sofa staring at Enid with nothing to say for a long time. Lit up a cigarette, just stared. Don't say a word! Enid begged. And what a sight Lizzie was at the moment—bone-bleached hair in pincurls, cold cream smeared on her face, eyebrows plucked half away but lips still luscious-red with lipstick.

Enid said goodbye, she wasn't going to stand there on exhibit, her sister's widened eyes moving up and down her body. Lizzie looking so blank and startled, so suddenly pitying! Enid got her coat, went to the door, the stairs, Lizzie followed slowly after her and when Enid was halfway down the stairs she called out, "Enid—all right. Yes. I'll help you. And you'll tell me how it turns out, will you? Let me know? Right away? *Will* you? As soon as you can?"

"I will," Enid said.

"Honey—you'll tell me everything?" Lizzie said.

"I will," Enid said.

Her relief was so immediate and so profound she felt no guilt hearing herself lie. She'd been telling lies for so long, it had become second nature.

This time there was a nurse as well as the doctor—a woman in her forties with a narrow mean face, grainy skin, watchful eyes very like Enid's own eyes or so it seemed to Enid in her trance of terror. But the office was a different office. Not in the suburbs but in the city somewhere below Grand Street, an older residential neighborhood, an older building of dull weathered brick, a clinic of sorts, a legitimate medical clinic, Enid guessed, though she and Felix had to enter it by way of a rear door off the parking lot. A single light burned above the entrance: it was past seven o'clock and very dark. The parking lot was empty except for Felix's car and two others. Felix walked Enid with his arm tight around her as if he thought she might slip on the icy pavement. Or break away from him suddenly.

He'd wanted to stay with her throughout the abortion, he said, but the doctor refused, said absolutely not.

"I wouldn't want you there either," Enid said, shocked. She drew back to look at him. "I wouldn't want you to see me like that."

"Like what?" Felix said.

"You know what I mean."

"Don't be childish," Felix said.

Enid began to laugh thinking of it—Felix Stevick in the same room with her observing her insides scooped out, seeing her bleeding like a stuck pig—Christ, wasn't it like him to want to make an extravagant gesture helpful to no one. Felix said irritably, "Don't get hysterical."

She was still laughing, trying to catch her breath, when the nurse led her away. Speaking to her in a hushed impatient voice telling her not to be afraid it was all routine, it wasn't major surgery, it would be over within an hour if there weren't complications, and she'd be home by ten o'clock and did she know she was lucky, damned lucky, to be in such good professional hands. Enid wanted to ask the woman what was her name—what was the doctor's name—how often did they perform such abortions—why did they do it, was it purely for money—were they worried about being caught—were they worried about one of their patients informing on them sometime, repentant and a little crazy having collaborated in a murder? But she couldn't get her breath. Fortunately! Slipping off her clothes, her fingers numb and dazed. Standing there with something clenched in her fist—her slip—the nurse had to take from her to lay on a chair.

Was she a real nurse, Enid wondered in her terror, or just a woman dressed in a nurse's costume—white rayon uniform crackling with static electricity, white transparent stockings, white shoes. Her coarse graying hair was caught back in a matronly bun so tight it seemed to have pulled her forehead into cruel lines, gave the skin an odd metallic sheen. Enid wondered had she any children. Had she a daughter Enid's age? She was staring at Enid as if sharing Enid's fright, despite herself she relented, even touched Enid's cool cheek with her fingers that too were chilly, perhaps trembling. But she tried to speak lightly: "Look—you're not going to die or anything. It really is routine. I promise."

Enid would remember afterward how close she'd come to throwing her arms around the nurse, begging her to take her home, take her away, it was all a mistake and she wasn't pregnant—Oh God she had no idea why she was here.

But she kept control of herself. Slipped the silly paper smock over her head as before. Climbed atop the table, which was exactly like the table on which she'd been examined in the other office except now she was being strapped down. Her heart thudding, her eyes opened wide staring at the squares of acoustical tile set in the ceiling. Now there was a curious sort of levity rising in her, a relief so vast as to be gay, too late to turn back, *irremeable* was one of her fancy dictionary words, December 28, 1955, and too late to turn back, *in vivo* she'd learned that morning and *in vitro* and *valediction* and *aborning* and *abortifacient,* which she'd spelled out again and again in calm graceful letters in fresh ink on clean white paper. Even as the doctor entered the room noiselessly and she shielded her face instinctively against him—didn't want to memorize *him*—she was thinking of the words she'd spelled out that morning to keep her sanity slowly and lovingly on sheets of tablet paper now crumpled in her wastebasket by her desk upstairs at 118 East Clinton. And if she died tonight on this table! if she died without waking! if she bled to death, as surely she deserved, the words would be there outliving her, inhabiting their own mysterious province without connection to her or to anything human. That was their special power—words, like music—like musical annotations precise on paper—to outlive us.

Her right arm was being lifted, something wet and cold dabbed on the tender flesh of the inside of the arm just below the elbow, then the needle's point entering so swiftly she hadn't time to feel pain. *Don't move,* the nurse whispered—but already Enid was gone.

In Felix's apartment in his bed, a thick sanitary pad fastened between her legs, she was to sleep for nearly twelve hours.

A deep unswerving tremulous sleep from which nonetheless she imagined she woke from time to time drenched in sweat, her heart beating hard, seeing Felix sitting beside her in the dark yet when she spoke he didn't seem to hear, desperately she called his name but he couldn't hear, reached out for him but he gave no sign of noticing. So she knew it was Felix who had died and not Enid.

The telephone was ringing. Then it was silent. Someone had answered it elsewhere in the apartment—she listened but heard nothing except the accelerated beat of her own blood.

"Felix . . . ?"

Around the edges of the tight-drawn blinds was a fierce white glow. Shadows in the corners of the rooms, a mirror aslant on one of the walls mirroring nothing. Enid's eyelids were heavy, it was an effort to keep them open. She was bleeding, she could feel it, a fascination in such sensation she couldn't be expected to control, like the heavy persistent discharge of menstrual blood she'd imagined years before would drain her white, anemic as Miss Holland had warned, for a while too in childish terror she'd frightened herself with thoughts of—was it leukemia?—her life's blood draining away soaked in ugly white cotton pads she was careful to wrap in Kleenex or toilet paper to hide. Such shame, such humiliation. Yet it was "normal": it was presumably desired. Now the cramps deep in her belly were no more severe than the most painful menstrual cramps, she supposed she could bear them, doped up as she was, dosed with codeine, the pain was real yet oddly distant like pain felt under nitrous oxide at the dentist's. She and Warren had tried to describe nitrous oxide— "laughing gas"—saying it was like murmuring or talking in another room you could hear but couldn't really follow, it was there, you were aware of it, but it hadn't anything specifically to do with you.

Her hair had been on fire. But she hadn't felt any pain. And that dove flying in wild maddened circles its feathers burning . . .

In a dim-lit room smelling of old linoleum and disinfectant she'd been lying on a couch trying to regain the strength in her legs. She was awake now and answering questions lucidly enough—always the bright girl, Enid Maria the honor student—still they were having some difficulty getting her to sit up, to stand, to walk. She could feel her legs but they gave way beneath her each time she tried to stand. Her head was heavy, rolling on her shoulders. The doctor was gone; Enid could hear the nurse's reedy voice worried and complaining, it wasn't good, she was telling Felix, for lights to be burning here this time of night. Finally Felix had to half carry Enid out into the parking lot, walking her with his arm tight around her waist in slow careful steps, murmuring words she couldn't quite hear. Felix had already turned on the Lincoln's motor, the heater turned full blast to warm the inside of the car for her, it was so bitter cold tonight, clouds of pale exhaust were rising spectacularly into the night air and Enid stared and stared transfixed. Was there some danger now they'd left the building?—the nurse had stayed behind, she'd locked the door after them. Enid's lips were numb as if she'd been injected there with Novocain, assuring Felix she was all right, she was fine. His face would have frightened her if she had really looked at it.

* * *

When she woke it was to a telephone ringing too loudly to be incorporated into her sleep. She understood she must be in Felix's bedroom in Felix's bed—she knew she wasn't in her own bed and that meant she must be here. There wasn't anywhere else.

A sudden warm seeping of blood, a thin trickle running down the inside of her thigh to soak into the sheet, the mattress. That meant the sanitary pad must be soaked through. One part of her mind responded quick and mean, telling her, Good: you deserve it. Another part of her mind urged her up, she'd have to get into the bathroom fast, except she was so groggy so woolly-headed, her mouth tasting like rust. She must have started crying or whimpering which was something she despised because Felix appeared, leaning over her, frightened himself, helping her up again half carrying her calling her sweetheart, honey, his baby girl telling her she was going to be all right if she could just hold on. In the bathroom she tried to push him away saying for Christ's sake she wanted to be alone would he get the hell out but he wouldn't, he had to help her on the toilet and with changing the sanitary pad as if she was a small child or a very sick dazed person not knowing what was happening from one second to the next, the bathroom lights aswim in her head. She was crying out of shame. She was crying she was so angry but hadn't any strength in her arms, her legs, her neck—her head rolled on her shoulders like crockery about to fall, to shatter. Felix said, Don't cry, don't cry, he was so close to breaking down himself and she knew it, she felt his hatred of her at that moment amounting almost to panic as if the touch of her frightened him, the look and the terrible smell of her, hadn't he hated her all along for arousing such weakness in him—he'd been ashamed all these years.

She swallowed down another of the chunky white pills Felix held out to her. Spilling water on the front of her nightgown, choking, coughing, through her sleep-encrusted eyelids she could see her uncle's face the pale creases at the corners of his mouth, nicks and discolorations in his skin, not so handsome seen up close in the unsparing light, the tiles reflecting light. Good, Enid was thinking, we both deserve it—blood all over our hands and splotched on the floor so that he'll have to clean it up afterward.

Then she was back in bed weeping in utter gratitude clutching at his hands, his arms, she loved him so, she loved him loved him so, she didn't sleep again but lay awake for hours exhausted in what she was to remember afterward as a mysterious suspension of time, the minutes uniform, one following another peacefully because everything was over, completed, all volition taken from her. She saw Felix in his silky white boxing trunks elevated in a brightly lit ring—it was the Armory, years ago, or was it now?—her father should not have taken her to see such a spectacle—Felix circling an opponent whose face was dim but the men were well matched, in superb condition, hot and oily with sweat, circling each other cautiously at first trying quick jabs, quick flying tentative left jabs, right crosses over the jabs, that terrible jarring, jolting, the head snapping back, the eyes momentarily dazed. She couldn't look: she hid her face. She loved him, loved him so, she didn't want to see what was going to happen to him.

Good, she thought calmly. He deserves it.

Calmly speculating on the effect an abortion—so extreme a physical trauma, as the medical book said—must have upon the female body with its arsenal of hormones in gear, in dumb preparation for the fetus to grow, to transform itself into an infant, now suddenly the fetus is gone—"removed"—what now does the body think, what does it do. She was running across Huron Street against the traffic light, the bright windy air filled with bits of paper and flying grit, always wind rushing into her face taking her breath away but she'd carried Felix's presence with her, he was always with her, inside her, he *was* her, now she'd be entirely alone, that was the knowledge her body would have to absorb. Jarring, jolting, the head snapped back with the terrible force of the blow. Felix frequently said the dangerous blows were the ones you hadn't seen coming and maybe they hadn't seen this one coming but maybe they had. She'd have the rest of her life to think about it.

Through a haze of pain she managed to dial Lizzie's number. Keeping her voice low, secret, so that Felix wouldn't hear. Lizzie sounded angry, saying she'd been waiting and *waiting* for Christ's sake, was Enid all right? and Enid said, Yes of course she was fine she was perfectly fine, Lizzie shouldn't have worried. It's not knowing what the hell is going on, Lizzie said. For instance—where *are* you? Enid said she couldn't say right at the moment, she'd tell Lizzie later. Her voice was nearly inaudible, Lizzie told her to speak louder asked was she really all right, Enid said, Yes of course, Lizzie said, Who is he?—are you in love with him? and Enid said, No, not really, it was just something that happened. Does he want to marry you or anything like that? Lizzie asked, and Enid said quickly, No, now she was going to hang up she'd call Lizzie tomorrow but Lizzie said she hadn't better hang up so fast goddamn it and Enid shut her eyes hearing her sister's voice rising in outrage wanting to cry the way she'd wanted to cry at the Cloverleaf Club amid the silly tacky Christmas decorations, the noisy customers, a drunken man at a nearby table Enid couldn't help but notice cupping his hands to his mouth to call out words to Lizzie Enid tried not to hear. Oh Lizzie sweetheart you're on your way, everybody saying afterward she was as good as Dinah Shore, a bombshell like Marilyn Monroe, Henri La Porte said; just look how the crowd loved her. In the powder room Geraldine and Enid and Lizzie talked excited and giggling, high on champagne, Geraldine said she was maybe just a bit jealous hugging Lizzie tight and Enid hugged her too, Oh Lizzie you're on your way, swallowing down the urge to cry, she remembered saying goodbye to Warren in his scratchy soldier's uniform but that was a long time ago. Now Lizzie was saying she had an appointment that morning she'd canceled on Enid's account she was worried sick about Enid the least Enid could do was tell her when they'd be seeing each other and Enid said maybe tomorrow or the next day, Enid was staring at the doorway waiting for Felix to appear to snatch the telephone from her hand he'd be incredulous he'd very possibly slap her but he wouldn't mean to hurt, it was just his reflex, his surprise: Felix Stevick was a man who hated being surprised in any wrong way. But he didn't appear. The door was ajar but he didn't appear. Finally Lizzie caught on, saying, Honey, can't you talk right now? and Enid said, Not too well, and Lizzie said, But you *are* all right? and Enid said, Yes, look did Momma call? and Lizzie laughed, saying, Yes in fact Momma called the night before, nothing serious and Nelia had answered saying Lizzie and Enid were both out at the movies seeing that movie at the Capitol with Audie Murphy and Momma said some boy from high school had called Enid some name she didn't know something about a New Year's Eve party but she'd managed to discourage him saying she didn't want her daughter going out on that night of the year of all nights when there were drunk drivers all over the city, people acting like they were crazy. Enid began to laugh quietly and Lizzie said, Wouldn't she just die if she knew, poor Momma!—and Enid said, choking back her laughter like a little girl, Poor Momma!—the last words she said before hanging up the phone.

She'd thought possibly Felix had been listening at the bedroom door but evidently not. She lay there in the smelly bed her fingers thrust in her mouth, trying not to laugh audibly, trying not to laugh.

* * *

When she woke she was still alone and she couldn't determine if it was the same day or another day. Or had she only slept five or ten minutes?

In the bedside table loose in the drawer was Felix's .45-caliber revolver, the sight of it always frightened her. Though there was comfort in it too, solace, she was beginning to understand the solace, that was why too Felix kept it there so close at hand and why he liked sometimes to tease her when she drove his car, out in the country where nobody was likely to catch them, Felix's gorgeous gleaming cream-colored Caddie now totaled holding the road at 85 miles an hour. Take it flat out, honey, he'd say. For the hell of it. See how high you can go. Enid's nervousness amused him, also her bravado, Enid Maria with her foot pressed down on the gas pedal nearly to the floor, Enid Maria with her lower lip caught in her teeth, staring, not daring to blink at the rushing pavement the crude black-topped country roads bracketed by woods and farmland. The faster you go the faster you want to go—it's that simple. The road straight and flat giving the illusion you can see to the horizon, you can see into the next few minutes, what can go wrong? An almost palpable excitement in the speeding car, Felix's closeness fueling Enid's daring, Enid's reckless-ness, he loved her wild and a little crazy scaring him now and then— but how rare it was, Felix Stevick scared! When it happened it was delicious as making love when he took his time sucking at Enid, teasing her with his tongue, all the time in the world, he'd inch her toward an orgasm so sharp and fierce she couldn't bear it. Oh Felix don't stop loving me, don't ever stop loving me, I can't live without you.

Someday you will, Felix said.

Then that won't be me, Enid said.

Mr. Stevick was in the habit of complaining jocularly about television. Programs like *I Love Lucy,* for instance, *I Remember Mama, The Honey-mooners*—he really did admire Jackie Gleason, couldn't deny it—on such shows the most simpleminded characters nevertheless possessed the words to speak easily and often shrewdly to one another, they were quick, witty, resourceful, their timing was always perfect and they were able to say what was in their hearts—seemed in fact to know what was in their hearts. While in real life on the wrong side of the television screen things were different: "They've got all the good lines," Mr. Stevick said. "We're stuck with the rest."

So Enid heard with vague groggy disbelief her question put to Felix—"Was it a boy or a girl—did they tell you?"—knowing it was a terrible thing to ask, knowing very likely it was senseless, she hadn't been that far along, had she?—for the baby to have any sex. She was doped up with codeine, that was the excuse. She'd surprised Felix sitting in the kitchen where he was drinking whiskey, smoking one cigarette after another judging by the ashtray heaped with ashes and butts, the air thick with smoke. His eyes narrowed with pain. The pupils were pinched. Christ she must have looked terrible leaning there in the doorway in her sweaty bloodstained nightgown, hair stuck to her damp forehead, her face creased tight and her eyes reddened, skin sickly white. His sweet little pretty little girl: and now look. On the table before him scattered newspaper pages and a near-empty bottle of Early Times, which Enid's wavering vision registered initially as Easy Times.

Was he drunk?—staring at her appalled as if he didn't trust himself to speak. She was frightened he'd reach out suddenly and strike her. She was frightened she would see the hatred in his face—then she'd never forget.

"Did they tell you? Did they tell you anything?" she persisted.

"Shut up," Felix said.

A glass in his hand, unshaven, in trousers and a soiled undershirt—a Felix Stevick Enid had never seen before. Looking so sick at heart, so weak. Like Lyle Stevick the other day leaning against the banister having coughed his guts out, Enid's mother shouting at him he *had* to give up his pipe, he *had* to see the doctor again, why did he want to kill himself! Was he doing it to spite her?

"Damn you, shut up," Felix whispered.

She was mesmerized by something in his face, couldn't turn away or hide her eyes though her eyes burned as if she were looking into a bright blinding light. Felix with his dark curly kinky body hair bristling through the thin white cotton fabric of his undershirt, swirls of hair on his forearms, beneath his arms, his flesh looking always slightly heated, urgent. He'd told her boxers loved to sweat, that was how they knew they were alive. Cooling off was bad, cooling off meant boredom, torpor. Now Felix's eyes were hooded, the lids puffy, his hair greasy and disheveled and Enid could see it had begun to recede at the temples, streaked too with gray like that "premature" gray in Geraldine's hair Neal teased her about, not knowing she didn't find it funny. It wasn't fair, Geraldine said, she was only twenty-six years old.

Enid wanted to know the answer to the question she'd asked Felix but already she had forgotten what it was. Before Felix could get up to come to her she went to him, leaning over him swaying dizzily pretending it was one of their flirtatious moments, she tried to read the headlines in the newspaper but her eyes slipped out of focus. "What's this?—for me?" Adroitly she took the glass of whiskey from him and had a swallow—the fiery liquid burned her throat, seemed to run lewdly up her nose. So fast! So potent! There was the old promise of comfort so she had another quick swallow before Felix intervened. "You'll make yourself sick," he said. She laughed because it was funny but he didn't laugh with her. Didn't smile. She swayed and would have fallen except for his arm braced against her belly. For a moment she couldn't remember if she was already drunk, if Felix had cagily gotten her drunk and why was he watching her so closely.

She'd never be able to leave his apartment, looking the way she did—her parents would call the police.

Enid judged by the slant of the wintry sunshine it was early afternoon. The bleached sky so cold it hadn't any color, might have been enamel, pewter. There was a dim unfocused look to Felix's kitchen or was it Enid's wayward vision—couldn't blink the moisture out of her eyes. The kitchen was a small purely functional room "modern" in design like something in a magazine advertisement, pebbly green Formica-topped counters on which dirty plates, glasses, silverware, old newspapers, and magazines had been set in no coherent order. The stainless steel sink heaped with dishes also, a small table at which Felix was accustomed to sit with his back to the wall: you could see how the tubular chair, tilted, had worn the paint off, made parallel indentations in the plaster. Enid had a sudden flash of her uncle sitting in this place alone, always alone, drinking black coffee without tasting it, smoking his Camels without tasting them, skimming newspapers finding nothing to engage his interest. He'd told her in his deadpan faintly bemused way that there was nothing in the world—in the larger world—that caught him up, excited him, made him angry or hopeful or disgusted or disappointed: what would it be? He'd fought in the war knowing he was on the right side, he'd done his soldier's duty you might say, but his deepest self, his soul, had never been involved as it had been involved in the least of his amateur boxing matches. As if he'd sleepwalked through those years in the

Pacific—Pvt. Felix Stevick in a fight too vast and too generalized to have any human significance.

Felix found it repellent, having to fire at men he didn't know, men who were the "enemy," killing the way you'd kill animals or vermin merely to erase them. Fighting a fair fight in such circumstances was impossible and would have been a joke in any case but it was the only kind of fighting he understood. And eventually he hadn't cared, hadn't given a damn. Your soul goes numb, Felix said, whatever it is there's inside you that's you, maybe it's extinguished like a candle flame and maybe it never comes back. He'd waited until the war ended to resume his own life but maybe by then it was too late.

Stirred by Warren's ideas Enid asked Felix did he have any political beliefs and Felix said sure, probably he did: if things went against the grain of what he wanted for himself then he'd start to think "politically." That was how everybody was, he said. That's what you mean by "political."

You're a cynical man, Enid said.

I don't ever want to be cynical, Enid said.

Felix just laughed.

Now he was going to make them a meal. Too late for breakfast so how about lunch?—if he wasn't too drunk to manage.

Eggs in the refrigerator, half a quart of milk, some cheese, bread, pickles—big tough salty briny Polish pickles; in the cupboard some cans of soup, did Enid like soup?—chicken noodle, cream of tomato, vegetable. Felix tried to cheer her up or was he trying to cheer himself up, holding the familiar red-and-white cans out for Enid's inspection, but Enid was fighting waves of nausea, trying to smile, thinking Oh Christ she never wanted to eat anything again, she'd punish the very marrow of her bones for the murder she and Felix had committed. Still, she heard herself giggling. Heard herself say, "Daddy has his bomb shelter stocked with Campbell's soup. Shelves and shelves of it. He's all prepared. He's waiting."

But Felix refused to be drawn into mocking his brother.

"Lyle means well," he said.

He splashed the contents of one of the cans into a battered saucepan, set it on the stove. His movements were slow and precise and not perfectly coordinated; he worked with a cigarette in his mouth. Enid watched him on the sly—his hawkish profile, his grainy skin, hair growing out unevenly at the nape of his neck. The muscular neck, muscular arms and shoulders—muscular so that he could absorb another man's blows and give strength to his own. It was all in the timing, in the leverage, he said. Whether a boxer had a real punch or not.

She recalled seeing a recent newspaper photograph—President Eisenhower admiring Rocky Marciano's enormous balled fist. Both men were in fact admiring the fist.

She laughed. Then felt overcome by a sense of despair, sorrow. She couldn't bear to look at Felix any longer: it was as if a part of herself stood before her, her own being in Felix, so *useless,* so *without purpose,* doomed.

He looked at her, frowning.

She cleared her throat and said, "It couldn't have been allowed to be born. It was never meant to be born."

Felix worked at the stove with a manly sort of clumsiness born out of contempt for what he did, the handling of saucepans, spoons, bowls. His whiskey glass had been set on the surface of the stove between the burners. If he heard Enid he gave no sign. The ugly scar over his eye was so familiar she realized she never saw it any longer. It was just there—she couldn't remember a time when it hadn't been there.

To offset the sensation of nausea Enid leafed through the scattered pages of the *Transcript.* Arms and defense appropriations, economic pronouncements by the National Association of Manufacturers, a photograph of a broadly smiling Vice-President Nixon disembarking from a jetliner. Only the comics gave her solace. You died, you came back, the comics remained unchanged—Dick Tracy, Blondie and Dagwood, Brenda Starr, Girl Reporter, Terry and the Pirates, Popeye, Olive Oyl, Wimpy. (Poor Wimpy: bleary-eyed and comical, so fat his shirt buttons were always popping off to be swallowed down by a mysterious attendant bird. Mr. Stevick said he understood Wimpy "from the inside.") A motley misfit world it was, immortalized in the comics. Enid said, "The comic strips go on forever, don't they?—do you remember a time when there wasn't Dick Tracy or Donald Duck?" Felix ignored her. Snubbing her, you might say: his girl bent over the comics, her hair in her face, a thick white cotton pad between her legs quietly soaking up blood.

This was Felix's kitchen yet he seemed scarcely familiar with it, banging around in the cupboards, in the refrigerator, swearing under his breath. He ate nearly all his meals out—he'd been eating out most of his life. "Don't you love the comics, Felix," Enid persisted, eyeing his stiff back, guessing how he was wary of her, fearful of looking directly at her. "Or don't you even read them?"

"Not since I was a kid," Felix said.

They sat down at the kitchen table together. The first meal Felix had ever prepared for Enid—tomato soup in twin bowls, slices of coarse Italian bread, a wedge of strong cheddar cheese—but neither had any appetite. Enid was afraid she'd start vomiting, sat with her hands clasped in her lap and her eyes half shut. Felix opened a new bottle of Early Times for himself and a bottle of red wine for Enid, poured her a generous glassful. She drank it gratefully. Her head swam. She was immediately at that point—how familiar the sensation, and Felix was very much a part of it—when she was about to cross over into another self, Enid Maria but drunk, giddy, forgiving.

She said, "We had to do it. We couldn't help it."

Felix said ironically, "That's right, honey."

13

New Year 1956. Felix Stevick was served a summons to appear downtown at police headquarters to be questioned by Albany detectives and by a prosecutor from the State Attorney General's office on the subject of Al Sansom of Sansom & Stevick, Inc. It seemed that Sansom had disappeared in Miami, Florida: he'd made arrangements to meet his wife Claudette in Kingston, Jamaica, on December 28, according to airline records he flew out of Albany at noon on December 26, arrived at La Guardia that afternoon, stayed overnight in Manhattan, then flew out from La Guardia to Miami the next morning, arrived in Miami but failed to pick up his ticket for the flight to Jamaica which left that afternoon at 1 P.M. And after that his whereabouts were said to be "unknown."

Felix told the detectives politely that he knew very little about his partner's private life. Though he wasn't that surprised that Sansom was missing—if he really was missing—since the man had been behaving strangely for a long time, drinking a good deal, hinting at some action he planned like packing up and leaving the country without notifying anyone, investing money—"hidden reserves of money" he called it—in the Caribbean. Felix believed that Sansom had been under pressure recently, nursing some secret worry or grief: there were frequent disappearances, weekends mainly but sometimes longer, he'd just—disappear: nobody knew where. He was a complex man, Felix said, you couldn't get close to him, he spoke of having secrets from everyone on earth including his wife—money in banks she didn't know of, places of residence in foreign countries.

Felix spoke frankly and openly but did express some surprise at their concern since his partner had not been missing for very long: hardly three weeks. Is this standard police procedure? he asked.

They questioned Felix for several hours, then released him, then summoned him back the next day and questioned him again, this time in the presence of his lawyer. But Felix had nothing to add to his testimony. He knew very little of Al Sansom's private life, he said, and he didn't know anybody who did. Business was business, they'd had some disappointment with their resort hotel investment but the 1956 season was expected to get them into the black and Felix knew of no one who might wish Al Sansom harm apart from Al Sansom himself—"He's the joker in the deck."

Still, Felix said, he found it hard to believe that anything serious had really happened to Al. He had a feeling, he said, that Al would turn up soon.

Said he'd telephone her but he put it off for a week, two weeks, finally he called from a pay phone in a hotel lobby in Philadelphia asking was she all right and she said yes and he asked her was she feeling bad and she said no, why should she feel bad, in this small thin cold voice he hated, so he asked her how was her health, her body, that sort of thing, he was embarrassed and she said did he mean was she menstruating normally now no she wasn't, she said, but the pain was gone, she said, and there really wasn't anything to worry about or think about, was there, now the pain was gone, the serious bleeding, the problem. Now the problem's gone, she said, and to this Felix could not reply, just stood there holding the receiver to his ear, and finally Enid said, Felix? Are you still there? and he said, Sure, where else would I be? and she said, I thought maybe you'd hung up and he said, Why would I do that?

A Saturday morning in February leaving the Locust Street Athletic Club—he never went to Mattiuzzios' now—Felix happened to see Lyle Stevick up the block peering in the window of a hardware store.

A windy day, grit and snow flying, Lyle in his old frayed camel's-hair topcoat that came to his knees, a black fedora jaunty on his head, hands thrust deep in his pockets and brow furrowed, Lyle staring into the window for so long Felix thought he must be aware of him, Felix, close by, standing there waiting for him to call out a greeting.

Y'know what?—we should go out drinking some night, get plastered some night, just us two. Got a lot of things to talk about accumulated over the years going back to old Karl, don't we? Lyle had said once and Felix had said, That's right.

Felix turned away before Lyle could speak if he meant to speak. His hair was damp from the shower; he was hatless and cold. Couldn't bring himself to shake his brother's hand, not right now. Go off and have a drink with his brother?—not right now.

Maybe he'd never see Lyle Stevick again? Alive? The survivor would see the other at the dead man's funeral and that might be soon enough.

Boy or girl she'd asked to torment him but it was a thought Felix didn't allow himself to think. A clump of flesh was all it would have been, flushed down a toilet.

That's what they did with these things, didn't they? Flushed down a toilet by the nurse.

It wouldn't have had any sex yet Felix was certain, wouldn't have been that far along, would it?—not that he knew, or cared to look up the information in a medical book. He'd have to go to the library for that and he wasn't going to make any special trip and in any case he really didn't want to know.

The doctor had told Felix Stevick all Felix had wanted to know, that night. The job was done and that's it.

Not a man of many words, no mention of fetus, embryo, baby, sex, only a quick run-through of the medical procedure—"a routine operation, D and C it's called"—sure, Felix had heard of that, Felix had had other girls after all and his friends had girls, if you knew your way around and had a little cash there was no problem. The abortion had cost Felix only $700, which he thought a bargain—Christ he'd have paid $7,000—and Enid had imagined it cost much more, showing how uninformed she was, or how she exaggerated things. Neither the doctor nor the nurse had showed the slightest surprise at the difference in his and Enid's ages, which Felix appreciated; they were skilled, experienced, knew what they were doing and did it. He'd never touch her again, he was thinking, he'd never see her again except with other people around and not for a long long time if that could be managed. I can't live without you she'd said, wet-eyed and pleading, and Felix said, Try.

In the Mid-City Café where he'd had a few too many drinks Felix told a man he'd struck up a conversation with that his younger sister had had a baby that died the week before and he couldn't say why it hit him so hard, made him feel so rotten, a baby weighing only one pound—it was born premature which was why it had died—wasn't far enough along to live. Shook his head, baffled, saying Christ it hit him hard, the way things go, fucking lousy bad luck and what can you say about it, Christ there's just nothing to say is there? And his drinking companion shook his head too and said, Yeah, I know.

Or maybe it was the Genesee Street Tavern, in the splotched mirror behind the shelves of bottles, his splotched reflection floating like a freak-show embryo in formaldehyde. Felix watched the last two rounds of the Gillette Friday Night Fight—Joey Maxim matched with a black light-heavyweight out of Cleveland walking away with a decision and the crowd booed and sure the fight was fixed, Maxim was one of the mob's boys and everybody knew it—but he didn't want to talk about the fucking fight he wanted to talk to this man Conroy or Connor, an older guy in the neighborhood, sympathetic and a good listener maybe sixty years old, and Felix found himself suddenly confiding in him things he hadn't known he had to confide, drunk or sober. This baby that had died, his sister's baby, just last week and how broken up the family was, they'd never get over it. Conroy listened saying yes he understood, the exact identical thing had happened to him and his wife a long time ago maybe thirty years ago a tiny little girl born three months premature with a defective heart so she couldn't get enough oxygen, poor thing, one of those blue babies you read about, the doctors put her on a respirator but she didn't make it, died in forty-eight hours. She'd weighed about a pound too, Conroy said, you can't imagine a baby that tiny, speaking in a slow serious voice, laying his hand on Felix's arm the way he guessed his father might have but never, maybe, did. The sad thing was his wife never even got to see the baby, Conroy said, like it wasn't even *her* baby she'd been carrying those months the hospital policy didn't allow it, she was screaming she wanted to see it, wanted to hold it, but they didn't let her so she got sort of crazy for a while after that but in the end—after a while—you get over it. You think maybe you won't get over it but you always do.

"You have other kids, you know? That's the only way."

Claudette was saying in her husky hurt voice so soft he could barely hear, It's some other woman, isn't it, and Felix said, No.

Thinking of how he wanted to be in motion—in his car in motion—taking solace from speed, from the phenomenon of moving rapidly forward in space simultaneously with moving forward in time, all his concentration his very soul fierce and reduced to what was immediately in front of him, that rushing pavement bounded by a blurred and insignificant world and he'd have a bottle close beside him not giving a fuck if one of the state troopers picked him out he'd have a fresh pack of Camels feeling his old kid's pride in the car this big-assed American car so finely tuned and expensive knocking your eye out a black Continental with the look of a sporty hearse that did in fact remind him now and then when the bourbon spread warmly through his veins of the old man's casket at the funeral parlor on Prudhoe the fancy white satin buttoned-in cushions like weird puckered mouths—Felix heard the hurt in the woman's voice, the appeal, the anger, Claudette loved him was crazy about him and he knew it and why didn't it seem to matter, why couldn't she now even make him hard as he'd always been so easily, aroused within seconds, and in her angry desperation she was behaving like a hooker moistening her hand with spit to stroke him sucking at him with her lovely satiny lips and mouth it was like trying to coax life into something basically dead, Felix thought, almost in pity for her—like prayer, doing the same anxious movements again and again when you know it isn't going to work but you keep doing it because there's nothing else to do. It's some other woman, isn't it, Claudette said in her hurt helpless voice, you're in love with some other woman, aren't you, why don't you tell me, we have to be honest with each other Felix, and Felix's reply would be, Why? but he said nothing, so empty so exhausted so guilty he'd tried to love this woman who was better than he or Al deserved but he'd failed and he didn't want to make love to her he didn't know when he would want to make love to her it wasn't just that the sensation wasn't there, nerve endings numb or dead, he'd been drinking much of the day and the day before, knowing he'd be called upon to make love to a dead man's wife and he might not be able to do it and he didn't want the woman to make love to him so he stroked her head, he gripped her neck, bunched her shining hair in his fingers, Jesus honey, he said—just let it go, let me go, it isn't worth all this.

Another time she slapped him, hard, on the face, screamed she hated him, she blamed him for everything, what kind of hell did he think it was not knowing if she was a man's wife or his widow?—but Felix backed away, hands raised, not wanting to strike out by instinct, letting her have it knocking her across the room with one punch, Jesus he wouldn't want to break her jaw or her nose, he wasn't the kind of man who hits a woman. But how could she tempt *him* how could she blame *him* for what had happened to her asshole husband!

Claudette's face was savage beneath its elaborate makeup, eyes wetly crazy fixed on him in terror of what he might do but he knew to do nothing. "Just take it easy, honey," he was saying. "Don't push it."

Since Al Sansom's disappearance Claudette had begun taking Seconal at night, drinking gin during the day. Talking now of committing herself voluntarily to a hospital in Albany, small private hospital someone recommended. It was ten weeks and she couldn't take the strain much longer not knowing if he was alive or dead, was she a wife, was she a widow?—every time the telephone rang her heart stopped and a knock at the door or even a noise outside, her nerves were gone, and she hated Felix for not giving a damn for her, not having time for her, all she'd gone through Jesus Christ didn't he have one ounce of human *pity.*

Felix said again, "Just take it easy."

Not that he minded her hitting him. At least not in private. The quick blow surprised him, stung like hell, brought tears to his eyes, waking him up, clearing his head as if he'd sniffed ammonia and he liked the feeling, to a degree. Even felt a tinge of excitement, sexual desire, Claudette Sansom a woman he hadn't met before and fucking her would be a way of really clearing his head, emptying out his skull. He loved the adrenaline rush but no he wasn't going to touch her he felt sorry for her she *was* damned better than he or Al deserved and seeing the look on his face she began to cry, let him hold her, okay, okay, he said, he'd see if he could find out for certain.

Knowing he never would. Wouldn't even ask.

Driving the Thruway snowswept and deserted at 2 A.M. the excitement was still with him, heartbeat quickened and a little erratic but now he knew he was safe, alone and in his car lighting up a cigarette inhaling luxuriously thinking maybe he'd finally had it with Claudette Sansom: slapping him across the face then wanting to be loved, that look of drowning in her eyes. Sure she'd have money when it was all settled but Felix didn't need that kind of money, how the hell was he to blame for anything that might have happened to Al Sansom in Florida or wherever it had happened—for all the police knew Sansom had been killed up north and another man had flown down to Miami using his plane ticket, that was a trick that nearly always worked, though Felix didn't know and didn't want to know. Without the body who did know. He'd spoken with Vince only once since December but the subject of Al Sansom had not come up. Vince called to ask whether Felix would like to join them in a deal bringing that Olympic heavyweight Floyd Patterson to the Armory, twenty-year-old black kid just turned pro and hot as a pistol and they could match him let's say with Joey Maxim moving up, maybe old Archie Moore, it was a bill that would sell tickets but Felix heard himself say no thanks he wasn't interested wasn't going to sink any more of his money in boxing. This must have shocked Vince because the line was quiet, then Vince said, I miss you, Felix, and Felix wasn't about to say, I miss you too, Vince, and he wasn't about to say, just let it go for Christ's sake, let me go. How he got off the line he couldn't remember.

Vince had been his only friend, might as well face it, now Vince was gone there weren't any and did he give a goddamn, he did not. And Enid was gone, his sweet little girl, he'd never be able to feel he was just a kid himself again telling himself those wild fantastical dreams of what's ahead, what's all to come. Oh sweet fucking Christ what Felix Stevick would do when he got his chance.

Driving west along the deserted Thruway the headlights of his car beaming out in the slow-falling snow, patches of ice, everything snowswept and clean looking like the Arctic, that was the place for him—the Arctic! Claudette cried too much these days, a woman has to be careful not to wear her face out Al Sansom once said and that was true. And Enid crying because she loved him and he'd harmed her. Because she'd trusted him and he was a shit. The stained mattress he'd have to get rid of one of these days but how do you get rid of something so big, the blood-soaked sanitary napkins she'd put in the bathroom wastebasket carefully wrapped in toilet paper so maybe he wouldn't notice. Grim little smile she gave him at the end as if trying to cheer him up, and recalling it Felix pressed his foot down hard on the accelerator, eager to get back home, or somewhere.

* * *

Avoided Lyle Stevick on the street that day and never telephoned them now but one February afternoon on his way to see one of his and Sansom's tax accountants Felix cruised north on Lock Street—that bleak derelict neighborhood—and at the corner of East Cadboro was his brother's store which he hadn't seen in years. Not the shabbiest place on Lock Street but sad enough, STEVICK'S BARGAIN & UNPAINTED FURNITURE (*Almost Anything Under the Sun Bought and Sold*), two big black men were hauling a sofa in the front entrance while Lyle gave orders in his shirt sleeves in the cold, oblivious of Felix passing close behind him.

Poor bastard.

Coming down here six days a week trying to make a living out of other people's discarded crap, degrading but he'd chosen to do it hadn't he?—a long time ago. Accounted for that smart-ass tone of his—defensive and jolly, "hearty"—eyeing the rest of the world with envy, his young half brother with envy, well, he'd envy him if he knew him wouldn't he, Felix thought ironically. Sure.

What he might do, Felix thought, suddenly cheered—surprise the s.o.b. so he'd *never* get over it: die and leave Lyle his money. And Lyle Stevick would spend the rest of his life trying to figure out how Felix had salted away so much, what the fuck had been his secret.

But he wasn't going to die for a long time.

Sold off some of his city property at a good profit and bought fifteen acres fronting Lake Oriskany on the south side—including the ancient brown-brick buildings of the old Huron Tanning Company, bankrupt and deserted for years. Went to Graham's Gentlemen's Haberdashery to be fitted for his first custom-made suit, the tailor told him the latest style was double-breasted, moderate-width lapels, he recommended a light wool flannel pinstripe in a bluish-gray material and Felix said, Sure, fine, how much?—hardly listening as the man quoted his price. Next he bought new shoes, $65 at Florsheim's on Main Street, then he went for a haircut at the barber's in the Onondaga Hotel lobby, left the barber a $5 tip because he was feeling good. For some time now he'd been shaving mornings without exactly looking at himself in the mirror, now he regarded his image in the barber's mirrors with a mild curiosity, thinking, Who's that? In a context of ordinary men Felix always looked taller than he was and in better condition than he was, shoulders and arms still muscular and that strong neck and the way he naturally carried himself pushing forward a little on the balls of his feet; instinct urged him forward off his heels; as they say, you're either going forward or retreating and it's hard to defend yourself in reverse. Felix stared fascinated at his own image, his own face, as the barber clipped and trimmed his hair—his cheek-bones chiseled as if he'd lost weight and his skin sallow and oddly dented beneath the eyes and of course the pearly-glinting scar tissue and the big snaky scar and he realized that no one ever looked at him without thinking, What the hell happened to *him?*—he'd been carry-ing the mark of his humiliation with him these many years. He had the steely concentrated look of an athlete past his prime guarding himself against being found out.

Still, he tipped the barber generously. Is there any mystery like who you finally turn out to *be,* Felix wondered.

Removed the bullets from both his guns, wrapped the guns carefully in newspaper, drove to the city dump to get rid of them. Had the canal been unfrozen he would have tossed the package into it, or the lake.

Shithead, Felix told himself, amused. You're really coming apart, aren't you.

Once Enid teased him saying what if he had an accident with one of his guns and shot himself and Felix said, You'd like that, sweetie?— and Enid quickly said no, no of course not. Fixing him with that hurt look he loved.

He never drove along East Clinton now, or Nine Mile. Avoided that part of town. And if he saw a group of teenagers on the sidewalk, particularly if he saw boys and girls walking together, he always looked away.

Had he done it on purpose?—maybe.

One evening the telephone rang and he decided to answer it instead of letting it ring as he usually did and it was Lizzie Stevick calling to say hello. Gay breathy chiding flirtatious, saying she hadn't seen her Uncle Felix in a long time, wasn't he going to come down and hear her sing at the Cloverleaf at all?

Sure, said Felix. Tell me when.

Felix despised the s.o.b.'s who ran the Cloverleaf but he dropped by anyway to catch his niece's act on a busy Saturday night. Stood at the rear of the noisy smoky room nursing a drink, assessing "Lizabeth Somers," who was husky-voiced and sultry, knowing how to move her body, her bare shoulders, her breasts, her ass, Jesus he'd have hardly recognized Lizzie with her hair bleached bone-white, all that elaborate makeup. Marilyn Monroe with the baby-doll glistening lips, Dinah Shore in the voice inflections, slow sexy breathless style. Felix joined in the enthusiastic applause—the isolated cheers, whistles—at the end of Lizzie's heartfelt rendition of "Stranger in Paradise" but didn't hang around to say hello. Didn't know if he was vaguely revulsed by what he'd seen and heard or just disoriented. In any case, Lizabeth Somers wasn't his type.

In early March it began.

"Hey, mister, how's about a good time?" a girl called out to Felix as he was unlocking his car on Genesee Street having some difficulty fitting the key in the lock and Felix looked up squinting to see a girl startlingly young maybe sixteen years old, cheaply stylish in a black leather coat, fake-fur-topped boots, a sequin-sprinkled pink chiffon scarf tied around her head. "Mister? Hey? How's about a good time?" in a drunk-belligerent voice and Felix said, "Okay, honey, how much?" looking her up and down. "Twenty-five," she said. Her smile was smeared and wet, rubbery, he saw her frightened eyes and wondered if she could be out here alone at 1:30 A.M. behind the railroad yards or was her pimp close by sitting warm and cozy in a parked car having a smoke, waiting. "Okay," said Felix in an amiable taunting voice, "where're you taking me?" He was drunk it might be said but his reflexes were unimpaired. Earlier in the evening he'd surprised himself overcome by a spasm of vomiting but it only lasted five minutes and now he felt all right. He felt good. He felt like himself more or less. "Around the corner?" said the girl, meaning the Flanders Hotel as it was called. "It's five dollars extra for the room." She was losing her edge on him now, which Felix liked, getting a little uneasy, seeing something in his face that worried her. Felix approached her smiling. "No need to bother with any hotel, get in the car and we'll do it in the car, just suck me off, honey, can you do that? For ten dollars." She blinked as if doubting she'd heard what she'd heard and said, "I don't know," in a weak voice. Her frightened eyes owlish inside the heavy black mascara and she'd outlined her eyebrows in charcoal gray, weird color, a pretty face though, fattish cheeks and baby fat under the chin, a pink valentine of a mouth. In the streetlight Felix saw she was older than sixteen—a lot older. Inside the coat she'd be busty, plump in the waist and hips, he couldn't have borne it fucking her having to smell her perfume and her hair and her face powder, all that. "Come on," he said, "Get in the car. Ten bucks or nothing." "No. I don't know," the girl said, backing off, unsteady on her high heels. Sure her pimp was sitting up the block watching them—the thought roused Felix to a sudden fury, hilarity too though he couldn't have said why. He made no move to take hold of the girl, he spoke calmly and politely, seeing the piggish-small eyes going smaller with fear of him though surely Felix Stevick looked good compared to her usual customers—this stretch of Genesee close by the truck docks had a half-dozen taverns, the patrons were rough, hard drinkers, unpredictable, mainly dock workers, truckers, men from the machine shops at GM, Chrysler, Ingersoll-Rand—it was an insult to Felix the girl should back off from *him.*

"Where's your pimp?" Felix asked. "Introduce me to your pimp."

"I don't have any—pimp! God damn you, who're you talking to?" the girl said, edging away. But Felix saw where she was looking and took hold of her arm and walked her in that direction. "Damn you! Fuck you! Fucker! Son of a bitch!"—her shrill silly voice he ignored, the hilarity rose in him, an excitement that had to do with the late hour, the freezing air, puffs of steamy breath around their mouths and the powerful smell of the lake close by. If ice had a smell. Did ice have a smell, like water? Something fresh and piercing clearing his head, mixed in with the smells of rubber, diesel fuel, factory smoke. The girl began screaming at him, trying to pry his fingers open, slapping and kicking, but Felix heard a car motor turn over just ahead, there he was, no headlights but the son of a bitch was going to take off leaving his girl behind, thinking probably Felix was a cop, which explained too why the guy didn't pull a gun or a knife why Felix was to have so little trouble—kicking in the door window, opening the door, dragging the fucker out and giving him the beating he deserved.

A guy Felix's age with a broad Bohunk look to his cheekbones, skin pitted, sideburns and an Elvis Presley pompadour smelling of hair oil, begging Felix not to hurt him, to let him go. He hadn't any strength in his legs he was so terrified, didn't even try to block Felix's blows, just whimpering and begging, gushing blood from his nose immediately with no instinct to defend himself, shielding his face like a woman as Felix stood flat-footed striking him methodically with punches that traveled no more than four or five inches, so tight, so economical, he felt the power radiate down from his shoulders into his chest as he hadn't felt it in a long time. The fucker! Pimp! Putting a girl out on the street to make a buck for him! Felix must have broken his nose with his first left, blood spraying over both of them and the girl hysterical but keeping her distance, farther up the street some men were leaving a tavern but they merely stood watching, they didn't intend to interfere. Felix was striking his man as he'd strike a heavy bag, timing and pacing himself, being sure to give the fucker a half-dozen body blows, the ones that really count and don't leave much visible damage, a cracked rib or two, punches to the liver and to the midriff, to the heart, a solid right to the solar plexus: any one of them a knockout punch but Felix had his man propped up against the side of the car where he couldn't fall, like being trapped in the ropes or in a corner, he'd never hit a man who was down, nobody refereeing, butting his nose into Felix's business, and Christ it felt good, that adrenaline rush and the power in his shoulders and chest and arms no matter he was panting open-mouthed—badly winded—badly out of condition—and reckless with his hands—why hadn't he at least put on his gloves!—reckless as a young kid and maybe he'd fractured his right hand on the bastard's jaw, what then.

He stepped back. Let the bastard fall. The beating hadn't lasted more than two or three minutes and Felix was shrewd enough to stop before something serious happened, before somebody was killed—that wasn't the point.

He turned to ask the girl did she need a ride anywhere?—but she was gone.

Little bitch, he'd done it for *her*.

Still he felt good. He felt like himself again driving away in the Lincoln high on adrenaline and he wouldn't come down for a long time, airy and floating and roused to perfect happiness though his heart was still kicking and thumping in his chest and he was still breathing through his mouth and his hands hurt like hell, scraped and raw, bleeding or maybe it was the other guy's blood—Felix's new cashmere topcoat splattered, his Florsheim shoes too, Christ his right hand hurt he hoped to hell he hadn't injured it and couldn't imagine why he hadn't put on his gloves—fur-lined leather gloves—they were lying on the seat beside him. Still he felt good. He felt damned good. Nobody to stop him in his big lovely car, he was taking the deserted streets at forty miles an hour, fifty miles an hour, hardly slowing for stop signs or blinking red lights, it was one of those times when you know you can't be hurt you know you're flying high you're going to live forever!—and Felix Stevick took a city boy's pleasure in the narrow grubby streets of south Port Oriskany, the darkened row-houses, tenements, vacant lots—St. Nicholas—Howard—Strick—Vandemere—South Stubb Boulevard bringing him uptown—crossing railroad tracks at a speed that made the car buck, skidding along old trolley tracks half hidden in the shiny packed-down snow—then a bridge—couldn't see the water—caught a glimpse of the domed basilica of the Polish Catholic church looking strange, ghostly—there was the Canal House Tavern he often patronized, neon lights still on—another tavern, Smitty's, on Fourth Street—then he was swinging out to Broad Street to the lakefront—warehouses and cement silos and small mountains of snow-covered gravel looking like something on the moon—boxcars—trucks—barges, freighters at the docks—even by night Felix's eye picked up details, he knew the city so well—Goodyear Tire Company—Quaker Cement—Atlas Storage—Fulton Sausage—Pittsburgh Paints—the dilapidated buildings of the old Huron Tanning Company which Felix Stevick owned!—and the scrubby acreage that went with them and was going to be worth hundreds of thousands of dollars someday. Miles away, factory smokestacks rimmed with flame sent up vast billowing clouds of smoke that gave a watercolor look to the sky—orangey yellow—a pink cast like dawn—beauty to the gray-layered winter sky like cotton batting laced with flame bleak and radiant simultaneously; and Felix in a rush of gratitude though his heartbeat was still erratic and his hands were sticky with blood could have wept seeing such beauty in all he'd been a witness to most of his life, thinking Oh Jesus he was going to miss these opaque surfaces of a world he knew so well, it was like his skull turned inside out, all he loved out there, he was missing them even now when he was still here, still alive.

Never got back to Graham's for a final fitting though they sent him a half-dozen notices, even tried to telephone—the hell with his custom-made suit. Let his hair grow long and shaggy, didn't shave sometimes for days nor did he drop by Sansom & Stevick any longer: "Stevick" too had had it.

Mail piling up in his mailbox downstairs, notices of special delivery letters, certified letters, Felix threw most of it away. The telephone ringing in his apartment threw him into a rage so he kept the receiver off the hook. Got into the practice of making his own calls out of pay phones or in hotel lobbies, recalling how Al Sansom was always joking about his phone conversations being tapped and it turned out he was right. And Al had been scared shitless about something happening to him and something had happened all right and Felix had had the audacity to tell the police about his partner's interest and even expertise in flying saucers—maybe he'd made contact with them? been taken away in one?—Felix looking deadpan at his interrogators who'd stared in turn at him for a long moment not knowing what to think. A smart-ass kind of thing to say and Felix's lawyer stiffened staring at the floor but the moment passed; for all they knew Al Sansom *had* made contact with creatures from another planet or dimension, maybe his body wasn't just dumped somewhere north of Albany in the mountains or in the Florida Everglades to be discovered in another few months and probably "suicide" would be named as the cause—there'd be a note somewhere, a safety deposit box. Why not think flying saucers just for now?—Felix stubbing out his cigarette, smiling mildly, saying, *"He'd* be damned happy if that was what it was."

Ursula was married as planned in a "small private nondenominational" ceremony in Miami Beach to her retired stockbroker whose name Felix made no effort to remember. His half brother Domenic— "Father" Domenic—died of a coronary thrombosis in Foxboro. Felix didn't attend either the wedding or the funeral, didn't in fact hear of them until afterward.

Aren't you happy for your mother, Felix.

Aren't you grieving for your brother, Felix.

A letter dated 11 March 1956 from Lyle Stevick—typed, the ribbon faint, some of the keys broken—*Let's the two of us get together soon please must talk to you—tried to telephone but the damn line is always busy or nobody answers and I'm hearing disturbing things about you around town, not that I want to butt my nose in your business—you know me better than that—but I am worried: so please call me soon? After all we're brothers, had the same father at least, that means something doesn't it.* Then two dense pages single-spaced about Domenic's death—the wake—the funeral—the man's "personal effects" at the rectory and his "meager pathetic" will: Felix skimmed it quickly forgetting even as he read. No mention of Enid, so he threw the letter away or lost it amid the crap piling up in his apartment.

Too late, Lyle. I don't give a shit.

Began to avoid Niagara Square entirely, his classy apartment building where if he entered the lobby at the wrong time of day people stared at him, the doorman with his fixed smile, the superintendent calling him "Mr. Stevick" in a tone he didn't like. If he wasn't looking his best. Or if he had a woman with him.

His preference was for cheap hotels, rooming houses as they were called—nothing fancy like the Onondaga, the Sheridan, the Oriskany Arms where people might know him. Or say he'd driven out of town on one of his impulsive excited aimless drives, he'd spend the night in a roadside motel sleeping fully clothed atop a bed, waking very late in the morning or past noon his head ringed with pain from hours of gym work—jumping rope shadow boxing sparring with a partner he didn't know whose face he couldn't see clearly and the guy was young, tough, wily, just slightly sneering, giving Felix Stevick a workout, showing him up with everybody looking on—and getting out of bed had to be plotted and rehearsed, how to get the leverage for his heavy torso then his legs positioned under him then to the bathroom if he made it. His body not a boxer's body now but an ordinary man's body, leaden with fatigue, its youth gone.

He'd wake to find himself in Fulton, or Marietta, or Oconee, or Pendleton. Or Spragueville. Or out in the country nowhere he could figure out or guess and it would require miles of driving—sober now, cautious—to discover which direction he wanted since he wasn't a man who asked questions. Not thinking of Enid or of the baby now not thinking of anything just feeling banged-up and rotten, two days' beard, stubble on his cheeks and chin with a strange silvery cast, eyes threaded with blood and sometimes one of his eyes swollen and discolored, cuts on his face, his mouth, his knuckles raw and swollen too and he rarely made the effort to remember exactly what had happened, what had precipitated an exchange of words into an exchange of blows—barrooms, lavatories, parking lots—skirmishes that never lasted more than a minute or two before some guy's buddies broke them up. There was always a good reason why he risked getting killed or risked killing another man or men just as there was always a name for the place he woke in next day—Bide-a-Wee, Traveler's Lodge, Spragueville Motor Court—but he'd stopped caring about the details.

Knowing he wouldn't remember them anyway, beyond the next time it happened.

Sober, Felix told himself he'd never do it again: never. Stop drinking and stop cold turkey, maybe give Dan Hickey a call, saying, Help me, he could get his body back into condition any time he wanted, couldn't he?—Felix Stevick's "body" always there waiting to be claimed. When he had his first drink of the day which was likely to be the first nourishment of the day at 9 A.M. or 3 P.M. he'd feel that sense of slipping, sliding, the solid earth was actually sand or bits of crumbly grit you couldn't get a decent footing on, a canvas you kept sliding on so why resist, why so much effort expended in resisting? Pack it in, Stevick, go where the current takes you.

There'd been a punchy ex-heavyweight named Zubrzycki who'd hung around the gym years ago, big slow-moving sweet-looking guy always in a sweatshirt, always smiling, showing a space where his front teeth were missing, good club fighter who'd actually gone eight rounds with Jimmy Braddock one night in the Armory but his career had ended abruptly and they said his brain was like a sieve, tell Zubrzycki something and he'd seem to be listening, then five minutes later he couldn't remember. Felix kept his distance from the poor son of a bitch but now he was beginning to see the advantage of being punchdrunk, life got simplified, didn't it, flat like a playing card with no depth, so thin you couldn't measure it, only one side up.

Mid-March, Felix Stevick was detained overnight in the Oconee County Jail in Pendleton for being involved in a "public disturbance" involving six other men; a week later he was arrested for "reckless" and "impaired" driving in the city speeding east on Grand, sixty-five miles an hour in a thirty-mile zone, so he was fined $500 and his license suspended for six months. Not that he gave a damn: told the judge right then he'd drive his fucking car whenever he wanted.

But a few days later he did give it up: left it parked in the street, walked away. He'd had a near-accident, a head-on collision averted at the last moment when driving on a busy street, he seemed to be drifting helpless as smoke, out of his body his head awash with dreams and only the frantic honking of other cars woke him. And another time he came close to running down some Negro children playing in the street, his reflexes mysteriously slow hitting the brake, the Lincoln skidded sideways for what must have been twenty feet and he sat behind the wheel cold sober feeling detached, bemused, as if he'd lived through all this before and knew the outcome.

That's it, Stevick.

By this time he was living a succession of days and nights not clearly distinguished from one another except in terms of consciousness and unconsciousness, the state of being awake and the state of being asleep and one shifted imperceptibly into the other and neither was more significant. He was never drunk by his own estimation and he was never sober. He'd moved out of the Niagara Towers without notifying his landlord, without having paid his March rent, leaving nearly everything behind, took up residence in the Mohawk Hotel, a room for $35 a week with a view of the waterfront near the wharves, warehouses, saloons. There was the Mid-City Café where he sometimes played poker, there was the Second Street Bar & Grill, there was Richie's, there was the Falcon Tavern on South Main and the nameless diner adjacent to the Greyhound terminal where he had many of his meals when he was in a mood for eating. Once or twice he made the rounds of the Genesee Street taverns, even asked at the Flanders Hotel about the girl in the black leather coat, but they claimed not to know who he was talking about. He never ran into her again. Or her pimp he'd beaten the shit out of: would they recognize each other? Felix wondered. There were large burnt-out patches in his brain he never entered. Why? To what purpose? Charred shapes you stumbled upon in the jungle, likely to be parts of human bodies or human heads or just tree limbs strangely blackened. Or the space in the brain you go when you're knocked out like nothing else on earth and the secret is, it's sweet. But he never entered, he didn't know and didn't want to know. He'd gone through all that. He did meet up with Jo-Jo Pearl's father though, somewhere on the South Side. Couldn't remember the man's name, then in a rush of sick feeling remembered: Leroy. Leroy Pearl swinging into a barroom on crutches cheery and belligerent, his hair like quills slicked back from his low fierce forehead and his face fuller than Felix recalled, cheeks ruddy from the cold. He saw Felix—stared at him—blinked stupidly trying to place him and Felix's heart kicked urging him to slip away, Christ yes he'd better get his coat and slip away, resisting the impulse to go up to Pearl to say, "Do you know me? Do you have any business with me?" He could see Jo-Jo's young unblemished face inside that older coarser face pushing through. A few nights later by accident they met again and this time Felix was sick-drunk, vomiting his guts out in the lavatory at the Second Street Bar & Grill, a long balmy late-winter day in a month he couldn't have named except suddenly it seemed people were walking around without coats bareheaded and squinting up at the sun, smiling, and icicles were melting and heaped-up filthy mounds of snow an unseasonal warm spell which depressed the hell out of him for some reason so he needed an early stiff drink since he'd learned finally to adjust to winter he'd understood what winter meant and now there was the danger of an abrupt change and Christ he wasn't ready and that night there was Leroy Pearl in the company of a big hook-nosed man wearing a soiled railroad cap backward on his head, both of them loud and pushy and feeling no pain and Felix was bent over a filthy sink soaking paper towels in cold water to press against his face and the mistake was Felix's eyes locking with Pearl's in the mirror—he might have ducked away if he hadn't made that mistake, might have avoided everything. But their eyes locked and this time Pearl knew who Felix was. This time Pearl was in control, leaning on his left crutch gesturing with his right, and you could see the ropey arm muscles inside the slacker flesh, his eyes rolling wild and wet, mouth curling like a scar into a smile and Felix was too weak to defend himself, his guts still sick and knees like water. Pearl said only, "You! I know you!" advancing on him but it seemed to take a very long time for the crutch to swing through the air, Felix was trying to shield his head thinking he'd slip the first blow then punch in over it a solid right to the man's jaw but the force of the blow astonished him, so hard, the edge of the crutch striking his skull, a hardness he'd never have anticipated and he fell against the sink, against one of the toilet stalls, and now his opponent stood over him in triumph shouting in manic glee striking any way he could—Felix's head, his arms, his chest, his groin—kicking him with the heel of his boot, half sobbing with the effort, "I know you! I know you! Stevick! Fucker! Bastard! Letting my boy die! Now it's your turn!"—and Felix was bleeding from the mouth, couldn't defend himself, now floating above his body looking down at the spectacle, a man lying on a filthy tile floor being kicked by two rummies, kicked and hit with a clumsy flying crutch, he didn't feel any pain or much surprise, hadn't he lived through all this before, a door opening slowly and he'd slip through and escape.

EPILOGUE

May 28, 1956

Dear Enid,

I am writing this quickly in a state of some agitation—I am afraid it will be disjointed and confusing. Not agitation perhaps but excitement and anticipation. I have not slept very well for the past week.

I want to say at once how much your letter meant to me. How much I wanted to call you. But you were right I think telling me not to call. I needed time.

I should explain my present circumstances—why I am here, in the company of 87 others, some of them strangers, approx. 25 miles south of Pueblo, Colorado, in a makeshift camp of tents, sleeping bags, trailers, vans, cars. In so beautiful yet so inhospitable a place. (As I write this I am looking over a plain stretching to the horizon—scrub grass, small stunted trees and shrubs, sweet clover in bloom and tiny yellow flowers, flowers to the horizon and a galaxy of bees and white butterflies. The sun is blazing but the air is cold and there's a constant numbing wind from the west.) By the time you receive this letter our mission will be over but I have no hope you will read of it; the U.S. Government (meaning specifically the Pentagon) is increasingly fearful of giving our efforts much publicity knowing that if we have access to the hearts and minds of the American people a rebellion of sorts might result. A mutiny—a revolution—in thought! I am speaking of our coalition's opposition to the U.S. war mentality. The U.S. preparation for war. The U.S. cultivation of the rhetoric of war. The U.S. manufacture of the weapons of war. Oh, Enid, aren't we all sick and disgusted, baffled—a military budget of $35.5 BILLION for next year even as the horror of what we are doing was brought home by last week's test in the Pacific and U.S. madness taking pride in the "first airborne" hydrogen bomb detonated 15,000 feet in the air. U.S. madness boasting of a "perfected" bomb of 10 megatons—*10 million tons of TNT.*

Our mission here—our demonstration/protest—begins tomorrow at 6 A.M. We are to post ourselves at strategic places blocking the construction site of the new Atlas intercontinental ballistics missile base of which you have doubtless read; our target is specifically missile launching "A" on which work was begun two weeks ago. A number of us will block all gateways and truck routes into the site, others will picket on the highway and along access roads. So many leaflets passed out and read—or not read!—so many speeches made and signs carried and "vigils of conscience" appealing only to those possessed of consciences—and now having seen the futility of such efforts some of us are impatient to move to action of a more dramatic nature, *dhurna* with its possibility of violence by the adversary. You would not know, Enid—for such facts are becoming systematically suppressed—but on May 15 a petition sponsored by the American Friends Service Committee consisting of 25,000 signatures demanding the United States cease its atomic testing in the Marshall Islands was delivered to the White House but not received by President Eisenhower in person. "The President is not available," the deliverers of the petition were told.

By trespassing on private land (the access routes are through property owned by local ranchers who have given permission for the military to use it) as well as on Government-owned land we are behaving in a way meant to disrupt services—not "peaceful noncooperation" any longer but active revolt—obstruction—the provocation of the "adversary" to react with force. But what is to be done otherwise? Many of us have discovered that words—the most forceful and logical arguments—seem to have no effect—is it the consequence of our very "freedom of speech" when *all* have speech and *no one* need listen?—but actions draw attention, actions cannot be ignored. In protest of U.S. global violence-to-be we must risk provoking violence against us, our very selves, at the present time. But SOMETHING is preferable to NOTHING—some action preferable to no action at all which is tantamount to assent.

The challenge we will be putting to the military guards at the site is one they cannot ignore—as leaflets, speeches, years of good intentions have been ignored. The challenge we will be putting to the truckers by blocking their roads is: KILL US—IN ORDER TO BUILD THIS MISSILE SITE. They will have the choice of (1) running some of us over, (2) stopping their trucks and dragging us away, (3) turning around and refusing to continue work on the site.

In any case—by the time this reaches you our efforts will be over. I'd ask you to pray for us, Enid, except you and I don't believe in prayer—do we.

As for your letter—sure I was shocked. I *am* shocked.

What can I say. That I'm profoundly relieved you are all right now as you claim to be—that nobody there knows about it—except the "father." ("Father" of what!) And that you aren't seeing him any longer.

I was shocked, Christ yes. And I was angry. It's good I didn't call you, I wasn't really in control. But maybe I couldn't have called you—afraid of hearing your voice. Or having to talk with Mother and Father. Being unable to say anything except the usual helpless things we say over the phone.

What *can* I say. (Did I ever mention I still have that paperweight you gave me? One of those glass globes with "snowflakes" inside, a souvenir of Shoal Lake. Back in my room in Philadelphia. On my desk. Or don't you remember?)

I began this letter over an hour ago. Wanting to say so much. Now I'm stalled. Tasting something like bile—self-disgust.

Maybe it's because my nerves are strung tight about tomorrow morning. Maybe it's because I don't want to say fatuous things to you after the fact. (And when we saw each other in April you seemed to avoid me. Or did I avoid you. Avoiding everybody asking me about law school, would I try again, etc. And poor Daddy so broken up so floored by his brother's death.) Maybe it's because I can think of you only as my sister Enid, my youngest sister, and it isn't credible that what happened happened. (As for me—after the woman who was supposed to be my fiancée left me I was diagnosed as having a "minor" venereal infection. Please don't laugh. But of course you

415

wouldn't laugh. And I'm not bitter, really—shall I be shameless and say I'm grateful nonetheless. Warren Stevick the lover!)

Strange isn't it—how "love" seems to carry with it no knowledge. The people I have loved most in my lifetime (including you) I haven't known at all. Nor have they known me.

The blood ties are so powerful and deep and mute. Something terrifying there. How we feel about one another—even about the house on East Clinton Street—so strange, helpless, paralyzing and exciting both. It's only away where people don't know me or haven't known me for very long that I am my*self.*

Next year when you go away to school you will know what I mean. And we'll write to each other, won't we? All through our lives? Promise me I won't lose you. Though I've been an inadequate brother to you.

Don't feel guilty. You speak of guilt and that's natural but *don't* feel it. (Does the "father" feel guilt? Does the "father" even know all you've told me?)

I should be ending this letter. We're driving one of the vans into Hershey in a half hour to pick up supplies, I can mail it at the Hershey P.O.

I *should* end . . . yet I can't. This is the most difficult letter I believe I have ever written! Each word coming so excruciatingly slowly it's as if I imagined the document Warren Stevick's "last will and testament." (Sheer vanity, paranoia. I may be knocked around a bit tomorrow by the guards, or the truckers, or the Colorado state police, but certainly I am in no danger of being killed. Warren Stevick's political significance is not of that scale.)

Put in mind suddenly of a fighter pilot I knew in Korea. Did I tell you about him—I think I must have—he'd gone beyond the 100-mission mark, sometimes did two missions a day. The strain was beginning to show but he claimed he thought of what he did as routine. His plane was an "aerial ammunition truck" and he drove the truck escorted by a spotter plane, then was told by radio what to do—bomb or strafe a hill, a forest, a village—then turn back, be back in time for lunch. He said sometimes in the briefing room he'd get nervous, even panicked, but once in the air he settled into the routine and things washed back and it was hypnotic in a way as flying always is, then when he came in actual sight of his target he'd wake up not feeling excitement exactly, not fear, a kind of certainty he was in the right place doing the right thing—hadn't he been brought from the other side of the world to do his mission?—drop a load of bombs according to instructions. There was just him, he said, and the target alone in the world—the entire war *was* him. So he couldn't fail. He couldn't make a mistake. So it was all right.

It's perverse to say this but I feel the same way. All my senses quickened as if they've been dead for months—my heart stirred with hope or is it *torn* with hope!

I love you. Pray for me anyway. In haste, your brother

Warren

You don't deserve this, the voice nudged, nagged, *you don't deserve any of this.* And Enid swallowed hard trying not to hear.

Murderer, how do you dare!

It was a new fierce voice, derisive and knowing. Enid tried not to hear.

In a dark-blue linen suit, a white silk blouse sewed by Mrs. Stevick, in stockings and high heels Enid went in late May by bus to Rochester, New York, to the Westcott School of Music where she was scheduled to meet with the professor who would be her faculty adviser in the fall. She'd been accepted at the school without having been interviewed; she'd won not only a New York State Regents scholarship but a matching scholarship from the music school. She was even to graduate salutatorian of her high school class.

You don't deserve this as with shaking fingers she'd ripped open the envelope from the Westcott School and began to scream, "Oh, Momma! Momma! Good news!" And Momma had tried to respond—you could see that. And Daddy too that evening though Enid could see the pinched look inside his broad smiling face, that look of hurt that gradually pushed forward. "What's wrong with the teachers' college right here in Port Oriskany?" he would ask repeatedly. "Then you could live at home, honey, you could save the cost of room and board"—reasonable and stubborn and beginning to be offended as if his daughter's rejection of the local state-funded school was in a way a rejection of him. Which, Enid supposed, it was. Enid said only, "Daddy, *no.*" And she said, "Daddy, *please.*" But she would not be drawn into arguing with him.

In the end he'd let her go. What choice had he?—all his children were going away.

This final season of her life in Port Oriskany in the house at 118 East Clinton and Enid was slow to acknowledge her happiness for fear it would slip from her—as in one of her dreams of exquisite misery she reached with childish expectation for something mysterious and tantalizing, and it eluded her, turned to smoke. *You don't deserve any of this,* the voice not Enid's own but an intimate voice close as her pulse—*murderer, and you know it.*

But she dared. She would do it. Leave Port Oriskany, leave home the way Warren had, go to college in another city and return only on vacations and never see her Uncle Felix again and never think of *it* again, all they'd done together. She believed she could do it because she believed she was strong enough but she knew she'd have to leave home and she was going to leave home, not even Mr. Stevick, pleading smiling hurt beginning to be angry, could dissuade her.

Daddy, *no.*

May 28 and Enid took the 7:15 A.M. bus out of the Greyhound terminal thinking nervously and excitedly it was the first time she'd traveled such a distance on her own, then she took a taxi from the bus station in Rochester to the Westcott campus a few miles away, some minutes' panic as she tried to find the building without success, then someone directed her and she hurried, climbed a flight of stairs and found the room, her heart thudding absurdly in her chest and the man who was her adviser shook her hand as if she were an adult and his equal—and Enid thought, almost faint with relief, It's all right.

At the conclusion of the half-hour conference it emerged that Enid's adviser knew Anton Lesnovich and thought highly of him—"an idiosyncratic teacher but an excellent one, and eminently reliable in his judgments"—in fact it was Mr. Lesnovich's unusually forceful recommendation of her that had been the determining factor in Enid's admission at the school. Enid sat blinking and smiling, struck dumb for a moment by this revelation so casually as if incidentally made—the glimpse it provided of a world of adult authority in which she was an object of others' judgments, assessments. In which there existed an Enid Stevick she didn't perhaps know and could not truly judge.

It was a thought—curious, unexpected—Enid had had months ago, sick as her parents were deceived into thinking with "flu," intestinal "flu," but nothing really serious nothing that would require, say, a visit to the doctor: not that. Sick and staying out of school for nearly two weeks, too weak to get out of bed most days and crying frequently, she claimed to have and perhaps truly did have a headache, fever, chills, most of all she was exhausted—lying in bed beneath an old quilt Mrs. Stevick had made for her years ago propped up against pillows with the intention of reading, keeping up with her schoolwork, listening to one of the records Felix had bought her which she knew by heart, following the score in her lap, but she'd realize after a while she was simply lying there thinking of—nothing: not even of *it*. Eyes open but sightless and even the ache in her loins dull and remote and in a way abstract, impersonal. For comfort rubbing the quilt—Momma's quilt, "double wedding ring" the pattern was called, interlocking circles of vari-textured white cloth on a plain white background with white appliqué and white embroidery so finely done it fairly astonished—so many hours of Hannah Stevick's life sewn into it, Enid was thinking, thinking too it was beyond her even to calculate the jigsaw puzzle of hundreds of subtly differing shades and textures of white. White upon white upon white, the wedding rings interlocking scarcely perceptible to the casual eye. She wondered if anyone in the family had ever *seen* this quilt Momma had sewed? Really *seen* it? Though looking wasn't enough, you had to touch too—like reading Braille.

Enid was ashamed recalling the times she and Lizzie had mocked their mother's sewing, not wanting to think maybe that Mrs. Stevick loved her daughters, that was why she sewed them things not always fashionable or to their taste, so many hours, so much love, how could *they* ever repay her?

The quilt was yellowed from numberless launderings but still warm, heavy, beautiful; Enid sleepily contemplated its interlocking circles, the ingenious pattern of rings, thinking that if Momma had sewn it for a child Enid no longer remembered, a child she'd never been, what did that matter really? What did it matter.

"You! How the hell *are* you!"

Lizzie in the doorway of what had been her room now oddly shy, self-conscious, as if Enid might not want company, or might not want her company. But she was brash, smiling, glamorous, filling the room with her presence and her perfume—it would linger in the air for hours, even downstairs, so that Mr. Stevick would be moved to ask when he came home that evening, What is that *smell,* some fancy new kind of Air-Wick?

Lizzie brought Enid sisterly things you might call them, a small stuffed panda, a paperback copy of *East of Eden*—"Since you're so crazy for reading long things"—some Ann Page chocolates. Couldn't stay long since Henri was waiting for her but she wanted to check in on Enid, see how things were; with a surreptitious glance out into the hall she asked how things *really* were, and Enid started to cry but Enid said quickly, "All right—really." "Really?" Lizzie asked skeptically. "Yes, really," Enid said. "What about the bleeding, is that all right too? I mean—is it over with?" "Yes, it's over with." "Do they give you stitches or anything?" "No." "What's it *like?*" "I was anesthetized when the doctor did it, I don't know what it's like," Enid said, "just that it hurt, sure, afterward." "Does it hurt now?" "Sometimes." "Does it hurt *bad?*" "Lizzie, I'd rather not talk about it right now, please—" "What about the guy, who *is* he? I'm dying to know." "Nobody you know." "Yes, but *who?*" Lizzie leaned over Enid, touching Enid's overheated face with surprisingly cool fingers but Enid said nothing. "I just can't get over it," Lizzie said finally. "Jesus. My kid sister of all people"—looking at Enid in that new way of hers that Enid guessed Lizzie would always look at her, thinking, Here is the one in the family who can't ever be trusted. Ever.

Sometimes half asleep or groggy from too much sleep, Enid could not recall was it now—or that other time?—when she'd wanted so badly to die, to extinguish herself utterly, but had failed and they brought her back and she lay in this very bed beside the secret wallpaper, so very tired, so very empty you can't imagine the emptiness. Then by degrees she began to feel better, stronger, one morning waking hungry for the first time in so long and she knew she'd had enough of being sick, enough of repentance, what she wanted to do now was get up and take a shower and wash her hair and get dressed and go downstairs and go out—no more of this bed with its familiar bumps and hollows, no more of the covers and the stained wallpaper at which she rarely glanced. She'd had enough too of grief, of mourning, of that din inside her skull telling her she too deserved to die, she'd killed her baby, hadn't she, the "baby" that in fact had never existed, and the thought of it like the ache in her loins gradually lightened, faded like an exercise at the piano she'd practiced so long that at a certain point merely to strike the initial note was to strike all the successive notes with no further conscious thought, only her fingers and nerve endings engaged.

When Felix was in the hospital for twelve days in late March ("an accident," Enid was told at first, "a beating," she subsequently learned), Enid was the only family member *not* to visit him.

Everyone else went, even Neal O'Banan. But not Enid Stevick who owed her uncle so much?

Enid told anyone who asked that she couldn't bring herself to enter that hospital again—just the smell of it would remind her of something she wanted to forget. So they asked nothing further: after all, Enid's own "accident" had nearly been forgotten in the family, was never mentioned now.

She was circumspect too about asking how Felix was, how serious were his injuries, not trusting her voice or her face or her hands which might suddenly begin to tremble, but Mr. Stevick said his brother would be all right, wasn't going to die, a few broken ribs, a broken nose "with his money he can get fixed easy enough," and Mrs. Stevick turned on him with startling violence saying his brother had been seriously injured for God's sake, hadn't they said at the hospital he'd been unconscious for hours? But Mr. Stevick held his ground stubborn and grudging: "Felix always lands on his feet—wait and see."

Mid-May Felix telephoned Enid for the first time in months. To tell her he was getting married.

Are you, Enid said faintly.

And moving out of Port Oriskany, to Albany for a while, then somewhere else—somewhere new. He was going into another line of business, another kind of investments, selling off the property in the Adirondacks et cetera but he hadn't yet decided what.

Mainly he wanted her to know he was getting married, he said.

He wanted her to be the first to know—before the woman herself knows, he said.

Enid laughed. The shock of hearing his voice went through her, leaving her weak, but she heard herself laugh as if he'd said something amusing, which perhaps he had. Felix spoke quickly, guiltily, saying he understood why she hadn't visited him in the hospital, he'd hoped she would stay away—better to forget all that.

Yes, said Enid.

He wasn't going to tell her who the woman was and she wasn't going to ask.

They weren't on the phone long, perhaps ten minutes. There were pauses, stretches of strained silence, Enid tried to muffle her sobs, she didn't want him to hear her cry and he wasn't going to acknowledge he heard her cry or guessed it or wished for it. Why hadn't he died, she was thinking. Beaten in a tavern down by the docks, beaten savagely, his wallet taken and his clothes ripped half off him even one of his shoes thrown into a toilet—he'd been taken by ambulance to Port Oriskany General and when he finally regained consciousness, when he was able to speak coherently, he told police he'd never seen his assailants, couldn't have identified them.

The other day on Main Street, Enid had happened to see a man resembling Felix Stevick crossing the street, hair dark and windblown, Felix's height, Felix's profile, that air of his of barely contained impatience, and Enid stood on the sidewalk staring after him feeling her strength run down like water, all her pride and resolve and hurt—even after she saw the man wasn't Felix, even then she continued to watch him, stricken to the heart, thinking she'd be seeing that man all her life and she must not allow him to turn and see her.

Now he was asking how she was and Enid said the usual things and he said he'd heard from Lyle she was going away to college to study music in the fall. If she ever needed money—

No, Enid said carefully. I won't need money.

If you do, said Felix, just let me know.

Why hadn't he died.
Why hadn't they both died.

She recalled as if she'd been present or seen it in a movie a man and a woman who were lovers desperately in love preparing to die, closing themselves in a car in some hidden secret place a length of hose running from the exhaust pipe into one of the windows, the radio on and turned low, sweet murmurous music to accompany their dying or would it be better to have no sound at all, everything silent, sacred, except for the car's motor and their slow purposeful breathing which eventually would become silent too. *Why hadn't they.*

―――――――――――

Following her conference on the twenty-eighth, Enid had an hour or more before her next appointment—she was to meet a former student of Mr. Lesnovich's for lunch, a girl who was majoring in music education as Enid planned to major—so she walked around the campus of the Westcott School curious and admiring. *Did* she deserve this, any of it, this place of cobblestone paths and green quadrangles, Gothic buildings, soaring arches, sudden surprising vistas of trees?—so many young people, intelligent-looking, she was thinking, and serious, attractive, her classmates-to-be. She looked like one of them even now, except for her dressy clothes.

The night before there'd been a thunderstorm and now the sky was a high clear enamel blue and all the earth, the grass in particular, the trunks and foliage of trees, seemed charged with light and vibrancy. Enid walked not knowing where she went, looking at everything hard, greedily. She was thinking how ironic, now she was here, she would come in time to believe she belonged here.

Wave upon wave of happiness washed over her. *You don't deserve it,* she knew but she didn't care, she *was* here.

She approached a building that must have been, at one time, a private residence, a mansion of sorts. She had been drawn to it hearing varying slightly discordant notes of music, the ground-floor windows were partway open and at one she could see a young woman at a piano, playing and replaying a few familiar bars, was it Beethoven, surely Beethoven; at the next window the sound of a violin, farther on an instrument that might have been a clarinet, then again a piano—this was the music practice building where, next year, Enid would herself practice piano. She entered it by way of a rear door that was propped open and found herself in a low-ceilinged corridor, the wooden floors smelling sharply of wax, the walls badly in need of paint, pipes and heating ducts exposed. It was an old building after all, homey, unpretentious. Through closed doors Enid could hear muffled sounds of music—piano, violin, woodwind—these secret languages, groping, tentative, urgent like currents of water rushing underground. At the end of the corridor Enid came to an empty room—went inside and shut the door after her and locked it. Why not? As if she'd stepped through time into the future where she belonged by rights in this small soundproofed room with a spinet piano, a Wurlitzer, for her use.

The piano was rather old, scarified, the keys discolored, but the tone was startlingly sharp and rich—as good as Mr. Lesnovich's piano. Enid adjusted the stool to her height and sat running her fingers along the keyboard, feeling still those waves of happiness rising, mounting, a giddiness that was like drunkenness as she thought how privileged she was, how privileged she'd been, merely sitting at a piano playing perfectly ordinary scales, chords—arpeggios in particular always soothed and calmed her, a consolation for any kind of loss, or nearly—the fact, so very simple, yet miraculous, that the piano's music was *there* inside the instrument waiting to be struck.

She played one of the little Mozart rondos she'd memorized for Mr. Lesnovich, she struck a wrong note and began again, another wrong note in her excitement and another beginning but there was no one to hear, no one to register her mistake so indeed it wasn't a mistake exactly. She was calmed by the rondo's sunny logic and by the mere act of moving her slightly stiffened fingers along the keys, hearing subtleties of sound in this particular piano new to her and intriguing. When she'd been sick and hadn't gone downstairs for days hadn't gone near the piano for weeks she'd thought in her fever delirium how lovely it would be—oh Christ, how lovely it always is—just to sit at that piano and depress a single key, to draw out that single clear extraordinary sound. But she hadn't had the strength. The will. Three months away from the instrument and three months away from Lesnovich and when she resumed her lessons she'd played badly, stupidly, it was as if she must begin again, Mr. Lesnovich was surprisingly sympathetic, didn't scold or chide, told her not to be impatient. He reassigned her old pieces, old familiar pieces she'd "mastered" the previous year. Told her that a single day away from his instrument is harmful for any musician, let alone so much time, did she understand?

Yes, she understood. She was willing to work, she was willing to humble herself starting over and beginning again, for what after all was the alternative.

At a family gathering years ago Enid had heard her father and one of her uncles complaining of work, working their asses off, Mr. Stevick had been eloquent and despairing and funny, saying in a drunken voice, *What is the alternative?*—and Enid had loved him at that moment for all he'd endured, she'd been embarrassed of course but she'd loved him too, knowing he was right. What after all is the alternative.

Playing the rondo another time Enid steeled herself for a mysterious resistance from the keyboard that sometimes balked her when she was feeling a piece begin to take hold, easing from her and her quick-darting thoughts, listening to herself playing as if from a distance—her fingers, her arms, her very breathing controlling the passage of notes while she herself stood apart, critical and attentive. But there was no resistance this time. The piece began to take hold, to fly. The composition fascinated her beyond her own exertion, Mozart so young when he'd written it, Mr. Lesnovich had told her, hardly more than a child but it's a work of genius, its wiry delicacy, its logic, simplicity, humor, these small graceful tricky turns and subtle resolutions, a piece of music written circa 1770 now being played on a morning in May 1956 with nothing intervening, or so it seemed—not the pianist, not the instrument itself.

For the second or third time that afternoon she said she didn't want to stay down there very long. Being underground like that made her nervous, she began to imagine she wasn't breathing right.

And Lyle Stevick controlling his impatience promised her they wouldn't stay long. Only a few minutes: he wanted to do a quick inspection after last night's rainstorm. And it would be nice to see how the bedspreads looked on the beds, wouldn't it?

They should brighten things a little, Hannah said, half smiling.

Down they climbed out of the whitish May sunshine, Lyle Stevick first, then Hannah—through the hatchway, slowly descending the metal ladder as if entering a submarine—below the solid-packed inches of soil and grass where Lyle's silver-foil walls glimmered and where an odor of damp, earth, sewage faintly arose. Lyle hoped Hannah would not complain. Certainly she noticed—she noticed everything—but he hoped she would not complain. The first time she'd visited the shelter after weeks of his cajoling they'd quarreled about the "smell" as she called it and Lyle made the point that there is always some sort of "smell" underground; then as their quarrel continued he insisted she was imagining it all—in fact there *was* no "smell." And by then Hannah was so accustomed to the air in the shelter she had to admit she no longer smelled it but being Hannah Stevick she couldn't let the matter rest: said the "smell" was there whether anybody smelled it or not. And Lyle said mockingly, Does a tree crash over in the forest if there's nobody there to see or hear it?—and Hannah stared at him as if he were crazy. Of course, she said. What a fool question.

This afternoon thank God the woman was tactful, protective of his feelings, made no comment on the odor, even murmured grudgingly that the floor *was* dry—wasn't it?—drier anyway than their cellar floor. At least the pump he'd bought was working, that was something. (Early in April Lyle Stevick had had the shock of his life—inspecting the shelter one morning after a severe rainstorm he'd found some six inches of dirty water in it!—he'd had to hurry over to Harry Poole's to get a secondhand sump pump for $45 to flush the water out by way of a hose flowing into the alley, like dirty soapy water from the women's washing machines, and neighbor children naturally gathered to watch, to ask insolent questions, but it couldn't be helped. But the damn pump *had* worked; as Hannah said, that was something.) She had become surprisingly sensitive to his moods lately, even rather worried about him—he'd had a health scare back in March—then his brother Domenic dying so suddenly so without

warning had devastated him and Felix's "accident" was a shock too—
and Lizzie, dear Christ just to think of Lizzie drove his blood pressure
up—one goddamned thing after another so Hannah was making an
effort to be kind, to be thoughtful, maybe even humoring him which
he certainly did not want; he'd come upon Hannah and his sister-in-
law Ingrid talking and they'd fall suspiciously silent, looking at him
he imagined with embarrassment if not actual guilt, pointedly waiting
for him to go away again—after so many years what *did* those women
find to talk about even granting they talked about him?

Today however Hannah herself was in a somber mood, the sisters
were having difficulties with one of their dressmaking customers but
primarily she was feeling melancholy about Enid's going off—Enid,
their youngest child, their last child, away in Rochester most of the
day preparing to leave home in the fall and nothing could dissuade
her: she had a special scholarship from the Westcott School of Music
and she was *going*. For perhaps the thousandth time Lyle Stevick told
his wife he didn't see why Enid couldn't go to school right here in Port
Oriskany and live at home, some of her high school friends were
going to the teachers' college, think of all the money she'd save, he'd
never known Enid was so willful, and Hannah said with an air of
resignation they were all willful—children. Whether you knew it or
not at the time.

Did the thought of no more children at home alarm Hannah as
frankly it alarmed Lyle Stevick?—he suspected it did. Just the two of
them alone in the house as in the beginning when they were newly
married but of course they weren't alone for long, the first baby came
fast. One after another after another of the children growing up and
leaving, which was only natural Lyle knew, it *was* nature, the distress-
ing thing was only Geraldine would be in Port Oriskany next year—
thank God for Neal O'Banan after all. But who would have predicted
Warren would turn out so oddly, so disappointing, now he'd even
dropped out of law school and was working in some city-financed job,
Children's Aid it was called, in a slum neighborhood in Philadelphia,
shied away from answering his father's questions about the job for a
damned good reason, Lyle suspected. And Warren had done so well
in high school! And Warren was Lyle Stevick's only son! And there
was Lizzie, about whom he hardly dared think—run off to Manhattan
to pursue her career and living in a residential hotel near Broadway
and 42nd Street and her fiancé La Porte was with her though as Lizzie
claimed they had separate rooms at the hotel—separate rooms!—did
she imagine Lyle Stevick could believe that for a minute?—and when

La Porte's divorce came through they were to be married, oh yes, they'd be married, Daddy could count on that. The message wasn't subtle and the message was, *Like it or not who gives a good goddamn about you.*

And there was Enid suddenly so stubborn, so undaughterly—

But no: he wasn't going to think about Enid right now. Not now with Hannah clearly making an effort to be agreeable, complimenting him on the look of the walls which, she said, took getting used to, the silvery sheen like the inside of something—she didn't know what. And the secondhand Armstrong linoleum tiles he'd laid on the concrete floor. With fussy wifely authority she checked the cupboard as if half thinking the supplies might be depleted. Then turned to shake out the corduroy bedspreads she'd made for the bunk beds, not smiling at Lyle as he might have wished but not frowning and severe either; she knew what the shelter meant to him, she was the only person on earth who seemed to know and he had to be grateful for that. For months bitter about the money he'd spent, then with the scare about his health she'd come round to seeing his side of things, or behaved as if she did. Didn't quarrel. Didn't object to him spending a few more dollars—on the sump pump for instance. Watching her fit the bedspreads on the bunk beds Lyle felt a stirring of affection for her, a curious mild stirring of desire, it had been kind of her after all to take the time to make the spreads to "brighten" the shelter as she suggested, though she shrugged off his thanks irritably, saying the bedspreads were nothing for heaven's sake—inexpensive corduroy, rust-colored, quickly made on the sewing machine, anybody could do it. In the dim light her face looked smoother, even the creases between her eyes, prominent in daylight, were softened; her downcast expression reminded Lyle of the Hannah Weir of years ago—a quarter century ago!—when as a young husband he'd been virtually ablaze with sexual desire—with love—guiltless in the knowledge that holy matrimony was a sacrament of the Church and that his shy young wife though often paralyzed with shame at what they did could not refuse him: was in fact pregnant anyway. Too late now! What harm, now! It had been physical desire pure and simple—and how *pure,* how *simple!*—that had bound Lyle Stevick to her twenty-five years ago, made them man and wife of one flesh as the eerie saying went, one flesh in sickness and in health forever and ever Amen.

The impulse came to Lyle suddenly and almost fearfully: Why not make love?

They were in the safest and most private of places. Nobody would know. Who would know?

Certainly Hannah was attractive for a woman of her age—fifty-three or was it fifty-four—though rather heavy, solid, so full in the bust it must be a hardship to her getting herself in and out of those wired support contraptions every day of her life, hooks, eyes, straps, elastic bands, the corsets were even worse, like armor and always hospital-white with the garters hanging down. Hannah had lost a few pounds, evidently as a result of the diet the doctor had put Lyle on (*Lyle* had lost twelve pounds since March but Jesus had he any choice after the scare Ritter put into him!), but still she was broad at the hips and he knew how the white-lardish flesh of her thighs and buttocks was wattled, the big breasts hanging low, her upper arms sadly flaccid so she never wore short sleeves any longer—a vanity there Lyle wouldn't have guessed, like her wearing lipstick sometimes, dabbing powder on her face, Hannah and Ingrid both conscious of their "outfits" now in public—and Lyle liked her hairdo too, permed, close-cropped, so light a brown you couldn't really see how much of it was gray.

Why not make love?

It was odd, it was unexpected, disturbing—since the various crises of the spring he'd begun to experience at wayward times pangs of sexual desire, moods that were frankly amorous, he was startled and ashamed to acknowledge them, damned glad he didn't believe in confession any longer since he'd have had to confess them like a kid of fifteen to Father Ogden. Jesus, think of that! But anything could arouse him no matter his conscious thoughts—seeing women in the street, waiting on women in his store, television every night, that sweet-faced very pretty woman who visited Felix in the hospital, dreams of Elvira French whom he'd have sworn he had forgotten. Worst of all a virtual attack of sexual desire he'd experienced at his brother's very funeral staring at a young white-skinned woman, a total stranger to him, one of Domenic's Foxboro parishioners, lucky nobody caught him looking so rapt with lust, so stupid in oblivion. He chastised himself for such folly but what was to be done!—years and years his cock limp and useless, ornamental you might say, so much bulk to a man's sexual equipment, then the redundancy makes it seem funny, something you should joke about but what's the joke?—it's all *you.* Giving up his pipe, giving up tobacco, had something to do with it probably, losing weight too, worry that he had cancer of the rectum, then it turned out to be only hemorrhoids, but still there was the emphysema, that beginning of the end Ritter'd scared him with. After Domenic's death he'd thought a lot, sitting at the kitchen table late at night drinking ale so slow he could nurse one for an hour thinking what the hell, what the hell. Domenic's dead and I'm alive and what the hell.

Seeing his expression Hannah turned slightly aside, purse-lipped and frowning, fussing with her task, she knew the drift of her husband's thoughts since in the past several weeks they'd tried—he had tried—to make love without much success, Lyle nervous and apologetic and soon giving up, he didn't want to impose upon her, didn't want to embarrass her—or himself! They had not made love after all for nearly eighteen years. Did I hurt you, dear, Lyle asked the last time they'd tried, and Hannah said quietly, No. Then, after a moment, in the same still quiet voice, Why don't you try again if you want to. But Lyle flushed and shamefaced and in any case no longer tumescent said, No, it's all right, never mind, let's go to sleep.

By day of course they never alluded to such matters, to what Hannah must be thinking of as Lyle's strange if not unnatural behavior, but Lyle himself couldn't help brooding: what a profoundly mysterious and unfathomable thing sexual desire was! The philosophers tried to analyze it in purely abstract terms, Schopenhauer claimed it was nothing but the striving of the Will, the mad blind unthinking desire of the species to reproduce itself, but surely there was more to it than that—else why such anguish? such hope?

Shyly Lyle said, "Hannah—?"

"Yes? What?" She was tucking the corners of the last bedspread tightly into place, he saw a faint sheen of perspiration on her upper lip.

"I'd like to make love," Lyle said. "Can we? Could we? Now? Right here? I promise I won't—" His voice trailed off, he'd lost the drift of his words. He saw that look of careful blank neutrality of hers but he wasn't to be so easily dissuaded—he was her husband after all. She had no reason to refuse him. As if impulsively he went to embrace her—tried to kiss her—stooped and pressed his mouth against the nape of her neck. The urgency of his desire was startling even as Hannah made a feeble effort to push him away, chiding him for being so rough, for joking about matters that weren't funny, and he said, protesting, he wasn't joking, he loved her and didn't she love him?— his voice raw and quavering. They were agitated and clumsy as young lovers who had never kissed. *Didn't* she love him? How could she refuse him? Wasn't Lyle Stevick a normal man still in the prime of life very nearly in the prime of health, prone to normal urges, needs, appetites, yes and love too, certainly love, hadn't he been a faithful husband to her these many years in sickness and in health? Clearing his throat, he said more aggressively than he intended, "I love you," and again, burying his face in her warm damp neck, "Hannah—*I love you.*" And she could not further object.

Now the mystery had a name—emphysema—that terrible constriction in the chest, that shortness of breath then the violent racking cough, not TB, not cancer as he'd feared, but emphysema, hadn't one of his Rossky great-uncles died of the disease years ago, the poor bastard having worked fifty-odd years in one or another steel foundry, then everything—heart, lungs, guts—collapsed within a week. And his years at Swale Cyanamid—breathing in that sharp chemical stink! *That* was to blame, wasn't it, Mr. Stevick demanded of Dr. Ritter, "malathion" fumes, don't hand me this business about the pipe, you don't inhale with a pipe, do you! Angry and ranting, not knowing what he said, the fear of the Lord in him, breaking out in icy sweat, and this weeks before he'd get the news of poor Domenic's death, finally pleading he asked, Is it too late for me? and Ritter said, We'll see, grim and unyielding, a man of no promises, a tight-assed son of a bitch Lyle Stevick had always disliked so why in hell had the Stevicks been going to him for twenty years?—you figure it.

What it meant was a certain percentage of his lungs not *gone* exactly but *out of commission.* X-rays showed the walls of the air sacs stretched thin, broken down, there were air pockets in the lung tissue hence swelling and enlargement, why hadn't he come in for x-rays years ago, why hadn't he spoken of his terrible coughing fits and so on and so forth, why had he continued to smoke when he must have known something was wrong? Well, now he'd quit smoking, for sure. Forever. Missing his pipe and the taste of the tobacco so keenly at first he couldn't sit still for more than five minutes, couldn't sleep for more than two or three hours at a stretch, he'd come downstairs barefoot and disheveled to sit staring at the TV screen all zigzags and shivery blue surface, the programs off the air and all sound gone as on the morning after the last day of earth—the morning after the big 10-megaton H-bomb is dropped and the enemy fires back with one or two or a dozen of their own. That's all, folks! Maybe he'd lived too long, knew too much. His brain circuits like his lungs overloaded. Last week the coverage of the H-bomb test in the Marshall Islands, this week TV jokes about Bikini "atomic cocktails," there was to be a

Bikini bathing suit for women as well, a scandalous suit maybe the size of two men's handkerchiefs. The other day he'd stared at the TV seeing the devastation some tornadoes had made in Illinois, Ohio, western Pennsylvania, family of six children wiped out, aerial shots of destroyed homes, barns, overturned cars, an elderly woman crying— why not *not* inform himself of the horrors of the world, Lyle Stevick thought.

When you're powerless to intervene anyway.

What had Domenic said one time—something to do with God's silence. (One of the few remarks of his Lyle could now recall. Over all those years.) Lyle'd been baiting him, saying people prayed to God all the time but God sure as hell never answered back, it was a one-way conversation, and Domenic said stiffly, yes, that was the beauty of God, He didn't answer back. His wisdom was silence. Lyle hadn't known how to reply—it was a queer uncomfortable moment. The beauty of God, that He didn't answer back? Where was the logic there?

Now that Domenic was dead things seemed subtly altered, but Lyle Stevick couldn't have said why. Like out-of-doors when an invisible cloud passes over the sun and the quality of the light is changed, the air suddenly colder. Not that the brothers had been close—they hadn't been. In boyhood they'd shared their unhappiness but as adults they'd rarely had a serious conversation, even when Enid nearly died that time, even when Warren was shot up in Korea. Much of it Lyle's own fault, he supposed—always a chip on his shoulder regarding the Church, the celibate priests telling the faithful what to do, where even to stick your cock, under what precise conditions, birth control absolutely forbidden like eating meat on Friday—mortal sins, not venial; if you died you went straight to Hell. (How white-lipped and furious Hannah got reading of women in the newspapers like those organizing something called Planned Parenthood: *she'd* had to suffer so why not everybody else?) Domenic had been only fifty-nine years old at the time of his death. Big Sunday dinner in the home of one of his parishioners—Virginia baked ham and scalloped potatoes, corn bread, applesauce, mince pie—then the heart attack, toppling over helpless in his chair, dead within minutes. *Requiescat in pace.*

Night after night following the funeral Lyle Stevick went out drinking, making the rounds of the neighborhood taverns talking to whoever was available, old friends, strangers, bartenders, speaking of the tragedy of losing a brother you never really had, like losing a father you never really had, and the worst of it is by *dying* the dead seem to be mocking the enterprise of *living,* showing it up in all its pettiness and vulgarity like Gulliver in his travels traveling right out of the human condition altogether.

He got to thinking: if you believe in Heaven maybe you go there after your death automatically, maybe poor Domenic *was* there somehow, didn't the Buddhists believe that?—or the Hindus?—the mind's tricks it plays on itself. His own thoughts now reverted almost all the time to the shelter, of which he was enormously proud, and the odd fact was since he'd built it his old nightmare of the white-tiled room had vanished—that terrible, terrible vision!—vanished.

Requiescat in pace.

As for Felix he'd written the s.o.b. a letter and never got an answer naturally enough, taken an entire morning to compose a perfect letter appealing to his brother's—*half* brother's—sense of responsibility and obligation, the blood tie between them et cetera, but the selfish bastard hadn't answered, naturally enough.

Serves him right was Lyle's judgment on the latest scrape Felix had got himself in except of course this was the worst ever, *he'd* been beaten half to death. A few days afterward Lyle had seen an item in the paper, Rocky Marciano retiring aged thirty-two, the first heavyweight champion to retire undefeated, and he'd torn the item out meaning to take it to Felix in the hospital. End of an era, Lyle thought, contemplating Marciano's battered smiling face. No more white champions.

Jesus!—that young woman with the pale skin, crimson lips, black tulle veil and black-feathered cloche hat, black coat with a mink collar, one of the mourners at Domenic's funeral but composed in her grief, aloof and unexpressive, damned good-looking and she must have known it, not batting an eyelash at Lyle's stare or was she accustomed to men looking at her?—did she enjoy it? Like Marilyn Monroe larger than life on the posters, preening herself, pursing those juicy red lips for a kiss or in a lewd sucking gesture, you had to imagine her breasts hanging heavy and perfect half out of her dress, the material of the dress tight and clinging, a bright electric red outlining every curve of her astonishing soft voluptuous body, and there'd been a nurse at St. Joseph's when he did his volunteer work during the war but he'd forgotten her, name Jean-Marie was it? So pretty with red hair and a pale freckled skin, brown eyes, Jesus the shock of seeing *that* one get out of an elevator with the nursing nuns, some of them plain and hefty as bull calves, he'd heard such things about her just to look at her excited him but he wasn't the kind of man to investigate, he was a responsible married man, a father, no matter if Hannah turned from him even then so many years ago in fear in revulsion in disgust—No, don't, please! don't! *please!*—and some nights trembling with hurt he slept downstairs on the couch all thoughts of love and of lovemaking dampened, his manhood limply silly between his legs but of course Hannah was right—she couldn't risk another pregnancy ever again.

Lying on her side her flannel nightgown gripped about her, knees to her breasts, even her bare feet tucked under, his young wife her eyes closed, her face tear-streaked, closed against him: *Don't. Please.*

He was losing his erection—he was desperate grinding and pumping against her, the folds of pulpy soft flesh, oddly cool, down below where he couldn't allow himself to imagine her crotch spread wide the wattled flesh of her hips and thighs, Oh dear Jesus help me, don't let me fail, and a faint trickling sound somewhere—*was* there leakage after all?—the bunk beds too small for their struggling bulk and Hannah's arms around him, a dead weight of duty obligation wifely resignation, her face screwed up and eyes tightly shut, he supposed he must be hurting her down there, chafing her, she was so dry, damn it, she was so dry as if to spite him!—he'd wetted his penis with spittle but it didn't help very much Oh Jesus there was sly Elvira French slipping her arms around him, teasing him with her lips and tongue, that heady smell of perfume her surprisingly ample breasts pushing against him through the filmy material of her dress—but no, better not, the woman was mad, treacherous, some sort of evil there and in any case Mrs. French was no longer young, better the hat-check girl at that restaurant in her provocative costume flirting with him eyeing him frankly and cheerfully as if knowing full well the drift of his desire, the heavy overripe fruit in his pants, probably she was a call girl? a high-class call girl? but of course Lyle Stevick wouldn't dare even inquire there was the possibility of disease after all but Christ don't start thinking of disease! and he tried to recall the girl's sinuous body, the way in which she inclined her head childlike yet knowing, lascivious, he tried not to think of poor Hannah enduring his exertions wordless and submissive, the cords in her neck taut and her mouth pursed and her eyes shut tight against him as of old, her fatty legs rudely asprawl, her dignity lost, she had just finished tucking in the corners of the bedspread when her amorous husband untucked them, laughing nervously kissing and nuzzling her saying, Can we? here?

433

now? why *not?* Surely he knew better but at the same time he couldn't help but feel she might be excited too, she might be gratified and flattered by how hard and stiff and urgent he was, yes he knew better, he wasn't a fool kid any longer but he hoped she might suddenly weaken, smiling in feminine consent, after all it had been so many years! so many years! Now his manhood returning in a fierce desperate plunge, his heart pounding in his chest his lungs straining his haunches exposed to the air his stiffened penis precarious as a lighted candle in a breeze, Oh Hannah I love you, Hannah can you help me?—her stiff fingers cold on his neck, her face closed as a fist but she was trying to cooperate she was unresisting allowing her legs to be spread her buttocks ground into the shallow mattress without protest and though he had some difficulty at first—had he forgotten how?— after so many years!—finally he was inside her grunting and sweating, a sweet shock of sensation in his groin exotic yet familiar, there it was, there, there it was, reclaimed. He tried not to think of the spectacle they made if for instance one of their children should peer down the hatchway staring and appalled, incredulous, he tried not to think of the aftermath—how they'd have to dress, return to the house, Hannah would prepare supper as always silent and chagrined and Lyle would eat it glancing at her, abashed, hopeful, shamefaced, grateful, just the two of them alone in the kitchen tonight, alone, alone at the supper table because all their children had fled them even sweet Enid Maria who Lyle had loved more than his own life but in the end love isn't enough!—but Christ he had better turn his thoughts elsewhere he was getting limp his heart knocking in his chest and the bed squeaking poor Hannah grunting beneath his weight and no doubt he was hurting her though she wouldn't say a word, not even a murmur of protest, he felt a surge of desire like a kick in the small of the back seeing again that good-looking woman leaving Felix's hospital room, something soft and sweetly appealing about her, her honey-colored hair in a pageboy falling over one eye, high-heeled shoes and the sheen of the nylons stretched tight against her calves, she was wearing a suit in some casual style good-looking too and probably expensive, the jacket swinging open, some sort of fine jersey, mauve-colored, and a blouse with bunched-up material at the throat, elegant you might say, yes, probably expensive, he caught the glitter of a diamond on her hand and the scent of her perfume and he'd stared covertly after her, resisting the impulse to speak to her, to introduce himself as Felix Stevick's brother, also he might have followed her into the elevator

434

and struck up a conversation with her there but of course he'd let her go but he'd cherished her image for days afterward, summoning it back at the furniture store during idle hours to warm and console him or driving his car in traffic or in bed with Hannah breathing quietly beside him, he recalled that sweet carefully made-up face, her gaze veiled over, not seeing him at all, her expression muted, unreadable—was she Felix's lover or just the wife of a friend as Felix said, not even volunteering her name though Lyle had hinted he'd like to know. Felix lay in the hospital bed calm and indifferent, probably doped up so he didn't give a damn, his upper face swollen and discolored, his lower face swathed in white bandages and a tube sticking into one nostril, poor Felix who'd taken quite a beating and didn't want to talk about it, not to the police or to Lyle Stevick, not to anybody, shrugging, saying, It's just one of those things.

Jesus he was losing it—the beat, the rhythm—couldn't seem to regain it, his penis growing limp, sweat running down his sides and his thighs aching with the unfamiliar strain slantwise, he was seeing himself like poor Lemuel Gulliver crouched atop an enormous breast, the nipple alone enormous, monstrous, everywhere so much bulbous fatty flesh you could sink into forever and be suffocated—but Oh sweet Jesus! suddenly there was Hannah Weir eighteen years old the girl from Olcottsport, so shy so faltering in her speech, glancing at him half smiling, love for him shining in her eyes, artless and uncritical, her brown hair neatly braided and wound around her ears, smiling suddenly; she had plump dimpled cheeks and he could make her laugh as if in surprise at her own laughter and one evening in Kilbirnie Park he overcame her protests with kisses, slow steady hypnotic caresses telling her he loved her of course he loved her, his mouth dry with excitement his heart hammering then suddenly unbelievably he was rubbing himself against her, half out of his mind, her white cotton underpants the damp tight crotch of the pants—dear God he lost control he couldn't stop, as naïve and virginal as she and shuddering he ground himself desperately against her, buried his face against her as if he was drowning, he scarcely knew what was happening nor did Hannah Weir seem to know, dazed and terrified, hugging him around the neck, sobbing after a long while, whispering words he couldn't hear and yes he did love her, and that was how it began and he'd do it again, he'd do it again, again—once begun it can't be stopped.

And now it was over. It was over. Lyle Stevick lay spent and panting beside his wife, jammed against the wall, his head bumping the bedframe but he didn't give a damn; his heart still pounding now in triumph, all his veins flushed with surprise and well-being and gratitude, he said, "Thank you, Hannah," he said, "I love you, Hannah," and after a moment came the quiet nearly inaudible reply, "I love you too."